THE BEST OF STEPHEN R. DONALDSON

THE BEST OF STEPHEN R. DONALDSON

STEPHEN R. DONALDSON

Edited by Bill Sheehan

Subterranean Press 2011

First Edition

ISBN
978-1-59606-367-9

Subterranean Press
PO Box 190106
Burton, MI 48519

www.subterraneanpress.com

TABLE OF CONTENTS

Daughter of Regals

Through a small, narrow window high up in one wall of the manor's great ballroom, I watched the last of the lesser guests arrive. They were families of consequence, scions of made or inherited fortune, maidens like myself and otherwise, searching for excitement or marriageable partners. They were dressed and decked in all their splendor, as befitted people who attended any ball given at the manor of the Regals. But only the youngest and least cognizant among them came here simply to dance and dine under the chandeliers ablaze with candles. Most attended this night's festivities to witness the Ascension of a new Regal to the rule of the Three Kingdoms. Or—if the Ascension failed—to play whatever parts they chose for themselves in the collapse of the realm.

I was surprised to find that I did not wish myself among them. They were safer than I—and I was not blind to the value of safety. But I was willing to forego such luxuries for the sake of my chance. And—a point which frankly dismayed Mage Ryzel—I was willing to risk the realm along with myself.

He stood near me at another window, watching the arrivals as I did: the Mage Ryzel, my teacher, guardian, and guide—and for the past half year, since the death of my father, regent of the Three Kingdoms. He was a short man with a hogshead chest emphasized by the fit of his Mage's cassock, hands better suited to work at a smithy than to display at table, and a bald pate on which sweat gleamed at any provocation: not a prepossessing figure. But his worth showed in the keenness of his eyes, the blunt courage of his features—and in the crooked and rough-barked Scepter which he gripped at his side.

His Scepter was true Magic, a branch of the Ash which grew high up in the forests of Lodan. Anyone with any education knew that the Ash was the only remaining Real Tree in the Three Kingdoms; and everyone who trusted or feared Ryzel wondered how an ordinary man, who was not Real himself, had contrived to claim a limb of the last Tree.

The Mages of the realm dealt in images of what was Real. These images had substance and effect; they could be shaped and controlled. Therefore they were powerful. But they were no more Real than simple wood or normal flesh-and-blood; true Magic could not be touched. Only the ancient Creatures were Real: the Cockatrice, Basilisk, and Gorgon, the Phoenix, Wyvern, and Banshee—only the Wood of the Ash—only the Fire buried in the mountains of Nabal—only the Wind which caressed or ruined the plains of Canna. Only the men who had founded and secured the line of the Regals, men who were somehow Creatures themselves, Magic men, the Basilisk-Regal and the Gorgon-Regal his son and the Phoenix-Regal my father. And only Mage Ryzel had a Magic Scepter.

He told no one how he had come by such a Scepter, or what uses it served. Secrecy helped secure his position. But I had the story from my father: the Phoenix-Regal himself had obtained that power for Ryzel when I was a young girl, in reward for the Mage's earlier regency.

As was to be expected in the Three Kingdoms, some had considered Ryzel a poor choice to stand as regent after the death of my father. After all, his detractors argued, did not the realm degenerate nearly to chaos during his previous regency, those awkward and perilous years between the failure of my grandmother and the Ascension of the Phoenix-Regal? Yet he was primarily resented because he was strong rather than because he was weak. In truth, no other man could have done what he did as regent for my father: he preserved some semblance of unity over the Three Kingdoms when every pressure of history and personality impelled them to warfare—preserved the realm despite my grandmother's failure of the Magic which alone had compelled the contending monarchs and factions to peace.

That failure had not been foreseen—the line of Regals was then too recent to have established precedents—and so the kings had taken scant advantage of it at first. With the Gorgon-Regal newly dead, no one had contested the Ascension of his daughter. And she had been a woman in middle life, her son just four years short of age. In her failure—and the realm's need—Ryzel had shown himself able to contain, if not quench, the hot struggle for power which followed. First he had demonstrated that my grandmother's son possessed the latent capacity for Magic which she had lacked, and then he had contrived to keep the youth alive and safe until my father grew old enough to attempt the Seat.

Then as now, it was Mage Ryzel who gave the line of Regals the chance to rule.

I was a young woman—this night was the eve of my twenty-first birthday—with no power and scant sources of hope. I was grateful to Ryzel from the bottom of my heart. But he had counseled me to flee rather than accept the hazard of my heritage, and I did not take his counsel. My father had warned me against him.

As indeed the Mage himself had warned me against everyone else. Below me, the influx of guests had ended to prepare for a more considerable arrival. Jeweled and lovely women were paraded by their escorts or admirers to stand against the warm wood of the walls. Families cleared the center of the ballroom, taking auspicious vantage points among the other spectators and leaving the polished tile of the floor to gleam its response to the bright chandeliers. Young gallants—some of them wearing rapiers in defiance of the etiquette which required that no weapons be brought to the manor of the Regals—posed themselves as advantageously as possible below the high windows and balconies. Then, when the doors and the hall were ready, the trumpeters blew a flourish; and my heart stirred because I dreamed of hearing such brave fanfares sounded for me. But this tantara was not mine: it belonged to the people who more than any others wished me dead—to the rulers of the Three Kingdoms.

As the doors rang open, the three entered together, unable to determine who among them should take precedence. On the right strode Count Thornden of Nabal, huge and bitter, and as shaggy as a wolf, with a wolf's manners and appetites. In the center, King Thone of Canna moved with more dignity: he was rotund, urbane, and malicious. And on his left came Queen Damia of Lodan, sylph-like and lambent in her unmatched finery, as well-known for beauty as for cunning. Into the silence of the assemblage they walked, commanding the respect of the guests. From my window, they appeared to catch and hold the light proudly. Variously and together, they seemed far more fit to manage the realm than I.

Behind them came their Mages, famous men in their own names: Cashon of Canna, Scour of Lodan, Brodwick of Nabal.

Any one of them would have attempted my life already if Ryzel had not stood by me since my father's passing, and if they had not secretly feared that I would yet prove myself a Creature, capable of holding the realm against them all.

The Ascension for which these festivities had been prepared would be the test. At midnight this night, I would rise to the Seat which the Basilisk-Regal had created for his line. Into that Seat had been set a piece of Stone, a Real span of slate on which nothing that was not also Real could rest its weight. If the Seat refused me, I would die at the hands of the forces arrayed against me—unless Ryzel contrived some means to save me. Perhaps I would be dead before dawn.

Ryzel believed that I would die. That was the source of his distress, the reason for the sweat on his pate. He believed that I would fail of

Magic as my grandmother had failed. And I would not be rescued by the factors which had spared her life—by the surprise of her failure, and by the presence of her son.

Therefore the Mage had spent a good portion of the afternoon arguing with me in my private chambers. While I had pretended indecision concerning what I should wear to the feast and the ball and the Ascension, he had paced the rich rugs from wall to wall and rehearsed all his former efforts to dissuade me. Finally, he had protested, "Chrysalis, give it up!"

But I had only smiled at him. Not often did he call me by my given name.

"If the thought of death will not sway you," he continued, glowering, "think of the realm. Think of the price which your fathers have paid to achieve some measure of peace for this contentious land. It is not yourself alone that you risk. We must act now. *Now,* while we retain some leverage—while the thought that you may yet succeed still causes fear. Once your failure is assured, we will be left with nothing—neither fear nor doubt, coercion nor promise—by which we may secure your life. And the Three Kingdoms will run to war like mad beasts."

I was tempted to retort that his point had not escaped me. He and the Phoenix-Regal had taught me well to consider such questions. But I held to my purpose. Fingering the elaborate satin of gowns I did not mean to wear, I replied only, "Mage, do you recall why my father chose the name he did for his daughter?"

In response, Ryzel made a rude noise of exasperation.

Again, I smiled. Among other things, I loved him for his lack of ceremony. "He named me Chrysalis," I answered myself, "because he believed that in me something new would be born."

A thin hope, as I knew. But the Mage saw it as less. "Something new, forsooth!" he snorted. His Scepter thumped the old stone of the floor under the rugs. "Have we not labored for five years in vain to discover some ground for that hope? Oh, assuredly, your father was a Creature, not to be questioned. But in this he was misled or mistaken."

I turned from my wardrobe to challenge him; but he was too angry to relent. In truth, he appeared angrier than the case deserved. "My lady, we have tested you in every possible way. I have taught you all that lies within my grasp. You are not Magic. You have no capacity for Magic.

"It is *known* that the ability which makes a Mage is not born to everyone. And where that ability is born, it may be detected, be it active or latent. No surer test is required than that you are unable to place hand to my Scepter." That was true: my fingers simply would not hold the wood, no matter how I fought for grip. "Thus it is shown that you are not Real in yourself—not a Creature such as your fathers before you—*and* that you lack the blood or flesh which enable a Mage to treat with the Real. But we have not been content with one test. We have assayed every known trial. You fail them all."

"All but one," I murmured falsely. "I have not yet attempted my Ascension."

"My lady," he replied, "that is folly. The need of the realm does not forgive folly. Do you doubt that the crisis is upon us? You cannot. Your father did not rear you to be a fool. Count Thornden openly musters his forces into readiness for war. King Thone hides his harvests in secret storages, defying the command of the first so that he may be prepared to starve both his foes and us. Queen Damia designs new ploys of every description. Uncertainty alone keeps these fine monarchs from our throats."

As he spoke, I sifted through my trays of jewelry and ornaments, holding baubles to the light and discarding them. But my apparent preoccupation only served to whet the Mage's anger. That was my intent: I wished him angrier and angrier—angry enough, perhaps, to betray his covert thoughts.

He did not, however, reveal anything of which I was ignorant. Grimly, he continued, "And that is not the full tale of the peril. Kodar and his rebels mount fiercer attacks with every passing season. They desire an end to all rulers, forsooth. Fools!" he growled. "They are blind to the fact that throughout history the Three Kingdoms have known no freedom from violence and bloodshed except through rulers—powers strong enough to impose peace."

I had no need to hear such lessons; but I let him go on while I sought the chink in his secrets.

"Canna has no wood. Lodan has no metals. Nabal has no food. This wild Kodar believes that each town—or each village—or each family— or perhaps each *individual*—will do well to fend alone. Does he credit that Canna will gift its harvests to all Lodan and Nabal? It will not; it never has. It will sell to the best buyer—the buyer of greatest resource. And how will such resources be obtained? Hungry towns and villages and families and individuals will attempt to wrest them from each other. Similarly Nabal with its mines and ores, Lodan with its great forests. Kodar seeks anarchy and ruin and names them freedom. The first Regal did not found his line in the realm because he sought power. He was a Creature and had no need for such trivialities. He brought the Three Kingdoms under his rule because he grew weary of their *butchery.*"

And Mage Ryzel himself hated that butchery. I knew him well enough to be sure of that. Yet my father had warned me against him. And I had seen my father rise from his man-form into a Creature of wings and Real glory, almost too bright to be witnessed. I could not believe that he had lied to me in any way. Even Ryzel's long-proven fidelity was less to be trusted than the least word of the Phoenix-Regal.

My father was vivid to me, never far from my thoughts. Remembering the whetted keenness of his eyes—as blue as the sky—and the wry kindness of his smile, my throat ached for him. I could not bring him back. But he had promised me—had he not?—that I would follow him in splendor.

No. He had not. But his hopes had the force of promises for me. He had named me Chrysalis. And he had spoken to me often concerning Ascension.

A Regal is both human and Creature, he had said—*fully human and fully Real. This state is not easily attained. It may be reached in one way, by the touch of Stone to one whose very blood and flesh are latent Magic—not merely capable of Magic, but Magic itself. In that way, the first Regal found himself. And for that reason he built the Seat, so that his heirs might be transformed publicly and formally and the realm might acknowledge them.*

But this blood and flesh must be ready. It must be mature in its own way and touched by the influences it requires, or else it will not trans-form. His smile was bemused and dear. *It would have been well for the realm if I had Ascended when your grandmother failed. But the Magic latent in me was not ripe, and so for four years Mage Ryzel was needed to sustain the peace of the Three Kingdoms.*

Was it wrong that I saw a promise in such talk? No. How could I not? I was his daughter. And he and Ryzel had reared me to be what I was. I was full of memories and grief as I turned at last to face the Mage.

Softly, I replied, "All this is known to me. What is your counsel?"

My father had said of Ryzel, *He is the one true man in the Three Kingdoms. Never trust him.* Now for the first time I began to sense the import of that caution.

He mopped at the sweat on his pate; for a moment, his gaze avoided mine as though he were ashamed. Then he looked at me. Roughly, he said, "Propose marriage to Count Thornden."

I stared at him so that he would not see that I had considered this path for myself. From Thornden I might get a son. And a son might prove to be a Creature where I was not.

"Assuredly he is a beast," said Ryzel in haste—the haste of a man who liked none of his words or thoughts. "But even he will not dare harm to a wife who comes to him from the line of Regals. Some at least in the Three Kingdoms know the value of peace, and their loyalty will ensure your safety. Also their support will enable Thornden to master the realm. Already he is the strongest of the kings, and the boldest. If you name him your husband—and ruler in your stead—Canna and Lodan will be taken unprepared.

"He will be an ill monarch"—Ryzel grimaced—"but at the least he will hold the realm from war while we pray for the birth of another true Regal."

I measured his gaze and watched his soul squirm behind the dour facade of his face. Then, slowly, I said, "This is strange counsel, Mage. You presume much. Have you also presumed to suggest such a course to Count Thornden, without my word?"

At that, he stiffened. "My lady," he said, striving to match my tone, "you know that I have not. I am no fool. To be managed, the lord of Nabal must be surprised. He prides himself too much on his force of arms. Only surprise and uncertainty will bend him safely to your will."

"Then hear me, Mage Ryzel," I said as if I were the Regal in truth rather than merely in aspiration. "I say to you clearly that I count death a kinder resting place than Count Thornden's marriage-bed."

If he had allowed me time to soften, I would have added, So you see that I truly have no choice. But at once he swore at me as if I were a child—as if I had denied him something which he prized. And before I could protest, he said, "Then you have but one recourse. You must attempt the Seat now, before the coming of the kings. You must learn the truth of your heritage now. If you succeed, all other questions fail. And if you do not—" He shrugged abruptly. "Perhaps you will be able to flee for your life."

Now I let him see that I was not taken aback. That, too, I had considered. How not? From girlhood, I had dreamed repeatedly of Ascending the Seat—in public or in secret, according to the nature of the dream—and becoming Regal. The right to do so was the gift from my father which I most valued. And he had spoken so often of the transforming touch of Stone.

But I did not tell the Mage the truth—that I had already done as he advised.

The previous night in secret, I had entered the Ascension hall. Commanding the guards briefly from their posts, I had crossed the strange floor and mounted the marble steps to the Seat. But the Stone had refused the touch of my hands.

Yet I met Ryzel on his own ground without flinching, though in my heart I winced—betrayed by myself if not by him. "And if I fail and must flee," I asked, "will you accompany me?"

He lowered his head. His grip was hard on the wood of his Scepter. "No, my lady. I will remain where I am."

I took a moment to wonder what he might hope to gain from my flight—what dream of his my abdication might make possible—and also to let him observe that I wondered. Then I said simply, "My father commanded that I Ascend the Seat at midnight on the eve of my twenty-first birthday, under the light of the full moon. You have said that I am not Magic, and in all truth it would seem that I am not. Yet I would heed the plain word of any Creature. Still more will I obey the wishes of my father, the Phoenix-Regal. At midnight and not sooner I will attempt my Ascension, let come what may."

My regret that I had already disobeyed was fierce in me; and it held me to my purpose in the place of courage and confidence.

Ryzel's eyes were bleak as he saw that I would not be swayed. He began pacing again between the walls of my chamber while he mastered himself; and his bald head shone wetly in the light of the lamps. *The one true man in the Three Kingdoms.* I studied him as he moved, but did not know how to disentangle his fear for me from his fear for the realm. *Never trust him.* His helplessness did not sit well with him. Often I had believed that I would still be able to take my place as Regal and rule the Three Kingdoms even though I was not Magic—if only the Mage Ryzel would put forth his full power to support my claim. For what other purpose had my father given him his Scepter? But his talk of flight showed that my belief was vain. If I Ascended the Seat and failed, he might attempt to save my life—but he would not pretend me Regal.

In my turn, I would not trust my decisions to him.

And I gave him no glimpse of the pain my aloneness caused, I could not now afford to let him know how much I needed him.

By degrees, he regained his familiar gruff balance. Still shaking his head, he came to stand before me. "Soon the arrival of the guests will begin," he said as if my refusals had not trapped him among his bitter secrets. "My lady, what will you wear?"

That was very like him. Often he had told me that no detail of behavior, attitude or appearance was irrelevant to the craft of rulers; and he had shown his belief by advising me on everything—how to bear myself at table, how much wine to drink, when and where to laugh. I was not surprised by his desire to know what I meant to wear. Beauty, like power, was vital to the position for which he had trained me.

I showed him my choice. Bypassing the wealth of beribboned and revealing and ornamental gowns which I had been given to mask my obvious shortcomings, I took from the wardrobe a simple white muslin dress, almost a shift, and held it for his inspection.

His exasperation came back with a snarl. "Paugh! Chrysalis," he rasped. "You are already the plainest woman in the Three Kingdoms. Do not seek to flaunt what you should disguise. You must at least appear that you are fit for Ascension."

There he hurt me. It was fortunate that I had been well-taught for self-command. With great care and coldness, I replied, "Mage, I will not conceal what I am."

Twisting his Scepter in his rough hands, he gave me a glare, then turned and strode from my chambers. But at the last he did not slam the door; he did not wish to give any public hint of his distress. And when I joined him to watch the coming of the guests, his manner toward me had become the proper bearing of a Mage toward a woman who would soon Ascend to take her place among the Regals.

Below us, the three rulers entered together. Then they separated, moved with their Mages and courtiers to opposing places in the large hall—as far as they could be from each other. Count Thornden's retinue was unmistakably military in character, obviously armed. By contrast, King Thone had come accompanied by sophistication and gaiety—by style-setters and known wits of every description. But Queen Damia had surrounded herself with the most beautiful maids she could glean from the comely people of Lodan, showing by the way she outshone her entourage that her own loveliness was astonishing.

Doubtless that accounted for Count Thornden's loathing of her. Doubtless he had once made advances toward her, driven by one of his many outsize lusts—and she had laughed in his face. But the antipathy of these two altered nothing: the one thing I did not need to fear this night was that any two of the three rulers would league together against the third—or against me.

When the arrival was finished, the great doors were closed and the musicians struck up a lively air of welcome. The sounds of talk began to rise toward my window. The rulers stirred where they stood without changing their positions; and the other guests flowed in conflicting directions around the walls, seeking safety, favorites, or excitement. Not raising his eyes from the scene, Mage Ryzel murmured, "It is time, my lady."

"Is it, forsooth? I responded to myself. From the moment when I joined that gathering, my future would rest squarely in my open hands, exposed to every conceivable assault—and preserved by no power or beauty or love, but only by my own resources. An altogether fragile estate, as Ryzel had often deigned to inform me. Yet I had found that I did not envy those who were not in my place. When the Mage at last looked to me for my answer, I discovered myself able to smile.

"Time indeed," I said. "Let us go."

Glowering because he did not approve—perhaps of me, perhaps of himself—he turned and strode along the passage toward the head of the formal stair which stretched from this level down into the ballroom.

I followed at a little distance, so that I would not be seen from below before he had announced me.

His appearance cast an instant silence over the assemblage. The music stopped; all conversation ended; every eye was raised toward him. He was beyond question an unprepossessing figure, yet his influence was felt in every corner of the Three Kingdoms. And the Scepter he held would have compelled respect in the grasp of a child. He did not need to lift his voice to make himself heard down the length of the stair and across the expanse of the hall.

"Monarchs and Mages," he said in a dry, almost acerbic tone. "Lords and ladies. All true friends of the Regals—and of the realm. This is the night of Ascension, when old things become new. I give you the Lady Chrysalis, daughter of the Phoenix-Regal and by his command heir to the rule of the Three Kingdoms."

A brave speech: one calculated to fan the doubts of my ill-wishers. It was not a flourish of trumpets, but it pleased me nonetheless. When Ryzel began to make his lone way down the long stair, I waited where I could not be seen in order to reinforce those doubts—waited until the Mage had descended into the ballroom, walked out into the center of the hall, and turned to present his Scepter toward my coming. Only then did I go to stand at the head of the stair.

The guests reacted with a sudden murmur—muffled expressions of surprise, approval, disapproval, perhaps of my person or dress, perhaps of myself. But it was quickly stilled. And in the silence I found that I could not say the words of welcome and confidence which I had prepared for the occasion. Hidden by white muslin, my knees were trembling; and I knew that my voice would betray me. Mutely, I remained motionless while I promised the memory of my father that I would not stumble as I descended the stair.

By no shift of his hands or flicker of his face did Ryzel express anything other than certainty. He almost seemed to dare the gathering to utter one breath of impatience. Grateful for that, I summoned my courage and started downward.

With such slow dignity as I could muster, I went to meet those who wished me dead.

When I saw that in fact I was not about to stumble, I smiled.

As I gained the foot of the stair, a man concealed at the rear of the crowd called, "Hail the coming Regal!" But no one seconded his shout.

Then Mage Ryzel's expression did change. Frowning dangerously, he lowered his Scepter, folded it to his chest, and began to clap applause for me.

At first tentatively, then with more strength, the guests echoed his welcome. Unsure as they were of me—and of their own future standing—the consequential people of the Three Kingdoms feared to insult me directly in Ryzel's presence.

As the applause faded, I looked to him, letting him see in my eyes that, whatever transpired later, much would be forgiven him for what he had done here. Then, before the assemblage, I said, "Mage, I thank you. The Phoenix-Regal held you to be the one true man in the Three Kingdoms. I am gladdened to learn that there are others like you here." I spoke brightly, so that no one would miss the threat I implied toward those who did not support me.

Bearing my smile and my plain white dress in the place of Magic, I moved to greet King Thone and his party, choosing him because he stood nearer to me than the other rulers.

Around the hall, another murmuring arose and subsided. Everyone wanted to hear what would pass between me and my principal enemies.

Thone considered himself a sophisticate, and he bowed over my hand in a courtly and suave manner, kissing the backs of my fingers— the only public display of homage which the Regals had ever required of the three rulers. Yet his eyes disturbed me as much as ever. They appeared milky, opaque, as though he were nearly blind. And their color concealed the character of his thoughts. As a result, the simple quality of his gaze seemed to give everything he said another meaning, a hidden intent.

Like several of his adherents, he wore at his side a slim sword as if it were merely decorative, a part of his apparel.

Nevertheless, I greeted him with an air of frankness, pretending that I had nothing to fear. And likewise I greeted his Mage, Cashon of Canna, though that man perplexed me. He was tall and straight; and until the passing of the Phoenix-Regal his repute had matched his stature, for both strength and probity—and perhaps also for a certain simplicity. Though his home was in Lodan—and though his arts would have been highly prized in Nabal, for the smelting and refining of ores—he contented himself with Canna, where the most arduous work asked of him was the clearing of stubbled fields, or perhaps the protection of frost-threatened orchards. This he did because he had wedded a woman of Canna. Doting on her extremely, he had set aside numerous opportunities to stand among the foremost folk of the realm. So I had been surprised—and Ryzel astonished—when Cashon had suddenly declared his allegiance to King Thone, displacing the monarch's lesser dependents. We had not thought that this Mage would have stomach for Thone's invidious pursuits.

He greeted me at his chosen lord's right hand and kept his gaze shrouded, hiding his thoughts. But he could not conceal the lines which marked his face. Some acid of sorrow or futility had cut into his visage, weakening his mouth, causing the flesh to sag from the line of his jaw. He had an aspect of secret suffering which both moved and alarmed me.

"My lord Thone," I said, still smiling, "I have not yet had opportunity to congratulate you on winning such a man as the Mage Cashon to your service. You are indeed fortunate."

"Thank you, my lady," Thone replied in a negligent tone, as if he were bored. "I have great need of him. He has made himself a master of Fire, as you know."

By this he meant, of course, that Cashon cast images of the Real flame that melted and flowed deep under the mountains of Nabal. There was much debate in the realm as to which form of magery was most powerful. The images of the great Creatures were certainly potent, but many argued that in practical application either Wind or Fire was the sovereign strength. No one comprehended the uses of Wood—no one except Ryzel, who said nothing on the subject—and Stone appeared too passive to be considered. King Thone's milky eyes gave the impression that he had offered me a hint which I was too obtuse to follow.

When I simply nodded, he changed his topic without discernible awkwardness or obvious relevance.

"Have you heard," he said in that same tone, "that Kodar and his rebels intend to commemorate this night with another attack? My spies are positive. They report that he means to put Lodan's largest warehouse to the torch. An entire season's timber will be lost." His fleshy lips smiled slightly. "Would it be wise, do you think, my lady, if I were to warn Queen Damia of her danger?"

"It would be useless, my lord of Canna," I replied. "I am certain that she has received the same report." Indeed, I suspected that every spy in the realm knew Kodar's plans and movements as well as Thone did.

"Have you observed," I went on, seeking to turn this king's hints and gambits another way, "that Kodar's many attacks are strangely ineffective? He challenges the Three Kingdoms often, but to little purpose. Word of his intent precedes him everywhere. Is it possible, do you think"—I mimed his tone as exactly as I could—"that his purpose against Lodan is a feint?"

His eyes revealed nothing; but one eyebrow twitched involuntarily. The storages of Canna were certainly as vulnerable as Queen Damia's warehouses.

Before he could reply, I bowed to him and moved away to give my greetings to Count Thornden. At the edge of my sight, I glimpsed Mage Ryzel. He looked like a man who frowned so that he would not smile.

But Count Thornden was more obviously a threat to me than either of the other rulers, and he demanded my full attention. He styled himself "Count" because he proclaimed that he would not be "King" until all the realm acknowledged him. But I considered that position to be the subtlest he had ever taken; he was not a subtle man. He stood head-and-shoulders over me and scowled as if I affronted him. When he spoke, his lips bared his teeth, which were as sharp and ragged as fangs. Pointedly, he refused to take my hand.

That insolence spread a stirring and stiffening of tension among the onlookers; but I ignored the lesser people who watched me, in hope or dread. Straightening my back, I met Thornden's stare. "My lord of Nabal," I said quietly, "I bid you welcome, though you offer me no good greeting. This night is the time of my Ascension, and many things will change. I suspect that before tomorrow's sun you will be content to name yourself King."

For a moment, I watched him grin at what he took to be my meaning. Then I had the satisfaction of seeing his brows knot as other possibilities disturbed his single-minded wits. His only retort was a growl deep in his throat.

For the sake of good manners—and good ruler-craft—I saluted Thornden's Mage as I had Thone's. Brodwick of Nabal was a shaggy lump of a man, large and misshaped, whose fawning was exceeded only by his known prowess. He appeared oddly dependent, perhaps because he shared appetites with Count Thornden which only the lord of Nabal could satisfy. Following his master's example, he refused my hand.

I dismissed the slight. Whatever motivations ruled Brodwick, he was still dangerous. Deliberately, I resumed my progress around the ballroom, nodding to those people who looked at me honestly, gauging those who did not—and moving toward the encounter I could not shun with Queen Damia.

Perhaps I had unconsciously left her to the last, hoping foolishly to avoid her altogether. In all truth, she daunted me—she and that quick ferret who served her, the Mage Scour. Perhaps I could have borne it that her loveliness and grace gave me the aspect of a scullion by comparison. Or that her finery would have made the grandest gown I might have worn appear frumpish and shabby. Or that even Ryzel was unable to speak of her without an undercurrent of longing in his voice. I envied such things, but they were not necessary to me. To those strengths, however, was added another which made my blood run cold in my chest because I was not equal to it. I could play games of implication and inference with King Thone and not lose my way. Count Thornden was obvious; therefore he could be thwarted. But Queen Damia's cunning ran far deeper than theirs—deeper and more dangerously. And I feared that I lacked the wit to fathom her. Certainly I lacked the experience to walk unscathed through the mazes she built for the bafflement of her antagonists. In such matters, she was ably aided by Mage Scour. He served her, it was said, because she put her nearly limitless wealth at his disposal, enabling him to pursue his experiments and researches wherever he willed. And it was also said that he came here this night prepared by what he had learned to alter the entire order of the realm.

Ryzel had scoffed at that rumor, but in a way which conveyed uncertainty. The casting of images of what was Real was a known art, varying only according to the skill, dedication and inborn capacity of the Mage. But Magic itself remained a mystery, transcending that which was known, mortal, or tangible. And the rumors surrounding Scour claimed that he had gone beyond images of the Real into Magic itself.

I felt myself more a lost girl than a lady of state as I drew near to Queen Damia and her retinue.

Her smile was as brilliant as one of the chandeliers—so brilliant that it made me feel the fault of manners was mine rather than hers when she declined to accept my hand. But the gracious sound of her voice— as haunting as a flute—covered the social awkwardness of her refusal. "Lady," she said sweetly, "I have seen the portraits of your line which hang in the gallery of the manor. Surely no paint which is not itself Real can hope to portray the virility of the Regals. But the painting of your grandmother well becomes her—or so I have heard from those who knew the mother of the Phoenix-Regal. You are very like her. Your dress is so simple and charming, it displays you to perfection."

As she spoke, I found myself watching the movement of her décolletage as if I were a man. It was an effective sight; I was so taken by it that a moment passed before I grasped that I had been insulted in several ways at once.

"You flatter me, my lady," I replied, schooling myself to calmness so that I would not redden before the guests of the manor. "I have seen my grandmother's portrait often. She was altogether handsomer than I am." Then the success of my efforts gave me enough reassurance to return her compliment. "In any case, all beauty vanishes when Queen Damia appears."

A small quirk twitched the corner of her soft mouth; but whether it indicated pleasure or vexation, I could not tell. Yet my response sufficed to make her change her ground. "Lady," she said smoothly, "it ill becomes me to discuss the business of the Three Kingdoms upon such a festive occasion—but the need of my subjects compels me to speak. The next Regal simply must reexamine the pricing structure of Lodan woods against the ores and gems of Nabal and the foods of Canna. In particular, our mahogany is scarce, and growing scarcer. We must have a higher return for it, before we sink into poverty."

To follow her cost me an effort of will—and of haste. With the same words, she prepared for any outcome to my test. If my Ascension to the Seat succeeded, she would turn to me sweetly and say, "May we now discuss the price of Lodan mahogany, my lady?" And at the same time she contrived to suggest to all who heard us that the next Regal would be none other than Queen Damia herself.

I could not match her in such conversation. To escape her—and also to show her that I was not swayed—I attempted a laugh. To my ears, it sounded somewhat brittle. But perhaps it did not entirely fail.

"Surely you jest, my lady of Lodan. Your people will never know want while you have jewels to sell for their succor."

From the gathering, I heard a muffled exclamation, a low titter, whisperings of surprise or approbation. With that for victory, I turned away.

But I felt little victory. As I turned, I saw clearly Mage Scour's sharp face. He was grinning as if he had the taste of my downfall in his mouth.

To his credit, Ryzel allowed the monarch of Lodan no opportunity for riposte. He made an obscure, small gesture which the servants of the manor knew how to read; and at once a clear chime rang across the hush of the ballroom.

"My lords and ladies," he said casually, as though he were unaware of the conflicting currents around him, "friends and comrades, the feast is prepared. Will you accept the hospitality of the Phoenix-Regal's daughter at table?"

With an unruffled demeanor, he offered me his arm to lead me to the banquet hall. I gripped it harder than I intended while I continued to smile somewhat fixedly at the people who parted before us. Entering the passage which connected the ballroom and the banquet hall, he whispered softly to me, "Thus far, it is well enough. I will wager that even that proud Queen has been somewhat unsettled in her mind. Do not falter now."

Perhaps I could not trust him. But he was still my friend; and while his friendship lasted, I clung to it. In reply, I breathed, "Ryzel, do not leave me to dine alone with these predators."

"It is the custom," he said without turning his head. "I will regale the Mages while their masters feast. Do not fail of appetite. You must show no fear." A moment later, he added, "Perchance I will glean some hint of what has wedded Cashon to King Thone's side."

With that I had to be content.

At the doors of the hall, he dropped his arm. I walked without him ahead of the guests into the feasting-place of the Regals.

It was resplendent with light and warmth and music and savory aromas. In the great hearths fires blazed, not because they were needed, but because they were lovely and comforting. Long ranks of candelabra made the damask tablecloths and the rich plate gleam. Playing quietly in one corner, musicians embellished a sprightly air. The scent of the incensed candles gave each breath a tang. But this night such things provided me neither pleasure nor solace. As it was custom that Mage Ryzel would not attend me here, so also was it custom that I must take my feast uncompanioned—at a table set only for me and placed in full view of all the guests. The long tables had been arranged in a rough semicircle; but my seat rested on a low platform within the arms of the formation, solitary and exposed, so that all in the hall might study me as we ate.

A barbarous custom, I thought sourly. Yet I understood it. Always better—so my father had often told me—to rule by confidence of personality than by display of strength. And how better to show my enemies that I did not fear them, than by taking a calm meal alone in front of them?

Gripping what courage I had, I moved to my place and stood there while the three kings and their followers, the chief families and minor nobility of the realm, all my principal friends and foes found their proper seats. For a moment as I watched them, I fervidly wished myself a Gorgon as my great-grandfather had been, capable of turning to stone those who sought my ill. But then I shook the thought away; it did not become one who aspired to Ascension. The Gorgon-Regal had been a grim and fatal monarch—and yet there was no record that he had ever used his Magic to harm any of his subjects.

When all the guests were in their places, I made the short, formal speech expected of me, inviting the company to feast and happiness in the manor of the Regals. I was steadier now, and my voice betrayed no tremor. According to custom, I stood until the people around me had seated themselves. Then the steward clapped his hands for the servants, and I lowered myself gratefully to my chair.

At once, the feast appeared. Again according to custom, the steaming trays and chafing dishes, platters of meats and flagons of mulled wine and tureens of rich soup were brought first to me. And with them came a servant to act as my taster. He would taste for me; and I would taste for the guests; and so both caution and courtesy were satisfied.

But there I was somewhat surprised. The man who came to serve me was not my accustomed taster, an old retainer of the manor whom I had known and loved from girlhood. Rather he was a tall and excellently made fellow perhaps ten years older than I. I knew him little; but I had noticed him about the manor since the death of my father—indeed, I could not have failed to notice him, for his handsomeness was extreme, and it plucked at my heart in a way no man had ever done. His name was Wallin. Now, in the light of the candles and the aura of the music, he appeared more than handsome: he seemed to glow with perfection.

Looking at him, I thought that girls dreamed of such men. Women would be well advised to distrust them.

The blessing of my isolated seat and the music was that I could speak without being overheard. Softly, I said, "This is not your accustomed duty, Wallin."

"Your pardon, my lady." His composure was a match for his appearance. "Do not be displeased. Your taster was taken ill this evening—a slight indisposition, but enough to keep him from his feet." He smiled self-deprecatingly. "I begged for his place until the steward granted it to me so that I would desist."

"You have curious desires, Wallin," I said, studying him narrowly. In all truth, I distrusted him less than my attraction to him. "Why are you avid for such perilous duty? The task of taster is not altogether ceremonial here. There is a tradition of poison in the Three Kingdoms."

Speaking as quietly as I did, he replied, "My lady, your guests await their feast."

A glance showed me that he was right. Many of the men and women at their tables were watching me curiously. Others appeared restive. But I made a dismissive gesture. "Let them wait." It would serve to heighten their uncertainty. "You interest me."

"Then, I must answer you frankly, my lady." His manner suggested diffidence, yet he was entirely unruffled. "It is said of the Regals that they take their mates from the common people rather than from the high families—or from the adherents of the three rulers. This is unquestionably wise, for it avoids any implication of favoritism or preference which might unsettle the realm." He glanced around us, assuring himself that there was no one within earshot. Then he concluded, "My lady, when you come to the choice of a mate, I wish to be considered. I serve you to gain your notice."

He astonished me. I was not the sort of woman whom handsome men found desirable—or any men at all, handsome or otherwise, in my experience. Somewhat bitterly, I responded, "Are you hungry for power, Wallin?"

"My lady"—his composure was extraordinary—"I am hungry for your person."

For an instant, I nearly laughed. But if I had laughed, I might also have wept. Without my will, he inspired a yearning in me to be loved rather than feared or hated; and the pain that I was not loved welled against my self-command. Mustering all the severity I possessed, I said, "You are bold. Perhaps you are too bold. Or your grasp of the risk you run is unclear. I have not yet proven myself Regal. If I fail, any man who dares ally himself with me will share my doom. In permitting such hazard to your life, I would demonstrate myself unworthy of the rule I seek." Then I relented a degree. Some weaknesses require utterance, or else they will seek admission in other ways. "You may be assured that you have gained my notice."

"With that I am content," he replied. But his eyes said candidly that he would not be content long.

He nonplussed me to such an extent that I felt gratitude when he went about his duties, enabling me to occupy myself with the first of my food—and to avoid meeting his gaze again. His attitude defied reason. Therefore I could not trust it—or him. And therefore the strength of my wish to defy reason appalled me.

Thus it was fortunate that I had no appetite for any of the food placed before me. I required a great concentration of will to sample each dish as if I were pleased by it; and that discipline schooled me to master myself in other ways. As the servants fanned away from me to the long tables, bearing rich fare and rare delicacies to the guests of the manor— not *my* guests, though Wallin had termed them so—I became better able to play my part with proper grace. Let those who studied me for signs of apprehension see what they willed.

Yet whenever I felt Queen Damia's gaze come toward me, I did not meet it. I was prepared to outface all the rest of the gathering if need be, alone or together. But I was not a match for Lodan's queen.

So the banquet passed. No toasts were proposed to me—a breach of good etiquette, but one easily forgiven, considering the vulnerability of those here who wished me well—and I offered none in return. Hostility and tension were covered by the gracious music, the plenty of the feast, the flow of superficial conversation and jests. And then the musicians set aside their instruments to make way for the minstrels.

The minstrels were perhaps the only people in the hall with nothing at hazard except their reputations. War provided them with material for songs; peace gave them opportunity to sing. As did this night, whatever the outcome of my Ascension. So they had come to the manor from around the Three Kingdoms, that they might establish or augment their fame, their standing in the guild. In consequence, their singing was exceptional.

Custom declared that the minstrel of the manor must perform first; and she regaled the guests with an eloquent and plainly spurious account of how the Basilisk-Regal had wooed and won the daughter of one of Canna's farmers, in defiance of the man's deathly opposition to all things Magic. Then came the turn of the minstrels of the three rulers. However, only two men stood forward—Count Thornden had no minstrel with him, either because he had none at all, or because he had not troubled to bring his singer here. King Thone's representative took precedence by virtue of his ranking in the minstrel's guild, and he delivered himself of an elaborate, courtly ballad, highly sophisticated in its manner but rather crude in its intent, which was to flatter the monarch of Canna. I felt no offense, however. I was willing to listen to him as long as possible. Even crude minstrelsy beguiled me as though it had power to hold back the future.

But Queen Damia's singer gave the banquet a song which caught in my throat. It was one I had not heard before, and it was at once passionate and poignant, fiery and grieving, as only the best songs can be. In brief, it described the slaying of the last Dragon by the Basilisk-Regal, my grandmother's grandfather.

That thought was frightening: Creature at war against Creature, kind-murder which bereft the world of something Real and therefore precious. In the known history of the realm, only the Mage-made images of the ancient Creatures fought and slew. The Magic beings themselves lived lives of their own, apart and untouched, ruled by interests and needs and commitments which took no account of that which was not

Real. But Queen Damia's minstrel sang that the Basilisk-Regal went out to rid the realm of the last Dragon because that great, grim Creature had conceived a corrupt taste for unReal flesh and had begun to feed upon the folk of the Three Kingdoms. Thus for the sake of his chosen people the Basilisk-Regal was forced to take the blood of one of his own kind, and the stain of that death had marked his hands until his own passing. It had soaked into his flesh until at the last he was compelled to keep his hands covered because they had become too hideous to be looked upon by ordinary human eyes.

When the song faded from the hall, I found myself with tears on my face and a hot ache in my heart. It is only a song, I protested against myself. It has no power over you. Do not act the girl in front of your enemies. But to myself I responded, The last Dragon! Oh father of Regals! The *last*! How did you bear it?

I paid no heed to the banqueters who watched me in my weakness, and I heard nothing of the songs sung by the remaining minstrels. I thought only of the fine Creatures which had filled my dreams from my earliest girlhoood—the fierce Wyvern and wild Banshee, the terrible Gorgon and subtle Cockatrice, the mystic Phoenix—of my dream that one day I would stand among them, a Creature myself. And of what the world had lost in the slaying of the last Dragon.

If the song were true.

At last I recollected myself enough to be firm: *if* the song were true. Mage Ryzel had told me all he knew of the history of Magic in the realm—and he had not spoken of any bloodshed among Creatures. And who had sung the song which had struck so deeply into my lone heart? Who, indeed, but the minstrel of Queen Damia?

Was this song some ploy of hers?

If it were, I could not fathom it. As in everything she did, her true intent lay hidden beneath a surface of immaculate innocence. Perhaps she mocked me—or perhaps warned. Whatever her purpose, I feared I had already fallen to the snare. But now I no longer sought to avoid her gaze; when she looked toward me, I let her see that there was a darkness in my eyes which she would be wise to interpret as cold rage.

Perhaps I should have made shift to prolong the banquet. Each new phase of the evening brought me closer to the time of my trial. But instead I wished for an escape from the masque of confidence I was required to perform. My smile felt brittle on my lips, and I had need for privacy in which to shore up my resolve. So when the minstrels had done I rose to my feet and thanked them formally. At this signal, the servants brought around brandies and richer wines to complete the meal;

and the guests also rose to stretch their legs and mingle and talk while the ball itself was made ready.

But as I turned to leave the banquet hall, a servant came to inform me quietly that King Thone desired an audience with me alone before the ball.

I swore to myself because beyond question I could not afford to shirk such a request. Then I set aside my ache for respite and asked the servant to guide Canna's king to one of the private meeting-rooms near the banquet hall.

There were several of these rooms in the manor—places where the Regals might hold discreet conversation with kings and counselors and messengers—and it was surely known to half the ambitious connivers in the Three Kingdoms that these chambers were not in truth private. A ruler who sought to hold sway without bloodshed preserved his own secrets while at all times suggesting to his opponents that their secrets were not safe. Therefore some of the meeting-rooms were behung with tapestries behind which eavesdroppers might be concealed; others had listening slits cunningly hidden in the walls; still others possessed covert doors which might give sudden entrance at need to the guards of the manor.

For my audience with King Thone, I selected a chamber which displayed a brave weaving of the Ascension of the Phoenix-Regal. But I set no one behind the tapestry, neither Mage Ryzel nor any guard. Let King Thone believe himself overheard or not, as he chose; I had a need to show myself capable of facing him alone. And if Ryzel were indeed untrustworthy, I would do well to withhold as many secrets from him as possible.

Entering the room, I succumbed to my anxieties so far as to glance behind the tapestry for my own reassurance. Then I seated myself in the ornately carved chair reserved for the use of the Regals and awaited Thone's coming.

He arrived shortly, unaccompanied by any of his courtiers or dependents. Since I did not invite him to sit, he remained standing. To make him wait and wonder, I instructed the servant to bring a decanter of the Gorgon-Regal's choice brandy, and I did not speak to the monarch of Canna until after the brandy had come and the servant had departed again. Then, deliberately, I poured out one glass of the deep amber drink—for King Thone, not for myself—and said as obtusely as I could, "My lord, you asked an audience. Do you have some complaint? Does the hospitality of the manor displease you?"

He held his glass and gazed at it in silence for a moment. I had given it to him as a test, to see how he would choose between the courtesy of setting the brandy aside and the discourtesy of drinking when I did not. So my heart sank somewhat when he raised the glass to his mouth and sipped delicately.

His milky orbs betrayed nothing as he looked toward me at last; but his way of savoring the taste of the brandy hinted at other pleasures. "My lady," he said slowly, "the hospitality of the manor is without flaw, as ever. You do not believe that I would trouble you on such a pretext."

"What matters the pretext," I replied, seeking to unsettle him, "if it gives us opportunity to speak openly to each other?"

His gaze held me as if he were blind, proof against what I did. Still slowly, he said, "My lady, what do you wish to say to me?"

I gave him a smile to suggest any number of possibilities; but I answered only, "My lord of Canna, you requested this audience. I did not."

"My lady," he said at once, as if nothing lay hidden behind his words, "at such balls it is often done that the Mages of the realm give demonstration of their prowess. I ask permission for my Mage to entertain you."

He surprised me, but I did not show it. "Cashon?" I asked in mild curiosity. "You have termed him a master of Fire."

Thone's plump lips implied a smile.

"Then his demonstration will be hazardous in this crowded hall, among so many guests. Why do you wish him to display his skill here?"

"My lady, you are not Regal. You are merely aspirant. You would be wise to understand the significance of my Mage's power."

His tone made me stiffen. I knew now that I was being threatened, but I did not yet grasp the nature of the threat. Carefully, I responded, "It is undeniable that I am merely aspirant. But I am also the daughter of my father, the Phoenix-Regal. I need not risk harm to the guests of the manor in order to understand Cashon's magery—or the meaning of Fire."

He played his gambit well. His voice was that of a polite man who sought to disguise his boredom, and his eyes gave away nothing, as he said, "Perhaps if you better understood the uses of Fire, you would not risk the entire realm on a foolish attempt at Ascension. Perhaps if your eyes were opened, you would see that there are others better placed than yourself to assume the rule of the Three Kingdoms."

You dare? I wished to retort. You dare say such things to me? I will have you locked in irons and left in the coldest cell of the manor, and you will never threaten man or woman again. *That* power I still have while this evening lasts!

But I uttered none of those words. I kept my anger to myself. Instead, I said quietly, "You speak of yourself, my lord Thone. Please continue."

As if he had already won, he emptied his glass, then refilled it from the decanter. The faint twist of his mouth suggested that I was a fool not to share this excellent brandy.

"My lady"—now he did not trouble to conceal his sarcasm—"I had not thought you in need of such instruction. Mage Ryzel has taught you ill if you do not understand me. But I will be plain. Canna feeds the Three Kingdoms. Lodan and Nabal provide them with luxuries; Canna gives them life. And I am served body and soul by a Mage who has mastered Fire."

I did not let my gaze waver from the milky secret of his eyes. "That much is plain. Be plainer."

King Thone could not stifle a grin. "My lady, you are charming. This girlish innocence becomes you. But it does not render you fit for rule. However, you have commanded plainness, and while this evening lasts, you must be obeyed. Plainly, then, you must not attempt to Ascend the Seat of the Regals. Rather, you must give way to those better suited for rule. If you do not—I speak plainly at your command—if you set even one foot on the steps to that Seat, my Mage will unleash his Fire.

"Not upon the manor," he said promptly, as if I had questioned him. "Assuredly not. That would be hazardous, as you have said. No, he will set Fire upon the fields and crops of Canna. My secret storages will be spared, but Nabal and Lodan will starve. They will *starve,* my lady, until they see fit to cede their crowns to me."

Happily, he concluded, "You will find yourself unwilling to bring that much death upon the realm by defying me."

He made me tremble with shock and anger; but I did not show it. For an instant, I feared that I would. I had been trained and trained for such contests—but training was not experience, and I was not yet twenty-one, and until this night Mage Ryzel had always stood at my side. The peril to the realm, however, demanded better of me. Here the only question which signified was not whether I would later prove Regal, but rather whether I would be able to serve the realm now.

From my seat, I said softly, "You are bold, my lord. Apparently you care nothing that by these tactics you will make yourself the most hated man in the history of the Three Kingdoms. And apparently also," I continued so that he would not interrupt, "you have given careful thought to this path. Very good. Perhaps, my lord"—my courtesy was precise— "you will tell me how you intend to respond if I summon the guards of the manor and have you thrown without ceremony into the dungeon."

He stared through me as though I were trivial; but his mouth betrayed a smirk. "That would be ill advised," he replied. "My commands to my

Mage have been explicit. If I do not shortly appear at the ball to restrain him, he will commence the razing of Canna."

"I see." I nodded once, stiffly, acknowledging his cleverness. "And if I imprison Cashon also, what then?"

"My lady," Thone said with elaborate patience, "I have told you that he is a master. And surely Ryzel has taught you that a Mage need not be free to wield his power. Neither distance nor dungeon can spare the realm from my will."

I paused for a moment, marshalling my thoughts. Thone's plotting depended upon Cashon—a man whose integrity and scruples had never been questioned. Yet the monarch of Canna was certain that Cashon would commit such massive wrong. The idea was appalling. Still I preserved my composure. Facing my antagonist squarely, I asked, "Would you truly commit that abomination, my lord of Canna?"

"My lady," he replied in his tone of patience, "do not insult me with doubt." His eyes concealed everything. "I mean to rule the Three Kingdoms, and you will not prevent me."

Waving my hand, I dismissed this assertion as if my ability to prevent him were sure. "And Cashon?" I inquired almost casually. "He has earned goodly reputation in the realm. Will he truly obey your atrocious commands?"

"You may rely upon it," said the king. I had not ruffled him.

"That is preposterous!" I snapped at once, probing hard for a point of weakness. "We speak of Cashon, my lord—not of Thornden's sycophant or Damia's ferret. He was not shaped in the same gutter which gave birth to your lordship. *Why* will he obey you?"

King Thone's response lacked the simple decency of anger. Pleased with himself, he said, "He will obey me because his wife and his three daughters are in my power. He knows not where they are—but he knows that I will have them slain if he fails me. And he fears that I will find other uses for them before they die. Do not doubt that he will obey me."

His wife and daughters? I wished to cry out. Are you so base? And do you call yourself fit to rule? The nature of Thone's machinations horrified me; his revelation explained much.

But the sheer intensity of my outrage served as self-command. "In that case," I said, my heart pounding, "perhaps you will be so kind as to summon a servant." I indicated a bell-pull near him.

A slight faltering exposed him. Behind the veil of his gaze, I felt him study me closely. But I offered him no reason, and my countenance told him nothing. Perhaps now he sensed his peril, yet he had come too far to retreat. After a moment, he shrugged slightly and gave a condescending tug to the bell.

When a servant answered, I said clearly, but without inflection, "Request the Mage Cashon to attend us."

I was pleased to see that Thone now found he could not speak again, in protest or in warning, without appearing foolish. To keep himself still, he chewed upon his lower lip.

Cashon came to the chamber promptly. As he entered, his bearing was wary. Now that I knew his plight, his pain and his fear were unmistakable. Beneath its flesh, the courage which sustained his face was being eaten away. In his life, he had given up much which a Mage might find desirable for simple love of his wife—and it was plain that he had never regretted the loss. But now she and their daughters were threatened, and fear for them consumed him. It ruled him. He did not look at me; the suffering in his eyes was fixed on King Thone. His hands at his sides closed and unclosed uselessly.

For his sake, I spoke as soon as the door had been closed behind him.

"Mage," I said evenly, "this unscrupulous king has told me of the means by which he thinks to make himself monarch of the Three Kingdoms. You are the sword which he thinks to hold at my throat. But my word is otherwise: I say to you that you need not fear for your loved ones."

At that, Cashon's attention wrenched toward me.

Thone opened his mouth to speak, then closed it again, waiting to hear what I would say.

"You are reputed a master of Fire, Mage," I continued. "Therefore King Thone seeks to compel you to his use. And therefore you are able to defy him. Turn your Fire upon *him,* Mage"—now at last I allowed my ire to rasp in my voice—"upon this heartless fop who threatens thousands of innocent lives merely to serve his own ambition. Should you simply surround him with flame and let him feel its heat, he will reveal where your family is held to save himself pain. And he will go further. He will give you his written command for their release, so that you may free them this night."

That was my gambit for the protection of the realm. But I saw no hope leap up in Cashon's eyes; dread had dissolved all his strength. And the lord of Canna did not falter. His gaze did not shift from the Mage as he addressed me softly.

"You are a fool. Do you conceive that Cashon has not considered such threats for himself? But he knows that my men have been given command to first rape and then slay his wife and daughters, should harm of any kind come to me. If they hear any report that I have been hurt or defied, they will act. And I will never command any release.

"Look upon him." Cashon appeared to wither under Thone's scorn, so acid was the Mage's fear. "He counts himself fortunate that I will permit him to save his family by obeying me." Then Thone turned to me. "And I will achieve the same fate for you"—the calm of his demeanor broke into a shout—"if you do not submit to me *now!*"

My heart went out to Cashon in pity; but the safety of the realm hinged on him, and I could not afford to spare him. He had once been stronger; I gambled that he had not forgotten.

For the second time this night, I mustered a laugh. Smoothly, I rose from my chair. As I moved toward the door, I said, "Cashon, I leave him to you. You are a master. I trust you will do no harm to the manor. His command against your family will not be obeyed.

"Canna has not forgotten that he came to kingship through the suspected murder of his uncle—and that from the first moment of rule all the laws and commands of the Kingdom were altered. When word of his death reaches those who hold your loved ones, they will not dare obedience for fear that they will lose favor with the next monarch." I threw my whole weight into the scales on Cashon's side. "And you will be the next monarch—should Thone fail to satisfy you here."

At the door, I paused to look again at the king of Canna and smile. "I trust you will enjoy the ball, my lord," I said in my sweetest way. Then I left the meeting-room and closed the door after me.

There my legs nearly failed me. Dismay at the risk I took made my head whirl with faintness. If Cashon did not take courage from my display of confidence—if he did not conquer his fear—! Hardly able to stand, I clung to the door and listened and did not breathe. Through the panelled wood, I heard the first muffled roar of Cashon's magery—and King Thone's first shout of panic.

A servant nearby looked toward me in alarm. To calm her, I said, "Be not concerned." In an instant, my faintness became the light-headedness of relief. "King Thone and the Mage Cashon will resolve their differences well enough alone." I wanted to shout with jubilation. "And I wager that when King Thone emerges he will be unscathed. Leave them to themselves."

Turning in the direction of the ballroom, I walked away. For the first time, I felt that perhaps I was fit to become Regal over the Three Kingdoms.

A moment later, Ryzel appeared in the passage and came hastening toward me, barely able to hold his dignity back from running.

"Chrysalis," he breathed urgently, "are you well? There is power at work in that chamber."

He was unusually sensitive to the vibrations which spread from any exertion or presence which touched upon the Real. Any magery or Magic anywhere in the manor was known to him instantly. By that means, among many others, he had determined that I was no Creature. Now as he approached his alarm was briefly plain in his face—concern for me, perhaps—or perhaps anxiety that something had transpired to undermine his own intentions. But when he saw that I was unharmed—and that I was grinning—he drew himself to a halt, stifled his haste. "My lady," he asked cautiously, "what has happened?"

Before I could consider my reply, the door of the meeting-room leaped open, letting the reek of brimstone wash into the passage; and Cashon came out, alive with energy and hope. In one hand, he gripped a scrap of paper. He waved it toward me, then sped in the opposite direction, running to gain his horse.

Firmly, I took Mage Ryzel's arm and turned him away from the aftersmell of Fire. Despite my inexperience, I knew that it would be unwise policy to humble King Thone further by forcing him to make his exit from the chamber before witnesses. Let him repair his appearance and attend the ball as he saw fit; the mere thought of how he had been weakened would give me hold enough over him.

To answer Ryzel, I said softly, "It would seem that Cashon is no longer bound to the lord of Canna." But I gave him no explanation. He had his own secrets; I would keep mine. Also—to be honest—I was young yet and did not wish to give him opportunity to chastise me either for the risk I had taken or for bragging.

My silence made him frown dourly, but he did not question it. Instead, he said, "Then I am no longer chagrined that I learned nothing of Cashon's circumstances to aid you."

As we walked, I asked, "Is it not the custom of Mages to talk at these rare gatherings?"

"It is," he replied. "But Cashon spoke no more than three words from first to last."

Something in his tone alerted me. In an instant, I set King Thone's defeat aside and turned my attention to the Mage. "If Cashon did not speak, who did?"

He mulled his answer for some time, chewing it around in his mouth as if he loathed the taste of it but feared to spit it out. Then, abruptly, he said, "Scour."

His dislike of Queen Damia's Mage was of long standing; but it did not account for his present vehemence. And my own apprehensions concerning the lady of Lodan were many. Carefully, I inquired, "And what did this Scour say?"

"My lady," Ryzel said, obscurely angered and unable or unwilling to say why, "he spoke nonsense—hints and jests to no purpose. He could not be silenced. His own cleverness was a source of vast amusement to him." The Mage snarled his vexation. "Only one thing did he say clearly: he revealed that at his request Queen Damia's minstrel would sing of the slaying of the last Dragon for your banquet."

The sudden tightening of my hand on his arm stopped him. His words brought the monarch of Lodan's unexplained subterfuge back to me. Almost involuntarily, I asked, "Is it true?"

He turned toward me at the doors to the ballroom. From beyond them came the sounds of musicians tuning their instruments. "That Scour requested that song for your banquet? I know not. Surely he wished me to believe it."

I met questioning look squarely. "Is it true that the last Dragon was slain by the Basilisk-Regal?"

He scowled as he studied me, trying to guess what was in my mind. "That tale is told," he said slowly. "Perhaps it is true. There are many who believe that one Dragon still lived in the world when the Basilisk-Regal's rule began—and that it was gone when his rule ended. But only one portion of the tale is known to be certain: for the last years of his reign, the Basilisk-Regal wore his hands covered."

Unwilling either to outface or to satisfy Ryzel's curiosity, I moved toward the doors. But as they were opened for me, I thought better of my silence. On the threshold of the ball, I turned back to the Mage and said, "Then his grief must have been as terrible as his crime."

A step or two ahead of him, I went forward to continue this night's festivities.

Most of the guests had preceded me. King Thone's retinue appeared somewhat unsettled by his absence; but Queen Damia presided over her portion of the ballroom in great state and glitter; Count Thornden and his attendants kept their backs to her as pointedly as possible; and around the hall moved those families, courtiers, eavesdroppers, and lovers of dancing or sport who were not restrained by allegiance or personal interest.

At my entrance the gathering was hushed. The musicians ceased their tuning; the rulers and their entourages looked toward me; after a last giggle or two, the more playful girls joined the general silence. For a moment, I gazed about me and tried to appear pleased. Taken together, these people were a gay and enchanting sight under the bright gleam of the chandeliers. They were comely and fashionable—and well-to-do. Indeed, hardly a person could be seen who did not display some form of wealth. Here was evidence that the realm had prospered mightily under the imposed peace of the Regals. The rule to which I aspired was manifestly worthy and admirable; yet all these gallant men and women bedecked in loveliness also served to remind me that I was the plainest woman in the Three Kingdoms, as Ryzel had said. For all my victory over King Thone, I was not the equal of the manor's guests.

Nevertheless, I played my part as I was able. Assuming a grace I did not possess, I advanced into the center of the ballroom and spread my arms in a gesture of welcome. "Please dance," I said clearly. "This is the night of my Ascension, and I wish all the realm happy."

At once, the musicians struck up a lively tune; and after a moment's hesitation the ball came to life. Commanding every opportunity for advantageous display, Queen Damia allowed herself to be swept into the arms of a fortunate swain and began to float around the floor. Quickly, other eager young men found themselves partners; dignified old noblemen and their wives made stately circles as they moved. From the corner of my eye, I saw King Thone enter the ballroom, unremarked amid the first swirl of dancing. To myself, I applauded the way he contrived to rejoin the festivities without calling attention to himself; and I noted that he had managed to change parts of his apparel, thus eliminating the marks of Cashon's persuasion. In a moment, he garnered a partner for himself—the wife of one of his dependents—and busied himself about the task of pretending that nothing had happened.

Even Mage Ryzel tucked his Scepter under his arm and took a woman to dance—a girl who gazed at him as if he were the highlight of her life. Thus he also played his part. Soon it appeared that only Count Thornden and I were not dancing. He remained aloof, too fierce for such pastimes. And I— Apparently there were no men in the room bold enough to approach me.

Stiffly, I turned to remove myself from the path of the dancers. My thought was to gain the edge of the whirl and there to watch and listen until I found my chance to slip away unobserved. I did not enjoy what I felt as I saw the youngest daughters of the least consequential families outshine me. But when I left my place in the center of the ballroom, I nearly collided with the servant Wallin.

He had exchanged his livery for a plain broadcloth coat, clean and well-fitting but neither formal nor festive—a garment which emphasized his extreme handsomeness by its very simplicity. He took advantage of my surprise by slipping one arm about my waist, grasping my hand, and pulling me into the music.

A servant. The same servant who had proclaimed a desire for my person. In my first confusion as he commandeered me, the only thing about him which was not surprising was the fact that he danced excellently. Whatever else he was, I did not take him for a man who would have placed himself in this position if he had lacked the appropriate graces.

For half a turn of the ballroom, I simply clung to him and let him lead me while I sought to clear my head. His physical nearness, the strength of his arms, the scent of him—half kitchen-sweat, half raw soap—all served to confound me. But then I caught Ryzel's eye as we danced past him, and his nod of approval brought me to myself. He conveyed the clear impression that he saw my dancing—and my partner— as a gambit I had prepared for the occasion, so that I would not appear foolish when no man freely asked my company. And the other guests who noticed me did so with curiosity, startlement, and speculation in their eyes, sharing Ryzel's assumption—or perhaps thinking that I had in fact chosen Wallin to be my husband.

The Mage gave me too much credit—and revealed that he had had no hand in Wallin's behavior. With an effort, I mastered my confusion. Leaning closer to Wallin, I said so that only he would hear me, "You are fond of risks."

"My lady?" I seemed to feel his voice through his broad chest.

"If the steward discovers that you have left your duties, you will lose them altogether. You are a servant, not the scion of some rich nobleman. Even men of goodly aspect and astonishing presumption must have work in order to eat."

He chuckled softly, almost intimately. "Tonight I do not covet either work or food, my lady."

"Then you are either a hero or a fool," I replied tartly, seeking an emotional distance from him. "Did you see Count Thornden's gaze upon us? Already he has marked you for death. King Thone surely will not wish you well. And Queen Damia—" Would not her blood seethe to see me dancing with a man who was handsomer than any who courted her? "You would be wiser to test your audacity upon her."

"Ah, my lady." His amusement seemed genuine; but his eyes were watchful as we circled. Watchful and brown, as soft as fine fur. "It would delight me to be able to thrill you with my courage. Unfortunately, I am in no such peril. I am merely a servant, beneath the notice of monarchs." Then he laughed outright—a little harshly, I thought.

"Also, Count Thornden is a great lumbering ox and cannot run swiftly enough to catch me. None of King Thone's hirelings are manly enough to meet me with a sword. And as for the queen of Lodan"—he glanced in Damia's direction—"I heard it said that Kodar the rebel has chosen her for his especial attention. While he occupies her, I will be secure, I think."

"And for more subtle dangers," I remarked, "such as poison or hired murder, you have no fear. You are a wonderment to me, Wallin. Where does such a man come from? And how does it chance that you are 'merely a servant'? I would be pleased to hear your life's tale as we dance."

For an instant, he looked at me sharply, and his arm about my waist tightened. More and more of the guests took sidelong notice of us as we followed the current of the dance. But whatever he saw in my face reassured him; his expression became at once playful and intent. "My lady, I am of common birth. Yet I have gleaned some education." His dancing showed that. "I am learned enough in the ways of the world to know that men do not seek to woo women by telling them tales of low parentage and menial labor. Romance requires of me a princely heritage in a far-off land—a throne temporarily lost—a life of high adventure—"

"No," I said; and the snap in my voice made him stop. I was on the verge of avowing to him that my Regal sires had all chosen their brides from the common people for reasons of policy—and for the additional reason that it was the common people whom the Regals loved, the common people who had suffered most from the constant warring of the Three Kingdoms. But I halted those words in time. Instead, I said, "If you truly wish to woo me"—if you are not toying with me—oh, if you are not toying with me!—"then you will speak of such things tomorrow, not tonight. Tonight I have no heart for them."

At once, he ceased dancing and gave me a formal bow. His face was closed; I could not read it. "My lady," he said quietly, "if you have any need that I may serve, call for me and I will come." Then he turned and left me, melting away into the gay swirl as discreetly as any servant.

I watched him go as if I were a mist-eyed maiden, but inwardly I hardened myself to the promise that I would not call for him—not this night. I could not afford to trust his inexplicable behavior; and if I failed at my Ascension, he would not deserve the consequences of aiding me.

Somehow, I found my way from the flow of the dance toward the wide stair to the upper levels. By the foot of the stair, a chair had been set for me on a low dais, so that I might preside over the ball in some comfort. There I seated myself, determined now to let any of the dancers who wished look at me and think what they willed.

Perhaps for those who had come to the ball simply because it was a ball, the time passed swiftly. For me it dragged past like a fettered thing. The musicians excelled themselves in variety and vivacity, the dancers glittered as if they were the jewels of the realm, bright and rich and enviable. At intervals, Mage Ryzel came to stand beside me; but we had little to say to each other. Diligently, he continued to play his part, so that all the gathering would know he was not at work elsewhere, laboring either to prevent my ruin or to preserve his own regency. And my exposed position required me at all costs to maintain my facade of surety. I could do nothing to satisfy my true need, which was to shore up my courage for the coming crisis. Blandly, I smiled and nodded and replied when I was addressed—all the while yearning for privacy and peace. I did not wish to die; still less did I wish to fail.

It happened, however, that when the evening was half gone Queen Damia grew weary of the ball and again took command of the occasion. During a pause between dances, she approached me, accompanied by Mage Scour. In a tone as gracious and lovely as her person, she said, "My lady, your guests must have some respite in which to refresh themselves, lest they lose their pleasure in dancing. If you will permit it, I will offer some small entertainment for their enjoyment."

Her voice and her suggestion chilled me. I feared her extremely. And—as ever—I was unable to fathom her intent. But I could hardly refuse her offer. The callowest youth in the ballroom would know how to interpret a denial.

I saw Ryzel shifting through the stilled assembly toward me. To temporize until he reached me, I replied, "You are most kind, my lady of Lodan. What entertainment do you propose?"

"A display of Magic," she answered as if every word were honey and wine. "Mage Scour has mastered an art which will amaze you—an art previously unknown in the Three Kingdoms."

At that, a murmur of surprise and excitement scattered around the ballroom.

Ryzel's eyes were wary as he met my glance; but I did not need his slight nod to choose my course. We had often discussed the rumor that Scour's research had borne remarkable fruit. That rumor, however, had always been empty of useful content, leaving us unable to gauge either its truth or its importance. An opportunity for answers was not to be missed.

Yet I feared it, as I feared Queen Damia herself. She did not mean me well.

My throat had gone dry. For a moment, I could not speak. A short distance away stood Count Thornden, glowering like a wolf while his

Mage, Brodwick, whispered feverishly in his ear. Scour's grin made him resemble a ferret more than ever. King Thone's milky eyes showed nothing; but he had no Mage to support him now, and he held himself apart from most of the guests. Until this moment, I had not realized that my white muslin might become so uncomfortably warm. Surely the night was cooler than this?

Though every eye watched me as if my fears were written on my face, I waited until I was sure of my voice. Then I said as mildly as I was able, "A rare promise, good lady. Surely its fulfillment will be fascinating. Please give Mage Scour my permission."

At once, Scour let out a high, sharp bark of laughter and hurried away into the center of the ballroom.

Around him, the people moved toward the walls, making space for his display. Gallants and girls pressed for the best view, and behind the thick circle of spectators some of the less dignified guests stood on chairs. Mage Ryzel ascended a short way up the stair in order to see well. With a conscious effort, I refrained from gripping the arms of my seat; folding my hands in my lap, I schooled myself to appear calm.

Scour was a small, slight man, yet in his black cassock he appeared capable of wonders: dangerous. The silence of the ballroom was complete as he readied himself for his demonstration. He used no powders or periapts, made no mystic signs, drew no pentacles. Such village chicanery would have drawn nothing but mirth from the guests of the manor. These people knew that magery was internal, the result of personal aptitude and discipline rather than of flummery or show. Yet Scour contrived to make his simple preparations appear elaborate and meaningful, charged with power.

It was said that the blood of a distant Magic man or woman ran in some veins but not others, gifting some with the ability to touch upon the secret essence of the Real, leaving the rest normal and incapable. Whatever the explanation, Scour possessed something which I lacked. And I had been so thoroughly trained by Mage Ryzel—and to so little avail—that I needed only a moment to recognize that Scour was a true master.

Step by step, I watched him succeed where I had always failed. First he closed his eyes and clasped his hands together before him. Such actions might be necessary or unnecessary, according to his gift for concentration. His mouth shaped complex words which had no sound—again an aid to concentration. Softly, then with more force, his left heel began to tap an unsteady rhythm against the floor. Another man might have done these same things and seemed merely preposterous. Queen

Damia's Mage had the look of a man who would soon be strong enough to consume the very manor of the Regals.

Slowly, he separated his hands. Holding his arms rigid, he spread them wider and wider by small increments. Across the gap between his hands ran a palpable crackle of power. It was neither a clear bolt such as lightning nor a diffuse shimmer such as heat, but rather something of both. It shot streaks of red within the reach of his arms then green, then red again.

And as the colors crackled and flared, a shape coalesced within them.

I should have known what was coming. I had been given hints enough; a child could have read them. But the queen of Lodan had been too subtle for me from the first.

The shape took on depth and definition as it grew larger. Its lines became solid, etched upon the air. Moment by moment, its size increased. At first, it might have been a starling—then a pigeon—then a hawk. But it was no bird of any description. Passion flashed in its eyes, light glared along its scales. Gouts of fire burst from its nostrils.

As it beat its wings and rose above Scour's head, it was unmistakably a Dragon.

In response, cries of alarm and astonishment rang across the ballroom. Doors were flung open and banged shut as men and women snatched their children and fled. Some of the guests retreated to the walls to watch or cower; others cheered like Banshees.

It was small yet. But it continued to grow as it soared and flashed; and the stretch of Scour's arms, the clench of his fists, the beat of his heel showed that he could make his Creature as large as he willed.

The sight of it wrung my heart with love and fear. I had risen to my feet as if in one mad instant I had thought that I might fly with it, forsaking my human flesh for wings. It was instantly precious to me—a thing of such beauty and necessity and passion, such transcending Reality and importance, such glory that for me the world would be forevermore pale without it.

And it was my doom.

Even as my truest nerves sang to the flight of the Dragon, I understood what I saw. Mage Scour had gone beyond all the known bounds of his art to make something Real—not an image but the thing itself. There was no Dragon in all the realm from which an image might have been cast. Scour might as easily have worked magery of me as of a Dragon which did not exist. He had created Reality, could summon or dismiss it as he willed. And thereby he had made himself mightier than any Magic or Mage or Regal in all the history of the Three Kingdoms.

Or else he had simply cast an image as any other Mage might—an image of a Dragon which had come secretly into being in the realm.

In a way, that was inconceivable. Knowledge of such a Creature would not have remained hidden; one Mage or another would have stumbled upon it, and the word of the wonder would have spread. But in another way the thought was altogether too conceivable: if some man or woman of Lodan—or Mage Scour—or Queen Damia herself—were a Creature such as the Regals had been? Capable of appearing human or Real at will? Then the knowledge might well have remained hidden, especially if the Magic had been latent until recently. That would explain all Queen Damia's ploys—her confidence, her choice of songs for her minstrel, Scour's talk at the Mages' dinner.

Whatever its meaning, however, the Dragon bearing itself majestically above Scour's head and snorting flame spelled an end for me. Any Mage capable of creating Reality was strong enough to take the realm himself at whim. And a Creature hidden among Queen Damia's adherent—no, in the queen herself, for how could she appear so certain if one near her were stronger than herself and therefore a threat to her?—would be similarly potent.

Yet for that moment the sight alone contented me. Regardless of the outcome, I was blessed that such beauty had come to life before me and stretched out its wings. But others in the ballroom were less pleased. With a distant piece of my attention, I heard Count Thornden's harsh cursing—and his sudden silence. Scour's display was as much a threat to the lord of Nabal as to me. Now I realized that Thornden had been demanding a response from Brodwick. And Brodwick had begun—

A gust tugged at the hem of my dress. With a cry of grief or anger, I tore my gaze from the splendid wheel of the Dragon and saw Thornden's Mage summoning Wind.

More guests fled the ballroom, some shrieking; an image of true Wind was not a form of entertainment. But already their cries were scarcely audible through the mounting rush of air, the loud, flat thud of the Dragon's wing-beats, the furnace-sound of flame, the Creature's roar. People called Ryzel's name, demanding or imploring intercession. The chandeliers swung crazily against their chains; whole ranks of candles were blown out. Thornden barked hoarsely for more strength from Brodwick.

The Dragon was far from its full size, and Brodwick's exertion was likewise less than the blast of which he was known to be capable, the hurricane-force powerful enough to flatten villages, to scythe down forests. But within these walls his Wind had no free outlet. Rebounding from all sides, it made such chaos in the air that the Dragon's flight was disrupted: the Creature was unable to challenge its attacker.

Scour had been buffetted from his feet; he lay facedown on the floor, his cassock twisted about his rigid form. Yet he had not lost concentration. His fists pounded out their rhythm—and the Dragon continued to grow. Soon Brodwick would need a full gale to hold back the Creature.

An instant later, Count Thornden staggered forward. As strong as a tree, he kept himself erect under the force of the Wind. His huge hands gripped the hilt of a longsword—he must have snatched it from one of his attendants. Struggling step after step, he moved toward Scour.

If he slew Queen Damia's Mage, it would be a terrible crime. Before the coming dawn, he would find himself in open warfare with Lodan— and perhaps also with Canna, for no ruler could afford to let such murder pass unavenged. Even a Regal would not be able to prevent that conflict—except by depriving Thornden of his throne in punishment. And yet I grasped during the space of one heartbeat that Scour's death would save me.

I did not desire safety at the price of bloodshed. During that one moment, I tried to call Thornden back by simple strength of will.

Then I saw that his attention was not fixed on Scour. Whirling his blade, he aimed himself at the Dragon. He meant to throw the sword, meant to pierce the Creature's breast while it wrestled against Brodwick's Wind, unable to defend itself.

The sight tore a cry from me: "Ryzel!" But I could not hear myself through the roar of Wind and Dragon.

Yet the regent loved all Creatures as I did, and he did not withhold his hand. From him came a shout such as I had never heard before—the command of a Mage in full power.

"ENOUGH!"

Wrenching my gaze toward him, I saw him upon the stair with his Scepter held high and his strength shining.

Without transition, the work of the other Mages disappeared. Between the close and open of a blink, both Scour's work and Brodwick's were snatched out of existence, dismissed.

The instant cessation of the blast pulled Count Thornden from his feet in reaction. Among the remaining onlookers, people stumbled against each other and fell. Of a sudden, there was no sound in the ballroom except muffled gasping and the high clink of the swinging chandeliers. Scour snatched up his head; Brodwick spun toward the stair.

For the first time, Ryzel had shown what could be done with a Scepter of true Wood. He had declared the best-kept of his secrets for all the plotters in the realm to witness: his branch of the Ash enabled him to undo magery.

Did it also enable him to unmake things which were Real?

Near me, Queen Damia continued smiling, but her smile appeared as stiff as a mask. King Thone stood motionless as if without Cashon's support or advice he feared to move. Unsteadily, Thornden regained his feet and began snarling curses.

Mage Ryzel lowered his Scepter, stamped his heel on the stair beside him. *"Enough,* I say!" He was fierce with anger. "A Dragon is a Creature, worthy of homage. Real Wind is among the first forces of the world. Such things should not be mocked by these petty conflicts. Are you not ashamed?"

"Paugh!" spat Thornden in retort, "Be ashamed yourself, Mage. Will you now pretend that you do not desire the rule of the realm for yourself?"

"I will pretend nothing to you, king of Nabal," Ryzel replied dangerously. "I am regent now, as I have been before. You know the truth of me. I will not accept warfare among the Three Kingdoms—neither here nor upon the realm."

He did not say that, if he had desired the rule for himself, he yet lacked means to take it. He had shown only that he could counter the actions of other Mages. The power to dismiss images was not the power to force others to his will. Such things did not need to be said; given time, even Count Thornden would understand them for himself.

The situation required me to speak, before Thornden provoked Ryzel further. Stepping away from my chair, I addressed the guests. I was relieved that my voice did not shake.

"My lords and ladies, we have all been astonished by what we have seen here. Wine and other refreshments will be brought to restore you." I knew that the steward would hear me—and would see that I was obeyed. "When we have recovered the spirit of the occasion—and when the chandeliers have been relit"—I glanced wryly up at the ranks of wind-snuffed candles and was rewarded with a scattering of nervous laughter—"the ball will be resumed.

"For the present, I will leave you a while. I must prepare myself for my coming test." Also I required time to think. My need to be alone with my thoughts was acute, so that I might try to find some grounds for hope.

Bowing to the assemblage, I moved to the foot of the stair and asked Ryzel, "Will you accompany me, Mage?"

"Gladly, my lady," he replied gruffly. He appeared grateful that I rescued him from a difficult circumstance. I took his arm, and together we ascended from the ballroom.

Behind us, the shrill rasp of Scour's voice rose suddenly. "Beware Mage! You tamper with that which you neither understand nor control."

Ryzel did not turn his head or hesitate on the stair, but his reply could be heard clearly from one end of the hall to the other. "I will always beware of you, Scour."

I felt a tremor of reaction start in the pit of my stomach and spread toward my limbs. So that I would not falter, I gripped his arm harder. He gave me a glance which might have been intended as reassurance or inquiry; but we did not speak until we had left the stair and traversed the passage to my private chambers.

There I stopped him. I did not mean to admit him again to my rooms—or to my thoughts—until this night was ended and all questions of trust had been answered. Yet some matters demanded discussion. Leaning against the door to steady my trembling, I studied his face and said, "Mage, you were able to dismiss Scour's Dragon. Therefore it was not Real."

He did not meet my gaze; his face appeared older than my conception of it. Dully, he said, "Only one who can make the Real can also dismiss it. Perhaps I succeeded only because the Reality of the Dragon was not yet complete."

"You do not credit that." I masked my fear with asperity. "If Queen Damia holds command of such Magic, why has she not simply proclaimed her power and demanded rule?"

He shrugged. "Perhaps Scour's discovery is recent and requires testing. Or perhaps his capacity to make and unmake a Creature is limited." Still he did not look to my face. "I am lost in this."

And you are afraid, I thought in response. Your plans are threatened. It may be that you seek to defend them by deflecting me from the alternative. Stiffly, I said, "No. If what you suggest is true, then I am altogether doomed. I will not waste belief on that which must slay me. Rather, I will concern myself with the casting of images.

"If Scour's Dragon is not Real, then there is indeed a true Dragon alive in the realm—a Creature such as the Regals were, capable of concealing itself in human form. Is that not true, Mage?"

He nodded without raising his head.

"Then who *is* this Dragon? Is it not Queen Damia herself? How otherwise would she dare what she has done?"

That brought Ryzel's eyes to mine. Fear or passion smoldered in his brown gaze. "No," he said as if I had offended his intelligence. "That is untrue. Damia is not such a fool, that she would play games when only direct action will avail her. There is some chicanery here. If she is a Creature, why has she not simply taken the realm for herself? No!" he repeated even more vehemently. "Her daring shows that the Dragon is neither someone she can control nor someone she need fear. Her caution demonstrates that she does not know who the Creature is whose image Scour casts."

It was a plausible explanation—so plausible that it nearly lifted my spirits. It implied that I might still have reason to hope and plan and strive. But I did not like the bleak hunger and dread in Ryzel's gaze; they suggested another logic entirely.

Abruptly, before I could find my way between the conflicting possibilities, he changed his direction. "My lady," he asked quietly—almost yearning, as if he wished to plead with me—"will you not tell me now how Thone and Cashon came to be parted from each other?"

He surprised me—and confirmed me in the path that I had chosen. If I had known of his power to dispel magery earlier, I would not have needed to outface King Thone. But Ryzel had kept his secret even from me. Carefully, I met his question with another.

"Before he died, the Phoenix-Regal spoke to me of you. He said, 'He is the one true man in the Three Kingdoms. Never trust him.' Mage, why did my father warn me against you?"

For an instant, his expression turned thunderous, and his jaws chewed iron as if he meant to drive a curse into my heart. But then, with a visible effort, he swallowed everything except his bitterness. "My lady, you must do as you deem best." His knuckles on his Scepter were white. "I have merely served the realm with my life—and you as well as I have been able. I do not pretend to interpret the whims of Regals."

Turning on his heel, he strode away from me.

He had always been my friend, and I would have called him back, but that I was unable to refute my own explanation for the apparently unnecessary indirection of Queen Damia's plotting. Her various ploys might be the caution of a woman who did not know the true source of Scour's Dragon. Or they might be the maneuvers of a woman who was still bargaining with Mage Ryzel for the rule of the Three Kingdoms.

In my heart, I did not accuse him of malice—or even of betrayal. His fidelity to the realm was beyond question. Yet he believed that my Ascension must fail. How then was he to prevent the Kingdoms from war? How, indeed, except by allying himself with one of the monarchs and settling the power there before the others could defend themselves?

Perhaps he was in all truth as true a man as my father had named him. But it was certain to me now that I could not trust him for myself.

So I went alone into my chambers; I closed and bolted the doors. Then I hugged my arms over my breasts and strove not to weep like a woman who feared for her life.

For a time, I was such a woman. Without Ryzel's support I was effectively powerless. And he had indeed been my friend. Every man or woman must place trust somewhere, and for years I had placed mine in him. In league with Damia against me? I would have felt great anger if I had been less afraid.

But then I thought of the Dragon Scour had evoked in the air of the ballroom; and I grew calmer. All Creatures were perilous, and among them a Dragon was surely one of the most fearsome. But the Real danger of that lovely strength made the more human risk of my plight seem small in contrast—wan and bearable. My life was a little thing to lose in a world where Dragons and Gorgons and Wyverns lived. And also—the thought came to me slowly—the restoration of any Dragon to the realm was a boon to the line of the Regals. If the Basilisk-Regal had in fact slain a Dragon, then that crime was now made less. My sires had less need for grief.

And while the identity or allegiance of the Creature remained hidden, I was not compelled to despair.

When I was steadier, I was able to think more clearly about what I suspected of Mage Ryzel.

I saw now that although my life was small my presumption had been large. For no other reason than that I was my father's daughter—and that he had named me Chrysalis in prophecy—I had been prepared to risk the realm itself on the test of my Ascension—the same realm for which the Basilisk-Regal had shed the blood of the last Dragon. But that willingness was indefensible; it was a girl's pride, not a woman's judgement. Ryzel was wiser: behind my back, he sought not to deprive me of hope, but to keep the Three Kingdoms from war if I failed.

Though it pained me to do so, I resolved that I would accept whatever he did and be content. If I were truly the daughter of Regals—in spirit if not in Magic—then I could do no less, so that the innocent of the Three Kingdoms would not be lost in an abhorrent contest for power.

I wished sorely to be a woman of whom no Creature would be ashamed.

I had intended to remain in my rooms until midnight drew near, but after only a short time a servant came to my door and knocked. When I replied, she reported that Count Thornden desired a private audience with me.

My new calm did not extend quite so far; but the matter could not be shirked. While I held any hope for my life, I was required to walk the narrow line of my position, and so I could not afford to deny the lord of Nabal a hearing which I had earlier granted King Thone.

To the servant, I named a meeting-room in which a tapestry concealed a door through which guards might enter if I had need of them; but I did not immediately leave my chambers. I gave the guards a moment to be made ready—and myself an opportunity to insist that I was indeed brave enough for what lay ahead. Then I unbolted my doors and walked trembling to Count Thornden's audience.

I trembled because he was as large and unscrupulous and lacking in subtlety as a beast. And because I could not imagine what prompted him to request speech with me.

At the door, I nearly faltered. It was unattended—and should not have been. But I did not wish to betray my fear by refusing to meet the lord of Nabal until I was sure of my protections. Gripping my courage, I lifted the latch and went inward.

At once, a large hand caught my arm, flung me into the room. The back of the hand was dark with black hair, and its force impelled me against the table. Regals had often sat there with kings and counselors; and the peace of the realm had been preserved. I stumbled, and the edge of the table caught my ribs so that I gasped.

The room was lit with only two candles. Their flames capered across my vision as I fought to regain my balance, turn toward my attacker. I heard the door slam. At the edge of my sight, a massive chair seemed to leap from the table to wedge itself against the door. As I turned, a backhand blow took the side of my face with such force that I felt myself lift from my feet and sail toward the wall. With my hands, I broke the impact; but it was strong enough to knock me to the floor.

While the room reeled and all my nerves burned with the pain in my face and chest, Count Thornden came looming over me.

Tall and bestial, he spat an obscene insult at me. Candlelight reflected in the sheen of sweat on his heavy forehead. I feared that he meant to kick me where I lay, yet I was slow to realize the danger. How does he dare this? I asked through the shock of my pain. Is he too stupid to fear my rescue by the guards of the manor?

But the door to the meeting-room had been unattended.

Glaring down at me, he snarled, "No, I will not do it. You are too plain and puny for any man's respect, *my lady.*" In his mouth, that *my lady* was a worse insult than his obscenities. "And you have no Magic, *my lady.* Your Ascension will fail. I have been advised to offer you marriage—so that we may rule in alliance—but I will not demean myself by wedding such baggage."

"Fool," I panted up at him. Still I did not understand the danger. "Fool."

"Rather," he rasped, "I will render you unfit for any man or marriage. Then you will cleave to me in simple fear and desperation, because no other will have you, and my kingship will be accomplished at the cost of one small pleasure"—fury and hate were lurid in his eyes—*my lady.*"

I was rising to my feet, off-balance, unable to dodge him. In one swift movement, he grasped the white muslin at my shoulders and stripped it from me as if it were only gauze, as meaningless as my pretensions to the rule of the Three Kingdoms,

"Guards!" I shouted, recoiling from him. Or tried to shout; my voice was little more than a croak. "Guards!"

No guards came. The tapestries in the chamber hung unruffled by the opening or closing of any door which might have brought men with swords and pikes to my aid.

Count Thornden grinned his corrupt hunger at me. "Already I am king in effect if not in name. None who consider themselves your friends dare oppose me. You are lost, *my lady.*"

Brutally, he grabbed at me.

I eluded him by diving under the table. I had none of the skills of a warrior, but I was well-trained at physical sports. Hone the body to sharpen the mind, Mage Ryzel had taught me. And he had betrayed me: no one else in the manor had authority to command the guards from their duty. I rolled under and past the table. There I flipped to my feet.

But then I did not run or cry out or seek to escape. Naked, I stood erect across from Thornden and faced him. Anger and pain and betrayal had taken me beyond fear. I had done Ryzel too much honor by thinking him in league with Queen Damia; doubtless he feared her too much to ally himself with her. Instead, he had chosen Thornden for his machinations—chosen to submit me to rape rather than accept the risks of my Ascension. The bones of my cheek flamed as if they had been splintered.

"Resist me!" Thornden snarled. "It increases the pleasure." He began to stalk me around the table.

With all my strength, I shouted, "NO!" and hammered both fists against the tabletop.

I was only a woman—and not especially strong. My blow did not so much as cause the candleflames to waver. Yet the sheer unexpectedness of it stopped him.

"You are a fool!" I snapped, not caring how my voice shook. "If you harm me further, the result will be *your* doom, not mine." For the moment, I had surprised him into motionlessness. He took his pleasure from harming the weak and fearful; he was not prepared for me. And while it lasted I took advantage of his amazement.

"First, my lord of Nabal," I said in a snarl to match his, "let us agree that you dare not kill me. If you do so, you will forge an unbreakable alliance between Canna and Lodan against you. In the name of survival—as well as of ambition—they will have no choice but to do their uttermost together in an effort to punish my slayer."

I did not allow him time to claim—or even to think—that he was ready to fight any opposition in order to master the realm. Instead, I continued, "And if you dare not kill me, then you also dare not harm me. Look upon me, my lord of Nabal. *Look!*" I slapped the table again to startle him further. "I am indeed plain and puny. But do you think that I am also blind and deaf? My lord of Nabal, I am *aware* of my appearance. I understand the consequences of such plainness. You cannot render me unfit for any man or marriage; I have long since given up all hope of such things.

"Therefore it will cost me nothing to denounce you to Canna and Lodan if you harm me. I will not be afraid or ashamed to proclaim the evil you have done me." If he had any more than half a wit in his head, he was able to see that I would not be afraid or ashamed. "The result will be the same as if you had slain me. In self-interest if not in justice, Canna and Lodan will join together to reave you of your crown so that I will be avenged."

His surprise was fading; but still I did not relent, did not allow him opportunity to think. I knew what his thoughts would be: they were written in the sweat and darkness of his face. He had reason to avoid anything which might ally Canna and Lodan against him. Why else had he given any credence to the counsel that he should offer me marriage?—why had he sought to rape rather than to murder me? But he also had reason to think that he might be strong enough to prevail even against the union of his foes—especially if Ryzel stood with him. I sought to deny his conclusions before he could reach them.

"And if you dare not murder me—and you dare not harm me—then you also dare not risk battle. Ryzel supports you now because you are the strongest of three. But if Canna and Lodan join against you, you will be the weaker of two, and so Ryzel will turn from you for the sake of the realm."

But in that I erred. Thornden's purpose was suddenly restored. His stance sharpened, a grin bared his teeth. Clearly, his hold upon Ryzel's support was surer than I had supposed, so the threats I had levelled against him collapsed, one after the other. As he saw them fall, he readied himself to spring.

Still I did not waver. I could not guess the truth between Ryzel and Thornden; but my ignorance only made my anger more certain.

"But if you are too much the fool," I said without pause, "to fear Ryzel's defection, then I will not speak of it. And if you are too much the fool to fear Queen Damia's Dragon, that also I will not discuss." Though Thornden's wits were dull, Brodwick's were as sharp as they were corrupt; and he had undoubtedly brought his lord to Ryzel's conclusion—that Damia's Dragon was an image of a Creature she could not identify, and that therefore it was not as dangerous as it appeared. "But are you also fool enough to ignore King Thone? Have you not observed that his Mage has left the manor?"

That shot—nearly blind though it was—went through Thornden like a shock. He stiffened; his head jerked back, eyes widened. I tasted a fierce relish for my gambit.

"My lord of Nabal, Cashon is a master of Fire. Without Brodwick to defend them, your armies are lost. Cashon will turn the very ground beneath their feet to lava and death."

He could not know that I was lying. With a howl of rage, he sprang toward the door, heaved the chair aside, burst from the chamber. From the outer passage, I heard the pound of his running and the echo of his loud roar: *"Brodwick!"*

Relief and dismay and anger and fear rose in me as nausea. I wanted to collapse into a chair and hug my belly to calm it. But I did not. Unsteadily, I walked to the concealed door which should have brought the guards to my aid.

When I thrust the tapestry aside, I found Mage Ryzel there. His eyes were full of tears.

The sight nearly undid me. I was so shaken that I could hardly hold back from going to him like a girl and putting myself into his arms for comfort. At the same time, I yearned to flay his heart with accusations and bitterness.

I did neither. I stood and stared at him and said nothing, letting my nakedness speak for me.

He was unable or unwilling to meet my gaze. Slowly, he shambled from his hiding place as if he had become unaccountably old in a short time and crossed the room to the door. Bracing himself on the frame as if all his bones hurt and his Scepter alone were not enough to uphold him, he called hoarsely for any servant within earshot to attend him.

Shortly, he was answered. His voice barely under control, he told the servant to go to my private chambers and fetch a robe. Then—still with that painful slowness—he closed the door and turned back to face me.

"All I proposed to him," he said with a husky tremor, "was that he ask your hand in marriage—or in alliance, if you would not wed him. I conceived that Scour's Dragon would teach you your peril so plainly that you would give up your reasonless pretensions."

"Oh, assuredly, good Mage," I replied at once, scathing him as much as I was able. I only kept myself from tears by digging my nails into the palms of my hands. "That was all you proposed. And then you commanded the guards away, so that he would be free to act violence against me if he chose."

He nodded dumbly, unable to thrust words through the emotion in his throat.

"And when he sought to harm me, you did not intervene. He was certain that you would not."

Again, he nodded. I had never seen him appear so old and beaten.

"Mage," I said so that I would not rail against him further, "what is his hold upon you?"

At last, he looked into my eyes. His gaze was stark with despair. "My lady, I will show you."

But he did not move—and I did not speak again—until a knock announced the return of the servant. He opened the door only wide enough to receive one of my robes.

Without interest, I noted that the robe was of a heavy brocade which had been dyed to highlight the color of my eyes, so that I would appear more comely than I was. While I shrugged it over my shoulders and sashed it tightly, Ryzel averted his head in shame. Then, when I had signified my readiness, he held the door for me, and I preceded him from the meeting-room.

I desired haste; I needed movement, action, urgency to keep my distress from crying itself out into the friendless halls of the manor. But somehow I measured my pace to Ryzel's new slowness and did not lose my self-command. The death of my father had left me with little cause for hope and no love; but at least it had given me pride enough to comport myself as a woman rather than as a girl. Moving at Ryzel's speed, I let him guide me to the upper levels and out onto the parapets which overlooked the surrounding hills.

The night was cold, but I cared nothing for that, I had my robe and my anger for warmth. And I took no notice of the profuse scatter of the stars, though their shining was as brilliant and kingly as a crown in the keen air; they were no more Real than I was. I had eyes only for the moon. It was full with promise or benediction; its place in the heavens showed me that little more than an hour remained before midnight.

The manor was neither castle nor keep, not built for battle; it had no siege-walls, no battlements from which it might be defended. The first Regal had designed it as a seat of peace—and as a sign to the Three Kingdoms that his power was not founded upon armies that might be beaten or walls that could be breached. In consequence, the Mage and I encountered no sentries or witnesses as we walked the parapets.

Still he had not spoken, and I had not questioned him. But after we had rounded one corner of the manor, he stopped abruptly. Leaning against the outer wall, he peered into the massed darkness of the hills. Sharply, he whispered, "There!" and pointed.

At first, I saw nothing. Then I discerned in the distance a small, yellow flicker of light—a traveler's lamp, perhaps, or a campfire.

"I see it," I murmured stiffly.

Moonlight caught the sweat on his bald head as he nodded. Without a word, he began walking once more.

Within ten paces he halted again, pointed—and again I saw a yellow flickering among the nearby hills.

Down the next stretch of the parapet, he showed me three more glimpses of light, and along the following section, two more—barely visible bits of flame at once as prosaic as torches and as suggestive as chimera. When we had completed a circuit of the manor, I had seen that we were surrounded at significant intervals by these uncertain lights.

Around me, the chill of the dark seemed to deepen. I knew from many strolls at night upon the parapets that the few villages among the hills were hidden in valleys, invisible. And in all truth these lights did not appear to be the lamps of travelers; I had not seen them moving— and in any case none of them lay on the roads which led to the manor.

Yet Ryzel did not speak. Hugging his Scepter to his chest, he stared in silence into the heart of the wide dark. I had resolved patience; but at last I could endure no more. "I have seen, Mage," I breathed tightly. "What have I seen?"

"Carelessness, my lady." His tone was distant and forlorn. "Count Thornden is shrewd in his way, but not meticulous. You have seen the ill-muffled lights of his armies."

I held myself still and listened, though his words made my blood labor fearfully in my temples.

"He cannot believe that a woman will prove Regal, and so he lacks one fear which constrains both King Thone and Queen Damia. It was his intent to besiege the manor this night—to put it to the torch if necessary—in order to rid himself of all opposition at one stroke. You know that we have no defense; I was hard-pressed to persuade him to hold back his hand, at least until after midnight. Only the promise of my support brought him to hear me at all, and only my offer of an opportunity with you—or against you—caused him to agree that he would first allow me chance to give him the rule, before grasping it himself with bloodshed."

Therefore my lies about Cashon had turned Thornden aside from my harm. Only the Fire which Cashon might cast could hope to protect the manor from the forces of Nabal.

That I understood. I understood many things; my thoughts were as clear as the cold night. And yet inwardly I was stricken with treachery and loss, scarcely able to hold up my head. The presence of those armies surpassed me.

"You knew this," I whispered like weeping. So many men could not have moved among the hills to surround the manor without the knowledge of Ryzel's spies. "You knew this—and did not tell me."

The sense of betrayed hope filled my throat. Only dismay restrained me from shouting. "There was no need to fear these armies. Cashon would easily have been persuaded to aid us, if I had known to ask him. Thornden would not have dared his forces against Fire—not if he had known that you were able to silence Brodwick's Wind. All this could have been forestalled. If you had told me."

But now the chance was lost. Proud of my victory over King Thone—and ignorant—I had in effect sent Cashon from the manor, thus unbalancing the powers arrayed against me, tilting the scales in Thornden's favor. Now I could only pray that Queen Damia would be able to counter him.

That thought was gall to me. I grew sick from the mere suggestion of it.

Ryzel's presence at my side had become insufferable. Gripping my voice between my teeth, I said, "Leave me, Mage."

"My lady—" he began—and faltered. He was old and no longer knew how to reply to his own regret.

"Leave me," I repeated, as cold as the night. "I do not desire your company in my despair."

After a moment, he went. The door opened light across the parapet, then closed it away again. I was alone in the dark, and there was no solace for me anywhere.

If he had stayed, I would have howled at him, You were my friend! Of what value is the realm, if it may only be preserved by treachery?

But I knew the truth. My father had gauged the Mage accurately: he could not have been driven to such falsehood, except by one thing.

By the fact that I had no Magic.

From the moment of the Phoenix-Regal's death, all other considerations had paled beside the failure of my heritage. Born of a Creature—
from a line of Creatures—I had nothing in common with them except
yearning and love. Ryzel would have been steadfast in my service if he
had held any hope at all for my Ascension.

I should have stopped trusting him much earlier. But he had told me
so much, taught me so much, that I had not once wondered if he had
indeed told or taught me everything. So I had been left to work my own
doom in ignorance.

Above me, the moon entered its last hour before midnight. The end
was drawing near. In me, the line of the Regals and all their works
would fail. Because I did not wish to flee, I had nothing left to do with
my life except approach the Seat as if it were an executioner's block.

Perhaps I would go to the Seat early, attempt my Ascension now,
before midnight, so that my part in the ruin of the realm would not be
protracted beyond bearing.

"My lady."

His voice startled me. He had not come through the door behind
me—I had seen no light. And I had not heard his steps.

Handsome as a dream in the moonlight, Wallin stood before me.

I tried to say his name, but my heart pounded too heavily. Clasping
my arms under my breasts, I turned my back so that he would not
observe my struggle for self-command. Then, to ease my apparent rejection, I said as well as I could, "You are a man of surprises. How did you
find me?"

"I am a servant." His tone conveyed a shrug. "It is an ill servant who
remains unaware of the movements of his lady." Now I felt rather than
heard him draw closer to me. He seemed to be standing within touch of
my shoulder. "My lady," he continued gently, "you are grieved."

Somewhere in the course of the night, I had lost my defense against
sympathy. Tears welled in my eyes. I was incapable of silence. "Wallin,"
I said in misery, "I am a dead woman. I have no Magic."

If he understood the implications of my admission—how could he
not?—he paid them no heed. From the beginning, he had done and said
things which I could not have expected from him; and now he did not
fail to take me aback.

"My lady," he said in his tone of kindness, "some have claimed that
your grandmother failed of Ascension because she was not virgin."

"That is foolish," I replied, as startled by his statement as by his sudden appearance. The Seat was a test of blood, a catalyst for latent Magic,

not a measure of experience. "None have claimed that the Regals were virgin, either before or after they carne into their power."

"Then, my lady"—he placed his hand firmly upon my shoulder and turned me so that I would look at him—"there can be no harm if you allow me to comfort you before the end."

The pressure of his kiss made the sore bones of my cheek burn; but I found in an instant that I welcomed that pain like a hungry woman, starving in the desert of her life. The smell and warmth and hardness of him filled my senses.

"Come," I said huskily when his embrace loosened. "Let us go to my chambers."

Taking his hand, I drew him with me back into the manor.

I had no reason to trust him. But everything trustworthy had been proven false, therefore it was not madness to place trust where none had been earned. And I was in such need—I cared for nothing now except that he should kiss me again and hold me during my last hour, so that I might die as a woman instead of as a girl.

In part because I wished to be circumspect—but chiefly because I did not want to be interrupted—I chose the back ways of the manor toward my chambers. As a result, we encountered some few servants busy about their last tasks, but no guests or revelers—and no one that I recognized as a minion of Ryzel's. During our passage, Wallin remained silent. But the clasp of his hand replied to mine; and when I looked to him, his smile made his features appear dearer than any I had seen since the death of my father. I did not know how such eyes as his had come to gaze upon me with desire. Yet—by a Magic I had not felt before—their regard seemed to make me less plain to myself, leaving me grateful for that distant taste of a loveliness I did not possess.

But at the door to my chambers I hesitated, fearing that I had mistaken him, that I had been misled by my need—that at the last he would think better of himself and recant. Yet now his eyes were dark and avid, and the muscles at the corners of his jaw bunched passionately beneath the skin, so powerful were the emotions which drove him.

To my surprise, the sight of his intensity increased my hesitation. Suddenly, I found myself truly reluctant for him. I was reconsidering the danger he represented.

That he was dangerous was manifest. A harmless man would not have dared the things he had done this night. And how was it possible for a woman with my face to believe seriously in his desire for me? Deliberately, I placed my hand on his chest to restrain him from the door and said, "Wallin, you need not do this." Somehow, I contrived to smile

as if I were not sorrowing. "Your life is too high a price for my consolation. I am content to think that perhaps you have cared for me a little.
That is enough. Accept my gratitude and go to procure what safety you
can for yourself."

Altogether, he was a surprise to me. At my words, his visage grew
abruptly savage. Snatching my hand from his chest, he jerked me around,
clamped his fingers over my mouth with my back gripped against his
side so that I could not break free. His free hand wrenched open the
door. "My lady," he panted as he impelled me inward, "you have not
begun to grasp the things I care for."

Though I kicked at him with my heels, tore at his arm with my fingers, he held me helpless. In my chambers, he closed the door and bolted
it. Then he lifted me from my feet and bore me to the bed.

Forcing my face against the coverlet, he knelt on my back to keep me
still while he pulled free the sash of my robe. Deftly, as if he had done
such things many times, he pinned my arms behind me and bound my
wrists with the sash. Only then did he remove his weight so that I might
roll over and breathe.

As I struggled up to sit on the edge of the bed, he stood before me
with a long, wicked knife held comfortably in his right hand.

Pointing his blade at my throat, he gave me a grin of pure malice.
"You may scream if you wish," he said casually, "but I advise against it.
You can do nothing to save your life—or to prevent our success. But
if you scream, we may be forced to shed more blood than we intend.
Consider what you do clearly. It will be the innocent guards and servants
of the manor who will die in your name, and the outcome will not be
altered."

Feverishly, I tugged at my hands but could not free them. My life
seemed to stick in my throat, choking me. I had been so easily mastered.
And yet the simple shame of it—that I had been beguiled from my wits
by nothing more than a handsome face and a bold promise—made me
writhe for some escape, some means to strike back. As if I were uncowed,
I glared at him and said, "You have lied and lied to me. It has been your
purpose from the start to kill me. Why do you delay? What do you fear?"

He barked a short laugh without humor or pity. "I fear nothing. I
have risen above fear. I wait only to share your dying with my companion—the one who will rule the realm for me—and will in turn be ruled
by me."

Still straining at my bonds, I mustered sarcasm to my defense in the
place of courage. "You dream high, Wallin. Servants are usually too wise
for such ambition."

His smile was handsome and malign. "But I am no servant," he replied. His eyes glittered like bits of stone. "I am Kodar the rebel, and my dreams have always been high."

He astonished me—not in what he said (though it had surprised me entirely) but in that I believed him instantly. "Kodar?" I snapped, not doubting him, or what he would say, but seeking only to cover my dismay while he spoke. "Again you lie. It is known to half the realm that even now Kodar and his rebels prepare an assault upon Lodan."

He appeared to find a genuine pleasure in my belligerence. Softly, he stroked the side of my neck with his knife. "Of a certainty," he smugly. "It has required great cunning of me to ensure that every spy in the Three Kingdoms knows what my forces will do. But my end has been accomplished. While lesser men fight and die in my name, attracting all attention to themselves, my best aides and I have found employment here, disguised as servants. Unsuspected, we have placed ourselves in readiness for this night.

"My companion and I will slit your throat." The tip of his blade dug in until I winced. "Then we will summon the other monarchs to private audiences with you, and we will slit their throats." He made no attempt to hide his relish. "Then my men will fall upon the Mages and noblemen loyal to my enemies. Your Ryzel will not be spared. Before dawn, the rule of the realm will be ours. In truth, the rule will be mine, though my companion will assume that place." He considered himself clever in concealing the identity of his ally from me. "In that way," he said with a smirk, "my success will be as high as my dreams.

"Lest you misunderstand at all," he concluded, "let me assure you that I have never felt the slightest desire for you or your person. You are a savorless morsel at best, and I would not sully myself with you."

I heard him in silence. But if he thought that his insults would hurt me, he had misjudged his victim. His contempt only brought me back to clarity. To all appearances, my attention remained transfixed upon him; but within myself I was gone, seeking help and hope in places where he could not follow.

He looked at me narrowly. His excitement or his arrogance required the vindication of a response. "You would do well to speak," he said with velvet menace. "If you plead with me, perhaps I will spare you briefly."

I did not speak; I did not risk provoking him. I did not want to die. I wanted to learn who his confederate was.

A frown pinched the flesh between his brows. His desire to see me grovel was unmistakable. But before he could attempt to dismay me by other means, a faint knocking at the door interrupted him.

Nothing kindled in me at the sound. It was clearly a signal—a coded sequence of taps for Kodar's benefit, not mine. He cocked his head, at once gratified and vexed—gratified that his plans developed apace, vexed that he had no abject victim to show for his pains. Yet he did not hesitate; he had not come so far by giving spite precedence over ambition. Lithe and virile, he strode to the door and tapped a response.

When his question was answered, he unbolted the door and opened it, admitting Queen Damia to my chambers.

She appeared more radiant than ever. As Kodar sealed the door again, she flung her arms around his neck and kissed him as if she were insatiable for him. His ardor in return was everything a woman could have wished, yet she broke off their embrace before he was done with it. Her gaze turned to me, and her eyes were bright.

"Kodar, my love." She beamed. "You have done well. She considers herself defiant, but she will make an apt sacrifice nonetheless. I am pleased."

Watching her, I wondered if Kodar had noticed the subtle way in which she had already taken command of the room, reducing him from mastery to the status of one who obeyed.

But I did not understand why she had allied herself with him. For desire? Perhaps. It was conceivable in his case, but I did not think so. And if she had at her disposal the power of a Dragon—either Real or Mage-made—what need had she of him?

Kodar and his knife were several paces from me. I might be able to say a few words before I was silenced. Meeting her gaze alone as though I were capable of ignoring her companion, I said, "My lady of Lodan, this Kodar has advised me that I should not scream. But now that he has told me how he has betrayed his cause to serve you, and how he means to give you the rule of the Three Kingdoms by slaying all those who stand against you, I find I no longer comprehend why I should not. His plan will be foiled by any forewarning, however slight. With one cry, I will deprive you of all that he offers. Why then should I not—?"

Gripping his knife, Kodar started toward me. I snatched a breath, filled my lungs to call out with all my strength.

My threat meant nothing to him, yet Queen Damia stopped him. "Withhold a moment, Kodar." Her command was certain. "For the sake of blameless lives which would otherwise be lost, I will answer her."

This game was hers, and I was outplayed. But in the face of death I could do nothing but strive for life. My eyes held her as if Kodar had no significance between us, and I prayed that he had wit enough to understand her—and me.

"My lady," she said with demeaning courtesy, "you have not failed to reason that Mage Scour is not in truth able to create Magic. If he possessed that power, he would not suffer any other to rule him. Assuredly he would not suffer *me*." Her tone said plainly that Scour was a man and would gladly have suffered anything for her sake. "Therefore his Dragon was but an image. And therefore it follows that there is a Creature in the realm that has remained hidden from all eyes."

She smiled gloriously. "All eyes but mine."

Kodar grinned at her. I wanted to curse him for the arrogance which blinded him to the queen's cunning; but I kept my gaze upon her and waited for her to continue.

"Lacking Ascension, his power has been latent," she went on, "but fortunately Mage Scour and I discovered it."

Doubtless that had indeed been fortunate for her.

"My lady, he is the reason you will not scream. Kodar and I pursue this plan against you because it will cost little bloodshed—and will enable us to assume rule swiftly. But if we are foiled in that, we will simply call upon the rebels concealed in the manor. They will assist the Dragon to the Seat, and he will take what we desire by greater violence. So you see," she said as though contradiction were impossible, "we cannot be defeated. You will accept your death quietly in order to spare a great many lives in the Three Kingdoms."

Perhaps I was too slow-witted for her. Perhaps I should have worked out much earlier what she wished me to understand. But at last I knew. I might have cried out in my anguish, had I not been too desperate for such weakness; she pushed me to the limit of what my sore heart could endure. That such beauty had come to such evil! I had no recourse but to prove myself equal to it or die.

"My lady," I said slowly, "you speak as if even a Dragon will be glad to serve you when you claim the rule. That is clever—to put a smiling face upon the fact that you will be merely a figurehead through which the Creature commands. If indeed he will not cast you off when he has gained his ends. You seek to distract me from the truth.

"But Kodar lacks so much wit. He has already vaunted himself outrageously before me. Your Dragon will teach him the worth of his arrogance.

"Unless the Creature is Kodar himself."

He was facing me now. He seemed deaf to insult. His face was alight, not with umbrage, but with a savage glee. He felt in himself the power of the coming transformation and was exalted.

But Queen Damia stood behind him and to one side. With his gaze upon me, he had no view of her. He did not see her smile broadly in my direction.

I did not take up her hint. Instead, I turned my attention to Kodar. Having failed to make him think better of his trust for Lodan's queen, I encouraged him to see my grave regard as a new deference. "My lord," I said quietly, "I do not understand." If I could have pulled my hands free at that moment, I would not have done so. They would have been of no help to me. "Possessing such strength, why have you troubled to mime rebellion?" I had no doubt now that the *lesser men* whose lives he spent to further his plans were the sincere ones, the honest rebels who believed—however wrongly—that the realm would be better without rulers. "Why do you persist in subterfuge now? And why do you accept the hand of this treacherous queen in your dealings? Why do you not declare yourself openly and claim what is yours by right? You require nothing but the touch of true Stone."

At once, I saw that he would not refuse to answer me. Where his Magic estate was concerned, pride outweighed judgment.

While Damia watched him with a loveliness which might have signified either adoration or scorn, he replied, "A hidden threat is stronger than a declared power. When first I conceived my intent to rule the realm, my nature was unknown to me. Therefore rebellion was the only path open. And now it is clear that I will be stronger if none know how I betray those who serve me. My queen will assume the throne—and an unknown Dragon will roam the Three Kingdoms, wreaking her will and its own—and my rebels will continue to strike where I choose, thinking that they still serve me. Stark fear and incomprehension will unman all resistance. The realm will be unified as no Regal has ever been able to master it, and every man and woman will tremble at my feet!"

His vision of sovereignty seemed to entrance him. But Queen Damia had no use for his transports. "Kodar, my love," she interposed, "this is pleasant—but the time flees before us." She was marvelously unafraid of him. "If the guests are called to the Ascension before we have dispatched Thone and Thornden, our opportunity will be lost. We must be at work. Will you accept the sacrifice of this daughter of Regals?"

He glanced down at his knife and smiled. "Gladly."

The unmistakable look of bloodshed on his face, he started toward me.

I had no time left. I had been meditating to the depths of my mind on what I must do in order to live—what must happen to save me. There was but one hope, and it was as scant as ever. But if I did not act upon it, I was lost.

Summoning every resource of will and passion and heritage, I sent out a silent cry of desperation and protest. Then I ducked under the knife and flipped forward, away from the bed.

I was hampered without the use of my hands; but I contrived to roll my feet under me and spring erect. Whirling around, I faced Kodar.

He charged after me. The knife swung. The unsashed brocade of my robe caught the blade, deflecting his thrust as I danced aside. Though my sandals were paltry as weapons, I swung my foot with all my strength against his knee. He answered with a grunt of pain.

Trusting that small hurt to slow him, I dove past his reach. He slashed at me and missed. Another flip and roll returned me to the bed. Nearly staggering for balance because I could not use my hands, I leaped onto the bed. From that position above him, I would be able to ward off his knife with my feet for a moment or two.

"Kill her, you fool!" Queen Damia hissed furiously.

A loud crash resounded through the chamber as the wood around the doorbolt splintered.

Another heavy blow burst both bolt and latch. The doors sprang inward and shivered against the walls.

Mage Ryzel strode into the room.

His bald head was flushed with exertion; but there was nothing weak or weary in the stamp of his feet, the stretch of his thick chest. His Scepter attacked the air; threats glared from his eyes.

My relief and jubilation at seeing him were so great that I nearly sagged to my knees—into Kodar's reach.

When he saw the knife, Ryzel stopped. "Wallin?" he demanded. "What means this?"

For a moment, Kodar's attention jerked from side to side as if he were a cornered animal. Damia appeared frozen by surprise or indecision. The four of us remained motionless, gauging the ramifications of Kodar's blade. Now Kodar would gain nothing by shouting for his rebels—not while Ryzel might fell him before help came. But the Mage was alone. Though he held his Scepter, its power would be useless against a knife. And he was no longer young. Would he be a match for the tall, strong rebel?

Kodar decided that the Mage would not. Turning his back to me, he advanced warily toward Ryzel.

Queen Damia stopped him without discernible effort, "You are timely come, Mage," she said calmly, defying anyone to credit that any threat or interruption could unsettle her. "This man is not Wallin the servant. He is Kodar the rebel. He means to slay both me and the lady

Chrysalis. And when we are dead, he intends to treat King Thone and Count Thornden similarly. Then he will claim the rule—"

With a snarl, Kodar launched himself toward her, aiming his blade for the deep hollow of her décolletage.

He did not reach her. Though Ryzel was old, his hands were swift. One sure jab drove the end of his Scepter into the pit of Kodar's stomach. Kodar tumbled to the floor and groveled there, retching for breath.

"I thank you, good Mage," Queen Damia murmured as if she thought that she could sway Ryzel.

He did not waste a glance on her. When he was sure that Kodar would be unable to move for a few moments, he came to me and helped me down from the bed. Only the trembling of his hands as he undid my bonds betrayed his fear.

"My lady," he said grimly, "I felt power here. Therefore I came."

"That was Kodar," the queen answered. "He thinks himself a Creature." Her scorn for her confederate was evident. "Some small capacity for magery there is in him. But for the most part it remains stubbornly trivial."

I did not look at her; I did not wish her to see my reaction to this new demonstration of mendacity. Doubtless Scour had been clever in persuading Kodar to think himself a Dragon, so that his plans for rule would serve Damia's ends. Yet she betrayed him in his turn without compunction. I did not question that her purpose against me remained unaltered. My hands shook like Ryzel's as I took the sash from him and knotted it about my waist to close my robe.

From his place on the floor, Kodar gagged on gasps and curses.

"Mage," I said, controlling my voice as well as I was able, "Queen Damia and her servant have done with me. Will you escort them to the Ascension hall?"

He opened his mouth to protest, then shut it again. The look in my eyes silenced him. Though his jaws chewed questions and fears, he bowed to me, then turned his attention to the monarch of Lodan and Kodar the rebel.

When he had plucked Kodar's knife from the floor and concealed it somewhere in the sleeve of his cassock, he bunched one heavy fist in the back of Kodar's coat and heaved him upright. Supporting Kodar with that grip, he said to Queen Damia, "My lady, will you accompany me?"

"Gladly," she replied. Wrapping her hands around his arm, she turned her back on me without farewell and clung intimately to him as they left my chambers. Still she treated me as if I signified nothing—and him as if she meant to seduce him before they gained the end of the passage.

Then I heard him shout a summons to the guards; and I had no more concern for him. On his own terms, at least, he was a match for Damia.

I needed time—and had none. Time to recover my courage from the close touch of death, time to think and to understand. Time to prepare myself for the attacks which would be directed against me in the Ascension hall. But no time remained. If I did not go now, I would risk missing the moment of midnight. More than once, my father had stressed the importance of midnight on the eve of my twenty-first birthday, when the moon would be full above the realm and I would attempt the Seat.

I was not concerned for my apparel; the robe I wore would do well enough for the occasion. But I went to my glass and expended a few moments with my hair, pinning it this way and that in an effort to give my appearance more grace if not more comeliness—striving by such small vanities to cover the hollow place which Kodar had opened in my heart. With a trace of rouge, I concealed the mark of Thornden's hand by matching its color upon my other cheek. However, I could not remove the memory of Kodar's kiss from my mouth. Schooling myself to steadiness, I gave up the attempt.

Alone and afraid and resolute, I left my chambers and went to meet my fate.

The hall in which the Seat of the Regals stood upon its pediment was at the far side of the manor. When I reached it, all the guests and personages of the realm had gathered there before me. I heard their excitement and anticipation in the hum of voices which issued from the open doors. And at the sound I nearly failed of courage. To meet King Thone alone did not seem to me a great matter. To strive for my life in private against Count Thornden and Queen Damia and Kodar had been necessary, inescapable. To bear the loss of Mage Ryzel's allegiance was a burden I could not avoid. But to risk failure and humiliation publicly, to prove unworthy of my heritage before the assembled lords and nobility of the Three Kingdoms—ah, that was another question entirely. I did not know how I would endure the shame.

While I remained hesitating outside the hall, Ryzel appeared in the passage and came toward me.

I believed that he meant to hinder or challenge me. There was a grimness in his face which spoke of anger and accusation. Therefore I prepared to rebuff him despite my gratitude. My fragile hold upon myself was not a thing which I could submit to the consideration of his uncertain loyalty.

He did not speak at once, however. Taking my arm, he steered me a few paces from the door, so that we would be unheard as well as unseen. And he did not meet my gaze as he asked, "Chrysalis, are you sure of what you do?"

That question I could answer honestly. "No," I said. "I am sure only that I must make the attempt."

The effort of will which brought his eyes to mine was plain in his visage. "Then trust me," he breathed, not in demand, but in appeal. "I have become a cause of shame to myself. I will support you to the limit of my strength."

With one touch, he drove home the linchpin of my resolve. And with that touch, all my thoughts concerning him turned. A moment earlier, I had determined that I would reject him, though he had saved my life. Now I made promise to myself that I would not risk him.

"The matter is mine to hold or let drop, Mage," I said, speaking at once in kindness and severity. "Whatever the outcome, the realm will have need of you. Do not intervene here. Only do as I command you— and stand aside. That will suffice for me."

His gaze sharpened; he regarded me as if he were unsure of what I had become. Then he turned his head aside, so that I would not see how he took my words. "As you will, my lady," he said. His frown was black and lost—the ire of a man who had been denied restitution for his faults. But I said nothing to ease him. Only by refusing his service could I hope to save him if I failed.

Because of his pain, I left him and moved toward the door. Midnight was drawing near, and I did not mean to miss it. The coming day would give time aplenty for regret or forgiveness, either in life or in death. Therefore I nearly did not hear the words he uttered after me:

"I have spoken with King Thone."

Almost I stopped to demand an explanation. His soft statement sent implications hosting at my back, dire and imprecise. Did he seek to warn me? Had he given himself new cause for shame? What role did he intend for the lord of Canna in my last crisis?

But I had no time, and I feared that if I halted now I would never move again. I had come to the last of my questions—to the one upon which all others depended. Though my stride faltered and my head flicked a glance backward, I continued on my way.

Unattended and unannounced, I entered the great Ascension hall, where the high Seat of the Regals stood empty.

The place had a stark majesty which consorted ill with the festive apparel and conflicting dreams of the gathered guests. The hall itself was round and domed, its ceiling beribbed and supported by the most massive timbers of Lodan. The light came from many wide, flaming censers, where the perfumed oils of Canna burned over the wrought metals of Nabal. Some sophisticates thought such things barbarous, but I considered them fit accompaniment for the grandeur of Creatures. Around the walls stood the spectators of my crisis in their anticipation. The floor had been formed of large but irregular slabs of basalt polished to a fine sheen and then cunningly fitted like the pieces of a puzzle, their cracks sealed with a white grout like tracery. It was said that these white lines across the basalt had a pattern which could only be discerned from the Seat. Some averred that the pattern was the image of a Basilisk, the first Regal; others, that the lines depicted the Creature which would be the last of its line, the end of the rule of Magic in the realm. But Ryzel had scoffed at such claims. He asserted bluntly that the floor of the hall was neither more nor less than a map of the Three Kingdoms.

And from the center of that floor rose the Seat.

Upon a stepped base of white marble—itself nearly as tall as I was—stood the heavy and rude-timbered frame which held the Stone. This frame was not properly a chair, had neither arms nor back; it had been built so that it might be approached from any side. But the frame itself was of no importance. All that mattered was the dull Stone of the Seat—the Magic slate to which nothing could be touched which was not also Magic. Upon occasion in the past, Ryzel had shown me that the Stone made no actual contact with the frame which supported it, but instead floated slightly among the members of ordinary wood that composed the Seat.

Upon that Stone I must place my hands or die.

Fully human and fully Real.

I had already made the attempt once and failed.

Count Thornden stood with Brodwick and his adherents not far from the door by which I entered the hall—and Mage Ryzel behind me, though he did not presume to move at my side. The lord of Nabal had taken his place because it was across the hall from Queen Damia and her entourage, Kodar among them, his arms pinned at his sides by two guards. But Thornden took the opportunity of my nearness to speak.

"You lied to me, girl," he growled, making no effort to conceal his anger. "My scouts report Cashon riding wildly away into Canna, with no other thought but flight." He seemed not to care how widely he was overheard. With a mounting tightness in my throat, I observed that he and all his men were now armed.

"I have sent out my orders," he continued. "You are lost."

I understood him. The heat of his scowl was plainer than his words. He meant that his armies had begun to march on the manor. I should not have attempted to provoke him. But I knew now that he had spurned Ryzel's support; and that thought gave my heart a lift of audacity. Also I was angered—though not surprised—that he and his men had come armed to my Ascension. So I turned on him a gaze which would have withered a wiser man, and I said, "No, my lord. The loss is yours. Until now, I have striven to spare you from the cost of your own folly."

I held his glare until I saw that at last it occurred to him to fear me. Then I swept past him with all the dignity which my slight form and uncomely face could convey.

Moving directly to the base of the Seat, I set myself before the three rulers.

Instantly, the murmurs of tension and curiosity and speculation in the hall were stilled. Every gaze and glance came to me. I had become the center of the night. Obliquely, I noticed how few nobles had brought their wives and children to witness my Ascension.

With Count Thornden and Queen Damia standing opposite each other, I expected to see King Thone somewhere equally distant from them both. But he was not; his party was beside Thornden's, so close that the two were almost intermingled. Thone's stance was turned toward the lord of Nabal rather than toward me.

A sizable number of Canna's courtiers had also procured weapons for themselves.

At once, I seemed to fall dizzy as a whirl of inferences passed through my head. Count Thornden had already set his forces into motion. Therefore he no longer cared for Ryzel's support. Or Ryzel had informed him that my Ascension must fail. And the Mage had spoken to King Thone. Deprived of Cashon's power, had Thone now been persuaded to cast his lot with Thornden as the lesser evil, so that Queen Damia would not gain ascendancy? The prospect affected me as if it were a form of vertigo.

But I had come too far for retreat—and was too close to fury. The truth I would disentangle if I lived. If I died, lies would lose their significance. Therefore I faced the assembled doubt and hope and hunger of the Three Kingdoms as though I could not be moved. And when I spoke, I did not quaver in any way.

"People of the realm," I said clearly, "the passing of the Phoenix-Regal has left a time of trial upon us all. The future of the peace which the Regals have wrought has been uncertain—and uncertainty breeds fear as surely as fear breeds violence. It is tempting to look upon those who are our foes and believe them evil, avid for our destruction. Therefore they must be slain, before they slay us. And no reason can put an end to this bloodshed, for how can we dare to set aside our fear when our enemies fear us and remain violent? For that reason do we need Regals. A Regal is a Creature and has no need or fear of us—and so is not driven to violence. Rather, a Regal's power gives us peace, for it frees us from the fear of each other which compels us to war."

To one side, Count Thornden's men watched each other and him tensely. King Thone made a studious portrait of a fop immersed in the contemplation of his manicure. Queen Damia breathed deeply, but gave no other sign of her expectations. One ringed and immaculate hand rested on Mage Scour's shoulder. Kodar glared murderously at her, but she did not deign to notice it.

I was a plain woman, alone, and powerless; but my enemies had lost the capacity to make me afraid. "This night," I said as if I could hear the fanfare of trumpets which had never been sounded in my name, "I will put an end to uncertainty."

Thus I brought down upon my own head the crisis of my Ascension. Without hesitation or haste, I turned to the Seat and placed my feet upon the marble steps.

If I had spoken less clearly or appeared more frail, the rulers might have withheld their hands, awaiting the verdict of the Seat as both wisdom and caution urged them to do. But I had foiled each of them in turn, giving them cause to estimate me more highly. And I went to meet my Ascension as if there were no doubt of its outcome. In that way, I inspired them to risk themselves against me. If I succeeded, how could they believe that they would survive the punishment for their recent actions?

I knew that I was still some few moments early, that midnight had not quite come. But I had set my decision in motion at last. Better to hazard myself in advance of the time than to be made late by any delay or opposition.

Before I gained the second step toward the Seat, I heard Count Thornden's harsh command—and felt Wind begin to gather at my back.

Brodwick's image appeared to leap from nothingness to the force of a Banshee during the space between one heartbeat and another. And the hall erupted in a clangor of shouts and iron.

Involuntarily, I started to turn. A mistake: the mounting gale came upon me without my feet planted. Flame from all the censers gusted toward the timbers of the ceiling. I made a small pirouette like an autumn leaf in the air and fell to the basalt.

Somehow, I regained my feet—and lost them again. I stumbled heavily against the base of the Seat. The edge of the first step hit sharply across the center of my back. Wind pulled my robe away from my legs. I saw that both my knees were split and bleeding.

Then Brodwick's blast became so strong that I could hardly hold up my head. But I saw Kodar twist his arms from his surprised captors and break free. With a wrench, he sprang beyond them. His cry rose over the tumult:

"Kodar and freedom! To me, rebels!"

At once, all the doors burst open, letting a dozen men into the gale. They were dressed as servants; but they bore swords and pikes, and they fought the Wind toward Kodar's side.

He did not await them. With a single blow, he struck down one guard; he snatched a long dagger from the man's belt. Slashing that blade about him, he kept Damia's defenders back as he hurled himself toward the lady of Lodan.

Her hand on Scour's shoulder pushed the Mage away, out of Kodar's reach. So great was Scour's concentration that he simply pitched to the floor, unconscious of his own fall. Damia's smile did not waver as she met Kodar's assault.

One flick of her wrist and a gleam of metal stopped him. As his knees failed, the Wind seemed to take hold of him and lower him gently to the basalt, blood spurting from his cut throat.

In the air above them, Scour's Dragon appeared.

Leaping into existence, the image pounded its wings and struggled for size as though it were already hot upon the spoor of its prey. At first, it was too small to advance against the buffeting Wind which Brodwick hurled from across the hall. But Brodwick's force was focused on me, not upon the Creature, and Scour did not need his lady's blandishments to impel him. Surely he understood as all in the hall did that he could not afford to fail now, either to Thornden's Mage or to me. Lying as if he were as lifeless as Kodar, he put all his soul into his magery, and the Dragon let out a blast of flame which defied the Wind halfway to the spot where I cowered. The heat touched my sore cheek and was torn away. Laboring tremendously, the Dragon began to beat forward in the teeth of the gale.

I could not move. My limbs felt pinned and useless, as if my spine were broken. All Brodwick's exertion centered on me—and he was a master. I had known that this would happen—that my enemies would attack me here in all their fury—but I had not known that I would prove so weak. The simple effort to turn myself so that I might crawl up the steps surpassed my strength. The blood running from my knees appeared to carry my will away; the courage drained from me as from a cracked cistern. The Dragon was lovely and terrible; even the Wind seemed as beautiful as it was savage. I was no match for them. In all truth, I had no reason to move.

Mage Ryzel could have stilled both Wind and Dragon, but he did not. In the end, he betrayed me.

I had commanded him not to intervene.

And still I had not entirely understood that the iron clashing which punctuated the shouts and passion around me was the sound of swords.

Forcing my face into the Wind, away from the Dragon, I saw Count Thornden and his men fighting for their lives—and for Brodwick's protection—against the guards of the manor and King Thone's courtiers.

An awkward melee was in progress. Cudgeled by the gale, Thornden's men and Thone's and the rebels and guards hacked at each other in confusion. The lord of Nabal's party was large and heavily armed, but was hampered by the necessity of defending the Mage; it could not gain the advantage.

To my astonishment, I beheld King Thone deliberately block Count Thornden's path toward me. Thone's decorative blade could not withstand Thornden's huge sword; but the lord of Canna used his point so adeptly that Thornden was thwarted—prevented from charging forward to assail me personally.

I have spoken with King Thone.

Ryzel had not betrayed me. He had persuaded Thone to this defense—for what hope would remain to Canna now if Thornden was victorious. And the Mage had not stilled the rising magery because I had commanded him to withhold.

Perhaps after all I would be able to move. The life at issue was my own—but in the end it was not mine alone. It was also the life of the realm. While I remained in my weakness, blood was being shed; and that killing would give inevitable rise to the warfare which I abhorred as a matter of birthright. Surely I could at least move.

But when I had shifted myself so that my hands and cut knees were under me against the force of the Wind and the hammering approach of the Dragon, I understood that movement was not enough. If I held true, I might perhaps gain the top of the marble base—but beyond question I would be unable to stand erect in order to place my hands upon the Stone.

This state is not easily attained. It may be reached in one way, by the touch of Stone to one whose very blood and flesh are latent Magic. And I had already failed once.

I required help.

I demanded it as if it also were my birthright. In my extremity, I cried out through the battle and the blast and the roar:

"Ryzel! Your Scepter!"

Again, he obeyed. Without hesitation, the one true man in the Three Kingdoms flung his Scepter toward me.

The Wind bore it so that it sailed in a long arc to the base of the Seat. Bounding upon the steps, it struck like a whiplash against my side.

But I felt no pain; I was done with pain. Wildly, I slapped my arms around the Scepter and hugged it so that it would not slip away.

I had always failed in my efforts to grasp the rough-barked Wood. It was Real, not to be handled by ordinary flesh, yet it was simpler and less perilous than the Stone. The Stone could not be touched by anyone who was not Magic; but the Scepter required only the capacity for magery. Therefore Ryzel held a Scepter though he could not claim the Seat. And therefore I clung to the true Wood for my life.

Its nature transcended my own. Even with my arms about it, it seemed to ooze from me as if it were fluid rather than solid—a Scepter composed of a substance I could not comprehend. Brodwick's Wind cut across the hall, yowling like lost hope through my heart. And the Dragon—! Surely it was near to its full size now, its natural power and fury. All the air was fire and roaring. Those people who had not joined the melee either cowered against the walls or wrestled with the gale-kicked doors.

Yet I held the Scepter. Cupping one hand about its end, I kept it from slipping away. Then I began to crawl and squirm like a belabored mendicant up the steps.

The Wind was brutal to me, battering my head upon the marble, clogging my limbs, tearing my vision to shreds. In fear that I would lose my eyes, I kept my face turned from Thornden's Mage—turned toward the Creature beating like a holocaust against the blast to devour me. Its great jaws fountained flame in tremendous exhalations; heat slapped repeatedly at me, scorching my cheek, spreading black stains down the side of my robe. Only Brodwick's force as he strove to prove himself stronger than Scour preserved me from incineration.

But I did not fear the Dragon. It was a wonder in the world, and the sight of it gave me strength.

With that strength, my legs thrust me up the steps while my left arm crooked the Scepter and my right hand cupped its end.

Like water running impossibly upward, black char spread from step to step as the Dragon loomed over me, howling fire. The gale threatened to burst the ceiling of the hall from its timbers. Nails and pegs and weight could not hold; boards were stripped away into the outer dark. A new sound like a scream from many throats joined the turmoil. Only the Stone itself, immovable within its supports, kept the ordinary wood of the Seat from being swept away in kindling and splinters.

I had no time to gauge what I would do. The Creature inhaled, fearsome and savage; its next spewing of flame would roast me to the bone. A cry for my father wrung me, but I made no sound that I could hear as I took my last gamble.

Guiding the Scepter with my left arm, I thrust the Wood upward, forward—toward the Seat.

At midnight under the full moon on the eve of my twenty-first birthday, I touched the end of the Scepter to the Stone.

At once ponderous and instant, slow and swift, the shock of that contact began in my left elbow and right hand and spread through me, ripples of passion bringing flesh and muscle and bone to power. Ignited by this unprecedented connection of Stone and Wood and birthright, the blood which the Basilisk-Regal had shed came to life in me. All my weakness was swept away in wild glory. A roar came from me like a tantara—a challenge against every foe and traitor to the realm.

Bounding from the marble, I turned to my image with flame and claws and tore it from the air, heedless of Scour's screams. Then I flung myself toward Brodwick until his concentration melted to panic and he stretched himself groveling before me and his Wind was stilled.

Then I left the hall and went in bright joy and power out into the night.

Before dawn, when I had measured my wings and my fierce ecstasy across the deep sky—and almost as an afterthought had routed Thornden's armies among the hills—I returned to the manor and the hall and accepted the homage of the three rulers. Then I dismissed them, along with the rest of my guests. Servants bore away the injured for care, the dead for burial, but I did not leave the hall myself. Sitting upon the Seat in my human form, with my weight resting against the comfortable strength of the Stone, I spoke for some time alone with Mage Ryzel.

He was plainly astonished by what had transpired—and more than ever shamed by the things he had done in the name of his doubt. But he was a brave man and made no effort to excuse his mistakes—or to abase himself. Instead, he stood before me grasping his Scepter as he had formerly stood before the Phoenix-Regal, my father.

Gruffly, he said, "My lady, how is this done, that a woman of no great beauty gives a lesson of humbling to a man of no mean knowledge or strength, and the teaching provides him pleasure? You have become a source of pride to the realm."

I smiled upon him. My heart was at rest, and my gladness covered all the errors and betrayals of the night. If the three kings had known how little harm I intended toward them, their fear of me would have grown greater still. But to answer the Mage—and to exculpate him to himself— I attempted an explanation.

"The blood of the last Dragon had sunk deep into the flesh of the Regals. An extraordinary conjunction of powers was required to awaken it. Therefore when I was born, and my father saw that I had no Magic, he procured for you a limb of the Ash, so that it might aid the birth of something new in me—the restoration of the last Dragon to the world, and restitution for the ill deed which was forced upon the Basilisk-Regal."

"That much is evident," replied Ryzel. I was pleased that his manner toward me had changed so little. "But why did the Phoenix-Regal not tell me the purpose of my Scepter, so that I might aid you?"

"For two reasons." My father's dilemma now seemed plain to me. "First, he was uncertain that the blood I had inherited had grown strong enough to be awakened. If it had not, then the one true hope of the realm was that you would betray me." The Mage began to protest, but I gestured him silent. "The Phoenix-Regal trusted that you would cobble together some manner of alliance after my failure—and that you would find means to preserve my life. There was his hope. If I lived long enough to wed and have a child, the blood of the slain Dragon would grow stronger yet and might be awakened in my child where it had failed in me. This hope he provided by holding secret the purpose of the Scepter.

"Second, he did not wish the blood awakened, however strong it might be, if I did not merit it enough to discover it for myself and prove worthy. He desired a test for me. If I lacked the need and the will and the passion to find my own way, then I would be a poor Regal, and the realm would be better served by my failure or flight. He sought to instill me with hope," I mused. It was curious that I did not resent the ordeal my father had required of me. Rather, I relished what he had done—and was grateful. "But for the sake of the realm he could not allow me to rise untested to power."

Ryzel absorbed this and nodded. But after a moment's thought he said, "You surpass me, my lady. I do not yet understand. If you grasped the Phoenix-Regal's intent so clearly—no, I will not ask why you did not speak of it to me. But why did you command me to stand aside? Had you permitted me to counter Scour and Brodwick, your approach to the Seat would have been free."

There I laughed—not at his incomprehension, but at the idea that I had known what I was doing. I had learned that no path of hope existed for me but one; therefore it was hardly surprising that I had chosen that path. But I had not known what would happen. I had known only that I did not mean to fail. The things I knew now had come to me with the transformation of my blood, shedding light in many places where I had been ignorant.

That point, however, I left unexplained. Instead, I said, "No, Mage. Had you stilled Brodwick and Scour, our plight would have been unaltered. We would simply have had to strive against swords and pikes rather than against magery. Perhaps we would both have been slain. And also," I said, holding his gaze so that he would understand me, "I desired to spare your life. If I failed, the realm would have no other hope than you."

In response, he passed his hand over his eyes and bowed deeply. When he raised his head again, I thought he would say that he had not earned my concern for his life. But he pleased me by dismissing such questions. In his blunt way, he asked, "What will you do now, my lady? Some action must be taken to consolidate your hold upon the realm. And the treacheries of the three rulers merit retribution."

I wanted to laugh again for simple happiness; but I restrained myself. Calmly, I replied, "Mage, I believe I will commence a sizable conscription. I will claim all of Thornden's soldiery. I will demand every blackguard who serves Thone's machinations. And"—a grin of glee shaped my mouth—"I will call upon every eligible man within a day's ride of Damia's allure.

"These men I will set to work. Much hard labor requires to be done to unify the realm, so that it will be less an uneasy balance of kingdoms and more a secure nation."

Ryzel mulled what I was saying; but his eyes did not leave mine. Carefully, he asked, "What labor is that, my lady?"

I gave him my sweetest smile. "I am certain, Mage, that you will think of something."

After a moment, he smiled in return.

Outside the manor, dawn was breaking. When I had dismissed my Mage and counselor, I took on my other form and went out into the world to make the acquaintance of my fellow Creatures.

Mythological Beast

Norman was a perfectly safe, perfectly sane man. He lived with his wife and son, who were both perfectly safe, perfectly sane, in a world that was perfectly sane, perfectly safe. It had been that way all his life. So when he woke up that morning, he felt as perfect as always. He had no inkling at all of the things that had already started to happen to him.

As usual, he woke up when he heard the signal from the biomitter cybernetically attached to his wrist; and as usual, the first thing he did was to press the stud which activated the biomitter's LED readout. The display gleamed greenly for a moment on the small screen. As usual, it said, *You are OK,* There was nothing to be afraid of.

As usual, he had absolutely no idea what he would have done if it had said anything else.

His wife, Sally, was already up. Her signal came before his so that she would have time to use the bathroom and get breakfast started. That way there would be no unpleasant hurrying. He rolled out of bed promptly, and went to take his turn in the bathroom, so that he would not be late for work and his son, Enwell, would not be late for school.

Everything in the bathroom was the same as usual. Even though Sally had just used it, the vacuum-sink was spotless. And the toilet was as clean as new. He could not even detect his wife's warmth on the seat. Everything was perfectly safe, perfectly sane. His reflection in the mirror was the only thing that had changed.

The tight lump in the center of his forehead made no sense to him. He had never seen it before. Automatically, he checked his biomitter; but again it said, *You are OK*. That seemed true enough. He did not feel ill—and he was almost the only person he knew who knew what "ill" meant. The lump did not hurt in any way, but still he felt vaguely uneasy. He trusted the biomitter. It should have been able to tell him what was happening.

Carefully, he explored the lump. It was as hard as bone. In fact, it seemed to be part of his skull. It looked familiar; and he scanned back in his memory through some of the books he had read until he found what he wanted. His lump looked like the base of a horn, or perhaps the nub of a new antler. He had seen such things in books.

That made even less sense. His face wore an unusual frown as he finished in the bathroom. He returned to the bedroom to get dressed, and then went to the kitchen for breakfast.

Sally was just putting his food on the table—the same juice, cereal, and soyham that she always served him—a perfectly safe meal that would give him energy for the morning without letting him gain weight or become ill. He sat down to eat it as he always did. But when Sally sat down opposite him, he looked at her and said, "What's this thing on my forehead?"

His wife had a round bland face, and its lines had slowly become blurred over the years. She looked at his lump vaguely, but there was no recognition in her eyes. "Are you OK?" she said.

He touched the stud of his biomitter and showed her that he was OK.

Automatically, she checked her own biomitter and got the same answer. Then she looked at him again. This time, she, too, frowned. "It shouldn't be there," she said.

Enwell came into the kitchen, and Sally went to get his breakfast. Enwell was a growing boy. He watched the food come as if he were hungry, and then he began to eat quickly. He was eating too quickly, but Norman did not need to say anything. Enwell's biomitter gave a low hum and displayed in kind yellow letters, *Eat more slowly.* Enwell obeyed with a shrug.

Norman smiled at his son's obedience, then frowned again. He trusted his biomitter. It should be able to explain the lump on his forehead. Using the proper code, he tapped on the face of the display, *I need a doctor.* A doctor would know what was happening to him.

His biomitter replied, *You are OK.*

This did not surprise him. It was standard procedure—the biomitter was only doing its job by reassuring him. He tapped again, *I need a doctor.* This time, the green letters said promptly, *Excused from work. Go to Medical Building room 218.*

Enwell's biomitter signaled that it was time for him to go to school. "Got to go," he mumbled as he left the table. If he saw the lump on his father's forehead, he did not think enough about it to say anything. Soon he had left the house. As usual, he was on time.

Norman rubbed his lump. The hard boney nub made him feel uneasy again. He resisted an urge to recheck his biomitter. When he had finished his breakfast, he said goodbye to Sally as he always did when he was going to work. Then he went out to the garage and got into his mobile.

After he had strapped himself in, he punched the address of the Medical Building into the console. He knew where the Medical Building was, not because he had ever been there before (in fact, no one he knew had ever been there), but because it was within sight of the National Library, where he worked. Once the address was locked in, his mobile left the garage smoothly on its balloon tires (a perfectly safe design), and slid easily into the perfectly sane flow of the traffic.

All the houses on this street were identical for a long way in either direction; and as usual Norman paid no attention to them. He did not need to watch the traffic, since his mobile took care of things like that. His seat was perfectly comfortable. He just relaxed in his safety straps and tried not to feel concerned about his lump until his mobile deposited him on the curb outside the Medical Building.

This building was much taller and longer than the National Library; but apart from that, the two were very much alike. Both were empty except for the people who worked there; and the people worked there because they needed jobs, not because there was any work that needed to be done. And both were similarly laid out inside. Norman had no trouble finding his way.

Room 218 was in the Iatrogenics Wing. In the outer office was a desk with a computer terminal very much like the one Norman used at the Library; and at the desk sat a young woman with yellow hair and confused eyes. When Norman entered her office, she stared at him as if he were sick. Her stare made him touch his lump and frown. But she was not staring at his forehead. After a moment, she said, "It's been so long—I've forgotten what to do."

"Maybe I should tell you my name," he said.

"That sounds right," she said. She sounded relieved. "Yes, I think that's right. Tell me your name."

He told her. She looked around the terminal, then pushed a button to engage some kind of program.

"Now what?" he said.

"I don't know," she said. She did not seem to like being so confused.

Norman did not know, either. But almost at once the door to the inner office opened. The woman shrugged, so Norman just walked through the doorway.

The inner office had been designed to be cozy; but something had gone wrong with its atmospherics, and now it was deep in dust. When Norman sat down in the only chair, he raised the dust, which made him cough.

"I'm Doctor Brett," a voice said. "You seem to have a cough."

The voice came from a console that faced the chair. Apparently, Doctor Brett was a computer who looked just like the Director of the

National Library. Norman relaxed automatically. He naturally trusted a computer like that. "No," he said. "It's the dust."

"Ah, the dust," the computer said. "I'll make a note to have it removed." His voice sounded wise and old and very rusty. After a moment, he went on, "There must be something wrong with my scanners. You look healthy to me."

Norman said, "My biomitter says I'm OK."

"Well, then my scanners must be right. You're in perfect health. Why did you come?"

"I have a lump on my forehead."

"A lump?" Doctor Brett hummed. "It looks healthy to me. Are you sure it isn't natural?"

"Yes." For an instant, Norman felt unnaturally irritated. He touched the lump with his fingers. It was as hard as bone—no, harder, as hard as steel, magnacite. It was as hard as tung-diamonds. He began to wonder why he had bothered to come here.

"Of course, of course," the doctor said. "I've checked your records. You weren't born with it. What do you think it is?"

The question surprised Norman. "How should I know? I thought you were going to tell me."

"Of course," said the computer. "You can trust me. I'll tell you everything that's good for you. That's what I'm here for. You know that. The Director of the National Library speaks very highly of you. It's in your records."

The machine's voice made Norman's irritation evaporate. He trusted his biomitter. He trusted Doctor Brett. He settled himself in the chair to hear what his lump was. But even that amount of movement raised the dust. He sneezed twice.

Doctor Brett said, "You seem to have a cold."

"No," Norman said. "It's the dust."

"Ah, the dust," Doctor Brett said. "Thank you for coming."

"'Thank you for—'?" Norman was surprised. All at once, he felt very uneasy. He felt that he had to be careful. "Aren't you going to tell me what it is?"

"There's nothing to worry about," the doctor said. "You're perfectly healthy. It will go away in a couple of days. Thank you for coming."

The door was open. Norman stared at the computer. The Director did not act like this. He was confused, but he did not ask any more questions. Instead, he was careful. He said, "Thank you, Doctor," and walked out of the office. The door closed behind him.

The woman was still sitting at the outer desk. When she saw Norman, she beckoned to him. "Maybe you can help me," she said.

"Yes?" he said.

"I remember what I'm supposed to do now," she said. "After you see the Doctor, I'm supposed to get his instructions"—she tapped the console—"and make sure you understand them. But nobody's ever come here before. And when I got this job, I didn't tell them"—she looked away from Norman—"that I don't know how to read."

Norman knew what she meant. Of course, she could read her bio-mitter—everybody could do that. But except for that, reading was not taught anymore. Enwell certainly was not learning how to read in school. Reading was not needed anymore. Except for the people at the National Library, Norman was the only person he knew who could actually read. That was why no one ever came to use the Library.

But now he was being careful. He smiled to reassure the woman and walked around the desk to look at her console. She tapped the display to activate the readout.

At once, vivid red letters sprang across the screen. They said:

> SECRET CONFIDENTIAL PRIVATE PERSONAL SECRET UNDER NO CIRCUMSTANCES REPEAT UNDER NO CIRCUMSTANCES SHOW THIS DIAGNOSIS TO PATIENT OR REVEAL ITS CONTENTS......................................

Then there was a series of numbers that Norman did not understand. Then the letters said:

> ABSOLUTE PRIORITY TRANSMIT AT ONCE TO GENERAL HOSPITAL EMERGENCY DIVISION REPEAT EMERGENCY DIVISION ABSOLUTE PRIORITY...............

"Transmit," the woman said. "That means I'm supposed to send this to the Hospital." Her hand moved toward the buttons that would send the message.

Norman caught her wrist. "No," he said. "That isn't what it means. It means something else."

The woman said, "Oh."

The bright red letters said:

> DIAGNOSIS...
> PATIENT SUFFERING FROM MASSIVE GENETIC BREAKDOWN OF INDETERMINATE ORIGIN COMPLETE REPEAT COMPLETE STRUCTURAL

TRANSITION IN PROGRESS TRANSMUTATION
IRREVERSIBLE..
PROGNOSIS...
PATIENT WILL BECOME DANGEROUS HIMSELF AND
WILL CAUSE FEAR IN OTHERS REPEAT WILL CAUSE
FEAR...
TREATMENT..
STUDY RECOMMENDED BUT DESTRUCTION
IMPERATIVE REPEAT IMPERATIVE REPEAT
IMPERATIVE EFFECT SOONEST................................

"What did it say?" the woman said.

For a moment, Norman did not answer. His lump was as hard as a magnacite nail driven into his skull. Then he said, "It said I should get some rest. It said I've been working too hard. It said I should go to the Hospital if I don't feel better tomorrow." Before the woman could stop him, he pressed the buttons that erased the terminal's memory. The terminal was just like the one he used in the National Library, and he knew what to do. After erasing, he programmed the terminal to cancel everything that had happened today. Then he fed in a cancel program to wipe out everything in the terminal. He did not know what good that would do, but he did it anyway.

He expected the woman to try to stop him, but she did not. She had no idea what he was doing.

He was sweating, and his pulse was too fast. He was so uneasy that his stomach hurt. That had never happened to him before. He left the office without saying anything to the woman. His knees were trembling. As he walked down the corridor of the Iatrogenics Wing, his biomitter was saying in blue reassuring letters, *You will be OK. You will be OK.*

▲▼▲

Apparently, his erasures were successful. In the next few days, nothing happened to him as a result of Doctor Brett's report. By the time he had returned home from the Medical Building, his readout had regained its placid green, *You are OK.*

He did this deliberately. He did not feel OK. He felt uneasy, but he did not want his biomitter to send him to the General Hospital. So while his mobile drove him home he made an effort to seem OK. The touch of his lump gave him a strange reassurance, and after a while his pulse, blood pressure, respiration, and reflexes had become as steady as usual.

And at home everything seemed perfectly sane, perfectly safe. He woke up every morning at the signal of his biomitter, went to work at the signal of his biomitter, ate lunch at the signal of his biomitter. This was reassuring. It reassured him that his biomitter took such good care of him. Without it, he might have worked all day without lunch, reading, sorting the mountain of discarded books in the storeroom, feeding them into the Reference Computer. At times like that, his uneasiness went away. He went home again at the end of the day at the signal of his biomitter.

But at home his uneasiness returned. Something was happening inside him. Every morning, he saw in the mirror that his lump was growing. It was clearly a horn now—a pointed shaft as white as bone. It was full of strength. When it was more than four inches long, he tested it on the mirror. The mirror was made of glasteel so that it could never shatter and hurt anybody; but he scratched it easily with the tip of his horn. Scratching it took no effort at all.

And that was not the only change. The soles of his feet were growing harder, and his feet seemed to be getting shorter. They were starting to look like hooves.

Tufts of pure white hair as clean as the sky were sprouting from the backs of his calves and the back of his neck. Something that might have been a tail grew out of the small of his back.

But these things were not what made him uneasy. He was not uneasy because he was thinking that someone from the Hospital might come to destroy him. He was not thinking that at all. He was being careful; he did not let himself think anything that might make his biomitter call for help. No, he was uneasy because he could not understand what Sally and Enwell were doing about what was happening to him.

They were not doing anything. They were ignoring the changes in him as if he looked just the same as always.

To them everything was perfectly sane, perfectly safe.

First this made him uneasy. Then it made him angry. Something important was happening to him, and they did not even see it. Finally at breakfast one morning he became too irritated to be careful. Enwell's biomitter signaled that it was time for him to go to school. He mumbled, "Got to go," and left the table. Soon he had left the house. Norman watched his son go. Then he said to Sally, "Who taught him to do that?"

She did not look up from her soyham. "Do what?" she said.

"Go to school," he said. "Obey his biomitter. We never taught him to do that."

Sally's mouth was full. She waited until she swallowed. Then she said, "Everybody does it."

The way she said it made his muscles tighten. A line of sweat ran down his back. For an instant, he wanted to hit the table with his hand—hit it with the hard flat place on the palm of his hand. He felt sure he could break the table.

Then his biomitter signaled to him. Automatically, he left the table. He knew what to do; he always knew what to do when his biomitter signaled. He went out to the garage and got into his mobile. He strapped himself into the seat. He did not notice what he was doing until he saw that his hands had punched in the address of the General Hospital.

At once, he canceled the address, unstrapped himself and got out of the mobile. His heart was beating too fast. His biomitter was saying without being asked, *Go to the Hospital. You will be OK.* The letters were yellow.

His hands trembled but he tapped onto the display, *I am OK.* Then he went back into the house.

Sally was cleaning the kitchen, as she always did after breakfast. She did not look at him.

"Sally," he said. "I want to talk to you. Something's happening to me."

"It's time to clean the kitchen," she said. "I heard the signal."

"Clean the kitchen later," he said. "I want to talk to you. Something's happening to me."

"I heard the signal," she said. "It's time to clean the kitchen now."

"Look at me," he said.

She did not look at him. Her hands were busy wiping scraps of soyham into the vacuum-sink, where they were sucked away.

"Look at me," he said. He took hold of her shoulders with his hands and made her face him. It was easy. He was strong. "Look at my forehead."

She did not look at him. Her face screwed up into tight knots and ridges. It turned red. Then she began to cry. She wailed and wailed, and her legs did not hold her up. When he let her go, she sank to the floor and folded up into a ball and wailed. Her biomitter said to her in blue, *You will be OK. You will be OK.* But she did not see it. She cried as if she were terrified.

Norman felt sick in his stomach, but his carefulness had come back. He left his wife and went back to the garage. He got into his mobile and punched in an address only ten houses away down the road. His mobile left the garage smoothly and eased itself into the perfectly sane flow of the traffic. When it parked at the address he had given it, he did not get out. He sat in his seat and watched his house.

Before long, an ambulance rolled up to it. Men in white coats went in. They came out carrying Sally in a stretcher. They loaded her carefully into the ambulance and drove away.

Because he did not know what else to do, he punched the address of the National Library into the console of his mobile and went to work. The careful part of him knew that he did not have much time. He knew (everyone knew) that his biomitter was his friend. But now he also knew that it would not be long before his biomitter betrayed him. The rebellion in his genes was becoming too strong. It could not stay secret much longer. And he still did not know what was happening to him. He wanted to use the time to find out, if he could. The Library was the best place for him to go.

But when he reached his desk with its computer console like the one in Doctor Brett's outer office, he did not know what to do. He had never done any research before. He did not know anyone who had ever done any research. His job was to sort books, to feed them into the Reference Computer. He did not even know what he was looking for.

Then he had an idea: he keyed his terminal into the Reference Computer and programmed it for autoscan. Then he tapped in his question, using the "personal information" code which was supposed to keep his question and answer from tieing up the general circuits of the Library and bothering the Director. He asked:

I HAVE HOOVES, A TAIL, WHITE HAIR, AND A HORN IN THE MIDDLE OF MY FOREHEAD. WHAT AM I?

After a short pause, the display ran numbers which told Norman his answer was coming from the 1976 *Encyclopedia Americana,* That Encyclopedia was a century out of date, but it was the most recent one in the Library. Apparently, people had not bothered to make Encyclopedias for a long time.

Then the display said:

ANSWER.......UNICORN...
DATA FOLLOWS...

His uneasiness suddenly became sharper. There was a sour taste in his mouth as he scanned the readout.

THE UNICORN IS A MYTHOLOGICAL BEAST USUALLY
DEPICTED AS A LARGE HORSE WITH A SINGLE HORN
ON ITS FOREHEAD..

Sweat ran into his eyes. He missed a few lines while he blinked to clear his sight.

> IT REPRESENTED CHASTITY AND PURITY THOUGH
> IT WOULD FIGHT SAVAGELY WHEN CORNERED IT
> COULD BE TAMED BY A VIRGIN'S TOUCH IN SOME
> INTERPRETATIONS THE UNICORN IS ASSOCIATED
> WITH THE VIRGIN MARY IN OTHERS IT REPRESENTS
> CHRIST THE REDEEMER..

Then to his surprise the display showed him a picture of a unicorn. It was prancing high on its strong clean legs, its coat was as pure as the stars, and its eyes shone. Its mane flew like the wind. Its long white horn was as strong as the sun. At the sight, all his uneasiness turned into joy. The unicorn was beautiful. It was beautiful. He was going to be beautiful. For a long time, he made the display hold that picture, and he stared at it and stared at it.

But after his joy receded a little, and the display went blank, he began to think. He felt that he was thinking for the first time in his life. His thoughts were clear and necessary and quick.

He understood that he was in danger. He was in danger from his biomitter. It was a hazard to him. It was only a small thing, a metasensor that monitored his body for signs of illness; but it was linked to the huge computers of the General Hospital, and when his metabolism passed beyond the parameters of safety, sanity, his biomitter would summon the men in white coats. For the first time in his life, he felt curious about it. He felt that he needed to know more about it.

Without hesitation, he tapped his question into the Reference Computer, using his personal information code. He asked:

ORIGIN AND FUNCTION OF BIOMITTER?

The display ran numbers promptly, and began a readout.

> WORLDWIDE VIOLENCE CRIME WAR INSANITY OF
> 20TH CENTURY SHOWED HUMANS CAPABLE OF
> SELF-EXTERMINATION OPERATIVE CAUSE WAS FEAR
> REPEAT FEAR RESEARCH DEMONSTRATED HUMANS
> WITHOUT FEAR NONVIOLENT SANE.......................
> POLICE EDUCATION PEACE TREATIES INADEQUATE
> TO CONTROL FEAR OF INDIVIDUAL HUMANS BUT
> SANE INDIVIDUAL HUMANS NOT PRONE TO VIOLENCE
> WAR TREATIES POLICE WEAPONS UNNECESSARY IF
> INDIVIDUAL IS NOT AFRAID...................................
> TREATMENT...
> BIOMITTER MEDICOMPUTER NETWORK INITIATED

FOR ALL INDIVIDUALS MONITOR PHYSIOLOGICAL
SIGNS OF EMOTION STRESS ILLNESS CONDITIONED
RESPONSES INBRED TO CONTROL BEHAVIOR
FEAR***CROSS REFERENCE PAVLOV BEHAVIOR
MODIFICATION SUB CONSCIOUS HYPNOTISM.........
SUCCESS OF BIOMITTER PROGRAM DEMONSTRATES
FEAR DOES NOT EXIST WHERE CONTROL ORDER

Abruptly, the green letters flashed off the display, and the terminal
began to readout a line of red.

DATA CANCEL REPEAT CANCEL...............................
MATERIAL CLASSIFICATION RESTRICTED NOT
AVAILABLE WITHOUT APPROVAL DIRECTOR
NATIONAL LIBRARY FILE APPROVAL CODE BEFORE
REACTIVATING REFERENCE PROGRAM....................

Norman frowned around his horn. He was not sure what had happened. Perhaps he had accidentally stumbled upon information that
was always restricted and had automatically triggered the Reference
Computer's cancellation program. Or perhaps the Director had just now
succeeded in breaking his personal information code and had found out
what he was doing. If the interruption had been automatic, he was still
safe. But if the Director had been monitoring him personally, he did not
have much time. He needed to know.

He left his desk and went to the Director's office. The Director
looked very much like Doctor Brett. Norman believed that he could
break the Director with one kick of his hard foot. He knew what to do.
He said, "Director."

"Yes, Norman?" the Director said. His voice was warm and wise, like
Doctor Brett's. Norman did not trust him. "Are you OK? Do you want to
go home?"

"I am OK," Norman said. "I want to take out some books."

"Take out some books'?" the Director said. "What do you mean?"

"I want to withdraw some books. I want to take them home with me."

"Very well," the Director said. "Take them with you. Take the rest of
the day off. You need some rest."

"Thank you," Norman said. He was being careful. Now he had what
he wanted. He knew that the Director had been watching him, knew that
the Director had deliberately broken his personal information code. He
knew that the Director had transmitted his information to the General

Hospital and had been told that he, Norman, was dangerous. No one was allowed to take books out of the National Library. It was forbidden to withdraw books. Always. Even the Director could not override that rule, unless he had been given emergency programming.

Norman was no longer safe, but he did not hurry. He did not want the General Hospital to think that he was afraid. The men in white coats would chase him more quickly if they thought he was afraid of them. He walked calmly, as if he were perfectly safe, perfectly sane, to the stacks where the books were kept after they had been sorted and fed into the Reference Computer.

He did not try to be thorough or complete. His time was short. He took only the books he could carry, only the books he was sure he wanted. He took *The Mask, The Unicorn, and the Messiah;* the *Index to Fairy Tales, Myths, and Legends; Barbarous Knowledge;* the *Larousse Encyclopedia of Mythology; The Masks of God;* and *The Book of Imaginary Beings.* He would need these books when his transformation was complete. They would tell him what to do.

He did not try to find any others. He left the National Library, hugging the books to his broad chest like treasure.

▲▼▲

The careful part of him expected to have trouble with his mobile; but he did not. It took him home exactly as it always did.

When he entered his house, he found that Sally had not been brought back. Enwell had not come home. He did not think that he would ever see them again. He was alone.

He took off his clothes because he knew that unicorns did not wear clothes. Then he sat down in the living room and started to read his books.

They did not make sense to him. He knew most of the words, but he could not seem to understand what they were saying. At first he was disappointed in himself. He was afraid that he might not make a very good unicorn. But then he realized the truth. The books did not make sense to him because he was not ready for them. His transformation was not complete yet. When it was, he would be able to understand the books. He bobbed his horn joyfully. Then, because he was careful, he spent the rest of the day memorizing as much as he could of the first book, *The Book of Imaginary Beings.* He wanted to protect himself in case his books were lost or damaged.

He was still memorizing after dark, and he was not tired. His horn filled him with strength. But then he began to hear a humming noise in the air. It was soft and soothing, and he could not tell how long it had been going on. It was coming from his biomitter. It found a place deep inside him that obeyed it. He lay down on the couch and went to sleep.

But it was not the kind of sleep he was used to. It was not calm and safe. Something in him resisted it, resisted the reassuring hum. His dreams were wild. His emotions were strong, and one of them was uneasiness. His uneasiness was so strong that it must have been fear. It made him open his eyes.

All the lights were on in the living room, and there were four men in white coats around him. Each of them carried a hypogun. All the hypoguns were pointed at him.

"Don't be afraid," one of the men said. "We won't hurt you. You're going to be all right. Everything is going to be OK."

Norman did not believe him. He saw that the men were gripping their hypoguns tightly. He saw that the men were afraid. They were afraid of him.

He flipped off the couch and jumped. His legs were immensely strong. His jump carried him over the heads of the men. As he passed, he kicked one of the men. Blood appeared on the man's forehead and spattered his coat, and he fell down and did not move.

The nearest man fired his hypogun. But Norman blocked the penetrating spray with the hard flat heel of his palm. His fingers curled into a hoof, and he hit the man in the chest. The man fell down.

The other two men were trying to run away. They were afraid of him. As they were running toward the door, Norman jumped after them and poked the nearest one with his horn. The man seemed to fly away from the horn. He crashed into the other man, and they both crashed against the door and fell down and did not move again. One of them had blood all over his back.

Norman's biomitter was blaring red: *You are ill. You are ill.*

The man Norman had punched was still alive, gasping for breath. His face was white with death, but he was able to tap a message into his biomitter. Norman could read his fingers: he was saying, *Seal the house. Keep him trapped. Bring nerve gas.*

Norman went to the man. "Why?" he said. "Why are you trying to kill me?"

The man looked at Norman. He was too close to dying to be afraid anymore. "You're dangerous," he said. He was panting, and blood came out of his mouth. "You're deadly."

"Why?" Norman said. "What's happening to me?"

"Transmutation," the man said. "Atavism. Psychic throwback. You're becoming something. Something that never existed."

"'Never existed'?" Norman said.

"You must've been buried," the man said. "In the subconscious. All this time. You never existed. People made you up. A long time ago. They believed in you. Because they needed to. Because they were afraid."

More blood came out of his mouth. "How could it happen?" he said. His voice was very weak. "We put fear to sleep. There is no more fear. No more violence. How could it happen?" Then he stopped breathing. But his eyes stayed open, staring at the things he did not understand.

Norman felt a deep sorrow. He did not like killing. A unicorn was not a killing beast. But he had had no choice: he had been cornered.

His biomitter was shouting, *You are ill.*

He did not intend to be cornered again. He raised his wrist and touched his biomitter with the tip of his horn. Pieces of metal were torn away, and bright blood ran down his arm.

After that, he did not delay. He took a slipcover from the couch and used it as a sack to carry his books. Then he went to the door and tried to leave his house.

The door did not open. It was locked with heavy steel bolts that he had never seen before. They must have been built into the house. Apparently, the men in white coats, or the medicomputers, were prepared for everything.

They were not prepared for a unicorn. He attacked the door with his horn. His horn was as hard as steel, as hard as magnacite. It was as hard as tung-diamonds. The door burst open, and he went out into the night.

Then he saw more ambulances coming down the road. Ambulances were converging on his house from both directions. He did not know where to run. So he galloped across the street and burst in the door of the house opposite his. The house belonged to his friend, Barto. He went to his friend for help.

But when Barto and his wife and his two daughters saw Norman, their faces filled with fear. The daughters began to wail like sirens. Barto and his wife fell to the floor and folded up into balls.

Norman broke down the back door and ran out into the service lane between the rows of houses.

He traveled the lane for miles. After the sorrow at his friend's fear came a great joy at his strength and swiftness. He was stronger than the men in white coats, faster than ambulances. And he had nothing else to be wary of. The medicomputers could not chase him themselves. With his biomitter gone, they could not even tell where he was. And they had no weapons with which to fight him except men in white coats and ambulances. He was free and strong and exhilarated for the first time in his life.

When daylight came, he climbed up onto the roofs of the houses. He felt safe there, and when he was ready to rest he slept there alone, facing the sky.

He spent days like that—traveling the city, reading his books and committing them to memory—waiting for his transformation to be complete. When he needed food, he raided grocery stores to get it, though the terror of the people he met filled him with sorrow. Gradually his food-need changed, so he did not go to the grocery stores anymore. He pranced in the parks at night and cropped the grass and the flowers and ran nickering among the trees.

And his transformation continued. His mane and tail grew thick and exuberant. His face lengthened, and his teeth became stronger.

His feet became hooves, and the horny part of his hands grew. White hair the color of moonlight spread across his body and limbs, formed flaring tufts at the backs of his ankles and wrists. His horn grew long and clean and perfectly pointed.

His joints changed also and began to flex in new ways. For a time, this gave him some pain; but soon it became natural to him. He was turning into a unicorn. He was becoming beautiful. At times, there did not seem to be enough room in his heart for the joy the change gave him.

Yet he did not leave the city. He did not leave the people who were afraid of him, though their fear gave him pangs of a loneliness he had never felt before. He was waiting for something. There was something in him that was not complete.

At first, he believed that he was simply waiting for the end of his transformation. But gradually he came to understand that his waiting was a kind of search. He was alone—and unicorns were not meant to be alone, not like this. He was searching the city to see if he could find other people like him, people who were changing.

At last one night he came in sight of the huge high structure of the General Hospital. He had been brought there by his search. If there were other people like him, they might have been captured by the men in white coats. They might be prisoners in the Emergency Division of the Hospital. They might be lying helpless while the medicomputers studied them, plotting their destruction.

His nostrils flared angrily at the thought. He stamped his foreleg. He knew what he had to do. He put his sack of books in a place of safety.

Then he lowered his head and charged down the road to attack the General Hospital.

He broke down the front doors with his horn and pounded into the corridors. People fled from him in terror. Men and women grabbed hypoguns and tried to fire at him; but he flicked them with the power of his horn, and they fell down. He rampaged on in search of the Emergency Division.

The General Hospital was designed just like the Medical Building and the National Library. He was able to find his way without trouble. Soon he was among the many rooms of the Emergency Division. He kicked open the doors, checked the rooms, checked room after room. They were full of patients. The Emergency Division was a busy place. He had not expected to find that so many people were ill and dangerous. But none of them were what he was looking for. They were not being transformed. They were dying from physical or mental sickness. If any people like him had been brought here, they had already been destroyed.

Red rage filled his heart. He charged on through the halls.

Then suddenly he came to the great room where the medicomputers lived. Rank on rank, they stood before him. Their displays glared evilly at him, and their voices shouted. He heard several of them shout together, "Absolute emergency! Atmospheric control, activate all nerve gas! Saturation gassing, all floors!"

They were trying to kill him. They were going to kill everybody in the Hospital.

The medicomputers were made of magnacite and plasmium. Their circuits were fireproof. But they were not proof against the power of his horn. When he attacked them, they began to burn in white fire, as incandescent as the sun.

He could hear gas hissing into the air. He took a deep breath and ran.

The gas was hissing into all the corridors of the Hospital. Patients began to die. Men and women in white coats began to die. Norman began to think that he would not be able to get out of the Hospital before he had to breathe.

A moment later, the fire in the medicomputers ignited the gas. The gas burned. Oxygen tanks began to explode. Dispensaries went up in flames. The fire extinguishers could not stop the intense heat of burning magnacite and plasmium. When the cylinders of nerve gas burst, they had enough force to shatter the floors and walls.

Norman flashed through the doors and galloped into the road leaving the General Hospital raging behind him like a furnace.

He breathed the night air deep into his chest and skittered to a stop on the far side of the road to shake the sparks out of his mane. Then he turned to watch the Hospital burn.

At first he was alone in the road. The people who lived nearby did not come to watch the blaze. They were afraid of it. They did not try to help the people who escaped the flames.

But then he saw a young girl come out from between the houses. She went into the road to look at the fire.

Norman pranced over to her. He reared in front of her.

She did not run away.

She had a lump on her forehead like the base of a horn or the nub of a new antler. There was a smile on her lips, as if she were looking at something beautiful.

And there was no fear in her eyes at all.

Animal Lover

— 1 —

I was standing in front of Elizabeth's cage when the hum behind my right ear told me Inspector Morganstark wanted to see me. I was a little surprised, but I didn't show it. I was trained not to show it. I tongued one of the small switches set against my back teeth and said, "I copy. Be there in half an hour." I had to talk out loud if I wanted the receivers and tape decks back at the Bureau to hear me. The transceiver implanted in my mastoid process wasn't sensitive enough to pick up my voice if I whispered (or else the monitors would've spent a hell of a lot of time just listening to me breathe and swallow). But I was the only one in the area, so I didn't have to worry about being overheard.

After I acknowledged the Inspector's call, I stayed in front of Elizabeth's cage for a few more minutes. It wasn't that I had any objection to being called in, even though this was supposed to be my day off. And it certainly wasn't that I was having a particularly good time where I was. I don't like zoos. Not that this wasn't a nice place—for people, anyway. There were clean walks and drinking fountains, and plenty of signs describing the animals. But for the animals...

Well, take Elizabeth, for example. When I brought her in a couple months ago, she was the prettiest cougar I'd ever seen. She had those intense eyes only real hunters have, a delicate face, and her whiskers were absolutely magnificent. But now her eyes were dull, didn't seem to focus on anything. Her pacing was spongy instead of tight; sometimes she even scraped her toes because she didn't lift her feet high enough. And her whiskers had been trimmed short by zoo keepers—probably because some great cats in zoos keep trying to push their faces between the bars, and some bastards who go to zoos like to pull whiskers, just to show how brave they are. In that cage, Elizabeth was just another shabby animal going to waste.

That raises the questions of why I put her there in the first place. Well, what else could I do? Leave her to starve when she was a cub?

Turn her over to the breeders after I found her, so she could grow up and go through the same thing that killed her mother? Raise her in my apartment until she got so big and feisty she might tear my throat out? Let her go somewhere—with her not knowing how to hunt for food, and the people in the area likely to go after her with demolition grenades?

No, the zoo was the only choice I had. I didn't like it much.

Back when I was a kid, I used to say that someday I was going to be rich enough to build a real zoo. The kind of zoo they had thirty or forty years ago, where the animals lived in what they called a "natural habitat." But by now I know I'm not going to be rich. And all those good old zoos are gone. They were turned into hunting preserves when the demand for "sport" got high enough. These days, the only animals that find their ways into zoos at all are the ones that are too broken to be hunters—or the ones that are just naturally harmless. With exceptions like Elizabeth every once in a while.

I suppose the reason I didn't leave right away was the same reason I visited Elizabeth in the first place—and Emily and John, too. I was hoping she'd give some sign that she recognized me. Fat chance. She was a cougar—she wasn't sentimental enough to be grateful. Anyway, zoos aren't exactly conducive to sentimentality in animals of prey. Even Emily, the coyote, had finally forgotten me. (And John, the bald eagle, was too stupid for sentiment. He looked like he'd already forgotten everything he'd ever known.) No, I was the only sentimental one of the bunch. It made me late getting to the Bureau.

But I wasn't thinking about that when I arrived. I was thinking about my work. A trip to the zoo always makes me notice certain things about the duty room where all the Special Agents and Inspectors in our Division have their desks. Here we were in the year 2011—men had walked on Mars, microwave stations were being built to transmit solar power, marijuana and car racing were so important they were subsidized by the government—but the rooms where men and women like me did their paperwork still looked like the squadrooms I'd seen in old movies when I was a kid.

There were no windows. The dust and butts in the corners were so old they were starting to fossilize. The desks (all of them littered with paper that seemed to have fallen from the ceiling) were so close together we could smell each other working, sweating because we were tired of doing reports, or because we were sick of the fact that we never seemed to make a dent in the crime rate, or because we were afraid. Or because we were different. It was like one big cage. Even the ID clipped to the lapel of my jacket, identifying me as *Special Agent Sam Browne*, looked more like a zoo label than anything else.

I hadn't worked there long, as years go, but already I was glad every time Inspector Morganstark sent me out in the field. About the only difference the past forty years had made in the atmosphere of the Bureau was that everything was grimmer now. Special Agents didn't work on trivial crimes like prostitution, gambling, missing persons, because they were too busy with kidnapping, terrorism, murder, gang warfare. And they worked alone, because there weren't enough of us to go around.

The real changes were hidden. The room next door was even bigger than this one, and it was full to the ceiling with computer banks and programers. And in the room next to that were the transmitters and tape decks that monitored Agents in the field. Because the Special Agents had been altered, too.

But philosophy (or physiology, depending on the point of view) is like sentiment, and I was already late. Before I had even reached my desk, the Inspector spotted me from across the room and shouted, "Browne!" He didn't sound in any mood to be kept waiting, so I just ignored all the new paper on my desk and went into his office. I closed the door and stood waiting for him to decide whether he wanted to chew me out or not. Not that I had any particular objection to being chewed out. I liked Inspector Morganstark, even when he was mad at me. He was a sawed-off man with a receding hairline, and during his years in the Bureau his eyes had turned bleak and tired. He always looked harassed—and probably he was. He was the only Inspector in the Division who was sometimes human enough, or stubborn enough, anyway, to ignore the computers. He played his hunches sometimes, and sometimes his hunches got him in trouble. I liked him for that. It was worth being roasted once in a while to work for him.

He was sitting with his elbows on his desk, clutching a file with both hands as if it was trying to get away from him. It was a pretty thin file, by Bureau standards—it's hard to shut computers off once they get started. He didn't look up at me, which is usually a bad sign; but his expression wasn't angry. It was "something-about-this-isn't-right-and-I-don't-like-it." All of a sudden, I wanted that case. So I took a chance and sat down in front of his desk. Trying to show off my self-confidence—of which I didn't have a hell of a lot. After two years as a Special Agent, I was still the rookie under Inspector Morganstark. So far he'd never given me anything to do that wasn't basically routine.

After a minute, he put down the file and looked at me. His eyes weren't angry, either. They were worried. He clamped his hands behind his head and leaned back in his chair. Then he said, "You were at the zoo?"

That was another reason I liked him. He took my pets seriously. Made me feel less like a piece of equipment. "Yes," I said. For the sake of looking competent, I didn't smile.

"How many have you got there now?"

"Three. I took Elizabeth in a couple months ago."

"How's she doing?"

I shrugged. "Fair. It never takes them very long to lose spirit—once they're caged up."

His eyes studied me a minute longer. Then he said, "That's why I want you for this assignment. You know about animals. You know about hunting. You won't jump to the wrong conclusions."

Well, I was no hunter but I knew what he meant. I was familiar with hunting preserves. That was where I got John and Emily and Elizabeth. Sort of a hobby. Whenever I get a chance (like when I'm on leave), I go to preserves. I pay my way in like anybody else—take my chances like anybody else. But I don't have any guns, and I'm not trying to kill anything. I'm hunting for cubs like Elizabeth—young that are left to die when their mothers are shot or trapped. When I find them, I smuggle them out of the preserves, and raise them myself as long as I can, and then give them to the zoo.

Sometimes I don't find them in time. And sometimes when I find them they've already been crippled by careless shots or traps. Them I kill. Like I say, I'm sentimental.

But I didn't know what the Inspector meant about jumping to the wrong conclusions. I put a question on my face and waited, until he said, "Ever hear of the Sharon's Point Hunting Preserve?"

"No. But there are a lot of preserves. Next to car racing, hunting preserves are the most popular—"

He cut me off. He sat forward and poked the file accusingly with one finger. "People get killed there."

I didn't say anything to that. People get killed at all hunting preserves. That's what they're for. Since crime became the top-priority problem in this country about twenty years ago, the government has spent a lot of money on it. A *lot* of money. On "law enforcement" and prisons, of course. On drugs like marijuana that pacify people. But also on every conceivable way of giving people some kind of noncriminal outlet for their hostility.

Racing, for instance. With government subsidies, there isn't a man or woman in the country so poor they can't afford to get in a hot car and slam it around a track. The important thing, according to the social scientists, is to give people a chance to do something violent at the risk of their lives. Both violence and risk have to be real for catharsis to take place. With all the population and economic pressure people are under, they have to have some way to let off steam. Keep them from becoming criminals out of simple boredom and frustration and perversity.

So we have hunting preserves. Wilderness areas are sealed off and stocked with all manner of dangerous beasts and then hunters are turned loose in them—alone, of course—to kill everything they can while trying to stay alive. Everyone who has a yen to see the warm blood run can take a rifle and go pit himself, or at least his firepower, against various assortments of great cats, wolves, wildebeests, grizzly bears, whatever.

It's almost as popular as racing. People like the illusion of "kill or be killed." They slaughter animals as fast as the breeders can supply them. (Some people use poisoned darts and dumdum bullets. Some people even try to sneak lasers into the preserves, but that is strictly not allowed. Private citizens are strictly not allowed to have lasers at all.) It's all very therapeutic. And it's all very messy. Slow deaths and crippling outnumber clean kills twenty to one, and not enough hunters get killed to suit me. But I suppose it's better than war. At least we aren't trying to do the same thing to the Chinese.

The Inspector said, "You're thinking, 'Hooray for the lions and tigers.'"

I shrugged again. "Sharon's Point must be popular."

"I wouldn't know," he said acidly. "They don't get Federal money, so they don't have to file preserve-use figures. All I get is death certificates." This time, he touched the file with his fingertips as if it were delicate or dangerous. "Since Sharon's Point opened, twenty months ago, forty-five people have been killed."

Involuntarily, I said, "Sonofabitch!" Which probably didn't make me sound a whole lot more competent. But I was surprised. Forty-five! I knew of preserves that hadn't lost forty-five people in five years. Most hunters don't like to be in all *that* much danger.

"It's getting worse, too," Inspector Morganstark went on. "Ten in the first ten months. Fifteen in the next five. Twenty in the last five."

"They're very popular," I muttered.

"Which is strange," he said, "since they don't advertise."

"You mean they rely on word-of-mouth?" That implied several things, but the first one that occurred to me was, "What have they got that's so special?"

"You mean besides forty-five dead?" the Inspector growled. "They get more complaints than any other preserve in the country." That didn't seem to make sense, but he explained it. "Complaints from the families. They don't get the bodies back."

Well, that was special—sort of, I'd never heard of a preserve that didn't send the bodies to the next of kin. "What happens to them?"

"Cremated. At Sharon's Point. The complaints say that spouses have to sign a release before the hunters can go there. A custom some of the spouses don't like. But what they really don't like is that their husbands or wives are cremated right away. The spouses don't even get to see the bodies. All they get is notification and a death certificate." He looked at me sharply. "This is not against the law. All the releases were signed in advance."

I thought for a minute, then said something noncommittal. "What kind of hunters were they?"

The Inspector frowned bleakly. "The best. Most of them shouldn't be dead." He took a readout from the file and tossed it across the desk at me. "Take a look."

The readout was a computer summary of the forty-five dead. All were wealthy, but only 26.67% had acquired their money themselves. 73.33% had inherited it or married it. 82.2% had bright financial futures. 91.1% were experienced hunters, and of those 65.9% had reputations of being exceptionally skilled. 84.4% had traveled extensively around the world in search of "game"—the more dangerous the better.

"Maybe the animals are experienced too," I said.

The Inspector didn't laugh. I went on reading.

At the bottom of the sheet was an interesting piece of information: 75.56% of the people on this list had known at least five other people on the list; 0.00% had known none of the others.

I handed the readout back to Inspector Morganstark. "Word-of-mouth for sure. It's like a club." Something important was going on at the Sharon's Point Hunting Preserve, and I wanted to know what it was. Trying to sound casual, I asked, "What does the computer recommend?"

He looked at the ceiling. "It says to forget the whole thing. That damn machine can't even understand why I bother to ask it questions about this. No law broken. Death rate irrelevant. I asked for a secondary recommendation, and it suggested I talk to some other computer."

I watched him carefully. "But you're not going to forget it."

He threw up his hands. "Me forget it? Do I look like a man who has that much common sense? You know perfectly well I'm not going to forget it."

"Why not?"

It seemed like a reasonable question to me, but the Inspector waved it aside. "In fact," he went on in a steadier tone, "I'm assigning it to you. I want you out there tomorrow."

I started to say something, but he stopped me. He was looking straight at me, and I knew he was going to tell me something that was important to him. "I'm giving it to you," he said, "because I'm worried about you. Not because you're a rookie and this case is trivial. It is not trivial. I can feel it—right here." He put his hand over the bulge of his skull behind his right ear, as if his hunches came from the transceiver in his mastoid process. Then he sighed. "That's part of it, I suppose. I know you won't go off the deep end on this, if I'm wrong. Just because people are getting killed, you won't go all righteous on me and try to get Sharon's Point shut down. You won't make up charges against them just because their death rate is too high. You'll be cheering for the animals.

"But on top of that," he went on so I didn't have a chance to interrupt, "I want you to do this because I think you need it. I don't have to tell you you're not comfortable being a Special Agent. You're not comfortable with all that fancy equipment we put in you. All the adjustment tests indicate a deep-seated reluctance to accept yourself. You need a case that'll let you find out what you can do."

"Inspector," I said carefully, "I'm a big boy now. I'm here of my own free will. You're not sending me out on this just because you want me to adjust. Why don't you tell me why you've decided to ignore the computer?"

He was watching me like I'd just suggested some kind of unnatural act. But I knew that look. It meant he was angry about something, and he was about to admit it to both of us for the first time. Abruptly, he picked up the file and shoved it at me in disgust. "The last person on that list of dead is Nick Kolcsz. He was a Special Agent."

A Special Agent. That told me something, but not enough. I didn't know Kolcsz. He must have had money, but I wanted more than that. I gave the Inspector's temper another nudge. ""What was he doing there?"

He jumped to his feet to make shouting easier. "How the hell should I know?" Like all good men in the Bureau, he took the death of an Agent personally. "He was on leave! His goddamn transceiver was off!" Then with a jerk he sat down again. After a minute, all his anger was gone and he was just tired. "I presume he went there for the hunting, just like the rest of them. You know as well as I do we don't monitor Agents on leave. Even Agents need privacy once in a while. We didn't even know he was dead until his wife filed a complaint because they didn't let her see his body.

"Never mind the security leak—all that metal in his ashes. What scares me"—now there was something like fear in his bleak eyes—"is that we hadn't turned off his power pack. We never do that—not just for a leave. He should have been safe. Wild elephants shouldn't have been able to hurt him."

I knew what he meant. Nick Kolcsz was a cyborg. Like me. Whatever killed him was more dangerous than that.

— 2 —

Well, yes—a cyborg. But it isn't everything it's cracked up to be. People these days make the mistake of thinking Special Agents are "super" somehow. This comes from the old movies, where cyborgs were always super-fast and super-strong. They were loaded with weaponry. They had built-in computers to do things like think for them. They were slightly more human than robots.

Maybe someday. Right now no one has the technology for that kind of thing. I mean the medical technology. For lots of reasons, medicine hasn't made much progress in the last twenty years. What with all the population trouble we have, the science of "saving lives" doesn't seem as valuable as it used to. And then there were the genetic riots of 1989, which ended up shutting down whole research centers.

No, what I have in the way of equipment is a transceiver in the mastoid process behind my right ear, so that I'm always in contact with the Bureau; thin, practically weightless plastene struts along my legs and arms and spine, so I'm pretty hard to cripple (in theory, anyway); and a nuclear power pack implanted in my chest so its shielding protects my heart as well. The power pack runs my transceiver. It also runs the hypersonic blaster built into the palm of my left hand.

This has its disadvantages. I can hardly flex the first knuckles of that hand, so the hand itself doesn't have a whole lot it can do. And the blaster is covered by a latex membrane (looks just like skin) that burns away every time I use it, so I always have to carry replacements. But there are advantages, too—sort of. I can kill people at twenty-five meters, and stun them at fifty. I can tear holes in concrete walls, if I can get close enough.

That was what the Inspector was talking about when he said I hadn't adjusted. I can't get used to the fact that I can kill my friends just by pushing my tongue against one of my back teeth in a certain way. So I tend not to have very many friends.

Anyway, being a cyborg wasn't much comfort on this assignment. That was all I had going for me—exactly the same equipment that hadn't saved Nick Kolcsz. And he'd had something I didn't have—something that also hadn't saved him. He'd known what he was getting into. He'd been an experienced hunter, and he'd known three other people on that list of dead. (He must've known some of the survivors, too. Or known of them through friends. How else could he have known the place was dangerous?) Maybe that was why he went to Sharon's Point—to do some private research to find out what happened to those dead hunters.

Unfortunately, that didn't give me the option of going to one of his friends and asking what Kolcsz had known. The people who benefit (if that's the right word) from an exclusive arrangement don't have much reason to trust outsiders (like me). And they certainly weren't going to reveal knowing about anything illegal to a Special Agent. That would hurt themselves as well as Sharon's Point.

But I didn't like the idea of facing whatever killed Kolcsz without more data. So I started to do some digging.

I got information of a sort by checking out the Preserve's registration, but it didn't help much. Registration meant only that the Federal inspector had approved Sharon's Point's equipment. And inspection only covers two things: fencing and medical facilities.

Every hunting preserve is required to insure that its animals can't get loose, and to staff a small clinic to treat injured customers (never mind the crippled animals). The inspector verified that Sharon's Point had these things. Its perimeter (roughly 133 km.) was appropriately fenced. Its facilities included a very well equipped surgery and dispensary; and a veterinary hospital (which surprised me); *and* a cremator—supposedly for getting rid of animals too badly wounded to be treated.

Other information was slim. The preserve itself contained about 1,100 square km. of forests, swamps, hills, meadows. It was owned and run by a man named Fritz Ushre. Its staff consisted of one surgeon (a Dr. Avid Paracels) and a half dozen handlers for the animals.

But one item was conspicuously absent: the name of the breeder. Most hunting preserves get their animals by contract with one of three or four big breeding firms. Sharon's Point's registration didn't name one. It didn't name any source for its animals at all, which made me think maybe the people who went hunting there weren't hunting animals.

People hunting people? That's as illegal as hell. But it might explain the high death rate. Mere lions and baboons (even rabid baboons in packs) don't kill forty-five hunters at an exclusive preserve in twenty months. I was beginning to understand why the Inspector was willing to defy the computer on this assignment.

I went to the programers and got a readout on the death certificates. All had been signed by "Avid Paracels, M.D." All specified "normal" hunting-preserve causes of death (the usual combinations of injury and exposure, in addition to outright killing), but the type of animal involved was never identified.

That bothered me. This time I had the computers read out everything they had on Fritz Ushre and Avid Paracels.

Ushre's file was small. Things like age, marital status, blood type aside, it contained only a sketchy resume of his past employment. Twenty years of perfectly acceptable work as an engineer in various electronics firms. Then he inherited some land. He promptly quit his job, and two years later he opened up Sharon's Point. Now (according to his bank statements) he was in the process of getting rich. That told me just about nothing. I already knew Sharon's Point was popular.

But the file on Avid Paracels, Ph.D., M.D., F.A.C.S., was something else. It was full of stuff. Apparently at one time Dr. Paracels had held a high security clearance because of some research he was doing, so the Bureau had studied him down to his toenails. That produced reams of data, most of it pointless, but it didn't take me long to find the real goodies. After which (as my mother used to say) I could've been knocked over with a shovel. Avid Paracels was one of the victims of the genetic riots of 1989.

This is basically what happened. In 1989 one of the newspapers broke the story that a team of biologists (including the distinguished Avid Paracels) working under a massive Federal grant had achieved a major breakthrough in what they called "recombinant DNA research"—"genetic engineering," to ignorant sods like me. They'd mastered the techniques of raising animals with altered genes. Now they were beginning to experiment with human embryos. Their goal, according to the newspaper, was to attempt "minor improvements" in the human being—"cat" eyes, for instance, or prehensile toes.

So what happened? Riots is what happened. Which in itself wasn't unusual. By 1989, crime and whatnot, social unrest of all kinds, had already become the biggest single threat to the country, but the government still hadn't faced up to the problem. So riots and other types of violence used to start up for any reason at all: higher fuel prices, higher food costs, higher rents. In other words (according to the social scientists), the level of general public aggression had reached crisis proportions. Nobody had any acceptable outlets for anger, so whenever people were able to identify a grievance they went bananas.

That newspaper article triggered the great granddaddy of all riots. There was a lot of screaming about "the sanctity of human life," but I suppose the main thing was that the idea of a "superior human being" was pretty threatening to most people. So scientists and Congressmen were attacked in the streets. Three government buildings were wrecked (including a post office—God knows why). Seven apartment complexes were wrecked. One hundred thirty-seven stores were looted and wrecked. The recombinant DNA research program was wrecked. And a handful of careers went down the drain. Because this riot was too big to be put down. The cops (Special Agents) would have had to kill too many people. So the President himself set about appeasing the rioters—which led, naturally enough, to our present policy of trying to appease violence itself.

Avid Paracels was one of the men who went down the drain. I guess he was lucky not to lose his medical license. He certainly never got the chance to do any more research.

Well, that didn't prove anything, but it sure made me curious. People who lose high positions have been known to become somewhat vague about matters of legality. So that gave me a place to start when I went to Sharon's Point. Maybe if I was lucky I could even get out of pretending to go hunting in the preserve itself.

So I was feeling like I knew what I was doing (which probably should've told me I was in trouble already) when I left the duty room to go arrange for transportation and money. But it didn't last. Along the way I got one of those hot flashes, like an inspiration or a premonition. So when I was done with Accounting I went back to the computers and asked for a readout on any unsolved crimes in the area around Sharon's Point. The answer gave my so-called self-confidence a jolt.

Sharon's Point was only 80 km. from the Procureton Arsenal, where a lot of old munitions (mostly from the '60s and '70s) were stored. Two years ago, someone had broken into Procureton (God knows how) and helped himself to a few odds and ends—like fifty M-16 rifles (along with five thousand loaded clips), a hundred .22 Magnum automatic handguns (and another five thousand clips), five hundred hand grenades, and more than five hundred antipersonnel mines of various types. Enough to supply a good-sized street mob.

Which made no sense at all. Any street mob these days—or terrorist organization, or heist gang, for that matter—that tried to use obsolete weaponry like M-16s would get cut to shreds in minutes by cops using laser cannons. And who else would want the damn stuff?

I didn't believe I was going to find any animals at Sharon's Point at all. Just hunters picking one another off.

Before I went home, I spent an hour down in the range, practicing with my blaster. Just to be sure it worked.

The next morning early I went to Supply and got myself some "rich" clothes, along with a bunch of hunting gear. Then I went to Weapons and checked out an old Winchester .30-06 carbine that looked to me like the kind of rifle a "true" (eccentric) sportsman might use—takes a degree of skill, and fires plain old lead slugs instead of hypodarts or fragmentation bullets—sort of a way of giving the "game" a chance. After that I checked the tape decks to be sure they had me on active status. Then I went to Sharon's Point.

I took the chute from D.C. to St. Louis (actually, it's an electrostatic shuttle, but it's called "the chute" because the early designs reminded some romantic of the old logging chutes in the Northwest), but after that I had to rent a car. Which was appropriate, since I was supposed to be rich. Only the rich can afford cars these days—and Special Agents on assignment (fuel prices being what tney are, the only time most people see the inside of a car is at a subsidized track). But I didn't enjoy it much. Never mind that I'm not much of a driver (I haven't exactly had a lot of practice). It was raining like hades in St. Louis, and I had to drive 300 km. through the back hills of Missouri as if I was swimming. That slowed me down so much I didn't get near Sharon's Point until after dark.

I stopped for the night at the village of Sharon's Point, which was about 5 km. shy of the preserve. It was a dismal little town, too far from anywhere to have anything going for it. But it did have one motel. When I splashed my way through the rain and mud and went dripping into the lobby, I found that one motel was doing very well for itself. It was as plush as any motel I'd ever seen. And expensive. The receptionist didn't even blush when she told me the place cost a thousand dollars a night.

So it was obvious this motel didn't get its business from local people and tourists. Probably it catered to the hunters who came to and went from the preserve. *I* might've blushed if I hadn't come prepared to handle situations like this. I had a special credit card Accounting had given me. Made me look rich without saying anything about where I got my money. I checked in as if I did this kind of thing every day. The receptionist sent my stuff to my room, and I went into the bar.

Hoping there might be another hunter or two around. But except for the bartender the place was empty. So I perched myself on one of the barstools and tried to find out if the bartender liked to talk.

He did. I guess he didn't get a lot of opportunity. Probably people who didn't mind paying a thousand dollars a night for a room didn't turn up too often. Once he got started, I didn't think I would be able to stop him from telling me everything he knew.

Which wasn't a whole lot more than I already knew—about the preserve, anyway. The people who went there had money. They threw their weight around. They liked to drink—before and after hunting. But maybe half of them didn't stop by to celebrate on their way home. After a while I asked him what kind of trophies the ones that did stop by got.

"Funny thing about that," he said. "They don't bring anything back. Don't even talk about what they got. I used to do some hunting when I was a kid, and I never met a hunter who didn't like to show off what he shot. I've seen grown men act like God Almighty when they dinged a rabbit. But not here. "Course"—he smiled—"I never went hunting in a place as pricey as Sharon's Point."

But I wasn't thinking about the money. I was thinking about forty-five bodies. That was something even rich hunters wouldn't brag about. Probably those trophies had bullet holes in them.

— 3 —

I promised myself I was going to find out about those "trophies." One way or another. It wasn't that I was feeling confident. Right then I don't think I even knew what confidence was. No, it was that confidence didn't matter any more. I couldn't afford to worry about it. This case was too serious.

When I was sure I was the only guest, I gave up the idea of getting any more information that night. There was no cure for it—I was going to have to go up to the preserve and bluff my way along until I got the answers I needed. Not a comforting thought. When I went to bed, I spent a long time listening to the rain before I fell asleep.

In the morning it was still raining, but that didn't seem like a good enough reason to postpone what I had to do. So I spent a while in the bathroom, running the shower to cover the sound of my voice while I talked to the tape decks in the Bureau (via microwave relays in St. Louis, Indianapolis, Pittsburgh, and God knows where else). Then I had breakfast, and went and got soaked running through the rain out to my car.

The drive to the preserve was slow because of the rain. The road wound up and down hills between walls of dark trees that seemed to be crouching there, waiting for me, but I didn't see anything else until my car began picking its way up a long slope toward the outbuildings of Sharon's Point.

They sat below the crest of a long transverse ridge that blocked everything beyond it from sight. Right ahead of me was a large squat complex; that was probably where the offices and medical facilities were. To the right was a long building like a barracks that probably housed the animal handlers. On the left was the landing area. Three doughnut-shaped open-cockpit hovercraft stood there. (Most hunting preserves used hovercraft for jobs like inspecting the fences and looking for missing hunters.) They were covered by styrene sheets against the rain.

And behind all this, stretching along the ridge like the promise of something deadly, was the fence. It looked gray and bitter against the black clouds and the rain. The chain steel was at least five meters high, curved inward and viciously barbed along the top to keep certain kinds of animals from being able to climb out. But it didn't make me feel safe. Whatever was in there had killed forty-five people. Five meters of fence was either inadequate or irrelevant.

More for my own benefit than for Inspector Morganstark's, I said into my transceiver, "Relinquish all hope, ye who enter here." Then I drove up to the squat building, parked as close as I could get to a door marked office, and ran through the rain as if I couldn't wait to take on Sharon's Point single-handedly.

I rushed into the office, pulled the door shut behind me—and almost fell on my face. Pain as keen as steel went through my head like a drill from somewhere behind my right ear. For an instant I was blind and deaf with pain, and my knees were bending under me.

It was coming from my mastoid process.

Some kind of power feedback in my transceiver.

It felt like one of the monitors back at the Bureau was trying to kill me.

I knew that wasn't it; but right then I didn't care what it was. I tongued the switch to cut off transmission. And, shoving out one leg, caught myself with a jerk just before I fell.

It was over. The pain disappeared. Just like that.

I was woozy with relief. There was a ringing in my ears that made it hard for me to keep my balance. Seconds passed before I could focus well enough to look around. Not think—just look.

I was in a bare office, a place with no frills, not even any curtains on the windows to keep out the dankness of the rain. I was almost in reach of a long counter.

Behind the counter stood a man. He was tall and fat—not over-weight-fat, but bloated-fat, as if he was stuffing himself to feed some grotesque appetite. He had the face of a boar, the cunning and malicious eyes of a boar, and he was looking at me as if he was trying to decide where to use his tusks. But his voice was suave and kind. "Are you all right?" he asked. "What happened?"

With a lurch, my brain started working again.

Power feedback. Something had caused a feedback in my transceiver. Must've been some kind of electronic jamming device. The government used jammers for security—a way of screening secret meetings. To protect against people like me.

Sharon's Point was using a security screen.

What were they trying to hide?

But that was secondary. I had a more immediate problem. The fat man had been watching me when the jammer hit. He'd seen my reaction. He would know I had a transceiver in my skull. Unless I did something about it. Fast.

He hadn't even blinked. "What happened?"

I was sweating. My hands were trembling. But I looked him straight in the eye and said, "It'll pass. I'll be all right in a minute."

Nothing could've been kinder than the way he asked, "What is the matter?"

"Just a spasm," I said straight at him. "Comes and goes. Brain tumor. Inoperable. I'll be dead in six months. That's why I'm here."

"Ah," he said without moving. "That is why you are here." His pudgy hands were folded and resting on his gut. "I understand." If he was suspicious of me, he didn't let it ruffle his composure. "I understand perfectly."

"I don't like hospitals," I said sternly, just to show him I was back in control of myself.

"Naturally not," he assented. "You have come to the right place, Mr...?"

"Browne," I said. "Sam Browne."

"Mr. Browne." He filed my name away with a nod. Gave me the uncomfortable impression he was never going to forget it. "We have what you want here." For the first time, I saw him blink. Then he said, "How did you hear of us, Mr. Browne?"

I was prepared for that. I mentioned a couple names off the Preserve's list of dead, and followed them up by saying squarely, "You must be Ushre."

He nodded again. "I am Fritz Ushre." He said it the same way he might've said, "I am the President of the United States." Nothing diffident about him.

Trying to match him, I said, "Tell me about it."

His boar eyes didn't waver, but he didn't answer me directly. Instead, he said, "Mr. Browne, we generally ask our patrons for payment in advance. Our standard fee is for a week's hunting. Forty thousand dollars."

I certainly did admire his composure. He was better at it than I was. I felt my face react before I could stop it. Forty—! Well, so much for acting like I was rich. It was all I could do to keep from cursing myself out loud.

"We run a costly operation," he said. He was as smooth as stainless steel. "Our facilities are the best. And we breed our own animals. That way, we are able to maintain the quality of what we offer. But for that reason we are required to have veterinary as well as medical facilities. Since we receive no Federal money—and submit to no Federal inspections"—he couldn't have sounded less like he was threatening me—"we cannot afford to be wasteful."

He might've gone on—not apologizing, just tactfully getting rid of me—but I cut him off. "Better be worth it," I said with all the toughness I could manage. "I didn't get where I am throwing my money away." At the same time, I took out my credit card and set it down with a snap on the counter.

"Your satisfaction is guaranteed." Ushre inspected my card briefly, then asked, "Will one week suffice, Mr. Browne?"

"For a start."

"I understand," he said as if he understood me completely. Then he turned away for a minute while he ran my card through his accounting computer. The ac-computer verified my credit due and printed out a receipt that Ushre presented to me for validation. After I'd pressed my thumbprint onto the identiplate, he returned my card and filed the receipt in the ac-computer.

In the meantime, I did some glancing around, trying nonchalantly (I hoped I looked nonchalant) to spot the jammer. But I didn't find it. In fact, as an investigator I was getting nowhere fast. If I didn't start finding things out soon, I was going to have real trouble explaining that forty-thousand-dollar bill to Accounting. Not to mention staying alive.

So when Ushre turned back to me, I said, "I don't want to start in the rain. I'll come back tomorrow. But while I'm here I want to look at your facilities." It wasn't much, but it was the best I could do without giving away that I really didn't know those two dead men I'd mentioned. I was supposed to know what I was doing; I couldn't very well just ask him right out what kind of animals he had. Or didn't have.

Ushre put a sheaf of papers down on the counter in front of me, and said again, "I understand." The way he said things like that was beginning to make my scalp itch. "Once you have completed these forms, I will ask Dr. Paracels to show you around."

I said, "Fine," and started to fill out the forms. I didn't worry too much about what I was signing. Except for the one that had to do with cremating my body, they were pretty much standard releases—so that Sharon's Point wouldn't be liable for anything that might happen to me. The disposal-of-the-body form I read more carefully than the others, but it didn't tell me anything I didn't already know. And by the time I was done, Dr. Avid Paracels had come into the office.

I studied him as Ushre introduced us. I would've been interested to meet him any time, but right then I was particularly keen. I knew more about him than I did about Ushre—which meant that for me he was the key to Sharon's Point.

He was tall and gaunt—next to Ushre he was outright emaciated. Scrawny and stooped, as if the better part of him had been chipped away by a long series of personal catastrophies. And he looked a good bit more than thirty years older than I was. His face was gray, like the face of a man with a terminal disease, and the skin stretched from his cheekbones to his jaw as if it was too small for his skull. His eyes were hidden most of the time beneath his thick, ragged eyebrows, but when I caught a glimpse of them they looked as dead as plastene. I would've thought he was a cadaver if he wasn't standing up and wearing a white coat. If he hadn't licked his lips once when he first saw me. Just the tip of his tongue circled his lips that once—not like he was hungry, but instead like he was wondering in an abstract way whether I might turn out to be tasty. Something about that little pink gesture in that gray face made me feel cold all of a sudden. For a second I felt like I knew what he was really thinking. He was wondering how he was going to be able to use me. And how I was going to die. Maybe not in that order.

"Dr. Paracels," I said. I was wondering if he or Ushre knew there was sweat running down the small of my back.

"I won't show you where we do our breeding," he said in a petulant way that surprised me, "or my animal hospital." The whine in his voice sounded almost deliberate, like he was trying to sound pathetic.

"We never show our patrons those facilities," Ushre added smoothly. "There is an element of surprise in what we offer." He blinked again. The rareness of that movement emphasized the cunning and malice of his eyes. "We believe that it improves the sport. Most of our patrons agree."

"But you can see my clinic," Paracels added impatiently. "This way." He didn't wait for me. He turned around and went out the inner door of the office.

Ushre's eyes never left my face, "A brilliant surgeon, Dr. Paracels. We are fortunate to have him."

I shrugged. The way I was feeling right then, there didn't seem to be anything else I could do. Then I went after the good doctor.

That door opened into a wide corridor running through the complex. I caught a glimpse of Paracels going through a set of double doors at the end of the corridor, but there were other doors along the hall, and they were tempting. They might lead me to Ushre's records—and Ushre's records might tell me what I needed to know about Sharon's Point. But this was no time for taking risks. I couldn't very well tell Ushre when he caught me that I'd blundered onto his records by mistake—assuming I even found them. So I went straight to the double doors and pushed my way into the surgery.

The registration inspector was right: Sharon's Point was very well equipped. There were several examination and treatment rooms (including x-ray, oxygen, and ophthalmological equipment), a half dozen beds, a pharmacy that looked more than adequate (maybe a lot more than adequate), and an operating theater that reminded me of the place where I was made into a cyborg.

That was where I caught up with Paracels. In his whining voice (was he really that full of self-pity?), he described the main features of the place. He assumed I'd want to know how he could do effective surgery alone there, and that was what he told me.

Well, his equipment was certainly compact and flexible, but what really interested me was that he had a surgical laser. (I didn't ask him if he had a license for it. His license was hanging right there on the wall.) That wasn't common at all, especially in a small clinic like this. A surgical laser is very specialized equipment. These days they're used for things like eye surgery and lobotomies. And making cyborgs. But a while back (twenty-two years) they were used in genetic engineering.

The whole idea made my skin crawl. There was something menacing about it. As innocently as I could, I asked Paracels the nastiest question I could think of. "Do you save any lives here, Doctor?"

That was all it took to make him stop whining. All at once he was so bitter I half-expected him to begin foaming at the mouth. "What're you," he spat, "some kind of bleeding heart? The men who come here know they might get killed. I do everything for them that any doctor could do. You think I have all this stuff just for the hell of it?"

I was surprised to find I believed him. I believed he did everything he could to save every life that ended up on his operating table. He was a doctor, wasn't he? If he was killing people, he was doing it some other way.

— 4 —

Well, maybe I was being naive. I didn't know yet. But I figured I'd already learned everything Paracels and Ushre were likely to tell me of their own free will. I told them I'd be back bright and early the next morning, and then I left.

The rain was easing, so I didn't get too wet on the way back to my car, but that didn't make me feel any better. There was no doubt about it: I was outclassed. Ushre and Paracels had given away practically nothing. They'd come up with neat plausible stories to cover strange things like their vet hospital and their independence from the usual animal breeders. In fact, they'd explained away everything except their policy of cremating their dead hunters—and that was something I couldn't challenge them on without showing off my ignorance. Maybe they had even spotted me for what I was. And I'd gotten nothing out of them except a cold sweat. I had an unfamiliar itch to use my blaster; I wanted to raze that whole building, clinic and all. When I reactivated my transmitter, I felt like telling Inspector Morganstark to pull me off the case and send in someone who knew what he was doing.

But I didn't. Instead, I acted just like a good Special Agent is supposed to. I spent the drive back to town talking to the tape decks, telling them the whole story. If nothing else, I'd accomplished something by finding out Sharon's Point ran a security screen. That would tell the Inspector his hunch was right.

I didn't have any doubt his hunch was right. Something stank at that preserve. In different ways, Ushre and Paracels reminded me of maneaters. They had acquired a taste for blood. Human blood. In the back of my head a loud voice was shouting that Sharon's Point used genetically altered people for "game." No wonder Paracels looked so sick. The M.D. in him was dying of outrage.

So I didn't tell Inspector Morganstark to pull me off the case. I did what I was supposed to do. I went back to the motel and spent the afternoon acting like a rich man who was eager to go hunting. I turned in early after supper, to get plenty of rest. I asked the desk to call me at 6 A.M. With the shower running, I told the tape decks what I was going to do.

When midnight came, and the sky blew clear for the first time in two days, I climbed out a window and went back to the preserve on foot.

I wasn't exactly loaded down with equipment. I left my .30-06 and all my rich-hunter gear back at the motel. But I figured I didn't need it. After all, I was a cyborg. Besides, I had a needle flash and a small set of electromagnetic lock-picks and jimmies. I had a good sense of direction. I wasn't afraid of the dark.

And I had my personal good-luck piece. It was an old Gerber hunting knife that used to be my father's. It was balanced for throwing (which I was better at than using a rifle anyway), and its edges near the hilt were serrated, so it was good for cutting things like rope. I'd taken it with me on all my visits to hunting preserves, and once or twice it had kept me alive. It was what I used when I had to kill some poor animal crippled by a trap or a bad shot. Now I wore it hidden under my clothes at the small of my back. Made me feel a little more self-confident.

I was on my way to try to sneak a look at a few things. Like Paracels's vet hospital and breeding pens. And Ushre's records. I really didn't want to just walk into the preserve in the morning and find out what I was up against the hard way. Better to take my chances in the dark.

I reached the preserve in about an hour and hunched down in the brush beside the road to plan what I was going to do. All the lights in the barracks and office complex were out, but there was a bright pink freon bulb burning next to the landing area and the hovercraft. I was tempted to put it out, just to make myself feel safer. But I figured that would be like announcing to Sharon's Point I was there, so I left it alone.

The barracks I decided to leave alone, too. Maybe that wasn't where the handlers lived—maybe that was where Paracels kept his animals. But if it was living quarters, I was going to look pretty silly when I got caught breaking in there. Better not to take that chance.

So I concentrated on the office building. Using the shadow of the barracks for cover, I crept around until I was in back of the complex, between it and the fence. There, about where I figured the vet facilities ought to be, I found a door that suited me. I wanted to look at that clinic. No matter what Ushre said, it sounded to me like a grand place to engineer "game." I tongued off my transmitter so I wouldn't run into that jammer again and set about trying to open the door without setting off any alarms.

One of my picks opened the lock easily enough. But I didn't crack the door more than a few cm. In the light of my needle flash, the corridor beyond looked harmless enough, but I didn't trust it. I took a lock-pick and retuned it to react to magnetic-field scanners (the most common security system these days). Then I slipped it through the crack of the door. If it met a scanner field, I'd feel resistance in the air—before I tripped the alarm (in theory, anyway).

Isn't technology wonderful (said the cyborg)? My pick didn't meet any resistance. After a minute or two of deep breathing, I opened the door enough to step into the complex. Then I closed it behind me and leaned against it.

I checked the corridor with my flash, but didn't learn anything except that I had several doors to choose from. Holding the pick in front of me like some kind of magic wand, I started to move, half expecting the pick to start bucking in my hand and all hell to break loose.

But it didn't. I got to the first door and opened it. And found floor-cleaning equipment—electrostatic sweepers and whatnot. The night was cool—the building was cool—but I was sweating.

The next door was a linen closet. The next was a bathroom.

I gritted my teeth, trying to keep from talking out loud. Telling the tape decks what I was doing was already an old habit.

The next door was the one I wanted. It put me in a large room that smelled like a lab.

I shut that door behind me, too, and spent a long time just standing there, making sure I wasn't making any noise. Then I broadened the beam of my flash and spread it around the room.

Definitely a laboratory. At this end there were four large work-tables covered with equipment: burners, microscopes, glassine apparatus of all kinds—I couldn't identify half that stuff. I couldn't identify the chemicals ranked along the shelves on this wall or figure out what was in the specimen bottles on the opposite side of the room (What the hell did Paracels need all this for?) But there was one thing I could identify.

A surgical laser.

It was so fancy it made the one in the surgery look like a toy.

When I saw it, something deep down in my chest started to shiver.

And that was only half the room. The other half was something else. When I was done checking over the lab equipment, I scanned the far end, and spotted the cremator.

It was set into the wall like a giant surgical sterilizer, but I knew what it was. I'd seen cremators before. This was just the largest one I'd ever come across. It looked big enough to hold a grizzly. Which was strange, because hunting preserves didn't usually have animals that size. Too expensive to replace.

But almost immediately I saw something stranger. In front of the cremator stood a gurney that looked like a hospital cart. On it was a body, covered with a sheet. From what I could see, it looked like the body of a man.

I didn't run over to it. Instead, I forced myself to locate all the doors into the lab. There were four—two opposite each other at each end of the room. So no matter what I did I was going to have to turn my back on at least one of them.

But there was nothing I could do about that. I went to the door across from me and put my ear to it for a long minute, listening as hard as I knew how, trying to tell if anything was happening on the other side. Then I went to the other two doors and did the same thing. But all I heard was the thudding of my heart. If Sharon's Point was using sound-sensor alarms instead of field scanners, I was in big trouble.

I didn't hear anything. But still my nerves were strung as tight as a cat's as I went over to the gurney. I think I was holding my breath.

Under the sheet I found a dead man. He was naked, and I could see the bullet holes in his chest as plain as day. There were a lot of them. Too many. He looked as if he'd walked into a machine gun. But it must have happened a while ago. His skin was cold, and he was stiff, and there was no blood.

Now I understood why Ushre and Paracels needed a cremator. They couldn't very well send bodies to the next of kin looking like this.

For a minute I just stood there, thinking I was right, Sharon's Point used people instead of animals, people hunting people.

Then all the lights in the lab came on, and I almost collapsed in surprise and panic.

Avid Paracels stood in the doorway where I'd entered the lab. His hand was still on the light switch. He didn't look like he'd even been to bed. He was still wearing his white coat, as if it was the most natural thing in the world for him to be up in his lab at 1 A.M. Well, maybe it was. Somehow that kind of light made him look solider, even more dangerous.

And he wasn't surprised. Not him. He was looking right at me as if we were both keeping some kind of appointment.

For the first couple heartbeats I couldn't seem to think anything except, Well, so much for technology. They have some other kind of alarm system.

Then Paracels started talking. His thin old voice sounded almost smug. "Ushre spotted you right away," he said. "We knew you would come back tonight. You're investigating us."

For some strange reason, that statement made me feel better. My Pick hadn't failed me after all. My equipment was still reliable. Maybe I was better adjusted to being a cyborg than I thought. Paracels was obviously unarmed—and I had my blaster. There was no way on God's green earth he could stop me from using it. My pulse actually began to feel like it was getting back to normal.

"So what happens now?" I asked. I was trying for bravado. Special Agents are supposed to be brave. "Are you going to kill me?"

Paracels's mood seemed to change by the second. Now he was bitter again. "I answered that question this morning," he snapped. "I'm a doctor. I don't take lives."

I shrugged, then gestured toward the gurney. "That's probably a real comfort to him." I wanted to goad the good doctor.

But he didn't seem to hear me. Already he was back to smug. "A good specimen." He smirked. "His genes should be very useful."

"He's dead," I said. "What good're dead genes?"

Paracels almost smiled. "Parts of him aren't dead yet. Did you know that? Some parts of him won't die for two more days. After that we'll burn him." The tip of his tongue came out and drew a neat line of saliva around his lips.

Probably that should've warned me. But I was concentrating on him the wrong way. I was watching him as if he was the only thing I had to worry about. I didn't hear the door open behind me at all. All I heard was one last quick step. Then something hit the back of my head and switched off the world.

— 5 —

Which just goes to show that being a cyborg isn't everything it's cracked up to be. Cyborgs are in trouble as soon as they do start adjusting to what they are. They don't rely on themselves anymore—they rely on their equipment. Then when they're in a situation where they need something besides a blaster, they don't have it.

Two years ago there wasn't a man or animal that could sneak up behind me. The hunting preserves taught me how to watch my back. The animals didn't know I was on their side, and they were hungry. I had to watch my back to stay alive. Apparently not any more. Now I was Sam Browne, Special-Agent-cyborg-hotshot. As far as I could tell, I was as good as dead.

My hands were taped behind my back, and I was lying on my face in something that used to be mud before it dried, and the sun was slowly cooking me. When I cranked my eyes open, all I could see was brush a few cm. from my nose. A long time seemed to pass before I could get up the strength to focus my eyes and lift my head. Then I saw I was lying on a dirt path that ran through a field of low bushes. Beyond the bushes were trees.

All around me there was a faint smell of blood. My blood. From the back of my head.

Which hurt like a sonofabitch. I put my face back down in the dirt. I would've done some cursing, but I didn't have the strength. I knew what had happened.

Ushre and Paracels had trussed me up and dropped me off in the middle of their preserve. Smelling like blood. They weren't going to kill me—not them. I was just going to be another one of their dead hunters.

Well, at least I was going to find out who was hunting what (or whom) around here.

Minutes passed before I mustered enough energy to find out if my legs were taped, too. They weren't. How very sporting. I wondered if it was Ushre's idea or Paracels'.

That hit on the head must've scrambled my brains (the pain was scrambling them for sure). I spent what felt like ages trying to figure out who was responsible for leaving my legs free, when I should've been pulling myself together. Getting to my feet. Trying to find some water to wash off the blood. Thinking about staying alive. More time passed before I remembered I had a transceiver in my skull. I could call for help.

Help would take time. Probably it wouldn't come fast enough to save me. But I could at least call for it. It would guarantee that Sharon's Point got shut down. Ushre and Paracels would get murder-one—mandatory death sentence. I could at least call.

My tongue felt like a sponge in my mouth, but I concentrated hard, and managed to find the transmission switch. Then I tried to talk. That took longer. I had to swallow several times to work up enough saliva to make a sound. But finally I did it. Out loud I said one of the Bureau's emergency code words.

Nothing happened.

Something was supposed to happen. That word was supposed to trigger the automatic monitors in the tape room. The monitors were supposed to put the duty room on emergency status. Instantly, Inspector Morganstark (or whoever was in charge) was supposed to come running. He was supposed to start talking to me (well, not actually talking—my equipment didn't receive voices. Only a modulated hum. But I knew how to read that hum). My transceiver was supposed to hum.

It didn't.

I waited, and it still didn't. I said my code word again, and it still didn't. I said all the code words, and it still didn't. I swore at it until I ran out of strength. Nothing.

Which told me (when I recovered enough to do more thinking) that my transceiver wasn't working. Wonderful. Maybe that hit on the head had broken it. Or maybe—

I made sure my right hand was behind my left. Then I tongued the switch that was supposed to fire my blaster.

Again nothing.

Twisting my right hand, I used those fingers to probe my left palm. My blaster was intact. The concealing membrane was still in place. The thing should've worked.

I was absolutely as good as dead.

Those bastards (probably Ushre, the electronics engineer) had found out how to turn off my power pack. They had turned me off.

That made a nasty kind of sense. Ushre and Paracels had already cremated one Special Agent. Probably that was where they had gotten their information. Kolcsz's power pack wouldn't have melted. With the thing right there in his hand, Ushre would've had an easy time making a magnetic probe to turn it off. All he had to do was experiment until he got it right.

What didn't make sense was the way I felt about it. Here I was, a disabled cyborg with his hands taped behind him, lying on his face in a hunting preserve that had already killed forty-five people—forty-six counting the man in Paracels's lab—and all of a sudden I began to feel like I knew what to do. I didn't feel turned off: I felt as if I was coming back to life. Strength began coming back into my muscles. My brain was clearing. I was getting ready to move.

I was going to make Ushre and Paracels pay for this.

Those bastards were so goddamn self-confident, they hadn't even bothered to search me. I still had my knife. It was right there—my hands were resting on it.

What did they think the Bureau was going to do when the monitors found out my transceiver was dead? Just sit there on its ass and let Sharon's Point go its merry way?

I started to move, tried to get up. Which was something I should've done a long time ago. Or maybe it wouldn't have made any difference. That didn't matter now. By the time I got to my knees, it was already too late. I was in trouble.

Big trouble.

A rabbit came out of the brush a meter down the path from me. I thought he was a rabbit—he looked like a rabbit. An ordinary long-eared jackrabbit. Male—the males are a lot bigger than the females. Then he didn't look like a rabbit. His jaws were too big; he had the kind of jaws a dog has. His front paws were too broad and strong.

What the hell?

In his jaws he held a hand grenade, carrying it by the ring of the pin.

He didn't waste any time. He put the grenade down on the path and braced his paws on it. With a jerk of his head, he pulled the pin. Then he dashed back into the bushes.

I just kneeled there and stared at the damn thing. For the longest time all I could do was stare at it and think: That's a live grenade. They got it from the Procureton Arsenal.

In the back of my head a desperate voice was screaming: Move it, you sonofabitch!

I moved. Lurched to my feet, took a step toward the grenade, kicked it away from me. It skidded down the path. I didn't wait to see how far it went. I ran about two steps into the brush and threw myself flat. Any cover was better than nothing.

I landed hard, but that didn't matter. One second after I hit the ground, the grenade went off. It made a crumping noise like a demolition ram hitting concrete. Cast-iron fragments went ripping through the brush in all directions.

None of them hit me.

But it wasn't over. There were more explosions. A line of detonations came pounding up the path from where the grenade went off. The fourth one was so close the concussion flipped me over in the brush, and dirt rained on me. There were three more before the blasting stopped.

After that, the air was as quiet as a grave.

I didn't move for a long time. I stayed where I was, trying to act like I was dead and buried. I didn't risk even a twitch until I was sure my smell was covered by all the gelignite in the air. Then I pulled up the back of my shirt and slipped out my knife.

Getting my hands free was awkward, but the serrated edges of the blade helped, and I didn't cut myself more than a little bit. When I had the tape off, I eased up onto my hands and knees. Then I spent more time just listening, listening hard, trying to remember how I used to listen two years ago, before I got in the habit of depending on equipment.

I was in luck. There was a slow breeze. It was blowing past me across the path—which meant anything upwind couldn't smell me, and anything downwind would get too much gelignite to know I was there. So I was covered—sort of.

I crawled forward to take a look at the path.

The line of shallow craters—spaced about a half dozen meters apart—told me what had happened. Antipersonnel mines. A string of them wired together buried in the path. The grenade set one of them off, and they all went up. The nearest one would have killed me if it hadn't been buried so deep. Fortunately the blast went upward instead of out to the sides.

I wiped the sweat out of my eyes and lay down where I was to do a little thinking.

A rabbit that wasn't a rabbit. A genetically altered rabbit, armed with munitions from the Procureton Arsenal.

No wonder Ushre and Paracels raised their own animals—the genes had to be altered when the animal was an embryo. No wonder they had a vet hospital. And a cremator. No wonder they kept their breeding pens secret. No wonder their rates were so high. No wonder they wanted to keep their clientele exclusive.

No wonder they wanted me dead.

All of a sudden, their confidence didn't surprise me any more.

I didn't even consider moving from where I was. I wasn't ready. I wanted more information. I was as sure as hell rabbits weren't the only animals in the Sharon's Point Hunting Preserve. I figured those explosions would bring some of the others to me.

I was right sooner than I expected. By the time I had myself reasonably well hidden in the brush, I heard the soft flop of heavy paws coming down the path. Almost at once, two dogs went trotting by. At least they should've been dogs. They were big brown boxers, and at first glance the only thing unusual about them was they carried sacks slung over their shoulders.

But they stopped at the farthest mine crater, and I got a better look. Their shoulders were too broad and square, and instead of front paws they had hands—chimp hands, except for the strong claws.

They shrugged off their sacks, nosed them open. Took out half a dozen or so mines.

Working together with all the efficiency in the world, they put new mines in the old craters. They wired the mines together and attached the wires to a flat gray box that must have been the arming switch. They hid the wires and the box in the brush along the path (fortunately on the opposite side from me—I didn't want to try to fight them off). Then they filled in the craters, packing them down until just the vaguest discoloration of the dirt gave away where the mines were. When that was done, one of them armed the mines.

A minute later, they went gamboling away through the brush. They were actually playing with each other, jumping and rolling together as they made their way toward the far line of trees.

Fifteen minutes ago they'd tried to kill me. They'd just finished setting a trap to kill someone else. Now they were playing.

Which didn't have anything to do with them, of course. They were just dogs. They had new shoulders and new hands—and probably new brains (setting mines seemed a little bit much for ordinary boxers to me)—but they were just dogs. They didn't know what they were doing.

Ushre and Paracels knew.

All of a sudden, I was tired of being cautious. I was mad, and I didn't want to do any more waiting around. My sense of direction told me those dogs were going the same way I wanted to go: toward the front gate of the preserve. When they were out of sight, I got up into a crouch. I scanned the field to make sure there was nothing around me. Then I dove over the path, somersaulted to my feet, and started to run. Covering the same ground the dogs did. They hadn't been blown up, so I figured I wouldn't be either. Everything ahead of me was upwind, so except for the noise nothing in those trees would know I was coming. I didn't make much noise

In two minutes, I was into the trees and hiding under a rotten old log.

The air was a lot cooler in the shade, and I spent a little while just recovering from the heat of the sun and letting my eyes get used to the dimmer light. And listening. I couldn't tell much at first because I was breathing so hard, but before long I was able to get my hearing adjusted to the breeze and the woods. After that, I relaxed enough to figure out exactly what I meant to do.

I meant to get at Ushre and Paracels.

Fine. I wanted to do that. There was only one problem. First I had to stay alive.

If I wanted to stay alive, I had to have water. Wash the blood off. If I could smell me this easily, it was a sure bet every animal within fifty meters could, too.

I started hunting for a tree I could climb—a tree tall enough to give me a view out over these woods.

It took me half an hour because I was being so cautious, but finally I found what I needed. A tall straight ash. It didn't have any branches for the first six meters or so, but a tree nearby had fallen into it and stuck there, caught leaning in the lowest branches. By risking my neck, and not thinking too hard about what I was doing, I was able to shinny up that leaning trunk and climb into the ash.

With my left hand the way it was, I didn't have much of a grip, and I learned quickly enough that I wasn't going to be able to climb as high as I wanted. But just when I figured I'd gone about as far as I could go, I got lucky.

I spotted a stream. It was a couple of km. away past a meadow and another line of trees, cutting across between me and the front gate. Looked like exactly what I needed. If I could just get to it.

I didn't waste time worrying. I took a minute to fix the territory in my mind. Then I started back down the trunk.

My ears must've been improving. Before I was halfway to the ground (which I couldn't see because the leaves and branches were so thick), I heard something heading toward me through the trees.

Judging by the sound, whatever it was wasn't in any hurry, just moving across the branches in a leisurely way. But it was coming close. Too close.

I straddled a branch with my back to the trunk and braced my hands on the wood in front of me, and froze. I couldn't reach my knife that way, but I didn't want to. I couldn't picture myself doing any knife-fighting in a tree.

I barely got set in time. Three seconds later, there was a thrashing above me in the next tree over, and then a monkey landed maybe four meters away from me on the same branch.

He was a normal howler monkey—normal for Sharon's Point. Sturdy gray body, pitch-black face with deep gleaming eyes; a good bit bigger and stronger than a chimp. But he had those wide square shoulders, and hands that were too broad. He had a knapsack on his back.

And he was carrying an M-16 by the handle on top of the barrel.

He wasn't looking for me. He was just wandering. He was lonely. Howler monkeys live in packs; in his dumb instinctive way, he was probably looking for company—without knowing what he was looking for. He might've gone right on by without noticing me.

But when he hit the branch, the lurch made me move. Just a few cm.—but that was enough. It caught his attention. I should've had my eyes shut, but it was too late for that now. The howler knew I had eyes—he knew I was alive. In about five seconds he was going to know I smelled like blood.

He took the M-16 in both hands, tucked the stock into his shoulder, wrapped a finger around the trigger.

I stared back at him and didn't move a muscle.

What else could I do? I couldn't reach him—and if I could, I couldn't move fast enough to keep him from pulling the trigger. He'd cut me to pieces before I touched him. I wanted to plead with him, Don't shoot. I'm no threat to you. But he wouldn't understand. He was just a monkey. He would just shoot me.

I was so scared and angry I was afraid I was going to do something stupid. But I didn't. I just stared and didn't move.

The howler was curious. He kept his M-16 aimed at my chest, but he didn't shoot. I could detect no malice or cunning in his face. Slowly he came closer to me. He wanted to see what I was.

He was going to smell my blood soon, but I had to wait. I had to let him get close enough.

He kept coming. From four meters to three. To two. I thought I was going to scream. The muzzle of that rifle was lined up on my chest. It was all I could do to keep from looking at it, keep myself staring straight at the howler without blinking, meter.

One meter.

Very, very slowly, I closed my eyes. See, howler. I'm no threat. I'm not even afraid. I'm going to sleep. How can you be afraid of me?

But he was going to be afraid of me. He was going to smell my blood.

I counted two heartbeats with my eyes closed. Then I moved.

With my right foot braced on the trunk under me, I swung my left leg hard, kicked it over the top of the branch. I felt a heavy jolt through my knee as I hit the howler.

Right then, he started to fire. I heard the rapid metal stuttering of the M-16 on automatic, heard .22 slugs slashing through the leaves. But I must have knocked him off balance. In that first fraction of a second, none of the slugs got me.

Then my kick carried me off the branch. I was falling.

I went crashing down through the leaves with M-16 fire swarming after me like hornets.

Three or four meters later, a stiff limb caught me across the chest, I saw it just in time, got my arms over it and grabbed it as it hit. That stopped me with a jerk that almost tore my arms off.

I wasn't breathing any more, the impact knocked all the air out of me. But I didn't worry about it. I craned my neck, trying to see what the monkey was doing.

He was right above me on his branch, looking right at me. From there he couldn't have missed me to save his life.

But he wasn't firing. As slowly as if he had all the time in the world, he was taking the clip out of his rifle. He threw it away and reached back into his knapsack to get another one.

If I'd had a handgun or even a blaster, I could have shot him dead. He didn't even seem to know he was in danger, that it was dangerous for him to expose himself like that.

I didn't wait around for him to finish. Instead I swung my legs under the branch and let myself fall again.

This time I got lucky. For a second. My feet landed square on another branch. That steadied me, but I didn't try to stop. I took a running step down onto another branch, then jumped for another one.

That was the end of my luck. I lost my balance and fell. Probably would have broken my leg if I hadn't had those plastene struts along the bones. But I didn't have time to worry about that, either. I wasn't any more than ten meters off the ground now. There only one branch left between me and a broken back, and it was practically out of reach.

Not quite. I got both hands on it.

But I couldn't grip with my left. The whip of my weight tore my right loose. I landed flat on my back at the base of the tree.

I didn't feel like the fall kicked the air out of me—I couldn't remember the last time I did any breathing anyway. But the impact didn't help my head much. I went blind for a while, and there was a long crashing noise in my ears, as if the only thing I was able to hear, was ever going to hear, was the sound of myself hitting the ground. I felt like I'd landed hard enough to bury myself. But I fought it. I needed air. Needed to see.

That howler probably had me lined up in his sights already.

I fought it.

Got my eyes back first. Felt like hours, but probably didn't take more than five seconds. I wanted to look up into the tree, try to locate the monkey, but something else snagged my attention.

A coughing noise.

It wasn't coming from me. I wasn't breathing at all. It was coming from somewhere off to my left.

I didn't have to turn my head much to look in that direction. It was practically no trouble at all. But right away I wished I hadn't done it.

I saw a brown bear. A big brown bear. He must've been ten meters or more away, and he was down on all fours, but he looked huge. Too huge. I couldn't fight anything like that. I couldn't even breathe.

He was staring at me. Must've seen me fall. Now he was trying to decide what to do. Probably trying to decide whether to claw my throat out or bite my face off. The only reason he hadn't done anything yet was because I wasn't moving.

But I couldn't keep that up. I absolutely couldn't help myself. I needed air. A spasm of carbon-dioxide poisoning clutched my chest, made me twitch. When I finally took a breath, I made a whooping noise I couldn't control.

Which told the bear everything he wanted to know about me. With a roar that might have made me panic if I hadn't already been more dead than alive, he reared up onto his hind legs, and I got a look at what Paracels had done to him.

He had hands instead of forepaws, Paracels certainly liked hands. They were good for handling weapons. The bear's hands were so human-like I was sure Paracels must have got them from one of the dead hunters. They looked too small for the bear. I couldn't figure out how he was able to walk on them. But of course that wasn't too much of a problem for a bear. They were big enough for what Paracels had in mind.

Against his belly the bear had a furry pouch like a kangaroo's. As he reared up, he reached both hands into his pouch. When he brought them out again, he had an automatic in each fist. A pair of .22 Magnums.

He was going to blow my head off.

There was nothing I could do about it.

I had to do something about it. I didn't want to die. I was too mad to die.

Whatever it was I was going to do, I had about half a second to do it in. The bear hadn't cocked his automatics. It would take him half a second to pull the trigger far enough to get off his first shot—and that one wouldn't be very accurate. After that, the recoil of each shot would cock the gun for him. He'd be able to shoot faster and more accurately.

I flipped to my feet, then jumped backward, putting the tree between him and me.

I was too slow. He was firing before I reached my feet. But his first shots were wild, and after that I was moving. As I jerked backward, one of his bullets licked a shallow furrow across my chest. Then I was behind the tree. A half dozen slugs chewed into the trunk, too fast for me to count them. He had ten rounds in each gun. I was stuck until he had to reload.

Before I had time to even wonder what I was going to do, the howler opened fire.

He was above me, perched on the leaning dead tree. He must've been there when I started to move.

With all that lead flying around, he took aim at the thing that was most dangerous to him and opened up.

Damn near cut the bear in half.

Nothing bothered his aim, and his target was stationary. In three seconds he emptied an entire clip into the bear's guts.

He didn't move from where he was. He looked absolutely tame, like a monkey in a zoo. Nothing could have looked tamer than he did as he sat there taking out his spent clip, throwing it away, reaching into his knapsack for a fresh one.

That was the end of him. His blast had knocked the bear backward until the bear was sitting on the ground with his hind legs stretched out in front of him, looking as human as any animal in the world. He was bleeding to death; he'd be dead in ten seconds. But bears generally are stubborn and bloody-minded, and this one was no exception. Before he died, he raised his guns and blew the howler away.

I didn't spend any time congratulating myself for being alive. All that shooting was going to draw other animals, and I was in no shape to face them. I was bleeding from that bullet furrow, the back of my head, and a half dozen other cuts and scrapes. And the parts of me that weren't bleeding were too bruised to be much good. I turned and shambled away as quietly as I could in the direction of the stream.

I didn't get far. Reaction set in, and I had to hide myself in the best cover I could find and just be sick for a while. Sick with anger.

I was starting to see the pattern of this preserve. These animals were nothing but cannon fodder. They were as deadly as could be—and at the same time they were so tame they didn't know how to run away. That's right: *tame*. Because of their training.

Genetic alteration wasn't enough. First the animals had to be taught how to use their strange appendages. Then they had to be taught how to use their weapons, and finally they had to be taught not to use their weapons on their trainers or on each other. That mix-up between the bear and the howler was an accident; the bear just happened to be shooting too close to the monkey. They had to be taught not to attack each other every chance they got. Paracels probably boosted their brainpower, but they still had to be taught. Otherwise they'd just butcher each other. Dogs and rabbits, bears and dogs—they don't usually leave each other alone.

With one hand, Paracels gave them guns, mines, grenades; with the other, he took away their instincts for flight, self-preservation, even feeding themselves. They were crippled worse than a cyborg with his power turned off. They were deadly—but they were still crippled. Probably Paracels or Ushre or any of the handlers could walk the preserve end to end without being in any danger.

That was why I was so mad.

Somebody had to stop those bastards.

I wanted that somebody to be me.

I knew how to do it now. I understood what was happening in this preserve. I knew how it worked; I knew how to get out of it. Sharon's Point was unnatural in more ways than one. Maybe I could take advantage of one of those ways. If I could just find what I needed.

If I was going to do it, I had to do it now. Noon was already past, and I had to find what I was looking for before evening. And before some animal hunted me down. I stank of blood.

My muscles were queasy, but I made them carry me. Sweating and trembling, I did my damnedest to sneak through the woods toward the stream without giving myself away.

It wasn't easy, but after what I'd been through, nothing could be easy. I spent a while looking for tracks—and even that was hard. After all the rain, the ground was still soft enough to hold tracks, but I had trouble getting my eyes focused enough to see them. Sweat made all my scrapes and wounds feel like they were on fire.

But the only absolutely miserable trouble I had was crossing the meadow. Never mind the danger of exposing myself out in the open. I was worried about mines. And rabbits with hand grenades. I had to stay low, pick my way with terrible care. I had to keep off bare ground, and grass that was too thin (grass with a mine under it was likely to be thin), and grass that was too thick (rabbits might be hiding there). For a while I didn't think I was ever going to make it.

After that, the outcome was out of my hands. I was attacked again. At the last second, my ears warned me: I heard something cutting across the breeze. I fell to the side—and a hawk went whizzing past where my head had been. I didn't get a very good look at it, but there was something strange about its talons. They looked a lot like fangs.

A hawk with poisoned talons?

It circled above me and poised for another dive, but I didn't wait around for it. A rabbit with a grenade probably couldn't hit a running target. And if I touched a mine, I was better off moving fast—or so I told myself. I ran like hell for the line of trees between me and the stream.

The hawk's next dive was the worst. I misjudged it. If I hadn't tripped, the bird would have had me. But the next time I was more careful. It didn't get within a meter of me.

Then I reached the trees. I stopped there, froze as well as I could and still gasp for breath. After a while the hawk went barking away in frustration.

When I got up the nerve to move again, I scanned the area for animals. Didn't spot any. But on the ground I found what looked like a set of deer tracks. I didn't even try to think about what kind of alterations Paracels might have made in a deer. I didn't want to know. They were like the few tracks I'd seen back in the woods; they came toward me from the left and went away to the right. Downstream.

That was what I wanted to know. If I was wrong, I was dead.

I didn't wait much longer—just long enough to choose where I was going to put my feet. Then I went down to the stream. There was a small pool nearby, and I slid into it until I was completely submerged.

I stayed there for the better part of an hour. Spent a while just soaking—lying in the pool with my face barely out of water—trying to get back my strength. Then with my knife I cut away my clothes wherever I was hurt. But I didn't use the cloth for bandages; I had other ideas. After my wounds had bled clean and the bleeding had stopped, I eased partway out of the water and set about covering myself with mud.

I didn't want to look like a man and smell like blood; I wanted to look and smell like mud. The mud under the banks was just right—it was thick and black, and it dried fast. When I was done, my eyes, mouth, and hands were the only parts of me that weren't caked with mud.

The solution wasn't perfect, but mud was the best camouflage I was likely to find. And it would keep me from bleeding some more, at least for a while. As soon as I felt up to it, I started to work my way downstream along the bank.

My luck held. Nothing was following my track out of the woods. Probably all that blood around the dead bear and monkey was enough to cover me, keep any other animals from recognizing the man-blood smell and nosing around after me. But other than that I was in as much trouble as ever. I wasn't exactly strong on my feet. And I was running out of time. I had to find what I was looking for before evening. Before the animals came down to the stream to drink.

Before feeding time.

I didn't know how far I had to go, or even if I was going in the right direction. And I didn't like being out in the open. So I pushed myself pretty hard until I got out of the meadow. But when the stream ran back into some woods, I had to be more careful. I suppose I should have been grateful I didn't have to make my way through a swamp, but I wasn't. I was too busy trying to watch for everything and still keep going. Half the time I had to fight myself to stay alert. And half the time I had to fight myself to move at all.

But I found what I was looking for in time. For once I was right. It was just exactly where it should have been.

In a clearing in the trees. The woods around it were thick and tall, so it would be hard to spot—except from the air. Paracels and Ushre certainly didn't want their hunters to do what I was doing. The stream ran along one edge. And the bottom had been leveled. So a hovercraft could land.

Except for the landing area, the clearing was practically crowded with feeding troughs of all kinds.

Probably there were several places like this around the preserve. Sharon's Point needed them to survive. The animals were trained not to hunt each other. But that kind of training wouldn't last very long if they got hungry. Animals can't be trained to just let themselves starve. So Ushre and Paracels had to feed their animals. Regularly. At places like this.

Now the only question remaining was how soon the 'craft would come. It had to come—most of the troughs were empty. But if it came late—if the clearing had time to fill up before it got here—I wouldn't have a chance.

But it wasn't going to do me any good to worry about it. I worked my way around the clearing to where the woods were closest to the landing area. Then I picked a tree with bark about the same color as my mud, sat down against it, and tried to get some rest.

What I got was lucky—one last piece of luck to save my hide. Sunset was still a good quarter of an hour away when I began to hear the big fan of the 'craft whirring in the distance.

I didn't move. I wasn't all that lucky. Some animals were already in the clearing. A big whitetail buck was drinking at the stream, and a hawk was perched on one of the troughs. Out of the corner of my eye I could see two boxers (probably the same two I'd seen before) sitting and waiting, their tongues hanging out, not more than a dozen meters off to my left. Hidden where I was, I was practically invisible. But if I moved, I was finished.

At least there weren't very many of them. Yet.

I almost sighed out loud when the 'craft came skidding past the tree-tops. Gently it lined itself up and settled down onto the landing area.

Now time was all against me. Every animal in this sector of the pre-serve had heard the 'craft coming, and most of them would already be on their way to supper. But I couldn't just run down to the 'craft and ask for a ride. If the handler didn't shoot me himself, he'd take off, leaving me to the mercy of the animals. I gripped myself and didn't move.

The handler was taking his own sweet time.

As he moved around in the cockpit, I saw he was wearing a heavy gray jumpsuit. Probably all the handlers—as well as Ushre and Paracels when they worked with the animals—wore the same uniform. It pro-vided good protection, and the animals could recognize it. Furthermore it probably had a characteristic smell the animals had been taught to associate with food and friends. So the man was pretty much safe. The animals weren't going to turn on him.

Finally he started heaving sacks and bales out onto the ground: hay and grain for the deer, chow for the dogs, fruit for the monkeys—things like that. When he was finished emptying his cockpit, he jumped out of the 'craft to put the food in the troughs.

I still waited. I waited until the dogs ran out into the clearing. I wait-ed until the hawk snatched a piece of meat and flew away. I waited until the handler picked up a sack of grain and carried it off toward some of the troughs farthest away from the 'craft (and me).

Then I ran.

The buck saw me right away and jumped back. But the dogs didn't. The man didn't. He was looking at the buck. I was halfway to the 'craft before the dogs spotted me.

After that, it was a race. I had momentum and a headstart; the boxers had speed. They didn't even waste time barking; they just came right for me.

They were too fast. They were going to beat me.

In the last three meters, they were between me and the 'craft. The closest one sprang at me, and the other was right behind.

I ducked to the side, slipped the first dog past my shoulder. I could hear his jaws snap as he went by, but he missed.

The second dog I chopped as hard as I could across the side of the head with the edge of my left fist. The weight of my blaster gave that hand a little extra clout. I must have stunned him, because he fell and was slow getting up.

I saw that out of the corner of my eye. By the time I finished my swing, I was already sprinting toward the 'craft again. It wasn't more than three running steps away. But I could hear the first dog coming at me again. I took one of those steps, then hit the dirt.

The boxer went over and cracked into the bulging side of the 'craft.

Two seconds later, I was in the cockpit.

The handler had a late start, but once he got going, he didn't waste any time. When I landed in the cockpit, he was barely five meters away. I knew how to fly a hovercraft, and he'd made it easy for me—he'd left it idling. All I had to do was rev up the fan and tighten the wind convector until I lifted off. But he was jumping at me by the time I started to rise. He got his hands on the edge of the cockpit. Then I yanked him up into the air.

The jerk took his feet out from under him, so he was just hanging there by his hands.

Just to be sure he'd be safe, I rubbed a hand along the arm of his jumpsuit, then smelled my hand. It smelled like creosote.

I leveled off at about three meters. Before he could heave himself up into the cockpit, I banged his hands a couple times with my heavy left fist. He fell and hit the ground pretty hard.

But a second later he was on his feet and yelling at me. "Stop! he shouted, "Come back!" He sounded desperate. "You don't know what you're doing!"

"You'll be all right," I shouted back. "You can walk out of here by tomorrow morning. Just don't step on any mines."

"No!" he cried, and for a second he sounded so terrified I almost went back for him. "You don't know Ushre! You don't know what he'll do! He's crazy!"

But I thought I had a pretty good idea what Fritz Ushre was capable of. It didn't surprise me at all to hear someone say he was crazy—even someone who worked for him. And I didn't want the handler along with me. He'd get in my way.

I left him. I gunned the 'craft up over the trees and sent it skimming in the direction of the front gate. Going to give Ushre and Paracels what I owed them.

— 6 —

But I didn't let myself think about that. I was mad enough already. I didn't want to get all livid and careless. I wanted to be calm and quick and precise. More dangerous than anything Paracels ever made—or ever even dreamed about making. Because I was doing something that was too important to have room for miscalculations.

Well, important to me, anyway. Probably nobody in the world but me (and Morganstark) gave a rusty damn what was happening at Sharon's Point—just as long as the animals didn't get loose. But that's what Special Agents are for. To care about things like this, so other people don't have to.

But I didn't have to talk myself into anything; I knew what I was going to do. The big thing I had to worry about was the lousy shape I was in. I was giddy with hunger and woozy with fatigue and queasy with pain, and I kept having bad patches where I couldn't seem to make the 'craft fly straight, or even level.

The darkness didn't improve my flying any. The sun went down right after I left the clearing, and by the time I was halfway to the front gate evening had turned into night. I suppose I should've been grateful for the cover: when I finally got to the gate, my bad flying probably wouldn't attract any attention. But I wasn't feeling grateful about much of anything right then. In the dark I had to fly by instruments, and I wasn't doing a very good job of it. Direction I could handle (sort of), and I already had enough altitude to get me over the hills. But the little green dial that showed the artificial horizon seemed to have a life of its own; it wouldn't sit still long enough for me to get it into focus. I spent the whole trip yawing back and forth like a drunk.

But I made it. My aim wasn't too good (when I finally spotted the bright pink freon bulb at the landing area, it was way the hell off to my left), but it was good enough. I went skidding over there until I was sitting almost on top of the light, but then I took a couple minutes to scan the area before I put the 'craft down.

I suppose what I should've done was not land there at all. I should've just gone until I got some place where I could call the Bureau for help. But I figured if I did that Ushre and Paracels would get away. They'd know something was wrong when their hovercraft didn't come back, and they'd be on the run before the Bureau could do anything about it. Then the Bureau would be hunting them for days—and I'd miss out on the finish of my own assignment. I wasn't about to let that happen.

So I took a good look below me before I landed. Both the other 'craft were there (they must've had shorter feeding runs), but nobody was standing around outside—at least not where I could see them. Most of the windows of the barracks showed light, but the office complex was dark—except for the front office and the laboratory wing.

Ushre and Paracels.

If they stayed where they were, I could go in after them, get them out to the 'craft—take them into St. Louis myself. If I caught them by surprise. And didn't run into anybody else. And didn't crack up trying to fly the 300 km. to St. Louis.

I didn't even worry about it. I put the 'craft down as gently as I could and threw it into idle. Before the fan even had time to slow down, I jumped out of the cockpit and went pelting as fast as I could go toward the front office.

Yanked open the door, jumped inside, shut it behind me.

Stopped.

Fritz Ushre was standing behind the counter. He must have been doing some work with his accomputer; he had the console in front of him. His face was white, and his little boar eyes were staring at me as if I'd just come back from the dead. He didn't even twitch—he looked paralyzed with surprise and fear.

"Fritz Ushre," I said with my own particular brand of malice, "you're under arrest for murder, attempted murder, and conspiracy." Then, just because it felt good, I went on, "You have the right to remain silent. If you choose to speak, anything you say can and will be used against you in a court of law. You have the right to be represented by an attorney. If you can't afford one—"

He wasn't listening. There was a struggle going on in his face that didn't have anything to do with what I was saying. For once, he looked too surprised to be cunning, too beaten to be malicious. He was trying to fight it, but he wasn't getting anywhere. He was trying to find a way out, a way to get rid of me, save himself, and there wasn't any. Sharon's Point was dead, and he knew it.

Or maybe it wasn't. Maybe there was a way out. All of a sudden the struggle was over. He met my eyes, and the expression on his face was more naked and terrible than anything he'd ever let me see before. It was hunger. And glee.

He looked down. Reached for something under the counter.

I was already moving, throwing myself at him. I got my hands on the edge of the counter, vaulted over it, hit him square in the chest with both heels.

He smacked against the wall behind him, bounced back, stumbled to his knees. I fell beside him. But I was up before he could move. In almost the same movement, I got my knife out and pressed the point against the side of his fat neck. "If you make a sound," I said, panting, "I'll bleed you right here."

He didn't act like he heard me. He was coughing for air. And laughing.

Quickly, I looked around behind the counter to find what he'd been reaching for.

For a second I couldn't figure it out. There was an M-16 lying on a shelf off to one side, but that wasn't it—he hadn't been reaching in that direction.

Then I saw it. A small gray box built into the counter near where he'd been standing. It wasn't much—just a big red button and a little red light. The little red light was on.

Right then, I realized I was hearing something. Something so high-pitched it was almost inaudible. Something keen and carrying.

I heard something like it before, but at first I couldn't remember where. Then I had it.

An animal whistle.

It was pitched almost out of the range of human hearing, but probably there wasn't an animal in 10 km. that couldn't hear it. Or didn't know what it meant.

I put my knife away and picked up the M-16. I didn't have time to be scrupulous; I cocked it and pointed it at Ushre's head. "Turn it off," I said.

He was just laughing now. Laughing softly. "You cannot turn it off. Once it has been activated, nothing can stop it."

I got out my knife again, tore the box out of the counter, cut the wires. He was right. The red light went off, but the sound didn't stop.

"What does it do?"

He was absolutely shaking with suppressed hilarity. "Guess!"

I jabbed him with the muzzle of the M-16. "What does it do?"

He didn't stop shaking. But he turned to look at me. His eyes were bright and wild and mad. "You will not shoot me." He almost giggled. "You are not the type."

Well, he was right about that, too. I wasn't even thinking about killing him. I wanted information. I made a huge effort to sound reasonable. "Tell me anyway. I can't stop it, so why not?"

"Ah," he sighed. He liked that idea. "May I stand?"

I let him get to his feet.

"Much better," he said. "Thank you, Mr. Browne."

After that, I don't think I could've stopped him from telling me. He enjoyed it too much. He was manic with glee. Some sharp appetite maybe he didn't even know he had was about to get fed.

"Dr. Paracels may be old and unbalanced," he said, "but he is brilliant in his way. And he has a taste for revenge. He has developed his genetic techniques to the point of precise control.

"As you may know, Mr. Browne, all animals may be conditioned to perform certain actions upon certain signals—even human animals. The more complex the brain of the animal, the more complex the actions which may be conditioned into it—but also the more complex and difficult the conditioning process. For human animals, the difficulty of the process is often prohibitive."

He relished what he was saying so much he was practically slobbering. I wanted to scream with frustration, but I forced the impulse down. I had to hear what he was saying, needed to hear it all.

"Dr. Paracels—bless his retributive old heart—has learned how to increase animal brain capacity enough to make possible a very gratifying level of conditioning without increasing it enough to make conditioning unduly difficult. That provides the basis for the way in which we train our animals. But it serves one other purpose also.

"Each of our animals has been keyed to that sound." He gestured happily at the air. "They have been conditioned to respond to that sound in a certain way. With violence, Mr. Browne!" He was bubbling over with laughter. "But not against each other. Oh no—that would never do. They have been conditioned to attack humans, Mr. Browne—to come to the source of the sound and then attack.

"Even our handlers are not immune. This conditioning overrides all other training. Only Dr. Paracels and myself are safe. All our animals have been imprinted with our voices, so that even in their most violent frenzies they will recognize us. And obey us, Mr. Browne. Obey us!"

I was shaking as bad as he was, but for different reasons. "So what?" I demanded. "They can't get past the fence."

"Past the fence?" Ushre was ecastatic. "You fool! The gate is open! It opened automatically when I pressed the button."

So finally I knew what that handler back in the preserve had been so scared about. Ushre was letting the animals out. Out to terrorize the countryside until God knows how many people were killed trying to hunt them down. Or just trying to get away from them. Or even just sitting at home minding their own business. I had to stop those animals. With just an M-16? Fat chance!

But I had to try. I was a Special Agent, wasn't I? This was my job. I'd signed up for it of my own free will.

I rammed the muzzle of the M-16 hard into Ushre's stomach. He doubled over. I grabbed his collar and yanked his head up again.

"Listen to me," I said very softly. "I didn't used to be the type to shoot people in cold blood, but I am now. I'm mad enough to do it now. Get moving."

I made him believe me. When I gave him a shove, he went where I wanted him to go. Toward the front door.

He opened it, and we went out together into the night.

I could see the front gates clearly in the light from the landing area. He was absolutely right. They were open.

I was already too late to close them. A dark crowd of animals was already coming out of the preserve. They bristled with weapons. They didn't hurry, didn't make any noise, didn't get in each other's way. And more came over the ridge every second, moving like they were on their way out of Fritz Ushre's private hell. In the darkness they looked practically numberless. For one dizzy second I couldn't believe Ushre and Paracels had had time to engineer so many helpless creatures individually. But of course they'd been working at it for years. Sharon's Point must have been almost completely stocked when they opened for business. And since then they'd had twenty months to alter and raise even more animals.

I had to move fast. I had one gamble left, and if it didn't work I was just going to be the first on a long list of people who were going to die.

I gave Ushre a shove that sent him stumbling forward.

Out in front of that surging crowd. Between them and the road.

Before he could try to get away, I caught up with him, grabbed his elbow, jabbed the M-16 into his ribs. "Now, Mr. Ushre," I said through my teeth. "You're going to tell them to go back. Back through the gates. They'll obey you." When he didn't respond, I gouged him viciously. "Tell them!"

Well, it was a good idea. Worth a try. It might even have worked—if I could've controlled Ushre. But he was out of control. He was crazy for blood now, completely bananas.

"Tell them to go back?" he cried with a laugh. "Are you joking?" There was blood in his voice—blood and power. "These beasts are mine! Mine! My will commands them! They will rain bloodshed upon the country! They will destroy you, and all people like you. I will teach you what hunting truly means, Mr. Browne!" He made my name sound like a deadly insult. "I will teach you to understand death!"

"You'll go first!" I shouted, trying to cut through his madness. "I'll blow you to pieces where you stand."

"You will not!"

He was faster than I expected. Much faster. With one quick swing of his massive arm, he smacked me to the ground.

"Kill him!" he howled at the animals. He was waving his fists as if he was conducting an orchestra of butchery. "Kill them all!"

A monkey near the front of the crowd fired, and all of a sudden Ushre's hell erupted.

All the animals that had clear space in front of them started shooting at once. M-16 and .22 Magnum fire shattered the air; bullets screamed wildly in all directions. The night was full of thunder and death. I couldn't understand why I wasn't being hit.

Then I saw why.

Two thin beams of ruby-red light were slashing back and forth across the front of that dark surge of animals. The animals weren't shooting at me. They were firing back at those beams.

Laser cannon!

I spotted one of them in the woods off to one side of the landing area. The other was blazing away from a window of the barracks.

They were cutting the animals to shreds. Flesh and blood can't stand up against laser cannon, no matter what kind of genes it has. Monkeys and bears were throwing sheets of lead back at the beams, but they were in each other's way, and most of their shooting was wild. And the people operating the cannon were shielded. It was just slaughter, that's all.

Because the animals couldn't run away. They didn't know how. They were conditioned. They reminded me of a tame dog that can't even try to avoid an angry master. But instead of cringing they were shooting.

The outcome wasn't any kind of sure thing. The animals were getting cut down by the dozens—but all they needed was a few hand grenades, or maybe a couple mines in the right places, and that would be the end of the cannon. And the dogs, for one, didn't have to be told what to do. Already they were trying to get through the fire with mines in their jaws. The lasers had to draw in their aim to get the dogs, and that gave the other animals time to spread out, get out of direct range of the lasers.

It was going to be a long, bloody battle. And I was lying in the dirt, right in the middle of it. I didn't know how I was going to live through it.

I don't know how Ushre lasted even that long. He was on his feet, wasn't even trying to avoid getting hit. But nothing touched him. There must've been a charm of madness on his life. Roaring and laughing, he was on his way to the hovercraft. A minute later he climbed into the one I had so conveniently left idling.

I wanted to run after him, but I didn't get the chance. Before I could move, a rabbit went scrambling past and practically hit me in the face with a live grenade.

I didn't stop to think about it. I didn't have time to ask myself what I was doing. I didn't want to ask. All those dogs and deer and rabbits and God knows what else were getting butchered, and I'd already gone more than a little bit crazy myself.

I picked up the grenade and threw it. Watched it land beside Ushre in the cockpit of the craft.

Blow him apart.

The 'craft would've gone up in flames if it hadn't been built around a power pack like the one that wasn't doing me any good.

I just turned my back on it.

The next minute, a man came running out of the barracks. He dodged frantically toward me, firing his blaster in front of him as he ran. Then he landed on his stomach beside me.

Morganstark.

"You all right?" he panted. He had to stop blasting to talk, but he started up again right away.

"Yes!" I shouted to make myself heard. "Where did you come from?"

"Your transceiver went off!" he shouted back. "Did you think I was going to just sit on my hands and wait for your death certificate?" He fired a couple bursts, then added, "We've got the handlers tied up in the barracks, but there's one missing. Who was that you just blew up?"

I didn't tell him. I didn't have time. I didn't want Paracels to get away.

What I wanted was to tell Morganstark to stop the killing. I was going wild, seeing all those animals die. But I didn't say anything about it. What choice did Morganstark have? Let Paracels' fine creations go and wreak havoc around the countryside? No, I was going to have to live with all this blood. It was my doing as much as anybody else's.

If I'd done my job right, Ushre would never have gotten a chance to push that button. If I'd killed him right away. Or if I hadn't confronted him at all. If I'd let that handler back in the preserve tell me what he was afraid of.

"Get those gates shut!" I yelled at Morganstark. "I'm going after Paracels!"

He didn't have a chance to stop me. I was already on my feet, running and dodging toward the office door.

I took the M-16 with me. I thought it was about time Dr. Avid Paracels had one of these things pointed at him.

$$- 7 -$$

I don't know how I made it. I was moving low and fast—I wasn't very easy to see, much less hit. And I had only about twenty meters to go. But the air was alive with fire. Bullets were ripping all around me. Morganstark and his men were answering with lasers and blasters. Ushre must not have been the only one with a charm on him. Five seconds later, I dove through the open doorway, and there wasn't a mark on me. Nothing new, anyway.

Inside the complex, I didn't slow down. It was a sure thing Paracels knew what was happening—he could hear the noise if nothing else. So he'd be trying to make some kind of escape. I had to stop him before he got out into the night. He was the only one left who could stop the slaughter.

But I was probably too late. He'd had plenty of time to disappear; it wouldn't take much at night in these hills. I ran like a crazy man down the corridor toward the surgery—like I wasn't exhausted and hurt and sick, and didn't even know what fear was. Slammed into the clinic, scanned it. But Paracels wasn't there. I went on, hunting for a way into the lab wing.

A couple of corridors took me in the right direction. Then I was in one of those spots where I had several doors to choose from and no way to tell which was right. Again. But now I was doing things by instinct—things I couldn't have done if I'd been thinking about them. I knew where I was in the building and had a relative idea where the lab was. I went straight to one of the doors, stopped. Touched the knob carefully.

It was unlocked.

I threw it open and stormed in.

He was there.

I'd come in through a door near the cremator. He was across the room from me, standing beside the lab tables. He didn't look like he'd even changed his clothes since last night—he didn't look like he had enough life in him to make the effort. In the bright white lights he looked like death. He should not have even been able to stand up, looking like that. But he was standing up. He was moving around. He wasn't hurrying, but he wasn't wasting any time, either. He was packing lab equipment into a big black satchel.

He glanced at me when I came in, but he didn't stop what he was doing. Taking everything he could fit in his bag.

I had the M-16 tucked under my right elbow and braced with my left hand. My index finger was on the trigger. Not the best shooting position, but I wasn't likely to miss at this range.

"They're getting butchered," I said. My voice shook, but I couldn't help it. "You're going to stop it. You're going to tell me how to shut down that goddamn whistle. Then you're going to go out there with me, and you're going to order them back into the preserve."

Paracels glanced at me again, but didn't stop what he was doing.

"You're going to do it now!"

He almost smiled. "Or else?" Every time I saw him he seemed to have a different voice. Now he sounded calm and confident, like a man who'd finally arrived at a victory he'd been working toward for years, and he was mocking me.

"Or else," I hissed at him, trying to make him feel my anger, "I'll drag you out there and let them shoot you themselves."

"I don't think so." I wasn't making any kind of dent in him. He surprised me when he went on. "But part of that I was going to do anyway. I don't want too many of my animals killed." He moved to the far wall, flipped something that looked like a light switch. All at once, the high-pitched pressure of the whistles burst like a bubble and was gone.

Then he really did smile—a grin that looked as if he'd learned it from Ushre. "Ushre probably told you it couldn't be shut off. And you believed him." He shook his head. "He wanted to make it that way. But I made him put a switch in here. He isn't very farsighted."

"Wasn't," I said. I don't know why. I didn't have any intention of bandying words with Dr. Avid Paracels. But something changed for me when the whistle stopped. I lost a lot of my urgency. Now the animals would stop coming, and Morganstark would be able to get the gates closed. Soon the killing would be over. All at once I realized how tired I was. I hurt everywhere.

And there was something else. Something about the good doctor didn't fit. I had a loaded M-16 aimed right at him. He didn't have any business being so sure of himself. I said, "He's dead. I killed him." Trying to shake his confidence.

It didn't work. He had something going for him I didn't know about—something made him immune to me. All he did was shrug and say, "I'm not surprised. He wasn't very stable."

He was so calm about it I wanted to start shooting at him. But I didn't. I didn't want to kill him. I wanted to make him talk. It took a real effort, but I asked him as casually as I could, "Did you know what you were getting into when you started doing business with him?"

"Did I know?" He snorted. "I counted on it. I knew I could handle him. He was perfect for me. He offered me exactly what I was looking for—a chance to do some research." For an instant there was something in his eyes that almost looked like a spark of life. "And a chance to pay a few debts."

"The genetic riots," I said. "You lost your job."

"I lost my career!" All of a sudden he was mad, furious. "I lost my whole future! My life! I was on my way to things you couldn't even imagine. Recombinant DNA was just the beginning, just the first step. By now I would have been able to synthesize genes. I would've been making supermen! Think about it. Geniuses smart enough to run the country decently for a change. Smart enough to crack the speed of light. Smart enough to create life. A whole generation of people that were immune to disease. People who could adapt to whatever changes in food or climate the future holds. Astronauts who didn't need pressure suits. I could have done it!"

"But there were riots," I said softly.

"They should have been put down. The government should have shot anybody who objected. What I was doing was too important. But they didn't. They blamed the riots on me. They said I violated the sanctity of life. They sent me out in disgrace. By the time they were finished, I couldn't get a legitimate research grant to save my life."

"That's why you want revenge," I said. Keep talking, Paracels. Tell me what I need to know.

"Retribution," He loved the sound of that word. "When I'm done, they're going to beg me to let them give me whatever I want."

I tried to steer him where I wanted him to go, "How're you going to accomplish that? So far all you've done is kill a few hunters. That isn't exactly going to topple the government."

"Ah"—he grinned again—"but this is just the beginning. In about two minutes, I'm going to leave here. They won't be able to find me—they won't know where I've gone. By the time they find out, I'll be ready for them."

I shook my head. "I don't understand."

"Of course you don't understand!" He was triumphant. "You spent the whole day in my preserve and you still don't understand. You aren't able to understand."

I was afraid he was going to stop then, but he didn't. He was too full of victory. "Tell me, cyborg"—the way he said *cyborg* was savage—"did you happen to notice that all the animals you saw out there are male?"

I nodded dumbly. I didn't have the vaguest idea what he was getting at.

"They're all male. Ushre wanted me to use females, too—he wanted the animals to breed. But I told him that the animals I make are sterile—that grafting new genes onto them makes them sterile. And I told him the males would be more aggressive if they didn't have mates. I knew how to handle him. He believed me.

"Ah, you're all fools! I was just planning ahead—planning for what's happening right now. The animals I make aren't sterile. In fact, they're genetically dominant. Most of them will reproduce themselves three times out of four."

He paused, playing his speech for effect. Then he said, "Right now, all the animals in my breeding pens are female. I have hundreds of them. And there's a tunnel that runs from this building to the preserve.

"I'm going to take all those females and go out into the preserve. Nobody will suspect—nobody will ever think I've done such a thing. They won't look for me there. And once the gates are shut, I'll have time. Nobody will know what to do with my animals. Humanitarians'll want to save them—they'll probably even feed them. Scientists'll want to study them. Nobody will want to just kill them off. Even if they want to, they won't know how. Time will pass. Time for my animals to breed. To breed, cyborg! Soon I'll have an army of them. And then I'll give you revenge that'll make the genetic riots look like recreation!"

That was it, then. That was why he was so triumphant. And his scheme just might work—for a while, anyway. Probably wouldn't change the course of history, but a lot more than just forty-six hunters would get killed.

I was gripping the M-16 so hard my hands trembled. But my voice was steady. I didn't have any doubt or hesitation left to make me sound uncertain. "First you're going to have to kill me."

"I'm a doctor," he said. He was looking straight at me. "I won't have to kill you."

With the tip of his tongue, he made a small gesture around his lips.

He almost got me for the second time. It was just instinct that warned me—I didn't hear anything behind me, didn't know I was in any danger. But I moved. Spun where I was, whipped the M-16 around.

I couldn't have messed it up any better if I'd been practicing for weeks. My turn slapped the barrel of the M-16 into the palm of a hand as big as my face. Black hairy fingers as strong as my whole arm gripped the rifle, ripped it away from me. Another arm clubbed me across the chest so hard I almost did a flip in the air. When I hit the floor, I skidded until I whacked into the leg of the nearest table.

I climbed back to my feet, then had to catch myself on the table to keep from falling. My head was reeling like a sonofabitch—the room wouldn't stand still. For a minute I couldn't focus my eyes.

"I call him Cerberus." Paracels smirked. "He's been with me for a long time.

Cerberus. What fun. With an effort that almost split my skull, I ground my eyeballs into focus, forced myself to look at whatever it was.

"He's the last thing I created before they kicked me out. When I saw what was going to happen, I risked everything on one last experiment. I took the embryo with me and built incubators for it myself. I raised him with my own hands from the beginning."

That must've been what hit me the last time I was here. I'd been assuming it was Ushre, but it must've been this thing all along. It was too quiet and fast to have been Ushre.

Basically, it was a gorilla. It had the fangs, the black fur, the ape face, the long arms. But it wasn't like any gorilla I'd ever met before. For one thing, it was more than two meters tall.

"You see the improvements I made," Paracels went on. I didn't think he could stop. He'd gone past the point where he could've stopped. "He stands upright naturally—I adjusted his spine, his hips, his legs. His thighs and calves are longer than normal, which gives him increased speed and agility on the ground.

"But I've done much more than that." He was starting to sound like Ushre. "By altering the structure of his brain, I've improved his intelligence, reflexes, dexterity, his ability to do what I teach him to do. And he is immensely strong."

That I could see for myself. Right there in front of me, that damn ape took the M-16 in one hand and hit it against the wall. Wrecked the rifle. And took a chunk out of the concrete.

"In a sense, it's a shame we turned you off, cyborg. The contest might've proved interesting—an artificial man against an improved animal. But of course the outcome would've been the same. Cerberus is quick enough to dodge your blaster and strong enough to withstand it. He's more than an animal. You're less than a human being."

It was coming for me slowly. Its eyes looked so vicious I almost believed it was coming slowly just to make me more scared. I backed away, put a couple of tables between us. But Paracels moved too— didn't let me get closer to him. I could hardly keep from screaming, Morganstark! But Morganstark wasn't going to rescue me. I could still hear shooting. He wasn't likely to come in after me until he was finished outside and the gates were closed. He couldn't very well run the risk of letting any of those animals go free.

Paracels was watching me, enjoying himself. "That's the one thing I can't understand, cyborg." I wanted to yell at him to shut up, but he went on maliciously, "I can't understand why society tolerates, even approves of mechanical monstrosities like you, but won't bear biological improvements like Cerberus. What's so sacred about biology? Recombinant DNA research has unlimited potential. You're just a weapon. And not a very good one."

I couldn't stand it. I had to answer him somehow.

"There's just one difference," I gritted. "I chose. Nobody did this to me when I was just an embryo."

Paracels laughed.

A weapon—I had to have a weapon. I couldn't picture myself making much of an impression on that thing with just a knife. I scanned the room, hunted up and down the tables, while I backed away. But I couldn't find anything. Just lab equipment. Most of it was too heavy for me to even lift. And I couldn't do anything with all the chemicals around the lab. I didn't know anything about chemicals.

Paracels couldn't seem to stop laughing.

Goddamn it, Browne! Think!

Then I had it.

Ushre had turned off my power pack. That meant he'd built a certain kind of magnetic probe. If that probe was still around, I could turn myself back on.

Frantically, I started hunting for it.

I knew what to look for. A field generator, a small field generator, something no bigger than a fist. It didn't have to be strong, it had to be specific; it had to make exactly the right magnetic shape to key my power pack. It had to have three antenna as small as tines set close together in exactly the right pattern. I knew what that pattern looked like.

But Paracels's ape wasn't giving me time to search carefully. It wasn't coming slowly anymore. I had to concentrate to stay away from it, keep at least a couple of tables between us. Any minute now it was going to jump at me, and then I was going to be dead. Maybe the generator wasn't even here.

I reached for my knife. I was going to try to get Paracels anyway, at least take care of him before that thing finished me off.

But then I spotted it.

Lying on a table right in front of the gorilla.

"All right, Cerberus," Paracels said. "We can't wait any longer. Kill him now."

The ape threw himself across the tables at me so fast I almost didn't see it coming.

But Paracels had warned me. I was already moving. As the gorilla came over the tables, I ducked and went under them.

I jumped up past the table I wanted, grabbing at the generator. I was in too much of a hurry: I fumbled it for a second. Then I got my right hand on it. Found the switch, activated it. Now all I had to do was touch those tines to the center of my chest.

The ape crashed into me, and everything went blank. At first I thought I'd broken my spine; there was an iron bar of pain across my back just under my shoulder blades. But then my eyes cleared, and I saw the gorilla's teeth right in front of my face. It had its arms around me. It was crushing me.

My left arm was free. But my right was caught between me and the ape. I couldn't lift the generator.

I couldn't reach the ape's eyes from that angle, so I just stuck my left hand in its mouth and tried to jam it down its throat.

The ape gagged for a second, then started to bite my hand off.

I could hear the bones breaking, and there was a metallic noise that sounded like my blaster cracking.

But while it gagged, the ape eased its grip on my chest. Just a fraction, just a few millimeters. But that was all I needed. I was desperate. I dragged the generator upward between us, upward, closer to the center of my chest.

There was blood running all over the ape's jaw. I wanted to scream, but I couldn't—I had my tongue jammed against the switches in my teeth. I just dragged, dragged, with every gram of force in my body.

Then the tines touched my sternum.

The blaster was damaged. But it went off. Blew the gorilla's head to pieces.

Along with most of my hand.

Then I was lying on top of the ape. I wanted to just lie there, put my head down and sleep, but I wasn't finished. My job wasn't finished. I still had Paracels to worry about.

Somehow I got to my feet.

He was still there. He was at one of the tables, fussing with a piece of equipment. I stared at him for the longest time before I realized he was trying to do something to the surgical laser. He was trying to get it free of its mounting. So he could aim it at me.

Strange snuffling noises were coming out of his mouth. It sounded like he was crying.

I didn't care. I was past caring. I didn't have any sentimentality left. I took my knife out and threw it at him. Watched it stick itself halfway to the hilt in the side of his neck.

Then I sat down. I had to force myself to take off my belt and use it for a tourniquet on my left arm. It didn't seem to be worth the effort, but I did it anyway.

Some time later (or maybe it was right away—I don't know) Morganstark came into the lab. First he said, "We got the gates shut. That'll hold them—for a while, anyway."

Then he said, "Jesus Christ! What happened to you?"

There was movement around me. Then he said, "Well, there's one consolation, anyway." (Was he checking my tourniquet? No, he was trying to put some kind of bandage on my mangled hand.) "If you don't have a hand, they can build a laser into your forearm. Line it up between the bones—make it good and solid. You'll be as good as new. Better. They'll make you the most powerful Special Agent in the Division."

I said, "The hell they will." Probably I was going to pass out. "The hell they will."

Unworthy of the Angel

Let no man be unworthy of the Angel who stands over him.

—UNKNOWN

▲▼▲

...And stumbled when my feet seemed to come down on the sidewalk out of nowhere. The heat was like walking into a wall; for a moment, I couldn't find my balance. Then I bumped into somebody; that kept me from falling. But he was a tall man in an expensive suit, certain and piti-less, and as he recoiled his expression said plainly that people like me shouldn't be allowed out on the streets.

I retreated until I could brace my back against the hard glass of a display window and tried to take hold of myself. It was always like this; I was completely disoriented—a piece of cork carried down the river. Everything seemed to be melting from one place to another. Back and forth in front of me, people with bitten expressions hurried, chasing disaster. In the street, too many cars snarled and blared at each other, blaming everything except themselves. The buildings seemed to go up for miles into a sky as heavy as a lid. They looked elaborate and hollow, like crypts.

And the heat—I couldn't see the sun, but it was up there somewhere, in the first half of the morning, hidden by humidity and filth. Breathing was like inhaling hot oil. I had no idea where I was; but wherever it was, it needed rain.

Maybe I didn't belong here. I prayed for that. The people who flicked glances at me didn't want what they saw. I was wearing a gray overcoat streaked with dust, spotted and stained. Except for a pair of ratty shoes, splitting at the seams, and my clammy pants, the coat was all I had on. My face felt like I'd spent the night in a pile of trash. But if I had, I couldn't remember. Without hope, I put my hands in all my pockets, but they were empty. I didn't have a scrap of identification or money to make things easier. My only hope was that everything still seemed to be melting. Maybe it would melt into something else, and I would be saved.

But while I fought the air and the heat and prayed, Please, God, not again, the entire street sprang into focus without warning. The sensation snatched my weight off the glass, and I turned in time to see a young woman emerge from the massive building that hulked beside the storefront where I stood.

She was dressed with the plainness of somebody who didn't have any choice—the white blouse gone dingy with use, the skirt fraying at the hem. Her fine hair, which deserved better, was efficiently tied at the back of her neck. Slim and pale, too pale, blinking at the heat, she moved along the sidewalk in front of the store. Her steps were faintly unsteady, as if she were worn out by the burden she carried.

She held a handkerchief to her face like a woman who wanted to disguise the fact that she was still crying.

She made my heart clench with panic. While she passed in front of me, too absorbed in her distress to notice me or anyone else, I thought she was the reason I was here.

But after that first spasm of panic, I followed her. She seemed to leave waves of urgency on either side, and I was pulled along in her wake.

The crowd slowed me down. I didn't catch up with her until she reached the corner of the block and stopped to wait for the light to change. Some people pushed out into the street anyway; cars screamed at them until they squeezed back onto the sidewalk. Everybody was in a hurry, but not for joy. The tension and the heat daunted me. I wanted to hold back—wanted to wait until she found her way to a more private place. But she was as distinct as an appeal in front of me, a figure etched in need. And I was only afraid.

Carefully, almost timidly, I reached out and put my hand on her arm.

Startled, she turned toward me; her eyes were wide and white, flinching. For an instant, her protective hand with the handkerchief dropped from the center of her face, and I caught a glimpse of what she was hiding.

It wasn't grief. It was blood.

It was vivid and fatal, stark with implications. But I was still too confused to recognize what it meant.

As she saw what I looked like, her fright receded. Under other circumstances, her face might have been soft with pity. I could tell right away that she wasn't accustomed to being so lost in her own needs. But now they drove her, and she didn't know what to do with me.

Trying to smile through my dirty whiskers, I said as steadily as I could, "Let me help you."

But as soon as I said it, I knew I was lying. She wasn't the reason I was here.

The realization paralyzed me for a moment. If she'd brushed me off right then, there would have been nothing I could do about it. She wasn't the reason—? Then why had I felt such a shock of importance when she came out to the street? Why did her nosebleed—which really didn't look very serious—seem so fatal to me? While I fumbled with questions, she could have simply walked away from me.

But she was near the limit of her courage. She was practically frantic for any kind of assistance or comfort. But my appearance was against me. As she clutched her handkerchief to her nose again, she murmured in surprise and hopelessness, "What're you talking about?"

That was all the grace I needed. She was too vulnerable to turn her back on any offer, even from a man who looked like me. But I could see that she was so fragile now because she had been so brave for so long. And she was the kind of woman who didn't turn her back. That gave me something to go on.

"Help is the circumference of need," I said. "You wouldn't be feeling like this if there was nothing anybody could do about it. Otherwise the human race would have committed suicide two days after Adam and Eve left the Garden."

I had her attention now, but she didn't know what to make of me. She wasn't really listening to herself as she murmured, "You're wrong." She was just groping. "I mean your quote. Not help. Reason. 'Reason is the circumference of energy.' Blake said that."

I didn't know who Blake was, but that didn't matter. She'd given me permission—enough permission, anyway, to get me started. I was still holding her arm, and I didn't intend to let her go until I knew why I was here—what I had to do with her.

Looking around for inspiration, I saw we were standing in front of a coffee shop. Through its long glass window, I saw that it was nearly empty; most of its patrons had gone looking for whatever they called salvation. I turned back to the woman and gestured toward the shop. "I'll let you buy me some coffee if you'll tell me what's going on."

She was in so much trouble that she understood me. Instead of asking me to explain myself, she protested, "I can't. I've got to go to work. I'm already late."

Sometimes it didn't pay to be too careful. Bluntly, I said, "You can't do that, either. You're still bleeding."

At that, her eyes widened; she was like an animal in a trap. She hadn't thought as far ahead as work. She had come out onto the sidewalk without one idea of what she was going to do. "Reese—" she began, then stopped to explain, "My brother." She looked miserable. "He doesn't like me to come home when he's working. It's too important. I didn't even tell him I was going to the doctor." Abruptly, she bit herself still, distrusting the impulse or instinct that drove her to say such things to a total stranger.

Knots of people continued to thrust past us, but now their vehemence didn't touch me. I hardly felt the heat. I was locked to this woman who needed me, even though I was almost sure she wasn't the one I was meant to help. Still smiling, I asked, "What did the doctor say?"

She was too baffled to refuse the question. "He didn't understand it. He said I shouldn't be bleeding. He wanted to put me in the hospital. For observation."

"But you won't go," I said at once.

"I can't." Her whisper was nearly a cry. "Reese's show is tomorrow. His first big show. He's been living for this all his life. And he has so much to do. To get ready. If I went to the hospital, I'd have to call him. Interrupt—. He'd have to come to the hospital."

Now I had her. When the need is strong enough—and when I've been given enough permission—I can make myself obeyed. I let go of her arm and held out my hand. "Let me see that handkerchief."

Dumbly, as if she were astonished at herself, she lowered her hand and give me the damp cloth.

It wasn't heavily soaked; the flow from her nose was slow. That was why she was able to even consider the possibility of going to work. But her red pain was as explicit as a wail in my hand. I watched a new bead of blood gather in one of her nostrils, and it told me a host of things I was not going to be able to explain to her. The depth of her peril and innocence sent a jolt through me that nearly made me fold at the knees. I knew now that she was not the person I had been sent here to help. But she was the reason. Oh, she was the reason, the victim whose blood cried out for intervention. Sweet Christ, how had she let this be done to her?

But then I saw the way she held her head up while her blood trickled to her upper lip. In her eyes, I caught a flash of the kind of courage and love that got people into trouble because it didn't count the cost. And I saw something else, too—a hint that on some level, intuitively, perhaps even unconsciously, she understood what was happening to her. Naturally she refused to go to the hospital. No hospital could help her.

I gave the handkerchief back to her gently, though inside I was trembling with anger. The sun beat down on us. "You don't need a doctor," I said as calmly as I could. "You need to buy me some coffee and tell me what's going on."

She still hesitated. I could hardly blame her. Why should she want to sit around in a public place with a handkerchief held to her nose? But something about me had reached her, and it wasn't my brief burst of authority. Her eyes went down my coat to my shoes; when they came back up, they were softer. Behind her hand, she smiled faintly. "You look like you could use it."

She was referring to the coffee; but it was her story I intended to use.

She led the way into the coffee shop and toward one of the booths; she even told the petulant waiter what we wanted. I appreciated that. I really had no idea where I was. In fact, I didn't even know what coffee was. But sometimes knowledge comes to me when I need it. I didn't even blink as the waiter dropped heavy cups in front of us, sloshing hot, black liquid onto the table. Instead, I concentrated everything I had on my companion.

When I asked her, she said her name was Kristen Dona. Following a hint I hadn't heard anybody give me, I looked at her left hand and made sure she wasn't wearing a wedding ring. Then I said to get her started, "Your brother's name is Reese. This has something to do with him."

"Oh, no," she said quickly. Too quickly. "How could it?" She wasn't lying: she was just telling me what she wanted to believe.

I shrugged. There was no need to argue with her. Instead, I let the hints lead me. "He's a big part of your life," I said, as if we were talking about the weather. "Tell me about him."

"Well—" She didn't know where to begin. "He's a sculptor. He has a show tomorrow—I told you that. His first big show. After all these years."

I studied her closely. "But you're not happy about it."

"Of course I am!" She was righteously indignant. And under that, she was afraid. "He's worked so hard...! He's a good sculptor. Maybe even a great one. But it isn't exactly easy. It's not like being a writer—he can't just go to a publisher and have them print a hundred thousand copies of his work for two ninety-five. He has to have a place where people who want to spend money on art can come and see what he does. And he has to charge a lot because each piece costs him so much time and effort. So a lot of people have to see each piece before he can sell one. That means he has to have shows. In a gallery. This is his first real chance."

For a moment, she was talking so hotly that she forgot to cover her nose. A drop of blood left a mark like a welt across her lip.

Then she felt the drop and scrubbed at it with her handkerchief. "Oh, damn!" she muttered. The cloth was slowly becoming sodden. Suddenly her mouth twisted and her eyes were full of tears. She put her other hand over her face. "His first real chance. I'm so scared."

I didn't ask her *why*, I didn't want to hurry her. Instead, I asked, "What changed?"

Her shoulders knotted. But my question must have sounded safe to her. Gradually, some of her tension eased. "What do you mean?

"He's been a sculptor for a long time." I did my best to sound reasonable, like a friend of her brother's. "But this is his first big show. What's different now? What's changed?"

The waiter ignored us, too bored to bother with customers who only wanted coffee. Numbly, Kristen took another handkerchief out of her purse, raised the fresh cloth to her nose; the other one went back into her purse. I already knew I was no friend of her brother's.

"He met a gallery owner." She sounded tired and sad. "Mortice Root. He calls his gallery The Root Cellar, but it's really an old brownstone mansion over on 49th. Reese went there to see him when the gallery first opened, two weeks ago. He said he was going to beg…He's become so bitter. Most of the time, the people who run galleries won't even look at his work. I think he's been begging for years."

The idea made her defensive. "Failure does that to people. You work your heart out, but nothing in heaven or hell can force the people who control access to care about you. Gallery owners and agents can make or break you because they determine whether you get to show your work or not. You never even get to find out whether there's anything in your work that can touch or move or inspire people, no matter how hard you try, unless you can convince some owner he'll make a lot of money out of you."

She was defending Reese from an accusation I hadn't made. Begging was easy to understand; anybody who was hurt badly enough could do it. She was doing it herself—but she didn't realize it.

Or maybe she did. She drank some of her coffee and changed her tone. "But Mr. Root took him on," she said almost brightly. "He saw Reese's talent right away. He gave Reese a good contract and an advance. Reese has been working like a demon, getting ready, making new pieces. He's finally getting the chance he deserves."

The chance he deserves. I heard echoes in that—suggestions she hadn't intended. And she hadn't really answered my question. But now I had another one that was more important to me.

"Two weeks ago," I said. "Kristen, how long has your nose been bleeding?"

She stared at me while the forced animation drained out of her face.

"Two weeks now, wouldn't you say?" I held her frightened eyes. "Off and on at first, so you didn't take it seriously? But now it's constant? If it weren't so slow, you'd choke yourself when you went to sleep at night?"

I'd gone too far. All at once, she stopped looking at me. She dropped her handkerchief, opened her purse, took out money and scattered it on the table. Then she covered her face again. "I've got to go," she said into her hand. "Reese hates being interrupted, but maybe there's something I can do to help him get ready for tomorrow."

She started to leave. And I stopped her, just like that. Suddenly, she couldn't take herself away from me. A servant can sometimes wield the strength of his Lord.

I wanted to tell her she'd already given Reese more help than she could afford. But I didn't. I wasn't here to pronounce judgment. I didn't have that right. When I had her sitting in front of me again, I said, "You still haven't told me what changed."

Now she couldn't evade me, couldn't pretend she didn't understand. Slowly, she told me what had happened.

Mortice Root had liked Reese's talent—had praised it effusively—but he hadn't actually liked Reese's work. Too polite, he said. Too reasonable. Aesthetically perfect, emotionally boring. He urged Reese to "open up"—dig down into the energy of his fears and dreams, apply his great skill and talent to darker, more "honest" work. And he supplied Reese with new materials. Until then, Reese had worked in ordinary clay or wax, making castings of his figures only when he and Kristen were able to afford the caster's price. But Root had given Reese a special, black clay which gleamed like a river under a swollen moon. An ideal material, easy to work when it was damp, but finished when it dried, without need for firing or sealer or glaze—as hard and heavy as stone.

And as her brother's hands had worked that clay, Kristen's fear had grown out of it. His new pieces were indeed darker, images which chilled her heart. She used to love his work. Now she hated it.

I could have stopped then. I had enough to go on. And she wasn't the one I'd been sent to help; that was obvious. Maybe I should have stopped.

But I wanted to know more. That was my fault: I was forever trying to swim against the current. After all, the impulse to "open up"—to do darker, more "honest" work—was hardly evil. But the truth was, I was more interested in Kristen than Reese. Her eyes were full of supplication and abashment. She felt she had betrayed her brother, not so much by talking about him as by the simple fact that her attitude toward his work had changed. And she was still in such need—

Instead of stopping, I took up another of the hints she hadn't given me. Quietly, I asked, "How long have you been supporting him?"

She was past being surprised now, but her eyes didn't leave my face. "Close to ten years," she answered obediently.

"That must have been hard on you."

"Oh, no," she said at once. "Not at all. I've been happy to do it." She was too loyal to say anything else. Here she was, with her life escaping from her—and she insisted she hadn't suffered. Her bravery made the backs of my eyes burn.

But I required honesty. After a while, the way I was looking at her made her say, "I don't really love my job. I work over in the garment district. I put in hems. After a few years"—she tried to sound self-deprecating and humorous—"it gets a little boring. And there's nobody I can talk to." Her tone suggested a deep gulf of loneliness. "But it's been worth it," she insisted. "I don't have any talent of my own. Supporting Reese gives me something to believe in. I make what he does possible."

I couldn't argue with that. She had made the whole situation possible. Grimly, I kept my mouth shut and waited for her to go on.

"The hard part," she admitted finally, "was watching him grow bitter." Tears started up in her eyes again, but she blinked them back. "All that failure—year after year—" She dropped her gaze; she couldn't bear to look at me and say such things. "He didn't have anybody else to take it out on."

That thought made me want to grind my teeth. She believed in him—and he took it out on her. She could have left him in any number of ways: gotten married, simply packed her bags, anything. But he probably wasn't even aware of the depth of her refusal to abandon him. He simply went on using her.

My own fear was gone now; I was too angry to be afraid. But held it down. No matter how I felt, she wasn't the person I was here to defend. So I forced myself to sound positively casual as I said "I'd like to meet him."

In spite of everything, she was still capable of being taken aback. "You want me to—?" She stared at me. "I couldn't!" She wasn't appalled; she was trying not to give in to a hope that must have seemed insane to her. "He hates being interrupted. He'd be furious." She scanned the table, hunting for excuses. "You haven't finished your coffee."

I nearly laughed out loud. I wasn't here for her—and yet she did wonderful things for me. Suddenly, I decided that it was all worth the cost. Smiling broadly, I said, "I didn't say I needed coffee. I said you needed to buy it for me."

Involuntarily, the corners of her mouth quirked upward. Even with the handkerchief clutched to her face, she looked like a different person. After all she had endured, she was still a long way from being beaten. "Be serious," she said, trying to sound serious. "I can't take you home with me. I don't even know what to call you."

"If you take me with you," I responded, "you won't have to call me."

This time, I didn't need help to reach her; I just needed to go on smiling.

But what I was doing made sweat run down my spine. I didn't want to see her hurt any more. But there was nothing I could do to protect her.

▲▼▲

The walk to the place where she and her brother lived seemed long and cruel in the heat. There were fewer cars and crowds around us now—most of the city's people had reached their destinations for the day—and thick, hot light glared at us from long aisles of pale concrete. At the same time, the buildings impacted on either side of us grew older, shabbier, became the homes of ordinary men and women rather than of money. Children played in the street, shrieking and running as if their souls were on fire. Derelicts shambled here and there, not so much lost to grace as inured by alcohol and ruin, benumbed by their own particular innocence. Several of the structures we passed had had their eyes blown out.

Then we arrived in front of a high, flat edifice indistinguishable from its surroundings except by the fact that most of its windows were intact. Kristen grimaced at it apologetically. "Actually," she said, "we could live better than this. But we save as much money as we can for Reese's work." She seemed to have forgotten that I looked worse than her apartment building did. Almost defiantly, she added, "Now we'll be able to do better."

That depended on what she called better, I was sure Mortice Root had no end of money. But I didn't say so.

However, she was still worried about how Reese would react to us. "Are you sure you want to do this?" she asked. "He isn't going to be on his good behavior."

I nodded and smiled; I didn't want her to see how scared and angry I was. "Don't worry about me. If he's rude, I can always offer him some constructive criticism."

"Oh, terrific," she responded, at once sarcastic and relieved, sourly amused. "He just loves constructive criticism."

She was hardly aware of her own bravery as she led me into the building.

The hall with the mail slots and the manager's apartment was dimly lit by one naked bulb. It should have felt cooler, but the heat inside was fierce. The stairs up to the fourth floor felt like a climb in a steambath. Maybe it was a blessing after all that I didn't have a shirt on under my coat. I was sweating so hard that my shoes felt slick and unreliable against my soles, as if every step I took was somehow untrustworthy.

When Kristen stopped at the door of her apartment, she needed both hands to fumble in her purse for the key. With her face uncovered, I saw that her nosebleed was getting worse. Despite the way her hands shook, she got the door open. After finding a clean handkerchief, she ushered me inside, calling as she did so, "Reese! I'm home!"

The first room—it would've been the living room in anybody else's apartment—was larger than I'd expected; and it implied other rooms I couldn't see—bedrooms, a kitchen, a studio. The look of dingyness and unlove was part of the ancient wallpaper and warped baseboards, the sagging ceiling, not the result of carelessness; the place was scrupulously kempt. And the entire space was organized to display Reese's sculptures.

Set on packing crates and endtables, stacks of bricks, makeshift pedestals, old steamer trunks, they nearly filled the room. A fair number of them were cast; but most were clay, some fired, some not. And without exception they looked starkly out of place in that room. They were everything the apartment wasn't—finely done, idealistic, painless. It was as if Reese had left all his failure and bitterness and capacity for rage in the walls, sloughing it away from his work so that his art was kind and clean.

And static. It would have looked inert if he'd had less talent. Busts and madonnas stared with eyes that held neither fear nor hope. Children that never laughed or cried were hugged in the arms of blind women. A horse in one corner should have been prancing, but it was simply frozen. His bitterness he took out on his sister. His failures reduced him to begging. But his sculptures held no emotion at all.

They gave me an unexpected lift of hope. Not because they were static, but because he was capable of so much restraint. If reason was the circumference of energy, then he was already halfway to being a great artist. He had reason down pat.

Which was all the more surprising because he was obviously not a reasonable man. He came bristling into the room in answer to Kristen's call, and he'd already started to shout at her before he saw I was there.

At once, he stopped; he stared at me. "Who the hell is *this*?" he rasped without looking at Kristen. I could feel the force of his intensity from where I stood. His face was as acute as a hawk's, whetted by the hunger and energy of a predator. But the dark stains of weariness and strain under his eyes made him look more feverish than fierce. All of a sudden I thought, Only two weeks to get a show ready. An entire show's worth of new pieces in only two weeks. Because of course he wasn't going to display any of the work I could see here. He was only going to show what he'd made out of the new, black clay Mortice Root had given him. And he'd worn himself ragged. In a sense, his intensity wasn't directed at me personally: it was just a fact of his personality. He did everything extremely. In his own way, he was as desperate as his sister. Maybe I should have felt sorry for him.

But he didn't give me much chance. Before I could say anything, he wheeled on Kristen. "It isn't bad enough you have to keep interrupting me," he snarled. "You have to bring trash in here, too. Where did you find him—the Salvation Army? Haven't you figured out yet that I'm busy?"

I wanted to intervene; but she didn't need that kind of protection.

Over her handkerchief, her eyes echoed a hint of her brother's fire. He took his bitterness out on her because she allowed him to, not because she was defenseless. Her voice held a bite of anger as she said, "He offered to help me."

If I hadn't been there, he might have listened to her; but his fever made him rash. "*Help* you?" he snapped. "This bum?" He looked at me again. "He couldn't help himself to another drink. And what do you need help…?"

"*Reese*," This time, she got his attention. "I went to the doctor this morning."

"What?" For an instant, he blinked at her as if he couldn't understand. "The doctor?" The idea that something was wrong with her hit him hard. I could see his knees trying to fold under him. "You aren't sick. What do you need a doctor for?"

Deliberately, she lowered her hand, exposing the red sheen darkening to crust on her upper lip, the blood swelling in her nostrils. He gaped as if the sight nauseated him. Then he shook his head in denial. Abruptly, he sagged to the edge of a trunk that held two of his sculptures. "Damn it to hell," he breathed weakly. "Don't scare me like that. It's just a nosebleed. You've had it for weeks."

Kristen gave me a look of vindication; she seemed to think Reese had just showed how much he cared about her. But I wasn't so sure. I could think of plenty of selfish reasons for his reaction.

Either way, it was my turn to say something. I could have used some inspiration right then—just a little grace to help me find my way. My emotions were tangled up with Kristen; my attitude toward Reese was all wrong. I didn't know how to reach him. But no inspiration was provided.

Swallowing bile, I made an effort to sound confident. "Actually," I said, "I can be more help than you realize. That's the one advantage life has over art. There's more to it than meets the eye."

I was on the wrong track already; a halfwit could have done better. Reese raised his head to look at me, and the outrage in his eyes was as plain as a chisel. "That's wonderful," he said straight at me. "A bum and a critic."

Kristen's face was tight with dismay. She knew exactly what would happen if I kept going.

So did I. I wasn't stupid. But I was already sure I didn't really want to help Reese. I wanted somebody a little more worthy.

Anyway, I couldn't stop. His eyes were absolutely daring me to go on.

"Root's right," I said. Now I didn't have any trouble sounding as calm as a saint. "You know that. What you've been doing"—I gestured around the room—"is too controlled. Impersonal. You've got all the skill in the world, but you haven't put your heart into it.

"But I don't think he's been giving you very good advice. He's got you going to the opposite extreme. That's just another dead end. You need a balance. Control and passion. Control alone has been destroying you. Passion alone—"

Right there, I almost said it: passion alone will destroy your sister. That's the kind of bargain you're making. All it costs you is your soul.

But I didn't get the chance. Reese slapped his hand down on the trunk with a sound like a shot. One of his pieces tilted; it would have fallen if Kristen hadn't caught it. But he didn't see that. He jerked to his feet. Over his shoulder, he said to her, "You've been talking to this tramp about me." The words came out like lead.

She didn't answer. There was no defense against his accusation. To catch the sculpture, she'd had to use both hands, and her touch left a red smudge on the clay.

But he didn't seem to expect an answer. He was facing me with fever bright in his eyes. In the same heavy tone, he said, "It's your fault, isn't it. She wouldn't do that to me—tell a total stranger what a failure I've been—if you hadn't pried it out of her.

"Well, let me tell *you* something. Root owns a gallery. He has *power.*" He spat the word as if he loathed it. "I have to listen to him. From you I don't have to take this kind of manure."

Which was true, of course. I was a fool, as well as being useless. In simple chagrin I tried to stop or at least deflect what was coming.

"You're right," I said. "I've got no business trying to tell you what to do. But I can still help you. Just listen to me. I—"

"No," he retorted. "You listen. I've spent ten years of my life feeling the way you look. Now I've got a chance to do better. You don't know anything I could possibly want to hear. I've *been* there."

Still without looking at his sister, he said, "Kristen, tell him to leave."

She didn't have any choice. I'd botched everything past the point where there was anything she could do to save it. Reese would just rage at her if she refused—and what would that accomplish? I watched all the anger and hope drain out of her, and I wanted to fight back; but I didn't have any choice, either. She said in a beaten voice, "I think you'd better leave now," and I had to leave. I was no use to anybody without permission; I could not stay when she told me to go.

I didn't have the heart to squeeze in a last appeal on my way out. I didn't have any more hope than she did. I studied her face as I moved to the door, not because I thought she might change her mind, but because I wanted to memorize her, so that if she went on down this road and was lost in the end there would be at least one man left who remembered. But she didn't meet my eyes. And when I stepped out of the apartment, Reese slammed the door behind me so hard the floor shook.

The force of his rejection almost made me fall to my knees.

▲▼▲

In spite of that, I didn't give up. I didn't know where I was or how I got here; I was lucky to know why I was here at all. And I would never remember. Where I was before I was here was as blank as a wall across the past. When the river took me someplace else, I wasn't going to be able to give Kristen Dona the bare courtesy of remembering her.

That was a blessing, of a sort. But it was also the reason I didn't give up. Since I didn't have any past or future, the present was my only chance.

When I was sure the world wasn't going to melt around me and change into something else, I went down the stairs, walked out into the pressure of the sun, and tried to think of some other way to fight for Kristen's life and Reese's soul.

After all, I had no right to give up hope on Reese. He'd been a failure for ten years. And I'd seen the way the people of this city looked at me. Even the derelicts had contempt in their eyes, including me in the way they despised themselves. I ought to be able understand what humiliation could do to someone who tried harder than he knew how and still failed.

But I couldn't think of any way to fight it. Not without permission. Without permission, I couldn't even tell him his sister was in mortal danger.

The sun stayed nearly hidden behind its haze of humidity and dirt, but its brutality was increasing. Noon wasn't far away; the walk here had used up the middle of the morning. Heatwaves shimmered off the pavement. An abandoned car with no wheels leaned against the curb like a cripple. Somebody had gone down the street and knocked over all the trashcans, scattering garbage like wasted lives. Somewhere there had to be something I could do to redeem myself. But when I prayed for help, I didn't get it.

After a while, I found myself staring as if I were about to go blind at a street sign at the corner of the block. A long time seemed to pass before I registered that the sign said, "21st St."

Kristen had said that Root's gallery, The Root Cellar, was "over on 49th."

I didn't know the city; but I could at least count. I went around the block and located 20th. Then I changed directions and started working my way up through the numbers.

It was a long hike. I passed through sections that were worse than where Kristen and Reese lived and ones that were better. I had a small scare when the numbers were interrupted, but after several blocks they took up where they'd left off. The sun kept leaning on me, trying to grind me into the pavement, and the air made my chest hurt.

And when I reached 49th, I didn't know which way to turn. Sweating, I stopped at the intersection and looked around. 49th seemed to stretch to the ends of the world in both directions. Anything was possible; The Root Cellar might be anywhere. I was in some kind of business district— 49th was lined with prosperity and the sidewalks were crowded again. But all the people moved as if nothing except fatigue or stubbornness and the heat kept them from running for their lives. I tried several times to stop one for them to ask directions; but it was like trying to change the course of the river. I got glares and muttered curses, but no help.

That was hard to forgive. But forgiveness wasn't my job. My job was to find some way to help Reese Dona. So I tried some outright begging.

And when begging failed, I simply let the press of the crowds start me moving the same way they were going.

With my luck, this was exactly the wrong direction. But I couldn't think of any good reason to turn around, so I kept walking, studying the buildings for any sign of a brownstone mansion and muttering darkly against all those myths about how God answers prayer.

Ten blocks later, I recanted. I came to a store that filled the entire block and went up into the sky for at least thirty floors; and in front of it stood my answer. He was a scrawny old man in a dingy gray uniform with red epaulets and red stitching on his cap; boredom or patience glazed his eyes. He was tending an iron pot that hung from a rickety tripod. With the studious intention of a halfwit, he rang a handbell to attract people's attention.

The stitching on his cap said, "Salvation Army."

I went right up to him and asked where The Root Cellar was.

He blinked at me as if I were part of the heat and the haze. "Mission's that way." He nodded in the direction I was going. "49th and Grand."

"Thanks, anyway," I said. I was glad to be able to give the old man a genuine smile. "That isn't what I need. I need to find The Root Cellar. It's an art gallery. Supposed to be somewhere on 49th."

He went on blinking at me until I started to think maybe he was deaf. Then, abruptly, he seemed to arrive at some kind of recognition. Abandoning his post, he turned and entered the store. Through the glass, I watched him go to a box like half a booth that hung on one wall. He found a large yellow book under the box, opened it, and flipped the pages back and forth for a while.

Nodding at whatever he found, he came back out to me.

"Down that way," he said, indicating the direction I'd come from. "About thirty blocks. Number 840."

Suddenly, my heart lifted. I closed my eyes for a moment to give thanks. Then I looked again at the man who'd rescued me. "If I had any money," I said, "I'd give it to you."

"If you had any money," he replied as if he knew who I was, "I wouldn't take it. Go with God."

I said, "I will," and started retracing my way up 49th.

I felt a world better. But I also had a growing sense of urgency. The longer I walked, the worse it got. The day was getting away me—and this day was the only one I had. Reese's show was tomorrow. Then Mortice Root would've fulfilled his part of the bargain. And the price would have to be paid. I was sweating so hard my filthy old coat stuck to my back; but I forced myself to walk as fast as the fleeing crowds.

After a while, the people began to disappear from the sidewalks again and the traffic thinned. Then the business district came to an end, and I found myself in a slum so ruined and hopeless I had to grit my teeth to keep up my courage. I felt hostile eyes watching me from behind broken windows and gaping entrances. But I was protected, either by daylight or by the way I looked.

Then the neighborhood began to improve. The slum became close-built houses, clinging to dignity. The houses moved apart from each other, giving themselves more room to breathe. Trees appeared in the yards, even in the sidewalk. Lawns pushed the houses back from the street, and each house seemed to be more ornate than the one beside it. I would have thought they were homes, but most of them had discreet signs indicating they were places of business. Several of them were shops that sold antiques. One held a law firm. A stockbroker occupied a place the size of a temple. I decided that this was where people came to do their shopping and business when they were too rich to associate with their fellow human beings.

And there it was—a brownstone mansion as elaborate as any I'd seen. It was large and square, three stories tall, with a colonnaded entryway and a glass-domed structure that might have been a greenhouse down the length of one side. The mailbox on the front porch was neatly numbered, 840. And when I went up the walk to the porch, I saw a brass plaque on the door with words engraved on it:

The Root Cellar

a private gallery

Mortice Root

At the sight, my chest constricted as if I'd never done this before. But I'd already lost too much time; I didn't waste any more of it hesitating. I pressed a small button beside the door and listened to chimes ringing faintly inside the house as if Mortice Root had a cathedral in his basement.

For a while, nothing happened. Then the door opened, and a flow of cold air from inside, followed by a man in a guard's uniform, with a gun holstered on his hip and a badge that said, "Nationwide Security," on his chest. As he looked out at me, what he saw astonished him; not many of Root's patrons looked like I did. Then his face closed like a shutter. "Are you out of your mind?" he growled. "We don't give handouts here. Get lost."

In response, I produced my sweetest smile. "Fortunately, I don't want a handout. I want to talk to Mortice Root."

He stared at me. "What in hell makes you think Mr. Root wants to talk to you?"

"Ask him and find out," I replied. "Tell him I'm here to argue about Reese Dona."

He would have slammed the door in my face; but a hint of authority came back to me, and he couldn't do it. For a few moments, he gaped at me as if he were choking. Then he muttered, "Wait here," and escaped back into the house. As he closed the door, the cool air breathing outward was cut off.

"Well, naturally," I murmured to the sodden heat, trying to keep myself on the bold side of dread. "The people who come here to spend their money can't be expected to just stand around and sweat."

The sound of voices came dimly through the door. But I hadn't heard the guard walk away, and I didn't hear anybody coming toward me. So I still wasn't quite ready when the door swung open again and Mortice Root stood in front of me with a cold breeze washing unnaturally past his shoulders.

We recognized each other right away; and he grinned like a wolf. But I couldn't match him. I was staggered. I hadn't expected him to be so *powerful*.

He didn't look powerful. He looked as rich as Solomon—smooth, substantial, glib—as if he could buy and sell the people who came here to give him their money. From the tips of his gleaming shoes past the expanse of his distinctively styled suit to the clean confidence of his shaven jowls, he was everything I wasn't. But those things only gave him worldly significance; they didn't make him powerful. His true strength was hidden behind the bland unction of his demeanor. It showed only in his grin, in the slight, avid bulging of his eyes, in the wisps of hair that stood out like hints of energy on either side of his bald crown.

His gaze made me fell grimy and rather pathetic.

He studied me for a moment. Then, with perfectly cruel kindness, he said, "Come in, come in. You must be sweltering out there. It's much nicer in here."

He was that sure of himself.

But I was willing to accept permission, even from him. Before he could reconsider, I stepped past him into the hallway.

As I looked around, cold came swirling up my back, turning my sweat chill. At the end of this short, deeply carpeted hall, Root's mansion opened into an immense foyer nearly as high as the building itself.

Two mezzanines joined by broad stairways of carved wood circled the walls; daylight shone downward from a skylight in the center of the ceiling. A glance showed me that paintings were displayed around the mezzanines, while the foyer itself held sculptures and carvings decorously set on white pedestals. I couldn't see anything that looked like Reese Dona's work.

At my elbow, Root said, "I believe you came to argue with me?" He was as smooth as oil.

I felt foolish and awkward beside him, but I faced him as squarely as I could. "Maybe 'contend' would be a better word."

"As you say." He chuckled in a way that somehow suggested both good humor and malice. "I look forward to it." Then he touched my arm, gestured me toward one side of the foyer. "But let me show you what he's doing these days. Perhaps you'll change your mind."

For no good reason, I said, "You know better than that." But I went with him.

A long, wide passage took us to the glass-domed structure I'd taken to be a greenhouse. Maybe it was originally built for that; but Root had converted it, and I had to admit it made an effective gallery—well-lit, spacious, and comfortable. In spite of all that glass, the air stayed cool, almost chill.

Here I saw Reese's new work for the first time.

"Impressive, aren't they," Root purred. He was mocking me.

But what he was doing to Reese was worse.

There were at least twenty of them, with room for a handful more—attractively set in niches along one wall, proudly positioned on special pediments, cunningly juxtaposed in corners so that they showed each other off. It was clear that any artist would find an opportunity like this hard to resist.

But all the pieces were black.

Reese had completely changed his subject matter. Madonnas and children had been replaced by gargoyles and twisted visions of the damned. Glimpses of nightmare leered from their niches. Pain writhed on display, as if it had become an object of ridicule. In a corner of the room, a ghoul devoured one infant while another strove urgently to scream and failed.

And each of these new images was alive with precisely the kind of vitality his earlier work lacked. He had captured his visceral terrors in the act of pouncing at him.

As sculptures, they were admirable; maybe even more than that. He had achieved some kind of breakthrough here, tapped into sources of energy he'd always been unable or unwilling to touch. All he needed now was balance.

But there was more to these pieces than just skill and energy. There was also blackness.

Root's clay.

Kristen was right. This clay looked like dark water under the light of an evil moon, like marl mixed with blood until the mud congealed. And the more I studied what I saw, the more these grotesque and brutal images gave the impression of growing from the clay itself rather than from the independent mind of the artist. They were not Reese's fears and dreams refined by art; they were horrors he found in the clay when his hands touched it. The real strength, the passion of these pieces, came from the material Root supplied, not from Reese. No wonder he had become so hollow-eyed and ragged. He was struggling desperately to control the consequences of his bargain. Trying to prove to himself he wasn't doing the wrong thing.

For a moment, I felt a touch of genuine pity for him. But it didn't last. Maybe deep down in his soul he was afraid of what he was doing and what it meant. But he was still doing it. And he was paying for the chance to do such strong work with his sister's life.

Softly, my opponent said, "It appears you don't approve. I'm so sorry. But I'm afraid there's really nothing you can do about it. The artists of this world are uniquely vulnerable. They wish to create beauty, and the world cares for nothing but money. Even the cattle who will buy these"—he gave the room a dismissive flick of the hand—"trivial pieces hold the artist in contempt." He turned his wolf-grin toward me again. "Failure makes fertile ground."

I couldn't pretend that wasn't true; so I asked bitterly, "Are you really going to keep your end of the bargain? Are you really going to sell this stuff?"

"Oh, assuredly," he replied. "At least until the sister dies. Tomorrow. Perhaps the day after." He chuckled happily. "Then I suspect I'll find myself too busy with other, more promising artists to spend time on Reese Dona."

I felt him glance at me, gauging my helplessness. Then he went on unctuously, "Come, now, my friend. Why glare so thunderously? Surely you realize that he has been using her in precisely this manner for years. I've merely actualized the true state of their relationship. But perhaps you're too innocent to grasp how deeply he resents her. It is the nature of beggars to resent those who give them gifts. He resents me." At that, Root laughed outright. He was not a man who gave gifts to anybody. "I assure you that her present plight is of his own choice and making."

"No," I said, more out of stubbornness than conviction. "He just doesn't understand what's happening."

Root shrugged. "Do you think so? No matter. The point, as you must recognize, is that we have nothing to contend for. The issue has already been decided."

I didn't say anything. I wasn't as glib as he was. And anyway I was afraid he was right.

While I stood there and chewed over all the things I wasn't able to do, I heard doors opening and closing somewhere in the distance. The heavy carpeting absorbed footsteps; but it wasn't long before Reese came striding into the greenhouse. He was so tight with eagerness or suppressed fear he looked like he was about to snap. As usual, he didn't even see me when he first came into the room.

"I've got the rest of the pieces," he said to Root. "They're in a truck out back. I think you'll like—"

Then my presence registered on him. He stopped with a jerk, stared at me as if I'd come back from the dead. "What're you doing here?" he demanded. At once, he turned back to Root. "What is he doing here?"

Root's confidence was a complete insult. "Reese," he sighed, "I'm afraid that this—gentleman?—believes that I should not show your work tomorrow."

For a moment, Reese was too astonished to be angry. His mouth actually hung open while he looked at me. But I was furious enough for both of us. With one sentence, Root had made my position impossible. I couldn't think of a single thing to say now that would change the outcome.

Still, I had to try. While Reese's surprise built up into outrage, I said as if I weren't swearing like a madman inside, "There are two sides to everything. You've heard his. You really ought to listen to mine."

He closed his mouth, locked his teeth together. His glare was wild enough to hurt.

"Mortice Root owes you a little honesty," I said while I had the chance. "He should have told you long ago that he's planning to drop you after tomorrow."

The sheer pettiness of what I was saying made me cringe, and Root simply laughed. I should have known better than to try to fight him on his own level. Now he didn't need to answer me at all.

In any case, my jibe made no impression on Reese. He gritted, "I don't care about that," like a man who couldn't or wouldn't understand.

"This is what I care about." He gestured frantically around the room. "*This*. My work."

He took a couple of steps toward me, and his voice shook with the effort he made to keep from shouting. "I don't know who you are—or why you think I'm any of your business. I don't care about that, either. You've heard Kristen's side. Now you're going to hear mine."

In a small way, I was grateful he didn't accuse me of turning his sister against him.

"She doesn't like the work I'm doing now. No, worse than that. She doesn't mind the work. She doesn't like the *clay*." He gave a laugh like an echo of Root's. But he didn't have Root's confidence and power; he only sounded bitter, sarcastic, and afraid. "She tries to tell me she approves of me, but I can read her face like a book.

"Well, let me tell you something." He poked a trembling finger at my chest. "With my show tomorrow, I'm alive for the first time ten years. I'm alive *here*. Art exists to communicate. It isn't worth manure if it doesn't communicate, and it can't communicate if somebody doesn't look at it. It's that simple. The only time an artist is alive is when somebody looks at his work. And if enough people look, he can live forever.

"I've been sterile for ten years because I haven't had one other soul to look at my work." He was so wrapped up in what he was saying, I don't think he even noticed how completely he dismissed his sister. "Now I am alive. If it only lasts for one more day, it'll still be something nobody can take away from me. If I have to work in black clay to get that, who cares? That's just something I didn't know about myself— about how my imagination works. I never had the chance to try black clay before.

"But now—" He couldn't keep his voice from rising like a cry. "Now I'm alive. *Here*. If you want to take that away from me, you're worse than trash. You're evil."

Mortice Root was smiling like a saint.

For a moment, I had to look away. The fear behind the passion in Reese's eyes was more than I could stand. "I'm sorry," I murmured. What else could I say? I regretted everything. He needed me desperately, and I kept failing him. And he placed so little value on his sister. With a private groan, I forced myself to face him again.

"I thought it was work that brought artists to life. Not shows. I thought the work was worth doing whether anybody looked at it or not. Why else did you keep at it for ten years?"

But I was still making the same mistake, still trying to reach him through his art. And now I'd definitely said something he couldn't afford to hear or understand. With a jerky movement like a puppet, he threw up his hands. "I don't have time for this," he snapped. "I've got five more pieces to set up," Then, suddenly, he was yelling at me. "And I don't give one lousy damn what you think!" Somehow, I'd hit a nerve. "I want you to go away. I want you to leave me alone! Get out of here and *leave me alone!*"

I didn't have any choice. As soon as he told me to go, I turned toward the door. But I was desperate myself now. Knotting my fists, I held myself where I was. Urgently—so urgently that I could hardly separate the words—I breathed at him, "Have you looked at Kristen recently? Really looked? Haven't you seen what's happening to her? You—"

Root stopped me. He had that power. Reese had told me to go. Root simply raised his hand, and his strength hit me in the chest like a fist. My tongue was clamped to the roof of my mouth. My voice choked in my throat. For one moment while I staggered, the greenhouse turned in a complete circle, and I thought I was going to be thrown out of the world.

But I wasn't. A couple of heartbeats later, I got my balance back.

Helpless to do anything else, I left the greenhouse.

As I crossed the foyer toward the front door, Reese shouted after me, "And stay away from my sister!"

Until I closed the door, I could hear Mortice Root chuckling with pleasure. Dear God! I prayed. Let me decide. Just this once. He isn't worth it. But I didn't have the right.

▲▼▲

On the other hand, I didn't have to stay away from Kristen. That was up to her; Reese didn't have any say in the matter.

I made myself walk slowly until I was out of sight of The Root Cellar, just in case someone was watching. Then I started to run.

It was the middle of the afternoon, and the heat just kept getting worse. After the cool of Root's mansion, the outside air felt like glue against my face. Sweat oozed into my eyes, stuck my coat to my back, itched maliciously in my dirty whiskers. The sunlight looked liked it was congealing on the walks and streets. Grimly, I thought if this city didn't get some rain soon it would start to burn.

And yet I wanted today to last, despite the heat. I would happily have caused the sun to stand still. I did not want to have to face Mortice Root and Reese Dona again after dark. But I would have to deal with that possibility when it came up. First I had to get Kristen's help. And to do that, I had to reach her.

The city did its best to hinder me. I left Root's neighborhood easily enough; but when I entered the slums, I started having problems. I guess a running man dressed in nothing but an overcoat, a pair of pants, and sidesplit shoes looked like too much fun to miss. Gangs of kids seemed to materialize out of the ruined buildings to get in my way.

They should have known better. They were predators themselves, and I was on a hunt of my own; when they saw the danger in my eyes, they backed down. Some of them threw bottles and trash at my back, but that didn't matter.

Then the sidewalks became more and more crowded as the slum faded behind me. People stepped in front of me, jostled me off my stride, swore angrily at me as I tried to run past. I had to slow down just to keep myself out of trouble. And all the lights were against me. At every corner, I had to wait and wait while mobs hemmed me in, instinctively blocking the path of anyone who wanted to get ahead of them. I felt like I was up against an active enemy. The city was rising to defend its own.

By the time I reached the street I needed to take me over to 21st, I felt so ragged and wild I wanted to shake my fists at the sky and demand some kind of assistance or relief. But if God couldn't see how much trouble I was in, He didn't deserve what I was trying to do in His name. So I did the best I could—running in spurts, walking when I had to, risking the streets whenever I saw a break in the traffic. Finally I made it. Trembling, I reached the building where Reese and Kristen had their apartment.

Inside, it was as hot as an oven, baking its inhabitants to death. But here at least there was nobody in my way, and I took the stairs two and three at a time to the fourth floor. The lightbulb over the landing was out, but I didn't have any trouble finding the door I needed.

I pounded on it with my fist. Pounded again. Didn't hear anything. Hammered at the wood a third time.

"Kristen!" I shouted. I didn't care how frantic I sounded. "Let me in! I've got to talk to you!"

Then I heard a small, faint noise through the panels. She must have been right on the other side of the door. Weakly, she said, "Go away."

"Kristen!" Her dismissal left a welt of panic across my heart. I put my mouth to the crack of the door to make her hear me. "Reese needs help. If he doesn't get it, you're not going to survive. He doesn't even realize he's sacrificing you."

After a moment, the lock clicked, and the door opened.

I went in.

The apartment was dark. She'd turned off all the lights, when she closed the door behind me, I couldn't see a thing. I had to stand still so I wouldn't bump into Reese's sculptures.

"Kristen," I said, half pleading, half commanding. "Turn on a light."

Her reply was a whisper of misery. "You don't want to see me."

She sounded so beaten I almost gave up hope. Quietly, I said, "Please."

She couldn't refuse. She needed me too badly. I felt her move past me in the dark. Then the overhead lights clicked on, and I saw her.

I shouldn't have been shocked—I knew what to expect—but that didn't help. The sight of her went into me like a knife.

She was wearing only a terrycloth bathrobe. That made sense; she'd been poor for a long time and didn't want to ruin her good clothes. The collar of her robe was soaked with blood.

Her nosebleed was worse.

And delicate red streams ran steadily from both her ears.

Sticky trails marked her lips and chin, the front of her throat, the sides of her neck. She'd given up trying to keep herself clean. Why should she bother? She was bleeding to death, and she knew it.

Involuntarily, I went to her and put my arms around her.

She leaned against me. I was all she had left. Into my shoulder, she said as if she were on the verge of tears, "I can't help him anymore. I've tried and tried. I don't know what else to do."

She stood there quivering; and I held her and stroked her hair and let her blood soak into my coat. I didn't have any other way to comfort her.

But her time was running out, just like Reese's. The longer I waited, the weaker she would be. As soon as she became a little steadier, I lowered my arms and stepped back. In spite of the way looked, I wanted her to be able to see what I was.

"He doesn't need that kind of help now," I said softly, willing her to believe me. Not the kind you've been giving him for ten years. "Not anymore. He needs me. That's why I'm here.

"But I have to have permission." I wanted to cry at her, You've been letting him do this to you for ten years! None of this would've happened to you if you hadn't allowed it! But I kept that protest to myself. "He keeps sending me away, and I have to go. I don't have any choice. I can't do anything without permission.

"It's really that simple." God, make her believe me! "I need somebody with me who wants me to be there. I need you to go back to The Root Cellar with me. Even Root won't be able to get rid of me if you want me to stay.

"Kristen." I moved closer to her again, put my hands in the blood on her cheek, on the side of her neck. "I'll find some way to save him. If you're there to give me permission."

She didn't look at me; she didn't seem to have the courage to raise her eyes. But after a moment I felt the clear touch of grace. She believed me—when I didn't have any particular reason to believe myself. Softly, she said, "I can't go like this. Give me a minute to change my clothes."

She still didn't look at me. But when she turned to leave the room, I saw determination mustering in the corners of her eyes.

I breathed a prayer of long-overdue thanks. She intended to fight.

▲▼▲

I waited for her with fear beating in my bones. And when she returned—dressed in her dingy blouse and fraying skirt, with a towel wrapped around her neck to catch the blood—and announced that she was ready to go, I faltered. She looked so wan and frail—already weak and unnaturally pale from loss of blood. I felt sure she wasn't going to be able to walk all the way to The Root Cellar.

Carefully, I asked her if there was any other way we could get where we were going. But she shrugged the question aside. She and Reese had never owned a car, and he'd taken what little money was available in order to rent a truck to take his last pieces to the gallery.

Groaning a silent appeal for help, I held her arm to give her what support I could. Together, we left the apartment, went down the old stairs and out to the street.

I felt a new sting of dread when I saw that the sun was setting. For all my efforts to hurry, I'd taken too much time. Now I would have to contend with Mortice Root at night.

Twilight and darkness brought no relief from the heat. The city had spent all day absorbing the pressure of the sun; now the walks and buildings, every stretch of cement seemed to emit fire like the sides of a furnace. The air felt thick and ominous—as charged with intention as a thunderstorm, but trapped somehow, prevented from release, tense with suffering.

It sucked the strength out of Kristen with every breath. Before we'd gone five blocks, she was leaning most of her weight on me. That was frightening, not because she was more than I could bear, but because she seemed to weigh so little. Her substance was bleeding away. In the garish and unreliable light of the streetlamps, shop windows, and signs, only the dark marks on her face and neck appeared real.

But we were given one blessing: the city itself left us alone. It had done its part by delaying me earlier. We passed through crowds and traffic, past gutted tenements and stalking gangs, as if we didn't deserve to be noticed anymore.

Kristen didn't complain, and I didn't let her stumble. One by one, we covered the blocks. When she wanted to rest, we put our backs to the hot walls and leaned against them until she was ready to go on.

During that whole long, slow creep through the pitiless dark, she only spoke to me once. While we were resting again, sometime after we turned on 49th, she said quietly, "I still don't know your name."

We were committed to each other; I owed her the truth. "I don't either," I said. Behind the wall of the past, any number of things were hidden from me.

She seemed to accept that. Or maybe she just didn't have enough strength left to worry about both Reese and me. She rested a little while longer. Then we started walking again.

At last we left the last slum behind and made our slow, frail approach to The Root Cellar. Between streetlights I looked for the moon, but it wasn't able to show through the clenched haze. I was sweating like a frightened animal. But Kristen might have been immune to the heat. All she did was lean on me and walk and bleed.

I didn't know what to expect at Root's mansion. Trouble of some kind. An entire squadron of security guards. Minor demons lurking in the bushes around the front porch. Or an empty building, deserted for the night. But the place wasn't deserted. All the rest of the mansion was dark; the greenhouse burned with light. Reese wasn't able to leave his pieces alone before his show. And none of the agents that Root might have used against us appeared. He was that sure of himself.

On the other hand, the front door was locked with a variety of bolts and wires.

But Kristen was breathing sharply, urgently. Fear and desire and determination made her as feverish as her brother; she wanted me to take her inside, to Reese's defense. And she'd lost a dangerous amount of blood. She wasn't going to be able to stay on her feet much longer. I took hold of the door, and it opened without a sound. Cool air poured out at us, as concentrated as a moan of anguish.

We went in.

The foyer was dark. But a wash of light from the cracks of the greenhouse doors showed us our way. The carpet muffled our feet. Except for her ragged breathing and my frightened heart, we were as silent as spirits.

But as we got near the greenhouse, I couldn't keep quiet anymore. I was too scared.

I caused the doors to burst open with a crash that shook the walls. At the same time, I tried to charge forward.

The brilliance of the gallery seemed to explode in my face. For an instant, I was dazzled.

And I was stopped. The light felt as solid as the wall that cut me off from the past.

Almost at once, my vision cleared, and I saw Mortice Root and Reese Dona. They were alone in the room, standing in front of a sculpture I hadn't seen earlier—the biggest piece here. Reese must have brought it in his rented truck. It was a wild, swept-winged, malignant bird of prey, its beak wide in a cry of fury. One of its clawed feet was curled like a fist. The other was gripped deep into a man's chest. Agony stretched the man's face.

At least Reese had the decency to be surprised. Root wasn't. He faced us and grinned.

Reese gaped dismay at Kristen and me for one moment. Then, with a wrench like an act of violence, he turned his back. His shoulders hunched; his arms clamped over his stomach. "I told you to go away." His voice sounded like he was strangling. "I told you to leave her alone."

The light seemed to blow against me like a wind. Like the current of the river that carried me away, taking me from place to place without past and without future, hope. And it was rising. It held me in the doorway; I couldn't move through it.

"You are a fool," Root said to me. His voice rode the light as if he were shouting. "You have been denied. You cannot enter here."

He was so strong that I was already half turned to leave when Kristen saved me.

As pale as ash, she stood beside me. Fresh blood from her nose and ears marked her skin. The towel around her neck was sodden and terrible. She looked too weak to keep standing. Yet she matched her capacity for desperation against Reese's need.

"No," she said in the teeth of the light and Root's grin. "He can stay. I want him here."

I jerked myself toward Reese again.

Ferocity came at me like a cataract; but I stood against it. I had Kristen's permission. That had to be enough.

"Look at her!" I croaked at his back. "She's your sister! Look at her!"

He didn't seem to hear me at all. He was hunched over himself in front of his work. "Go away," he breathed weakly, as if he were talking to himself. "I can't stand it. Just go away."

Gritting prayers between my teeth like curses, I lowered my head, called up every ache and fragment of strength I had left, and took one step into the greenhouse.

Reese fell to his knees as if I'd broken the only string that held him upright.

At the same time, the bird of prey poised above him moved.

Its wings beat downward. Its talons clenched. The heart of its victim burst in his chest.

From his clay throat came a brief, hoarse wail of pain.

Driven by urgency, I took two more steps through the intense pressure walled against me.

And all the pieces displayed in the greenhouse started to move.

Tormented statuettes fell from their niches, cracked open, and cried out. Gargoyles mewed hideously. The mouths of victims gaped open and whined. In a few swift moments, the air was full of muffled shrieks and screams.

Through the pain, the fierce current forcing me away from Reese, and the horror, I heard Mortice Root start to laugh.

If Kristen had failed me then, I would have been finished. But in some way she had made herself blind and deaf to what was happening. Her entire soul was focused on one object—help for her brother—and she willed me forward with all the passion she had learned in ten years of self-sacrifice. She was prepared to spend the last of her life here for Reese's sake.

She made it possible for me to keep going.

Black anguish rose like a current at me. And the force of the light mounted. I felt it ripping at my skin. It was as hot as the hunger ravening for Reese's heart.

Yet I took two more steps.

And two more.

And reached him.

He still knelt under the wingspread of the nightmare bird he had created. The light didn't hurt him; he didn't feel it at all. He was on his knees because he simply couldn't stand. He gripped his arms over his heart to keep himself from howling.

There I noticed something I should have recognized earlier. He had sculpted a man for his bird of prey to attack, not a woman. I could see the figure clearly enough now to realize that Reese had given the man his own features. Here, at least, he had shaped one of his own terrors rather than merely bringing out the darkness of Mortice Root's clay.

After that, nothing else mattered. I didn't feel the pain or the pressure; ferocity and dismay lost their power.

I knelt in front of Reese, took hold of his shoulders, and hugged him like a child. "Just look at her," I breathed into his ear. "She's your sister. You don't have to do this to her."

She stood across the room from me with her eyes closed and her determination gripped in her small fists.

From under her eyelids, stark blood streamed down her cheeks.

"Look at her!" I pleaded. "I can help you. Just look"

In the end, he didn't look at her. He didn't need to. He knew what was happening.

Suddenly, he wrenched out of my embrace. His arms flung me aside. He raised his head, and one lorn wail corded his throat:

"Kristen!"

Root's laughter stopped as if it'd been cut down with an axe.

That cry was all I needed. It came right from Reese's heart, too pure to be denied. It was permission, and I took it.

I rose to my feet, easily now, easily. All the things that stood in my way made no difference. Transformed, I faced Mortice Root across the swelling force of his malice. All his confidence was gone to panic.

Slowly, I raised my arms.

Beams of white sprouted from my palms, clean white almost silver. It wasn't fire or light in any worldly sense; but it blazed over my head like light, ran down my arms like fire. It took my coat and pants, even my shoes, away from me in flames. Then it wrapped me in the robes of God until all my body burned.

Root tried to scream, but his voice didn't make any sound.

Towering white-silver, I reached up into the storm-dammed sky and brought down a blast that staggered the entire mansion to its foundations. Crashing past glass and frame and light fixtures, a bolt that might have been lightning took hold of Root from head to foot. For an instant, the gallery's lights failed. Everything turned black except for Root's horror etched against darkness and the blast that bore him away.

When the lights came back on, the danger was gone from the greenhouse. All the crying and the pain and the pressure were gone. Only the sculptures themselves remained.

They were slumped and ruined, like melted wax.

Outside, rain began to rattle against the glass of the greenhouse.

Later, I went looking for some clothes; I couldn't very well go around naked. After a while, I located a suite of private rooms at the back of the building. But everything I found there belonged to Root. His personal stink had soaked right into the fabric. I hated the idea of putting his things on my skin when I'd just been burned clean. But I had to wear something. In disgust, I took one of his rich shirts and a pair of pants. That was my punishment for having been so eager to judge Reese Dona.

Back in the greenhouse, I found him sitting on the floor with Kristen's head cradled in his lap. He was stroking the soft hair at her temples and grieving to himself. For the time being, at least, I was sure his grief had nothing to do with his ruined work. Kristen was fast asleep, exhausted by exertion and loss of blood. But I could see that she was going to be all right. Her bleeding had stopped completely. And Reese had already cleaned some of the stains from her face and neck.

Rain thundered against the ceiling of the greenhouse; jagged lines of lightning scrawled the heavens. But all the glass was intact, and the storm stayed outside, where it belonged. From the safety of shelter, the downpour felt comforting.

And the manufactured cool of the building had wiped out most of Root's unnatural heat. That was comforting, too.

It was time for me to go.

But I didn't want to leave Reese like this. I couldn't do anything about the regret that was going to dog him for the rest of his life. But I wanted to try.

The river was calling for me. Abruptly, as if I thought he was in any shape to hear me, I said, "What you did here—the work you did for Root—wasn't wrong. Don't blame yourself for that. You just went too far. You need to find the balance. Reason and energy." Need and help. "There's no limit to what you can do, if you just keep your balance."

He didn't answer. Maybe he wasn't listening to me at all. But after a moment he bent over Kristen and kissed her forehead.

That was enough. I had to go. Some of the details of the greenhouse were already starting to melt.

My bare feet didn't make any sound as I left the room, crossed the foyer, and went out into…

The Conqueror Worm

And much of Madness, and more of Sin,
And Horror the soul of the plot.
—EDGAR ALLAN POE

Before he realized what he was doing, he swung the knife.

▲▼▲

The home of Creel and Vi Sump. The living room.
Her real name is Violet, but everyone calls her Vi. They've been mar-
ried for two years now, and she isn't blooming.
Their home is modest but comfortable. Creel has a good job with his
company, but he isn't moving up. In the living room, some of the fur-
nishings are better than the space they occupy. A good stereo contrasts
with the state of the wallpaper. The arrangement of the furniture shows
a certain amount of frustration: there's no way to set the armchairs and
sofa so that people who sit on them can't see the waterspots in the ceiling.
The flowers in the vase on the endtable are real, but they look plastic. At
night, the lights leave shadows at odd places around the room.

▲▼▲

They were out late at a large party where acquaintances, business
Associates, and strangers drank a lot. As Creel unlocked the front door
and came into the living room ahead of Vi, he looked more than ever
like a rumpled bear. Whisky made the usual dullness of his eyes seem
baleful. Behind him, Vi resembled a flower in the process of becoming
a wasp.

"I don't care," he said, moving directly to the sideboard to get himself
another drink. "I wish you wouldn't do it."

She sat down on the sofa, took off her shoes. "God, I'm tired."

"If you aren't interested in anything else," he said, "think about me. I have to work with most of those people. Half of them can fire me if they want to. You're affecting my job."

"We've had this conversation before," she said. "We've had it eight times this month." A vague movement in one of the shadows across the room turned her head toward the corner. "What was *that*?"

"What was what?"

"I saw something move. Over there in the corner. Don't tell me we've got mice."

"I didn't see anything. We haven't got mice. And I don't care how many times we've had this conversation. I want you to stop."

She stared into the corner for a moment. Then she leaned back on the sofa. "I can't stop. I'm not *doing* anything."

"The hell you're not doing anything." He took a drink and refilled his glass. "If you were after him any harder, you'd have your hand in his pants."

"That's not true."

"You think nobody sees what you're doing. You act like you're alone. But you're not. Everybody at that whole damn party was watching you. The way you flirt—"

"I wasn't flirting. I was just talking to him."

"The way you *flirt*, you ought to have the decency to be embarrassed."

"Oh, go to bed. I'm too tired for this."

"Is it because he's a vice-president? Do you think that's going to make him better in bed? Or do you just like the status of playing around with a vice-president?"

"I wasn't *flirting* with him. I swear to God, there's something the matter with you. We were just talking. You know—moving our mouths so that words could come out. He was a literature major in college. We have something in common. We've read the same books. Remember *books?* Those things with ideas and stories printed in them? All you ever talk about is football—and how somebody at the company has it in for you—and how the latest secretary doesn't wear a bra. Sometimes I think I'm the last literate person left alive."

She raised her head to look at him. Then she sighed, "Why do I even bother? You're not listening to me."

"You're right," he said. "There *is* something in the corner. I saw it move."

They both stared at the corner. After a moment, a centipede scuttled out into the light.

It looked slimy and malicious, and it waved its antennae hungrily. It was nearly ten inches long. Its thick legs seemed to ripple as it shot across the rug. Then it stopped to scan its surroundings. Creel and Vi could see its mandibles chewing expectantly as it flexed its poison claws. It had entered the house to escape the cold, dry night outside—and to hunt for food.

She wasn't the kind of woman who screamed easily; but she hopped up onto the sofa to get her bare feet away from the floor. "Good God," she whispered. "Creel, look at that. Don't let it come any closer."

He leaped at the centipede and tried to stamp one of his heavy shoes down on it. But it moved so fast that he didn't come close to it. Neither of them saw where it went.

"It's under the sofa," he said. "Get off of there."

She obeyed without question. Wincing, she jumped out into the middle of the rug.

As soon as she was out of the way, he heaved the sofa onto its back. The centipede wasn't there.

"The poison isn't fatal," Vi said. "One of the kids in the neighborhood got stung last week. Her mother told me all about it. It's like getting a bad bee-sting."

Creel didn't listen to her. He lifted the entire sofa into the air so that he could see more of the floor. But the centipede was gone.

He dropped the sofa back onto its legs, knocking over the end-table, spilling the flowers. "Where did that bastard go?"

They hunted around the room for several minutes without leaving the protection of the light. Then he went and got himself another drink. His hands were shaking.

She said, "I wasn't flirting."

He looked at her, "Then it's something worse. You're already sleeping with him. You must've been making plans for the next time you get together."

"I'm going to bed," she said. "I don't have to put up with this. You're disgusting."

He finished his drink and refilled his glass from the nearest bottle.

▲▼▲

The Sumps' game-room.

This room is the real reason why Creel bought this house over Vi's objections: he wanted a house with a game-room. The money which could have replaced the wallpaper and fixed the ceiling of the living room has been spent here. The room contains a full-size pooltable with all the trimmings, a long, imitation leather couch along one wall, and a wet-bar.

But the light here isn't any better than in the living room because the fixtures are focused on the pooltable. Even the wet-bar is so ill-lit that its users have to guess what they're doing.

When he isn't working, traveling for his company, or watching football with his buddies, Creel spends a lot of time here.

▲▼▲

After Vi went to bed, Creel came into the game-room. First he went to the wet-bar and refilled his glass. Then he racked up the balls and broke so violently that the cueball sailed off the table. It made a dull, thudding noise as it bounced on the spongy linoleum.

"Fuck," he said, lumbering after the ball. The liquor he had consumed showed in the way he moved but not in his speech. He sounded sober.

Bracing himself with his custom-made cuestick, he bent to pick up the ball. Before he put it back on the table, Vi entered the room. She hadn't changed her clothes for bed, but she had put her shoes back on. She scrutinized the shadows around the floor and under the table before she looked at Creel.

He said, "I thought you were going to bed."

"I can't leave it like this," she said tiredly. "It hurts too much."

"What do you want from me?" he said. "Approval?"

She glared at him.

He didn't stop. "That would be terrific for you. If I approved, you wouldn't have anything else to worry about. The only problem would be, most of the bastards I introduce you to are married. Their wives might be a little more normal. They might give you some trouble."

She bit her lip and went on glaring at him.

"But I don't see why you should worry about that. If women aren't as understanding as I am, that's their tough luck. As long as I approve, right? There's no reason why you shouldn't screw anybody you want."

"Are you finished?"

"Hell, there's no reason why you shouldn't screw *all* of them. I mean, as long as I approve. Why waste it?"

"Damn it, are you *finished*?"

"There's only one thing I don't understand. If you're so hot for sex, how come you don't want to screw me?"

"That's not true."

He blinked at her through a haze of alcohol. "What's not true? You're not hot for sex? Or you do want to screw me? Don't make me laugh."

"Creel, what's the matter with you? I don't understand any of this. You didn't used to be like this. You weren't like this when we were dating. You weren't like this when we got married. What's happened to you?"

For a minute, he didn't say anything. He went back to the edge of the pooltable, where he'd left his drink. But with his cue in one hand and the ball in the other, he didn't have a hand free. Carefully, he set his stick down on the table.

After he finished his drink, he said, "You changed."

"*I* changed? *You're* the one who's acting crazy. All I did was talk to some company vice-president about *books.*"

"No, I'm not," he said. His knuckles were white around the cueball. "You think I'm stupid. Because I wasn't a literature major in college. Maybe that's what changed. When we got married, you didn't think I was stupid. But now you do. You think I'm too stupid to notice the difference."

"What difference is that?"

"You never want to have sex with me anymore."

"Oh, for God's sake," she said. "We had sex the day before yesterday."

He looked straight at her. "But you didn't want to. I can tell. You never *want* to."

"What do you mean, you can tell?"

"You make a lot of excuses."

"I do not."

"And when we do have sex, you don't pay any attention to me. You're always somewhere else. Thinking about something else. You're always thinking about somebody else."

"But that's *normal,*" she said. "Everybody does it. Everybody fantasizes during sex. *You* fantasize during sex. That's what makes it fun,"

At first, she didn't see the centipede as it wriggled out from under the pooltable, its antennae searching for her legs. But then she happened to glance downward.

"Creel!"

The centipede started toward her. She jumped back, out of the way.

Creel threw the cueball with all his strength. It made a dent in the lineoleum beside the centipede, then crashed into the side of the wet-bar.

The centipede went for Vi. It was so fast that she couldn't get away from it. As its segments caught the light, they gleamed poisonously.

Creel snatched his cuestick off the table and hammered at the centipede. Again, he missed. But flying splinters of wood made the centipede turn and shoot in the other direction. It disappeared under the couch.

"Get it," she panted.

He shook the pieces of his cue at her. "I'll tell you what I fantasize. I fantasize that you *like* having sex with me. You fantasize that I'm somebody else." Then he wrenched the couch away from the wall, brandishing his weapons.

"So would you," she retorted, "if you had to sleep with a sensitive, considerate, imaginative *animal* like you."

As she left the room, she slammed the door behind her.

Shoving the furniture bodily from side to side, he continued hunting for the centipede.

▲▼▲

The bedroom.

This room expresses Vi as much as the limitations of the house permit. The bed is really too big for the space available, but at least it has an elaborate brass headstead and footboard. The sheets and pillowcases match the bedspread, which is decorated with white flowers on a blue background. Unfortunately, Creel's weight makes the bed sag. The closet doors are warped and can't be closed.

There's an overhead light, but Vi never uses it. She relies on a pair of goose-necked Tiffany reading lamps. As a result, the bed seems to be surrounded by gloom in all directions.

Creel sat on the bed and watched the bathroom door. His back was bowed. His right fist gripped the neck of a bottle of tequila, but he wasn't drinking.

The bathroom door was closed. He appeared to be staring at himself in the full-length mirror attached to it. A strip of fluorescent light showed past the bottom of the door. He could see Vi's shadow as she moved around in the bathroom.

He stared at the door for several minutes, but she was taking her time. Finally, he shifted the bottle to his left hand.

"I never understand what you *do* in there."

Through the door, she said, "I'm waiting for you to pass out so I can go to sleep in peace."

He looked offended. "Well, I'm not going to pass out. I never pass out. You might as well give up."

Abruptly, the door opened. She snapped off the bathroom light and stood in the darkened doorway, facing him. She was dressed for bed in a nightie that would have made her look desirable if she had wished to look desirable.

"What do you want now?" she said. "Are you finished wrecking the game-room already?"

"I was trying to kill that centipede. The one that scared you so badly."

"I wasn't scared—just startled. It's only a centipede. Did you get it?"

"No."

"You're too slow. You'll have to call an exterminator."

"Damn the exterminator," he said slowly. *"Fuck* the exterminator. Fuck the centipede. I can take care of my own problems. Why did you call me that?"

"Call you what?"

He didn't look at her. "An animal." Then he did. "I've never lifted a finger to hurt you."

She moved past him to the bed and propped the pillows up against the brass bedstead. Sitting on the bed, she curled her legs under her and leaned back against the pillows.

"I know," she said. "I didn't mean it the way it sounded. I was just mad."

He frowned. "You didn't mean it the way it sounded. How nice. That makes me feel a whole lot better. What in hell *did* you mean?"

"I hope you realize you're not making this any easier."

"It isn't easy for *me.* Do you think I like sitting here begging my own wife to tell me why I'm not good enough for her?"

"Actually," she said, "I think you do like it. This way, you get to feel like a victim."

He raised his bottle until the tequila caught the light. He peered into the golden liquid for a moment, then transferred the bottle back to his right hand. But he didn't say anything.

"All right," she said after a while. "You treat me like you don't care what I think or how I feel."

"I do it the way I know how," he protested. "If it feels good for me, it's supposed to feel good for you."

"I'm not just talking about sex. I'm talking about the way you treat me. The way you talk to me. The way you assume I have to like everything you like and can't like anything you don't like. The way you think my whole life is supposed to revolve around you."

"Then why did you marry me? Did it take you two years to find out you don't really want to be my wife?"

She stretched her legs out in front of her. Her nightie covered them to the knees. "I married you because I loved you. Not because I want to be treated like an object for the rest of my natural life. I need friends. People I can share things with. People who care what I'm thinking. I almost went to grad school because I wanted to study Baudelaire. We've been married for two years, and you still don't know who Baudelaire is. The only people I ever meet are your drinking buddies. Or the people who work for your company."

He started to say something, but she kept going. "And I need freedom. I need to make my own decisions—my own choices. I need to have my own life."

Again, he tried to say something.

"And I need to be cherished. You use me like I'm less interesting than your precious poolcue."

"It's broken," he said flatly.

"I know it's broken," she said. "I don't care. This is more important. I'm more important."

In the same tone, he said, "You said you loved me. You don't love me anymore."

"God, you're dense. *Think* about it. What on earth do you ever do to make me feel like *you* love me?"

He shifted the bottle to his left hand again. "You've been sleeping around. You probably screw every sonofabitch you can get into the sack. That's why you don't love me anymore. They probably do all kinds of dirty things to you I don't do. And you're hooked on it. You're bored with me because I'm just not exciting enough."

She dropped her arms onto the pillows beside her. "Creel, that's *sick.* You're *sick.*"

Disturbed by her movement, the centipede crawled out between the pillows onto her left arm. It waved its poison claws while it tasted her skin with its antennae, looking for the best place to bite in.

This time, she did scream. Wildly, she flung up her arm. The centipede was thrown into the air.

It hit the ceiling and came down on her bare leg.

It was angry now. Its thick legs swarmed to take hold of her and attack.

With his free hand, he struck a backhand blow down the length of her leg that slapped the centipede off her.

As the centipede hit the wall, he pitched his bottle at it, trying to smash it. But it had already vanished into the gloom around the bed. A shower of glass and tequila covered the bedspread.

She bounced off the bed; hid behind him. "I can't take any more of this. I'm leaving."

"It's only a centipede," he panted as he wrenched the brass frame off the foot of the bed. Holding the frame in one hand for a club, he braced his other arm under the bed and heaved it off its legs. He looked strong enough to crush one centipede. "What're you afraid of?"

"I'm afraid of you. I'm afraid of the way your mind works."

As he turned the bed over, he knocked down one of the Tiffany lamps. The room became even darker. When he flipped on the overhead light, he couldn't see the centipede anywhere.

The whole room stank of tequila.

▲▼▲

The living room again.

The sofa sits where Creel left it. The endtable lies on its side, surrounded by wilting flowers. The water from the vase has left a stain that looks like another shadow on the rug. But in other ways the room is unchanged. The lights are on. Their brightness emphasizes all the places they don't reach.

Creel and Vi are there. He sits in one of the armchairs and watches her while she rummages around in a large closet that opens into the room. She is hunting for things to take with her and a suitcase to carry them in. She is wearing a shapeless dress with no belt. For some reason, it makes her look younger. He seems more awkward than usual without a drink in his hands.

▲▼▲

"I get the impression you're enjoying this," he said.

"Of course," she said. "You've been right about everything else. Why shouldn't you be right now? I haven't had so much fun since I dislocated my knee in high school."

"How about our wedding night? That was one of the highlights of your life."

She stopped what she was doing to glare at him. "If you keep this up, I'm going to puke right here in front of you."

"You made me feel like a complete shit."

"Right again. You're absolutely brilliant tonight."

"Well, you look like you're enjoying yourself. I haven't seen you this excited for years. You've probably been hunting for a chance to do this ever since you first started sleeping around."

She threw a vanity case across the room and went on rummaging through the closet.

"I'm curious about that first time," he said. "Did he seduce you? I bet you're the one who seduced him. I bet you begged him into bed so he could teach you all the dirty tricks he knew."

"Shut up," she muttered from inside the closet. "Just shut up—I'm not listening."

"Then you found out he was too normal for you. All he wanted was a straight screw. So you dropped the poor bastard and went looking for something fancier. By now, you must be pretty good at talking men into your panties."

She came out of the closet holding one of his old baseball bats.

"Damn you, Creel. If you don't stop this, so help me God, I'm going to beat your putrid brains out."

He laughed humorlessly. "You can't do that. They don't punish infidelity, but they'll put you in jail for killing your husband."

Slamming the bat back into the closet, she returned to her search.

He couldn't take his eyes off her. Every time she came out of the closet, he studied everything she did. After a while, he said, "You shouldn't let a centipede upset you like this."

She ignored him.

"I can take care of it," he went on. "I've never let anything hurt you. I know I keep missing it. I've let you down. But I'll take care of it. I'll call an exterminator in the morning. Hell, I'll call ten exterminators. You don't have to go."

She continued ignoring him.

For a minute, he covered his face with his hands. Then he dropped them into his lap. His expression changed.

"Or we can keep it for a pet. We can train it to wake us up in the morning. Bring in the paper. Make coffee. We won't need an alarm clock anymore."

She lugged a large suitcase out of the closet. Swinging it onto the sofa, she opened it and began stuffing things into it.

He said, "We can call him Baudelaire."

She looked nauseated.

"Baudelaire the Butler. He can meet people at the door for us. Answer the phone. Make the beds. As long as we don't let him get the wrong idea, he can probably help you choose what you're going to wear.

"No, I've got a better idea. You can wear *him*. Put him around your neck and use him for a ruff. He'll be the latest thing in sexy clothes. Then you'll be able to get fucked as much as you want."

Biting her lip to keep from crying, Vi went back into the closet to get a sweater off one of the upper shelves.

When she pulled the sweater down from the shelf, the centipede landed on the top of her head.

Her instinctive flinch carried her out into the room. Creel had a perfect view of what was happening as the centipede dropped to her shoulder and squirmed inside the collar of her dress.

She froze. All the blood drained out of her face. Her eyes stared wildly.

"Creel," she breathed. "Oh my God. Help me."

The shape of the centipede showed through her dress as it crawled over her breasts.

"Creel."

At the sight, he heaved himself out of his armchair and sprang toward her. Then he jerked to a stop.

"I can't hit it," he said. "I'll hurt you. It'll sting you. If I try to lift your dress to get at it, it might sting you."

She couldn't speak. The sensation of the centipede creeping across her skin paralyzed her.

For a moment, he looked completely helpless. "I don't know what to do." His hands were empty.

Suddenly, his face lit up.

"I'll get a knife."

Turning, he ran out of the room toward the kitchen.

Vi squeezed her eyes shut and clenched her fists. Whimpering sounds came between her lips, but she didn't move.

Slowly, the centipede crossed her belly. Its antennae explored her navel. All the rest of her body flinched, but she kept the muscles of her stomach rigid.

Then the centipede found the warm place between her legs.

For some reason, it didn't stop. It crawled onto her left thigh and continued downward.

She opened her eyes and watched as the centipede showed itself below the hem of her dress.

Searching her skin every inch of the way, the centipede crept down her shin to her ankle. There it stopped until she looked like she wasn't going to be able to keep herself from screaming. Then it moved again.

As soon as it reached the floor, she jumped away from it. She let herself scream, but she didn't let that slow her down. As fast as she could, she dashed to the front door, threw it open, and left the house.

The centipede was in no hurry. It looked ready and confident as its thick legs carried it under the sofa.

A second later, Creel came back from the kitchen. He carried carving knife with a long, wicked blade.

"Vi?" he shouted. "Vi?"

Then he saw the open door.

At once, a snarl twisted his face. "You bastard," he whispered. "Oh you *bastard*. Now you've done it to me."

He dropped into a crouch. His eyes searched the rug. He held the knife poised in front of him.

"I'm going to get you for this. I'm going to find you. You can bet I'm going to find you. And when I do, I'm going to cut you to pieces. I'm going to cut you into little, tiny pieces. I'm going to cut all your legs off, one at a time. Then I'm going to flush you down the disposal."

Stalking around behind the sofa, he reached the place where the endtable lay on its side, surrounded by dead flowers.

"You utter bastard. She was my wife."

But he didn't see the centipede. It was hiding in the dark water-stain beside the vase. He nearly stepped on it.

In a flash, it shot onto his shoe and disappeared up the leg of his pants.

He didn't know the centipede had him until he felt it climb over his knee.

Looking down, he saw the long bulge in his pants work its way toward his groin.

Before he realized what he was doing—

Ser Visal's Tale

The prospect of a tale from Ser Visal drew us as a flame draws moths, though only the most timid goodwoman—or the most rigorous Templeman—would claim that there was any danger in stories. And we were young, the sons of men of station throughout the region. Naturally, we scoffed at danger. The thought that we might hear something profane or even blasphemous—something that would never cross our hearing in the Temple or in the bosoms of our generally cautious families—only made the attraction more compelling. When the inns reopened between nones and vespers, we gathered, as eager as boys, in the public room of the Hound and Whip and opened our purses to provide Ser Visal with the lubrication his tongue required. The keeper of the Hound and Whip had the particular virtue of being as deaf as iron; he responded only to the vibrations he felt when we stamped our boots upon the boards, and he served us whatever wines God or inattention advised. For our part, we made certain that there were no tattlers among us in the public room before we urged Ser Visal to begin.

"Disorderly louts!" he responded, glaring around at us with a vexation which we knew to be feigned. He relished our enthusiasm for his stories. "Our God is a God of order. Confusion is abominable. Good King Traktus himself worships in the Temple of God. Twice a day he meets with High Templeman Crossus Hught to study and pray, that Heaven may defend us from evil. Have you nothing better to do with your time than to gaggle around me like puppies and loosen a fat old man's tongue with wine?"

One of our fellows giggled unfortunately at this brief jape of the Temple's teachings. But an elbow in the ribs silenced him before Ser Visal was diverted into a lecture on piety. He was prone to such digressions, perhaps thinking that they would whet our attention for his stories—and we dared not interrupt him, for fear that he would grow vexed in truth and refuse to continue. He demanded a rapt audience, and we sought to satisfy him.

Ser Quest Visal was indeed *a fat old man*—as fat as a porker, with eyes squeezed almost to popping in the heavy flesh of his face, arms that appeared to stuff his sleeves like sausages, and fingers as thick and pale as pastries. His grizzled hair straggled like a beldame's. Careless shaving left his jowls speckled with whiskers, Though he sat in the corner of the hearth—the warmest spot in the Hound and Whip—he wore two robes over his clothing, with the result that sweat ran from his brows as from an overlathered horse. Yet every gesture of his hands beyond his frilled cuffs held us, and every word he uttered was remembered. We were familiar with his storytelling.

He had returned to town after an absence of some days. In fact, it was rumored that he had fled to his estates immediately following the unprecedented—and unexplained—turmoil which had resulted from the most recent sitting of the judica. It was known to all that the judica had assembled to pass judgment upon a suspected witch, but no judgment had been announced. The disruption of the sitting had been followed by a rough and bitter search of the town, such as only the Templemen had the power and determination to pursue. Since then, the mood had been one of anger. Men who did not like the implied distrust of the search were further irked by the righteous frustration of the searchers. And finally—a development piquant to us all—no accounts of the judica, no high condemnations of witchcraft, no exhortations to shun for our souls the fires of damnation had been issued from the pulpits of the Temple. Instead, we had heard read out for the first time in our lives a writ of excommunication.

Its object had been Dom Sen Peralt.

You are cut off, the Templemen had thundered or crowed, according to their natures, *cut off root and trunk, branch and leaf, cut off from God and Temple, Heaven and hope. You are shunned by all men, blighted by all love. The sun will not warm your face. Shade will not cool your brow. Water and food will give you no sustenance. You are cursed in your mind and in your heart, in your blood and in your loins. Your loves will die, and your offspring will wither, and all that you have touched will be destroyed. This is the will of God.*

We knew that Ser Visal—like every other man of his rank—had attended the judica. And we prayed that he would reveal what had happened.

"Disorderly louts," he repeated, wiping wine from his chins. "Impious lovers of freedom and romance, which seduce souls to perdition." If his words were to be believed, he had always been one of the staunchest supporters of the Templemen. And surely none of us had ever heard him accused of courage. Yet we did not take his admonitions seriously. His voice had a special quaver which he used only to protest his devotion, and his eyes appeared to bulge with astonishment at what he heard himself say. "Well, attend me for your hope of Heaven. I will instruct you."

We settled ourselves on the long wooden benches of the Hound and Whip, hunched over the wide, planked tables, and listened.

"Boys are fools all," he began, and his fat fingers waggled at us. "I include you, every one. Fools! Lovers of dreams and freedom. And I count every man who has not set aside such toys a boy, whatever his age. You will learn better from me. I will lesson you in order and justice, in the folly of human passion against God's Temple and God's judgment. Your fathers will thank me for it." Without looking at any of us in particular, he remarked, "My flagon is empty."

Several of us stamped our feet. The son of Dom Tahl scattered coins onto the table. In response, the keeper brought a small cask of an unusually drinkable canary wine and left it for us to deal with as we saw fit.

Refreshed by a long draught, Ser Visal set down his flagon and sighed. "Boys and fools," he said, "surely none will deny that life has been much improved since good King Traktus became concerned for his salvation and turned to the Temple of God—and to High Templeman Crossus Hught—for spiritual assistance. The Templemen have become the right hand of the King as well as of God, and our lives are cleansed and straitened and made wiser thereby. Consider our prior state. Young whelps such as yourselves, Domsons and Sersons all, spent their lives riotously while their sires plotted for advantage or land. Farmers priced their produce as they chose and grew fat. Merchants wandered from town to town, spreading gossip and dissension with their wares. Gypsies and carnivals flourished upon credulity wherever it was found. The poor lined the streets as beggars, and when they died they were not left in the mud as they deserved, but were rather buried at public expense. Minstrels purveyed lies of heroism and great deeds, of thrones to be won in faraway lands, of adventures and dreams. Goodwomen who should have tended hearths and spinning left their homes to command shops and crops and men. And there were witches—

"The Temple has taught us that there are witches. We have learned to see the evil of a flashing glance"—Ser Visal rolled his eyes in mimicry—"the touch of a white hand, the smile of an unveiled face. We have learned that some women possess power to disorder men's minds as they disorder life, doing things which cannot be done and imposing their wills on those around them, weaving damnation and all foul perversion. For this reason we have the judica, to hunt that evil and root it out. So, good louts, you will hardly credit that there was once a time when some men and perhaps a few goodwomen did not believe in witches.

"Yet witches there were." He rubbed his hands through the sweat on his brow, then flicked his fingers negligently, as though aping a holy sign for our silent amusement. "This is excellent canary." The candles of the inn were new and bright because there were no windows, and the dancing flames made his eyes appear to stare from his face. "Witches, indeed. They lived quietly among the dark woods, or secretly in barrows which few could find beneath the hedgerows, or openly with the gypsies and the minstrels. And woe to any man who went near them with his heart unguarded by righteousness, for they were strange and powerful and lovely as only evil can be, and that man would never again look upon his own goodwoman or his promised maid with quite the same—shall we say, quite the same enthusiasm?"

On the word, his plump lips twisted into a sardonic expression. But before we could laugh, he raised his gaze to the smoke-stained ceiling and went on devoutly, "Praise the Temple of God that the danger is no longer what it was! Oh, some witches yet live. Some have fled where men cannot follow. And some have learned to pass in covert among us, concealing their powers. But forewarned is forearmed. And most witches have gone to judgment and the hot iron of the judica, destroyed by Temple zealotry. Many of them, you puppies—more than you imagine. So many, it is astonishing that we are able to live without them—gone to feed the cauldron with their bones and their sins and their terrible cries. And"—he lowered his voice portentously—"not one of them innocent. Not *one*. The judica has condemned every creature with a slim leg and a pert breast which the Templemen have brought for judgment."

He paused to refill his flagon and toss off another draught, then said, "Of course, I have not mentioned the many other amendments which good King Traktus has imposed upon our lives at the counsel of the High Templeman. Prices and merchants have been wisely regulated. Carnivals where such louts as you are were led into folly have been banned, on pain of slavery. And slavery itself—!

"It is an admirable institution, is it not? At one stroke, we are rid of all miscreants—the poor, the idle, the wicked—we are provided with cheap service which any honest tradesman or farmer or man of station may afford, and the coffers of the Temple of God are enriched, to the benefit of our immortal souls, for by the King's edict all the fees of the slavers are shared with the Templemen. An *admirable* institution.

"So you see, my eager young gallants, it is not surprising that the tale of Dom Peralt began with a slave and ended with a witch."

At that, we all stiffened. Our attention grew even sharper, if that were possible. The sound of excommunication was in our ears. This story was precisely the one we most wished to hear. Ser Visal smiled at the effect of his announcement. Then—perhaps recollecting that it was unwise to smile on any subject associated with the disfavor of the Temple—he frowned and slapped a fat hand to the table. "Be warned, whelps! This is not the tale of daring and passion you expect. It is sordid and foolish, and I tell it to caution you, so that you will be wiser than mad Dom Peralt, who was nothing more than a boy some few years older than yourselves."

But we were not daunted. We watched Ser Visal brightly, our breathing thick with anticipation in our chests. And slowly his face appeared to refold itself to lines of sadness. His gaze receded, as though he were now seeing the past rather than the public room of the Hound and Whip. We knew that look. If we did not interrupt now, he would tell his story.

"Dom Sen Peralt," he sighed. "I knew his father. The old Dom was a goodly man, as all agreed—perhaps somewhat too little concerned for the state of the public weal, somewhat too much immersed in the private affairs of his estates and dependents, but hale of heart and whole of mind nonetheless. And grown like a tree!" The memory made Ser Visal chuckle voluminously within his robes. "An oak of a man. He bore no weapons; the threat of his fist was as good as a broadsword." Then he relapsed to sadness. "And many folk flourished under the shade of his care. He was more interested in the commonest babe born in the farthest cottage on his lands than in all the affairs of kings and counselors. A goodly man, greatly grieved in his passing.

"By ill chance, however, young Sen Peralt's mother died during his babyhood, and the old Dom was too occupied elsewhere to attend closely to the rearing of his son. He trusted, I believe, that a decent heart would be inherited—and that his example would supply what his attention did not. In young Sen's early youth, his father had no cause to complain. But as the boy came toward manhood, he fell among ill companions"—Ser Visal gave us a glare—"shiftless whelps and roisterers such as yourselves, Serson Nason Lew and Domson Beau Frane chief among them, and he discovered the pleasures of folly. The old Dom was not a man to enforce his will upon others, and he knew not how to intervene. To his sorrow, his son become a tremendous gallant, dedicated to wine and minstrelsy and compliant women. Sen Peralt's brawls became matters of legend. I shudder to think of the inns he wrecked, the virgins he—"

Abruptly, Ser Visal stopped. "You are too young to understand virgins," he said severely. "Refill my flagon."

But when he had replaced some of the fluid he sweated away, he resumed his tale. "Unfortunately, the old Dom died while helping one of his farmers clear a field of boulders. In his mourning, the new Dom was consoled as he had been entertained by his boon companions, Serson Lew and Domson Frane. I will say of him that he gave fit respect to his father. But when he had taken upon himself his father's station, he showed no inclination to follow his father's path. He did not altogether neglect his duties. And he took no slaves, as his father had taken none. But the greater part of his time was spent in carouse, defying both the advice of his father's friends"—Ser Visal's expression suggested that he had given Dom Peralt hogsheads of good advice—and had helped him drink them—"and the strict attention of the Templemen. He was a scandal in the region, though doubtless you louts admired him. Templeman Knarll himself let it be known that sermons would soon be preached against Dom Peralt from every pulpit within a day's ride, if young Sen did not begin to take better care of his salvation. It was, said Templeman Knarll, precisely to protect good people from such sins that the Temple of God had become so rigorous."

Ser Visal shrugged his round shoulders. "And it was precisely in this state of ill grace that Dom Peralt came to town on slaving day.

"You are familiar with slaving day. It is most instructive—*most* instructive. A lesson to us all. There in the marketplace gather the slavers to sell their wares—and the Templemen to collect their fees. The streets are thick with mud, as rank as sewers, and pickpockets work happily among the crowds, and merchants hawk all manner of commodities, and every townsman comes to consider what may be bought. It is as near to festivity as the Temple of God permits. Goodwomen remain in their homes, but jades wear their brightest colors, and gallants preen, and money seeps everywhere from hand to hand, more subtle than the mud but not less tainted." Perhaps we saw anger in Ser Visal's eyes—or perhaps he was simply spinning the mood of his story. "And amid it all are the new slaves for purchase.

"They are chained to each other like cattle, hardly able to lift their fetters for exhaustion or hunger, and dressed as much in muck as in rags. In their eyes—when their eyes are open and their heads raised— are every kind of hate and fear and despair, but no love. I have seen children of no more than four summers manacled to known molesters of children—and the parents bound elsewhere for their debts, helpless. I have seen the sons of impoverished farmers coupled by iron to desperate whores. I have seen innocent travelers pleading for release from the slavers' quotas. Their filth and degradation exemplify all the evils which have brought slavery among us. The Templemen accompany them, garnering fees from the slaves—and so the world is cleansed. *Most instructive. Learn its lesson well, puppies.*"

With one long pull, Ser Visal emptied his flagon, then glowered at us as though he were outraged. But almost at once the flesh swelled around his eyes, and he smiled humorlessly.

"To slaving day," he said, "came Dom Sen Peralt and his two cohorts in debauch, Domson Frane and Serson Lew.

"He had not the full size of his father, but still he was *large* of frame, and neither wine nor feast had softened the edges of his strength. He bore his head high, as if he were of regal birth. The black curls which crowned his head gleamed darkly. His gaze shone in the sunlight. His stride was strong, immune to the mud sucking at his boots. His fine mouth above his chin showed a bemused contempt for all the human ruin enchained around him. And his comrades slogged at his side, struggling to match him and appearing only foolish.

"Do I make him seem grand?" asked Ser Visal acidly. "He was as drunk as a tinker. Only the prospect of more drink kept him on his feet. If he had tripped, he might have lain face down in the mud and been trampled without noticing it."

At once, however, our instructor reverted to piety. "But God's will was otherwise. Before Dom Peralt had crossed the marketplace to the inn he sought, he was accosted by a man nearly as large as himself—by Growt, most feared of the slavers.

"It is said of Growt—but such tales are told everywhere, especially among boys. Well, my puppies, the tales are true. Growt is feared because he asks no questions concerning those he hales into slavery. If the Templemen desire a man or woman punished, they merely give the name to Growt. If a miller comes to loathe his goodwoman's shrewish tongue, he gives her name to Growt. If a usurer covets the property of a debtor, he gives the name to Growt. And when he has not enough commissions to fill his quota, Growt takes minstrels and travelers and gypsies where he finds them.

"Now among slavers, as in the Temple of God, such men as Dom Peralt are looked upon with resentment—and perhaps also with fear—because they take no slaves. Their wealth is denied to those who most merit it. And on this slaving day Growt's resentment had grown beyond its usual blackness. His wares were in little demand. It will not surprise you that innocent travelers and shrewish goodwomen are not always docile slaves. Growt's wares were rendered suspect by his means of obtaining them. Therefore it was in no mood of good fellowship that he set himself in the way of Dom Sen Peralt.

"Burly as a bear, but entirely hairless from the knob of his pate to the tops of his toes, and dressed in his slavers' leathers, he was a formidable obstacle to be found in any man's path, were the man drunk or sober. But he was not content merely to bar Dom Peralt's way. When the young Dom neared him, Growt thrust out an arm as heavy as an axletree and jolted Dom Peralt in his tracks.

"It appeared momentarily that Dom Peralt would go sprawling at the feet of Growt's slaves. But he regained his balance. Young Nason and Beau Frane gaped at Growt as if he had been translated from the nether regions to appall them. Indeed, he was blackened and dirty enough to be a fiend—but of course he was not, being about the Temple's business. Arms akimbo, he stood his ground and awaited Dom Peralt's reaction.

"Hauling himself upright, Dom Peralt turned a smile upon Growt. For a moment, he seemed to study this barrier—though in truth he was hardly able to focus his eyes for drink. Then he said in a friendly manner, 'Slaver, you stand between me and a flagon of ripe sack. Already it languishes for me, and I mean to relieve it of its longing.' His cohorts giggled at this. 'Do not hinder me,' Dom Peralt concluded, 'in my errand of mercy.' To which Domson Frane, the bolder of the two, added, 'You mustn't hinder him, no, you mustn't. Hinderance makes him bilious.'

"'Your pardon,' replied Growt with admirable insincerity. 'Buy a slave, and I will let you pass.'

"Dom Peralt blinked in response, his smile unaltered. 'A slave?' he asked, betraying the impairment of his wits. 'You wish me to buy a slave? Heinous custom. Why should I buy a slave?'

"Growt had the trick of appearing to bristle with menace instead of hair. 'You insult me, Dom,' he answered. 'I do the work of the Temple of God. It is not heinous. And I do not *wish* you to buy a slave. I *mean* you to buy a slave.'

"Sunlight or some other gleam kindled in Dom Peralt's eyes. 'You are mistaken, slaver,' he said affably. 'I have not insulted you. It is not possible to insult you.'

"Growt glowered. Again, his great arm jabbed Dom Peralt, nearly depriving him of balance. Serson Lew retreated a step. Beau Frane looked to his leader for some hint of what was to be done. But Growt ignored those whelps as he would ignore you. 'Nevertheless,' he repeated, 'I mean you to buy a slave.' As Dom Peralt steadied himself, the slaver gestured toward his wares. 'I have young ones and old ones. I have women with open legs and men with strong backs. I have skilled laborers and dumb cattle. I even have one'—his mouth leered, but his eyes did not—'who will tune a lute—and a song with it—if you know the way to twist his thumbs.' Then, abruptly, his manner changed, and he used the voice which kept his charges cowering by day and pliant by night. *'Buy one.'*

"Again, Dom Peralt contrived to regain his bearing. On his lips was the smile which made maidens blush and caused women some weakness in their knees. He paid no regard to his companions, though Nason Lew whispered for retreat and young Beau silently urged fight. To Growt, he said sweetly, 'Now it is I who must ask your pardon. The cries of lorn sack from yonder inn are piteous, filling my ears. I fear I have been remiss in my attention—I did not hear you clearly. Will you be so kind as to repeat? I believe you began by begging my pardon. Continue from there.'

"Well, he had audacity. That I will say for him. But a playful mood was on him. In any other mind, he might simply have put his fist to Growt's face and chanced the outcome. And *that,* you louts, would have gone hard for him. He was roundly drunk—and Growt was not notably scrupulous in the use of his hands. But it is commonly said that God watches over drunkards; and so Dom Peralt sought contest with his sodden wits rather than with his equally sodden strength.

"For his part, however, Growt had no wit. He replied with a growl which bared what remained of his rotten teeth. Grabbing at the front of Dom Peralt's fine jacket, he wrenched young Sen from his feet to his knees in the mud. There Growt bent him backward and demanded softly, 'Buy a slave.'

"A crowd had gathered. Witnesses abounded, all hungry for excitement. In their hearts, most of the townspeople would have cheered for Dom Peralt to rise up and repay some of Growt's great debt of grief. But there were Templemen present, watching and wary for sins to be punished—and so most of the spectators kept the nature of their eagerness to themselves. Serson Lew hopped from one foot to the other, wanting to run. And his fellow had come to be of a similar mind. They were accustomed to observe Dom Peralt's brawls and applaud them, not to participate in them. No one considered intervention.

"For all his follies, however, Dom Peralt had been formed in another mold. On his knees in muck, and nearly falling backward under the pressure of Growt's grasp, he betrayed no whit of consternation. His smile remained sweetly upon his lips—his gaze did not waver from Growt's. 'Buy a slave?' he said, articulating carefully through his drunkenness. 'Splendid idea. Why have I never done so before? Truly, my own thoughtlessness astonishes me. I am in your debt, slaver. I will buy a slave at once.'

"This nonplussed Growt. He sensed Dom Peralt's sport, but could not fathom it. Clearly, the slaver wished to grind Dom Peralt's smile into the mud. But how could he do so, when Dom Peralt had just offered to meet his demand? 'Do not toy with me,' he snarled, attempting to recapture his menace. 'Buy a slave.'

"'But of course,' replied Dom Peralt. 'I said the same myself. Just now, as I recall. A splendid idea. Altogether splendid. Did I say that also?' There was laughter in his eyes, but none in his voice.

"Growt's whole face twisted as he strove to guess young Sen's game. Bending over him, he hissed, 'One of mine—or I will break your back where you kneel.'

"Dom Peralt flung his arms wide in a gesture of appeal. 'Slaver, you wound me. I have not deserved this doubt. I cannot deny that I am young and thoughtless. But none accuse me of ingratitude. You have awakened me to my error. What other wares should I consider, except yours?' In a subtle way, his tone turned harder as he spoke. But his smile belied all hint of anger. 'However,' he continued reasonably, 'you must allow me to rise. I cannot inspect your merchandise from here.'

"Growt was snared and knew it. Titterings and chuckles arose from the crowd, galling him—but he was compelled by his own demand to release Dom Peralt's jacket and stand back. He did so with a muttered curse and a black look that stilled some of the mirth of the onlookers. Then he pointed to the nearest chained line and said harshly, 'There. Choose.' And he named a price which was twice what any of his prisoners was worth.

"But Dom Peralt was a match for Growt's ill grace, and his sport had only begun. 'I thank you slaver,' he said with a glance at the slaves. Instead of moving to make selection, he drew a linen handkerchief from his sleeve. With the slow care of the drunken, he wiped the clots of mud from his breeches and boots. While Growt fretted and waited furiously, young Sen made a great show of cleaning himself. Then, when Growt was nearly frustrated enough to strike him again, he tossed his handkerchief aside and swayed toward the slaves.

"They were an unprepossessing lot—as you have perhaps seen on other occasions. Filth and poor food and fear had deprived them of their charms. To be frank, those charms might once have been substantial, considering the sources from which Growt obtained his merchandise. But where other slavers naturally attempted to put the best face possible upon their wares, Growt reveled in demonstrating the extent to which men and women created in God's image might be degraded. Dom Peralt could not keep a frown from his face as he surveyed his choices.

"Domson Frane and Serson Lew watched him with the honest astonishment of too much wine, as unable as Growt to fathom Dom Peralt's game. They did not fear that their leader would abandon his principles. What did they know of principles? *Their* fathers had slaves. Perhaps they owned slaves themselves. Doubtless they considered Dom Peralt's former refusals a harmless affectation—part of the jesting and fun of his company. No, they feared only that his reputation for courage would be tarnished, thus diminishing his stature—and theirs—in the eyes of other young roisterers like yourselves.

"Similarly the other onlookers. They did not wish Dom Peralt to fight for his beliefs—if he had any. They wished him to fight because they feared Growt. Only the Templemen felt otherwise. For the most part, Dom Peralt was surrounded by disappointment as he contemplated his selection.

"But he was blind and deaf to all concerns except his own, and his concern was to make his choice. Or perhaps it was simply to keep himself from falling on his face. Resisting unsteadiness, he moved along the chained line, stopping here before a girl still too young to live without her mother, there before a man so old that he could hardly lift his manacles—and yet he made no choice. One cynic among the townspeople offered wagers as to whether Dom Peralt would succeed at picking out a slave and paying before he lapsed into unconsciousness.

"Perhaps therefore it is open to question whether God watches over drunkards. Instead of lapsing into unconsciousness, Dom Peralt found a young woman locked to the chain between two battered fellows who had the look of dispossessed farmers. That she was young could be discerned through the grime. And the tatters which remained of her raiment suggested that she had lived for some time among gypsies—as guest, not gypsy herself, for her blue eyes and the shape of her face lacked the swart sullenness of that kind. But nothing of beauty survived the treatment she had received. A swollen cheek and blood showed that some teeth had been knocked from her jaw. Even the shade of her hair could not be determined through the muck. Oh, she was unsavory. Faugh! I know not what attracted Dom Peralt to her. Her wrists were gouged and infected from the efforts she had made to twist free of her fetters. Only her eyes—Their blue was startling in her smudged and beaten face. They suggested that she was better acquainted with anger than with fear.

"Dom Peralt roused himself as if he had dozed while studying her. With a nod, he said, 'This one. I want her.' Then he turned to Growt, and his smile was resumed. 'Hear you, slaver? I want this one.'

"Growt grinned and glowered because he had triumphed—and did not like the taste of Dom Peralt's manner, which deprived this triumph of the salt Growt preferred. Sourly, he named his price again. It was twice what he had already demanded.

"Still in all the sum was a trifle to a man with Dom Peralt's properties. From his purse he fumbled out coins which approximated the amount of Growt's price and tossed them to the slaver. So unsteady was young Sen now that Growt could not claim insult in the way the coins were thrown so that he could not catch them all. Anger corded his neck as he retrieved his earnings from the mud, but he had no choice left. Even the Templemen would not smile on him if he harmed a purchaser of his wares. Snarling and vicious, he went to unlock Dom Peralt's selection from the chains.

"When the clasp was undone and the chain dropped from the manacles, a peculiar shudder ran through the woman, as if a weight had been lifted from her soul. Perhaps there were tears amid the grime on her cheeks. Stepping forward, she raised her ironbound wrists to Dom Peralt, dumbly asking that he have those fetters removed as well.

"Whenever he met her gaze, his smile failed him. 'Free her wrists,' he commanded Growt. 'I want her arms free.' A sharp edge had entered his voice. To disguise it, he pretended a jest. 'Have no fear that she will escape me.'

"Cursing continuously under his breath, Growt complied. From a pouch at his belt, he took a chisel of hardened iron—from among his tools, a hammer and a rude anvil. He was not gentle, but he did nothing which might be protested—nothing which would require even the justice of the Templemen to compel the return of some portion of the price for damaged merchandise—as he set first one wrist and then the other against the anvil and struck away the manacles. The task finished, however, he could not resist thrusting the slave so that she stumbled at Dom Peralt, staining his clothes with her filth. She trembled against him as though the removal of the iron had made her feverish.

"'There,' growled the slaver. 'She is yours. Another rape or two, and she will be well suited to you.'

"'No,' replied Dom Peralt. His smile was restored, and his eyes laughed as his game ended. Setting the woman away from him, he turned to Growt and gave the slaver a mocking bow. 'She is free. I want no slaves. I have purchased her, and now I set her free. It is my right. *Hear you?*' he demanded of the crowd, his witnesses—a shout perhaps of pleasure, perhaps of concealed outrage. '*I set her free!*'

"That was his triumph over Growt the slaver. Heed me well, you louts—and learn. Thus passes the romance of the world. To the dismay of his cohorts—and the great glee of the crowd—his eyes rolled back in his head and he toppled into the mud.

"When anyone thought to look toward the woman he had freed— well, she was gone. Before so many onlookers, she disappeared as if she were merely mist and dream. No sign of her remained but her fetters lying at Dom Peralt's feet.

"Are you blind? My flagon is empty."

Abashed by our negligence, we stamped our feet, shoveled coins from our purses. This time, the keeper saw fit to bring us a wine which God had intended to be malmsey but which man had reduced to something approaching vinegar. Ser Visal, however, quaffed it without protest. Sweat poured from him so profusely that the collar of his outer robe had turned dark and the shoulders were spotted. He, too, had a look of fever about him. While he drank, we held our breath and prayed in silence that he would not cease his tale.

For a moment, his pale, plump hands trembled on the flagon. Wine dribbled from the corners of his mouth to diversify the stains on his robe. But slowly the drink—rank though it was—appeared to ease or mask his discomfort. He refilled his flagon and drank again, spilling less. When at last he looked around at us once more, his bulging eyes had a whetted aspect, a sharpness which might have been mockery or cunning.

"So much"—he snapped his fingers, a fat, popping sound—"for the gallantry of Dom Sen Peralt. A grand figure, is he not? Face down and drunken in the mud, having risked himself in sport with a man who might have taken a hammer to his thick skull—altogether worthy of your emulation. I am pleased to see that I have your attention. Perhaps you will learn something which will do you credit. Have I spoken to you concerning witches?"

We nodded, hoping to deflect him from a digression. But he ignored us. "It is said," he mused, "in the stories that goodwomen tell around their hearths of a winter's evening that iron is the bane of all witches. A witch's power is over flesh and plant, and with both she works many things which the Templemen abominate—but iron blocks her strength, reducing her to mortal helplessness. This, my puppies, chances to be true. Every witch brought before the judica comes with her wrists bound in iron, and none escape. Escape would surely be without difficulty for a woman capable of turning the minds of the men around her, causing them to see in her place the goodwoman who mothered them or married them, the daughter of their loins—or perhaps to see no woman at all, but only a chamber full of men gathered about a cauldron of molten metal to no purpose. But that does not transpire, though the women haled before the judica are never innocent. Their wrists are manacled, and so they are seen to be what they are, witches deprived of power. Thus the efficacy of iron is proven."

Ser Visal drank again, then looked at us and smiled. "When Dom Sen Peralt awakened from his stupor, he found himself in a windowless cell on a pallet of foul straw. The walls were of blocked granite—the door, barred iron. He was alone except for the light of one small tallow candle and the scurrying sound of rats.

"This was no little surprise to him, as you may perhaps imagine"— Ser Visal grinned sardonically—"and in his fuddled state he was slow to comprehend it. He was afire with thirst, and his first thought was for wine to quench the burning—his second, for water if he could not have wine. Lurching up from the pallet, he blundered from wall to wall of the cell as though it were the public room of an inn and shouted for the keeper to attend him until the pain of effort threatened to split his skull. But he was young and hale, and when he had rested a few moments he became conscious that it was cold stone to which his face was pressed, rather than honest planking. Still he did not understand. Slowly, however, he mastered himself enough to grasp the meaning of the single candle left burning in the center of the earthen floor—and of the barred door.

"His head hurt horridly. His tongue was a dry sponge in his mouth, and the back of his throat was hot with acid. Rats came sniffing about his boots, but he ignored the vermin. He stood with his back to the stone while his mind turned like a rusted and squalling millwheel. Then he went back to the pallet, seated himself there, folded his arms about his knees, and strove to will the pain from his head.

"Much time passed, but he endured it as though he were stoic, sitting upon the pallet and moving only to fend away the rats. I have said—have I not?—that he had wit. Despite his debauched state, he employed that wit to some purpose. Rather than ranting about the cell and howling from the door and expending himself wildly, he attempted instead to clear his mind and conserve his strength.

"Gradually, his hurt eased, but his thirst did not. At last, he left the pallet and searched the dark corners of the cell, hoping to find that his captors possessed humanity enough to have left him some water. But they had not. Outwardly calm—and inwardly raging, both with thirst and with other passions—he resumed his seat and his waiting.

"Without a window, he had no measure for the time. The hour-bells were not audible. But he was familiar enough with drink to estimate the duration of his unconsciousness. Eventually, he judged that vespers and compline had rung and passed. Despite his thirst, which grew upon him like a rage, he set himself to endure the night as well as he was able.

"But his captors were accustomed to darkness, and they came for him when he did not expect them. He heard the striding of boots outside his cell. In such cases, men hope unreasonably. It was, with great difficulty that he refrained from springing to the door and croaking for help. He possessed himself upon the pallet, however, and shortly a key groaned in the lock of his cell. Armed guards entered. They bore with them a writing desk lit by several candles and a chair, which they set facing their prisoner. Then they withdrew to the walls on either side of the door, so that Dom Peralt would be prevented from either violence or escape.

"Into the cell came Templeman Knarll himself, highest of all servants of the Temple of God in this region.

"He wore his formal robes, which were customarily reserved for the pulpit of the Temple. Resplendent in white surplice and gold chasuble, symbolizing Heavenly purity and worldly power, he would have appeared impressive if—Well, Templeman Knarll is known to you. He is a devout and searching man, worthy of admiration." Ser Visal employed his pious tone to good effect. "He is not to be mocked for his appearance. That he has the form of a toad and the face of a hedgehog is the will of the Almighty—surely not of Templeman Knarll. Nevertheless, it is not to be wondered at that he has little patience for those better made by their Creator than he.

"Without a glance at Dom Peralt, he seated himself at the desk, produced parchment, quill, and ink, and began to write.

"As he listened to the scratching of Templeman Knarll's pen, Dom Peralt had opportunity to inquire what he had done to expose himself to the Temple's anger—and the King's justice. He was surely imprisoned in the Temporal Office of the Temple of God, where crimes both physical and spiritual were perse—that is to say, prosecuted since good King Traktus joined hands with High Templeman Crossus Hught. But for what reason? Doubtless any of you would have asked that question, were you brave enough to address Templeman Knarll before gaining his permission to speak. Dom Peralt was formed in another mold. He allowed his spiritual father a few moments' silence. Then he said as clearly as his parched throat permitted, 'Templeman, I thirst. I must have water.'

"Templeman Knarll raised his head and scowled—no comforting sight. Releasing his pen, he began to read aloud what he had written. 'Dom Sen Peralt, son of—and so on, on such-and-such date, in the following place—'by authority of the Temple of God, and of His Royal Highness'—as you might imagine"—Ser Visal waggled his plump fingers as though conducting music—"'you are adjured on your soul, and in the sight of God, to answer the questions put to you herewith.'

"But young Sen had not given Templeman Knarll the courtesy of rising to his feet, and his reply was similarly respectful. 'Have done, Templeman,' he interposed. 'I will answer your questions. I will pay whatever price you require for absolution. But I must have water. Slake my thirst, and I will give you no cause to complain of me.' He was a fool, as I have said.

"'You misunderstand your plight,' replied Templeman Knarll. He was angered, but too certain of his power to give way to vexation. 'First you will satisfy me. Then perhaps I will grant you water—or vinegar, if I see fit. For the sake of your soul, I will have no pity on your poor flesh.' Glancing at the parchment before him, he said formally, 'Dom Sen Peralt, you are a carouser and a wastrel, a source of sin and shame to the Temple of God and the community of believers. But such faults may be forgiven, if they are fully and abjectly repented. The crime of which you are accused knows no absolution. It is an offense against Heaven and must be cleansed with blood. That blood will be yours rather than another's, if you fail to answer me truthfully and contritely.

"'Dom Peralt, for how long have you been in consort with the witch Thamala?'

"During his wait, Dom Peralt had readied himself for many things—but he was not prepared for *that* accusation. In astonishment, he demanded, '*Who?*'

"'For how long,' Templeman Knarll repeated heavily, 'have you been in consort with the witch Thamala?'

"'No,' muttered young Sen. 'No.' He now had some glimmering of his true plight—and yet he could not understand it at all. In something akin to panic, he stumbled to his feet and steadied himself against the wall, swallowing at the taste of brimstone in his dry mouth. 'I know nothing of witches.' Fervidly, he gathered his strength. 'I do not consort with witches. I have never met one. If did, I would shun her. You err with me, Templeman.'

"Templeman Knarll's regard did not waver. 'Denial is foolish—and dangerous,' he replied. 'Innumerable witnesses will attest that you freed her of your own will, when she was ironbound and helpless. That was not the act of one who knows nothing of witches. It was the act of a man who saw his debauched lover in peril and sought to free her, so that he would not be deprived of the evil for which he had bartered his soul.'

"Hungry, thirst-ravaged, and frightened, Dom Peralt could not stifle his trembling. Yet he held his gaze firm. 'I repeat. I do not consort with witches. I have never met one. You have been gulled with lies, Templeman.'

"'Lies!' snorted Templeman Knarll. 'You are glib, Dom Peralt. Do you deny that of all the slaves proffered by the slaver Growt you chose none other than the witch Thamala? Do you deny that you willingly paid an exorbitant price for her? Do you deny that you commanded the iron struck from her wrists? Do you deny,' concluded the Templeman, chewing upon each word, 'that you set her free?'

"Dom Peralt stared at his interrogator and for a moment had no answer. He had wit, as I have said—he was not blind to the gulf yawning at his feet. Oh, he was young and strong and cocksure, not much prone to the fears which bedevil those of weaker flesh. But he was not faulty of mind. So he did not protest that he had purchased and freed that woman merely upon a whim, to mock Growt. Instead, he said carefully, 'It appears that I must make some defense. Questions occur to me, Templeman.'

"'Do not think to play with me,' snapped Templeman Knarll, 'I am not come here to answer your questions. You will answer mine—and feel gratitude that I deign to ask them.'

"'If this Thamala was a witch,' insisted Dom Peralt, 'why was she not haled before the judica rather than granted to Growt for sale? Is it the custom of Templemen to sell proven witches as merchandise, in order to trap and damn the innocent man who makes purchase?'

"Young whelps, it is well that the Temple of God is served by able men such as Templeman Knarll rather than by ignorant louts such as yourselves. He also is not blind. He saw that this question was one which he must answer. It would be asked again before the judica, when Dom Peralt was brought for judgment—and the men of land and station and power there would not look kindly upon an affirmative reply. Restraining his ire, Templeman Knarll responded, 'Thamala was not known to be a witch. She was merely a finding of Growt's, nothing more. And he took her asleep in a camp of gypsies, where she was in hiding from the justice of the Temple. His iron blocked her wiles before she had opportunity to employ them. Therefore he was unaware of her—and did not report her. Had she been known to us, we would have taken her from him at once, to protect the innocent.'

"At this, Dom Peralt bowed. 'Your integrity relieves me greatly,' he said. 'It does, however, inspire another question. By what means have you now determined that this Thamala was indeed a witch? Have you taken her captive? Has the judica already pronounced judgment upon her?'

"From this unseemly inquiry Templeman Knarll stepped back. Dom Peralt's second question did not appear as dangerous as his first. 'I caution you,' said the Templeman. 'I will have no more of your insolence. It is in my power to deprive you of water until your flesh screams for it, if I choose. For how long have you been in consort—?'

"Dom Peralt made no movement which might attract the force of the guards. He stood against the stone, his hands still at his sides—no threat in him. Yet he interrupted Templeman Knarll in a voice which caused that worthy to flinch as though he had been struck. 'Have you named this Thamala a witch merely because I set her free?'

"Provoked to fury, the Templeman pounded a fist on the top of his writing desk, so that the candleflames wavered and danced and his eyes echoed the fires of damnation. 'She *vanished!*' he roared. 'No Godly goodwoman simply disappears before townspeople and Templemen— but your consort did! With her foul power, she veiled her flight from all around her. And that was *witnessed!* It was witnessed by *Templemen!*' By degrees, he regained his composure. 'You freed her,' he said in a tone at once soft and venomous. '*You.* Of all the slaves offered you, you chose her and freed her—her and no other. I notice you do not protest your innocence. Why her, Dom Peralt? Why her and no other?'

"Dom Peralt smiled as well as the growing anguish of his thirst permitted. 'You say that she has vanished, and you have not recaptured her. Therefore you cannot present her as evidence of my wrong-doing to the judica. You have no case against me, Templeman.'

"Templeman Knarll did not blink or turn aside. Why should he permit this degraded youth to anger him? His power was sure. More softly still, he repeated, 'Why her and no other?'

"But Dom Peralt also did not turn aside. His smile in no way softened the hardness in his eyes. 'When I looked at her,' he answered, 'I saw that her spirit was greater than her fear. Though she was enslaved— and enslaved by Growt!—she was not cowed. For that reason, I chose her.' Then he said again, 'Templeman, you have no case against me.'

"Abruptly, Templeman Knarll stood from his chair. With great care, he set aside his quill, stopped his inkpot, then gathered up his sheets of parchment and tucked them away within the sleeve of his surplice. As he did so, he said, 'Dom Sen Peralt, you are an impious wretch, careless of your soul, and a hazard to all who love salvation. Praise God, the Temple is stronger. And we who serve the will of Heaven will never permit such as you to disorder our good work. If you think to defy me, you are a fool. I will return to question you when thirst has lessened your haughtiness somewhat.

"'Understand me well,' he continued as he moved to the door. 'By the word of the Temple, you are bound—and by the word of the Temple, your bones will burn in molten iron if you refuse to answer me. Tell me how you came into the company of this witch—how she wove her wiles upon you—and how we may find her again, recapture her so that her evil can be destroyed—and you will be spared from agony if not from death. Hear you? The Temple is *stronger* than you. You have no escape. Your soul is in our care, whether you are determined for Heaven or Hell, and we will wrest you from evil at any cost. You are bound to us as all are bound, from the meanest slave to King Traktus himself, and *we will rule our own*. Think upon it and recant.'

"A stirring speech," Ser Visal commented after a fresh draught of that vile malmsey. "You would do well to heed it. But I regret to say that Dom Peralt was not swayed by such chaff. Perverse man, he faced Templeman Knarll as he had earlier faced Growt the slaver and was not abashed.

"'I think not,' he said. 'For the most part, the folk under your rule are cattle, and so you misjudge all others. But to condemn me you must try me before the judica—and the judica is composed of men like myself, men of my own station. Do you believe they will pass judgment upon me? They will not dare. For the safety of their own skins, they will not dare. You have no case against me,' he said for the third time. 'And if any Dom or Ser may be sent to the cauldron on such a pretext, then none of their lives are secure. They will not permit it.'

"'They will not be asked to permit it,' replied Templeman Knarll almost mildly, 'Before the judica sits, I will obtain your confession. Thirst and pain, Dom Peralt. I will obtain all the answers I require. In simple mercy for a confessed consort of witches, the judica will condemn you— and all your insolence will avail you nothing.'

"This Dom Peralt chose to ignore. His thirst was already severe, and he did not wish to consider its consequences. 'Further,' he continued as if Templeman Knarll had not spoken, 'my friends will support me. Serson Nason Lew and Domson Beau Frane will testify that I have no knowledge of witches. Especially they will testify that I had never beheld the woman Thamala until I purchased her—and that I purchased her while drunk—*and* that I did so only under Growt's bullying, so that he would not break my skull. It is plain that I will be freed. You will know how you are feared if no one of the judica laughs in your face.'

"But Templeman Knarll was no longer to be baited. He gestured the guards to retrieve his writing desk and chair. As they obeyed, he said,

'Your friends have already spoken.' Now he did not trouble to meet Dom Peralt's gaze. 'They understand the error of their ways and are prepared to be truthful. They will testify that frequently you left them at night, to go they knew not where. But always when you returned you bore the marks of blood and debauch upon your person. And always when you returned you proposed some new revel, prank, or crime, each more degrading and vile than the one before. They will testify that they have long suspected your involvement with witchcraft—and that only their fear of you impelled them to hold their tongues until now.

"'Dom Peralt, I advise confession.' Brusquely, Templeman Knarll waved the guards from the cell. He stood aside in the passage as the door was locked. Then through the bars he concluded, 'You will earn a kinder death.'

"Without further word, he strode away. The boots of his escort knelled upon the hard earth as they departed.

"'*Whoresons!*' Dom Peralt shouted after them—and had the satisfaction of hearing his anger echo from the walls. But the echoes faded rapidly, and he was left alone.

"Doubtless," said Ser Visal abruptly, disdaining transition, "you are all agog with curiosity concerning the witch Thamala." There he misjudged us—or judged us better than we knew. For the moment, we were not concerned with Thamala at all. Our first thought was a righteous indignation that Dom Peralt had been betrayed by his trusted friends. What manner of men were they, to be so spineless? *We* would have been braver. But then we thought again. At one time or another, all of us had tasted the severity of the Temple in small ways, and from our cradles we had learned an abiding fear of Templemen. Their authority ruled our lives. Would any of us truly have defied them to champion a friend who had fallen under their disfavor? If we were honest, we admitted that we had doubt of ourselves.

Therefore we felt Dom Peralt's plight the more poignantly. Imprisoned by Templemen, intended for torture and death—and betrayed by his friends! How had he borne it? Alone and without hope, how had he borne it?

But Ser Visal told his tales in his own way, and he chose to misinterpret our avid attention. Bracing his hands upon the table, he shifted his weight to settle his hams more comfortably. Then he leaned again into the warmth of the hearth. "Well," he continued, "there is little I can profitably relate to you. All witches conceal their homes, parentage, and skill, striving in that way to preserve themselves from the cauldron of the judica. I may say of her only that her mother was also a witch—and unlucky, unable to elude the grasp of the Templemen. In bitter flight because she could not aid her mother—for were not her mother's wrists bound in iron, proof against witchery?—Thamala turned to the gypsies for sanctuary. And there she indeed found safety for a time. But at last some trifling display of witchcraft concerning a young man and a girl incurred the hostility of the crone who ruled the band. Jealous of her authority, that old beldame made occasion to drug Thamala's food and sell her, helpless, to Growt.

"As for her escape when Dom Peralt had freed her—an ordinary woman might have crept away to safety, avoiding the notice of the townspeople. Their attention was elsewhere—upon Dom Peralt's fall into the mire. But the Templemen are more vigilant. Suspicious of him for his carousing, his refusal of slaves, his scorn toward the Temple, they would not have failed to watch the woman he freed, hoping that she would provide them opportunity against him. Thamala would not have escaped them without employing the evil of her wiles.

"Yet she was safe. That was the thought with which Dom Peralt consoled his thirst and his fear. I do not credit him with any selfless concern for her person. He had freed her only on a whim, to spite Growt the slaver, not for love or conviction. But in this matter, he reflected, her safety was his. Though it was an uncertain hope at best, it enabled him to master the anger of his betrayal. After his first outrage, a number of regrettably sacrilegious oaths, and a time of tense pacing, he found some comfort in the knowledge that the case against him was composed entirely of inference and malice. Lacking Thamala, the Templemen lacked the sure evidence which would compel the judica to enact judgment. And if it were not compelled, the judica might think better of the precedent it was asked to establish—a precedent potentially dangerous to all its members.

"With that hope, Dom Peralt urged himself to conserve his strength. An undertaste of vinegar lurked in the wine of his reasoning. If a confession were wrung from him, by whatever coercions the Templemen chose, then no evidence would be required to consign him to the cauldron. It was utterly necessary that he keep up his courage, husband his resources.

"I assure you—though I doubt you fully understand me—that this was not easily done. To remain calm alone in a hard and rat-infested cell is certainly difficult. To remain calm in the face of unjust accusation and betrayal would test the patience of a saint. But thirst is a terrible thing, destructive to the self-possession of its victims." Ser Visal snatched up his flagon and drank deeply as though to ward away the mere thought of true thirst. "Before midnight, Dom Peralt began to doubt that his resolve would hold.

"In due time, it occurred to him to wonder whether the blood of rats were fit for human drink."

His eyes squeezed and glittering in the flesh of his face, Ser Visal cast a glance around the public room, then said with unexpected sanctimony, "Perhaps it would have been well for his immortal soul if he had been driven to that extremity. But what is done may not be undone. It is the will of Heaven—not to be questioned. Midnight was well gone by Dom Peralt's reckoning when he was startled to hear a key labor once again in the lock of the door. And he was more than startled when the door opened, admitting the witch Thamala to his cell."

Though our astonishment was plain, Ser Visal appeared to take no pleasure in it. For the moment, his story held him as it did us, and he did not note our reaction.

"The witch Thamala," he repeated softly. "She had made shift to bathe herself and obtain clean clothing, so that she little resembled the begrimed wretch he had freed. Her bruises and swellings had already begun to heal, allowing the beauty of her face to show itself. Her hair was a soft and generous brown, a color which invites the touch of a man's hand. In simple justice, she should have been unrecognizable. But Dom Peralt stared and stared at her and could not be mistaken.

"She entered the cell as if it were free of access to all. No hue arose behind her—no guard came to watch what she did. As she had once vanished, so she now reappeared.

"In her hands, she bore the iron ring, as large around as a fist, from which jangled the keys of the jailer. But when she had ascertained that it was indeed Dom Peralt who sat, dumbfounded, before her, she cast the ring from her, spurning that metal as though its touch burned her. Then she knelt before him, so that her gaze met and studied his.

"What she saw satisfied her. Placing her hands on his arms where they folded across his knees, she said, 'Come. We must flee this dire place.' A smile touched her lips. 'Even with my aid, the guards will not sleep forever. Come.'

"Dom Peralt stared at her and did not respond. He felt that he had somehow fallen into drunkenness again—his wits refused to function. That she had come here, he thought stupidly. A witch. Had come here. It required understanding, but he had none to give. Her gaze called him down the road to his soul's ruin, and he could not understand.

"Some of his plight she was able to see for herself. After a moment, she released one hand from his arm and raised it to his temple. Her fingertips stroked the tight skin there, where the pulse of his life beat—and—

"Faugh!" Ser Visal muttered. "A murraine upon you all. Words will not convey it. Such things defy utterance. She touched her fingers to his temple, and his thirst was gone. Impossible! Yet it was true. In an instant, all that pain left him. And the relief was sweet! Surely even such louts as you are may grasp that the relief was sweet.

"But its sweetness came to Dom Peralt commingled with flavors of horror. Some wit returned to him at last. He grabbed at Thamala's wrist, pulled her hand from his temple. 'Why are you here?' he demanded in his dismay.

"His grip hurt her iron-scored skin, and she did not like the look of his consternation. But she answered him bravely. 'To free you, as you freed me. For all its faults, life remains desirable. Come.' Gently, she attempted to tug him out of his amazement.

"She was unprepared for violence. He flung her from him, so that she sprawled among the rats. Heaving himself up from the pallet, he crouched on his feet, ready to spring after her. As she regained her legs—more lithe and strong of movement than Growt's treatment of her would have augured—he panted at her, 'Witch! *Why are you here?*'

"'Witch, is it?' she replied. 'I know that tone. I had expected better of you, Dom Sen Peralt.' Straightening her hair with her fingers, she faced him angrily. 'Well, be answered. I am indebted to you for my freedom— and I pay my debts. I have come to give you that which you gave me.'

"Too horrified to realize that now it was she who did not understand, he raged at her—but softly, softly, so that the guards would not be roused. 'You damn me,' he hissed. 'There is no debt. Your freedom was only a matter of a few coins. A paltry sum. Trivial. I could make a hundred such purchases and not feel the price. Your freedom cost me *nothing*. And you damn me for it.'

"'No,' she retorted. She had been much abused in recent days, and her temper was somewhat short. 'This I will not endure.' Power curled in her fingers as she raised her hands against him. 'Murder and treachery have become the constant lot of my kind, and I accept those things as well as I am able. At the least, I have turned my back on revenge. But insult I do *not* accept—not while I am still able to defend myself. If there are evil and damnation here, they are *your* doing, not mine.

"'We whom you call witches commit no crimes. We desire only to live in peace among the leas and woodlands that we love—and to expand our knowledge of the weaving of true dreams—and to barter our help for the simple necessities we lack. And for that we are *slaughtered*.

You and your precious Templemen abhor us because we are free in spirit—and because we possess knowledge which you are too cowardly to share.'

"Dom Peralt sought to interrupt her indignation, but she did not permit him. 'Do you believe,' she continued, 'that I need only wave my hands to steal clothes and cleansing and access to your cell from anyone I choose? No! The first I obtained honestly, healing the walleye of a child and the abcessed teeth of a goodwoman in trade. And for my appearance here—by good fortune, the outer street was deserted. But two guards hold the door of this building. Scribes labor at desks everywhere, lettering indictments. Four more guards dice with the jailer, thinking themselves secret. Three Templemen confer together nearby. And between that chamber and this, six guards more. For all of them, *all,* I spin the dreams which enable them to believe they have not seen me. No harm to them— but women like myself have gone mad under such strains.

"'Heed me well, you who despise the aid of witches. I pay my debts. But you will accompany me without insult, or I will cramp the tongue in your mouth until it chokes you.'

"Here at last Dom Peralt's wit caught up with him. By a great effort, he reined his growing frenzy. Under careful control, he rose from his crouch, straightened his back. 'Your pardon,' he said, his voice at once hard-edged and quiet. 'I meant no insult. When I bought your freedom, I cared not what you were. I care not now. And I believe that you have come here honestly, intending to help me.' Then his urgency returned, too strong to be stifled. 'But you know not what you do. Whatever is done now, you have damned me. The escape you offer must be seen as the work of witchcraft. No other explanation will occur to the minds of the Templemen. Therefore they will hound us until I falter, lacking your powers—and my life will be forfeit upon the spot. Or we will be taken in the attempt, and your involvement will give proof of my guilt, dooming me without defense to the cauldron.'

"Now she saw the import of his fear. Her anger fell away. Dismay softened her face. But he was not done. The vision of his plight drove him. 'While you remained free, there was hope for me. The Templemen might harm and harass me, but they could not procure the judgment of the judica without evidence—without you, without proof of your witchery, without demonstration of complicity between us.' For the moment, he believed that Templeman Knarll would never wrest a confession from him. 'My friends who speak against me would alter what they say, when they were given time to see that they would imperil their own fathers by witnessing falsely. I had hope.

"'It is gone. You give the Templemen the demonstration they desire. Your freedom truly cost me nothing more than discomfort and inconvenience. Your help costs me my life.'

"There he stopped. I have said that he was not blind. How could he close his eyes to the bitter grief which welled up in her at his words? As grim as talons, her hands covered her face. Her shoulders stretched the fabric of her blouse, knotting to restrain sobs. She had been *much* abused—too much to be endured. Helpless and alone, her mother had been taken to the cauldron, and Thamala had fled for her life. The gypsies had betrayed her to Growt. And Growt's record of rapes and beatings," commented Ser Visal mordantly, "would daunt a lesser man. Her sufferings transcend your imaginations, whelps. And now the one act of kindness she had received she repaid with ill. You are taught, all of you, I do not doubt, that women weep easily and often, for any reason. But I tell you, it is no small matter when such a woman as Thamala weeps. She was at once fierce and pitiable to behold, and the sight would have touched a harder heart than Dom Peralt's.

"But while he stood there like a lout, shuffling his feet in shame and groping desperately to conceive some new hope for them both, she returned to herself. The pity went out of her—the fierceness remained. Meeting his gaze, not as a woman who wished for counsel, but as one who desired to know his mind, she asked, 'What would you have me do?'

"Dom Peralt was a young man—a youth and a fool, as I have said. But he was growing older swiftly. The thought of what he might expect from the tender mercies of Templeman Knarll came to him with some force, but he put it aside. Swallowing his fear, he replied, 'Escape. Relock the door, return the keys. Preserve your freedom. Ignorant that you have come here, the Templemen will remain without evidence. Eventually, I will be released.'

"Perhaps she was unaccustomed to such answers. For a long moment, her clear eyes searched him. Then she asked softly, 'Do you believe that?'

"In response, he made shift to appear certain and resolute. 'Yes.'

"She shook her head. 'No. You think it. You reason it. But you do not believe it.' Briefly, a shadow of her own fear showed in her face—a face not formed for fear. But she took a deep, shuddering breath and dismissed what she felt. Her arms hung at her sides, the strength gone from them. Yet there was strength enough in her voice. 'I pay my debts,' she said. 'Summon the guards.'

"He gaped at her. If he had spoken, he would have protested that she had lost her wits. The Templemen would bind her over to the judica for certain and terrible death—after they had tortured her enough to sate them. But he was too astonished to reply at once. Mad—she was unquestionably mad.

"'You will capture me,' she continued. The look in her eyes was bleak and dire. 'You will deliver me to the Templemen. That will ascertain your innocence. You will be freed.'

"Thinking her mad, Dom Peralt sought to reason with her. 'It will not be believed. You are a witch. I have no means to capture you. The Templemen will suspect some trick. They will believe that we have agreed together to obtain my release—so that I may in turn contrive to rescue you. The fact that you came to me will damn us both.'

"For an instant, thought furrowed her brow. She glanced toward the keys which she had thrown to the floor. Then she shrugged. 'You will slip the key-ring over my wrists. That will give you means. If I am held powerless, none will doubt that you have captured me.' Her loathing for the touch of cold iron was evident, but she did not let it sway her. 'My debt will be paid.'"

Ser Visal coughed, cleared his throat, drank. Sitting slumped in his chair, he resumed with a sigh, "Ah, the strange courage of witches. She put Dom Peralt to the test in a way which humbled Templeman Knarll's threats. He saw at once that her plan would succeed. Some lie would be required to account for her presence in the cell, but the evidence of iron held about her wrists by his own hand would defeat all suspicion. He would be freed. And she—why, she would go to the doom which God demands of all witches. Though he was young and debauched, he understood that his soul hung in the balance here. If he captured her, he would be saved.

"It was not in him. He had purchased her freedom with a few coins. She meant to purchase his with her life. The simple injustice of it was more than he could stomach.

"'No,' he replied, though his head reeled with fear and his guts knotted sickly. 'I will not. There is no debt. Do you hear me? I deny that there is any debt. I did not buy your freedom. You were evilly used—whatever the Temple teaches. With a few coins, I merely restored what was yours by birth and decency. And the blame of my plight does not fall to you. It is on my head. I was too drunk to do what any sane man would have done—to take you with me and release you only when you might better profit from your freedom. I *will not* accept the sacrifice of your life in so small a cause.'

"Thamala waited until he was done. Then she said, 'You are brave, Dom Sen Peralt.' Her tone suggested both mockery and respect, 'But no coin measures the value I place upon my life. How do you intend to prevent me?'

"For his pride—if for no other reason—he attempted to match her. 'I need do nothing,' he said, 'nothing other than wait. When next the guards come to this cell, they will find us together—and then we will both be undone.' He smiled wryly through his fear. 'To avert that outcome—so that your life will be preserved, and I will be able to hope— you will depart before the guards come, relocking the door after you to protect my protestations of innocence. Of what worth is my life,' he concluded, 'if it may only be saved by your death?'

"The witch shook her head again. 'You are mistaken,' she said. 'The world has need of such men.' For no evident reason, her voice now seemed to come to him from a great distance. The candlelight blurred, as if his eyes were failing. 'Therefore,' she uttered in a tone which could not be refused, 'it will be necessary for you to dream.'

"Then the flame of the candle shrank away, and the cell's darkness closed over his head. He heard nothing beyond the promise she had made, at once fierce and gentle. 'I pay my debts.'

"But in the dream…

"Faugh!" spat Ser Visal. "Dream, indeed. *Witchcraft*. With her wiles, she deprived him of will and choice. *Faugh!*" Hawking up phlegm, he grabbed for his flagon and drank. But he did not stop his tale. Despite his apparent indignation, he sounded weak and in some way frightened as he said, "I shudder for his soul. In the dream he was not himself.

"In the dream, he raised his voice and shouted lustily for the guards. He kicked the door so that it rang against the wall. He shouted again. Then he went to the key-ring.

"She held her hands behind her back for him, but they would not both fit through the ring. No matter—one sufficed. With iron closed about any part of her, she was caught.

"At that moment, he felt that he began to awaken. But still the dream persisted. He could not break free of it. He could only watch with the taste of horror in his mouth as guards came to the cell at a run and he called out to them, saying, 'Here is the witch Templeman Knarll seeks. She sought to seduce me to her foul ends, but I have captured her with iron,' and Thamala made pretense of struggling against him while he clasped the ring over her wrist.

"He did not return to himself entirely until the Templemen had taken her from him, to bind her with surer fetters, and Templeman Knarll had grudgingly granted his release. Then he found that there were tears in his eyes, and they would not be stanched, for the deed was done, and he could not now afford to cry out in anger or protest.

"I must have more wine."

The candles had begun to wane, a reminder that afternoon was on its way to evening and all of us were required by our God-fearing families—and by Temple curfew—to be in our homes before vespers rang. But none of us thought of such things. For a long moment, none of us thought to stamp our feet and produce money so that the keeper would bring more wine. We were held. All our attention was centered on Ser Visal. He appeared oddly shrunken in the fading candlelight, his eyes glazed by what he saw in his mind, his stubbled cheeks ashen and sagging from the bones of his skull. At another time—during another tale—we might have nudged each other and winked, thinking in silent laughter that the heat of the hearth made him melt, that his fat flesh was composed of nothing but tallow and wine, which he sweated away. But not now. We were held. And he seemed hardly to be aware of us.

There was one thought in all our minds. *He is afraid. This tale is dangerous, and he fears to tell it.*

Nevertheless, he soon restored a sense of our duties. Without fore-warning, he crashed his flagon down upon the tabletop and bellowed, "Are you deaf? I must have more wine!"—a mere croak of his normal roar, but enough to startle us from our stupefaction. Hastily, we labored the boards with our boots. From our purses, we dredged up coin for another cask. The keeper responded without interest or hurry, as if when he had lost his hearing all other questions had been answered for him. Upon this occasion, he produced a cask of liquid which only a Templeman who did not drink would have called wine. It smelled of cattle and tasted as if it had been fermented by wringing the moisture from Ser Visal's sodden robe. Yet we made no protest—we cared only that he should finish his tale. And he showed his disfavor only by frown-ing as he tossed two measures of the vile stuff past his avid lips and began on a third.

Despite its faults, however, the drink amended his appearance some-what. In his piggish eyes, a dull smoldering glower hinted at angers he did not choose to explain. Yet he smiled, and his voice took on its particular quaver of piety as he resumed.

"In an age of remarkable institutions," he said, "and outstanding men, when the Temple of God gives us order, morality, and slavery, and a figure such as High Templeman Crossus Hught aids in the management of the kingdom, the judica is especially worthy of note. Founded upon the highest principles, for the highest purpose—to defend the innocent and the honorable from evils which would otherwise deprive them of Heaven—the judica has prosecuted the sinners haled before it—primar-ily witches—with unflagging rigor. For lesser crimes, men and women are sold into slavery, their property confiscated, their homes burned. But for witchcraft and all its abominations, only one punishment is deemed just—the cauldron.

"You have not seen that black pot, or the chamber which holds it. None who do not belong are admitted there. And I wager that your fathers have not spoken of it, just as they have not told you the outcome of Thamala's judgment. Such things are too holy and severe to be discussed lightly.

"It is a high chamber, and round, housed in the same Temporal Office where malefactors are imprisoned. From tiered seats circling the walls, Templemen and judges look down on two doors—one heavily barred and timbered to prevent escape to the outside, the other opening to the guards and passages of the Temporal Office—and on the cauldron itself.

"It resembles an immense stewpot in which three or four men—or I alone—might stand comfortably. But its victims find little comfort there. Somewhat precariously balanced, I fear, upon its bricks, it sits over a kiln in the floor, in which the fire is never "permitted to fade, and it is full to its middle with bubbling iron, melted for the doom of witches. The pot itself does not melt only because its sides have been hardened with alloys. The heat is tremendous! Its victims feel its force as they are questioned and judged, and it causes them to sweat in terror.

"From the floor to the rim on one side rises a ramp of masonry. There the evil are led when they have been judged. For a moment or two, they are suspended over the cauldron, so that they may have opportunity to repent and pray, perhaps—or to name those who consort with them. Then, when they have screamed enough, they are let drop."

Ser Visal drank again, urgently, and refilled his flagon. But almost at once he continued, "As is right and fitting, the judica is led by Templemen. The spiritual welfare of the kingdom is in their care. But to that august body also belongs each Dom and Ser of the region, every man of station. It is they who pronounce the judgment when the Templemen have produced the evidence and searched the witnesses. And these men of station do not—I may say, *dare* not—fail of attendance. The calling of their duty is too high. And the consequences of failure may not be contemplated calmly.

"The more so in the present case. The matter of Thamala was of unusual importance, offering especially bold evidence of witchery—so bold as to make all virtuous souls tremble—and touching as it did upon the honor of a high family. That was rare. In all the years that I have attended the judica, I do not remember a similar case. It is generally true that those who consort with witches come from among the poor and unenlightened.

For that reason, as I am sure you have heard, High Templeman Crossus Hught himself elected to preside over Thamala's judgment.

"It is rumored—I know not why—that Templeman Knarll made a special appeal for the presence of good King Traktus' counselor. That is of no importance. The judica was delayed several days to permit the High Templeman to settle his affairs and make the journey—also a matter of no importance. The point I wish you to grasp is that this judica transcended all others in authority and significance.

"Do you understand me, puppies? Are your minds clear enough for thought? *This* judica was one which Dom Peralt was required to attend. By virtue of his new station—and of the High Templeman's presence— he had no choice. The woman who had purchased his life with her own would be consigned to the cauldron, and he was required to assist in the judgment.

"This, of course, he understood. Perhaps he understood it from the moment when Thamala first proposed to save his life with hers." Ser Visal's sanctimony had given way to muffled sarcasm. "He was young and gallant, and he had something of a reputation for boldness, which he prized. And yet a woman whom he had not known for the total of an hour repaid a debt which had cost him nothing by sacrificing everything. When at last Templeman Knarll released him from the Temporal Office, Dom Peralt went back to his estates in mortal shame to await the sitting of the judica.

"In shame? you ask. Why in shame?" Ser Visal glared around at us. It became increasingly difficult to distinguish between his piety and his sarcasm. "For no good reason. The woman was a *witch*, offensive to God and Temple. If she chose to do one honorable thing before she died, perhaps her soul would be the better for it. And I repeat that he had not known her for the total of an hour. He knew nothing about her at all, except her power.

"Yet he *was* shamed. His skin burned with it, and his heart ached. Every twist of his thoughts squeezed sweat from his brow. It was a cauldron more subtle than iron, but no less compulsory. Hiding himself within the walls of his manor, he drank wine by the barrel to slake the fire—but it only burned higher. All about him were reminders of his father, that strong and just man who had filled his life with care for those dependent upon him—memories which gave young Sen no ease. In desperation, he turned from strong wine to clear water and became sober, hoping that cold reason would succeed where besottedness failed. But the flame did not subside. He consulted those who still named themselves his friends—not young Beau Frane and Serson Lew,

I assure you, but older heads and wiser—and obtained no relief. He attempted every solace but one, the strict comfort of the Temple. All failed him, as all things human and prone to sin must fail. His shame would not be quenched. One thought tormented him: *it was not just.* He had purchased Thamala with a few coins—his father's earnings, not his own. It was not just.

"In due time, word was brought to him that the High Templeman had arrived, and that therefore the judica would meet upon the morrow. According to custom, the sitting would commence promptly at the third hour, so that the remainder of the day would be purified by its labors. Again he searched his conscience and consulted his friends. Then he returned a somewhat terse message to Templeman Knarll, saying that he would surely attend the judica, as God and duty required of him.

"That night"—Ser Visal had turned his glower to the tabletop, avoiding our rapt eyes—"the slaver Growt was put out of work with two broken legs. And the next morning, Dom Sen Peralt was among the first to enter the chamber of the judica after the ringing of the time.

"He and your fathers engaged in no idle conversation upon such a solemn occasion. In silence, they entered the chamber and took their proper seats—Dom Peralt and those of like station around the middle tiers, men of lesser rank above them, near the walls. In silence, they awaited the coming of the Templemen. Dom Peralt bore himself gravely, his eyes downcast with a humility new to him. But the cauldron's heat flushed his face. This was not a place in which any man sat at ease. The sound of the fire was loud in the stillness, as was the closing of the bolts as the outer door was sealed, so that no rescue of the witch might be attempted.

"There was some small delay. Then the inner doors were opened, and the Templemen entered.

"All were clad in the black cassocks which signalized the dark work they meant to do, the wrestling with evil—black contrasted only by the scarlet ropes knotted at their waists and the strict pallor of their faces. All appeared as dour as the day of God's doom. Half a score of those who served under Templeman Knarll's jurisdiction took their seats around the lowest tier. After them came Templeman knarll himself, bearing in his hands the iron crozier of his office—and looking more than ever like a creature born in a swamp. And when he had assumed his place, he was followed by High Templeman Crossus Hught.

"Though he was similarly black-clad, the High Templeman did not need the golden miter which he carried in the crook of his arm to distinguish him from the other servants of the Temple. He was tall, strong despite his years, and commanding. Much of his authority was in his eyes, which seemed to have no color at all. Indeed, at first glance his face itself appeared to have no color. His thin, close-cropped hair was white—his skin, pale with the translucence of old age. Upon nearer inspection, however, a faint red hue could be seen, for every blood vessel was visible beneath the skin, as distinct as madness—I mean, of course, that purity of mind which the sinful world might term madness, but which is in truth the most exalted devotion to God. Seeing him, it was at last possible to understand his importance to good King Traktus. He was not a man who would be easily refused.

"As he entered, the Templemen began to chant the appropriate orisons against evil. But no special homage was demanded by the High Templeman. Here judgment was in the hands of the men of station, not of the Temple—though the guidance and authority of the Templemen were properly plain to all. When High Templeman Crossus Hught had assumed his place—he and Templeman Knarll stood opposite each other on either side of the ramp leading up to the lip of the cauldron—he joined the chanting, his colorless gaze fixed upon Heaven. 'God damn all witches. Punish all presumption. Preserve the purity of the Temple.' If I were able, I would recite each prayer for your edification. It is a fault of mine—which I rue daily—that I have no memory for such holy things.

"During the chants, Dom Peralt bore himself as a man who had sworn a great oath that he would not fidget. Rather, he watched the door as we all did, awaiting the arrival of the prisoners.

"Did I say prisoners? Well, we had assumed that the witch would not be brought to judgment without company. The Templemen had had several days in which to question her—and it was a rare woman who could not be persuaded by righteous interrogation to name consorts or other witches. But when the prayers were ended, and Templeman Knarll called for Thamala to be brought into the chamber, she was alone.

"Two guards bore her between them, supporting her because she was hardly able to stand. They took her to the foot of the ramp and left her there, withdrawing from the chamber and closing the doors after them. Somehow, she remained on her feet. Iron manacles still clasped her wrists behind her. The guards had positioned her 'with her back to the cauldron—perhaps deliberately—so that she faced Dom Peralt. But she did not meet his brief glance. Weakly, she turned so that her doom was directly before her, as though she wished to see it for what it was and prepare herself to meet it.

"But Dom Peralt did not need a long look to see what the Templemen had done to her. Her hair was torn and ragged, leaving bloody patches upon her scalp and giving her a frenzied aspect. One eye was closed with swelling—the other, raw and aggrieved. Indeed, all her face had been beaten to a new shape. Dirt and hunger outlined the bruises. Her clothing had been torn in various places—some of them indecent—and through the rents showed wounds and welts. Blood crusted her fetters. Plainly, her evil was stronger than her flesh, for how else was it possible for her to keep her feet—or to gaze upon the cauldron without terror?

"Yet she had given no other name to her questioners. The Templemen had not succeeded at wringing the answers they desired from her. As he looked at the places where blood caked her clothing to her back, Dom Peralt began to smile—the same smile with which he had faced Growt's bullying.

"At once, High Templeman Crossus Hught snapped, 'You.' His voice struck like the cut of a whip through the cauldron's heat and the silence. All eyes sprang to him. With his long arm, he pointed his miter straight at Dom Peralt's face. 'Why do you smile?'

"'That is Dom Sen Peralt,' whispered Templeman Knarll to his temporal lord. 'The same who bought and freed the witch.'

"The High Templeman ignored Templeman Knarll. He seemed to know by Divine inspiration whom he addressed. His miter did not waver. 'Are you,' he demanded, 'amused by the plight of wickedness in the hands of the Temple of God?'

"Dom Peralt—fool that he was—shook his head, but his smile remained.

"'You have been familiar with this foul woman,' pursued Crossus Hught. 'Now you betray her, and you smile because you think to escape her fate. Evil is weak against the will of Heaven for many reasons, but most because it knows no virtue except treachery. So the very demons sacrifice each other, to procure their own safety. Do not think that we who serve the Temple are blind.'

"Dom Peralt lowered his eyes, bowing his head so that his smile would be less plain. 'Your pardon, High Templeman,' he said softly. His voice conveyed a tremor which might have been fear. 'I mean nothing unseemly, I smile only at the thought of justice.'

"'Justice, is it?' returned the High Templeman. Abruptly, he settled his miter once again in the crook of his arm. 'You do not appear to be a man who is much concerned for such pure matters. If you care for justice, why have you not set foot in the Temple of God from the day of the witch's capture to this, seeking remission for your mortal faults from the justice of Heaven?'

"When Dom Peralt raised his eyes again, they were full of darkness, and his smile was gone. With elaborate care, he replied, 'In the matter of the witch Thamala I have committed no fault. Before this last slaving day, I had never seen her. I purchased her because the slaver Growt demanded it of me. I chose her from among all his slaves because she caught my whim. And for that same whim I set her free. I had no knowledge of her evil.' With more wisdom than I had credited to him, he refrained from claiming that the Templemen had imprisoned him unjustly. Instead, he said, 'When she came to me in my cell, I snared her and delivered her to the Templemen, fulfilling my duty to both God and man.

"'High Templeman,' he concluded in a tone which might have been mistaken for humility, 'will you declare here, before the judica, that I must repent what I have done?'

"*That* was foolish. A child could have warned Dom Peralt that such men as Crossus Hught are not notoriously forgiving of wit in others. But the High Templeman had no present recourse but to ignore that wit. Turning from Dom Peralt, he said stiffly to Templeman Knarll, 'Let us commence.'

"Sighing between battered lips, the witch Thamala sank to her knees. Were it not sacrilege to consider her honorable, one might have thought that she retained strength enough—in spirit, if not in body—to care what happened to Dom Peralt.

"Templeman Knarll glowered his disfavor at her. Perhaps now he regretted the impulse which had led him to request the High Templeman's attendance. Thamala had resisted his most searching interrogations. Her reticence—like Dom Peralt's affrontery—did not speak well for Templeman Knarll's stewardship over the region. There was a particular grimness in his voice as he began the ceremonies of the judica.

"First he welcomed us to the performance of our duty. He asked for the names of any men of our station who were not present. Then he charged us to adjudge the heinous crime of witchcraft strictly, according to the will of Heaven, for the safety of our own souls. Faugh! It is well that the Temple is served by abler men than I. My fat head will not hold half the proper admonitions. Templeman Knarll's memory, however, did not fail. And that was well for him. He did not wish to appear foolish before High Templeman Crossus Hught.

"After the appropriate invocations, he proceeded to deliver the Temple's formal accusation against the witch Thamala. 'It is charged'—or some such phrase—'that you have abandoned the teachings of Heaven. That you have consorted with witches, participating in their most foul practices. That you have studied witchcraft, knowing it to be evil—a defiance of God and His Temple.' A fulsome list, truly. It was plain that Thamala had never drawn a breath which was not deliberate and mortal sin. But that, of course, was merely the ritual accusation cited against all witches. A listing of Thamala's particular evils followed. 'That you have lived among gypsies, the outcast of Heaven. That you have worked your abominable wiles upon them, whose souls have no defense.' And so on. Such an impressive recital would justly have won confession from the first mother of all witches.

"Certainly we were impressed. Experienced as we were with the judica and its work, we were still impressed. It is an impressive thing to hear a helpless woman damned in every item of her life, every corner of her soul. For good reason, no one accused by the Temple has ever been found innocent.

"Dom Peralt listened attentively, his eyes on Templeman Knarll's face, his smile faintly upon his lips. But he appeared unmoved, as though his innocence were complete. And Thamala remained on her knees and showed no reaction, as though she were deaf to what was being said against her.

"But when Templeman Knarll came to his conclusion and asked of her, 'What do you say to these things?' she gave him an answer. With great difficulty because of her weakness—and because her hands were bound with iron at her back—she rose to her feet. On her face was a look of strange yearning, as though she wished as keenly as love for the strength to mount the ramp at once and cast herself into the cauldron, before she could be condemned. In a voice hardly audible around the highest tier, she replied, 'You have murdered my mother and all who held her dear. Now you mean to murder me. Do it and have done. God in His Heaven gazes down upon you with abhorrence.'

"'Vile wretch!' snarled Templeman Knarll, raising his hand to strike her. But High Templeman Crossus Hught snapped at once, 'Hold! Here she may say whatever she will. Her words purify the judica of doubt and false pity.' Then he turned toward Thamala and touched his miter to her shoulder.

"Dumbly, she gazed at him as though he had power to command her. Bending his look of madness over her, he said softly, almost fondly, 'Woman, you are my daughter in the spirit. The care of your immortal soul is my duty and my great treasure. You believe that we mean to deal with you harshly—and perhaps by mortal standards we *are* harsh. But there is God's love for you in what we do. By the standards of Heaven, only the harsh mortification of the flesh may hope to free the soul. The

sufferings of your body will soon end. But the sufferings of your soul—
Ah, your soul cries out for forgiveness, though you do not heed it.

"'Woman, you say that we have murdered your mother. What was
she, that the judica required her death?'

"Thamala did not reply. Crossus Hught seemed to hold her eyes so
that she could not turn away. But she did not speak.

"In response, his manner became more stern. 'If you confess humbly
and repent your life, there is hope of Heaven's smile. But if you harden
your heart, the torment which awaits your soul will make child's play
of your present pain.' Had I been in her place, I would have admitted
to all that he desired. Truly! Though I sat in the highest tier and had no
part of her crimes, I could hardly hold my tongue. 'Your mother met her
death,' he continued, 'because she pursued the fiendish power of witchcraft. Knowing her fate—the fate which God wills for all evil—why did
you choose the way of witchery for yourself? Did you wish to revenge
yourself upon those who judged her? Or did you love the lascivious ill
of witches?'

"Still she made no answer. Around the chamber, strong, good men
sweated in the heat of the cauldron—and in plain dread of what they
witnessed—but she was not swayed. The bruises and swellings on her
face distorted her expression, so that it could not be read. But her eyes
held life yet, and they were not cowed by Crossus Hught.

"For a moment, he glanced around the chamber. Perhaps he wished
to see that we judged her silence as it deserved. His colorless gaze rested
briefly on Dom Peralt. Then he returned his attention to Thamala.

"Setting the end of his miter to her cheek, he pressed her to face the
cauldron. Standing at the foot of the ramp below the pot, she could not
see its contents. But the fire in the kiln made a steady roaring, and at
intervals the molten iron could be heard to bubble.

"'There is your doom, witch,' said the High Templeman. 'Look for
hope and mercy there, not from me. You will find that the agony is terrible. But it will be brief. A moment's anguish—a few screams. Nothing
more. The agony of your soul will endure. Fiercer than any physical
hurt, it will go on and on without let, and you will never escape. Only
by confession and repentence may you hope to ameliorate the fire which
awaits you.

"'Answer but one question, and God may be moved to hear you.
Thamala, why did you enter the cell of Dom Sen Peralt when he had set
you free? Was he not your paramour in witchcraft? Did you not attempt
to rescue him because you had need of him, in love and in power?'
Crossus Hught's voice had become a lash again, cutting at her. 'And did

he not betray you in an effort to save himself, snaring you for the judica because he feared to risk his life in flight with you?'

"In the chamber, the silence of the judica became intense. The High Templeman had found his way around Dom Peralt's protestations of innocence. Now with one word Thamala could damn Dom Peralt, and nothing that he might say in his own defense would save him. He sat rigidly, heedless of the sweat standing on his brow. A greater fool might have made objections, but he had wit enough to avoid that pitfall. Clenching his silence between his teeth, he watched Thamala's blood-crusted back and waited. We all watched and waited, knowing that if Dom Peralt could be thus implicated in witchery none of us would ever again be safe. At last we saw why High Templeman Crossus Hught had accepted Templeman Knarll's invitation. Here the High Templeman sought to extend his power into new territory.

"And Thamala did answer. Facing the cauldron with Crossus Hught's miter jabbed against her bruises, she said in tight outrage, 'Do you never wonder how witches breed? You murder us and murder us—and yet we endure. But there are no male witches. We must seduce men to beget children upon us, so that we will continue.

"'When Dom Peralt purchased me, I saw that he was strong and goodly—a fit man to father a child. Therefore I sought to rescue him, thinking that he would find me desirable. But he did not. In his eyes, I was evil, and he spurned me.'

"Thus she paid her debt. Damning herself, she defeated the accusation against Dom Peralt.

"For a moment, an appearance of consternation reigned over the judica as your fathers disguised their relief with surprise and indignation. High Templeman Crossus Hught's face grew red, his blood enflamed by the failure of his ploy. Perhaps he saw a vision of good King Traktus's reaction when our monarch learned that the High Templeman had attempted to embroil an innocent Dom in the judgment of a witch. Dom Peralt's jaws knotted with the effort he made to suppress what he felt.

"'Godless wretch!' cried Templeman Knarll. With the end of his crozier, he struck Thamala so that she fell to the stone. 'Will you utter falsehood in the teeth of doom?" He had good reason for his dismay. Whatever chagrin afflicted the High Templeman because of this failure would be visited doubly upon Templeman Knarll. But his eyes—and Crossus Hught's—watched Dom Peralt avidly.

"That snare Dom Peralt also avoided. By no movement or expression or word did he betray any concern for the witch. Let all her bones be broken there before him, and let her be damned! Raising his head, he said in a loud voice, 'Praise be to God and the justice of the Temple! I am vindicated!'

"The glare which High Templeman Crossus Hught fixed upon Dom Peralt was murderous and wild. The blood beat so furiously beneath his pale skin that we feared a seizure, but there remained nothing that he could do. Not one of us would now vote death upon Dom Peralt. If the High Templeman persisted, he would appear to have lost his reason. And that report must surely damage him in the eyes of good King Traktus. Therefore he put the best face possible upon his defeat. Trembling in voice and limb, he turned his back toward Dom Peralt and addressed the judica.

"'It is our work to judge and punish evil,' he said. 'An accusation of witchcraft has soiled the good name of Dom Sen Peralt'—he cast a dire glance at Templeman Knarll, who appeared to shrink under it like a depleted wineskin—'and that accusation has been found false. In this the high purpose of the judica shows itself, winnowing the honest from the ill. For this was the judica instituted, so that the innocent would be spared when the guilty are adjudged.

"'But this woman is condemned out of her own mouth.' As he spoke, his passion rose. 'Out of her own mouth! She admits herself the daughter of a witch. She admits herself vulnerable to the judgment of the judica, and she offends Heaven by naming that judgment murder. She admits her intent to seduce Dom Peralt, so that she might breed her evil! She refuses repentence. She denies the just interrogation of the judica. And to this must be added that she entered Dom Peralt's cell when none but a witch might do so, bypassing the guards with her wiles.

"'No other evidence is required.'

"When he chose to unleash it, his voice was indeed an admirable instrument—at once clarion and cutting. By such men, even Kings may be daunted. 'It remains to us,' he continued, 'to consider who we are and why we are here by the will of Heaven. We are the spiritual servants of the Temple of God and the temporal servants of our estates and towns and peoples. To us belongs the duty to protect and purify what we serve. We give the world order! Around us lurk fiends and darknesses of every kind—demons of seduction, souls that know not God, terrifying powers. Threatened by such perils, no honorable man or devout goodwoman may set foot from home without fear. At any moment, any good thing may be devoured in evil. Only *we*—we who serve God in spirit and in body—only we stem the world's ill.

"'To do so, we must acknowledge that pity and forgiveness are in God's hands, not ours. They are too high for us. We cannot ask whether this crime or that may be let pass. On our souls, we cannot! We can only call evil by its true name and consign it to fire, as the will of Heaven demands.

"'The name of the evil which we are called upon to judge this day is witchcraft, *witchcraft*! The woman Thamala is a *witch*, self-confessed and abominable, defiant of all things holy. And no ordinary witch! So cunning is her malice that she nearly dragged down an innocent young man with her.' As I have said, the High Templeman put the best face possible upon his defeat. Thamala had risen again to her knees. New blood seeped from the wounds which Templeman Knarll had opened on her back. But Crossus Hught had already dispensed with pity and forgiveness. 'Men of the judica,' he concluded, 'the judgment is yours. What is your word?'

"For a moment, your fathers remained mute under the High Templeman's gaze—not doubting what their word would be, of course, but wondering who would be the first to speak it. By virtue of his years and his great wealth, Dom Tahl often took precedence. But upon this occasion both Ser Lew and Dom Frane had cause to stand forward, if for no other reason than simple gratitude that their sons had not been called to give evidence against Dom Peralt. Had I wished to call attention to myself, I might have spoken. Thamala's guilt was certainly plain to me. It was awkward for Crossus Hught that no man sprang up at once to offer verdict.

"But the moment was short—too short to do more than gall the High Templeman. Then Dom Peralt stood slowly from his seat.

"'High Templeman,' he said, 'no word is required here but mine. All have heard the witch's confessions. But only I have experienced her seductions. Only I have felt her foul power. *My* judgment is sufficient to doom her.' As he spoke, Thamala bowed her head, but gave no other sign that she heard him. 'And I proclaim that she is the most evil of all witches, deserving of excruciation and death.' His voice had the sound of a man who had been truly humbled. His gaze, however, did not waver from Crossus Hught's hot glower. 'High Templeman,' he continued, 'if you will permit it, I will give her to the cauldron myself. Her vileness has besmirched me, and I wish to aid in her punishment. By so doing, I hope to cleanse her touch from my soul.'

"At this, High Templeman Crossus Hught studied Dom Peralt narrowly. He did not know what to make of the young man's offer. It has always been the Templemen themselves who cast witches to the cauldron. But almost at once he saw the benefit to himself. Thus far, the tale of this judica did not promise to augment his stature with good King Traktus. But if he could report that the honor of a reckless young

Dom had been questioned by an over-zealous subordinate—and that he, Crossus Hught, had determined the young man's innocence during the judica—and that the young man had been allowed to deliver the witch to death himself, thereby restoring his good repute beyond all doubt—why, then the High Templeman would have no reason to fear that he might lose by the tale.

"But he was too wise to sanction such a breach of custom without encouragement. Holding Dom Peralt's gaze, he asked softly, 'Men of the judica, what say you to this?'

"Dom Frane and Ser Lew responded instantly, 'Permit him!' It could be seen in their faces that they did not mean to deal gently with their offspring when the judica was done.

"Other men promptly added their voices. Every proof of Dom Peralt's innocence secured their own safety further. In moments, the will of the judges was plain.

"The High Templeman nodded gravely, but betrayed no satisfaction. 'Very well,' he said to Dom Peralt. 'The deed is yours. Her death will indeed go far to cleanse your soul.'

"It would have been seemly if Dom Peralt had spoken a word of thanks or obeisance to the High Templeman. But perhaps the solemn duty he had undertaken confused his sense of fitness. Or perhaps he was serious now as he had not been before the slaver Growt, and so did not see the wit in thanking Crossus Hught. He glanced once around the upper tiers of the chamber, then left his seat to approach the witch Thamala.

"She had not moved from her knees. When he set his hand to her shoulder, she stiffened as if expecting to be struck again. But she did not resist him. She had reconciled herself to death. As he lifted her, she assisted him as well as she could.

"In the heat of the kiln and the molten iron, with all the eyes of the judica upon them, they climbed the ramp toward the rim of the cauldron.

"Starved and beaten as she was, she had no strength for the ascent. The reflected glow of the metal showed fiercely upon her swellings and bruises. Dom Peralt was compelled to support her, one arm around her back, one hand on her shoulder. For that reason, he did not resemble a man who intended to hurl her into agony when they gained the head of the ramp.

"At the rim of the cauldron, they halted. She leaned, half stumbling, toward the terrible heat, as though he had already thrust her to fall. But he caught her back. A smile made savage by the direct radiance of the iron twisted his mouth. He gazed into her face—but she would not raise her eyes. He was her slayer, and she had chosen this death to pay her debts.

"Roughly, he turned her away from him. His hands clamped her sore shoulders. If she had tried to struggle—even if she had been healthy—she could not have escaped his young strength. Her head hanging weakly, she did not struggle.

"'Thamala,' he said in a voice which we all heard, 'you are doomed. This I do for justice.'"

Ser Visal lifted his flagon to his lips—and lowered it without drinking. "My puppies," he said slowly, "you will not be more surprised than your fathers were by what transpired." Several of the candles had failed, and the dimmer light seemed to give his face a grim intensity, almost a keenness, as though he were not as fat and soft as he appeared. "As you may imagine, the attention of every man in the chamber was fixed upon Dom Peralt and the witch. None who witnessed the event were able to account for what they saw.

"From somewhere about the tiers, a goatskin full of water was hurled into the cauldron. Striking the molten iron, it burst with such an eruption of steam and noise that the onlookers ducked their heads. High Templeman Crossus Hught and Templeman Knarll recoiled against each other. The cauldron and the head of the ramp were obscured from view.

"When the vapor cleared—before any Templeman could call out— Dom Peralt and Thamala became visible again. She lay on her side on the ramp, her manacles held against the stone. In one hand, he gripped a hammer which he had worn hidden under his belt—in the other, a hardened chisel that he had borrowed from Growt. As the judica watched in astonishment and horror, he struck the iron from Thamala's left wrist.

"Templeman Knarll gaped to shout, but Crossus Hught was quicker, 'Guards!' he thundered. Treachery! Beware of witchcraft! *Guards!'* A thrust of his thin arm impelled Templeman Knarll toward the ramp.

"Nevertheless, Dom Peralt might have succeeded in his attempt. Only a moment was required. But he was inexperienced with Growt's tools. His first blow was luckier than he deserved—his second, unluckier. As he swung the hammer, the chisel slipped from the manacle. Striking the stone, it twisted from his grasp, skidded away, and fell to the floor beside the kiln.

"At that moment, the inner doors crashed open. A company of guards charged into the chamber, waving their swords—ready to butcher a whole host of helpless witches and weaponless young fools. Templemen dove into the tiers to clear the path of the guards.

"Dom Peralt did not hesitate. At the last, his wit—or his bravado—did not fail him. Pulling Thamala with him, he jumped after the fallen chisel.

"But when he had regained the tool, he made no effort to use it. Rather, he gave it to Thamala and thrust her to the floor. He had no time to break her remaining fetter. The guards were too near.

"To counter that threat, he did what no sane man would have done, regardless of his courage. He put his shoulder to the side of the cauldron and pushed."

Ser Visal wiped the sweat from his face, scrubbed his hands on the front of his robe. His eyes stared amazement at remembered visions. "It was plain to all in the chamber," he said softly. "Every man of the judica witnessed it. And no wonder that we fear to speak of it now! We saw the pressure of his great frame against the iron. We saw his clothing take fire from the heat. We smelled his flesh as it burned. We heard the howl wrung from him in hideous pain.

"And we saw the brick which held the cauldron upright crumble.

"After that"—Ser Visal threw up his hands—"chaos. The cauldron tilted and fell, pouring molten iron at the guards. In instant panic, they did their utmost to avoid that liquid agony. Some sprang to safety among the seats. Others were hurt only by the spattering droplets. But a few were too slow. They lost feet and limbs before they were pulled free.

"Amid the shouts and screams and confusion, only a few of us saw that Dom Peralt retained consciousness, despite his tremendous hurt. Tharnala held the chisel against her manacle as he raised the hammer and brought it down with his last strength.

"She had been tortured and starved for days, reduced to such frailty that she could hardly stand. But she did not fail him. As the iron fell from her waist, she called up her power—and both she and Dom Peralt seemed to vanish as though they had ceased to exist.

"A moment later, all the wood of the outer doors burst from the hinges and bolts.

"At once, the High Templeman roared, 'They flee!' Brandishing his miter like a club, he sent every guard and Templeman within reach chasing outward in a rush. And we followed, half thinking that we might yet recapture the witch and her rescuer, half desiring only to escape the pain and ruin of the judica.

"But Dom Peralt and Thamala were gone."

Abruptly, Ser Visal tossed down the dregs of the bitter wine and thumped his flagon to the table. "The rest you know," he said brusquely. In a surge of flesh and robes, he gained his feet. "The witch and her consort were not found. A great search was made, and many men and goodwomen were offended by it. A writ of excommunication was read against Dom Peralt. But no sign of him or the witch was found.

"The breaking of the outer door was a ruse, of course. Neither he nor Thamala had the strength for flight. They remained in the judica, and she kept them from being seen, until the chamber was left empty. Then they made their way to whatever means of escape he had prepared for them.

"That is enough. Vespers will be rung soon. You must go." Balancing his bulk on his stout legs, Ser Visal started toward the door.

Consternation stopped our mouths. He was not done—surely he was not done? There was so much we wished to know. Yet he was on his way to the door without a backward glance.

The son of Dom Tahl, however, was accustomed to leadership among us, and he spoke when the rest of us could not. "Ser Visal, how do you know all this?" Was there a hint of warning in his voice—a threat? Perhaps he meant to tell his father what he had heard. "How do you know what ruses Dom Peralt and the witch used?"

Ser Visal turned. In the failing light, the gaze he cast toward Domson Tahl appeared furtive, frightened. "It needs no great wit," he replied with an effort of blandness. "I have heard that the injured guards are recovering remarkably well. Without exception, they suffer less than expected—and heal more rapidly. And some admit that they felt a beneficent influence while they waited for succor." He shrugged his mounded shoulders. "Witches are known to be healers."

Domson Tahl frowned and nodded. But at once he asked, "And how do you know what Dom Peralt and the witch said to each other in his cell?"

Bulging in his fat cheeks, Ser Visal's eyes shifted among us warily. Still slick with sweat, his skin had a pasty color. Twice he opened his thick lips and closed them again, gaping like a fish. Some of us nudged Domson Thal warningly. Others clenched their fists. We wanted no harm to come to Ser Visal for the things he had revealed to us. But at last he swallowed his fear and accepted the full risk of his tale.

"Do you louts have minds of stone?" he retorted acidly. "Who do you suppose threw the goatskin of water into the cauldron?"

Turning on his heel, he left the Hound and Whip.

We followed him out into the dusty street and the evening. Some of us staggered a little from the wine we had consumed, but drink had no effect on Ser Visal. He was as steady on his feet as a sack of grain as he walked away.

Reave the Just

Of all the strange, unrelenting stories which surrounded Reave the Just, none expressed his particular oddness of character better than that concerning his kinsman, Jillet of Forebridge.

Part of the oddness was this—that Reave and Jillet were so unlike each other that the whole idea of their kinship became difficult to credit.

Let it be said without prejudice that Jillet was an amiable fool. No one who was not amiable would have been loved by the cautious people of Forebridge—and Jillet was loved, of that there could be no doubt. Otherwise the townsfolk would never have risked the unpredictable and often spectacular consequences of sending for Reave, merely to inform him that Jillet had disappeared. And no one who was not a fool would have gotten himself into so much trouble with Kelven Divestulata that Kelven felt compelled to dispose of him.

In contrast, neither Reave's enemies—of which his exploits had attracted a considerable number—nor his friends would have described him as amiable.

Doubtless there were villages across the North Counties, towns perhaps, possibly a city or two, where Reave the Just was admired, even adulated: Forebridge was not among them. His decisions were too wild, his actions too unremitting, to meet the chary approval of the farmers and farriers, millers and masons who had known Jillet from birth.

Like a force of nature, he was so far beyond explanation that people had ceased trying to account for him. Instead of wondering why he did what he did—or how he got away with it—the men and women of Forebridge asked themselves how such an implausible individual chanced to be kinsman to Jillet, who was himself only implausible in the degree to which likable character was combined with unreliable judgment.

In fact, no one knew for certain that Reave and Jillet were related. Just recently, Jillet had upon occasion referred to Reave as "Reave the Just, my kinsman."

That was the true extent of the information available in Forebridge. Nothing more was revealed on the subject. In an effort to supply the lack, rumor or gossip suggested that Jillet's mother's sister, a woman of another town altogether, had fallen under the seduction of a carnival clown with delusions of grandeur—or, alternatively, of a knight-errant incognito— and had given Reave a bastard birth under some pitiful hedgerow, or perhaps in some nameless nunnery, or conceivably in some lord's private bedchamber. But how the strains of blood which could produce Reave had been so entirely suppressed in Jillet, neither rumor nor gossip knew. Still it must have been true that Reave and Jillet were related. When Reave was summoned in Jillet's name, he came.

By the time Reave arrived, however, Jillet was beyond knowing whether anyone valued him enough to tell his kinsman what had become of him.

How he first began to make his way along the road to Kelven's enmity was never clearly known. Very well, he was a fool, as all men knew— but how had he become enmeshed in folly on this scale? A few bad bargains with usurers were conceivable. A few visits to the alchemists and mages who fed on the fringes of towns like Forebridge throughout the North Counties were conceivable, in fact hardly to be wondered at, especially when Jillet was at the painful age where he was old enough to want a woman's love but too young to know how to get it. A few minor and ultimately forgettable feuds born of competition for trade or passion were not only conceivable but normal. Had not men and women been such small and harmless fools always? The folk of Forebridge might talk of such matters endlessly, seeking to persuade themselves that they were wiser. But who among them would have hazarded himself against Kelven Divestulata? Indeed, who among them had not at one time or another suspected that Kelven was Satan Himself, thinly disguised by swarthy flesh and knotted muscle and wiry beard?

What in the name of all the saints had possessed Jillet to fling himself into such deep waters?

The truth—which no one in Forebridge ever divined—was that Jillet brought his doom down on his own head by the simple expedient of naming himself Reave's kinsman.

It came about in this fashion. In his early manhood, Jillet fell victim to an amiable, foolish, and quite understandable passion for the widow Huchette. Before his death, Rudolph Huchette had brought his new bride—foreign, succulent, and young—to live in the manor house now occupied by Kelven Divestulata, thinking that by keeping her far from the taints and sophistication of the cities he could keep her pure. Sadly for him, he did not live long enough after settling in Forebridge to learn that his wife was pure by nature and needed no special protection. And of course the young men of the town knew nothing of her purity.

They only knew that she was foreign, young, and bereaved, imponderably delicious. Jillet's passion was only one among many, ardent and doomed. The widow Huchette asked only of the God who watched over innocence that she be left alone.

Needless to say, she was not.

Realistically considered, the only one of her admirers truly capable of disturbing her was dour Kelven. When she spurned his advances, he laid siege to her with all the cunning bitterness of his nature. Over the course of many months, he contrived to install himself in the manor house which Rudolph had intended as her lifelong home; he cut off her avenues of escape so that her only recourse was to accept the drudgery of being his housekeeper since she steadfastly refused the grim honor of being his wife. And even there he probably had the best of her, since he was no doubt perfectly capable of binding and raping her to satisfy his admiration.

However, Jillet and the other men enamored of the widow did not consider her circumstances—and their own—realistically. As men in passion will, they chose to believe that they themselves were the gravest threat to her detachment. Blind to Kelven's intentions, Jillet and his fellow fools went about in a fog of schemes, dreaming of ways to persuade her to reveal her in evitable preference for themselves.

However, Jillet carried this scheming farther than most—but by no means all—of his peers.

Perhaps because of his amiability—or perhaps because he was foolish—he was not ordinarily successful in competitions over women. His face and form were goodly enough, and his brown eyes showed pleasure as openly as any man's. His kindness and cheery temper endeared him throughout Forebridge. But he lacked forthrightness, self-assertion; he lacked the qualities which inspire passion. As with women everywhere, those of Forebridge valued kindness; they were fond of it; but they did not surrender their virtue to it. They preferred heroes—or rogues.

So when Jillet first conceived his passion for the widow Huchette, he was already accustomed to the likelihood that he would not succeed.

Like Kelven Divestulata after the first year or so of the widow's bereavement—although no one in Forebridge knew at the time what Kelven was doing—Jillet prepared a siege. He was not wise enough to ask himself, Why am I not favored in the beds of women? What must I learn in order to make myself desirable? How may I rise above the limitations which nature has placed upon me? Instead, he asked, Who can help me with this woman?

His answer had already occurred to a handful of his brighter, but no less foolish, fellows. In consequence, he was no better than the fifth or sixth man of Forebridge to approach the best-known hedgerow alchemist in the County, seeking a love potion.

According to some authorities, the chief distinction between alchemists and mages was that the former had more opportunities for charlatanism, at less hazard. Squires and earls consulted mages; plowmen and cotters, alchemists. Certainly, the man whom Jillet approached was a charlatan. He admitted as much freely in the company of folks who were wise enough not to want anything from him. But he would never have revealed the truth about himself to one such as Jillet.

Charlatan or not, however, he was growing weary of this seemingly endless sequence of men demanding love potions against the widow Huchette. One heart sick swain by the six-month or so may be profitably bilked. Three may be a source of amusement. But five or six in a season was plainly tedious. And worrisome as well: even Forebridge was capable of recognizing charlatanism when five or six love potions failed consecutively.

"Go home," the alchemist snapped when he had been told what Jillet wanted. "The ingredients for the magick you require are arduous and expensive to obtain. I cannot satisfy you."

But Jillet, who could not have put his hand on five farthings at that moment, replied, "I care nothing for the price. I will pay whatever is needed." The dilemma of cost had never entered his head, but he was certain it could be resolved. The widow Huchette had gold enough, after all.

His confidence presented an entirely different dilemma to the alchemist. It was not in the nature of charlatans to refuse money. And yet too many love potions had already been dispensed. If Providence did not inspire the widow to favor one of the first four or five men, the alchemist's reputation—and therefore his income—would be endangered. Perhaps even his person would be endangered.

Seeking to protect himself, the alchemist named a sum which should have stunned any son of a cotter.

Jillet was not stunned. Any sum was acceptable, since he had no prospect of ever paying it himself. "Very well," he said comfortably. Then, because he wished to believe in his own cleverness, he added. "But if the potion does not succeed, you will return that sum with interest."

"Oh, assuredly," replied the alchemist, who found that he could not after all refuse money. "All of my magicks succeed, or I will know the reason why. Return tomorrow. Bring your gold then."

He closed his door so that Jillet would not have a chance to change his mind.

Jillet walked home musing to himself. Now that he had time to consider the matter, he found that he had placed himself in an awkward position. True, the love of the widow Huchette promised to be a valuable investment—but it was an investment only, not coin. The alchemist would require coin. In fact, the coin was required in order to obtain the investment. And Jillet had no coin, not on the scale the alchemist had mentioned. The truth was that he had never laid mortal eyes on that scale of coin.

And he had no prospects which might be stretched to that scale, no skills which could earn it, no property which could be sold for it.

Where could a man like Jillet of Forebridge get so much money?

Where else?

Congratulating himself on his clarity of wit, Jillet went to the usurers.

He had had no dealings with usurers heretofore. But he had heard rumors. Some such "lenders" were said to be more forgiving than others, less stringent in their demands. Well, Jillet had no need of anyone's forgiveness; but he felt a natural preference for men with amiable reputations. From the honest alchemist, he went in search of an amiable usurer.

Unfortunately, amiable, forgiving usurers had so much kindness in their natures because they could afford it; and they could afford it because their investments were scantly at risk: they demanded collateral before hazarding coin. This baffled Jillet more than a little. The concept of collateral he could understand—just—but he could not understand why the widow Huchette did not constitute collateral. He would use the money to pay the alchemist; the alchemist would give him a love potion; the potion would win the widow; and from the widow's holdings the usurer would be paid. Where was the fallacy in all this?

The usurer himself had no difficulty detecting the fallacy. More in sorrow than in scorn, he sent Jillet away.

Other "lenders" were similarly inclined. Only their pity varied, not their rejection.

Well, thought Jillet, I will never gain the widow without assistance. I must have the potion.

So he abandoned his search for an amiable usurer and committed himself, like a lost fish, to swim in murkier waters. He went to do business with the kind of moneylender who despised the world because he feared it. This moneylender feared the world because his substance was always at risk; and his substance was always at risk because he required no collateral. All he required was a fatal return on his investment.

"One fifth!" Jillet protested. The interest sounded high, even to him. "No other lender in Forebridge asks so much."

"No other lender in Forebridge," wheezed the individual whose coin was endangered, "risks so much."

True, thought Jillet, giving the man his due. And after all one fifth was only a number. It would not amount to much, if the widow were won swiftly. "Very well," he replied calmly. "As you say, you ask no collateral. And my prospects cannot fail. One fifth in a year is not too much to pay for what I will gain, especially"—he cleared his throat in a dignified fashion, for emphasis—"since I will only need the use of your money for a fortnight at most."

"A *year*?" The usurer nearly burst a vessel. "You will return me one fifth a *week* on my risk, or you can beg coin of fools like yourself, for you will get none from me!"

One fifth in a week. Perhaps for a moment Jillet was indeed stunned. Perhaps he went so far as to reconsider the course he had chosen. One fifth in a week, each and every week—And what if the potion failed? Or if it were merely slow? He would never be able to pay that first one fifth, not to mention the second or the third—and certainly not the original sum itself. Why, it was ruinous.

But then it occurred to him that one fifth, or two fifths, or twenty would make no difference to the wealth of the widow Huchette. And he would be happy besides, basking in the knowledge of a passion virtuously satisfied.

On that comfortable assumption, he agreed to the usurer's terms.

The next day, laden with a purse containing more gold than he had ever seen in his life, Jillet of Forebridge returned to the alchemist.

By this time, the alchemist was ready for him. The essence of charlatanism was cunning, and the alchemist was nothing if not an essential charlatan. He had taken the measure of his man—as well as of his own circumstances—and had determined his response. First, of course, he counted out Jillet's gold, testing the coins with spurious powders and honest teeth. He produced a few small fires and explosions, purely for effect: Like most of his ilk, he could be impressive when he wished. Then he spoke.

"Young man, you are not the first to approach me for a potion in this matter. You are merely the first"—he hefted the purse—"to place such value on your object. Therefore I must give you a magick able to supersede all others—a magick not only capable of attaining its end, but in fact of doing so against the opposition of a—number—of intervening magicks. This is a rare and dangerous enterprise. For it to succeed, you must not only trust it entirely, but also be bold in support of it.

"Behold!"

The alchemist flourished his arms to induce more fires and explosions. When an especially noxious fume had cleared, he held in his palm a leather pouch on a thong.

"I will be plain," said the alchemist, "for it will displease me gravely if magick of such cost and purity fails because you do not do your part. This periapt must be worn about your neck, concealed under your"—he was about to say "linen," but Jillet's skin clearly had no acquaintance with finery of that kind—"jerkin. As needed, it must be invoked in the following secret yet efficacious fashion." He glared at Jillet through his eyebrows. "You must make reference to 'my kinsman, Reave the Just.' And you must be as unscrupulous as Reave the Just in pursuing your aim. You must falter at nothing."

This was the alchemist's inspiration, his cunning at work. Naturally, the pouch contained only a malodorous dirt. The magick lay in the words *my kinsman, Reave the Just*. Any man willing to make that astonishing claim could be sure of one thing: he would receive opportunities which would otherwise be impossible for him. Doors would be opened, audiences granted, attention paid anywhere in the North Counties, regardless of Jillet's apparent lineage, or his lack of linen. In that sense, the magick the alchemist offered was truer than any of his previous potions. It would open the doors of houses. And conceivably, if the widow Hucherte were impressionable enough, it would open the door of her heart; for what innocent and moony young female could resist the enchantment of Reave's reputation?

So, of course, Jillet protested. Precisely because he lacked the wit to understand the alchemist's chicanery, he failed to understand its use. Staring at his benefactor, he objected, "But Reave the Just is no kinsman of mine. My family is known in Forebridge. No one will believe me."

Simpleton, thought the alchemist. *Idiot.* "They will," he replied with a barely concealed exasperation born of fear that Jillet would demand the return of his gold, "if you are bold enough, *confident* enough, in your actions. The words do not need to be true. They are simply a private incantation, a way of invoking the periapt without betraying what you do. The magick will succeed if you but *trust* it."

Still Jillet hesitated. Despite the strength which the mere idea of the widow Huchette exercised in his thinking, he had no comprehension of the power of ideas: he could not grasp what he might gain from the idea that he was related to Reave. "How can that be?" he asked the air more than the alchemist. No doubt deliberately, the alchemist had challenged his understanding of the world; and it was the world which should have answered him. Striving to articulate his doubt, he continued, "I want a love potion to change the way she looks at me. What will I gain by saying or acting a thing that is untrue?"

Perhaps this innocence explained some part of the affection Forebridge felt for him; but it did not endear him to the alchemist. "Now hear me," *clod, buffoon half-wit,* said the alchemist. "This magick is precious, and if you do not value it I will offer it elsewhere. The object of your desire does not desire you. You wish her to desire you. Therefore something must be altered. Either she must be made to"—*stifle her natural revulsion for a clod like you*—"feel a desire she lacks. Or you must be made more desirable to her. I offer both. Properly invoked, the periapt will instill desire in her. And bold action and a reputation as Reave the Just's kinsman will make you desirable.

"What more do you require?"

Jillet was growing fuddled: he was unaccustomed to such abstract discourse. Fortunately for the alchemist's purse, however, what filled Jillet's head was not an idea but an image—the image of a usurer who demanded repayment at the rate of one fifth in a week, and who appeared capable of dining on Jillet's giblets if his demands were thwarted.

Considering his situation from the perspective not of ideas but of images, Jillet found that he could not move in any direction except forward. Behind him lurked exigencies too acute to be confronted: ahead stood the widow Huchette and passion.

"Very well," he said, making his first attempt to emulate Reave's legendary decisiveness. "Give me the pouch."

Gravely, the alchemist set the pouch in Jillet's hand. In similar fashion, Jillet hung the thong about his neck and concealed the periapt under his jerkin.

Then he returned to Forebridge, armed with magick and cunning—and completely unshielded by any idea of what to do with his new weaponry.

The words *trust* and *bold* and *unscrupulous* rang in his mind. What did they mean? *Trust* came to him naturally; *bold* was incomprehensible; *unscrupulous* conveyed a note of dishonesty. Taken together, they seemed as queer as a hog with a chicken's head—or an amiable usurer. Jillet was altogether at sea.

In that state, he chanced to encounter one of his fellow pretenders to the widow Huchette's bed, a stout, hairy, and frequently besotted fletcher named Slup. Not many days ago, Slup had viewed Jillet as a rival, perhaps even as a foe; he had behaved toward Jillet in a surly way which had baffled Jillet's amiable nature. Since that time, however, Slup had obtained his own alchemick potion, and new confidence restored his goodwill. Hailing Jillet cheerfully, he asked where his old friend had been hiding for the past day or so.

Trust, Jillet thought. *Bold. Unscrupulous.* It was natural, was it not, that magick made no sense to ordinary men? If an ordinary man, therefore, wished to benefit from magick, he must require himself to behave in ways which made no sense.

Summoning his resolve, he replied, "Speaking with my kinsman, Reave the Just," and strode past Slup without further explanation.

He did not know it, of course, but he had done enough. With those few words, he had invoked the power, not of the periapt, but of ideas. Slup told what he had heard to others, who repeated it to still others. Within hours, discussion had ranged from one end of the village to the other. The absence of explanation—When had Jillet come upon such a relation? why had he never mentioned it before? how had *Reave the Just,* of all men, contrived to visit Forebridge without attracting notice?—far from proving a hindrance, actually enhanced the efficacy of Jillet's utterance. When he went to his favorite tavern that evening, hoping to meet with some hearty friend who would stand him a tankard of ale, he found that every man he knew had been transformed— or he himself had.

He entered the tavern in what was, for him, a state of some anxiety. The more he had thought about it, the more he had realized that the gamble he took with Slup was one which he did not comprehend. After all, what experience had he ever had with alchemy? How could he be sure of its effectiveness? He knew about such things only by reputation, by the stories men told concerning alchemists and mages, witches and warlocks. The interval between his encounter with Slup and the evening taught him more self-doubt than did the more practical matter of his debt to the usurer. When he went to the tavern, he went half in fear that he would be greeted by a roar of laughter.

He had invoked the power of an idea, however, and part of its magick was this—that a kinship with Reave the Just was not something into which any man or woman of the world would inquire directly. No one asked of Jillet, "What sort of clap-brained tale are you telling today?" The consequences might prove dire if the tale were true. Many things were said about Reave, and some were dark: enemies filleted like fish; entire houses exterminated; laws and magistrates overthrown. No one credited Jillet's claim of kinship—and no one took the risk of challenging it.

When he entered the tavern, he was not greeted with laughter. Instead, the place became instantly still, as though Reave himself were

present. All eyes turned on Jillet, some in suspicion, some in speculation—and no small number in excitement. Then someone shouted a
welcome; the room filled with a hubbub which seemed unnaturally
loud because of the silence that had preceded it; and Jillet was swept
up by the conviviality of his friends and acquaintances.

Ale flowed ungrudgingly, although he had no coin to pay for it. His
jests were met with uproarious mirth and hearty backslappings, despite
the fact that he was more accustomed to appreciating humor than to
venturing it. Men clustered about him to hear his opinions—and he
discovered, somewhat to his own surprise, that he had an uncommon
number of opinions. The faces around him grew ruddy with ale and
firelight and pleasure, and he had never felt so loved.

Warmed by such unprecedented good cheer, he had reason to congratulate himself that he was able to refrain from any mention of alchemists
or widows. That much good sense remained to him, at any rate. On the other
hand, he was unable to resist a few strategic references to *my kinsman,
Reave the Just*—experiments regarding the potency of ideas.

Because of those references, the serving wench, a buxom and lusty
girl who had always liked him and refused to sleep with him, seemed
to linger at his elbow when she refreshed his tankard. Her hands made
occasion to touch his arm repeatedly; again and again, she found herself
jostled by the crowd so that her body pressed against his side; looking
up at him, her eyes shone. To his amazement, he discovered that when
he put his arm around her shoulders she did not shrug it away. Instead,
she used it to move him by slow degrees out from among the men and
toward the passageway which led to her quarters.

That evening was the most successful Jillet of Forebridge had ever
known. In her bed and her body, he seemed to meet himself as the man
he had always wished to be. And by morning, his doubts had disappeared; what passed for common sense with him had been drowned in
the murky waters of magick, cunning, and necessity.

Eager despite a throbbing head and thick tongue, Jillet of Forebridge
commenced his siege upon the manor and fortune and virtue of the
widow Huchette.

This he did by the straightforward, if unimaginative, expedient of
approaching the gatehouse of the manor and asking to speak with her.

When he did so, however, he encountered an unexpected obstacle.
Like most of the townsfolk—except, perhaps, some among his more recent
acquaintance, the usurers, who had told him nothing on the subject—
he was unaware of Kelven Divestulata's preemptive claim on Rudolph's
widow. He had no knowledge that the Divestulata had recently made

himself master of the widow Huchette's inheritance, possessions, and person. In all probability, Jillet would have found it impossible to imagine that any man could do such a thing.

Jillet of Forebridge had no experience with men like Kelven Divestulata.

For example, Jillet knew nothing which would have led him to guess that Kelven never made any attempt to woo the widow. Surely to woo was the natural action of passion? Perhaps for other men; not in Kelven's case. From the moment when he first conceived his desire to the moment when he gained the position which enabled him to satisfy it, he had spoken to the object of his affections only once.

Standing before her—entirely without gifts or graces—he had said bluntly, "Be my wife."

She had hardly dared glance at him before hiding her face. Barely audible, she had replied, "My husband is dead. I will not marry again." The truth was that she had loved Rudolph as ardently as her innocence and inexperience permitted, and she had no wish whatsoever to replace him.

However, if she had dared to look at Kelven, she would have seen his jaws clenched and a vein pulsing inexorably at his temple. "I do not brook refusal," he announced in a voice like an echo of doom. "And I do not ask twice."

Sadly, she was too innocent—or perhaps too ignorant—to fear doom. "Then," she said to him gravely, "you must be the unhappiest of men."

Thus her sole interchange with her only enemy began and ended.

Just as Jillet could not have imagined this conversation, he could never have dreamed the Divestulata's response.

In a sense, it would have been accurate to say that all Forebridge knew more of Reave the Just, who had never set foot in the town, than of Kelven Divestulata, whose ancestral home was less than an hour's ride away. Reave was a fit subject for tales and gossip on any occasion: neither wise men nor fools discussed Kelven.

So few folk—least of all Jillet—knew of the brutal and impassioned marriage of Kelven's parents, or of his father's death in an apoplectic fury, or of the acid bitterness which his mother directed at him when her chief antagonist was lost. Fewer still knew of the circumstances surrounding her harsh, untimely end. And none at all knew that Kelven himself had secretly arranged their deaths for them, not because of their treatment of him—which in fact he understood and to some extent approved—but because he saw profit for himself in being rid of them, preferably in some way which would cause them as much distress as possible.

It might have been expected that the servants and retainers of the family would know or guess the truth, and that at least one of them would say something on the subject to someone; but within a few months of his mother's demise Kelven had contrived to dispense with every member of his parents' establishment, and had replaced them with cooks and maids and grooms who knew nothing and said less. In this way he made himself as safe from gossip as he could ever hope to be.

As a result, the few stories told of him had a certain legendary quality, as if they concerned another Divestulata who had lived long ago. In the main, these tales involved either sums of money or young women who came to his notice and then disappeared. It was known—purportedly for a fact—that a usurer or three had been driven out of Forebridge, cursing Kelven's name. And it was undeniable that the occasional young woman had vanished. Unfortunately, the world was a chancy place, especially for young women, and their fate was never clearly known. The one magistrate of Forebridge who had pursued the matter far enough to question Kelven himself had afterward been so overtaken by chagrin that he had ended his own life.

Unquestionably, Kelven's mode of existence was secure.

However, for reasons known only to himself, he desired a wife. And he was accustomed to obtain what he desired. When the widow Huchette spurned him, he was not daunted. He simply set about attaining his goal by less direct means.

He began by buying out the investments which had been made to secure the widow's future. These he did not need, so he allowed them to go to ruin. Then he purchased the widow's deceased husband's debts from the usurer who held them. They were few, but they gave him a small claim on the importing merchantry from which Rudolph Huchette's wealth derived. His claim provided him with access to the merchantry's ledgers and contacts and partners, and that knowledge enabled him to apply pressure to the sources of the merchantry's goods. In a relatively short time, as such things are measured, he became the owner of the merchantry itself.

He subsequently found it child's play to reveal—in the presence of a magistrate, of course—that Rudolph Huchette had acquired his personal fortune by despoiling the assets of the merchantry. In due course, that fortune passed to Kelven, and he became, in effect, the widow Huchette's landlord—the master of every tangible or monetary resource on which her marriage had made her dependent.

Naturally, he did not turn her out of her former home. Where could she have gone? Instead, he kept her with him and closed the doors to the manor house. If she made any protest, it was unheard through the stout walls.

Of all this, Jillet was perfectly innocent as he knocked on the door of the manor's gatehouse and requested an audience with the widow. In consequence, he was taken aback when he was admitted, not to the sitting room of the widow, but to the study of her new lord, the Divestulata.

The study itself was impressive enough to a man like Jillet. He had never before seen so much polished oak and mahogany, so much brass and fine leather. Were it not for his unprecedented successes the previous evening, his aching head, which dulled his responses, and his new warrant for audacity, he might have been cowed by the mere room. However, he recited the litany which the alchemist had given him, and the words *trust, bold,* and *unscrupulous* enabled him to bear the air of the place well enough to observe that Kelven himself was more impressive, not because of any greatness of stature or girth, but because of the malign and unanswerable glower with which he regarded everything in front of him. His study was ill-lit, and the red echo of candles in his eyes suggested the flames of Satan and Hell.

It was fortunate, therefore, that Kelven did not immediately turn his attention upon Jillet. Instead, he continued to peruse the document gripped in his heavy hands. This may have been a ploy intended to express his disdain for his visitor; but it gave Jillet a few moments in which to press his hand against his hidden pouch of magick, rehearse the counsel of the alchemist, and marshal his resolve.

When Kelven was done with his reading, or his ploy, he raised his grim head and demanded without preamble, "What is your business with my wife?"

At any former time, this would have stopped Jillet dead. *Wife?* The widow had already become Kelven Divestulata's *wife?* But Jillet was possessed by his magick and his incantation, and they gave him a new extravagance. It was impossible that Kelven had married the widow. Why? Because such a disappointment could not conceivably befall the man who had just earned with honest gold and courage the right to name himself the kinsman of Reave the Just. To consider the widow Huchette Kelven's wife made a mockery of both justice and alchemy.

"Sir," Jillet began. Armed with virtue and magick, he could afford to be polite. "My 'business' is with the widow. If she is truly your wife, she will tell me so herself. Permit me to say frankly, however, that I cannot understand why you would stoop to a false claim of marriage. Without the sanction of the priests, no marriage can be valid—and no sanction is possible until the banns have been published. This you have not done."

There Jillet paused to congratulate himself. The alchemist's magick was indisputably efficacious. It had already made him *bolder* than he had ever been in his life.

In fact, it made him so *bold* that he took no notice of the narrowing of Kelven's eyes, the tightening of his hands. Jillet was inured to peril. He smiled blandly as the Divestulata stood to make his reply.

"She is my wife," Kelven announced distinctly, *"because* I have claimed her. I need no other sanction."

Jillet blinked a time or two. "Do I understand you, sir? Do you call her your wife—and still admit that you have not been wed?"

Kelven studied his visitor and said nothing.

"Then this is a matter for the magistrates." In a sense, Jillet did not hear his own words. Certainly, he did not pause to consider whether they would be pleasing to the Divestulata. His attention was focused, rather, on alchemy and incantations. Enjoying his new boldness, he wondered how far he could carry it before he felt the need to make reference to his kinsman. "The sacrament of marriage exists to protect women from those who are stronger, so that they will not be bound to any man against their will." This fine assertion was not one which he had conceived for himself. It was quoted almost directly from the school lessons of the priests. "If you have not wed the widow Huchette, I can only conclude that she does not choose to wed you. In that case"—Jillet was becoming positively giddy—"you are not her husband, sir. You are her enslaver.

"You would be well advised to let me speak to her."

Having said this, Jillet bowed to Kelven, not out of courtesy, but in secret delight. The Divestulata was his only audience for his performance: like an actor who knew he had done well, he bowed to his audience. All things considered, he may still have been under the influence of the previous evening's ale.

Naturally, Kelven saw the matter in another light. Expressionless except for his habitual glower, he regarded Jillet. After a moment, he said, "You mentioned the magistrates." He did not sound like a man who had been threatened. He sounded like a man who disavowed responsibility for what came next. Having made his decision, he rang a small bell which stood on his desk. Then he continued, "You will speak to my wife."

The servant who had conducted Jillet to the Divestulata's study appeared. To the servant, Kelven said, "Inform my wife that she will receive us."

The servant bowed and departed.

Jillet had begun to glow inwardly. This was a triumph! Even such a man as Kelven Divestulata could not resist his alchemy—and he had not yet made any reference to Reave the Just. Surely his success with the widow was assured. She would succumb to his magick; Kelven would withdraw under threat of the magistrates; and all would be just as Jillet had dreamed it. Smiling happily at his host, he made no effort to resist as Kelven took him by his arm.

However, allowing Kelven to take hold of him may have been a mistake. The Divestulata's grip was hard—brutally hard—and the crush of his fingers upon Jillet's arm quickly dispelled the smile from Jillet's lips. Jillet was strong himself, having been born to a life of labor, but Kelven's strength turned him pale. Only pride and surprise enabled him to swallow his protest.

Without speaking—and without haste—Kelven steered Jillet to the chamber where he had instructed his wife to receive visitors.

Unlike Kelven's study, the widow's sitting room was brightly lit, not by lamps and candles, but by sunshine. Perhaps simply because she loved the sun, or perhaps because she wished herself to be seen plainly, she immersed herself in light. This made immediately obvious the fact that she remained clad in her widow's weeds, despite her new status as the Divestulata's *wife*. It also made obvious the drawn pallor of her face, the hollowness of her cheeks, the dark anguish under her eyes. She did nothing to conceal the way she flinched when Kelven's gaze fell upon her.

Kelven still did not release Jillet's arm. "This impudent sot," he announced to the widow as though Jillet were not present, "believes we are not wed."

The widow may have been hurt and even terrified, but she remained honest. In a small, thin voice, she said, "I am wed to Rudolph Huchette, body and life." Her hands were folded about each other in her lap. She did not lift her gaze from them. "I will never marry again."

Jillet hardly heard her. He had to grind his teeth to prevent himself from groaning at Kelven's grip.

"He believes," Kelven continued, still addressing the widow, "that the magistrates should be informed we are not wed."

That made the widow raise her head. Sunlight illuminated the spark of hope which flared in her eyes—flared, and then died when she saw Jillet clearly.

In defeat, she lowered her gaze again. Kelven was not satisfied. "What is your answer?" he demanded.

The widow's tone made it plain that she had not yet had time to become accustomed to defeat. "I hope he will inform the magistrates," she said, "but I believe he was a fool to let you know of his intentions."

"Madam—my lady." Jillet spoke in an involuntary gasp. His triumph was gone—even his hope was gone. His arm was being crushed. "Make him let go of me."

"Paugh!" With a flick of his hand, Kelven flung Jillet to the floor. "It is offensive to be threatened by a clod like you." Then he turned to the widow. "What do you believe I should do when I am threatened in this fashion for your sake?"

Despite her own distress, Rudolph's widow was still able to pity fools. Her voice became smaller, thinner, but it remained clear. "Let him go. Let him tell as many magistrates as he wishes. Who will believe him? Who will accept the word of a laborer when it is contradicted by Kelven Divestulata? Perhaps he is too shamed to tell anyone."

"And what if he is not shamed?" Kelven retorted instantly. "What if a magistrate hears him—and believes him enough to question you? What would you say?"

The widow did not raise her eyes. She had no need to gaze upon her *husband* again. "I would say that I am the prisoner of your malice and the plaything of your lusts, and I would thank God for His mercy if He would allow me to die."

"That is why I will not let him go." Kelven sounded oddly satisfied, as though an obscure desire had been vindicated. "Perhaps instead I will put his life in your power. I wish to see you rut with him. If you do it for my amusement, I will let him live."

Jillet did not hear what answer the widow would have made to this suggestion. Perhaps he did not properly hear anything which the Divestulata and his *wife* said to each other. His shame was intense, and the pain in his arm caused his head to throb as though it might burst; and, in truth, he was too busy cursing himself for not invoking the power of alchemy sooner to give much heed to what was said over him. He was a fool, and he knew it—a fool for thinking, however briefly, that he might accomplish for himself victories which only magick could achieve.

Therefore he struggled to his feet between Kelven and the widow. Hugging his arm to his side, he panted, "This is intolerable. My kinsman, Reave the Just, will be outraged when he learns of it."

Despite their many differences, Kelven Divestulata and the widow Huchette were identical in their reactions: they both became completely still, as though they had been turned to stone by the magick of the name *Reave the Just.*

"My kinsman is not forgiving," Jillet continued, driven by shame and pain and his new awareness of the power of ideas. "All the world knows it. He has no patience for injustice or tyranny, or for the abuse of the helpless, and when he is outraged he lets nothing stand in his way." Perhaps because he was a fool, he was able to speak with perfect conviction. Any man who was not a fool would have known that he had already said too much. "You will be wiser to come with me to the magistrate yourself and confess the wrong you have done this woman. He will be kinder to you than Reave the Just."

Still united by the influence of that name, the widow and Kelven said together, "You fool. You have doomed yourself."

But she said, "Now he will surely kill you."

His words were, "Now I will surely let you live." Hearing Kelven, Jillet was momentarily confused, misled by the impression that he had succeeded—that he had saved the widow and himself, that he had defeated the Divestulata. Then Kelven struck him down, and the misconception was lost.

When he awakened—more head-sore, bone-weak, and thirst-tormented than he had ever been in his life—he was in a chamber from which no one except Kelven himself and his own workmen had ever emerged. He had a room just like it in his ancestral home and knew its value. Shortly, therefore, after his acquisition of the manor house he had had this chamber dug into the rock beneath the foundations of the building. All Forebridge was quite ignorant of its existence. The excavated dirt and rock had been concealed by being used in other construction about the manor house—primarily in making the kennels where Kelven housed the mastiffs he bred for hunting and similar duties. And the workmen had been sent to serve the Divestulata in other enterprises in other Counties, far from Forebridge. So when Jillet awakened he was not simply in a room where no one would ever hear him scream. He was in a room where no one would ever look for him.

In any case, however, he felt too sick and piteous to scream. Kelven's blow had nearly cracked his skull, and the fetters on his wrists held his arms at an angle which nearly dislocated his shoulders. He was not surprised by the presence of light—by the single candle stuck in its tallow on a bench a few feet away. His general amazement was already too great, and his particular discomfort too acute, to allow him the luxury of surprise about the presence or absence of light.

On the bench beside the candle, hulking in the gloom like the condensed darkness of a demon, sat Kelven Divestulata.

"Ah," breathed Kelven softly, "your eyes open. You raise your head. The pain begins. Tell me about your *kinship* with Reave the Just."

Well, Jillet was a fool. Alchemy had failed him, and the power of ideas was a small thing compared to the power of Kelven's fist. To speak frankly, he had lived all his life at the mercy of events—or at the dictates of the decisions or needs or even whims of others. He was not a fit opponent for a man like the Divestulata.

Nevertheless he was loved in Forebridge for a reason. That reason went by the name of *amiability,* but it might equally well have been called *kindness* or *openheartedness.* He did not answer Kelven's question. Instead, through his own hurt, he replied, "This is wrong. She does not deserve it."

"'She'? Do you refer to my wife?" Kelven was mildly surprised. "We are not speaking of her. We are speaking of your kinsman, Reave the Just."

"She is weak and you are strong," Jillet persisted. "It is wrong to victimize her simply because she is unable to oppose you. You damn yourself by doing so. But I think you do not care about damnation." This was an unusual insight for him. "Even so, you should care that you demean yourself by using your strength against a woman who cannot oppose you."

As though Jillet had not spoken, Kelven continued, "He has a reputation for meddling in other men's affairs. In fact, his reputation for meddling is extensive. I find that I would like to put a stop to it. No doubt his reputation is only gossip, after all—but such gossip offends me. I *will* put a stop to it."

"It is no wonder that she refuses to wed you." Jillet's voice began to crack, and he required an effort to restrain tears. "The wonder is that she has not killed herself rather than suffer your touch."

"*Simpleton!*" spat Kelven, momentarily vexed. "She does not kill herself because I do not permit it." He promptly regained his composure, however. "Yet you have said one thing which is not foolish. A strong man who exerts his strength only upon the weak eventually becomes weak himself. I have decided on a more useful exercise. I will rid the world of this 'Reave the Just.'

"Tell me how you propose to involve your *kinsman* in my affairs. Perhaps I will allow you to summon him"—the Divestulata laughed harshly—"and then both you and my wife will be rescued."

There Jillet collapsed. He was weeping with helplessness and folly, and he had no understanding of the fact that Kelven intended to keep him alive when the widow Huchette had predicted that Kelven would kill him. Through a babble of tears and self-recrimination and appeals for pity, he told the Divestulata the truth.

"I am no kinsman of Reave the Just. That is impossible. I claimed kinship with him because an alchemist told me to do so. All I desired was a love potion to win the widow's heart, but he persuaded me otherwise."

At that time, Jillet was incapable of grasping that he remained alive only because Kelven did not believe him.

Because Kelven did not believe him, their conversation became increasingly arduous. Kelven demanded; Jillet denied. Kelven insisted; Jillet protested. Kelven struck; Jillet wailed. Ultimately Jillet lost consciousness, and Kelven went away.

The candle was left burning.

It was replaced by another, and by yet another, and by still others, so that Jillet was not left entirely in darkness; but he never saw the old ones gutter and die, or the new ones set. For some reason, he was always unconscious when that happened. The old stumps were not removed from the bench; he was left with some measure for his imprisonment. However, since he did not know how long the candles burned he could only conclude from the growing row of stumps that his imprisonment was long. He was fed at intervals which he could not predict. At times Kelven fed him. At times the widow fed him. At times she removed her garments and fondled his cold flesh with tears streaming from her eyes. At times he fouled himself. But only the candles provided a measure for his existence, and he could not interpret them.

How are you related to Reave?

How do you contact him?

Why does he meddle in other men's affairs?

What is the source of his power?

What *is* he?

Poor Jillet knew no answer to any of these questions.

His ignorance was the source of his torment, and the most immediate threat to his life; but it may also have saved him. It kept Kelven's attention focused upon him—and upon the perverse pleasures which he and the widow provided. In effect, it blinded Kelven to the power of ideas: Jillet's ignorance of anything remotely useful concerning Reave the Just preserved Kelven's ignorance of the fact that the townspeople of Forebridge, in their cautious and undemonstrative way, had summoned Reave in Jillet's name.

Quite honestly, most of them could not have said that they knew Reave had been summoned—or that they knew how he had been summoned. He was not a magistrate to whom public appeal could be made; not an official of the County to whom a letter could be written; not a lord of the realm from whom justice might be demanded. As far as anyone in Forebridge could have said for certain, he was not a man at all: he was only a story from places far away, a persistent legend blowing on its own queer winds across the North Counties. Can the wind be summoned? No? Then can Reave the Just?

In truth, Reave was summoned by the simple, almost nameless expedient of telling the tale. To every man or woman, herder or minstrel, merchant or soldier, mendicant or charlatan who passed through Forebridge, someone sooner or later mentioned that "Reave the Just had a kinsman here who has recently disappeared." Those folk followed their own roads away from Forebridge, and when they met with the occasion to do so they told the tale themselves; and so the tale spread.

In the end, such a summons can never be denied. Inevitably, Reave the Just heard it and came to Forebridge.

Like a breeze or a story, he appeared to come without having come *from* anywhere: one day, not so long after Jillet's disappearance, he was simply *there*, in Forebridge. Like a breeze or a story, he was not secretive about his coming: he did not lurk into town, or send in spies, or travel incognito. Still it was true that he came entirely unheralded, unannounced—and yet most folk who saw him knew immediately who he was, just as they knew immediately why he was there.

From a certain distance, of course, he was unrecognizable: his clothing was only a plain brown traveler's shirt over leather pants which had seen considerable wear and thick, dusty boots; his equally dusty hair was cropped to a convenient length; his strides were direct and self-assured, but no more so than those of other men who knew where they were going and why. In fact, the single detail which distinguished him from any number of farmers and cotters and wagoneers was that he wore no hat against the sun. Only when he drew closer did his strangeness make itself felt.

The dust showed that he had walked a long way, but he betrayed no fatigue, no hunger or thirst. His clothing had been exposed to the elements a great deal, but he carried no pack or satchel for food or spare garments or other necessities. Under the prolonged pressure of the sun, he might have developed a squint or a way of lowering his head; but his chin was up, and his eyes were open and vivid, like pieces of the deep sky. And he had no knife at his belt, no staff in his hand, no quiver over his shoulder—nothing with which to defend himself against hedgerow robbers or hungry beasts or outraged opponents. His only weapon, as far as any of the townspeople could see, was that he simply appeared *clearer* than any of his surroundings, better focused, as though he improved the vision of those who looked at him. Those who did look at him found it almost impossible to look away.

The people who first saw him closely enough to identify him were not surprised when he began asking questions about "his kinsman, Jillet of Forebridge." They were only surprised that his voice was so kind and quiet—considering his reputation for harsh decisions and extreme actions—and that he acknowledged the implausible relation which Jillet had claimed for the first time scarcely a week ago.

Unfortunately, none of the people questioned by Reave the Just had any idea what had become of Jillet.

It was characteristic of the folk of Forebridge that they avoided ostentation and public display. Reave had the effect, however, of causing them to forget their normal chariness. In consequence, he did not need to go searching for people to question: they came to him. Standing in the open road which served Forebridge as both public square and auctioneer's market, he asked his questions once, perhaps twice, then waited quietly while the slowly growing crowd around him attracted more people and his questions were repeated for him to the latecomers until a thick fellow with the strength of timber and a mind to match asked, "What's he look like, then, this Jillet?"

The descriptions provided around him were confusing at first; but under Reave's influence they gradually became clear enough to be serviceable.

"Hmm," rumbled the fellow. "Man like that visited my master t'other day."

People who knew the fellow quickly revealed that he served as a guard for one of the less hated usurers in Forebridge. They also indicated where this usurer might be found.

Reave the Just nodded once, gravely.

Smiling as though they were sure of his gratitude, knew they had earned it, the people crowding around him began to disperse. Reave walked away among them. In a short time, he had gained admittance to the usurer's place of business and was speaking to the usurer himself.

The usurer supplied Reave with the name of the widow Huchette. After all, Jillet had offered her wealth as collateral in his attempt to obtain gold. Despite his acknowledged relation to Jillet, however, Reave was not satisfied by the information which the usurer was able to give him. Their conversation sent him searching for alchemists until he located the one he needed.

The alchemist who had conceived Jillet's stratagem against the widow did not find Reave's clarity of appearance and quietness of manner reassuring: quite the reverse. In fact, he was barely able to restrain himself from hurling smoke in Reave's face and attempting to escape through the window. In his wildest frights and fancies, he had never considered that Reave the Just himself might task him for the advice he had sold to Jillet. Nevertheless, something in the open, vivid gaze which Reave fixed upon him convinced him that he could not hope for escape. Smoke would not blind Reave; and when the alchemist dived out the window, Reave would be there ahead of him, waiting.

Mumbling like a shamed child—and inwardly cursing Reave for having this effect upon him—the alchemist revealed the nature of his transaction with Jillet. Then, in a spasm of defensive self-abnegation, attempting to deflect Reave's notorious extravagance, he produced the gold which he had received from Jillet and offered it to Jillet's "kinsman."

Reave considered the offer briefly before accepting it. His tone was quiet, but perfectly distinct, as he said, "Jillet must be held accountable for his folly. However, you do not deserve to profit from it." As soon he left the alchemist's dwelling, he flung the coins so far across the hedgerows that the alchemist had no hope of ever recovering them.

In the secrecy of his heart, the alchemist wailed as though he had been bereft. But he permitted himself no sound, either of grief or of protest, until Reave the Just was safely out of hearing.

Alone, unannounced, and without any discernible weapons or defenses, Reave made his way to the manor house of the deceased Rudolph Huchette.

Part of his power, of course, was that he never revealed to anyone precisely how the strange deeds for which he was known were accomplished. As far as the world, or the stories about him which filled the world, were concerned, he simply did what he did. So neither Jillet nor the widow—and certainly not Kelven Divestulata—were ever able to explain the events which took place within the manor house after Reave's arrival. Beginning with that arrival itself, they all saw the events as entirely mysterious.

The first mystery was that the mastiffs patrolling within the walls of the manor house did not bark. The Divestulata's servants were not alerted; no one demanded admittance at the gatehouse, or at any of the doors of the manor. Furthermore, the room in which Jillet was held prisoner was guarded, not merely by dogs and men and bolted doors, but by ignorance: no one in Forebridge knew that the chamber existed. Nevertheless after Jillet's imprisonment had been measured by a dozen or perhaps fifteen thick candles, and his understanding of his circumstances had passed beyond ordinary befuddlement and pain into an awareness of doom so complete that it seemed actively desirable, he prised open his eyelids enough to see a man standing before him in the gloom, a man who was not Kelven Divestulata—a man indeed, who was not anyone Jillet recognized.

Smiling gravely, this man lifted water to Jillet's lips. And when Jillet had drunk what he could, the man put a morsel or two of honeycomb in his mouth. After that, the man waited for Jillet to speak. Water and honey gave Jillet a bit of strength which he had forgotten existed. Trying harder to focus his gaze upon the strange figure smiling soberly before him, he asked. "Have you come to kill me? I thought he did such things himself. And liked them." In Jillet's mind, "he" was always the Divestulata.

The man shook his head. "I am Reave." His voice was firm despite its quietness. "I am here to learn why you have claimed kinship with me."

Under other conditions, Jillet would have found it frightening to be confronted by Reave the Just. As an amiable man himself, he trusted the amiability of others, and so he would not have broadly assumed that Reave meant him ill. Nevertheless, he was vulnerable on the point which Reave mentioned. For several reasons, Jillet was not a deceptive man: one of them was that he did not like to be *found out*—and he was always so easily *found out*. Being discovered in a dishonest act disturbed and shamed him.

At present, however, thoughts of shame and distress were too trivial to be considered. In any case, Kelven had long since bereft him of any instinct for self-concealment he may have possessed. To Reave's inquiry, he replied as well as his sense of doom allowed, "I wanted the widow."

"For her wealth?" Reave asked.

Jillet shook his head. "Wealth seems pleasant, but I do not understand it." Certainly, wealth did not appear to have given either the widow or Kelven any particular satisfaction. "I wanted her."

"Why?"

This question was harder. Jillet might have mentioned her beauty, her youth, her foreignness; he might have mentioned her tragedy. But Reave's clear gaze made those answers inadequate. Finally, Jillet replied, "It would mean something. To be loved by her."

Reave nodded. "You wanted to be loved by a woman whose love was valuable." Then he asked, "Why did you think her love could be gained by alchemy? Love worth having does not deserve to be tricked. And she would never truly love you if you obtained her love falsely."

Jillet considered this question easy. Many candles ago—almost from the beginning—the pain in his arms had given him the feeling that his chest had been torn open, exposing everything. He said, "She would not love me. She would not notice me. I do not know the trick of getting women to give me their love."

"The 'trick,'" Reave mused. "That is inadequate, Jillet. You must be honest with me."

Honey or desperation gave Jillet a moment of strength. "I have been honest since he put me in this place. I think it must be Hell, and I am already dead. How else is it possible for you to be here? You are no kinsman of mine, Reave the Just. Some men are like the widow. Their love is worth having. I do not understand it, but I can see that women notice such men. They give themselves to such men.

"I am not among them. I have nothing to offer that any woman would want. I must gain love by alchemy. If magick does not win it for me, I will never know love at all."

Reave raised fresh water to Jillet's lips. He set new morsels of honeycomb in Jillet's mouth.

Then he turned away.

From the door of the chamber, he said, "In one thing you are wrong, Jillet of Forebridge. You and I are kinsmen. All men are of common blood, and I am bound to any man who claims me willingly." As he left, he added, "You are imprisoned here by your own folly. You must rescue yourself."

Behind him, the door closed, and he was gone. The door was stout, and the chamber had been dug deep: no one heard Jillet's wail of abandonment.

Certainly the widow did not hear it. In truth, she was not inclined to listen for such things. They gave her nightmares—and her life was already nightmare enough. When Reave found her, she was in her bedchamber, huddled upon the bed, sobbing uselessly. About her shoulders she wore the tatters of her nightdress, and her lips and breasts were red with the pressure of Kelven's admiration.

"Madam," said Reave courteously. He appeared to regard her nakedness in the same way he had regarded Jillet's torment. "You are the widow Huchette?"

She stared at him, too numb with horror to speak. In strict honesty, however, her horror had nothing to do with him. It was a natural consequence of the Divestulata's lovemaking. Now that he was done with her, he had perhaps sent one of his grooms or serving men or business associates to enjoy her similarly.

"You have nothing to fear from me," her visitor informed her in a kindly tone. "I am Reave. Men call me 'Reave the Just.'"

The widow was young, foreign, and ignorant of the world; but none of those hindrances had sufficed to block her from hearing the stories which surrounded him. He was the chief legend of the North Counties: he had been discussed in her presence ever since Rudolph had brought her to Forebridge. On that basis, she had understood the danger of Jillet's claim when she had first met him; and on that same basis she now uttered a small gasp of surprise. Then she became instantly wild with hope. Before he could speak again, she began to sob, "Oh, sir, bless Heaven that you have come! You must help me, you must! My life is anguish, and I can bear no more! He rapes me and rapes me, he forces me to do the most vile things at his whim, we are not wed, do not believe him if he says that we are wed, my husband is dead, and I desire no other, oh, sir! you must help me!"

"I will consider that, madam," Reave responded as though he were unmoved. "You must consider, however, that there are many kinds of help. Why have you not helped yourself?"

Opening her mouth to pour out a torrent of protest, the widow stopped suddenly, and a deathly pallor blanched her face. "Help myself?" she whispered. "Help myself?"

Reave fixed his clear gaze upon her and waited.

"Are you mad?" she asked, still whispering.

"Perhaps." He shrugged. "But I have not been raped by Kelven Divestulata. I do not beg succor. Why have you not helped yourself?"

"Because I am a woman!" she protested, not in scorn, but piteously. "I am helpless. I have no strength of arm, no skill with weapons, no knowledge of the world, no friends. He has made himself master of everything which might once have aided me. It would be a simpler matter for me to tear apart these walls than to defend myself against him."

Again, Reave shrugged. "Still he is a rapist—and likely a murderer. And I see that you are not bruised. Madam, why do you not resist him? Why do you not cut his throat while he sleeps? Why do you not cut your own if his touch is so loathsome to you?"

The look of horror which she now turned on him was unquestionably personal, caused by his questions, but he was not deterred by it. Instead he took a step closer to her.

"I offend you, madam. But I am Reave the Just, and I do not regard who is offended. I will search you further." His eyes replied to her horror with a flame which she had not seen in them before, a burning of clear rage. "Why have you done nothing to help Jillet? He came to you in innocence and ignorance as great as your own. His torment is as terrible as yours. Yet you crouch there on your soft bed and beg for rescue from an oppressor you do not oppose, and you care nothing what becomes of him."

The widow may have feared that he would step closer to her still and strike her, but he did not. Instead, he turned away.

At the door, he paused to remark, "As I have said, there are many kinds of help. Which do you merit, madam?"

He departed her bedchamber as silently as he had entered it, leaving her alone.

The time now was near the end of the day, and still neither Kelven himself nor his dogs nor his servingmen knew that Reave the Just moved freely through the manor house. They had no reason to know, for he approached no one, addressed no one, was seen by no one. Instead, he waited until night came and grew deep over Forebridge, until grooms and breeders, cooks and scullions, servingmen and secretaries had retired to their quarters, until only the hungry mastiffs were awake within the walls because the guards who should have tended them had lost interest in their duties. He waited until Kelven, alone in his study, had finished readying his plans to ruin an ally who had aided him loyally during a recent trading war, and had poured himself a glass of fine brandy so that he would have something to drink while he amused himself with Jillet. Only then did Reave approach the Divestulata's desk in order to study him through the dim light of the lamps.

Kelven was not easily taken aback, but Reave's unexpected appearance came as a shock. "Satan's balls!" he growled shamelessly. "Who in hell are *you*?"

His visitor replied with a smile which was not at all kindly. "I am grieved," he admitted, "that you did not believe I would come. I am not as well known as I had thought—or men such as you do not sufficiently credit my reputation. I am Reave the Just."

If Reave anticipated shock, distress, or alarm in response to this announcement, he was disappointed. Kelven took a moment to consider the situation, as though to assure himself that he had heard rightly. Then he leaned back in his chair and laughed like one of his mastiffs.

"So he spoke the truth. What an amazing thing. But you are slow, Reave the Just. That purported kinsman of yours has been dead for days. I doubt that you will ever find his grave."

"In point of fact," Reave replied in an undisturbed voice, "we are not kinsmen. I came to Forebridge to discover why a man of no relation would claim me as he did. Is he truly dead? Then I will not learn the truth from him. That"—in the lamplight, Reave's eyes glittered like chips of mica—"will displease me greatly, Kelven Divestulata."

Before Kelven could respond, Reave asked, "How did he die?"

"How?" Kelven mulled the question. "As most men do. He came to the end of himself." The muscles of his jaw bunched. "You will encounter the same fate yourself—eventually. Indeed, I find it difficult to imagine why you have not done so already. Your precious reputation"—he pursed his lips—"is old enough for death."

Reave ignored this remark. "You are disingenuous, Kelven. My question was less philosophical. How did Jillet die? Did you kill him?"

"I? Never!" Kelven's protest was sincere. "I believe he brought it upon himself. He is a fool, and he died of a broken heart."

"Pining, no doubt," Reave offered by way of explanation, "for the widow Huchette—"

A flicker of uncertainty crossed Kelven's gaze. "No doubt."

"—whom you pretend to have married, but who is in fact your prisoner and your victim in her own house."

"She is my *wife!*" Kelven snapped before he could stop himself. "I have claimed her. I do not need public approval, or the petty sanctions of the law, for my desires. I have claimed her, and she is *mine.*"

The lines of Reave's mouth, and the tightening about his eyes, suggested a variety of retorts, which he did not utter. Instead, he replied mildly, "I observe that you find no fault with my assertion that this house is hers."

Kelven spat. "Paugh! Do they call you 'Reave the Just' because you are honest, or because you are 'just a fool'? This house was awarded to me publicly, by a *magistrate*, in compensation for harm done to my interests by that dead thief, Rudolph Huchette."

The Divestulata's intentions against Reave, which he had announced to Jillet, grew clearer with every passing moment. For some years now, upon occasions during the darkest hours of the night, and in the deepest privacy of his heart, he had considered himself, to be the natural antagonist of men like Reave—self-righteous meddlers whose notions of virtue cost themselves nothing and their foes everything. In part, this perception of himself arose from his own native and organic malice; in part, it sprang from his awareness that most of his victories over lesser men—men such as Jillet—were too easy, that for his own well-being he required greater challenges.

Nevertheless, this conversation with his natural antagonist was not what he would have wished it to be. His plans did not include any defense of himself: he meant to attack. Seeking to capture the initiative, he countered, "However, my ownership of this house—like my ownership of Rudolph's relict—is not your concern. If you have any legitimate concern here, it involves Jillet, not me. By what honest right do you sneak into my house and my study at this hour of the night in order to insult me with questions and innuendos?"

Reave permitted himself a rather ominous smile. As though he were ignoring what Kelven had just asked, he replied, "My epithet, 'the Just,' derives from coinage. It concerns both the measure and the refinement of gold. When a coin contains the exact weight and purity of gold which it should contain, it is said to be 'just.' You may not be aware, Kelven Divestulata, that the honesty of any man is revealed by the coin with which he pays his debts."

"Debts?" Involuntarily, Kelven sprang to his feet. He could not contain his anger sitting. "Are you here to annoy me with *debts?*"

"Did you not kill Jillet?" Reave countered.

"I did *not!* I have done many things to many men, but I did not kill that insufferable clod! *You,*" he shouted so that Reave would not stop him, "have insulted me enough. Now you will tell me why you are here—how you *justify* your actions—or I will hurl you to the ground outside my window and let my dogs feed on you, and *no one* will dare criticize me for doing so to an intruder in my study in the dead of night!"

"You do not need to attack me with threats." Reave's self-assurance was maddening. "Honest men have nothing to fear from me, and you are threat enough just as you stand. I will tell you why I am here.

"I am Reave the Just. I have come as I have always come, for blood—the blood of kinship and retribution. Blood is the coin in which I pay my debts, and it is the coin in which I exact restitution.

"I have come for your blood, Kelven Divestulata."

The certainty of Reave's manner inspired in Kelven an emotion he did not recognize—and because he did not recognize it, it made him wild. *"For what?"* he raged at his visitor. "What have I done? Why do you want my blood? I tell you, *I did not kill your damnable Jillet!"*

"Can you prove that?"

"Yes!"

"How?"

Shaken by the fear he did not recognize, Kelven shouted, "He is still alive!"

Reave's eyes no longer reflected the lamplight. They were dark now, as deep as wells. Quietly, he asked, "What *have* you done to him?"

Kelven was confused. One part of him felt that he had gained a victory. Another knew that he was being defeated. "He amuses me," the Divestulata answered harshly. "I have made him a toy. As long as he continues to amuse me, I will continue to play with him."

When he heard those words, Reave stepped back from the desk. In a voice as implacable as a sentence of death, he said, "You have confessed to the unlawful imprisonment and torture of an innocent man. I will go now and summon a magistrate. You will repeat your confession to him. Perhaps that act of honesty will inspire you to confess as well the crimes you have committed upon the person of the widow Huchette.

"Do not attempt to escape, Kelven Divestulata. I will hunt you from the vault of Heaven to the pit of Hell, if I must. You have spent blood, and you will pay for it with blood."

For a moment longer, Reave the Just searched Kelven with his bottomless gaze. Then he turned and strode toward the door. An inarticulate howl rose in Kelven's throat. He snatched up the first heavy object he could find, a brass paperweight thick enough to crush a man's skull, and hurled it at Reave.

It struck Reave at the base of his neck so hard that he stumbled to his knees.

At once, Kelven flung himself past his desk and attacked his visitor. Catching one fist in Reave's hair, he jerked Reave upright: with the other, he gave Reave a blow which might have killed any lesser man.

Blood burst from Reave's mouth. He staggered away on legs that appeared spongy, too weak to hold him. His arms dangled at his sides as though he had no muscle or sinew with which to defend himself.

Transported by triumph and rage and stark terror, the Divestulata pursued his attack.

Blow after blow he rained upon Reave's head: blow after blow he drove into Reave's body. Pinned against one of the great bookcases which Rudolph Huchette had lovingly provided for the study, Reave flopped and lurched whenever he was struck, but he could not escape. He did not fight back; he made no effort to ward Kelven away. In moments, his face became a bleeding mass; his ribs cracked; his heart must surely have faltered.

But he did not fall.

The utter darkness in his eyes never wavered. It held Kelven and compromised nothing.

Reave's undamaged and undaunted gaze seemed to drive Kelven past rage into madness. Immersed in ecstasy or delirium, he did not hear the door of the study slam open.

His victims were beyond stealth. In truth, neither the widow Huchette nor Jillet could have opened the door quietly. They lacked the strength. Every measure of will and force she possessed, she used to support him, to bear him forward when he clearly could not move or stand on his own. And every bit of resolve and desire that remained to him, he used to hold aloft the decorative halberd, which was the only weapon he and the widow had been able to find in the halls of the manor house.

As weak as cripples, nearly dying from the strain of their exertions, they crossed the study behind Kelven's back.

They were slow, desperate, and unsteady in their approach. Nevertheless, Reave stood patiently and let his antagonist hammer him until Jillet brought the halberd down upon Kelven Divestulata's skull and killed him.

Then through the blood which drenched his face from a dozen wounds, Reave the Just smiled.

Unceremoniously, both Jillet and the widow collapsed.

Reave stooped and pulled a handkerchief from Kelven's sleeve. Dabbing at his face, he went to the desk, where he found Kelven's glass and the decanter of brandy. When he had discovered another glass, he filled it as well; then he carried the glasses to the man and woman who had rescued him. First one and then the other, he raised their heads and helped them to drink until they were able to sit and clutch the glasses and swallow without his support.

After that, he located a bellpull and rang for the Divestulata's steward.

When the man arrived—flustered by the late summons, and astonished by the scene in the study—Reave announced, "I am Reave the Just. Before his death, Kelven Divestulata confessed his crimes to me, in particular that he obtained possession of this house by false means, that he exercised his lusts in violent and unlawful fashion upon the person of the widow Huchette, and that he imprisoned and tortured my kinsman, Jillet of Forebridge, without cause. I will state before the magistrates that I heard the Divestulata's confession, and that he was slain in my aid, while he was attempting to kill me. From this moment, the widow is once again mistress of her house, with all its possessions and retainers. If you and all those under you do not serve her honorably, you will answer both to the magistrates and to me.

"Do you understand me?"

The steward understood. Kelven's servants were silent and crafty men, and perhaps some of them were despicable; but none were stupid. When Reave left the widow and Jillet there in the study, they were safe.

They never saw him again.

As he had promised, he spoke to the magistrates. When they arrived at the manor house shortly after dawn, supported by a platoon of County pikemen and any number of writs, they confirmed that they had received Reave's testimony. Their subsequent researches into Kelven's ledgers enabled them to validate much of what Reave had said; Jillet and the widow confirmed the rest. But Reave himself did not appear again in Forebridge. Like the story that brought him, he was gone. A new story took his place.

This also was entirely characteristic.

Once the researches and hearings of the magistrates were done, the widow Huchette passed out of Jillet's life as well. She had released him from his bonds and the chamber where he was imprisoned; she had half carried him to the one clear deed he had ever performed. But after Rudolph Huchette she had never wanted another husband; and after Kelven Divestulata she never wanted another man. She did one thing to express her gratitude toward Jillet: she repaid his debt to the usurer. Then she closed her doors to him, just as she did to all other men with love potions and aspirations for her. In time, the manor house became a kind of nunnery, where lost or damaged women could go for succor, and no one else was welcome.

Jillet himself, who probably believed that he would love the widow Huchette to the end of his days, found he did not miss her. Nor, in all candor, did he miss Reave, After all, he had nothing in common with them: she was too wealthy; he was too stringent. No, Jillet was quite content without such things. And he had gained something which he prized more highly—the story; the idea.

The story that he had struck the blow which brought down Kelven Divestulata.

The idea that he was kinsman to Reave the Just.

The Woman Who Loved Pigs

Fern loved pigs, but in all the village of Sarendel-on-Gentle she may have been the only woman who did not own one.

Gentle's Rift down which the river ran was at once fertile and isolated. The wains of the merchanters came through in season, trading salt by the pound and fabric by the bolt for wheat and barley by the ton; there were no other visitors. And the good people along the river wanted none—especially after they had listened to the merchanters' tales of the larger world, tales of wars and warlocks, princes and intrigues. Their lives in the Rift were like the Gentle itself, steady and untroubled. Whether poor or comfortable, solitary or gregarious, the villages and hamlets had only four essential activities—their children, their farms, their animals, and their ale. Pleasure produced their children, work in the fields and with the animals produced their food, and ale was their reward.

Among the fields and meadows, cows were precious for their milk, as well as for their strength at the plow. And pigs made better meat. For that reason, sows and porkers were common.

It may have been because they were raised for meat—because they were such solid creatures, and so doomed—that Fern loved them, although they were not hers.

In Sarendel she knew them all by their size and coloring, their personalities and parentage. Recognizing her love, they came to her whenever they could. And she adored their coming to her, as though she were a great lady visited by royalty.

Yet she took nothing which was not granted to her, and so she returned them. Before she returned them, however, she pampered them as best she could in the brief time her honesty allowed her, tending their small sores and abrasions, offering them the comfits and comforts she was occasionally able to scavenge for them, scratching their ears when she had no treats to offer. She wept for the porkers and flattered the sows. Since she had no language of her own, their throaty voices were articulate enough for her; she knew how to warm her heart with their snorts and grunts of affection.

When they strayed among the hills, she could divine where they were, and so she was able to recover them. When they misplaced their piglets, she found the young and brought them home—her ear for the thin squeals of the lost was unerring. When the sows suffered farrowing, she came to them from wherever her scavenging took her, bringing poultices and caresses which eased the piglets out.

The good people of Sarendel could not comprehend the sounds which came from her mouth, but they understood the importance of gratitude and kindliness in a small village. When Fern had performed her small services for the creatures she loved, the farmwives and alemaids to whom they belonged thanked her with gifts of food, which did more to keep breath in her body than the sustenance she scavenged.

Indeed, in gratitude one of her fellow villagers would almost certainly have given her a pig, had she been capable of raising it. Alas, that steady nurturance would have been beyond her. In a village where poverty was common but active want was rare, Fern was destitute. If Yoel the aleman had not allowed her a disused storeshed to serve as her hovel, she would have had no place to live. If the farmwives had not given her scraps of weaving and discarded dresses, she would have had no clothes. If Sarendel-on-Gentle had not granted her the freedom of its refuse, she would have lacked food more often than had it. Her parents had been poor—her father a farm laborer, her mother a scrubwoman—able to feed and clothe and shelter her, but little more; and they were long dead. From dawn to dusk she was friendless as only those to whom words meant nothing could be, comforted only by the affection of the sows and porkers.

If she owned a pig—so the village believed—she would have fed it before she fed herself; and so she would have died.

Even with only herself to keep alive, no one would have been surprised to find her dead one morning among the fields or beside the river. Her life was a small thing, even by the ordinary standards of Sarendel-on-Gentle. The village in turn was a small thing along the verdant Rift. And the Gentle's Rift itself was a small thing within the wide world of Andovale, where princes and warlocks had their glory.

No one took note—or had cause to take note—when Fern of Sarendel-on-Gentle was adopted by a pig.

He was not a handsome pig, or a large one. Indeed, she saw as soon as she looked at him that he was dying of hunger. His brindled skin showed splotches of disease, as well as of scruffy parentage. Stains and gashes marked his grizzled snout. One eye appeared to be nearly blind;

the other was flawed by a strange sliver of argent like a silver cut. In the early dew of dawn, he shouldered his way into her hovel as though he had traveled all night for many nights to reach her, lay himself down at her feet, rolled his miscolored eyes at her weakly, and began at once to sleep like the dead.

Fern had only seen that sleep once before—a sleep without the twitches and snuffles, the unconscious rootings of a pig's dreams. She had no measure of time, and so she did not know when it was, but on some prior occasion she had found a lost sow far from the village. The sow had broken her leg crossing a streambed. The disturbance of the rocks and mud showed that she had struggled for hours, perhaps for days; then she had lost heart. She was asleep when Fern found her, and Fern could not rouse her; she slept until she died.

Fern understood instantly that the pig now asleep at her feet was like that sow—brokenhearted and near to dying.

As she looked at him, however, an image formed in her mind. It was unfamiliar because she was a creature of instinct and did not think in images.

Rueweed.

Rueweed and pigsbane.

Also carrots.

Rueweed was poison to both pigs and cattle, as everyone knew. And pigsbane was presumed to be poison, for the simple reason that pigs refused to eat it—and pigs were known to be clever in such matters. Nevertheless Fern did not hesitate. The images which had come into her head were like the voiceless promptings that told her when one of the pigs of the village was in need of her. She did not question them any more than she questioned why this pig had come to her—or where he had come from. She had seen Meglan, one of the farmwives, working in her carrot patch yesterday. Perhaps there would be carrots in Meglan's refuse-tip today. And Fern knew where to find rueweed and pigsbane. Hurrying because a pig had come to her for his life, she clutched the scraps which served as her cloak around her and ran from her hovel.

Along the one street which passed over the hills and became Sarendel-on-Gentle's link to the other villages of the Rift, past both alehouses, into a little lane which separated thatch-roofed shacks from more prosperous homes of timber and dressed stone, she made her way in a scurry of haste. An observer who did not know her would have thought she looked furtive. However, the villagers were accustomed to her crouching gait and her habitual way of keeping to the walls and hedges as if she feared to be accosted by someone who might expect her to speak, and so she passed as unremarked as a wraith among the dwellings to Meglan's home on the outskirts of the village.

Apparently unaware of Meglan spading her vegetables outside the house, Fern went directly to the refuse-tip beyond the fence and began rooting in her human fashion among the farmwife's compost.

Meglan paused to watch. She was a kindly woman, and Fern's haste suggested extreme hunger. When she saw how Fern pounced on the remaining peels and tassels of yesterday's stew, the farmwife unthinkingly pulled up a fresh handful of carrots, strode to the fence, and offered the carrots over the rails to Fern.

Too urgent to be gracious, Fern snatched the carrots, snuffled a piggy thanks, and scuttled away toward the hills as fast as her scrawny, unfed limbs could carry her.

Pigsbane. Rueweed. Meglan's generosity had already fallen into Fern's vague past, in one sense vividly remembered, in another quite forgotten. In her present haste she could not have formed any conception of how she had come by so much largesse as a handful of fresh carrots. Her head held nothing except rueweed and pigsbane and the need for speed.

It did not occur to her to fret over the fact that centuries of habitation had cleared all such plants away around the village for at least a mile in any direction. She did not fret over facts. They simply existed, unalterable. Yet she was afraid, and her fear pushed her faster than her strength could properly carry her. A pig had come to her, heartbroken and dying. She did not understand time, but she understood that when the pig's broken heart became cold death it would be a fact, as unalterable as the location of pigsbane and rueweed on the distant hillsides. Therefore she was afraid, and so she ran and stumbled and fell and ran again faster than she could endure.

Scarcely an hour had passed when she returned to her hovel, clutching the fruits of her scavenging in the scraps of her clothes. Sweat left streaks in the grime of her cheeks, and her eyes were glazed with exhaustion; she could have collapsed and slept and perhaps died without a moment's pause. Nevertheless she was still full of fear. And when she looked at the pig sprawled limp and hardly breathing in the dirt of her hovel, new images entered her mind.

She had no fire for heat, no mortar and pestle for grinding; she made do with what she had. First she tore the pigsbane to scraps. Scrubbing one stone over another, she reduced the scraps to flakes and shreds. Then she set them to soak in a bowl of water.

Shaking with tiredness and fear, she broke open the leaves of rue-weed and rubbed their pungent odor—the tang of poison—under the pig's snout.

With a snort and a wince, the pig pulled his head back and blinked open his eyes. One of his eyes was unquestionably blind, but the other flashed its slice of silver at her.

At once, Fern set her bowl of soaking pigsbane in front of him. In relief rather than surprise—how could she be surprised, when all facts were the same to her?—she watched him drink.

When he had emptied the bowl, she gave him the carrots.

That was all she could do. If she had understood time, she would have known that she herself had eaten nothing for at least a day and a half. Her fear and strength were used up. Curling herself against the pig's back to keep him warm, she sank into sleep.

She did not think of death. Her heart was not broken.

Sleep was a familiar place for her, full of colors which might have been emotions and the affectionate snuffling of sows suckling their young. But after a time the colors and sounds became more images, and these were not familiar.

She saw the silver cut of the pig's eye rising like a new moon over the night of her mind.

She saw herself. How she knew it was herself was unclear, since her only knowledge of her appearance came from reflections in the moving waters of the Gentle, yet she did know it. And she knew also that it was herself beaten and weary, nearly cold with extinction.

Although the image was of herself, however, it did not disturb her. She gazed at it the same way that she gazed at all the world, as a fact about which there were no questions.

A crimson hue which might have been vexation or despair washed the image away, and another took its place.

In this image, she rose from her hovel and went to the nearest ale-house. There she scratched at the rear door until the aleman opened it. Then she dropped to her knees and made supplicating gestures toward her belly and mouth.

This image did disturb her. It came to her clad in the yellow of lament. She was Fern. She accepted gifts, but she did not ask for anything which was not hers. The image of pleading sent tears across the trails of sweat on her sleeping cheeks.

Nevertheless the thin sliver of argent in her mind and in the pig's eye bound her to him. He had come to her, adopted her: she was already his. When she awoke, she pulled her scraps of clothing about her and crept weeping along the street to Jessup's alehouse, where she scratched at the door behind the building until he answered. Filled with yellow and tears, she fell to her knees and begged for food with the only words she knew—the movements of her hands.

From his doorway Jessup peered at her and frowned. He was not known for Meglan's unthinking generosity. Stern and plain in all his dealings, he had used his father's alehouse to make himself wealthy—as such things were measured in Sarendel—and he liked his wealth. He made good ale and expected to be paid for it. Farmers and weavers, potters and laborers, men and women who wished to drink their ale today and settle their scores tomorrow were strictly required to take their custom to Yoel's alehouse, not Jessup's. In some other village, in some other part of Andovale, Jessup would have closed his door in Fern's face and thought no more about it.

But here, in Sarendel-on-Gentle, beggary was unknown. Jessup had not learned to refuse an appeal as naked as hers. Fern herself *was* well-known, however: both her destitution and her honesty were as familiar as the village itself. On this occasion, her plight was as plain as emaciation and grime, tears and rags could make it. And finally, at Jessup's back door there were no witnesses. No one would see what he did and think that he had become less strict. With a black scowl, he retreated to his kitchen and brought out a jug of broth, a slab of bread, and an earthen flask of ale, which he thrust into Fern's unsteady hands.

Snuffling grief instead of thanks, she returned to her hovel.

She did not want to eat the bread or drink the broth and ale. She felt that a violation had taken place. She had been hurt in some way for which she had no words and no understanding. She took nothing which was not granted to her. But as soon as she reentered her dwelling the brindled pig fixed his eyes upon her. He could scarcely lift his head; he clearly had no strength to stand. His exhaustion was as profound as hers, and as fatal. The danger that he would starve had been only briefly postponed. And the scabs and splotches which marked his hide were plain signs of illness rather than injury. Yet he fixed his eyes upon her—the one blind, the other flawed with silver—and she found that she could not refuse to eat. Did she not love pigs? And had he not come to her in his last need?

Held by his gaze, she chewed the bread and drank the broth. With a pig's cleverness she knew that the ale was too strong for her, so she did not touch it. Instead she poured it out in a bowl and set it under his snout so that he could have it.

When he had consumed it all, he drew a shuddering breath which she interpreted as pleasure. And that in turn pleased her more than any amount of food or drink for herself.

Together they slept again.

So Fern became a beggar—and so her pig's life was saved. Each time she slept, the images came to her: more scratching at doors, more supplication. And each time she awoke she acted on them with less sorrow. The loss of her honesty had become a fact, unalterable. Instead of grieving, she used the strength of new sustenance to scavenge for her pig. She was able to roam more widely, root more deeply. She found grains and vegetables for him, as well as herbs from which she concocted healing poultices and balms. Steadily, if slowly, he drew vitality from her care and began to mend.

After several nights, the images stopped. They were no longer needed. In their place, her head was filled with the soothing cerulean and emerald which she had always gained from the affection of pigs, and occasionally she heard sounds—silent except within her head—which might have been, *My thanks*. She felt the gratitude in them; but the sounds themselves meant nothing to her, so at last she concluded that they were the pig's name, and she took to calling him "Mythanks." That was the first word she had ever spoken, the only word she knew. She hugged him morning and night, and caressed him whenever the mood came upon her, and whispered fondly in his ears, "Mythanks, Mythanks," and her regret for the woman she had once been became vague with the uncertainty of all time.

When perhaps a fortnight had passed, Mythanks was well enough to join her in her scavenging. Although he was still weak, he trotted briskly at her side, scenting the air and scanning the vistas like a creature which had come to a new world. Uncharacteristically for a pig, he sniffed and snorted at every grass and herb and shrub they encountered as though he were teaching himself to know them for the first time. He surveyed the hillsides as though he were measuring distances and possibilities. He shied away from passing herd-dogs and farmers as though they might be his enemies, despite the fact that no one in Sarendel-on-Gentle would harm a pig—until the time came to slaughter the porkers and the aging sows. And when the herd-dogs and farmers were gone, he rubbed his bristled back against Fern's legs with a pig's desire for reassurance. Because he was not yet fully hale, he could not roam far; and so the day's scavenging found him less food than he wanted. This worried Fern. She thought she saw a look of discouragement—or was it calculation?—in Mythanks' strange eyes. However she petted and coddled him, he did not nuzzle her fondly, or fill her head with the hues of gratitude. He had adopted her. He was her responsibility, and her care of him was inadequate. When a tear or two of remorse caught and spread on her muddy cheeks, he ignored them.

But the next day he went with her while she begged.

Prompted by her instinct to creep from place to place, calling as little attention to herself as possible, she had taken her unwonted supplications to a different villager each day. After the gift of carrots, she had not dared return to Meglan. Certainly she had not approached Jessup again. Rather she had been to Yoel's alehouse, then to widower Horrik's tannery, then to Salla and Veil among the farmwives, then to Karay the weaver and Limm the potter; and so to a new benefactor on every occasion.

On this occasion, however, Mythanks had his own ideas. Directly, as though he had lived in Sarendel all his life and knew it well, he led Fern back to Jessup's alehouse.

Wordlessly alarmed, she could not put her hand to the door at the rear of the alehouse. Jessup's sternness frightened her. If she had not been so near to starvation on that first day, she would not have dared go there at all. She could only watch and wince as Mythanks lifted a foreleg and scratched at the door with his hoof.

When Jessup opened the door and saw her, he did not take the sight kindly.

"You!" he snapped. "Begone! Do not think you can take advantage of me a second time. All the village is talking about your beggary. You have acquired a pig, and now you beg. Did you beg him as well, or have you fallen as low as theft? I would not have fed you so much as once, but I believed that you were honest. I will not make that mistake again."

Fern understood none of his words, but his tone was plain. It hurt her like a blow. Cringing, she tried to shrink down into herself as she turned away.

Mythanks snorted once, softly, and fixed Jessup with his eyes, the one blind, the other flawed by silver.

Jessup made a noise in his throat which frightened Fern more than shouts and abuse. To her ears, it was the strangling gurgle of death.

As if he were stunned, Jessup moved backward into the alehouse and out of sight. Then he returned, carrying a bushel of barley and a large basket overflowing with bread and sausages. These he set at Mythanks' feet without a word. Backward again, he reentered the alehouse and closed the door.

Mythanks sniffed the barley, looked over at Fern where she crouched in alarm, and snorted a pig's laughter.

Fern was astonished. She had never seen so much food. "Mythanks," she murmured because she had no words with which to express her surprise. "Mythanks, Mythanks."

At once his laughter became vexation. New sounds formed in her mind. *My name is not Mythanks, you daft woman. It is Titus. Titus! Do you hear me? TITUS!*

"Ti-tus." Staring at him, she tried the word in her mouth. "Titus. Titus." In her amazement, she failed to notice that she had understood him.

Blue pleasure and green satisfaction came into her head as she said his name. *That,* he replied, *is a distinct improvement.* But her instant of comprehension had passed, and she had no idea what the sounds meant. "Titus."

Hardly aware of what she did, she set the basket of bread and sausages on his back, steadied it with one hand, then propped the bushel of barley on her hip and returned to her hovel. That day they feasted and slept. And the next morning Titus nudged her awake with his snout. When she met his blind and piercing gaze, she heard more sounds in the silence of her mind.

It is time we began. Bread and sausages will feed your body, but they will do nothing to nourish your intelligence. I must have intelligence. Also you are filthy—and filth wards away help. There are many lessons that a pig could teach you. Today we will make a start.

This meant nothing to Fern. The sounds came from him—she accepted that as a fact—but they communicated less than the grunts of pigs. Nevertheless she hugged him happily because he seemed so brisk and whole. Yesterday's fear and surprise were forgotten. She was simply glad that Titus had come to her, and that she had been able to help him, and that she knew his name.

Never mind, he said while he nuzzled her neck. *Perhaps you will understand me in time. For the present, you are willing. I will make that suffice.*

Again he fixed her with the argent sliver of his good eye, and now in images she saw herself leaving her hovel and walking to a secluded bank of the Gentle, where she removed her shreds of clothing, immersed herself in the water, and scrubbed herself with sand until her skin became a color which she had never before seen in her own reflection.

It is a risk, he said as she rose to obey the image. *Change attracts attention, and attention is dangerous. But I need help. We must begin somewhere. Cleanliness will do much to improve your place in this misbegotten pigsty of a village.*

"Titus," she answered, dumbly pleased. "Titus."

Snuffling encouragement, he accompanied her down to the Gentle.

The image he had placed in her mind amazed her entirely, but her compliance did not. She had accepted her obedience to him as a fact. And she was not afflicted with modesty. Her impulse to cower, to avoid notice, grew from other fears than bodily shame. So it was not a hard thing for her to do as Titus directed. Hidden by the overarching boughs of a thirsty willow at the river's edge, she set aside her scraps and entered the water.

Here the Gentle was cool but not cold, and it had worn a fine sandy bottom for itself off the hard edges of time. Under Titus' watchful eye, Fern splashed and bubbled and rubbed until the color of her skin and the feel of her hair were transformed. As she did so, she was filled with a light blue pleasure as quiet and steady as the water. And the blue deepened to azure—she did not know or ask why—when the pig said to her like a promise, *Someday you will ask me what loveliness is, and I will tell you.*

Next he gave her an image in which she scrubbed her clothes as she had cleaned herself. Washing them did not make them whole, but it did give them a gentler touch on the unfamiliar tingle of her skin.

At last she rose from the water as if on this day she had been made new.

As she dressed, two of Yoel's small sons scampered past the willow, looking to avoid the chores which Nell alewife, their mother, had in mind for them. They may have seen Fern or they may not; in either case, their attention was elsewhere. Nevertheless she crouched instinctively against the bole of willow, so that whatever the boys saw would be as unobtrusive as possible.

At once the pleasure in her head changed to the hue of vexation. Perhaps all the colors of her mind were no longer hers, but now belonged to Titus.

Blast you, he muttered, *you have too far to go. And I am helpless.*

Almost as if he wished to punish her for her timidity, he urged her to scavenge all day for wood. And the next day he pushed her to accost one of Yoel's small sons while the boys played truant from Nell's chores. Fern herself did nothing except to put out her hand to pause the boy as he ran, and that was enough to make her heart beat in her throat. Titus did the rest. After he had gazed at the boy for a moment or two with his silver-marred eye, he turned away. Snorting in satisfaction, he led Fern back to their hovel.

Because she loved his satisfaction, she hugged and caressed him and fed him barley-mash. When Yoel's small son and two of his brothers arrived at her storeshed a short time later carrying a firepot full of flame, her ability to grasp that they might have been doing the pig's bidding had already faded. She understood them only because the farmwives sometimes sent her a firepot as an act of kindness, knowing that she had no other flame to keep her alive if the night turned bitter across the Gentle's Rift.

Before she lost her honesty, she had been able to accept gifts. But now kindness dismayed her. She cowered away from the children as though they frightened her.

The youngest boy set the firepot in the dirt beside Fern's woodpile. Staring at her, he asked, "Is she sick, then?"

"You're daft," the middle brother snorted with the contempt of his greater age. "That ain't sick, that's clean."

"Cor!" breathed the oldest. "Who'd have thought she looked like that?" Then he flushed and ducked his head.

While Fern tried to sink out of sight against the wall, Titus stepped in front of her. Standing proudly in the center of the space as if the hovel were a mansion and his, he fixed his eyes on each of the boys until they all nodded in turn. Then he dismissed them with a grunt and a jerk of his head.

"Titus," Fern murmured because she had no other name for her dismay. "Titus."

He looked at her. As if her distress were a question, he said, *Yes, they would be easier—for a time. But then they would begin to fear me, and then I would be lost. However, I seriously doubt that any of these clods and clowns is capable of fearing you. And the children even less than the adults. So I will ask only children for help—and only for you. The rest must be kept between the two of us.*

Seeing that she was not comforted, he nuzzled at her until she came away from the wall to scratch his ears. Then he added, *I will take it as a personal triumph if you are ever able to say* yes *to me of your own accord.*

Yes, Fern thought to herself. Yes. It was a strange sound. If it had been the name of a pig, she would have understood it. As matters stood, however, the sound could only trouble her with hints of significance; it could not reach her.

Never mind, he told her again. *For today we have gained enough. When those whelps return, we will cast our net wider.*

She heard sadness in his voice, and so she hugged him with all her strength, seeking to reassure him. *You or no one,* Titus whispered to her embrace, *You must suffice, I have no other hope.*

The boys did not return until evening. While Fern and Titus warmed themselves beside her unaccustomed fire—which she built and tended and kept small according to the images he placed in her mind—hands tugged at the burlap curtain that served as her door, and children entered her hovel. During the day the three had become five, and two of them were girls. They came to her carrying small sacks and tight bundles of herbs.

Here her acceptance of facts failed her. Herbs? For her and Titus? Children did not do such things. Her vague experience of time did not contain those actions. Typically children ignored her; on occasion they teased and tormented her; sometimes they were as kind as a warm breeze. But they did not bring her gifts of witch hazel and thyme, rueweed and coriander, sloewort, and marjoram, and vert. And Titus had not prepared her with images. Whatever she knew and needed in order to live seemed to totter when Yoel's familiar sons and daughters offered her herbs.

In order to grasp what had happened, to accommodate it so that it could be borne, she had to make a leap across time; for her, a profound leap. She had to connect the fact that Titus had looked into Yoel's sons' eyes at some point in the imprecise past with the fact that these children had come here now with herbs. This was a leap greater than understanding that a sow broached in farrow must be helped to release her piglets. It was a leap greater than knowing that the farmwife who offered her a cloak after she had eased the birth pangs of the farmwife's sow did so in thanks. Those events were self-contained, each within its own sequence. But *this*—

As though he sensed her distress, Titus began to fill her head with images.

One of them showed her herself as she nodded in thanks and smiled for the children; it showed her rising from the protection of the wall to surprise them with her cleanliness, and to touch each of them gratefully upon the cheek, and to let them know that it was time for them to return home.

But she obeyed without noticing what she did: her attention was on other images, images which explained what the children had done. In those images, he spoke to them, and they complied. When they brought the herbs he needed to her hovel, they were acting on his instructions.

Yes, Titus told her firmly, almost urgently, as soon as the children were gone, *there* is *a connection. You guessed that, and you were right. You do not understand time, but you can understand that it is no barrier to sequence. If you touch the flame, will you not be burned? If Jessup at the hearth of his alehouse touches the flame, will he not be burned, even though you do not see it? If I ask you to bathe, do you not go to the river and cleanse yourself? It is not otherwise with these whelps, or with time. One thing will lead another because it must.*

Yes, Fern repeated because that was the only sound she recognized. Yes, Titus.

She meant neither *yes* nor *no,* but only that she knew no other response. Nevertheless she saw clearly what he gave her to see: he had spoken to the boys as he spoke to her, silent and silver; those sounds conveyed images to them, which they had heeded; obediently they had hunted the hills for herbs and brought them to her, telling no one what they did. Again and again the events played through her, showing her the links between them, until she fell asleep; sleeping, she dreamed of nothing else. And when she awakened, the connection had become secure.

Across time, and against all likelihood, Yoel's children had brought these herbs because Titus had asked it of them.

At her side, Titus snored heavily, sleeping as though he had been awake all night to weave images. He did not rouse when she scratched his throat; dreams and images were gone from her head.

But the connection remained.

"Yes," she said aloud, although he did not hear her.

The sound *Titus* meant this pig. The sound *Yes* meant the connection. One thing will lead to another because it must.

She had no idea what all these herbs were for, so she left them where they lay. After a fine breakfast of bread and sausages and clear water, she spent the morning hunting wood; then she returned to her hovel to find Titus awake at last.

About time, he snorted. *Did you think I gathered all these herbs for my health?* But the hue of his mood was reassuring, and the images he wove for her had an itch of excitement in them.

She set to work promptly under his watchful gaze. When she had built up her fire from its embers, she turned to the gifts Yoel's children had brought. In a bowl of water she mixed marjoram *(Not too much),* vert *(Just so),* coriander and thyme *(More than that, more),* and sloe-wort *(Only a pinch, you daft woman, I said only a **pinch**).* This she settled in the flames to boil, and as it heated she crushed rueweed *(Better if it were dry, but it will have to serve)* and a little witch hazel into a smaller pot. Once she had ground the leaves as fine as she could, she stirred in enough water to make a paste with a smell so acute that her nose ran.

Wipe it on a rag, not your hand, he told her imperiously. *You already need another bath.* However, he gave her no images to compel her. His attention was on the bowl steaming among the coals.

At his behest, she stirred the herbs vigorously while they boiled; then she pulled the bowl from the flames and set it in the dirt to cool.

Hints of green and blue and a strange, raw crimson flickered at the edges of her mind while she and the pig waited. Titus was excited, she felt that. And expectant, awaiting another connection. And anxious—

Anxious? Was it possible for the connection to fail? Had he not told her that one thing will lead to another?

Because it must, he finished brusquely. *Yes. But it is possible to misunderstand or misuse the sequence. And it is possible for the sequence to be obstructed. It may be that you are too stupid, even for me.*

His tone saddened her, but she did not know how to say so.

Instructed by images, she stirred the herb broth again, then scooped a measure of the thick liquid into a broken-rimmed cup—the last container she owned. New images followed. Titus showed her drinking from the cup, showed her face twisting in disgust showed her spitting the broth into the dirt. Then, so vehemently that her head rang and her limbs flinched, he forbade her to do what she had just seen. Instead she must swallow the broth, no matter how it gagged her. After that she must dip one finger into the paste of rueweed and witch hazel, and place a touch of it upon her tongue. That would cure her need to gag.

He was Titus, the pig who had adopted her; he was her only connection in all the world. She wished to shy away from the broth, but she did not do so. Thinking, Yes, with her peculiar understanding of the word, she gulped down the contents of the cup.

It felt like thistles in her throat; it stung her stomach like thorns and immediately surged back toward her mouth. Her face twisted; she hunched to vomit. Yet Titus' images held her. Obeying them, her finger stabbed at the paste, carried it to her tongue.

That flavor was as acrid as gall, but it accomplished what he had promised: instantly it stilled her impulse to gag. Her body felt that it had suffered another violation; however, the sensation faded swiftly. By the time her heart had beat three times, she was no longer in distress.

The pig rewarded her with a vivid display of pleasure and satisfaction, as bright as the sun on the waters of the Gentle and as comforting as dawn on her face. *Well done,* he breathed, although she did not know those words. *You are indeed willing. The fault will not be yours if I fail.* Then he added, *As you grow accustomed to it, it will become less burdensome.*

"Yes?" she murmured, asking him for the sequence, the connection. Without words or knowledge, she wished to comprehend what he did.

Now, however, he did not appear to understand her.

He required her to drink the broth again at sunset, and again at dawn and noontime. And when the sun had set once more, Yoel's children returned, bringing four or five of their young friends as well as more and firewood. They also brought bread and carrots, corn and bacon, butter and apples and sausages and beans, which they had appropriated from their parents' kitchens. Now Fern was not a beggar: she was a thief. But she did not see the connection, and so she was not disturbed by it. Instead she was simply gladdened that she did not need to abase herself for so much good food.

For perhaps another fortnight, Titus impelled her to do nothing new or strange. Indeed, her life became simpler than it had ever been, so simple that she hardly regarded its unfamiliar ease. Apparently he was now content. Three times a day she drank the broth and touched her tongue with the paste. Often she bathed in the Gentle. And she stopped pressing her bones against the wall when the children—at least a dozen of them now at various intervals—came to her hovel. More than often, she smiled; once she was so filled by pleasure that she laughed outright. The rest of her days and nights were spent sleeping with Titus, roaming the hills with him, caressing and cozying him, or perhaps watching the games and play of the children, and then studying the images in her mind while Titus showed her the sequences which explained what the children did.

She owned a pig, and she was happy. Only her lack of self-consciousness prevented her from knowing that she was happy. If other pigs needed her, she failed to hear their cries or feel their distress. And they no longer came to her when they succeeded at wandering away from their homes. But her knowledge of time was still uncertain, and she did not notice the change. Of course, the village noticed. With the selective blindness of adults, the farmers and farmwives, the weavers and potters declined to recognize the surreptitious activities of their children; but they had known Fern long enough to mark the change in her. They saw her new cleanliness, her new health; they saw the gradual alteration in the way she walked. When she raised her head, the brightness in her eyes was plain. And all Sarendel could hardly fail to observe that wherever she went she was accompanied by a pig which belonged to no one else.

Strange things were rare in Sarendel-on-Gentle. They were worthy of discussion.

"A beggar!" Jessup protested in his taproom. "That pig has made her a beggar, I swear it."

"Be fair, Jessup," rumbled widower Horrik the tanner. He was a large man with large appetites. He still missed his wife, but because of Fern's cleanliness he had begun to see her in new ways, ways which did not altogether distress him. "She was only a beggar for a short time. Was it as much as a fortnight? Now she lives otherwise."

He looked around the taproom, hoping that someone would tell him how Fern lived.

No one did. Instead, Meglan's husband, Wall, said, "In any case, Jessup, you must be sensible." To counteract his softheartedness, Wall placed great store on sense. "The creature is only a pig—and not a prepossessing one, you must admit. How can a pig make her do anything?

Jessup might have retorted sourly, Because she is daft and dumb. She cannot care for a pig with her own wits. However, Karay the weaver was already speaking.

"But where does he come from?" she asked. "That's what I wish to know. Pigs do not fall from the sky—or climb the sides of the Rift. No village is nearer than Cromber, and that is three days distant for a man in haste. At their worst pigs do not wander so far."

Wall and the other farmers nodded sagely. None of them had ever heard of a pig lost more than three miles from home.

Like Wall's, Karay's question was unanswerable. Glowering blackly, Jessup muttered, "I mean what I say. You mark me. That pig is an ill thing, and no good will come of him." He had no name for the silver compulsion which had caused him to give bread, sausages, and barley to Fern. "If she no longer feeds herself by beggary, it is because she has learned a worse trick."

"Be fair," Horrik said again, and Wall repeated, "Be sensible." Nevertheless the men and women gathered in the taproom squirmed uncomfortably at Jessup's words. All Sarendel had heard the tales of the merchanters on their annual drive down the Rift, tales of intrigues and warlocks and wonders. The villagers could adjudge with confidence any matter which was familiar along the Gentle, but who among them could say certainly what was and what was not possible in the wider world?

No more than a day or two later, the wider world offered them an opportunity to ask its opinion. Unprecedented on a white horse, with a rapier at his side and a tassel in his hat, a man entered Sarendel-on-Gentle from the direction of Cromber. In the center of the village, he dismounted. Stamping dust from his boots and wiping sweat from his brow, he waited until Limm the potter and Vail the farmwife came out from their homes to greet him; until every child of the village had arrived as if drawn by magic to the surprise of a stranger; until Yoel and Jessup had left their alehouses, Horrik his tannery, Karay her weaving, and the other farmwives their kitchens and gardens to join the crowd he attracted. Then he swept off his hat, bowed with a long leg, and spoke.

His eyes were road-weary and skeptical, but he smiled and spoke cheerfully. "Good people of Sarendel-on-Gentle, I am Destrier, of the Prince's Roadmen. Lately it has come to Prince Chorl, the lord of all Andovale, that his domain would profit if its many regions and holdings were bound together by a skein of tidings and knowledge. Therefore he has commissioned his Roadmen to travel throughout the land. It is the will of my Prince that I spread the news of Andovale down the Gentle's Rift, and that I bear back to him the news of the Rift's villages and doings. Good people, will you welcome me in Prince Chorl's name?"

Yoel tugged at his leather apron. Because he was an affable man who had shown during the visits of the merchanters that he was not chagrined by strangers, he sometimes spoke on behalf of the village. "Surely," he replied in a slow rumble. "We welcome any man or woman who passes among us. Why should we not? We mean no harm, and expect none." He might have added, We do not require the bidding of princes to extend courtesy. However, his good nature worked against such plain speaking. Instead he continued, "But I fear I do not understand. What manner of news is it that you seek?"

"Why, change, of course," Destrier replied as I though he found Yoel's affability—or his perplexity—charming. "I seek news of change. Any change at all. Change is of endless interest to my Prince."

Yoel received this assertion with some concern, "Change?" He dropped his eyes, and a frown crossed his broad face. Around him, people shifted on their feet and looked away. Children stared at the Roadman as though he might begin to spout poetry. At last Yoel met Destrier's gaze again and shook his head.

"We are as you see us—as we have always been. Along the Gentle we know little of change. Surely the other folk of the Rift have said the same?

"However, it is of no great moment," he went on quickly. "You are road-weary, no doubt thirsty and hungry as well. I must not ask you to remain standing in the sun while I inquire in what way your Prince believes we might have changed. Will you accept the hospitality of my alehouse?" He gestured toward it with an open palm. "Your horse will be cared for. We have no horses here, as you surely know, but the merchanters have taught us how to care for their beasts."

At once Wall stepped forward to place a hand on the reins of the Roadman's mount. "I have a stall to spare in my barn." During the visits of the merchanters, he often profited in a small way by tending their horses.

Smiling with less cheer and more skepticism, Destrier bowed and answered, "My thanks." To Yoel he added, "Aleman, I will gladly accept a flagon and a meal. I do not mean to overstay my welcome, but if you will house and feed me until the morrow, you will earn Prince Chorl's gratitude."

"In plain words," Jessup muttered softly to the farmwife standing near him, "the Prince's Roadman does not propose to pay for his fare. Let Yoel have his custom—and my gratitude as well."

If Destrier heard this remark, he did not acknowledge it. Instead he followed Yoel to the alehouse.

In turn, a good half of the villagers—Jessup among them—followed the Roadman. They desired to hear the tales he would tell of the wide world. And his talk of "change" had made them apprehensive; they wished to know what would come of it. The rest of Sarendel's folk herded their children away and returned to their chores.

While these events transpired, Fern and Titus knew nothing about them. Together they had roamed farther than usual, and they came home late for her midday dose of herbs. However, during the afternoon some of the smaller children made their way to her hovel with the tidings.

The pig responded as though he had been wasp-stung. Fern saw flashes of anger and fear in the air as he turned his one blind eye and his marred one commandingly on the children. Unfortunately, they were too young to give a cogent account of what had happened. Strangers and strangeness caught their attention more than names or words. One child remembered "Roadman." Another babbled of "Prince Chorl." But none of them could say what brought a Roadman to Sarendel, or what Prince Chorl had to do with the matter.

Fools, Titus snorted bitterly. *Guttersnipes. Children. Why has that meddling Prince invented Roadmen? And what damnable mischance has brought this pigsty to his attention? Curse them, I am not ready. I need more time.*

In a voice so harsh that Fern was shocked by it, he cried, *I need more* **time***!*

"Yes," she murmured incoherently, trying to console him. "Yes, Titus." The pig turned on her. Thin silver ran like a cut into her brain.

For an instant she saw an image of herself approaching Yoel's alehouse, entering it to witness what was said and done. She saw herself hearing voices and remembering what they said, remembering words—

But before it was complete the image frayed away, tattered by despair.

You will understand nothing, he groaned. *And they will not allow a pig to enter.*

I must—I must—

He did not say what he must.

But when he had fretted Fern to distraction through the afternoon and evening, his fortunes improved. Late enough to find her yawning uncontrollably and barely able to keep wood on the fire, more children came to her hovel and nudged the curtain to announce themselves. When they entered, she recognized two of the older boys, one Yoel's tallest son, the other Wall and Meglan's boy, who was nearly of a size to begin working in his father's fields. She knew without knowing how she knew that their names were Levit and Lessom.

Titus jumped up to face them. With the familiarity of frequent visits, they dropped to the dirt beside the fire. Fatigue and excitement burned on their faces; their eyes were on a level with his. As if they no longer noticed the oddness of what they did, they spoke to the pig rather than to the woman.

"They told us not to go," Lessom panted, out of breath from running. "We are too young for ale, and we had no business there. But we sneaked into the cellar—Levit knew the way—and found a crack in the floorboards where we could hear. Cor, my legs hurt. We stood for hours and hours.

"Do all grown men talk so, of everything and nothing in the middle of the day, as if they had no work—?"

Titus stopped the rush of words with a flash of his eyes. *Slowly,* Fern heard. *Be complete. I must know everything. Begin at the beginning. Who is he? Where does he come from? What does he want?*

Every line and muscle of the pig's body was tight with strain, as though he were about to flee.

"He is Destrier," Levit offered, "Prince Chorl's Roadman. He said Prince Chorl commissioned the Roadmen to carry news everywhere in Andovale. He said he wants to hear the news from all the villages in the Rift. And he told tales—"

"Cor, the tales!" Lessom breathed. "Better than the merchanters tell. Is it true that there are wars—that warlocks and princes fight each other for power beyond the Rift?"

No! Titus grunted. *Warlocks do not fight princes. The ruling of lands requires too much time and attention. Any warlock who neglects his arts for such things becomes weak. Warlocks reserve their struggles for each other.*

What "news" does this Roadman want?

"Change." Levit's eyes were as round and solemn as a cow's. "He said he wants news of change. Any change. For Prince Chorl."

Impelled by the pig's tension, Fern added more wood to the fire.

Titus held the boys with his gaze. *Now pay attention,* he insisted. *Make no mistake. My life depends on this. What did they tell him? Your fathers—all those self-satisfied clodhoppers who talk of everything and nothing when there is work to be done—what did they tell him?*

Did they betray me? Have I been betrayed?

Levit glanced sidelong at Lessom. "Your father talked about the weather. I've never heard so many words about wind and sun. The weather! I thought I would die of impatience. I wanted to hear what the Roadman would say."

"Yes." Lessom was too excited to take offense. "And your father repeated everything everyone has ever known about brewing ale."

Levit nodded. "And then Karay mentioned every birth or death in, cor, it must have been ten years. My knees were trembling before the Roadman so much as began his tales."

Continue.

"But the tales were worth it," Lessom said, "were they not?"

Again Levit nodded.

"You say that warlocks do not fight princes," Lessom continued, "but the Roadman said otherwise. He spoke of a time when the enemies of Andovale mustered a great army of soldiers and warlocks to march against Prince—"

"Prince Chrys," Lessom put in.

"—Prince Chrys, and were defeated by—"

Titus stopped him. *Old news. Ancient history. That war is why warlocks no longer meddle in the affairs of princes. Preparing for war, the warlocks of Carcin and Sargo neglected their true arts. They made themselves weak, and so were defeated by the warlocks of Andovale. In magic, those who do not grow must decline.*

Hearing another connection, Fern thought softly, Yes.

But, *Think!* the pig was saying. *This Roadman did not ride the length of the Rift to relate old news. He must have spoken of more recent matters—events which have transpired since the last visit of the merchanters. Tell me that tale!*

Titus' vehemence disconcerted Levit. "He spoke of a war among warlocks," the boy began. "But Prince Chorl was also involved—" He broke off as though he feared to displease the pig.

That one, Titus demanded.

"He was called Suriman," Lessom began abruptly. The small cut of silver in the pig's gaze seemed to take hold of him. His body tightened in ways which distressed Fern. From the corners of his mind he brought out the Roadman's tale just as Destrier had told it. "That was his title— men do not speak his name. He was a prince among warlocks, ancient in magic as well as years. That he was called Suriman shows the respect in which he was held by all his brother warlocks. When the masters of magic gathered in council, he was often the first to speak. When Prince Chorl or the other lords of Andovale needed either the help or the coun- sel of a warlock, they often approached Suriman first. Indeed, it was Suriman himself who devised the means by which the warlocks of Sargo and Carcin were defeated.

"Yet there were some in Andovale, warlocks as well as ordinary men, who spoke ill of Suriman behind his back. They were thought jealous or petty when they hinted that he practiced his arts in ways which the masters of magic in council had proscribed many generations ago. They said—though they were not believed—that he had violated the foremost commandment of the councils, which is that the study and practice of magic is the responsibility of warlocks and must not be imposed on ordi- nary men against their will. If a warlock requires a man for experimen- tation or study, he must perform his researches upon himself, or upon some other warlock, not on men who can neither gauge nor accept—and certainly cannot prevent—the consequences.

"Those who spoke ill against Suriman said that he had performed his studies upon ordinary men, making some less than they were and others more, but always depriving his victims of choice in his research- es. By so doing, he had gained for himself powers unheard of among warlocks for many generations. Thus his might, his stature, and his very title were founded upon evil." Titus snorted in disgust, but did not interrupt.

"At first, those who spoke ill against Suriman were ignored. Then they were criticized and scorned. From time to time, one or another of them died, perhaps because they erred in their own experimentation, perhaps because they were punished for their indiscretions, perhaps because Suriman himself took action against them. Such deaths belonged to the province of warlocks, however, not to the jurisprudence of princes, and masters of magic found Suriman faultless in them.

"But Prince Chorl had a daughter. Her name was Florice, and she was renowned throughout Andovale for her beauty and her sweetness—and her simplicity. In truth, she was not merely simple. She was a child of perhaps eight or nine years in a woman's body, unfit for a woman's life.

For some time this was a cause of great grief to Prince Chorl. But when his grief was done, he cherished her for her beauty, for her sweet nature, and also for her simplicity. Therefore she was unwed—and unavailable. The Prince kept her as a child in his household, both protecting and loving her for what she was."

Abruptly, Fern found that she could see Prince Chorl's daughter— a woman clad in white as pure as samite, with silken hair, eyes like sunshine, and a form which Titus might have called *lovely*. Her image in Fern's mind was as precise as presence. Yet Fern knew more of her through the colors of the image than from the image itself. They were the hues of a complex and insatiable hunger.

"So she would have remained," Lessom related in Destrier's tones, "until old age claimed her, if she had not caught Suriman's eye. To Prince Chorl's amazement, and all Andovale's astonishment, Suriman asked to wed Florice.

"'No,' said the Prince in his surprise.

"'Why not?' Suriman countered calmly. 'Do you fear that I will not cherish her as you do? I swear by my arts that her sweetness and happiness are as precious to me as my life, and I will find great joy in her.'

"Dumbfounded, Prince Chorl seemed unable to think calmly. 'It is absurd,' he protested. 'You do not know what you are asking. You—' Because he was not thinking calmly, he turned to his daughter. 'Florice, do you wish to wed this man?'

"Florice gazed at Suriman and smiled her sweetest smile. 'No, Father,' she said. 'He is bad.'

"Neither the Prince nor Suriman knew how to respond to such a remark. However, the warlock was less disconcerted than his Prince. Laughing gently, he said, 'Really, my lord, I am too old to be a jilted suitor. I have lost my appetite for appearing foolish. Please permit me to remain as your guest for a season. Permit me to speak to your daughter for a few minutes each day—in your presence, of course. If you see nothing ill in my comportment toward her, perhaps you will not believe that I am "bad." And if at the end of the season she does not desire me, I will accept my folly and depart the wiser.'

"This proposal Prince Chorl accepted. He is not to be blamed for his mistake—although he blames himself mightily. Suriman was held in high esteem throughout Andovale. And those who spoke ill against him could prove nothing."

The colors in Fern's mind were ones of hope and possession, of a grasped opportunity. She could not image why Titus showed them to her: they were simply a fact, as all his images were facts—or became facts. Perhaps they came from him involuntarily or unconsciously while he heard Destrier's tale in Lessom's mouth.

"Yet if the Prince erred, he did not err blindly. He made certain that Suriman had no contact with Florice outside his own presence. And he watched her closely while Suriman spoke with her, studying her dear face for understanding. Before a fortnight passed, he saw that her face had changed.

"Tightness pulled at the corners of her mouth, straining her smiles. Her eyes lost their forthright sweetness and turned aside from her father's gaze. She asked questions which the Prince had never heard from her before. 'Father, why do men and women marry?' 'Father, why do you treat me like a child?' By these signs, he understood that his beloved daughter was in peril.

The image Fern saw conveyed satisfaction and excitement, whetted desire. Nevertheless, unbidden, she made a connection which did not come to her either from the image or through its colors. Rather it came from her own emotions—and from her growing sense of time.

Yes, she thought, not in acceptance, but in dismay. What she saw on the face of the Prince's daughter was violation.

Florice was not willing.

Perhaps Titus wished her to understand this, so that she would understand what followed.

"Yet Suriman was Suriman, respected everywhere. Prince Chorl felt that he could not send the warlock from his house. Instead, he took other precautions. In secret he summoned one of the warlocks—a man named Titus"—again the pig snorted—"who was known to think ill of Suriman, and he told Titus of his fears. He gave Titus the freedom of his house, and charged Titus to find proof that Suriman wrought evil against Florice.

"With Prince Chorl's support and assistance, Titus did as he was charged. Before another fortnight was ended, Florice announced to her father her settled intention to wed the warlock who courted her—and Titus announced his accusation that Suriman had flouted the most urgent commandment of the councils, that he had betrayed Florice by using his arts to alter her to his will.

"Consternation! In an instant, the peace of Andovale became chaos and distress. Flinging defiance at her father, Florice sought to flee the house with Suriman." Fern saw a hunger on her face which echoed the hunger of the colors surrounding her—a hunger she had not chosen and could not refuse. "Prince Chorl countered by imprisoning her, his daughter whom he cherished. Suriman attacked her prison, wreaking havoc in the Prince's house, and was only prevented from freeing Florice by the foresight of Titus, who had prepared defenses against the greater warlock—and had also demanded the attention of the council in what he did. The masters of magic gave Titus their aid until they could learn the truth of his accusations, and so Suriman's onslaught was beaten back. Even as the masters of magic met in council to examine Titus' proofs, Suriman ran.

"Inspired by his loathing of the crimes he attributed to Suriman, Titus had found sure proof. With gossamer incantations and webs of magic, he had followed Suriman's movements throughout the Prince's house. He had traced Suriman daily to the kitchens, where the delicacies which Florice most loved were prepared. And in the foods she was given to eat he found the herbs and simples, the poisons and potions, which Suriman would need to make Florice something other than she was against her will.

"Outraged, the council declared anathema on Suriman and went to war against him.

"He was mighty—oh, he was mighty! He could stand alone against any half dozen of his peers. And the dark tower where he studied his arts was mightily protected. But all the masters of magic in Andovale moved against him. They brought out fire from the air to crack his tower and drive him forth. Then he fled, and they gave chase. He took refuge in castles and towns. They scorched the very walls around him until he fled again. He hid himself in forests and villages. They shook the stones under his feet, so that he could not stand, but only run. And at last, on one of the farms at the end of the Gentle's Rift, they brought him to bay.

"The masters of magic do not speak of the final battle, but it was prodigious. In desperation, Suriman wove every power and trick at his vast command. Warlocks fell that day, and some never rose again. When the fire and passion had ended, however, Suriman lay dead among the wreckage of the farm. The beasts had scattered, and the fields were blasted, but the council had triumphed.

"That is to say, the masters of magic believed that they had triumphed. Suriman's corpse lay before them. Only Titus insisted that the evil was not done—Titus and Florice. Crying in wild hunger, the Prince's daughter claimed that the warlocks were too little to kill a man of Suriman's greatness. And Titus, whom loathing for Suriman had made cunning, spoke of texts and apparatus in Suriman's tower which pertained to the transfer of intelligences from one body to another. He told all who would hear him that Suriman could have escaped the last battle cloaked inside another man, or even concealed within a beast. If what he said were true, then Suriman might well remain alive—and might return.

"So the council watches for Suriman constantly, seeking any sign that the most evil of warlocks yet lives. And Prince Chorl watches also. His daughter is little better than a madwoman now, sorrowing over the loss of the man who changed her, and because the Prince blames himself his anger cannot be assuaged.

"All considered," the Roadman concluded his tale in Lessom's voice, "it has been a tumultuous time. Surely you have felt it here? Magic and battles on such a scale have repercussions. Has nothing changed at all—nothing out of the ordinary? Do not the cows talk, or the pigs sprout wings? Has no thing occurred which you might call strange? Is everything truly just as it has always been?"

With a gasp, Lessom sagged as the pig's gaze released him. Titus turned his eyes on Levit.

Now think! he demanded. *Make no mistake. What answer was this Roadman given?*

Yoel's son appeared to search his memory. "They were silent," he said slowly. "I could not see them, but I heard their boots on the floor, and the benches shifting. Then Horrik said, 'You came. That was strange. We have never seen a Roadman before.'

"Everyone laughed, and the Roadman with them. After that my father took Destrier to a room for the night, and people left the alehouse. I heard nothing else."

Think, Titus grunted urgently. *Nothing was said of me? Of Fern? Did not that clod-brain Jessup speak against me?*

Levit glanced at Lessom. "Nothing."

Lessom nodded and echoed, "Nothing." For a time, the pig did not speak. Both boys slumped on the dirt, wearied by Titus' coercion. Beside them Fern tended the fire uncomfortably; she wanted sleep, but she was full of a fear she could not name. Images of Florice seemed to resonate for her like wind past a hollow in a wall, as though they might convey another connection; yet the connection eluded her. Such things were matters of time, and her grasp on them remained imprecise.

Then Titus snuffled, *Ah, but they squirmed, I can see it. They dropped their eyes and twisted in their seats. And this Destrier noticed it. He was sent to notice such things.*

Hell's blood! I must have time!

Like Titus, Lessom and Levit needed time. Their parents would not speak kindly to them for staying out so late. Yawning and shuffling, they left the hovel.

But Titus continued to fret. He paced the floor as though his hooves were afire. Fern tried to rest, but she could not be still when the pig she loved was in distress. "Yes?" she murmured to him, "yes?" hoping that the sound of her concern would comfort him.

No, he retorted harshly. *You do not know what you are saying. It is not enough.*

As though he had judged and dismissed her, he did not speak again that night.

The next morning, however, he ventured out early to watch Prince Chorl's Roadman ride away from Sarendel-on-Gentle. And when he returned to the hovel, he was full of grim bustle. *I must take action,* he informed her. *Any delay or hindrance now will be fatal.* And he showed her an image which instructed her to prepare a double—no, a treble—portion of the herbs and paste with which he fed her thrice daily.

She obeyed willingly, because he instructed her. When his concoctions were done, she bathed thoroughly; she combed out her hair and let the sun dry it until it shone. Then, guided by images, she draped her limbs with her scantest, most inadequate rags.

Cold, she thought when she saw how ill she was covered. A moment later, she thought another word, which might have been, Shame.

Shame? The pig's disgust was as bright as fire. *Shame will not kill you. My need is extreme. Extreme measures are required.* Nevertheless he allowed her to remain concealed in her hovel while he roamed the village; when he returned, they remained there together until the sun had set.

By that time, Sarendel had newer, more personal news to replace Destrier's unexpected visit. Meglan's husband, Wall, had fallen ill. According to the children who brought the tale, he writhed on his bed like a snake, vomiting gouts of bile and blood, and his skin burned as though his bones were ablaze. Meglan and her children were beside themselves, fearing his death at any moment.

Meglan? Fern had little impression of Wall, but Meglan farmwife was vivid to her. Meglan's kindnesses, of which Fern had known many, came to her through veils of time—carrots and shawls, cabbages and sandals and smiles. She felt tugging at her the same concern, the same impulse to respond, which she had often felt for Sarendel's pigs.

Good, Titus said. *Such concern looks well.* And he showed her an image in which she went alone to Meglan's home, bearing small portions of her broth and paste. Alone she knocked at the door until she was answered. Alone she repeated Meglan's name until Meglan was brought to her. Then, still alone, she spoke to Meglan. In words, she explained how the broth and paste should be administered to save Wall.

Alone?

Spoke? In words?

Explained—?

Fern flinched against the wall of the hovel as though Titus had threatened to strike her. *I will teach you,* Titus replied patiently. *If you are willing, you will be able to do it.*

"No," she protested in fright.

Come now, Fern, Titus went on, filling her mind with the colors of calm. *You will be able to do it. I have made you able. Did you not hear yourself speak just now? That was a word. You know both "yes" and "no." And you know names. Each new word will be a smaller step than the one before—and you will not need many to save Wall.*

Alone? she cried fearfully.

If you love me, you will do this. Meglan will have no tolerance for pigs at such a time.

Fern did not know how she understood him; yet she comprehended that he needed her—and that his need was greater than she could imagine. With her crumbling resistance, she gestured toward the rags she wore.

You will feel no shame, he promised her. *There can be none for you, when you do my bidding.*

There: another connection. Through her fright and distress, an involuntary excitement struck her. She had always contrived to cover herself better than this; but now she did not because Titus had instructed her. His bidding—She acted according to his wishes, not her own.

Other connections trembled at the edges of her mind, other links between what he wished and what people did. However, his urgency and his steady promises distracted her. While she readied her small portions of herbs and paste, he taught her the words she would need.

When she left the hovel, she went in a daze of fear and shame and excitement. No, not shame—*There can be none for you, when you do my bidding.* What she felt was the strange, uneasy eagerness of comprehension, the unfamiliar potential of language. Ignoring how her breasts and legs showed when she walked, she crossed the village and did as Titus had instructed her.

She was almost able to recognize what she gained by wearing her worst rags. They caught the attention of the farmer who opened the door, a friend of Wall's; they trapped him in pity, embarrassment, and interest, so that he was not able to send her away unheard. Instead, he went to fetch Meglan, thinking that Meglan would be able to dismiss Fern more kindly.

And when Meglan came to the door, Fern astonished her with words.

"I know herbs," said Fern, slurring each sound, and yet speaking with her utmost care, because of her love for Titus. "These can heal Wall. A spoonful of the broth. A touch of the paste on his tongue. Four times during the night. His illness will break at dawn."

Meglan stared as though the sounds were gibberish. All Sarendel knew Fern did not speak; she could not. Then how could these sounds be words?

But Titus had taught her one more: "Please."

"'Please'?" Meglan cried, on the verge of sobs. "My husband whom I love dies here, and you say, 'Please'?"

Fern could not withhold her own tears. Meglan's grief and the burden of words were too great for her to bear. Helpless to comfort the good farmwife—and helpless to refuse her pig—she could only begin again at the beginning.

"I know herbs. These can heal—" Another woman appeared at Meglan's shoulder, a neighbor. "Is that Fern?" she asked in surprise. "Did I hear her speak?"

Grief twisted Meglan's face. If Fern could speak, the farmwife could not. Taking both broth and paste, she turned her back in silence and closed the door. Fern went weeping back to her hovel. Titus had no patience for her nameless sorrows. When she entered the hovel and stumbled to the scraps and leaves which she used as a pallet, he fixed her with his eyes, compelling her with silver and blindness until he had seen what was in her mind.

After that, however, his manner softened. *It was hard, I grant,* he told her. *But you have done a great thing, though you do not know it. The next steps will be less arduous. That is a better promise than the one I gave you earlier.*

Then he nuzzled and comforted her, and filled her head with solace, until at last she was able to stop crying and sleep.

While she slept, new connections swam and blurred, seeking clarity. She had gone to Meglan because Titus bade her. She had bathed her body and combed her hair and donned her worst rags on his instructions. She had prepared new stores of broth and paste at his behest. Were all these things connected in the same way? One thing will lead to another because it must. Had the pig foreseen Wall's illness? Was time no barrier to him, neither the past nor the future?

For a moment, as if time were no barrier to her as well, she seemed to see through the veils of the past. She saw that the ease and comfort and companionship of her life were new—that her life itself had changed. How did it come about that all her needs were supplied by children who had taken no notice of her until Titus adopted her?

What had he done? He had filled her with images. And she had done his bidding. One thing will lead to another— Did the children also find images in their minds, new images which instructed them in Titus' wishes?

These connections were like the surface of the Gentle. They caught the sun and sparkled, gems cast by the water, but they were too full of ripples and currents to be seen clearly.

And they vanished when the pig awakened her. *It is morning,* he informed her intently. *You must be prepared to speak again soon.* His concentration was acute; his eyes seemed to focus all of him on her. *Hear the sounds. They are words. When I have given them to you, they will be yours. At first, they will be difficult to remember. Nevertheless they will belong to you, and you will be able to call on them at need.*

Words? she thought. More words? But he left her no opportunity for protest. When she tried to say, "No," he brushed that word aside. *It will become easier, I tell you,* he snapped. *And I have no time for subtlety.*

She surrendered to his bidding scant moments before a tentative scratching at her door curtain announced a visitor. Held by his gaze, she spoke the first of his new words.

"Enter."

Expecting children, she was filled with chagrin when she saw Meglan come into her hovel. Only the strength of her love for her pig—or the strength of his presence in her mind—enabled her to rise to her feet instead of cowering against the wall.

Meglan herself appeared full of chagrin. Fern could look at the farmwife because Meglan was unable to look at Fern. Her gaze limped aimlessly across the floor, lost among her pallid features, and her voice also limped as she murmured, "I know not what to say. I can hardly face you. My husband is saved. You saved him—you, who speaks when none of us knew you could—you gave no hint—You, whom I have treated with little concern and no courtesy. You, who came in rags to offer your help. You, whom I have considered at worst a beggar and at best a half-wit. You and no other saved my husband.

"I cannot—I do not know how to bear it. You deserve honor, and you have been given only scorn.

"Fern, I must make amends. You have saved Wall, who is as dear to me as my own flesh. Because of you, he smiles, and lifts his head, and will soon be able to rise from his bed. I must make amends." Now she looked into Fern's eyes, and her need was so great—as great as

Titus'—that Fern could not look away. "I will tell the tale. That I can do. I will teach Sarendel to honor you. But it is not enough.

"I have brought—" Meglan opened her hands as if she were ashamed of what they held, and Fern saw a thick, woolen robe, woven to stand hard use and keep out cold. "It is plain—too plain for my heart—but it is what I have, and it is not rags. And still it is not enough.

"If you can speak—if you are truly able to speak—please tell me how to thank you for my husband's life."

Fern, who had never owned a garment so rich and useful, might have fallen to her knees and wept in gratitude. To be given such a gift, without begging or dishonesty—! But Titus' need was as great as Meglan's. He did not let her go.

Instead of bowing or crying, she answered, "Thank you." The words stumbled in her mouth; they were barely articulate. Yet she said them— and as she said them she felt an excitement which seemed like terror. "I helped Wall because I could. I do not need tales."

That is safe, Titus commented. *She will talk in any case.*

"Or gifts," Fern went on. Belying the words, she gripped the robe tightly. "Yet it would be a kindness if I were given an iron cookpot and a few mixing bowls."

Damnation! Titus grunted. *That came out crudely. I must be more cautious.*

Ashamed to be begging again, Fern could no longer face the farmwife. Because Titus required it, however, she gestured at her fire and her few bowls. "My knowledge of herbs is more than I can use with what implements I have. If I could cook better, I could help others as I have helped your husband."

Tears welled in Meglan's eyes. "Thank you. You will have what you need." Impulsively, she leaned forward and kissed Fern's cheek. Then she turned and hurried from the hovel as though she were grieving— or fleeing.

There. Titus sounded like Jessup rubbing his hands together over an auspicious bargain. *Was that not easier? Did I not promise that it would be less arduous? Soon we will be ready.*

For the second time, Fern felt her own tears reply to Meglan's. "No." She had no recollection that she had ever been kissed before. Her surprise at Meglan's gesture startled another surprise out of her—an unfamiliar anger. "No," she repeated. Almost in words, almost using language for herself, she faced the pig's strange gaze and showed him her shame.

Titus shook his head. *You did not beg.* Now he sounded condescending and desirous, like Horrik the tanner. *You answered her question—a small act of courtesy and self-respect. Consider this.* He showed Fern an image of Meglan coming to the hovel to offer gratitude, carrying not a robe but a cookpot and some bowls. *Would you have felt shame then?* he asked. *No. You were not shamed by the gift she chose to give you. It is only because you named your own need that you think you have done wrong.*

But it was not wrong. It was my bidding.

Perhaps we will have enough time. Perhaps you will be able to save me. Take comfort in that, if you cannot forget your shame. Perhaps you will be able to save me.

As I saved Wall? she almost asked. Was that not also your doing?

But she lacked the language for such questions. And the pig distracted her, nuzzling her hand to express his affection and gratitude, wrapping her mind in azure and comfortable emerald; and so the connection was lost.

After that, her life changed again. The roaming and scavenging which had measured out her days came to a complete end. Feeling at once grand and unworthy in her new robe, she sat in her hovel while Titus went out alone and came back; while children supplied her with food and water and firewood and herbs; while first one or two and then several and finally all of Sarendel's good people came to visit her. Some scratched at her curtain and poked their heads inside simply to satisfy their curiosity or resolve their doubt. But others brought their needs and pains to her attention. Meglan's tale had inspired them to hope that Fern could help them.

Red-eyed from sleeplessness, and strangely abashed in the presence of a woman whom she had scarcely noticed before, Salla farmwife brought her infant son, who squalled incessantly with colic. Had the boy been a pig, Fern would have known what to do. However, he was a boy, and so it was fortunate that Titus stood at her side to instruct her. *(A bit of the paste, diluted four times. Mint and sage to moderate the effect. There.)* When Salla left the hovel, she added her son's smiles and his sweet sleep to Meglan's tale.

And later Salla brought Fern the gift which Titus had told Fern to request—a mortar and pestle, and a set of sturdy wooden spoons.

Horrik came, bearing an abscessed thumb. After Fern had treated it with a poultice which she had never made before, he lingered to stare and talk like a man whose mind drooled at what he saw. Yet he did not take it unkindly when at last Titus succeeded at urging her to dismiss him. Smiling and bowing, the tanner left; still smiling, he brought to her the gift she had requested, a keen flensing knife.

Karay's daughter had been afflicted with palsy from birth. The weaver was so accustomed to her daughter's infirmity that she would not have thought to seek aid were it not for the strange fact that Fern could now speak. Perhaps if a mute half-wit could learn language and healing, a palsy could be cured. So Karay set her forlorn child in the dirt beside Fern's fire and asked bluntly, "Can you help her?"

In response, Fern prepared a broth not unlike the one she ate herself, a paste not unlike the one she had given Salla's infant. "And ale," she added. "Mix it in ale. Let her drink at her own pace until she has drunk it all."

Once Karay had seen that this rank brew indeed put an end to her daughter's palsy, she gave Fern a curtain of embroidered velvet to replace the hovel's burlap door. And also, because she was asked, she delivered to Fern a cupful each of all the dyes she used in her weaving.

Herded by his angry wife and four angry daughters, Sarendel's blacksmith entered her hovel, carrying *so* much pain that he could hardly move. He had fallen against his forge and burned away most of the flesh on one side of his chest; his wife and daughters were angry because they feared that he would die. Fern gave him a salve for healing, herbs to soften the hurt, and other herbs to resist infection. When her husband began to mend, the blacksmith's wife at last allowed herself to weep. She cried ceaselessly as she brought Fern several small flakes of silver.

A farmer was given a cure for gout; he expressed his thanks with a lump of ambergris which he had treasured for years without knowing why. Over her father-in-law's vociferous objections, Jessup's eldest son's wife asked for and received an herb to ease the severity of her monthly cramps; her gratitude took the form of two pints of refined lard. One of the blacksmith's daughters believed that she was unwed because her beauty was marred by a large wen beside her nose; when Fern supplied her with a poultice which I caused the wen to shrink and fall away, she—and her father—gave Fern an iron grill to hold Meglan's cookpot.

In the course of a fortnight, Fern seemed to become the center of all Sarendel-on-Gentle, the hub on which the village turned. Children cared for her needs, and adults visited her at any hour. Resplendent in her new robe—of all the gifts she had been given, this one alone warmed her heart—she sat in state to receive all who came to her. With Titus at her side, as well fed and well tended as herself, she made new concoctions and spoke new words as though those separate actions were one and the same, bound to each other in ways she could not see. She no longer cowered against her walls in fright or chagrin. Instead she gave her help with the same unstinting openheartedness which she had formerly shown only to pigs. Helping people made her love them. She disliked only the gifts she was given in thanks, never the efforts she made to earn that thanks.

Her life had indeed changed. This time, however, she recognized the change for what it was. She neither chose it nor resisted it, but she saw it. And when she watched the change, comparing it to what her life had once been, she made new connections.

She understood why she could speak, why she could understand the people around her and reply, why she could prepare complex salves and balms, why she could look her fellow villagers in their faces. It was because of the broth and paste which Titus caused her to eat three times daily. Those herbs had wrought a change within her as profound as the change in her life.

One thing will lead to another because it must.

And she understood that she did not deserve Sarendel's gratitude for her cures and comforts. That was why gifts gave her no pleasure, but only sorrow. She healed nothing, earned nothing. Like her new ability to speak, all the benefits she worked for others came from Titus: the credit for them was his, not hers.

She did not resent this. The pig had come to her in his extremity, and she loved him. Nor could she wish the lessons he had taught her unlearned. Nevertheless she grieved over her unworth.

In addition, she understood without knowing she understood that Titus himself caused a certain number of the hurts she treated. Too frequently to be unconnected, his forays away from her hovel coincided with the onset of injuries and illnesses in the village. The same powers with which he had raised her from her familiar destitution, he used to create the conditions under which Sarendel needed her.

He was trying to speed the process by which she accumulated gifts.

This troubled her. It offended her honesty more than begging; it seemed a kind of theft. But she did not protest against it. Other, similar connections crouched at the edges of her understanding, waiting for clarity. When she grasped one, she would grasp them all.

Ready, she thought to herself, using words instead of images. We must be ready. We are becoming ready.

We are, Titus assented. She could hear pride and hope in his voice, as well as anger and more than a little fear.

Before the end of another fortnight, Sarendel had learned to accept Fern in her changed state; the village had begun to live as though she had always been a healer rather than a half-wit. And Titus had finished accumulating the gifts he required.

Now she noted the passing of time. Around her the seasons had moved along the Gentle's Rift, turning high summer to crisp fall. Hints of gold and crimson appeared among the verdure; at their fringes the leaves of the bracken took on rust. Slowly the labor of tending fields and beasts eased. Soon would come a time she dreaded, a time she now knew she had always dreaded—the time when porkers were slaughtered for food and hide and tallow. She did not fear for Titus in that way: because he was hers, no villager would harm him. And yet she feared for him now, just as she had always feared for the porkers.

True, she could hear his own fear in the way he spoke. But she also saw it in the tension of his movements, in the staring of his flawed eyes; she smelled it in his sweat. It confirmed her apprehension for him when she might have been able to persuade herself that she had no reason for alarm.

One sharp fall morning, he poked his snout past her hovel's velvet curtain, scented the air—and recoiled as though he had been stung.

Hell's blood! he panted. *Damn and blast them!*

An unnamed panic came over her. She surged up from her pallet to throw her arms about his neck as though she believed that she could ward him somehow. He shivered feverishly, hot with dread.

"Titus?" She needed words for her fear, but only his name came to her. "Titus?"

He appeared to take comfort from her embrace. After a moment, his tremors eased. The confused moil of images and hues which he cast into her sharpened toward concentration.

Now we must hurry in earnest, he breathed. *There is a stink of princes and warlocks in the air. That damnable Roadman has betrayed me, and I have little time. As I am, I can neither flee nor fight.*

Oh, Fern, my Fern, if you love me, help me. Give me your willingness. Without it, I am lost.

"Who?" she asked with her face pressed to his neck. "Who comes to threaten you?"

Princes, warlocks, does it matter? he snapped back. *They are frightened, even more than I—therefore they will be enough. They would not come if they were not enough. I tell you, we must* **hurry***!*

She could not refuse him. She gave him a last hug, as though she were saying farewell. After that, she dropped her arms and seated herself by the fire.

"Then tell me what to do."

She seemed to take his fear from him; he seemed to leach all calm and quiet out of her. The words and images which he supplied to instruct her were precise and unmistakable, as clear as sunlight on green leaves; yet her hands shook, and her whole heart trembled, while she obeyed. She was Fern of Sarendel-on-Gentle, a half-wit who loved pigs. What did she know of language or time, of magic or warlocks? Nevertheless Titus needed her, as he had needed her once before, and she did not mean to fail him.

Throughout the day she labored under his guidance, trying to do several things at once. As she heated her new cookpot until the iron shone red, she also ground rueweed and fennel and sloewort and garlic and vert and silver flakes to fine powder; at the same time, she gripped the lump of ambergris between her thighs to soften it. While she warmed lard to liquid in one of her mixing bowls, she also kneaded the ambergris until it became as workable as beeswax. And when her hands were too tired for kneading, she busied herself dividing her powders into ever more meticulous quantities and combining them with pinches of dried dyes.

Children came to scratch at her curtain, but she sent them away without caring whether she was brusque. She would have sent all Sarendel away. Horrik the tanner came as well; he seemed to want nothing more than an opportunity to sit and look at her. But she told him "No," calling the word past Karay's heavy curtain without raising her head from her work. "If you meant to speak to me, you should have done so long ago." She hardly heard herself add, "I am too far beyond you now."

Morning lapsed to afternoon; afternoon became evening. Still she worked. Now her hands were raw and her arms quivered, and sweat splashed from her cheeks to the dirt. Fire and red iron filled the hovel with heat until even the slats of the walls appeared to sweat. The smells of powders and dyes in strange combinations made her head wobble on her neck. But Titus did not relent. His instructions were unending, and she labored with all her willingness to obey them.

At last he let her pause. While she rested, panting, he surveyed her handiwork, squinting blind and silver at what she had done.

Now, he announced distinctly. *Now or never.*

With the hem of her robe, she mopped sweat from her face. Fatigue blurred her sight, so that she could no longer see the pig clearly.

"Have they come yet?" she asked in a whisper. "Are they here?"

I cannot tell, he responded. *Even a pig's senses cannot distinguish between those scents and what we do.*

But it does not matter. Whether they are poised around us or miles away, we must do what we can.

Fern, are you ready?

Because all his fear was hers, she countered, "Are you?"

To her surprise, he filled her mind with laughter. *No,* he admitted, *not ready at all.* Then he repeated, *But it does not matter. For us there is only now or never.*

"Then," she repeated in her turn, "tell me what to do."

Now his instructions were simple. She obeyed them one at a time, as carefully as she could.

The lump of ambergris she divided in two parts, each of which she molded with her fingers until it was shaped like a bowl. Into these bowls she apportioned the powders she had prepared, the mixtures of herbs and dyes and metal. Using Horrik's knife, she pricked at the veins in her forearm until enough blood flowed to moisten the powders. Then quickly, so that nothing spilled, she cupped one bowl over the other to form a ball. With water warmed in a pan at the edge of the fire, she stroked the seam of the ball until the ambergris edges were smeared together and sealed.

Good. Titus studied her hands while she worked as though he were rapt. His breathing had become a hoarse wheeze, and sweat glistened among the bristles on his hide. *The ball. The lard. My water dish. And some means to remove that cookpot from the fire.*

Fern flinched at the thought. The fatal glow of the iron seemed to thrust her back. She was not sure that she could go near enough to the pot to take hold of it. A shaft of anger and fear broke through Titus' calm; he grunted a curse. But then, grimly, he stilled himself. Reverting to images, he made her see herself taking two brands from her dwindling woodpile and bracing them under the handles of the cookpot to lift it out.

She picked up the brands, set them in front of her beside the half-full water dish, the lard, and the ambergris ball.

The pig stood facing her as though nothing else existed—as though all the world had shrunk down to one lone woman. He had told her more than once to hurry, but now he gave her no instructions, and did not move himself.

Fear crowded her throat. "Titus," she breathed "why do you delay?"

Like you, he told her, *I am afraid.*

After a moment, he added, *Do you remember your first name for me? It was Mythanks. At the time, I was not amused. But now I consider it a better name than Titus.*

So swiftly that she could not distinguish them, images rang through her head. In one motion, she rose to her feet and dropped the ball into the cookpot.

Ambergris hit the red iron with scream of scalding wax. But before the ball melted entirely away, she snatched up the lard and poured it also into the pot.

Instantly the smoke and stench of burning fat filled the hovel. The walls seemed to vanish. Tears burst from Fern's eyes. She could no longer see Titus.

She could see his images still, however. They guided her hands to the brands, guided the brands to the cookpot; they made her strong and sure as she lifted out the pot and tilted it to decant its searing contents into the dish.

Gouts of steam spat and blew through the reeking smoke. Nevertheless Titus did not hesitate now. The potion would lose its efficacy as it cooled.

Plunging his snout into the fiery dish, he drank until he could no longer endure the agony. Then he threw back his head and screamed.

Fern cried out at the same instant, wailed, "Titus!" She had never heard such a scream. The pain of cattle was eloquent enough. And pigs could squeal like slaughtered children. But this was worse, far worse. It was the pure anguish of a pig and the utter torment of man in one, and it seemed to shake the hovel. The walls bowed outward; smoke and stink filled the air with hurt.

And the scream did not stop. Shrill with agony and protest, it splashed like oil into the fire, so that flames blazed to the ceiling. The smoke itself caught fire and began roaring like the core of the sun. Conflagration limned each slat of the walls and roof, etched every scrap and leaf of her pallet against the black dirt. The scream became fire itself. Flames ate at Fern's robe, her face, her hair. In another instant it would devour her, and she would fall to ashes—

But it did not. Instead it seemed to coalesce in front of her. Flames left the walls to flow through the air; flames drained off her and were swept up into the center of the hovel. The fire she had made lost heat. Her pallet ceased burning. Every burst and blaze came together to engulf Titus.

At the same time, another fire burned in Fern's head, as though she, too, were being consumed.

Outside her, beyond her, he stood in the middle of the floor, motionless. Like wax, he melted in the flames. And like wax, he fed the flames, so that they mounted higher while he was consumed. From his pig's body they grew to a pillar which nearly touched the roof. Then the pillar changed shape until it writhed and roiled like a tortured man.

Abruptly he stopped screaming.

The fire went out.

A deep dark closed over Fern. The smoke and stench blinded her with tears; echoes of flame dazzled her. She could see nothing until he took hold of her arms and lifted her to her feet.

Lit by the last embers of her fire, a man stood in the hovel with her. Clad only in a faint red glow and shadows, he released her arms and stepped back so that she could see him more clearly.

He was tall and strong. Not young—she saw many years in the lines of his face and the color of his beard. Prominent cheekbones hid his eyes in caves of shadow. Beneath a nose like the blade of a hatchet, his mouth was harsh.

Looking at him, she was hardly able to breathe. She knew him without question—he was Titus, the pig who had chosen her, the one she loved—and the sight of him struck her dumb, as though he had stepped out of her dreams to meet her. Was he handsome? To her, he was so handsome that she quailed in front of him.

"Fern," he murmured softly, "oh, my Fern, we have done it." His voice was the voice she had heard in her mind, the voice which had taught her words—the voice which had changed her life. "We have *done* it."

Before she could fall to her knees in hope and love and astonishment, another voice answered him. As hard as the clang of iron, it called out, *"But not in time!"*

"Damnation!" A snarl leaped across Titus' face; embers and silver flashed from his hidden eyes. His strong hands reached out and snatched Fern to him as though he meant to protect her.

In that instant, a bolt like lightning shattered the hovel. Argent power tore the air apart. A concussion too loud for hearing knocked the walls to shards and splinters, and swept them away. Embers and rags scattered as though they had been scoured from the dirt. Fern was only kept on her feet amid the blast by Titus' grasp. She clung to him helplessly while her home ceased to exist. Then they found themselves with their arms around each other under the open sky at the edge of the village. This was the spot where her hovel had stood, but no sign of it remained: even her iron cookpot had been stricken from the place. Dimmed by glaring coruscation, a few stars winked coldly out of the black heavens.

A circle of fire the color of ice surrounded her and Titus. It blazed and spat from the ground as though it marked the rim of a pit which would open under their feet. At first it was so bright that her abused eyes could not see past it. But gradually she made out figures beyond the white, crystal fire. On the other side of the ring, she and Titus were also surrounded by men and women on horseback, as well as by the people of Sarendel-on-Gentle.

She saw Jessup and Yoel there, Veil and Nell and Meglan, Horrik and Karay, all the folk she had known throughout her life. Only the children were absent, no doubt commanded to their homes with the best authority their parents could muster. The strange, chill light seemed to leech the familiar faces of color; they were as pallid as ghosts. Their eyes were haunted and abashed, full of shame or fear.

Among them towered the riders. These figures also were spectral in the icy glow. Nevertheless they masked their fear and betrayed no shame. Their eyes and mouths showed only anger and determination, an unremitting outrage matched by resolve.

Fern had never seen such men and women before. Their armor and cloaks and caps, their weapons and apparatus, were outlandish, at once regal and incomprehensible. Yet she seemed to recognize them as soon as she caught sight of them. There was Prince Chorl—there, with the blunt forehead, the circlet in his curling hair, and the beard like a breastplate. He was accompanied by his lords and minions, as well as by his Florice— her plain riding habit, wild hair, and undefended visage made her unmistakable. And among the others were Andovale's masters of magic come to carry out the judgment of the council against one of their own.

All of them had ridden here for no reason except that the people of Sarendel had squirmed when Destrier had asked them about change. And those people had squirmed because they had known of a change which they had not wished to name. Out of loyalty or pity, they had declined to mention that she, Fern, had been adopted by a pig none of them had ever seen before. And yet their very desire to protect Fern had betrayed the man who now held her in his arms. He was snared in this circle by his enemies because of her.

She did not ask how she knew such things. She knew a great deal which had been vague to her before: the fire which had transformed Titus had altered her in some way as well. Or perhaps in his desperation for her help he had altered her more than he intended. She made connections easily, as though the pathways of new understanding had been burned clear in her brain.

One among the riders was fiercer than the others; his rage shone more hotly. He lacked the sorrow which moderated Prince Chorl's anger. Alone of the warlocks—the men who bore apparatus and periapts instead of arms were surely warlocks—he rode at his Prince's side, opposite Florice. He appeared to command the ring of riders as much as the Prince did.

"So, Suriman," this warlock barked across the fire, "you are caught again—and damned as much for new crimes as for old. How you escaped

us to work your evil here, I do not fully understand. But we are prepared
to be certain that you do not escape again."

Suriman? Fern thought. Suriman?

The man in her arms loosened his embrace so he could bow. If he
felt any dismay at his nakedness, he did not deign to show it. His lips
grinned sardonically over his teeth, and silver glinted like a threat in his
eye. "My lord Prince." His voice was as clear and harsh as the night. "My
lady. Titus. You are fortunate to catch me. In another hour I would have
been beyond the worst that you can do."

Fern felt a pang around her heart. "Titus?" she asked aloud.
Connections twisted through her, as ghostly and fatal as the riders, "You
said *your* name was Titus."

"He is called Suriman because we do not speak his name," the warlock barked. "I am Titus. If he told you his name is mine, that is only
one lie among many."

"Titus?" Fern asked again. Surrounded by cold fire, she sounded
small and lost. Ignoring the warlock, she faced the man who had been
her pig. Unprotected from the cold, he had begun to shiver slightly.

He did not look at her; his gaze held the Prince and the warlock.
When he spoke, his voice cut like a whip. "Her name is Fern, Titus. You
will address her as 'my lady.' Regardless of your contempt for me, you
will show her courtesy. "

Fern flung a glance at this unfamiliar Titus in time to see him flinch
involuntarily. All the power here was his—and still he feared his enemy.

Prince Chorl lifted his head. His eyes were as deep as the night.
"Show her courtesy yourself, Suriman. Answer her."

For a moment, the man hesitated. But then, slowly, he turned in
Fern's grasp so that he could face her. Again his eyes were hidden away
in shadows. Yet he seemed abashed by her needy stare, as if he were
more vulnerable to her than to any of the circled riders. Tightly, he said,
"I am Suriman."

She could not still the pain twisting in her. "Then why did you teach
me to call you Titus?"

His brows knotted. "I feared such stories as the Roadman told. I
thought that if I gave myself another's name I was less likely to be
betrayed—and what name would protect me more than the name of the
man who most wished me dead? But I misjudged you, my Fern. I misjudged your willingness. If I had known then what you are now, I would
have risked the truth."

At his words, anger stirred the ring. Flames of ice leaped higher, as
though the warlocks fed them with outrage. And Titus cried in a loud

voice, *"Willingness?* She is not *willing.* She is a *half-wit*—the poorest and most destitute person in all the Rift. These folk love her—they do not speak against her—but at least one of them has told us what he knows."

Fern did not doubt that this was Jessup. The other villagers ached to have no part in her downfall. Yet they could not turn away. Fire and fury held them.

"We can surmise the rest," Titus continued. "She had no *choice,* Suriman. You took her life from her; without her consent. You altered her for your own purposes, not knowing and not caring what she wished or desired. She is not willing because she chose *nothing."*

Suriman did not shift his gaze from Fern. She felt the appeal in his eyes, although she could not see them.

"That is false," he said softly. "She is willing because she *is,* not because I made her so. She was willing when I found her. She loves pigs, and I was a pig. She would have given her life for me from the first moment she saw me."

Then the Prince's daughter spoke for the first time. In a voice made old by too much weeping, "But *I* was not willing. When you first asked to wed me, I knew your evil. I told my father of it as best I could. You did not heed that, or anything I might have desired for myself. Now I crave you, I cannot stop desiring you, and I chose none of it.

"Was that not a crime, Suriman? Have you not betrayed me? Tell me that you have not betrayed me."

Like Suriman's fire, Florice's pain burned through Fern, making new connections.

He turned to face this accuser. "I did not betray you, my lady," he answered. He seemed to hold the lords and warlocks at bay with harshness. To Fern, he looked strong enough for that. "I failed you. The distinction is worth making. If I had not failed, you would have craved me utterly. Prince Chorl would have lost a half-wit daughter, and all Andovale would have gained a great lady. You would have been as willing as my Fern is now, and you would have regretted nothing.

"It was my folly that I could not win your father's trust—and his that he asked this Titus to act in his name."

Titus reared back to launch a retort, but Fern stopped him by raising her hand. All her attention was focused on Suriman; she hardly noticed that Titus had stopped, or that all the ring fell silent as though she were a figure of power.

"I was not willing."

Suriman swung back toward her like a man stung. "Not?" The word was almost a cry.

If she could have seen his eyes, she might have told him, Do not be afraid, I must say this, or else I will say nothing. But they remained shadowed, unreadable. She knew nothing about him except what he had chosen to reveal.

"You made me a beggar." Her voice shook with fright; she felt overwhelmed by her own littleness in the face of these potent men and women. Yet she did not falter. "Oh, I helped you willingly enough. As you say, I love pigs. But in all my life I have taken nothing that was not mine. That shamed me."

"We would have died!" he countered at once, gently. "You lacked the means to keep us alive. It is not a crime to ask for help—or to need it. Do you think less of me because I came to you when I was in need?"

She shook her head. "But Jessup did not choose to feed us the second time. The children did not choose to feed us. You chose for them. You cast images into their minds which they did not understand and so could not refuse. You made me a thief."

"A thief?" Suriman sounded incredulous—and daunted. "You stole nothing!"

"But I lived on stolen things. I grew healthy and comfortable on stolen things. The fault is yours—but you feel no shame, and so the shame is mine."

"What are you saying?" His voice came close to cracking. "You did not know the food was stolen because you could not comprehend it." He had another nakedness, which signified more than his lack of garments. "It was beyond your abilities to see consequences which did not take place before your eyes—and you could not remember them when they were past.

"I do not say this in scorn, Fern. You simply were not able to understand. And now you are. I have given you that. You accuse me of a fault which would have meant nothing to you if I had not given you the capacity to see it."

His need touched her so deeply that tears came to her eyes, and the ring of fire blurred against the dark night. And still she did not falter.

"But you could see it," she replied. "You knew all that I did not, and more besides. You knew me—you knew my mind. You saw the things which shamed me. And yet you caused the children of this village to go thieving for my benefit."

As though she had pushed him beyond his endurance, he snapped back, "Fern, I was *desperate*. I was a *pig*, in hell's name! If I did not die on the road to be devoured by dogs, I would be slaughtered in the village to be eaten by clods and fools!"

At the same time, she heard his voice in her mind, she had heard it so often when he could not speak.

Fern, I implore you.

"So is the lady Florice desperate," she answered. "So am I."

Florice could no longer keep silent. "Yes, desperate, Suriman—as desperate as you were. I am desperate for you, though it breaks my heart. But more than that, I am desperate to understand.

"What is this *willingness* you prize so highly? Why must you extract it from women who can neither comprehend nor refuse? You do not desire us as women—you desire only tools, subjects for research. Why must you make us to be more than we were, when what you wish is that we should be less?"

Suriman did not turn from Fern. He concentrated on her as though the circle of riders and villagers and fire had ceased to have any import. When he responded to Florice, his words were addressed to Fern.

"Because, my lady, no woman but a half-wit is able to give herself truly. You say I do not desire you as women, but I do. If I had not failed, you would have lost your flaws—the limitations which prevent you from sharing my dreams and designs—but you would have retained your open heart, your loveliness of form and spirit.

"If that is a crime, then I am guilty of it." Finality and fear ached in his tone. "Do what you came to do or leave me be. I am defenseless against you."

At the same time, his silent voice said beseechingly, *Oh, my Fern, tell me I have not failed.*

"We will," Titus announced loudly. And Prince Chorl echoed, more in sorrow than in anger, "We will.

"I care nothing for your protests or justifications, Suriman," the Prince continued. "We are not here to pass judgment. That has been done. Our purpose is only to see you dead."

"Dead," the warlocks pronounced. "Finally and forever."

"Yes," growled the lords and minions on their mounts.

The silver fire leaped up, encircling Suriman more tightly.

"Do not harm Fern!" a farmwife cried out. It was Meglan. Fern could no longer see her: all the villagers were hidden by flames of ice, "She has done nothing wrong!" Then, abashed by her own audacity, she pleaded more quietly, "My lords and ladies, if you say that he is evil and must die, we do not protest. We have no knowledge of these matters. But she is ours. There is no harm in her. Surely you will not hold her to account for his crimes?"

Titus might have answered, but Prince Chorl stopped him with a gesture. "Good woman," he replied to Meglan, "that is for her to say. Until now, she has made no choices. Here she will choose for herself.

"My lady Fern," the Prince said across the fire, "the warlock at your side is condemned for precisely such crimes as he has committed against you. Knowing what he has done, and having heard his answers, would you stand between him and his punishment? Or will you stand aside?"

Fern had been changed by fire. Even now, she could not stop making connections which had never occurred to her before. She had said what she must: that was done. Now she took the next step.

Letting go of Suriman, she backed away.

"No!" At the sight of her withdrawal, he flinched and crouched down as though his destruction had already begun; he covered his face with his hands. Spasms of cold shook and twisted his naked limbs. To abandon him wrung her heart. Softly, so that he might hear her, she murmured, "My thanks."

He must have heard her. A moment later, he lowered his arms and drew himself erect. For the first time in the ring of fire, she saw his eyes clearly—the one almost blind, the other marred by a slice of silver. Shivers mounted through him, then receded. He could not smile, but his voice was gentle as he said, "I regret nothing. You were worth the risk. You have not asked me what loveliness is—in that I was wrong, as in so many other things—but still I will tell you.

"It is you."

Because he did not try to compel her with images or colors or supplications, Fern answered, "Yes."

"*Suriman!*" Florice wailed in despair.

She was too late. The masters of magic had already raised their periapts and apparatus, summoned their powers. In silence the white fire raged abruptly into the heavens: mutely the flames towered over the ring and then crashed inward, falling like ruin upon the warlock.

He did not scream now, as he had when he was transformed. The force mustered against him surpassed sound. As voiceless as the conflagration, he writhed in brief agony while retribution and cold searched him to the marrow of his bones, the pit of his chest, the gulf of his skull. Then he was lifted out of the circle in a swirl of white embers and ash. The fire burned him down to dust, which the dark swallowed away. Soon nothing remained of him except the riders in their triumph, the shocked faces of the villagers and Florice's last wail.

As though bereft of language, images, and will Fern sprawled on the ground with her face hidden in her arms. Her heart beat, her lungs took air. But she could not speak or rise or uncover her face—or would not. At Prince Chorl's bidding, two of his minions and one of the warlocks came forward to offer their assistance. Meglan, Karay, and others had already run to Fern's side, however, and they spurned help. Unexpectedly dignified in the face of lords and magic, Meglan farmwife said, "She is ours. We will care for her."

"I understand," said the Prince sadly. "But I give you this promise. At any time, in any season, if you desire help for her, only send to me, and I will do everything I can."

"And I," Florice added through her grief. "I promise also."

Titus was too full of fierceness and vindication to find his voice; yet he nodded a promise of his own.

When the riders were gone, Meglan and the others lifted Fern in their arms. Like a cortege, they bore her to Wall's house, where a clean room with a bed and blankets was made ready for her. There she was comforted and cosseted as she had once cared for Sarendel's pigs. Unlike the pigs, however, she did not respond. She lay with her face covered—as far as anyone knew, she slept with her face covered. And before dawn, she left the house. Meglan searched for her, but to no avail, until the farmwife thought to look out toward the refuse-tip beyond her garden.

There she saw Fern scavenging.

After Meglan had wept for a time, she bustled out to the village. She told what she had seen; men and women with good hearts—and no knowledge of warlocks—heard her. Before Fern returned from her scavenging, a new shed had been erected on the exact spot of her former hovel. A new curtain swung as a door; a new pallet lay against one wall; new bowls and cups sat on the pallet. And the bowls were full of corn and carrots, cured ham and bread.

Fern did not seem surprised to find her hovel whole. Perhaps she had forgotten that it was gone. Yet the sight of Meglan and Horrik, Veil and Salla, Karay and Yoel standing there to greet her appeared to frighten her. With a familiar alarm which the village itself had forgotten, she cowered at the nearest hedge, peering through her hair as though she feared what would happen if she were noticed.

In rue and shame, the villagers left the hovel, pretending that they had not noticed her. At once she took the fruits of her scavenging inside and closed the curtain.

From that moment onward, her life in Sarendel-on-Gentle became much the same as it had been before she had been adopted by a pig. From dawn to dusk she roamed the village refuse-tips and the surrounding hills, scavenging scraps and herbs, and storing them against the coming winter. The changes which marked her days were few—and no one spoke of them. First out of kindness, then out of habit, Sarendel's folk gave her as many gifts as she would accept. The children learned to ignore her; but if any of the younger ones thought to tease or torment her, the older ones put a quick stop to it. As the days became fortnights, even Horrik forgot that he had once desired her. And she no longer seemed to know or care anything about pigs. Her love for them had been lost among the stars and the cold white fire. By slow degrees the present became so like the past that men and women shook their heads incredulously to think the continuity had ever been disturbed.

In this way she regained the peace and safety which had been lost to her.

If the villagers had looked more closely, however—if Fern had worn her mud-thick and straggling hair away from her face, or if she had not ducked her head to avoid meeting anyone's gaze—they might have noticed one other change.

Since the night when she had transformed her only love from a pig to a man, just in time to see him caught and taken by his doom, one of her eyes had grown warmer, brighter, belying her renewed destitution. The other bore a strange mark across the iris, a thin argent scar, as though her sight had been cut by silver.

The Kings of Tarshish
Shall Bring Gifts

> *People who dream when they sleep at night, know of a special kind of happiness which the world of the day holds not, a placid ecstasy, and ease of heart, that are like honey on the tongue. They also know that the real glory of dreams lies in their atmosphere of unlimited freedom. It is not the freedom of the dictator, who enforces his own will on the world, but the freedom of the artist, who has no will, who is free of will. The pleasure of the true dreamer does not lie in the substance of the dream, but in this: that there things happen without any interference from his side, and altogether outside his control.*
>
> *[The dreamer is] the privileged person to whom everything is taken. The Kings of Tarshish shall bring gifts.*
>
> —ISAK DINESEN, *OUT OF AFRICA*

I have often wondered why there are tyrants, and I have come to the conclusion it is because some men remember their dreams. For what do we know of dreams? What is the truest thing to be said of them? Surely it is that we forget them. And therefore it is also sure that this forgetting must have a purpose. Hungers are conceived in dreams in order to be forgotten, so that the dreamer and his life may go on without them. That is why most men remember nothing—except the sensation of having dreamed.

But men who do not forget are doomed. Such a man was Prince Akhmet, the only son of the Caliph of Arbin, His Serene Goodness Abdul dar-El Haj.

After a reign enviable in every respect except the birth of male offspring, in his declining years His Serene Goodness at last produced an heir. This, as may be imagined, was a great relief to the Caliph's wives, as well as a great joy to the Caliph himself. Thus it is easily understood that from the first young Akhmet was coddled and pampered and indulged as though he came among us directly from the gods. In later years, during the Prince's own brief reign, men looked to his childhood as an explanation for his tyrannies. After all, Arbin had no tradition of tyranny. His Serene Goodness Abdul dar-El Haj, like his father before him, and his father's father, was a man in whom strength exercised itself in the service of benevolence. Some explanation was needed to account for Prince Akhmet's failure to follow the path of his sires.

But I do not believe that a childhood of indulgence and gratification suffices to explain the Prince. For with his pampering and coddling young Akhmet also received example. The Caliph was demonstrably benign in all his dealings. Therefore he was much beloved. And the Prince's mother was the sweetest of all the Caliph's sweet young wives. Surely Akhmet tasted no gall at her breast, felt none at his father's hand.

His Serene Goodness Abdul dar-El Haj, however, remembered none of his dreams. His son, on the other hand—

Ah, Prince Akhmet remembered everything.

This was not, of course, a salient feature of his childhood. For him, in fact, childhood was what dreams are for other men—something to be forgotten. But his ability to remember his dreams was first remarked soon after the first down appeared on his cheeks, and he began to make his first experiments among the odalisques in his father's harem.

That is always an exciting time for young men, a time of sweat at night and fever in daylight, a time when many things are desired and few of them are clearly understood. It is, however, a strangely safe time—a time when attention to the appetites of the loins consumes or blinds or transmutes all other passions. Men of that age must think about matters of the flesh, and if the flesh is not satisfied they are rarely able to think about anything else. So it was only after he had more than once awakened in the bed of a beautiful girl about whom he had believed he dreamed, thus at once deflating and familiarizing such visions, that his true dreams began their rise to his notice, like the red carp rising among the lilies to bread crumbs on the surface of his father's ornamental pools.

"I had the most wonderful dream," he announced to the girl with whom he had slept. "The most wonderful dream."

"Tell me about it, my lord," she replied, not because she had a particular interest in dreams, but because his pleasure was her fortune. In truth, she already knew how to be enjoyed in ways which had astonished him. But she was also prepared to give him the simple satisfaction of being listened to.

He sat up in her bed, the sheets falling from the graceful beauty of his young limbs. His features were still pale with sleep, but his eyes shone, and they did not regard his companion.

"I can see it now," he murmured distantly. "I can see it all. It was of a place where there are no men."

"No men?" the girl asked with a smile, "or no people?" Her fingertips traced his thigh to the place where her notion of manhood resided.

The Prince heard her question, but he did not appear to feel her touch. "No people," he answered. "A place where there are no people, but only things of beauty."

The girl might have said again, "No people?" with a pout, thinking herself a thing of beauty. But perhaps she knew that if she had done so he would not have heeded her. All his attention was upon his dream.

"The place was a low valley," he said, showing the angle of the slopes with his hands, "its sides covered by rich greensward on which the early dew glistened, as bright in the sunshine as a sweep of stars. Down the vale-bottom ran a stream of water so clean and crystal that it appeared as liquid light, dancing and swirling over its black rocks and white sand. Above the greensward stood fruit trees, apple and peach and cherry, all in blossom, with their flowers like music in the sun, and their trunks wrapped in sweet shade. The air was luminous and utterly deep, transformed from the unfathomable purple of night by the warmth of the sun.

"The peace of the place was complete," murmured young Akhmet, "and I would have been content with it as it was, happy to gaze upon it while the dream remained in my mind. But it was not done. For when I gazed upon the running trance of the stream, I saw that the dance of the light was full of the dance of fish, and as my eyes fell upon the fish I saw that while they danced they became flowers, flowers more lovely than lilies, brighter than japonica, and the flowers floated in profusion away along the water.

"Then I gazed from those blooms to the flowers of the trees, and they, too, changed. Upon the trees, the flowers appeared to be music, but in moments they became birds, and the birds were music indeed, their flights like arcs of melody, their bodies formed to the shape of their song. And the shade among the tree trunks also changed. From the sweet dark emerged rare beasts, lions and jacols, nilgai deer with fawns among them, oryx, fabled mandrill. And the peace of the beasts, too, was complete, so that they brought no fear with them. Instead, they gleamed as the greensward and the stream gleamed, and when the lions shook their manes they scattered droplets of water, which became chrysoprase and diamonds among the grass. The fawns of the nilgai wore a sheen of finest silver, and from their mouths the mandrill let fall rubies of enough purity to ransom a world.

"I remember it all." A sadness came over the Prince, a sadness which both touched and pleased the girl. "I would have been content if the dream had never ended."

"Why are there no such places in the world?"

His sadness brought him back to her. "Because we do not need them," she replied softly. "We have our own joys and contentments." Then she drew him to her. She was, after all, only a girl, ignorant of many things. She took pleasure in the new urgency with which he renewed his acquaintance with her flesh, and saw no peril in it.

But I must not judge her harshly. No one saw any peril in it. I saw none in it myself, and I see peril everywhere. "When he came later into the cushion-bestrewn chamber of his father's court, interrupting the business of Arbin with a young and indulged man's heedlessness in order to describe his dream again for the benefit of the Caliph and his advisers, none of those old men took it amiss.

His Serene Goodness, of course, took nothing that his beloved son did amiss. The sun shone for his son alone, and all that his son did was good. And he was entranced by the Prince's dream, full as it was with things which he had himself experienced, but could not remember. The truth was that the Caliph was not an especially imaginative ruler. Common sense and common sympathy were his province. For new ideas, unexpected solutions, unforeseen possibilities, he relied upon his advisers. Therefore he listened to young Akhmet's recitation as if in telling his dream the Prince accomplished something wondrous. And he cozied the sadness which followed the telling as if Akhmet had indeed suffered a loss.

With the Caliph's example before them, Abdul dar-El Haj's advisers could hardly have responded otherwise themselves. Each in his own way, all of us valued our suzerain. In addition, we were accustomed to the indulgence which surrounded the Prince. And lastly we enjoyed the dream itself—at least in the telling.

We listened to it reclining, as was the custom in Abdul dar-El Haj's court. His Serene Goodness was nothing if not corpulent, and liked his ease. He faced all the duties of Arbin recumbent among his cushions. And because none of his advisers could lay even a distant claim to youth, he rebuked us all to do as he did. We were stretched at Prince Akhmet's feet like admirers while the young man spoke.

When the telling was done, and His Serene Goodness had comforted his son, the Vizier of Arbin, Moshim Mosha Va, stroked his thin gray beard and pronounced, "You are a poet, my lord Prince. Your words give life to beauty."

This was not a proposition to which the High Priest of the Mosque, the Most Holy Khartim a-Kul, would have assented on theological grounds. Beauty was, after all, a creation of the gods, not of men. As a practical matter, however, the High Priest nodded, shook the fringe around his cap, and rumbled, "Indeed."

For myself, I primarily wondered whether it was the recitation itself which enabled Akhmet to remember his dream so vividly. Nevertheless I expressed my approval with the others, unwilling to launch a large debate on so small a subject.

But the Prince was not complimented. "No," he protested, at once petulant and somewhat defensive. "Words have nothing to do with it. It was the dream. The beauty was in the dream."

"Ah, but the dream was yours, my lord Prince, not ours." The Vizier was disputatious by nature, sometimes to his own cost. "We would not have been able to know of its beauty, if you had not described it so well."

"No!" young Akhmet repeated. He was still close enough to his childhood to stamp his foot in vexation. "It was the dream. It has nothing to do with me."

"Of course," His Serene Goodness put in soothingly. He liked nothing which vexed his son. "But Moshim Mosha Va is quite correct. He only means to say that your words are the only way in which we can share the beauty of what you have seen. Perhaps there are two beauties here—the beauty of your dream, and the beauty of your description."

For some reason, however, this eminently reasonable suggestion vexed the Prince further. His dream had made him sad. It had also made him fierce. "You do not understand!" he cried with an embarrassing crack in his young voice. "I remember it all!" Then he fled the court.

In puzzlement, the Caliph turned to his advisers after his son had gone and asked plaintively, "What is it that I have failed to understand?"

The Vizier tangled his fingers among his whiskers and pulled them to keep himself still, a rare effort of self-restraint. Perhaps he knew better than to venture the opinion that Prince Akhmet behaved like a spoiled brat.

"My lord Prince is young," commented the Most Holy Khartim a-Kul in his religious rumble, "It may be that his ideas are still too big for his ability to express them. It may be that his dream came to him from the gods, and he rightly considers it false worship to compliment the priest when praise belongs only to Heaven."

This notion "rightly" made His Serene Goodness uneasy. A son whose dreams came to him from the gods would make an uncomfortable heir to the rule of Arbin. The Caliph's eyes shifted away from his advisers, and he resumed the business of the court without much clarity of thought.

As for the Prince, when he returned to his apartments he kicked his dog, a hopeless mongrel on which he had doted for most of his boyhood.

At the time, no one except the dog expressed any further opinions on the subject.

But of course it was inevitable that the Prince would dream again.

Not at once, naturally. In him, the carp had only begun to rise. The bread crumbs on the surface were few, or the fish did not see them. He was in a sour humor, and his attention was fixed, not on the hope of new dreams, but on the failure of other people to understand the significance of the first one. For a time, he lost interest in women—at least to the extent that any young man can be said to have lost interest in women. At the same time, he experienced an increased enthusiasm for the manly arts of Arbin, especially for hunting, and most especially for the hunting of beasts of prey, creatures of disquiet, feasters on blood. Arbin is a civilized country. Nevertheless the great forests do not lack for leopard and wild pig, with tusks which can gut a horse with one toss of the head, and packs of hungry langur often harry the flocks on the plains. By the standards accepted for a young lord of the realm and his father's son, Akhmet expended a not-unreasonable amount of time upon matters of bloodshed. Until he dreamed again.

He and his companions, several young men of the court and a commensurate number of trusted retainers and hunters, had spent the night camped among the thick trunks and overarching limbs of a nearby forest. In this forest was said to live a great ape which had learned a taste for human flesh—a small matter as the affairs of the world are considered, but by no means trivial to the villagers whose huts bordered the trees—and for three days Prince Akhmet with his entourage had been hunting the beast under conditions which can best be described as gracious hardship. Apparently, fatigue enabled him to sleep especially well. On the morning of the fourth day, he sprang from his bedding like a dust devil, chasing in all directions and shouting incoherently for his horse. When his companions inquired as to the meaning of his urgency, he replied that he had had another dream. His father must know of it immediately.

Clattering like madmen in their haste—a haste which no one but the Prince himself actually comprehended—Akhmet and his entourage raced homeward.

Now when he burst among us, hot and flurried from his ride, with stubble upon his cheeks and a feverish glare in his eyes, and announced, "I have dreamed again. I remember it all." I felt a serious skepticism. To remember one dream is merely remarkable, not ultimately significant. To remember a second, however, so soon after the first—if a few weeks may be called soon—as well as after the confusion of a hard ride, and without the exercise of relating the dream to anyone else—

Well, in all honesty, I doubted young Akhmet. I watched him closely for signs of stumbling or invention, which would call the accuracy of his memory into question.

In contrast, His Serene Goodness appeared to feel no skepticism at all. Perhaps he was simply delighted to see his son after an absence of a few days. Perhaps he was delighted by the idea of dreams. Or perhaps he saw in Akhmet's eyes that the Prince would brook no opposition. Unlike his advisers, who exchanged uneasy glances as unobtrusively as possible, the Caliph only beamed pleasure at his son and said, "Another dream! Tell us at once. Was it also wonderful?"

"It was," the Prince pronounced, "wonderful beyond compare."

Steadying himself as well as his excitement allowed, he said, "I stood upon a great height, and below me lay the city of Arbin at night, unscrolled with all its lights as legible as any text, so that the movements of the least streetsweeper as well as the activities of the mightiest house were plain to be read. Indeed, the city itself was also alive, breathing its own air, flexing its own limbs, adding its own superscript to the writing of the lights. I knew that the truth and goodness and folly of all our people were written there for me to read.

"Yet as I began to read, the height on which I stood grew even greater, and the city itself expanded, and I shrank to a mote among them—a mote without loss or grief, however, but rather a part at once of the lights and of the darkness between the lights, much as a particle of blood partakes of all blood while it surges through the veins." The Prince spoke with a thrill in his voice which answered my skepticism, a blaze in his eyes which bore me with him. "Thus at the same time I rose and shrank, losing myself within a greatness that transformed and illumined me. I rose and shrank, and the city grew, and the lights became stars and suns and glories, lifting every living heart to heights which we have never known. And the darkness between the lights was the solace in which every living heart rests from wonder.

"While I dreamed, I was among the heavens and the gods."

There he stopped. His chest rose and fell with the strength of his breathing, and the fever in his eyes abated slowly.

"This is truly a wonder," said His Serene Goodness when he had collected his thoughts, "a wonder and wonderful." Like his advisers, he had no intention of repeating the mistake of the previous occasion. "Is this not so, Vizier?"

"It is, my lord," replied Moshim Mosha Va sagely. He tugged at his beard for a moment, then ventured to add, "Perhaps it is also something more."

"More?" The Prince and his father spoke at once, but in differing tones. Abdul dar-El Haj was naturally delighted by anything which would enable him to think even better of his son. Young Akhmet, however, appeared strangely suspicious.

"To remember one dream, my lord," said the Vizier, echoing my earlier ruminations, "is pleasant and desirable. More so when the dream itself is peaceful and lovely. But to remember two—two such dreams in so short a time—is unusual. It may be that Prince Akhmet has been given a gift. It may be that he has been touched by wisdom or prophecy. In that case, his dreams may have meaning which it would be folly to ignore.

"Perhaps we would do well, my lord, to seek interpretation for his dreams."

Both the Caliph and his son were startled by this suggestion, and now their expressions were nearly identical. His Serene Goodness had too much common sense—and too little imagination—to believe that a gift of wisdom or prophecy would be a good thing in an heir. And the Prince seemed to dislike any deflection of attention from the dream itself. Nevertheless he held his peace, and his father turned to the Most Holy Khartim a-Kul.

"Do you concur, High Priest?"

Khartim a-Kul waggled the fringe on his hat to conceal his squirming. Wisdom and prophecy were matters of religion, and did not belong to spoiled young princes. Yet he could not ignore his responsibility to His Serene Goodness, or to Arbin.

"Two dreams are only two dreams, my lord," he murmured judiciously. "It is, however, better to search for meaning where meaning is absent, than to ignore it where it is present."

Sadly, Abdul dar-El Haj was not judicious where his son was concerned, and so did not enjoy judiciousness in others. Somewhat sourly, he demanded, "Then interpret this dream for us, High Priest. Give us the insight of the gods."

The Most Holy Khartim a-Kul rumbled inchoately past the dangles of his hat. He did not enjoy being made to squirm. Neither did he like to fail either his religion or his ruler. After a moment, he said, "The language of dreams, my lord, is private, and requires study. There are interpreters who make a specialty of such matters." Seeing the Caliph's mounting vexation, however, he hastened to add, "Yet I might hazard to say, my lord, that this dream speaks of Prince Akhmet's future. At that forever-to-be-lamented day when your Serene Goodness ceases to be Caliph in Arbin, and Prince Akhmet ascends to his inheritance, he will be one in spirit as well as in body with all his people—'much as a particle of blood partakes of all blood.' He will see the good of the whole as well as the good of each individual, and will rule with the same selfless benevolence which has made Abdul dar-El Haj beloved throughout this land."

Thus the High Priest of the Mosque extricated himself from his lord's displeasure.

While I, who see peril everywhere, saw peril not in Khartim a-Kul's interpretation, but in young Akhmet's reaction.

So vehemently that spittle sprang from his lips, he snapped, "Nonsense, Priest. You rave. Dreams have no meaning. Only the memory of them has meaning."

In fury, he withdrew himself from the court.

The Caliph was shocked. "*Now* what have we done amiss?" he inquired plaintively.

None of his advisers answered. Apparently we had once again misunderstood Prince Akhmet's reasons for relating his dream.

Later, we learned that the Prince had gone straight to his father's harem, where he had covered one of his favorite women savagely, leaving the marks of his teeth on her breasts—marks which took weeks to heal.

So the seeds of concern were planted.

Those seeds did not sprout, however, until the Prince dreamed again, despite the fact that during the interval he tended them in a desultory fashion, giving them occasional water and fertilizer. In a time of unusual application to the study of weapons, he presumed upon his favored station to do one of his instructors an injury. He became increasingly rough in his treatment of women. His commands to his servants were sometimes far-fetched—and sometimes his anger was extreme when those commands were not carried out to his satisfaction. Such signs, however, such bubbles rising from the depths of the pool, were generally ignored. We are taught to be indulgent of the behavior of princes. And he was still young. In the words of one of his grooms, he had conceived an itch which he did not know how to scratch. Therefore he was irritable. And he had not yet learned the benefits of self-restraint.

Finally, Akhmet's actions passed unheeded because our fears were focused elsewhere. After many years of health, His Serene Goodness Abdul dar-El Haj began to fail. A cough which the physicians could not ease brought blood to his lips in flecks. His appetite left him, and his flesh began to sag from his bones. His wives lost the capacity to comfort him. Often he needed assistance to rise from his cushions. Because he was so much beloved, the sight of his decline filled his advisers and all his people with grief. We had little heart to spare for the vagaries of the young Prince.

So he committed small hurts without reprimand, performed small acts of unreason without restraint, caused petty vexations throughout the court and was ignored. Too little notice was taken of him until he dreamed again.

This time, his dream brought him out of sleep in the lonely hours of the night. Such was the power he remembered that he could not contain himself until morning. He must relate what he had seen. Regardless of the Caliph's weakness, Prince Akhmet hurried at once to his father's chamber, where physicians stood watch at his father's bedside, and maidens dabbed away the blood as it came to his father's lips.

"I have dreamed again," he announced peremptorily, ignoring his father's weakness, his father's uneasy sleep, "the most wonderful dream."

With difficulty, His Serene Goodness opened his eyes. Perhaps because he was still partly in sleep, or perhaps because his pain ruled him, or perhaps because he could not be blind to his son's inconsideration, he replied in a weary tone, "I, too, have had a dream. I dreamed that I had a son who loved me."

At this time, young Akhmet was still within reach of chagrin. He seemed to see his father's illness for the first time, and all his demand left him. Falling to his knees at the bedside, he cried, "Father, forgive me. You are ill, and I have been heedless, heartless. What can I do to comfort you? Why do these physicians not heal you? Why do you tolerate them, if they have no power to heal you? I will do everything I can."

This at once dispelled whatever anger the Caliph may have felt toward his son. Stroking the youth's beautiful head, he said, "You will give me ease if you tell me of your dream. Only be still while my advisers are summoned, so that they may hear you also. And permit the High Priest to bring his interpreters, so that the truth of your wonderful dream may be understood."

Prince Akhmet bit his lips, plainly distraught. Yet he acceded to his father's wishes.

And so the advisers of the court were summoned to Abdul dar-El Haj's chamber, along with interpreters roused and admonished by the Most Holy Khartim a-Kul himself.

In the corridors of the palace, upon the way to the Caliph's sickchamber, I encountered Moshim Mosha Va. The High Priest of the Mosque strode some paces ahead of us with his interpreters. We were able to speak quietly.

"This is unseemly," said the Vizier, with disgust hidden under his beard. "I am old. I need more sleep."

"You are old," I replied, "and need less sleep, not more. You have no more use for dreams."

He snorted to me. "You are glib, wizard. I know of no other reason why the Most Pompous Khartim a-Kul has not branded you a heretic. But glibness will not save you when that little shit becomes Caliph. For myself, I believe I will put an end to my life. I do not wish to spend my waning years tormented by his fancies."

I smiled at the thought that the disputatious Vizier would ever consent to death. Pleasantly, I answered, "That is because you do not understand him."

He paused to peer closely into my face. "Do you?"

"No," I admitted. "But I will." I must. Have I not said that I see peril everywhere?

Together, we followed the High Priest into the sickchamber of His Serene Goodness Abdul dar-El Haj.

The young Prince still knelt at his father's side. The Caliph's fingers stroked his son's fine hair. In that pose, the lord appeared to be passing his blessing to his heir.

"Come and hear what my son has dreamed," said His Serene Goodness when we had gathered around him. "This is the third dream, and must have meaning." It seemed that the Caliph had reconciled himself to the idea of a gods-gifted scion. Or perhaps he realized, in his unimaginative way, that Prince Akhmet must be reconciled to himself in order to become a fit lord for Arbin. "High Priest, are these men the interpreters of dreams?"

"They are, my lord," answered the Most Holy Khartim a-Kul, sounding more than ever like a subterranean mishap. "We have prayed over the young Prince and consulted the stars."

I knew for a fact that this was pious falsehood. Khartim a-Kul had had no attention to spare for Akhmet. All his hours had been spent in preparation for the rites and ceremonies of the Caliph's passing, and of the installation of a new lord. I kept this knowledge to myself, however.

"We are ready," the High Priest concluded, "to bring you our best insight."

"Very well," said His Serene Goodness as though his breath were fading. "Let my son speak his dream." At the Caliph's bedside, Prince Akhmet rose to his feet and told us what he had dreamed.

"In my dream, I saw a mighty suzerain, a nameless caliph in a land I have never known. He was in the time of his best youth, and though I did not know him and could not name him, his features were the features of the Caliph of Arbin, His Serene Goodness Abdul dar-El Haj, my father."

Had the Prince been more of a politician, I would have believed this beginning false. But it was impossible to mistake the ardor of his stance, or the growing hunger in his gaze.

"His head was crowned with light," said young Akhmet, "and love lived in his eyes, and his limbs were of such beauty that all hearts were drawn to him. He was the center of the storm, where peace lives untouched by pain. He was the pause between the beats of the pulse, the rest between respirations, and his gift to all who knew him was balm.

"Yet he was more than this. Indeed, when he spread out his hands, the world was shaped by his gestures, so that nature itself took on the form of his will. He stretched his fingers, and plains were made. He shrugged his shoulders, and mountains grew. Where he pointed, there were rivers. The seed of his loins gave birth to new peoples, and his caress left all women faint with pleasure."

While he spoke, I observed, as I should have observed weeks ago, that he had changed. His lips had grown pinched like a simoniac's, and his cheeks hinted at hollowness, and his form was as gaunt as his youth and beauty permitted. Regret is useless, but still I regretted that I had not turned my attention to him earlier.

"And in my dream," he continued, "the storm of pain which drives all men, but which could only run in circles of folly around the nameless caliph, took notice of him and grew wrathful, for it is not given to men that they should be free of pain, or that they should free others, or that the world should shape itself to their will. Therefore the storm moved against him. Great was its wrath, and terrible, and whole lands and peoples were bereaved by its power. The reach of his beneficence was constricted as pain bore peace away and his place in the center of the storm shrank.

"Then there was grief everywhere, for all men were hurt, and so all men believed that the nameless caliph could not endure against pain.

"At last the storm withdrew, thinking itself victorious.

"And yet the caliph stood as he had stood before, with light upon his brow and beauty in his limbs. Nothing about him was changed, except his eyes. There love still shone, love for all peoples and all lands, love which healed all it saw. But with the love was also knowledge of pain, understanding for the injuries and losses which drive men to do ill, forgiveness for frailty. He had accepted pain into his being and searched it to its heart and taken no hurt.

"That was my dream," concluded the Prince. For a moment, he seemed overcome by sorrow. Then, however, he lifted his head, and in his eyes was a look which might have signified both love and the knowledge of pain. Or perhaps it was only madness. Softly, he added, "It was wonderful. It lives with me still, and will live always. I will forget nothing."

His Serene Goodness did not reply. But his eyes also shone, and there were tears upon his cheeks, and his hand clung to his son's until it trembled.

"Such dreams must be valued," murmured the Most Holy Khartim a-Kul. He may conceivably have been sincere. "To have such dreams is surely a gift from Heaven. We are blessed to be in your presence, my lord."

During the pause between one heartbeat and the next, Prince Akhmet's face lost its look of love and knowledge. At once, it became as tight and miserable as a miser's.

"Wonderful," breathed the Caliph past the blood on his lips. "Wonderful. Oh, my son.

"High Priest." A fit of coughing gripped him. When it passed, it left fresh red upon his chin. Nearly gasping, he asked, "How is this dream to be interpreted?"

Khartim a-Kul was nothing if not a politician. Graciously, he deferred to his chief interpreter, not because he doubted what to say, but because he knew the words would carry more weight if they came from a professed student of dreams.

The chief interpreter was a plump individual with more oil in his manner than most men can comfortably digest. "My lord Caliph," he began, "I pray devoutly that you will live forever. The reading of dreams is at once a mystery and a science. This is because the language of dreams is a language not of words but of images, and images do not speak. They only show themselves and leave their meaning to the insight of the observer. And yet they *are* a language, and all languages must be coherent. Their meaning can be learned, much as other men learn to speak foreign tongues."

This disquisition left the Prince shifting his weight from one foot to the other like a man restraining outrage. For his father's sake, however, he did not speak.

"Usually, my lord Caliph," the chief interpreter went on, "we do not presume to explain dreams until we have studied them, until we have had time to learn the language of their images." Nevertheless even he could see that His Serene Goodness was losing patience. He hastened to say, "But the present case is exceptional. Prince Akhmet's dream is so precise that its import is unmistakable.

"My lord Caliph, your son has been given a vision of the journey of man from life to paradise. The nameless suzerain of the dream bore your face as a symbol of goodness, of the virtue and value which the gods intend for all men. If all men were ruled by goodness, the world would be remade into a place of joy. Thus the nameless suzerain has the power to shape the world. He is opposed, however, by the storm of pain, the storm of death, by the conflicting and petty intentions which assail goodness out of fear. And against this storm goodness cannot prevail because it is mortal and must die.

"But when goodness has faced death and understood it, when goodness has learned the true compassion of experience for all fear, all pain, then goodness itself becomes paradise, the perfect and healing home of the soul. Pettiness and hurt are made whole, conflicts are swept away, and joy becomes the heart's demesne."

As the chief interpreter spoke, the impatience faded from His Serene Goodness' face. The strain of his illness also seemed to fade, and peace filled his eyes. He was pleased by what he heard. Who would not have been pleased? Watching him, however, I believed that he would have been pleased by any interpretation which did not falsify the tone of the dream. For a moment, I was fascinated by the contrast between the two lords, father and son. The father thought of reasons to go to his death unafraid. The son could barely contain his fury. At the sight, I was struck by the odd notion that the true benefit of dreams comes, not to those who have them, but rather to those who hear about them.

Then the Most Holy Khartim a-Kul began to intone a prayer, and the notion was forgotten.

But Prince Akhmet had come to the end of his restraint. Despite the prayer—despite the necessity of reverence for the High Priest, or of respect for his father's pain and contentment—he left the Caliph's bedside and swept across the chamber to confront the chief interpreter. Knotting his fists in the plump man's robes, he hissed so that his father would not hear him, "You are a fool! You are all *fools*. You will not demean my dreams with your unctuous pieties. Do you hear me? When I am Caliph, I will have you *beheaded*."

The Vizier Moshim Mosha Va cast me a look which said, I mean what I say. When this little shit becomes Caliph, I will put an end to my life.

Standing much closer to the chief interpreter than to the bedside, Khartim a-Kul heard the Prince's words. He was shocked, of course, and outraged. But he could not stop his prayer without drawing the Caliph's attention to the fact that something was amiss. Grinding his teeth, he continued his unheeded appeal to the gods to its end.

By that time, young Akhmet had left the sickchamber.

He kept his word. As soon as his father's corpse began to blacken and shrivel on the pyre, he commanded the beheading of the chief interpreter. The man was dead before sundown.

Abdul dar-El Haj's death was still some days away, however. His son's dream seemed to give him respite in his illness. He rested well that night, and for a day or two he grew stronger. And when his decline resumed, drawing him steadily toward his death, he remained contented, blessed with peace. He, too, believed the Prince's dream.

During those days, Akhmet had a number of dreams.

He remembered them all and told them to whoever would listen. The only restraint he exercised was that he did not trouble his father again—and did not permit his dreams to be interpreted in his presence. Yet his look of simony worsened. More and more, I came to think that he was paying the price for his father's ease.

And at last His Serene Goodness Abdul dar-El Haj died.

At once, all Arbin was plunged into a veritable apotheosis of mourning. That is to say, the entire land was seized by such a frenzy of religious prostration, ceremonial grief, and ritualized emotional flagellation that it became nearly impossible for men like the Vizier and myself to remember that the love underlying the Mosque's extravagances was genuine. The advisers of suzerains become cynics of necessity, and the Most Holy Khartim a-Kul was surely the most cynical among us. Therefore Moshim Mosha Va and I were hard-pressed to perceive the relationship between show and substance, between the public display of grief and its private truth. But we were grieved ourselves, perhaps not at our best. And, like the High Priest, we had reason to wonder what would become of us with the loss of our lord—but, unlike the High Priest, we had no outlet for our uncertainty.

We were not made less uncertain by the beheading of Khartim a-Kul's chief interpreter. For that act of tyranny, however, we had been forewarned. We had had time to accustom ourselves to the concept, if not to the actuality. As a consequence, we were more deeply disturbed by young Akhmet's other contribution to his father's funerary commemorations.

In tribute to His Serene Goodness, Khartim a-Kul revived a number of extreme liturgies and worships which had not been used for several generations—had not been used, in fact, precisely because they were so extreme. Like several of his fathers before him, Abdul dar-El Haj had become Caliph not as a youth, but as a man, and as a man, with the common sense of his forebears, he had forbidden the exercise of any liturgies or worships which he considered excessive.

Doubtless the Most Holy Khartim a-Kul deserved blame for his breach of recent custom, even though his decisions were made understandable by his fear of his new lord. But he could not have been blamed for the use young Akhmet made of his example.

Entirely to the High Priest's surprise, the new Caliph revived the old custom of suttee.

As an idea, suttee was alive among the people of Arbin. Upon the death of a caliph, all the ruler's wives and odalisques were expected to join his corpse in cremation. And this harsh practice was not utterly unjustified. It preserved the succession of rule from the confusion which could result if one of those women bore a son after her lord's death. For several generations, however, no wife or odalisque had actually been required to commit suttee. Each new caliph of Arbin had spared his father's women by the simple expedient of claiming them for himself, thus at once establishing his own reputation for benevolence and resolving any questions of legitimacy in his father's offspring.

The consternation among Abdul dar-El Haj's harem must have been profound when young Akhmet announced that he would not follow the path of his predecessors. Specifically, he refused to claim or exempt any woman with whom he had shared carnal pleasure. He wished, he said, to begin his rule in Arbin pure. As a demonstration, he said, of his devotion to virtue and the Mosque.

The Most Holy Khartim a-Kul looked as ill as a fish as his priests led the beautiful and innocent women whom Akhmet had loved up onto Abdul dar-El Haj's pyre. The High Priest was only cynical, not heartless. Primarily to contain his own anger, the Vizier Moshim Mosha Va insisted that the High Priest deserved his distress. I found, however, that I had lost my taste for things which distressed Khartim a-Kul.

When the funerary rites and ceremonies were concluded, the new Caliph disposed of the rest of his father's wives by divorce. Doubtless he had no interest in hearing what his mother or the other older women might say about his purity or virtue.

The question in Arbin was not, What manner of caliph will Akhmet become? It was, Whom will he kill next?

The necessity of understanding him had become imperative.

"How long will it take, do you think?" asked the Vizier when we were alone. "You are a wizard. You have strange arts." His tone was bitter, although I knew he meant me no harm. "Read the signs. How long will it take before he has one of us beheaded? How long will it take before he has *me* beheaded?

"*Suttee*, by my beard! We are all disgraced. No civilized people will have dealings with us again for a hundred years."

Well, I am no prophet. I do not see the future. In the case of young Akhmet, I could hardly see my hand before my face. Nevertheless I had seen Arbin flourish under a line of benevolent rulers. I had watched Arbin's people grow in tolerance, as well as in religion and wealth. And I had loved His Serene Goodness as much as any man.

"Moshim Mosha Va," I said formally, so that the Vizier would heed me, "your death is already written—but it is written in the heart of the rock, where I cannot read it. Yet you are the Vizier of Arbin. Safe or doomed, you must uphold your duty."

"Oh, truly?" he snapped at me. "And must I uphold *suttee*? Must I uphold the murder of interpreters? Must I uphold the whims of a spoiled whelp who remembers his dreams?"

"No," I snapped back, pretending to lose patience with him simply to conceal my own fear. "You must uphold the succession in Arbin. You must uphold the integrity of the realm. Leave this new Caliph to me."

The Vizier Moshim Mosha Va studied me until I dropped my gaze. Then he breathed softly, "Yes. Wizardry and dreams. I will leave this new Caliph to you. And may the gods pity your soul."

"If you will prevent the Most Holy Khartim a-Kul from interfering with me," I replied, speaking half in jest to dispel the seriousness of the moment, "my soul will venture to fend for itself."

Moshim Mosha Va nodded without hesitation. Still studying me, he asked for the second time, "Wizard, do you understand our lord?"

"No," I answered for the second time. "But I will."

The truth was that I did not need understanding to know that Caliph Akhmet would come to me when he had dreamed again. He had already rejected the interpretation and counsel of the Mosque. And he surely had little use for the Vizier's manner of wisdom. Where else would he turn?

He did not dream again for some weeks. During the same period, he did nothing outrageously cruel. Apparently, the beheading of the chief interpreter and the burning of all his lovers had sated him in some way. The state and luxury of his new position he enjoyed. The responsibilities he ignored, except as they gave him opportunity to demonstrate new powers or obtain new satisfactions. For the most part, his time was spent replenishing his harem, and there his instinct for tyranny showed itself most plainly, for he seemed to choose his women, not because they were ripe for love, but because they were apt for humiliation. Nevertheless in the eyes of Arbin women were only women. Unthinking people began to believe that perhaps Caliph Akhmet's rule would not prove intolerable.

I did not make that mistake. I readied my arts and waited.

At last, in the small hours of the night, when even such men as I am must sleep, I was summoned to the Caliph's chambers.

I arrived to find him busy atop one of his women, and it was clear from the sound of her moans and whimpers that she did not relish the nature of his attentions. I would have withdrawn, of course, but I was commanded to attend and watch.

Had I been Moshim Mosha Va, I might have withdrawn regardless and accepted the consequences. Sadly, I lack the Vizier's pragmatic soul. Therefore I stood where I was until the Caliph had achieved his satisfaction. Then I risked saying, "It appears that I have misunderstood your summons, my lord. I believed you wished to discuss the matter of dreams. If I had known you wished me to comment on your performance, I would have prepared myself differently."

"Wizard," Caliph Akhmet replied as if I had not spoken, "my advisers are fatuous in all things, but especially where the wonder of my dreams is concerned. Pious Khartim attempts to interpret what I dream. Sour Moshim attempts to interpret the fact that I dream—and remember. Only you have not made a fool of yourself on this subject. Why is that?"

"Two reasons, my lord," I said at once. "First, I am a wise man. I understand that there are powers which lie beyond mortal interpretation. There the Vizier makes his mistake. He sees nothing which surpasses his own mind. Second, I am a wizard. I know that those powers will not allow themselves to be limited or controlled. There the High Priest makes his mistake. He fails to grasp that religion is not an explanation or a control for that which transcends us, but is rather an explanation or a control for how we must live in the face of powers which will not be defined or interpreted."

"Very good," said the Caliph, and his eyes glittered with the confused penetration of the simoniac, at once insightful and blind. "I see that you want to live. Now you will earn your life.

"I have dreamed the most wonderful dream. I remember it all. Every detail lives in my soul, shining and immaculate, never to be lost. No man has ever remembered such things as I remember them.

"Wizard, I will tell you what I have dreamed. Then you will tell me what to do."

I bowed my acquiescence calmly, although my mouth was dry with fear, and my heart trembled. I had not come to this crisis adequately prepared. I still did not understand.

"I dreamed of wine," said the Caliph, his gaze already turning inward to regard his dream, "of strange wine and music. There were colors in the wine which I have seen in no wine before, hints of black with the most ruby incarnadine, true gold and yellow among straw, regal purple swirling to azure in my cup. There were depths to the liquid which my eyes could not pierce. Its taste was at once poppy and grape, at once fermented and fresh, and all its colors entered my body through my tongue, so that my limbs lived and burned and grew livid because of what was in my mouth. My member became engorged with such heat that no mere female flesh could cool it.

"And while my nerves sang with ruby and gold and cerulean, the music about me also sang. At first it was the music of lyre and tambour, plucked and beating. But as the colors of the wine filled my ears, the music became melody, as if strings and drum had voices full of loveliness, sweet as nectar, rich as satin. Those voices had no words for their song and needed none, for the song itself was as clean as air, as true as rock, as fertile as earth. And the music entered my body as the wine had entered it, came through my ears to live and throb in every muscle and sinew, transporting all my flesh to song. It was promise and fulfillment, carrying comfort to the core of my heart.

"Then the heat of my member grew until it became all heat, all passion, and my whole body in its turn became a part of my member, engorged with the same desire, aching with the same joy. And because of the wine and the music, that desire, that joy, were more precious to me than any release. I knew then that if my member were to spend its heat, all my flesh would experience the climax as part of my member, and the sense of ecstasy and release which would flood my being would be glorious and exquisite beyond any climax known to men— and yet that ecstasy and release, despite their greatness, would be only dross compared to the infinite value of the engorged desire, the aching joy.

"Therefore I was not compelled to seek release, as men are compelled by the lesser passions of wakefulness. Transformed by wine and music, I hung suspended in that place of color and glory and song until the dream ended and left me weeping."

The Caliph was weeping now as he remembered his dream, and his voice was husky with sadness when he again addressed me.

"Wizard, tell me what to do."

He might have been a small boy speaking to his father. Yet his need was not for me, but for a father wiser than I or all the old men of Arbin.

It is conceivable that I could have helped him then. But still I did not understand. I have lived too long in the world, away from dreams.

"My lord," I said, "you are the Caliph. You will do what you wish."

He strove to master his emotion, without success. "And what is it that I wish?"

There I failed him. As if I were wise and sure, I replied, "You wish to make your dreams live. That is why you have summoned me."

He stared at me while the tears dried in his eyes, and his mouth drew down into lines of simony, and I knew then that I had failed him. "Explain yourself, wizard," he said in the tone of a man who hurt women for pleasure.

Now, unfortunately, I could not stop or recant. "My lord," I answered as well as I could, "dreams and wizardry have much in common."

From within my robes, I produced a bouquet of rich flowers.

"Both are composed of illusion and freedom."

When I spread my hands, the flowers became butterflies and scattered themselves about the chamber.

"Yet the freedom and illusion of dreams are internal and may only be reached in sleep, without volition."

Again I spread my hands, and now music could be heard in the air, soft voices whispering melodiously of magic and love.

"The freedom and illusion of wizardry are external, matters of choice."

A third time I spread my hands, and this time flame bloomed in my palms, rising toward the ceiling as I spoke.

"You wish the power of wizardry to make the wonder and glory of your dreams accessible to your waking mind, to make wonder and glory matters of choice."

When I lifted my arms, the flame enveloped me entirely, causing me to disappear from his sight. Only a pillar of fire remained before him, burning the air, consuming nothing. From out of the flame, like the voice of the music, I said, "Wizardry is the path you must follow to pursue your dreams. You must turn away from cruelty and become my disciple. You will find no true happiness in the pain of helpless girls."

Then I stepped from the flame and let the fire go.

"My lord," I said, speaking quietly to contain my fervor, "allow me to serve you. I have knowledge which will enable you to make your dreams live."

That was my best effort, yet I had already lost him. He held a harsh bit clenched between his teeth, and his eyes were as wild as an overdriven mount's.

"So you are a fool after all, wizard," he snarled. "You do not understand. For all your knowledge, you cannot comprehend the worth of my dreams."

The truth must be told. Behind my aged composure, I was near to panic. Nevertheless fright has its uses. It gave me the courage to say, "You are mistaken, my lord. I comprehend very well. Dreams have no worth in themselves. Their only value is the value we find in them, the value we bring to them with our waking eyes and hearts. Because they stir us or move us or teach us, they are precious. Otherwise they are nothing."

The Caliph regarded me, a twist of loathing on his, lips. "Do you believe that?"

I made some effort to hold up my head. "I do, my lord."

"Then, wizard," he said grimly, "you will have the satisfaction of dying for your beliefs. They are a fool's beliefs, and they become you."

I could think of no way to appeal to him as his guards dragged me from the chamber.

For reasons which I did not grasp at the time, however, he let me keep both my head and my life. Instead of sending me to the block—or to the lion pits, or to any other more imaginative or painful death—he sealed me in my workrooms, with little food and water, less light, and no companionship. Indeed, the only contact I had with the court or Arbin came daily at noon, when for a brief time the Vizier Moshim Mosha Va was permitted to stand outside my door and report on the state of Caliph Akhmet's rule.

At first, of course, I believed that I was simply being held in my rooms until a suitable torture and death could be devised. By the second day, however, I began to think that young Akhmet had other intentions. When the Vizier came to my door, I asked him, "Why am I not dead? Does the Caliph imagine I fear death so extremely that I will go mad here among my arts and tools?"

In a sour tone, Moshim Mosha Va replied, "He is not done with you, wizard."

"What remains?" I inquired, daring to hope that I would be given one more chance.

"Who can say?" The Vizier's words were deferential, but his manner of speaking was savage. "Our illustrious lord surpasses us all. There are signs, however, which perhaps you will read better than I can. This morning he commanded one of his wives to be stretched upon the rack. And while her limbs strained with agony, he mounted her. His thrusts caused her to bleat like a sheep."

"Indeed," I muttered to myself. "How quaint."

Then I asked, "And what pleasure did the Caliph take in this action?"

"He appeared blissful," retorted the Vizier, "if such fierceness may be called bliss, until he had spent himself. But then his joy curdled. He ordered the torturer racked until he died, as though the fault lay in the instrument of his will. I think, however, that he meant the man no harm. He was merely vexed."

Perhaps that was the point at which I began to understand Caliph Akhmet and his distress.

"Indeed," I said again. "You have become sagacious since the passing of His Serene Goodness, Vizier. You have grasped an important truth. He means harm to none of us. He is merely vexed."

Moshim Mosha Va made a noise which would have been a curse if the Caliph's guards had not stood beside him, listening. After a moment, he resumed, "Nevertheless the hand of our good lord's vexation is heavy. Why do you not free yourself, wizard? Surely wizardry is good for that, if not for Arbin."

It may have been possible for me to do as he suggested. I could have conjured an affrit to appear before the guards and command them to unlock my prison. Perhaps they would have obeyed instead of fleeing. Freedom lay no farther away than the other side of the heavy door. Yet the distance was too great for me. I had loved Abdul dar-El Haj. I loved Arbin. And I had begun to hope again.

"Wizardry is illusion," I replied to the Vizier, "It is not power. And it is assuredly not freedom. I will await my Caliph's pleasure."

Then, whispering to reduce the hazard that the guards would overhear me, I added, "In the meantime, you must provide for the succession."

The Vizier snorted in disgust and went away.

For a number of days subsequently, he came at noon as he was permitted, bringing me the news of Arbin, which was essentially the news of Caliph Akhmet's attempts to achieve the sensation of his dreams through the exercise of power. He caused considerable pain and occasional death, striving to grasp a knowledge of mortal hurt. At unexpected intervals, he was generous, even benign, so that he could see gratitude on the faces of his subjects and compare it to the look of their distress. Well, he was young, and the young are foolish. He had had too few years in which to learn that power binds rather than releases. It was little wonder that he was vexed.

Therefore I readied myself for the time when he would summon me again.

He did not summon me again, however. Instead, covered by a bright blaze of daylight and torches, he came to see me in my workrooms. The door was flung open, allowing me light for the first time during my captivity. Among guards armed with lamps, Caliph Akhmet strode forward to confront me.

I endeavored to hold up my head, but failed. My old eyes could not bear the brightness. As if I were weeping and ashamed, I bowed and hid my face before my lord.

"Wizard."

I was unable to see him. I could only hear the strain in his voice, the struggle against frailty and grief.

"I need you."

"My lord," I mumbled as if I had become decrepit, "I will serve you."

"Tell me what to do."

"You are the Caliph. You will do what you wish."

"I do not know what I wish."

Indeed. This I had already grasped. Softly, I said, "Tell me what troubles you, my lord."

Out of the light blurred by my tears, young Akhmet answered, "Wizard, I am only myself."

There at last I became sure that I had gleaned the truth. "The same may be said of all men, my lord," I responded gently.

"But all men do not remember their dreams!" If a tyrant can suffer anguish—if such pain can be ascribed to a man who causes so much pain in others—then the Caliph deserved pity. "They are the most wonderful dreams! And I remember them all. Every touch, every color, every joy. Nothing is lost. I have with me now the first dream as clearly as the last, and both are desirable beyond bearing.

"But when I have dreamed, I awake, and I am only myself.

"Help me, wizard."

"I will, my lord." My voice shook, and I cursed the blindness of so much light, but I did not falter. "You wish to live your dreams. You desire to be possessed by dreaming, to give yourself to that glory and freedom always. You wish to cease to be yourself. Therefore you resent anything that takes you from your dreams, any interpretation, any distraction, any release which restores you to your mortality. Waking, you strive for joy and accomplish only dross.

"My lord, I can make you dream always, waking or sleeping. I can enable you to be entirely the dreamer who remembers, beyond interpretation or distraction or release."

I felt his hands clutch at my robes, felt his fingers grip my shoulders to implore. "Then do so. Do so. Do it now."

"Very well, my lord. Give me a moment in which to prepare myself."

In order to gather my strength, as well as to draw the attention of the guards to me, I stepped back from Caliph Akhmet.

Rising to my full height, although I was still effectively blind, I said in the resonant voice of wizards, "Let all witness that what I do now, I do at my lord's express command. He has made his wishes known. I seek only to fulfill them. By my arts he will become his dreams, become dreaming incarnate."

Before the guards could ask whether it lay within their duty to permit this to happen to their lord, I spread my arms and filled the room with fires I could not see.

I did not need to see them, of course. I knew them well. Their suddenness made them seem hotter than they were, and they blazed among my tables and periapts and apparatuses if Caliph and wizard and guards were about to be consumed in conflagration. They did no hurt, however. Instead, as they leaped, roaring silently toward the ceiling, they began to spew out the known stuff of young Akhmet's dreams. Mandrill leaped and snarled, spitting rubies and blood. Nilgai chased silver fear among the flames. City lights unfolded maps of tyranny across darknesses implied by the cruel gaps between the fires. His Serene Goodness Abdul dar-El Haj stretched his mouth to let out a cry of love or pain. Akhmet's swollen member ached for the most glorious and rending ejaculation. To all appearances, my workroom had been filled with dreams come to madness and destruction.

Caliph Akhmet saw those fires no more than I did. They were intended for the edification and appeasement of his entourage. He saw, rather, that I reached among my vials and flasks, uncorked a dusty potion, and poured a liberal draught into a goblet ready with arrak.

"Drink this, my lord," I said as my arts distracted the spectators. "It will enable you to live your dreams even while you are awake."

Young Akhmet had not been a tyrant long enough to learn the fear which corrupts and paralyzes hurtful men. He took the goblet and drank. I could not see the expression on his face.

▲▼▲

Several days later, after Akhmet had died, and I had outfaced the accusation that I had killed him, and a previously forgotten relation of His Serene Goodness Abdul dar-El Haj, discovered and prepared by the Vizier, had been installed as the new Caliph in Arbin, Moshim Mosha Va took me aside and challenged me.

"The truth, wizard," he demanded. "You killed that little shit, did you not?"

"I did not," I replied in feigned indignation. "Did not the guards declare that I gave our lamented lord no draught or potion, but only a vision of his dreams? Did not the best physicians in Arbin proclaim that our lamented lord showed no evidence of poison? This truth is plain, Vizier. Caliph Akhmet brought about his own death by refusing to eat or drink. He died of thirst, I believe, before he could have died of hunger. Can I be blamed for this?"

"Apparently not," growled the vexed Vizier. "Yet I will continue to blame you until you answer me. By what miracle have we been freed of him? What wizardry did you use? What power do you have, that you do not reveal?"

"Moshim Mosha Va," I responded piously, "I gave our lamented lord exactly what he desired. I gave him the capacity to dream his wonderful dreams while he remained awake. Sadly, his dreams so entranced him that he neglected to live."

The Vizier treated this answer with disdain. He could not obtain a better, however, and in time he grew to be content with it.

Wizardry is illusion. I put the potion which had drugged Caliph Akhmet away in my workroom and made no use of it again. I am a man, and all men dream. But I have forgotten my dreams. I have no wish to become a tyrant.

Penance

The previous evening, I had restored the Duke's son and heir, the Lord Ermine, bringing him back from the deep mortality of his wounds. For safety's sake, I had given of my life in the strict privacy of the Duke's chambers. Indeed, I was attended only by Duke Obal himself, so that no lord of the Duchy, no official of the court, no commander from the field, and no servant in the palace would witness what I did. And when I had infused the young man with my vitality, his death had withdrawn from him, allowing him to rest and grow strong again. Then, depleted and grieving, I had crept quietly from the palace, observed by none except those whom the Duke had commanded to protect me.

Now, in the dusk of the battlefield, I scavenged to restore myself.

All day, Duke Obal's forces had labored against the High Cardinal's siege. Sorties had ridden forth from the walls of Mullior, probing for weakness in the Cardinal's holy persecution. Feints and forays had spent their lives and their horse to protect the Duke's fervent efforts to shore up his defenses, as well as his attempts to ensnare or sabotage the Cardinal's siege engines. Arrows of flame had flown the sky among heavy stones arching from the trebuchet, their flights punctuated by the blaring of the Duke's few cannon, the flatter shouts of his fusils, and the more brazen replies of the Cardinal's harquebus. Now gunpowder added its reek to the stench of charred flesh and garments, the odor of opened bowels, the stink of sweat and pain. On such days, death and bodies seemed to fall like rain, although they fed no harvest on the churned ground. The only crop of so much killing was blood.

Yet it suited me, in its way. To my cost, I gained sustenance from it, and grew strong again. Giving my life to the Duke's son had left me famished and forlorn—so near collapse that my daily resolve to wait until dusk nearly drove me mad.

I had vowed that I would feed from no man or woman except those to whom God had already given death. And in daylight the battlefield was too hazardous for me. I could be hacked apart as easily as any other man, or killed by shot, or burned to death. Nothing warded me except the brief strength which I had already spent in Duke Obal's name. Until

I fed, I was as frail as I appeared—and no less contemptible. Indeed, daylight itself threatened me. It encouraged witnesses and denunciation. Therefore I awaited the sun's decline, although my hunger and weakness were anguish.

When the sun at last dipped from the heavens, however, drawing daylight westward off the plain of battle, I presented myself to the secret portal in Mullior's outer wall. There the guards had been commanded to let me pass—and to admit me again when I was done. This, too, was hazardous. If ever the guards had refused my reentry, I would surely have fallen prey to the High Cardinal's retribution. But they were ignorant of what I was, and had never scrupled to fulfill their lord's instructions. Piously they gave me Godspeed when I departed, and welcomed me when I returned. Doubtless they considered me a spy, charged with some small, regular mission for the Duke, and for that reason they wished me well. Duke Obal was well loved in Mullior, as in the Duchy at large.

My own love resembled theirs, although I did not demean the Duke by speaking of it. Even in Mullior, my esteem would have brought him execration, if I were known.

Concealed by twilight and battle fume, I emerged from the portal and followed failing light across the human wreckage of the siege. Crouching as I went, I scurried among the corpses and the dying—as timorous as the vermin which now thronged the field, and as ravenous.

It was commonly said of my kind that we drank blood. The High Cardinal himself had pronounced anathema upon me in those terms, calling me "blood-beast" and "spawn of Satan." We were misunderstood, however. I did not drink blood. I did not consume blood at all. I drew life from blood—and I drew it by touch. The vitality in the blood of any man or woman who still lived could sustain me.

It was a fact of my nature that I absorbed nourishment and strength more quickly and easily, and with more pleasure, through the touch of my tongue than of my fingers. But at need any portion of my flesh would suffice. Life passed by blood from the one who bled to me, and I was made whole.

As for those who bled— Their lives became mine, so they died.

For that reason, I fed only from the doomed.

Because their vitality was diminished, tainted with death and therefore noxious, they sustained me ill. I was forced to range widely to preserve myself, groaning with the nausea of my kind.

Nevertheless I was scrupulous, careful of my vow, although it was commonly believed that my kind had no souls and no conscience, and existed beyond the reach of God's redemption. I had joined my heart to Mother Church, and to the sweet maid Irradia, for whom I still wept, and what I had sworn to do I did. I took no life which had not already been claimed by God. Any of the fallen for whom the faintest hope of rescue or healing still breathed, I passed by.

However, Mullior was at war with Mother Church, in the person of the High Cardinal, His Reverence Straylish Beatified. And each day of the contest harvested enough soldiers and commanders, camp followers and lords, to sate me several times over. I did not lack for sustenance, despite my scruples.

Yet I may indeed have lacked a soul, or the impulse for redemption. I kept my vow—and all this carnage did not content me. Touching my hand to a torn side here, my tongue to a gutted chest or a ripped throat there, I skulked among the bodies and the charnel stench, feeding abundantly—and still I desired more. Nausea hindered my satisfaction.

This night, trouble found me in spite of my caution. My foraging had drawn me nearer than I realized to one of the Cardinal's encircling camps, and their tents and fires stood no more than an arrow's shot distant. I heard the unsteady crunch of boots among bones and mud as a heavy tread approached me, but the warning came too late. I could not slip away among the shadows and corpses before I was observed.

The man's presence was dangerous enough. More fatal to me, however, was the lantern in his fist. He had shielded its light so that it would not expose him to hostile eyes, but when he turned its radiance directly toward me he could not fail to see the blood upon my hands and lips— the stigmata of my unalterable damnation.

Hunching among the fallen, I stared up at him, unblinking, transfixed by the cruelty of illumination.

"Ho, carrion-crow," he snorted as he regarded me. "Eater of the dead." His tone held no fear. Rather it suggested the amiable malice of a soldier who took pleasure in killing and meant well by it. His grin showed teeth the color of stones. "Straylish told us Mullior's foul Duke harbored such as you, but I doubted him. I doubted such fiends existed. Now I see the virtue of this war more clearly."

I made to rise, so that I might better defend myself. At once, the soldier snatched at his falchion. In the light of the lantern, its notched and ragged edge leered toward me, eager for butchery.

"Stay where you are, hellspawn," the man warned. "There will be promotion in it when I deliver you to the High Cardinal. He will be pleased if you are presented to him alive—but he will find no fault with me if you are dead."

And Straylish the High Cardinal would certainly recognize me. This war attested daily to the enmity between us.

The soldier's grin sharpened as I sank back. His lantern reflected sparks of greed in his gaze—for advancement, for pain. Directing his falchion at my neck, and confident of his authority, he shouted over his shoulder toward his camp, "Ho, you louts! Here! On the run!"

While his head was turned, I rose.

Here was one of the High Cardinal's captains, brutal and righteous—and rich with life. I had fed enough, and could overmatch him, striking a blow against my accuser in the person of his servant. Within my stained robes, behind my tattered beard and shrouded eyes, I was no longer the frail figure who skulked the shadows of Mullior, or crept tottering in prostration from the Duke's chambers. I had become strong again. This man's blood would exalt me.

Yet I had forsworn such measures. In my heart, I had accepted the accusation.

Instead I leaped upon him, sweeping his sword aside as I sprang. My unexpected bulk staggered him, hampered his reactions. In that instant of advantage, I struck him senseless to the ground.

Shouts carried across the field, answering his call. His men had heard him, and hastened to respond. But they would not catch me now. With nourishment I had grown fleet as well as strong, and the dark was my ally in all its guises.

Before I could flee, however, I saw that the captain's lantern had fallen with him, spilling its oil over him as it broke. Already flames licked at his side. In another instant he would begin to burn.

His men might save him. Or they might reach him too late.

And I had sworn that I would take no life not first claimed by God. Uncertain of my own soul, I had sworn it on the maid Irradia's, in the name of Mother Church.

The soldiers of the Cardinal charged toward me, yelling. Their weapons caught the unsteady light of the campfires and shed it in slivers of ruin. Although I was frantic for my life, I spent a precious moment stamping out the flames. Then I turned and ran.

The captain had named me "carrion-crow," and so I was. Threadbare, my robe fluttered and snapped about me like wings as I raced among the dead. I stooped and turned like a raven assailed by hawks. My only haven was Duke Obal's secret portal, distant before me, but I did not aim for it. I feared betraying its existence to the High Cardinal's forces. Instead I directed my flight elsewhere.

Blood I encountered aplenty as I ran. My senses discerned it acutely, despite my haste through the enfolding darkness, I knew it by its aroma, and its luminescence, and its aura of life. Its sweetness clad the fallen wherever they lay. Yet I did not pause to feed.

There was purpose to my path—and hope. Although the soldiers pursued me perilously, I trusted the Duke's defenses, and bent my flight ever nearer to his walls. Like their captain, the men on my heels carried lanterns, as revealing as corpse-light, else they would have lost me at once. And those shielded flames were apparent from the walls. Soon I heard shouts from the city, a quick fusillade, cries at my back.

Several of the soldiers dropped, shot-struck. Cursing, the rest fell back and let me go.

Those who had been mortally wounded died at my hands. Cardinal Straylish was my enemy, and when my vows permitted it I did him what harm I could. By choice, I accepted the taint of Hell with each flicker of life I consumed from the dying.

Once I had fed deeply, I turned away.

Ashamed of the carelessness which had led me into difficulty, and haunted by the ceaseless fear of my kind—the alarm that I had not fed enough to sustain me until I could feed again—I returned to my portal and signaled for admittance.

Had I possessed a soul, its sickness might have driven me to madness or suicide. I had embraced the teachings of Mother Church, and knew my own evil. From Irradia's sweet love I had learned to yearn for Heaven. With the eye of my heart, I saw clearly the baffled distress and—perhaps—revulsion she would have felt at my actions since her tormented death. Although I had not caused this war, I used it to serve me. Duke Obal and all Mullior unwittingly carried out my contest with the High Cardinal. Grieving, Irradia might have begged me to surrender, as she would have surrendered in my place.

I, too, grieved. I had no hope for the redemption which had surely enfolded her in God's grace. But I had chosen another road, and did not turn aside from it.

Because I grieved, however, I resolved to spend this night in the hospital where the Duke's surgeons tended those who had been injured in battle—both Mullior's men and the soldiers of High Cardinal Straylish. There I could repay in some small measure the life I had stolen from the battlefield. I was familiar to the surgeons and nurses, although they knew nothing of my nature. I had moved among them often, when Duke Obal did not require my service. Where the portal guards considered me a minor spy, the hospital's attendants believed me a holy man of an obscure sect, visiting the injured and dying in expiation for my sins—a man whose piety and prayers gave rest to pain, healing for fevers, and relief from infections. I was subtle and circumspect, so that no one grasped what I did. The small restorations which helped the victims of this war survive their hurts passed unremarked.

I felt the need for expiation. My carelessness had led to deaths which might not have occurred otherwise, and that burden I did not bear easily.

But at the portal a new trouble awaited me, more ominous than my encounter with the Cardinal's captain. The guards informed me that Duke Obal required my presence. I was instructed to obey swiftly.

That he saw fit to risk my aid two nights running was highly unusual. It was also profoundly unwise. The "miracles of healing" which I performed in his service endangered us both. They attracted notice. Members of the Duke's court, as well as of his army, could hardly fail to observe that men such as Lord Ermine—or one of the field commanders—or indeed the Duke himself—were borne, dying, from the day's carnage, only to return entirely whole. In sooth their recovery was so remarkable that even the opposing forces noted it. No ordinary surgeon or priest could account for the new health of those men, except by miracle—or by Satanic intervention. And Straylish preached that God's judgment would permit no miracles in the name of an excommunicate like Mullior's Duke. Thus were spread the rumors that fiends and hellspawn served Duke Obal empowering his resistance to the righteous authority of Mother Church in the person of the High Cardinal.

This notion was so fearsome to the devout of the Duchy that it undermined Obal's position and strength, despite the fact that his people loved him. To all appearances, I alone bore the cost of the arduous restorations which I wrought on the Duke's behalf. I passed stored vitality to those of his most precious adherents who had been sorely wounded—a transaction fraught with pain for me, as well as with the weakness of deep loss, all compounded by the unannealed visceral terror of giving away my own life. While it drew its recipients back from death, the infusion left me drained and frail, scarcely able to provide for my own continuance. Thus the core of the Duke's support in Mullior was preserved. All the suffering of the stricken became mine.

Nevertheless Duke Obal also paid a price for my aid. It may have been more subtle than that which I endured, but it was no less grievous.

The High Cardinal and others of his ilk argued that I was the whole cause of the war which had set the Duke against Mullior's more pious neighbors. Priests damned me with their prayers even when they supported Duke Obal. Religious families shuddered at the thought of

Satan in their midst. And ambitious men, men who might perhaps have made their fortunes and their futures by replacing those whom the Duke trusted, advancing to positions of power from which they could conceivably have delivered Mullior and all its riches to the Cardinal—ah, such men loathed me where I stood.

It was more than unwise for Duke Obal to call upon my service too often or too frequently, it was foolish and fatal.

I considered refusal. I sensed a crisis in Mullior which might prove lethal to me. And at all times I lived in fear that the Duke might be persuaded by his advisers, or by his people's need for peace, to turn against me—to deliver me to Cardinal Straylish so that the siege might be lifted. I had saved his life twice—that of his beloved son, thrice—his dearest and staunchest friends half a score of times. For all men, however—and even more for Dukes and Cardinals—necessity was the mother of cruelty. I could too easily imagine that the Duke might decide my life, like his own most prized convictions, was too expensive to merit so much death.

Perhaps I had expended my last hope, and only flight remained to me.

Yet I knew I could not deny Duke Obal's summons. He had earned my unflagging service by the simple expedient of accepting it from me. I had seen the maid Irradia tortured, and heard the High Cardinal pronounce anathema upon me. How could I not love a man who opposed such evils?—a man who did not fear my nature because he trusted my honor?

Escorted as much for my own protection as to ensure my haste, I left the portal and found my way to the Duke's low-lying palace in the heart of Mullior.

There another surprise deepened my dread. Necessarily cautious, I turned my steps toward the private gate and the unfrequented corridors through which I customarily approached my lord. But my escort redirected me. A guard at either shoulder led me to the ornate portico which gave formal entrance to the hereditary domicile and seat of Mullior's rulers. Before I was announced to the fusiliers at the polished and engraved doors, I grasped the significance of this development.

Despite the peril to us both, Duke Obal had commanded me to a public audience.

Holding my breath to contain my fear, I listened narrowly to the terms in which my escort had been instructed to announce me. I understood that the Duke had chosen to place my damned head on the executioner's block of his court's opprobrium. Apart from the danger, this violated the unspoken terms of my service. Only the form of my announcement offered any hint as to whether or not I could hope to survive the night.

The leader of my escort clearly found the occasion tedious. If I was doomed, he did not know it. In a tone of bluff boredom, he stated, "Here is Duke Obal's faithful handservant Scriven. By the Duke's express wish, he presents himself to attend upon his lord."

The reaction of the palace fusiliers was more ominous. As if involuntarily, they flinched and crossed themselves. One of them muttered, "Carrion-eater." Others breathed fervent oaths.

This caused my escort to look at me askance. Unlike the fusiliers, however, they were familiar with me, comfortably convinced that I was a minor spy serving their lord. They were veterans of the siege, hardened to it, and reserved their fear for the enemy. Surprised at my reception, they did not step back from my shoulders.

"'Carrion-eater'?" one of them demanded. "Where?"

The fusiliers did not reply. Their captain silenced them. Stiff with disapproval and alarm, he spoke a prepared welcome. "The lord of Mullior welcomes all who serve him faithfully." Between his teeth, he added, "I am to say that the Duke himself awaits his handservant Scriven's arrival."

His obedience did not comfort me. "Scriven" was not my name. Straylish Beatified knew me otherwise. However, it was the name I had chosen for the Duke's use. While I lived, I bore Irradia's fate written on my soul.

Covering my unsteadiness, I required myself to draw breath. My danger was as great as I had feared. Already rumor had run ahead of the Duke's intent, hinting at worse within.

At the captain's word, my escort bowed themselves haphazardly away. Eager to be rid of me, the captain detached a fusilier to accompany me into the palace, presumably so that I would not wander astray. I was hastened forward. For the first time, I stood accursed and dismayed in the formal entry hall of Duke Obal's home.

It was not the opulence of the space which daunted me. I had little use for wealth myself, and saw no value in the devout tapestries, woven of gilt and verdigris, which behung the walls, the sheened marble of the floor, the lamps burning scented holy oils in their stands of gold and mahogany, the sculpted and pious busts of Mullior's lords. Rather, I was chagrined by the fact that such luxuriance existed. An effort I could not conceive had gone into the creation of Duke Obal's ornaments—and the work had not been done by men or women of my kind. Our lives were fixed on survival, and from day to day we had neither leisure nor inclination for embellishment. The palace's wealth daunted me because it reminded me that I was vastly outnumbered by souls accepted by God and Mother Church, souls who could hope for Heaven—and who could afford to spend their existence on decoration.

Each step I took in such a place increased my peril. I did not belong there. I belonged in servants' entrances and private passages, small rooms secreted from scrutiny, lofts and stables and mud. The farther I intruded here, the greater grew the certainty that my nature would be discovered. And each bust and weaving seemed to mock the idea that I would ever be free to depart.

Clutching to my breast the faith which Irradia had taught me—the faith that some among humankind understood loyalty and honor as well as they grasped war and anathema—I followed my fusilier toward the Duke.

Chamber succeeded chamber, some high and stately, others smaller and more discreet. Servants tended a few, but most were vacant, and their emptiness troubled me. It suggested that their usual occupants and attendants had been called elsewhere. Therefore I feared that Duke Obal meant to make me known to the entire palace.

Instinctively I yearned to cower and skulk forward as though I had come to haunt a battlefield. The strain of walking erect tested me sorely. Only the wisdom of my kind restrained me from creeping—the given knowledge that the more I showed my fear the more I would empower my enemies to act on their own.

Before me loomed a set of doors as high as those which guarded the portico, but at once less massive and more ornate. There the fusilier led me. Anxiously bidding me to wait, he tapped his knuckles on the wood, then stepped back to compose himself.

At once, the doors were jerked partly aside, and a man slipped between them to confront us, closing them swiftly behind him so that we might not see inward or enter.

He wore the rich braid and tooled leather of Duke Obal's livery, although his costume was more elaborate than those I knew by sight. A pectoral cross hung by a chain of heavy gold from his neck, and a short satin cloak of midnight purple with the Rose of Obal picked out in crimson thread draped one shoulder. In his hand he held a slender staff surmounted by Mullior's Eagle in silver and gems. This rod proclaimed him the Duke's majordomo.

He did not look at me. Indeed, he seemed determined to avoid sight of me. Vexed by trepidation, he snapped waspishly at the fusilier, "Who is this?"

Too loudly, the fusilier replied, "By your grace, this is Duke Obal's handservant Scriven." Sweat stood on his brow, although the night was cool. "His presence has been commanded."

At last the majordomo flicked a frightened glance at me, then swore in a whisper. "I know that, fool. You would have done the Duke and all

Mullior a service if you had failed to find him, no matter how strenuously his presence was commanded."

The fusilier retreated a step from the majordomo's anger. "I'm sorry," he murmured uncertainly. "We didn't know—"

The majordomo swore again. "Return to your duties. Say nothing." Flapping his hand, he dismissed my escort. Then he demanded of me, "You are Scriven? You and no other?" Again his eyes evaded my face.

Alarm closed my throat. Unable to speak, I nodded awkwardly. His manner foretold that I was doomed as well as damned.

Staring past my shoulder, he breathed, "On my soul, and for the sake of this House, I pray that the horrors rumored of you are false."

Before I could attempt a reply, he returned to the doors. "Enter," he commanded as he drew them aside. "The Duke awaits you."

I could not believe that I would have been greeted in this fashion, hostile though it was, if the Duke openly meant to harm me. He could have easily had me brought before him in irons, disavowing me without subterfuge. Yet any direct rejection would have called into question the acceptance which had preceded it. Therefore, my terror suggested, I would be asked to betray myself. If I did so, I would spare Duke Obal the censure of Mother Church and his own lords for his former acquiescence in my designs.

Even then I might have changed my mind and fled. I was strong enough. I could have run like the wind—overpowered most ordinary opposition—broken from the palace and dashed into the dark streets and alleys of Mullior, outdistancing immediate pursuit. And if I set my scruples aside so that I remained strong, I might prolong my life for days. On the brink of the fate Duke Obal had prepared for me, I nearly turned aside.

But I did not. I had sworn my vows to myself and to God, and to Irradia's memory, and they held me.

Duke Obal opposed the High Cardinal. In the Cardinal's person, he opposed the worldly might of Mother Church. And he did not do so because that course was convenient for him, or expedient, or free of peril. Already he had been excommunicated. Worse would befall him if Mullior fell. Therefore I would trust him, and remain true to the service I had chosen to give him.

Hunching within my robes, I stepped between the doors and joined the majordomo in the hall beyond.

Although my eyes had grown accustomed to the profuse illumination within the palace, I was not prepared for the brilliance of the Duke's ceremonial chamber. Intricate chandeliers depended thickly from the ceiling.

Candelabra without number lined the walls. And they were enhanced at intervals by braziers and glittering lamps. In two high hearths blazing logs cast back the evening's chill. From end to end, light searched the space, seeking fears and effacing concealment. By preference and necessity, I was a creature of the night, inclined to coverts and darkness—dismayed by so much flame-shine. I quailed at the majordomo's side, despite my resolve to show no fright.

That the hall was crowded with people only augmented my alarm.

Here apparently were gathered all the highborn and significant citizens of Mullior. Among the Duke's servants and fusiliers, I saw folk that I knew—lords and ladies, captains and commanders, priests and officials, merchants and moneylenders—and at least twoscore men and women that I did not. Some wore the garb of their duties and rank. Others displayed their finery, their wealth, or their charms, as those who courted suzerains were inclined to do at any provocation, claiming their stature by right of ostentation or appearance.

As palpable to me as the vitality of blood, their tension gave flesh to my apprehensions.

It was a singular assembly—and not a disinterested one. All Mullior stood excommunicate. Highborn and low, lords and streetsweepers, ladies and whores—all Mullior's inhabitants faced anathema from the High Cardinal's indignation and ruin for their immortal souls. Here were gathered, however, those whose riches and power—as well as salvation—were either threatened or enhanced by the siege of Mother Church. According to their factions and loyalties, to the sources of their wealth and standing, these men and women had tangible, worldly reasons to support resistance, or to encourage surrender. They might speak of evil and redemption—some of them sincerely—but they had other concerns as well.

As did I. I did not think ill of them for their personal considerations. I had no right—and no soul to give my judgments worth. But I also did not trust them. None of their concerns were mine.

They would not hesitate to sacrifice me.

After a moment I caught sight of Duke Obal, some distance from me. He stood in a cluster of his supporters and adherents, among them Lord Ermine, heir to the Duchy, Lord Vill, who commanded the Duke's forces in the field when the Duke himself was absent, Lord Rawn, Master of Mullior's Purse, and several captains noteworthy for their daring in battle. Another observer might not have remarked the particular company surrounding the Duke, but I was struck by it.

They were all men whom I had restored, in the name of my vow.

The rest of the assembly appeared less deliberately composed—grouped more by family or rank than by faction—although the Bishop of Mullior, His Reverence Heraldic, kept the company of his priests and confessors close about him. Yet the general flow and eddy of social intercourse preserved a discreet space around those who stood with the Duke, I judged that these folk were discomfited by the occasion, chary of seeming uncritically allied to the House of Obal. Perhaps under the troubled gaze of the Bishop they did not wish to appear impious by too obviously supporting a man accused of sacrilege and threatened with anathema.

A low murmur of taut conversation and uneasy riposte filled the hall, softened by the rugs which overlay much of the marble floor. The majordomo had ushered me inward quietly. At first we attracted no notice. But clearly my escort had been given instructions which defied his preferences. With his head turned from me and his shoulders clenched in distaste, he struck his staff against the floor. By some trick of the light, Mullior's Eagle appeared to flap its wings, barking for attention. Almost instantly, every voice in the hall was stilled, and every eye swung toward us, some with interest, others in trepidation.

The impulse to cower multiplied within me. If I had not fed so recently, I would not have been strong enough to refuse it.

Clearing his throat, the majordomo declaimed unsteadily, "My lords and ladies, here is Duke Obal's faithful handservant Scriven." The decreed litany of my peril had already grown ominously familiar. "By the Duke's express wish, he presents himself to attend upon his lord."

The growl of opprobrium which at once greeted this announcement shriveled my heart in my chest. I heard "carrion-crow" muttered and "blood-beast" moaned. Priests and devout ladies crossed themselves or clutched their beads, their lips busy with prayer. Fusiliers gripped their guns or their falchions. Lords closed their hands on their sabers. Every man and woman near me drew back, looking to each other for protection.

Somehow my nature had become known—or suspected—despite all my caution. I was now a threat to the Duke. He had called me here to resolve the matter.

All that remained was to discover what form my doom would take.

I told myself that I was merely suspected, not known. Otherwise some righteous soul would have struck me where I stood, compelled by his devotion to Mother Church. But that was cold comfort, and tenuous. I could not long endure the scrutiny of so much light.

From the cluster amid which he stood, Duke Obal turned his head. Blinded by the illumination, I could not descry his features, or his expression. When he spoke, his tone was neutral, rigidly controlled.

"Scriven." He did not seem to raise his voice. Yet nature had made him potent, despite his years. And he was no longer the wracked invalid to whom I had first offered my service. Both disease and injury had been lifted from him. His voice carried easily. "You are welcome here. My thanks for your promptness.

"Approach me." He beckoned firmly. "You are needed."

His self-command was evident. Still his words did not suggest that he meant me ill.

Before I could comply, however, Bishop Heraldic intervened. A hush fell over the hall as he stepped forward.

He was a fleshy individual, disinclined to asceticism. That may have explained his acquiescence to the moral ambiguity of serving Mother Church without supporting the High Cardinal's siege. Any serious effort to denounce the Duke would have cost him considerable comfort. Nevertheless he made an imposing presence, resplendent in his vestments and miter, the gold of their stitching, and of his heavy pectoral cross, agleam with reflected lampshine. His protuberant eyes glowered, and his pendulous jowls quivered, giving the indignant authority of his office corporeal form. It seemed that his conscience had reached its limits.

Disdaining to glance at me, he confronted Duke Obal across an interval of rugs and marble.

"No, my lord," he proclaimed, sententious with virtue. "I must protest. By my cloth, and in the name of Mother Church, I forbid this sacrilege. Fiends and demons give no service to Heaven, whatever they pretend. A life is a small price to pay for the sanctity of an immortal soul."

The Duke raised his chin. "So you have said, my lord Bishop." Although he owed deference to Mother Church and all Her representatives, he permitted himself an acerbic reply. "I have heard you. I have *understood* you. But I am the Duke of Mullior, and within these walls my will rules. I will address your concerns—later.

"Approach me, Scriven," he repeated. Again he beckoned, but with more force, "I am impatient of delay. There is much at issue between us."

Murmuring, "Yes, my lord," I left the majordomo's side and ventured into the expanse of the hall.

Whispers of renewed execration followed me as I moved—a miasma of revulsion and alarm. Ladies and their lords retreated to avoid my proximity. Half the assembly glared at me as though I had arrived in an eruption of brimstone and flame. The rest watched His Reverence Heraldic, hoping—or perhaps fearing—that he would call upon their righteousness to join him in protest or revolt.

For his part, the Bishop withdrew to await events. What he hoped to gain, I did not know. I could not conceive how Duke Obal meant to resolve the dilemma of my presence in Mullior.

Approaching the Duke, I crossed luxurious rugs over a floor of burnished marble, but they had no value to me. I would have preferred to walk in mud.

My lord wore the full regalia of his station—the ornamental hauberk chased with silver, the sash gathered in a rosette at his waist, the tooled greaves and boots, the saber on his hip, and beneath it all a blouse and hose of blackest silk. Rings studded his fingers. The gems of a circlet glittered in his hair. Clearly he intended a commanding display, so that he would be difficult to contradict.

In that he succeeded, for his demeanor and visage conveyed as much authority as his attire. An iron beard shot with gray sculpted the line of his jaw, and the sun-hued planes of his face might have been cast in bronze. When I had first offered him my service, he had been a mere husk of himself, drained by consumption and time, as well as by half a dozen wounds. And even then, he had sustained the High Cardinal's siege and held the loyalty of Mullior by the unbroken force of his will. Now, however, he was whole and well, and his spirit shone with renewed vitality. He appeared as merciless as his blade.

Only the gentle intelligence of his gaze—the troubled, accessible color of his eyes—revealed the man who was loved more than feared in his Duchy, the man who could defy the edicts of Cardinal Straylish and still trust the hearts of his people. The man whose easy justice and open concern had taught me that not all rulers and powers were cast in the High Cardinal's mold.

As I neared him, his companions stepped apart, making way for me, and I received a new surprise, a blow so sudden and unexpected that it nearly halted the labor of my heart. For the first time I glimpsed the nature of Duke Obal's purpose. With his lords and captains, and his son, he had placed himself to conceal a cot on which lay a man of middle years, plainly dying.

I did not recognize him. And he was not identified by attire, for he wore only a cloth wrapped about his loins. Yet I saw his death beyond mistake in the waxen hue of his flesh, the sheen of sweat strained from the pores of his brow, the flecks of blood on his ashy lips. It was my nature to feed on life, and I knew its passing with an intimacy which other men reserved for their lovers, or for God. His soul would achieve its culmination before dawn, and then he would know only bliss or torment forevermore.

And Duke Obal meant—he wished—

The brightness of the hall seemed to gather about me, multiplying on the pale flesh of the dying man, so that my vision blurred, and my mind with it. Here before scores of witnesses rife with censorious piety, Duke Obal intended—

Hardly conscious of what I did, I stumbled in my alarm, and would have fallen if Lord Ermine had not caught my arm.

"Calm your fear, Scriven," he breathed in my ear. Born late, he little resembled his father. His features did not yet bear the stamp of his character. He had the Duke's eyes, however, and had recovered his life at my hand. "This is necessary. You have not been abandoned."

His reassurance was kindly meant. I did not believe him—I was wise enough to fear dukes and lords when they spoke of what was "necessary"—but I drew courage from his words and his grasp, and regained my legs.

Beckoning yet again, the Duke urged me to the side of the cot.

I had expected denunciations and curses—at the worst, I had expected a doomed battle to preserve my life—but in my gravest terrors I had never dreamed that I would be asked to betray my nature before all the powerful of Mullior. The prospect appalled me. But it also shamed me. Mother Church taught that my kind had no souls, and could never win release from anguish. Now I was asked to demonstrate the lack. I would not have been more distressed if Duke Obal had commanded me to rape a child in the hall.

The Duke's Commander joined Lord Ermine beside me. He, too, whispered for no ears but mine. "Come, Scriven. We cannot endure delay. Mullior is a powder keg this night, and every moment the fuse burns shorter."

I turned toward him in my weakness. "My lord Vill," I murmured, "I have not deserved this from you."

Impatiently Lord Rawn, the Master of Mullior's Purse, snapped his fingers. "What you deserve," he hissed softly, "is not at issue. Duke Obal's rule *is*. He will stand or fall here, and your hesitancy weakens the ground under him. Step forward, or recant your service, as you wish—but do it *now*."

At once, however, the Duke intervened, sparing me an immediate response. "You are mistaken, my lord Rawn," His tone was mild despite its tension. "We can afford a few moments."

Turning from the men at my sides, I concentrated my attention on the lord to whom I had sworn my service against Cardinal Straylish.

"Scriven," he informed me softly, "you have become known. I cannot explain it. I will not believe that you have been betrayed here." He meant within his palace. "Those who serve me have earned my trust. But rumor is a powerful foe. And I doubt not that the High Cardinal's spies are among us"—a sneer curled his lip—"spreading any tale Straylish desires.

"The charge that I countenance a scion of Hell is one I must confront." The set of his jaw bespoke anger and restraint. "If I fail, I will fall, as Lord Rawn suggests. Until now, as you know, Bishop Heraldic has withheld the condemnation of Mother Church from my actions, preaching that it is not the duty of God's servants to judge worldly princes. If he turns against me—if he persuades Mullior's more devout lords to make cause with the Cardinal—I am done."

I considered it significant that Bishop Heraldic did not preach—as Irradia had taught me—that Scripture urged all souls to embrace love and meekness rather than to practice execration or crave power. In my heart, I deemed him no better than the High Cardinal. He was merely more indolent.

"Scriven," Duke Obal concluded urgently, "you have trusted me until now. Trust me still, and we will do what we can to defuse this powder keg."

I could hardly refuse him. He had set my head on the block, and no one else could deflect the executioner's stroke. Bowing weakly, I replied, "How may I serve you, my lord?" although I knew the answer all too well.

The cast of his features suggested gratitude, but he did not express it. Instead he indicated the man recumbent before us.

"This is Lord Numis. He is Bishop Heraldic's chancellor—the Bishop's adviser and agent in all things which pertain to the legal affairs of Mother Church in Mullior. As you see, he is dying. Surgeons and physicians without number have failed to relieve his illness." The Duke's gaze held mine. "I ask you to restore him."

He confirmed my gravest dread. Doubtless his actions were necessary, as I had been told. Still I hesitated, fearing the outcome of any public declaration of my nature.

While I faltered, Lord Rawn offered sourly, "It may interest you that among Bishop Heraldic's advisers, Lord Numis is the High Cardinal's most vigorous and vehement supporter."

Frozen by apprehension, I temporized. "My lord," I murmured, "I do not understand. He is my enemy—and yours."

In fact, I understood perfectly. Terror rendered me acute. But I wished to hear Duke Obal's reply.

He spread his hands as though to reveal their openness—their honesty. "Scriven," he admitted, "I cannot defeat these rumors by pretending that they are false. With contradiction, they will swell until they burst, and their putrefaction overwhelms me." He shrugged. "Yet if I acknowledge that they are true, I must also name myself damned. Accepting the service of Satan's minions, I cannot escape the conclusion that I number among them."

He paused as though to consult his conscience, then continued, "This conundrum offers only two outlets. I might denounce you now, swearing that I lacked prior knowledge of your nature. By joining Mother Church in your condemnation, I might save myself.

"This course has been urged to me." Duke Obal did not glance at anyone present. "But I will not do it." Anger roughened his tone. "It is cowardly and dishonorable. I have promised otherwise. In addition, however, it is impolitic. It would undermine my plain opposition to the High Cardinal."

Then with an effort he seemed to set his ire aside. More gently, he said, "The other outlet is more difficult. We must demonstrate to this gathering that whatever your nature may be, you are not in truth a scion of Hell. If you are seen to heal, these folk will be hard-pressed to name you a killer. And any demonstration will convey more conviction if it benefits your enemies, rather than those who condone your presence." A nod indicated Lord Numis, "The healing of the Bishop's chancellor will not be marred by any appearance of self-interest."

Sore of heart, I noted that he did not advance an argument which might have touched me more deeply—the maid Irradia's belief that in God's name we were commanded to cherish those who reviled and persecuted us. If her sufferings had permitted it, she would have prayed for the Cardinal's soul while she died—

Still the fact remained that I had no choice. I could not hope to survive by flight or struggle, despite my strength. And until this night Duke Obal had given me no cause to doubt his given word. Bowing my head, I acquiesced.

"I will do what I can, my lord."

Again his expression suggested gratitude, but he did not voice it. Firmly he gestured me toward the chancellor's cot.

Dry of mouth, and trembling in all my joints, I approached the invalid. Lord Ermine and Lord Vill remained protectively at my sides. All others stepped back.

At the cot's edge, I knelt. The assembly might think that I prayed—or that I feigned prayer to disguise my malice—but in truth I lacked the will to stand. Fear loosened my joints. And I was also, suddenly, filled by the hunger of my kind, avid and ceaseless. Despite my strength, I desired more sustenance. And here lay a life apt to be consumed—a life already claimed by God—nourishment my vows permitted.

Further, Lord Numis was my enemy. Although his ribs started from his chest, and his flesh held the waxen pallor of death, I detected the heartless exigencies of the law in the shape of his mouth, and under his grizzled beard his jaw had a fanatic's strict cruelty. Hating such men, I burned to hasten his passage to Heaven or Hell.

Then, however, he turned a gaze dull with fever toward me. Despite his illness, he seemed to know himself and where he was—he seemed to know me—for he moistened his lips with blood in order to murmur hoarsely, "Stay back, fiend. Taint me not. Touch me not. I die because I must." He coughed thinly. "I will not go to God with your foulness upon me."

After he had spoken so, I could no more have taken his life than I could have turned my back on Irradia's memory. I had no soul, and knew myself damned. Nevertheless I had sworn vows I meant to keep.

Above my head, Duke Obal addressed the gathering. His voice grew in force and conviction, yet I hardly heard him. References were made to "tests" and "healing" and "Heaven," but I did not regard them. Shamed by my unrepentant appetites—and grieving at my own cruelty—I made a show of what I did, so that my actions would be visible to the whole gathering.

From within my robe, I drew out an inquisitor's dirk, a blade as keen and well pointed as necessity and a whetstone could make it. For a moment I brandished it above my head as though I might plunge it into the chancellor's breast, or my own. Then, swiftly, I drew a thin cut across the pad of my middle finger—one new cut among the lattice of scars I had acquired in Duke Obal's service.

Bright and precious in the intense illumination, a drop of rich ruby swelled from my wound.

By blood I devoured life—and restored it. Just as I consumed a man's vitality through the touch of his vein's fluid, so I returned it with the touch of my own. Lord Numis moved his lips in supplication, but I did not heed him. A last moment I hesitated, gazing at the gem of blood upon my finger—a bead of purest ruin—and dreading what was to come. Then I set all pity aside. Deliberately I slid my finger between the chancellor's jaws and stroked his tongue with my strength.

Whatever the reaction behind me may have been, I did not witness it. The instant Lord Numis tasted my blood, I felt the life pour from me like oil from a broken amphora, to be replaced by weakness and despair—and by a near-murderous hunger. My substance withered within my robes, the pliancy fled my muscles, and hope dwindled in my veins. Between one heartbeat and the next, I passed from vitality to utter sorrow. Now a child might have slain me—if I did not first contrive to snatch a touch of his blood. I had become no more than the sum of what I had lost.

For a brief time, I failed of consciousness. Fainting, I slumped into the depths of the Duke's rugs.

Yet the very richness of my bed seemed to spurn me. Stricken by panic and inanition, I heaved up my head and clawed my limbs under me, thinking to see swords high in the harsh light, men rabid with execration, guards and lords armed for slaughter—

Apparently, however, the interval of my stupefaction had been too brief for so much motion. Indeed, no one present had lifted a hand. Caught in a hush of mortal trepidation, none spoke or breathed. Duke Obal and his adherents remained poised like inquisitors about me. Lord Numis had not shifted on his cot.

Then the chancellor raised his head—and a hoarse sigh spread across the assembly.

Frowning bitterly, he considered his circumstances. His eyes held an unappeased glitter, which showed that his fever had left him. In its place, disgust twisted his lips, and his jaws seemed to chew the fouled meat of his restoration as though its rank savor pleased him obscurely.

When his abhorrence had collected all the force of my gift—my spent life—he swung his legs from the cot's edge and stood, trembling and strict, clad only in his loincloth and his righteousness.

At once Lord Ermine swept a cloak from his own shoulders and wrapped it about the rigid chancellor. But Lord Numis shrugged it aside as though he craved the humiliation of his nakedness—as though he wished all the gathering to see how he had been abased.

"Abomination," he croaked. "Abomination and sin."

Clearly he meant to shout, but at first his disused voice betrayed him. He did not falter, however. Swallowing the residue of fever from his throat, he began again, more strongly.

"Abomination, I say!" he declared, claiming the right to dispense Heaven's judgment. "Abomination and *sin!*"

"My lord, you forget yourself," put in Lord Rawn quickly. At a sign from the Duke, he and Lord Vill moved to interpose themselves between Lord Numis and the assembly. "You have been most gravely ill. You do not grasp the wonder of your recovery."

But the chancellor thrust them away. Fired by the force I had given him, he confronted his shocked audience.

"I have been most foully harmed!" he cried. "This vile minion of Satan has placed his taint upon my soul!" With one grim arm he aimed his accusation at my bowed head. "My God whom I have served with my life called me to the bliss of my just reward, and I answered gladly. But this blood-beast, this *hellspawn*, this eater of *death*, has snatched me back from Heaven! With the Duke's knowledge and consent, he has practiced his evil upon me, and I am prevented from peace."

I made an attempt to rise, and found that I could not. My weakness outweighed me. No other voice was raised, yet the atmosphere in the hall fairly crackled with apprehension, as furious and frantic as a fusillade. I had heard similar denunciations before. They carried the pang of sweet Irradia's death, and of my helplessness to save her, and in my despair I was filled by such a fury of weeping that I could scarcely suppress it.

Lord Numis swung toward me. His ire blazed from him in the excruciating light. "Carrion-crow," he ranted over my kneeling form, *"slave of evil.* I will know no rest until I have seen you *slain!"* Then he turned to the assembly again. "My lord Bishop, for my soul I beg you. I implore. Command his death. Instruct all Mullior on peril of damnation to hack him limb from limb and heart where he kneels. Anele me of this corruption before my soul is consumed by it."

Under the lash of his fanaticism, the highborn of the Duchy stirred and fretted. Some glanced uncertainly at their comrades, perhaps perturbed to hear such violence urged in the wake of unexpected healing. A number of them, I believed—those most sincere in their love for the Duke—disliked and distrusted Lord Numis. But others began to mutter encouragement for the chancellor's demand. Clergymen crossed themselves, and ladies prayed. Guards and fusiliers clutched at their weapons. Merchants and officials drew back in dread, or edged forward angrily. My kind was easily feared. And the strictures of Mother Church, harsh in the name of God's love, multiplied that alarm. Men and women who would have risked their own souls without hesitation to postpone death assented eagerly to the legalist's righteous umbrage.

They had never known my weakness, and could not conceive how my kind treasured life.

For a moment every eye was fixed on His Reverence Heraldic. Every heart awaited his response.

I would not have called the Bishop courageous. However, he was not a man who shirked precedence and power when they were offered without apparent cost—or apparent hazard. He put himself forward a step or two, announcing his authority. With both hands, he held high the wealth of his pectoral cross so that it shone like a beacon in the acute illumination.

"Guards," he called—and more loudly, "servants of Mother Church!" In stentorian tones, he proclaimed, "I name this Scriven damned. He is an eater of death, vile in the sight of the Almighty, and must be destroyed. The gifts of fiends are corrupt, and the more precious they appear the greater their corruption must be. Acceptance leads to damnation. The will of Heaven is plain. He must be destroyed now."

Irradia would have asked Heaven to forgive him. I did not.

Half the assembly shouted an acclamation at once, eager to see the source of their fear exterminated. Released from their tension, guards and lords surged to assail me, drawing their swords as they advanced.

I strove anew to gain my feet. "Do it yourself, my lord Bishop," I panted as I rose. "If you dare." But my defiance was so frail that even those near me did not hear it.

Instead Duke Obal compelled their attention. With a feral stride, he moved to confront those who meant my death. Closing one hard fist on the back of the chancellor's neck, he drove Lord Numis forcibly to his knees. The other he raised in threat.

"Hold!" he commanded, his voice ringing off the walls. "Stop where you stand!" The fury and force which made him dreadful in battle emanated palpably from him. "I have promised Scriven safety. He serves me, and is under my protection. Any man who lifts a hand against him will answer for it with blood."

Lord Ermine closed with his father, as did Lord Vill and the Duke's captains, forming a barrier to shield me. Accustomed to obey their lord, the hostile throng paused. While a few judicious voices called for restraint, men in the grip of righteous fervor looked uncertainly toward the Bishop, seeking his support.

To this Lord Numis croaked a protest. But the Duke's hard grasp on his neck prevented him from speaking clearly.

At another time, His Reverence might have regretted his hasty opposition. However, the chancellor's outrage had touched on the most sensitive part of Bishop Heraldic's posture of accommodation toward Duke Obal's apostasy. On other points, the Bishop could argue that he sought to prevent a rift between Mother Church and the people of Mullior. On this point, however, on the subject of tolerance for the creatures of Satan—

"No, my lord Duke," he retorted with apparent courage. "I know my duty to Mother Church, and to God. This Scriven is an abomination! We have witnessed his vile power, and must not endure it. In the name of Heaven, he must—"

Harshly the Duke interrupted His Reverence. "Have I not made myself plain?" he blared. *"Scriven has my protection.* If any hand rises against him, I will *lop it off! Even yours, my lord Bishop.*

"Have you forgotten where you are? This is the ducal palace of Mullior. *I rule here."*

To my amazement and chagrin, and to my vast sorrow, Duke Obal bound his fate to mine inextricably. He had spoken words which could not be recalled. If Mullior accepted Bishop Heraldic's denunciation now, the lord I served would share my doom.

And he was not done. "Perhaps it has escaped your notice," he continued acidly, "that this 'abomination' has saved a life. In fact"— here he jerked Lord Numis upright, so that the energy of the legalist's struggle was displayed for all to see—"he has saved the life of a man dedicated to Mother Church." Then he released Lord Numis so that the chancellor staggered away toward Bishop Heraldic and the shelter of the Bishop's retinue.

"I was taught by clergymen," stated the Duke, "that those who heal do God's work. I am no theologian, but I will venture to assert that the condition of my lord Chancellor's soul is not determined by the illness or health of his flesh."

The assembly stirred in confusion and thwarted ire. Fearful of their own temerity, and of their lord's wrath, the guards retreated to their duties. Bishop Heraldic did not fall back, however. Supported by some score of Mullior's most devout folk, he bore the withering force of Duke Obal's scorn.

Nevertheless he moderated his manner. "My lord," he answered carefully, "you cannot so lightly set aside Heaven's revulsion. Yes, Mother Church teaches that healing is God's work. But She also teaches that the stalking fiends of night, all werebeasts and succubi, vampyrs and ghouls, are scions of Hell. Merely to encounter them is to hazard damnation. To treat with them—to accept their service—to cover them with your protection—"

Piously rueful, His Reverence shook his head. "Perhaps you believe you have the strength to endure such evil, my lord. But you do not. It is not given to men to be greater than evil. Only by God's grace, and by the strict intervention of Mother Church, do we withstand Satan's depredations."

I had gained my feet, but I retained scarcely enough vitality to keep them. The blaze of the illumination seemed to bear down upon me as though I were a blot to be effaced from the hall. Nevertheless in my frailty and grief I sought for words potent enough to fend off Duke Obal's doom.

"My lord," I might have urged him, "withdraw your protection. My service will cost you more than it merits. If you turn against me now, you may yet retain the countenance of Mother Church in this siege. Without it, you must fall, and the Cardinal's triumph will be inevitable."

I could conceive no other salvation for him.

Yet I remained mute. My vows precluded surrender. And I had not yet been granted opportunity for supplication or defiance. Duke Obal did not hesitate to answer His Reverence.

"My lord Bishop, I am not a fool." He spoke as though to the emissary of a mortal enemy. "And I am a good son of Mother Church, whatever the High Cardinal may preach, or you may think. I am not careless of my soul's sanctity, or of my hope of Heaven. If I have accepted Scriven's service, with all its perils—*I*, Obal, Duke of Mullior"—vehemence flew like spittle from his lips—"then you must bow to the knowledge that *I have good reason!*"

At first His Reverence appeared shaken by this rejoinder. He could not reiterate his demands without insulting Duke Obal—and that would have been gravest folly at any time. While the Bishop searched his uncertainty for a reply, however, Lord Numis called fiercely, "Name them, my lord! Name your reasons."

The Duke gave a bark of harsh laughter. "Thank you, my lord Numis," he returned, his tone trenchant. "That is precisely why I have called my handservant Scriven to this assembly. I have had enough of rumor and innuendo and baseless defamation. Mullior has been sickened by them, and they must cease. Tonight their place will be taken by plain speech—and plain truth."

Felled by the import of what I heard, I found myself on my hands and knees. The senseless intricacy of the rug confronted me blindly. If the Duke desired "plain speech," "plain truth," he could ask it of but one man here—and that burden was greater than I could bear.

From the hour when I had first entered Mullior, I had told my tale to no living soul. Duke Obal himself had no knowledge of it. He had inquired into it, of course. He had inquired often. But I had answered him with evasions—evasions which he had accepted because my service to him was precious.

He did not know what I might say if he searched me now. In my worst nightmares, I had not dreamed that he might place us both in a danger so extreme.

And I had given up my strength to Lord Numis. I could not survive by flight or struggle. Scant moments ago, I had tried to envision how I might save Duke Obal. Now I could grasp no salvation for myself.

Despite my despair, however, I was forced to acknowledge the Duke a man of honor, worthy of service. With all Mullior at stake, he meant to place himself in my hands. If I told the truth and was damned for it, he would be damned as well.

When the gathering had fallen silent, he turned to me. At the sight of my huddled posture, he scowled. Glancing toward his son, he breathed, "Help him. He must stand. He must answer."

Joined by Lord Rawn, Lord Ermine hastened to my side. Together they supported me upright, their concern evident on their faces. Upon occasion they had witnessed my weakness, just as they had benefited from my strength, but they had never seen me so profoundly drained. In me sorrow and dread altogether surpassed my kind's more ordinary fear of hunger and frailty.

"Hold up your heart," Lord Ermine urged me. "We will prevail somehow. My father is unaccustomed to failure. And we believe that he has rightly judged Mullior's mood—and Mullior's needs."

He sought to fortify me, but I was unable to hear him. The light seemed to leave me deaf as well as blind. I could not blink my sight clear, or lift my heart.

"My lord," the Master of Mullior's Purse whispered to the Duke, "he is too weak for this. Look." Lord Rawn shook me so I staggered, although his grasp was gentle. "He is prostrate where he stands. If he does not feed, he will collapse before us, and then we are lost."

"That," stated Lord Vill through his teeth, "is impossible. If he feeds, someone must die for it. We cannot countenance such an act in front of these pious cowards. They will rise against us. We will be garroted before we can gain the doors."

That, too, was plain truth. In the name of my vows, and of my debt to Irradia, I summoned the resolve to raise my head. Although I failed to drive the blur of tears from my gaze, I faced Duke Obal and said for the second time, "I will do what I can, my lord."

He appeared to nod. "Good," he remarked privately. "I ask only the truth. Grant that, and I will abide the outcome."

Then he continued more strongly, so that the hall could hear him. "Speak openly, and fear nothing, Scriven. I have named you my handservant. As you restored Lord Numis, so you have also renewed my own life, and that of my son, as well as many others. For yourself, you have drawn sustenance solely from the fallen of this cruel siege. My lord Bishop calls you an abomination, but I have seen no sign of evil in you. I have felt no harm at your touch.

"The time has come for an accounting between us. Scriven, why do you serve me?"

I had said that I would do what I could, but dismay mocked my given word. The compulsion to dodge and feint in the face of peril ruled me. Rather than answering honestly, I countered, "My lord, why do you oppose the High Cardinal?"

The Duke's eyes narrowed, and a glower darkened his visage. I felt impatience through his urgency. He had not brought me to this hall in front of these witnesses in order to watch me scurry aside. Yet his self-mastery was greater than mine. Despite his vexation, he responded as I had asked.

"All Mullior knows my reasons. You know them yourself, Scriven. I oppose High Cardinal Straylish on both worldly and spiritual grounds."

In a formal voice, Duke Obal declared, "His Reverence Beatified has made plain that he considers it the province of Mother Church to dictate both law and policy to such states as Mullior. I do not." Each word he articulated with the force of a decree. "Where the duties of my station and my birth are concerned, I will be no man's puppet. The soul and its salvation are the proper care of Mother Church. Worldly circumstances are not. It is not the place of Mother Church to judge or control the actions of suzerains. Such matters as whether I form an alliance with one neighbor, or welcome refugees from another, are not resolved by theological debate. And I take it as a transgression—as a personal affront—when Cardinal Straylish commands me to enact laws which restrict or punish those citizens of Mullior who have not entrusted their souls to Mother Church. I grieve when my people do not recognize the light of Heaven, but I will not in any fashion deny them the freedom of such determinations."

Lord Vill and Lord Rawn nodded their approval, but no one in the hall spoke. All Mullior's highborn had often heard Duke Obal assert his convictions. They waited restively for the outcome of his peroration.

"These are worldly questions," the Duke continued. "On spiritual issues also I am not persuaded by the service His Reverence Beatified gives to God. Its tenor disturbs me.

"I was taught by the clergy of Mullior, Bishop Heraldic among them"—subtly he undermined the Bishop's censorious disapproval—"that God is a God of love, that Heaven is a place of joy, and that the task of Mother Church is to teach us to open our hearts to such beneficence. Therefore I believe that the true sign of those who serve Mother Church is that their hearts *are* open. Filled with God, they are neither condemnatory nor cruel.

"Yet the High Cardinal has closed his heart to all who do not honor his dominion. He *persecutes* any and all who do not share his beliefs, or his nature. He does not ask if they are *accessible* to salvation. Rather, he *coerces* them to it. And if he deems them beyond coercion, he seeks their destruction."

Duke Obal made no effort to disguise his bitterness. "In this His Reverence Beatified does not count the cost. Because he loathes evil, he prefers to torment and maim, to make war, to spill the blood of the harmless like water, and to impose his will by terror, rather than to suffer the existence of hellspawn. Better, he believes, to excruciate and murder an innocent—or a thousand innocents—than to risk letting one blood-beast escape him.

"I disagree," the Duke pronounced harshly. "I do not believe that coercion and torture are the proper instruments of love and joy. While I live, I will oppose them. If I am wrong, I will answer for it before Heaven. But I will not answer to His Reverence Straylish Beatified."

There he stopped. He had said enough to demean my evasion, and I was ashamed of it. Yet I strove to conceal myself still. Across the expectant silence of the assembly, I answered softly, "And does that not suffice to account for my service, my lord?"

He shook his head. "It does not."

And Bishop Heraldic echoed behind him, "It does not."

Their eyes held me. Every gaze in the hall was fixed toward me. Although I could not stanch my grief enough to see clearly, I felt horror and fascination from my witnesses—revulsion accentuated by the secret excitement of proximity to forbidden things.

"Very well," I sighed. "If I must."

And still I temporized. Of the Duke's son I inquired, "May I have wine, my lord? It will not restore me, but it will ease my throat."

I meant that I hoped it would ease my abasement.

"Certainly," answered Lord Ermine. He left my side. I heard murmuring, and a low voice asked, "Where is the wine which the Duke requires?" For a reason that eluded me, Lord Ermine was answered by a priest of the Duke's retinue—he may have been the Duke's personal confessor. The tension of the gathering grew sharper still. But I gave no heed. I cared only that when Lord Ermine returned he placed in my hands a goblet brimming with the sacred color of deep rubies and blood.

I preferred water, but I drank the wine, praying that it might have an effect upon one of my kind—that it might serve to blunt the edge of my distress, as it did for other men. And if it did not lift my weakness, or soften my woe, perhaps it would sanctify my penance.

With what strength I had, I declared, "I serve you, my lord, because His Reverence Straylish Beatified instructed me to do so."

My audience reacted with disbelief and indignation, and also with a kind of febrile mirth, heated by alarm. Bursts of harsh laughter punctuated shocked expressions of virtue and rejection, I was accused of "sacrilege," "Satanic cunning," and—more kindly—"madness." However, Duke Obal dominated the response.

"Explain yourself, Scriven," he demanded. "Are you a spy?"

I shook my head. "No, my lord. You will understand—"

As best I could, I hardened my heart.

Directing my gaze into the red depths of the goblet, I told my tale for the first and only time.

▲▼▲

"Like others of my kind," I explained, "I am commonly homeless. We cannot nourish each other, and none sustain us willingly. We are cursed to isolation. Therefore we wander.

"Perhaps a year ago, my roaming took me to Sestle"—the birthplace of the Cardinal, and the seat of his power. "There I settled to fend for survival as unobtrusively as I could.

"I cannot tell how others of my kind make their way. I suspect that we are diverse as ordinary men, and that some of us cut as wide a swath as they may, while others covet more timid existence. For myself, I had learned as I roved that places of worship provided congenial feeding grounds. In such places men are plentiful—and careless of their safety, thinking themselves protected by their gods. For the same reason, when a community comes to fear one of my kind, it seldom searches its sanctuaries and chapels. In lands to the east and south of Sestle"—lands which had not been enfolded by Mother Church—"I had lived well and long by secreting myself and selecting my prey within places of worship.

"That was my intention in Sestle. Avoiding the great cathedrals, I chose a decrepit chapel immured among the city's multitudinous poor, in a region named Leeside, where the worshipers were at once devout and defenseless, and where any number of unexplained deaths might pass unremarked. At first I made my home among the nameless graves in the chapel basement. Later, however, I learned that the chapel's builders, dreaming of grander sanctuaries, had given the edifice lofts and attics among the high rafters, and there I eventually took up residence. From above I could watch and hear what transpired below me, among the worshipers. This greatly improved the efficacy of my position.

"I believed that I had found a place where I might live for many years and be secure.

"However, its effect was not what I had imagined. From my lofty perch, I watched and heard—too much.

"The congregation I observed comprised little more than human refuse, more ruined than their house of worship, reduced by poverty and near-starvation to the semblance of vermin. And yet the devotion on their faces, the simplicity revealed through their grime and pain, the untrammeled trust of their hymns and prayers—these things touched me as I had never been touched before.

"Must I speak the truth, my lords? Then I will acknowledge that I saw myself in them. My homelessness and wandering, and my ceaseless isolation, had taught me to understand their deprivation. And my kind is always hungry.

"As I watched my intended prey, there reawakened in me a yearning which I had ignored for so long that it seemed to have no name, a longing of the heart to stand among other men, other folk, and call them mine."

Hearing whispered opprobrium and doubt, I admitted, "I am well aware that I revolt you, my lords. Throughout my life I have known only revulsion. It is the fact around which my existence revolves. Yet the truth remains. In that chapel I ached to join the congregation, and give myself up to be healed."

Then I resumed.

"As I say, I saw too much when I watched. And when I listened I heard too much. For the first time, I attended to the conduct and attitudes of my prey. Their priest—an old man called Father Domsen—was no less ruined than they, no less tattered and besmirched, no less stricken by want. But he was also no less devout, and his love of Heaven seemed to shine like a beacon in the dim sanctuary. Again and again, day after day, he spoke of love and acceptance and peace, and of an immortal joy beyond the smallest taint of earthly suffering, and in his faith I heard intimations of an ineffable glory. I was persuaded by it, my lords, when I had not known that I could be moved at all.

"The alteration in me was gradual, but it brooked no resistance. At first I was hardly conscious of the change. Then I found that I had grown loath to prey on those who worshiped in my chosen home. This required me to search more widely for sustenance, and to accept more hazard. Nevertheless I gained a comfort I could not explain from the knowledge that the chapel's congregation was in no peril. And for a time that contented me.

"As I listened to the priest's kind homilies, however, and to his gentle orisons, and heard the heartfelt goodwill of his blessings, I came to desire a deeper solace. I wished for the more profound balm of standing shoulder to shoulder with men and women who did not abhor me, and of sharing their simplicity.

"So it was that perhaps three months after I had arrived in Sestle I left my high covert in order to join the congregation when it gathered to worship.

"That was difficult for me, my lords. As I say, I had known only revulsion from ordinary men—only hatred, and a lust to see me exterminated. To mingle with folk who would avidly rend me limb from limb under other circumstances cost me severely. My pulses burned with fear, and at intervals my hunger swelled with feverish urgency. Yet I endured. Having entered among the congregation, I could not withdraw without drawing notice. At all times, notice threatens me. And in that gathering to be noticed would block any relief from the yearning which had driven me there.

"I did not know the prayers or the hymns, and the liturgy itself was new to me. But I mimicked those around me until I had secured a rote knowledge of their service. So I avoided the notice I dreaded. Men granted me the same vague nods they gave their fellows, children laughed or squalled in my presence, women and maids curtsied to me without recognition or concern. By small increments I began to feel that I was accepted."

I gripped my goblet weakly. "This was an illusion, I understood its ephemeral nature. The folk around me did not know what I was.

"Yet there was truth in it also. The poor of Sestle feared no one who was not better born, or wealthier, or more predatory than they. Within its plain limits, their acceptance of me was sincere.

"And I valued it for what it was. Soon I learned to treasure it.

"Determined to pose no danger in Leeside, I hunted ever more widely for sustenance. Consequently disturbances and rumors began to circulate in the neighborhoods of the rich and the wellborn, causing guards and watchmen to increase their vigilance—and my difficulties. Yet I regretted nothing that I did. The illusion of acceptance eased and nurtured me. I would willingly have incurred far greater hazards to preserve it.

"Still it *was* illusion. It taught me to crave more substantial consolations.

"However, I found that I could not glean what I sought by rote and mimicry. The forms of the chapel's worship were potent in my heart, but their content—I could not comprehend it. Apparently my life and my nature had precluded essential insights or assumptions which the devout of Mother Church shared with their priest, but which conveyed nothing to me. What was 'God'—or 'Heaven'—or 'soul?' I had no experience of their import. I knew only life and death. And death terrified me because it was not life. When the priest spoke of 'sin' and 'forgiveness' and 'salvation,' I could not imagine his meaning. I could only mouth the hymns and the prayers, and feel true acceptance slipping from my grasp.

"Eventually my desire to stand among those worshipers in their sanctuary might have curdled to darkness. My yearning had been reawakened, and its frustration could well have driven me to other extremes. However, I was spared that loss.

"Men say that my kind have no souls, and it may be true. But if we do not, I am unable to explain why God deigned to lift the burden of my isolation before it grew too cumbersome for me to bear."

Sighing, I drank from my goblet. In some measure, the wine did ease me. It cleared my throat for speech. But it did little to disperse the thunderheads of weeping and fury which threatened to overwhelm my fragile composure with storms. I had never told my tale because it gave me too much pain.

Nevertheless I did not stop. I hungered for expiation, despite its cost.

In the silence of the assembly, I continued my litany of woe.

"Like 'Heaven' and 'sin,' 'love' was a word I did not comprehend. I had no experience of it. I could not have explained 'kindness' to a passing cur. How then could I grasp the higher concerns of the spirit? But I was taught—

"One day as I entered the sanctuary among the worshipers, a maid curtsied to me. I hardly regarded her, except that I feared all notice, and so I replied with a bow, not wishing to call down attention by rudeness. Then I passed her by.

"However, she found a place near mine in the sanctuary. The hood of her threadbare cloak covered her hair, but did not conceal her face from me. During the first hymns, she met my gaze and smiled whenever I chanced to glance toward her.

"Instantly I feared her. How had I drawn her notice? And how could I deflect it elsewhere? Attention led to death, as I knew too well. Yet I was also intrigued by her. I saw no revulsion in her soft eyes—and no malice. No cunning. No knowledge of what I was. Rather, I seemed to detect a shy pleasure in my confusion, my muffled alarm. Although I knew nothing of such matters, I received the impression that she wished me to repay her notice.

"Covertly, I studied her during the prayers and readings. To me, she was comely—smooth of cheek and full of lip, alive with the vitality of youth, yet demure and pious in her demeanor. Her poverty was plain in the wear and patching of her attire, but if she understood want—as did all Sestle's poor—she had not been dulled by it. No taint of bitterness or envy diminished her radiance. In the depth and luster of her gentle gaze, I caught my first glimpse of what Father Domsen meant when he spoke of the soul, for her eyes seemed to hold more life than mere flesh could contain.

"Her smiles teased me in ways which disturbed me to the heart."

Within myself I wailed at the memory. But I did not voice my sorrow.

"The priest delivered his sermon earnestly, but I did not heed him. I could not. I felt a mounting consternation which closed my ears. I wished only to flee the maid's nearness—and dared not, fearing to attract still more notice. Through the final hymns and prayers, and the priest's distant benediction, I stumbled. Then I sought my departure with as much speed as I could afford.

"To my chagrin, she accosted me in the aisle before the doors. Avoidance was impossible. Curtsying again, she stepped near and laughed to me softly, 'Sir, you sing very badly.'

"To my chagrin, I say—and yet I felt a far greater dismay when I found myself unable to turn away from her jest. She meant no harm by it, that was plain. No insult sullied her mirth. She simply wished to speak with me. And the impulse gave her pleasure.

"By that soft enchantment she held me, despite my knowledge of death, and my fear. I might safely have stepped past her there, urged ahead by the moving throng, but I did not. Instead I bowed to conceal my face, murmuring, 'The melodies are new to me.'

"While I spoke, I cursed myself because I did not flee. But I cursed myself more because I could not match her smile. The pain of my loneliness had become greater than I knew.

"'You are a stranger then,' she remarked.

"'I am,' I told her. Because my discomfort seemed rude to me, I added, 'My lady.'

"She laughed again. '"My lady"? You are truly a stranger. No native of Sestle would attempt such excessive courtesy here. I am not so wellborn, sir.

"'I am called Irradia. Those who desire more formality name me "Irradia-of-the-Lees," for I was discovered as an infant among the dredgings of the river, and raised by the good folk of Leeside. This chapel is my home.' She glanced fondly about the edifice.

"Her enchantment did not release me. Awkward with difficulty, I strove to answer her. 'You honor me,' I said gruffly. 'As for me, I am so far from my birthplace that I have no name. But you will honor me further if you call me Aposter.'"

Unable to face my audience, I gazed into the darkness of my goblet. "My lords, that is not my name," I told the last of my wine. "Nor is Scriven. But it is the name I chose to give her. And it is the name by which I am known to His Reverence Straylish Beatified."

Hardening my sorrow, I resumed.

"She accepted it without demur. How could she have known that it was false? That I was false myself?" Or that she would die in anguish because she could name me? "So commenced my true conversion to the teachings of Mother Church. Until that day, I had stood among the worshipers, singing and praying attentively, but I had only aped their devotion, not shared it. I desired it, but could not grasp its import. From that moment forward, however, the maid Irradia became my teacher, and I began to learn.

"At first, of course, she did not know that she taught me. She did not know what I was—and I gave her no glimpse of my ignorance. She merely offered me her friendliness and courtesy. Perhaps she did so because she could see that I was lost in loneliness despite my mimicry. Perhaps she was guided to me by the hand of Heaven. Or perhaps the flawless bounty of her heart surpassed the ordinary bounds of flesh and blood. I could not account for her actions then, and cannot explain them now. But in the days which followed she showed me what friendship and kindness were. By example she gave me my first instruction in righteousness.

"And with every taste of her companionship, I found that my hunger for it swelled. I grew eager for her smiles and mirth. I gave her occasion to tease me because her jests brought me pleasure. I accompanied her on the rounds of charity, the innumerable generosities, which filled her days as an adopted daughter of the chapel, and my small part in them warmed my heart. And when we were apart—as naturally we were more than we were together—I craved the sight of her as I craved survival. Her presence was like the vitality I drew from my victims. It elevated me, it made me strong and whole, it added a sparkle to the light of day and a glow to the depth of night—but it did not satisfy me. I desired more. I had been lonely too long. Her company became as necessary to me as blood, and I grew insatiable for it.

"So I began to reveal myself to her, hoping to strengthen the bonds between us—bonds which I had never felt before, and had no wish to break. I did not tell her what I was. But when I had known her for a month or more, I unfolded my ignorance to her. Embarrassed and cunning, I described the yearning which caused me to stand among the congregation and sing—badly—although I lacked all comprehension of what my worship signified.

"My ploy succeeded better than I could have dreamed. It drew Irradia to me, for she was pure in her faith and the thought of healing the breach which separated me from Heaven enchanted her. At the same time, however, it increased my own attraction to the teachings of Mother Church. As my companion exemplified them, they seemed entirely lovely to me, worthy of all devotion. The idea that my long experience of revulsion might be redeemed transported me. Hopes and desires beyond imagination took root in my once-barren heart, and sprouted richly.

"The more I knew of Irradia, the more I longed for her. And the more I learned from her, the more I desired the solace and acceptance of Mother Church."

The assembly stirred, restive with distress—indignant tinder smoldering toward outrage. They had seen that I was fearsome, a creature of powers miraculous to them, and therefore cruel. That I now laid claim to the teachings of Mother Church, which they held as their own, affronted them mortally. The Duke himself appeared disturbed, and his supporters with him. I heard whispers of "blasphemy" and "carnal evil." No doubt the gathering thought that I expressed a wish for Heaven in order to disguise my lust.

But Duke Obal had cornered me in his bright hall. I was as ready to give battle as any trapped beast. And the pain of Irradia's loss—and of my part in her torment—gave me a kind of strength. Briefly I could raise my voice.

"Do you question my *sincerity,* my lords?" In sudden fury I flung my goblet so that it bounded, soundless and empty, across the rugs. "Do you believe that I *dissemble?*"

My vehemence shocked the whispers to silence.

"It may be that I have no soul," I cried. *"But I have a heart."* There my flare of force consumed itself, and died. Ash and regret seemed to fill my mouth as I repeated, "I have a heart. I wish daily that I did not."

Then I rallied against my weakness. "But I do not ask God to take it from me. It is *mine.* My life is only my life. Doubtless you will slay me, when I am done with my tale. But you cannot erase my pain, or stifle my yearning—or avoid the cost."

The Duke covered his eyes. Perhaps he lacked the courage to regard me directly. "Continue, Scriven," he murmured as though he had been moved. "Fear nothing. I am as mortal as any man, and as flawed. But I am not so easily turned aside from my promises."

He could not truly believe that I would "fear nothing" at his command. He was not such a fool. But I had set my feet to this path, and did not mean to step back now. Bowing my head, I answered, "As you wish, my lord."

All the influential of Mullior watched me as they would a serpent. Under the bale of their fascination, I pursued my tale.

"I have said, the maid Irradia gave me instruction, binding me to her with every lesson—and her to me. Indeed, the growing warmth of her regard taught me the truth of her words, for it demonstrated God's forgiveness. In the name of Mother Church, she offered me a life which was not defined and circumscribed by revulsion.

"And when she believed that I had understood her, she took me to Father Domsen, so that he might further my edification."

Bishop Heraldic and his confessors crossed themselves in self-protection, warding away heresy, but I paid them no heed.

"That good man welcomed me," I said without pause, as though I had seen no reaction. "He taught me gladly. He was Irradia's father—in a manner of speaking—both temporally and spiritually, and at first I thought that he extended his kindness to me for her sake. Later, however, I understood him better. His love for her enriched but did not determine his acceptance. The simplicity of his faith, and the embrace of his heart, were wide enough to enfold all who worshiped with him.

"Sooner than I would have thought possible"—and altogether too soon for my dismayed auditors—"he and Irradia began to speak of my baptism—of my union by water and sacrament with Mother Church." Despite the moisture in my gaze, I held up my head as though I meant to stare down the assembly. But I needed more valor to confront my memories than to outface my enemies. Word after word, my tale gathered its anguish.

"My lords, I know now that I should have feared baptism. Belatedly I have heard that holy water is agony to my kind, scalding us with Heaven's rejection. At the time, however, I had no such concern. Irradia and Father Domsen had taught me to trust God's utter benison. Having no soul, I was unaware that I was damned.

"Yet I was troubled in my mind—and in my heart, if I have no soul. Throughout my life, I had known only abhorrence. And from abhorrence I had learned shame, although I did not realize it until I had recognized my loneliness. I am what I am, and life is life, and I had not ceased to feed. No creature of flesh endures without its proper sustenance. I studied the will of Heaven openly, desiring it as I desired Irradia's love. Yet still I preyed widely in Sestle so that I would not perish.

"Ashamed, I feared that Irradia—and Mother Church—would repulse me if they learned the truth.

"Further, I knew that I had been careless, although I had not yet imagined the consequences. Blinded by yearning, I had fed too often upon the fat and the wellborn, the wealthy and the publicly devout. And in so doing I had drawn notice.

"A child might have foreseen this, yet I did not. Ignoring the hazard of my actions, I had brought myself unwittingly to the awareness of His Reverence Straylish Beatified."

And the High Cardinal had completed my instruction. I abided by his precepts still.

"From his spies and informants," I explained, "as well as from more common sources, he heard tales of unexplained deaths, sudden passings. And some of the lost were his supporters, vital to his stature in the affairs of Sestle. Inspired by righteousness, he guessed the truth.

"So he searched for me." Relentless as a death-watch, my tale progressed toward its doom. "With every resource at his command, he hunted the byways and coverts, the dens and hovels, the inns and stables, the markets and middens, seeking some sign of my presence. As yet he did not know who I was, or where I resided, or how I selected my victims. But he knew *what* I was, and he bent the annealed iron of his loathing toward me."

I sighed so that I would not groan aloud. "Yet I was oblivious, immersed in my hunger for salvation. Only the sanctuary of my loft protected me, for I had lost the true habit of self-regard. While Cardinal Straylish stalked me with all his priests and allies, I concentrated on the impending crisis of my baptism.

"As I have said, I was ashamed. I saw my nature as an obstacle to my baptism—a bar to my union with Mother Church, and to Irradia's love, and to all good. Yet for that same reason I was loath to speak of my dilemma. The rejection of the congregation I might survive. I had endured for many long years without a place among ordinary men, and might do so again. But the thought that Irradia might hear my revelation with horror—that her outpouring love might curdle against me—caused such pain that I did not think I could bear it.

"At last, however, I accepted the risk. How could I ask for love if I did not honor truth? Irradia and Father Domsen preached that the welcome of Heaven knew no end or limit—that all life was of Divine creation, born of God to seek God's glory through Mother Church, How then could anyone who saw the worth of that worship be refused?

"On the eve of the day appointed for my baptism, I told Irradia what I was."

Inwardly I flinched at the memory. Yet I suffered it alone. Only the ceaseless blurring of my sight and the quavering of my voice betrayed my distress to the assembly.

At first her response was all I had dreaded. Her dear features paled, and she shrank from me as though I had become loathsome to her. She trembled, feverish with alarm. And she avoided the supplication of my touch, hid her face from my gaze. Weeping threatened to overtake her.

"The blow was a devastation to me, my lords. My life in Sestle, and my heart, cracked wide at the impact. In another moment, I would have begun to tear my garments and wail in despair. And when that was done, I might have turned my thoughts to ruin. She was the foundation upon which my dream of love and Heaven rested, and she could not stand.

"However, she rallied. Groaning my name, she turned toward me. Pain in runnels streaked her face. 'Have you lied to me all this time?' she cried out. 'Are this chapel and this congregation no more than a trough at which you mean to feed? Am I nothing more to you than meat and drink?'

"I knew not how to answer her. I cannot prove my sincerity to you, my lords, and could not to her. But at last I said, 'All my days, Irradia, I have spent alone. I have known only fear and abhorrence. Your regard, your gentleness, Father Domsen, this congregation, the teachings of Mother Church—they are sacred to me. Ask me to sacrifice myself for your preservation, and I will do it.' My desire for life had never been greater, yet I spoke truly. 'Death would be kinder to me than the loss of Heaven's blessing, which I have tasted only from you.'

"Gradually she calmed. Her innocent heart and her faith defended me when her mind quailed. Doubt still held her, but her revulsion had passed. When she had composed herself, she sighed, 'Oh, Aposter. This matter is too grave for me. A darkness has fallen over me, and I cannot see. I must speak to Father Domsen.' She studied me sidelong. 'Will you accompany me?' In that way she tested my protestations. 'Will you tell him what you are?'

"I felt the burden of her request. It weighed heavily upon my scant courage, my slight hopes. I esteemed the priest highly—but I trusted only her. However, I did not hesitate. 'I will,' I told her shortly. 'I will abide his judgment.'

"'Then I will believe you, while I may,' she replied with a wan smile. 'You have given me no cause to fear you. I have met no harm in you, and no malice.' Then she added, 'I, too, will abide his judgment.

"'Come.'

"I complied. Together we sought out the good Father."

Shading my eyes to ease the sting of the light, I walked that path again in my mind, dreading what followed.

"The hour was late, and he had retired, for he was old. When her knock summoned him to the door, however, he welcomed us into his dwelling.

"His quarters had been erected against the side of the chapel as an afterthought, and they were draughty, ill lit, and damp. Still his congregation had given what they could for his comfort. A fire burned in the hearth of his small study, warming the moist stones. At his invitation, we seated ourselves on hard lath chairs softened by pillows.

"He asked Irradia to speak of her plain distress, but I forestalled her. Seeking to spare her as much as I could, I blurted without grace or apology, 'Father, I have concealed what I am. I am not of your flesh—not an ordinary man, as I seem. Because I hunger to be united with Mother Church, and to earn Irradia's esteem, I feared to reveal myself.'

"He regarded me in confusion. Quailing within myself, I continued weakly, 'Yet I must speak the truth, or set aside my hope of Heaven.'"

Remembering that moment, I uncovered my eyes again so that the Duke's assembly might see my pain. "'Father,' I told him, 'I am called "vampyr" and "death-eater."' Among much harsher names. 'I do not feed on beasts or growing things that have no souls. I sustain myself on the lives of men and women formed in God's image.'

"At my words, he fell back in his seat, overtaken by clear shock and apparent horror. Watching him, I felt my hopes shift from under me, as though they rested on sand. How had I so entirely misconstrued his instruction? Had God created me and my kind solely so that innocent maids and gentle priests could name us evil?

"His hands clasped each other around his crucifix. For a moment it seemed that he would not speak—that he could find no words sufficient to denounce me. But then he asked, whispering terribly, 'Do these men and women die to feed you? Do you slay them?'

"I wished to cry out against his revulsion. But I did not. Irradia's need for his guidance was vivid in her gaze, and it restrained me. Instead I answered, 'I do not slay them in order to feed. Yet they are slain. They die at my hand. Their life becomes mine as they nourish me, and they fall.'

"His voice trembled. 'Then how can it be that you desire baptism?—that you seek the embrace of Mother Church?'

"There he saved me, although he did not know it. Despite my distress, and his, I heard his bafflement—and his sincerity. I had misread him. He had been profoundly disturbed, shaken to the core, but not by abhorrence. His nature may have lacked that capacity. He had asked an honest question. His dilemma was one of incomprehension.

"And Irradia clung to his every word, as though it issued from the mouth of Heaven.

"I replied as well as I could, like a man who had been snatched back from the rim of perdition. 'I did not cause what I am. I cannot alter it.

But I have met kindness from you, and from Irradia, I have learned to know love. And I ache for the teachings of Mother Church. If the grace of Heaven is without end or limit,' I pleaded softly, 'surely it holds a place for such as me?'

"At first he did not answer my gaze. Raising his hands, he fixed his eyes upon the crucifix. Prayers I could not distinguish murmured from his lips. Unsteady light from the hearth colored his features, and Irradia's. Together they appeared to contemplate the flames of everlasting torment.

"When he had finished his prayer, however, he turned toward me. Tears reflected in the lines of his face, but he did not waver.

"'Then, my son,' he avowed, 'I will baptize you tomorrow.'

"I heard him without moving, without breath. Trained to apprehension, I feared that if I stirred his promise would be snatched away.

"'Father—' protested Irradia. Perhaps he had answered his own uncertainty, but he had not yet relieved hers. 'If he is a vampyr—'

"He silenced her gently. 'Whatever he is, my daughter, he has been created by God, for God's own reasons. It is not our place to judge what the Almighty has made. In baptism Heaven will accept or reject him, whatever we do. But if for the sake of our own fears and ignorance we refuse that which Heaven welcomes, our sin will be severe. Mother Church does not empower us to withhold the hope of redemption.

"'If he is accepted, the flock we serve will see it. That will do much to ease his way among us.' His tone darkened. 'And if he is rejected, they will be forewarned.

"'But there is a condition, my son,' he told me before I could speak. 'You must cease from slaying.'

"My hopes had blazed up brightly. Now they dwindled again, doused by Father Domsen's words. 'Then I will die,' I retorted bitterly. 'Does Heaven honor self-murder?'

"He shook his head. 'It does not. Yet you must cease,' he persisted. 'Since you require sustenance, as do all things living, seek it from those whose lives have already been claimed by God. Nourish yourself among the dying. It will—' He faltered momentarily, and I saw a new sorrow in his gaze. Yet he did not relent. 'I fear it will not be pleasant,' he continued more harshly. 'But I cannot condone any other course for you. To take lives which have not yet been called by Heaven is more than murder. It is blasphemy. It offends the sacredness of God's creation.'

"At once a great relief washed through me. The restriction he required would *not* be pleasant. In that he spoke more truly than he knew. Yet its difficulties were within my compass. In Heaven's name, I could bear them gladly.

"'Father,' I vowed, 'I will do as you say.'

"Irradia stared at me with wonder, as though she hardly dared to believe that her doubts had been lifted.

"Father Domsen showed no relief, however. He accepted my oath without question, but it did not ease him. Wincing, he bowed his head and slowly slumped into his seat. Perhaps he had seen visions in the firelight, and Irradia's face, and mine—sights which wracked him.

"'Leave me now, my children,' he breathed thinly. 'I must pray.' His sorrow did not abate. 'I must pray for us all. Tomorrow the will of Heaven will be made plain.'

"I heard his grief well enough. Yet I did not understand it. He had glimpsed a future which lay beyond my comprehension. And," I admitted ruefully, "knowing the aftermath—knowing my failure, and its cost—made no attempt to grasp it. As Irradia and I departed, my heart arose, and an unwonted joy seemed to chirp and warble in my blood's vitality. My deepest dreams had become real to me again, brought back from transience and illusion by the good Father's willingness to hazard my baptism. His restriction I welcomed, for it provided a reply to my shame. And—most joyous of all things—I saw hope in Irradia's gaze again. He had restored her dreams also. She clasped my arm as we made our way from the chapel, and her smile held a hint of its familiar pleasure.

"Before our ways parted, she addressed me gravely.

"'Aposter, I said that I would abide Father Domsen's judgment. Now I say that I will stand with you when you are baptized.' Her tone was firm, and clarity shone from her eyes. 'I do not believe that God's face will be turned away. If my trust has worth in Heaven—as it must, for God is good—it will weigh on your behalf.'

"Laughing, she kissed my cheek to forestall any return for her generosity. Then she was gone.

"As I returned to my loft, I sang her name as I would the most sacred of the hymns. Before Heaven she had taken a vow of her own, and I cherished it. After all my fears, I was avid for the morrow, and for my sacramental union with Mother Church, and for her."

My own grief welled up in me. I had come to understand Father Domsen's sorrow. I did not think that he had foreseen his own weakness. Rather, I conceived that he knew the public life of Sestle, and the worldly affairs of Mother Church, better than his innocence could tolerate. For that reason, he had sequestered himself in Leeside chapel, hoping that broader, more hurtful concerns would pass him by.

Past my pain, I sighed, "But the time appointed for my baptism never came."

Involuntarily I paused, striving to master myself.

"It did not," interjected Bishop Heraldic suddenly, "because Heaven spoke to your priest—your Father Domsen—and gave him better wisdom."

No doubt His Reverence believed that he had been silent too long. Fearing the effect of my tale, he wished to assert himself in the hall. But I had no patience for him.

"*No*," I retorted harshly. "It did not because Cardinal Straylish found me."

When my ire had stifled the Bishop's interruption, I added, "Or I should say that he found Irradia."

Of all my victims, my prey, she was the most blameless—and the most dear.

"Later," I told Mullior's assembled lords and authorities, "I learned of the wide net which he had cast over the city, searching for me. I heard how he had become suspicious of Leeside, for that region seemed exempt from my activities. And I was informed that rumors of a stranger had at last reached the ears of his agents—a stranger who seemed to have no dwelling place, but who had been befriended by the maid Irradia, the chapel's adopted daughter.

"On the morn of my intended baptism, however, I knew none of this. Ignorant of the ruin prepared for me, I readied myself gladly, singing her name, and remembering all the words I must say in the liturgy of the sacrament. When the time came, I crept from my loft so that I could join the worshipers gathering before the doors of the chapel, as was my custom.

"Entranced by excitement, and by the prospect of Irradia, I was slow to notice my peril.

"The doors remained shut, although the time of worship was near. That in itself was strange, and should have alerted me. But there were other signs also. Men on horseback crowded the approaches to the chapel. Ruffians unlike the Leeside congregation in both aspect and comportment shifted among more familiar men and women, attentive as hounds. And Father Domsen stood at the doors as though he meant to address his flock in the street. His old eyes hunted the growing throng anxiously.

"When he saw me, he beckoned. The gesture appeared to cause him pain.

"I approached to discover what he wished of me. As I drew near, I heard him speak the name I had given myself. 'Aposter. There he is.'

"Finally I grasped that there was something amiss. Events had gone awry in Sestle. Perhaps I should have fled. But I did not conceive that I was in peril. I could not. At that moment I feared only for Irradia, and for the priest.

"Pointing toward me, he repeated, 'There he is.' I saw now that weeping filled his face.

"Then some blow or bludgeon seemed to take away the back of my head, and I stumbled into darkness."

There I paused. I had reached the crux of what I must relate, and I faltered. "My lord Duke," I inquired hoarsely, "may I have more wine? I thirst." After a moment, I added, "And I am afraid."

Duke Obal flicked his fingers, a brusque command. His strained gaze did not leave my face.

At once a fresh goblet was given to Lord Ermine at my side. He offered it to me, frowning in solicitude. I accepted it and drank. With the wine I swallowed cries I did not mean to utter, fury and woe I could not afford to express. Only my tale stood between me and death. And only my tale held back Obal's fall. Bracing my heart, I continued.

"I awoke to a dazzle of illumination"—light as acute as my distress in the Duke's hall—"and the sound of screaming. I found myself seated erect, but my limbs were bound so that I could not move. The pain of damaged bone filled my head. And hunger— A considerable time must have passed since I had last fed. Two days? As much as three? I had not drawn sustenance the night before I was to have been baptized. Now the yearning to survive blazed in all my veins. My weakness was such that I could not have stood if my arms and legs had been free—could not have remained upright if my bonds had not held me.

"The voice that screamed was one I knew well. It had grown dear to me, a treasure of sweetness, now betrayed to agony.

"In frailty and desperation, I labored to clear my sight so that I might determine the nature of my plight."

Some among my auditors must have guessed what I would relate— and anticipated it with relish.

"I sat, secured by ropes, in a chair of iron which had been placed on a low dais against one wall of a stone chamber, windowless and cold. By its shape, the room was an oubliette. But if it was, then night had fallen on the world, for no hint of sun or sky showed above me. Instead the chamber was lit by torches and braziers by the score, leaving nothing unrevealed.

"Arrayed around the space and awaiting use were objects and devices which chilled my chest, instruments of torture—I saw racks and thumbscrews, an iron maiden, eye-gouges, flails and lancets and brands, flaying tables, cruel gibbets where a body might hang for days without death, castrators, rape-engines, alembics a-fume with acid. By such means was Hell made tangible, temporary flesh given its first taste of eternal excruciation.

"Clearly the room was a testing chamber, where the servants of Mother Church searched for truth among the wracked limbs and torn flesh of Heaven's foes. I had heard that clergymen and inquisitors employed such instruments against evil, but I had given the matter no thought—no credence. It had no place in Father Domsen's teachings, or in Irradia's beliefs, and I had put it from my mind.

"Now I saw that I must expand my understanding of Mother Church."

Bishop Heraldic might take offense at my words, but I did not care. Closing my eyes against illumination and memory, I went on.

"At the center of the room, a man stood beside a long table with his work displayed before me as though for my inspection. Despite my weakness, and my damaged head, I knew him at once for a clergyman. He wore the robes and chasuble, as crimson as anguish, of the lords of Mother Church, but he had set aside the miter of his office, leaving his head unrestricted, and his hands were flecked with blood. His features had been formed for piety, strict of mouth and nose, lean of cheek, his brow lined with denunciations. Rue and eagerness defined his gaze. Two ebon-clad men, bulky and muscular, awaited his commands, but did not put themselves forward to assist him.

"With each touch he lifted new screams from Irradia's raw throat.

"She lay naked on the table." The memory was vivid to me, etched so deeply into the passages of my brain that I believed it would endure when my flesh had fallen to worms and corruption. Merely closing my eyes did not shut it out. "Her arms had been drawn above her head and clamped in iron fetters, and her ankles were knotted to rings set into the wood. Thus outstretched, she might shift her hips and writhe, but could do nothing to avoid her tormentor's touch. Already blood and pain in profusion marked her helpless flesh.

"In one hand the clergyman employed a curiously serrated blade—in the other, pincers gripping a sponge damp with vitriol. As I watched, he stroked his blade tenderly across her belly toward her breasts, laying bare her nerves, then squeezed his sponge to drip acid into the streaming wounds. Her skin and tissues steamed with liquid fire as she shrieked out her hurt to the high ceiling and the unattainable sky.

"Appalled beyond bearing, I croaked, 'Stop'—and again, 'Stop.'

"Her tormentor lifted his head. Setting aside his implements, he seemed to regard me kindly. After a moment, he addressed me.

"'I see that you have regained consciousness.' His voice was husky and avid, a voice of passion—as well suited as his long fingers to caress or flay. 'That is well. You must attend what transpires here.

"'I am Straylish,' he continued, 'High Cardinal of Mother Church, and worldly suzerain of all this land in the name of Heaven. What you are'— he appeared to smile—'will be made plain to God's judgment.'

"He confused me. Living in Sestle, I had heard him spoken of often, yet I did not comprehend his power—or his intent. Did he not already know me? 'Father Domsen—' I began. But there my voice, or my heart, faltered. I meant to say that the priest had already betrayed me. Cardinal Straylish knew perfectly what I was.

"How had Father Domsen turned against me? And *why*? I had seen sorrow in him, but not distrust. His grief had given me no hint—

"And if Father Domsen had turned against me, why did the High Cardinal now inflict such suffering upon Irradia?

"'I am not done with him,' replied His Reverence sternly. 'Like this maid—her name is Irradia, I believe?—he also has countenanced the presence of evil among us.

"'It is true that he served me in the end. Repenting his folly—or so he said—he identified you to my men, so that you would work no more abomination. I doubt his sincerity, however. I do not know how long he was aware of you. Later you will confess the truth, so that I may pursue Heaven's judgment accurately.' The High Cardinal flexed his fingers in anticipation. 'But he did not come forward until after I had taken her.' A gesture indicated Irradia. 'I fear for him that he was moved to aid my search, not by genuine repentance, but rather by a desire to spare this weak daughter of his congregation God's wrath.

"'That doubt I will resolve later, however. For the present, her guilt compels me.' He spoke as lovers do, in eagerness and intimacy.

"Now I understood Father Domsen, although His Reverence still baffled me. At the time, I gave the matter no further thought. I cared only for Irradia—cared only that I might find some means to halt her great pain.

"Nevertheless between that day and this I have ached with regret over the good priest's plight—yes, and burned with shame for my part in it. I find no fault with him that he chose to sacrifice me as he did. For Irradia's sake, I would have done the same.

"Yet he did betray me, and I am certain that his gentle heart bore the burden heavily. Irradia I had apparently doomed by the simple sin of accepting her goodwill. But if I had not revealed myself to Father Domsen, he would have been spared the necessity of denouncing me."

It seemed that my confession meant nothing to my auditors. Their silence had closed against me, unyielding as the doorstone of a sepulchre. Even the Duke and his adherents stood motionless, almost breathless, as though snared in dismay.

Sighing, I labored onward.

"As I say, however, such considerations came later. At the time, every faint scrap of my remaining energy and attention was concentrated toward His Reverence. I knew how I had come to be where I was. But I could not conceive why my captor continued to harm Irradia after I had fallen into his power.

"'Father Domsen has told you what I am,' I countered through my weakness. 'She is no longer needed. What do you want from her?'

"'What do I want?' My question appeared to pique the Cardinal. 'For myself, nothing.' With the tip of his tongue, he moistened his lips. 'For my God, however, I desire the utter extirpation of Satan and all his minions. And toward that end, one small step will be taken here.

"'It came to my attention,' he explained, 'that a vampyr preyed in Sestle—a vile spawn of Hell, devouring souls to feed its own damnation. For some weeks I hunted him in vain. Infidels and scum, apostates and heretics I sifted without number, seeking Heaven's foe. And at last I gleaned the tale of a Leeside maid befriended by a stranger—a man without apparent homeland, history, employment, or domicile. By degrees I learned to believe that this stranger was indeed the abomination I sought—that this lost maid knew who and what he was—and that she had condoned his evil by concealing his identity. Therefore I gathered her to me.'

"Sadly he shook his head over her. 'Her sin is as great as her innocence. I suspect that she has been cruelly misled. By God's grace, however, her soul has been granted to my care. Guided by Heaven, I will win truth from her, purging her fault with pain.

"'Then,' he finished gently, 'I will deal with you.'

"Still I did not understand. I failed to comprehend his doctrine, as I had failed to grasp Father Domsen's. By nature I knew nothing of 'forgiveness' or 'repentance.' But Irradia's cries had at last subsided to quiet sobbing while the Cardinal spoke with me, and I could not endure to think that he would torment her anew—that she would scream again.

"'No,' I protested. 'Deal with me now.

"'I will confess,' I told him, gathering urgency as I went. 'Release her. *Stop* this cruelty. I will confess'—I hardly knew what—'everything. She was ignorant of me. I hid the truth. I tricked her—I will tell you how I practiced on her innocence, so that she learned to trust me. Whatever you wish—

"'Only release her,' I pleaded.

"The High Cardinal replied with laughter. 'You will surely confess,' he promised. 'In your turn, you will reveal the depth and breadth of your foulness in every particular. But first I must redeem this maid.

"'Without repentance she cannot hope for Heaven's forgiveness. She must see her sin and turn from it. She must turn from you. In mercy and love, I will not spare her one item or instance of agony until she surrenders her fault by speaking your name.'

"Smiling, he retrieved his implements. A stroke of the sponge wiped her blood from his blade, refreshing its serrations. His hands were those of an adept, certain of their purpose, and made cunning by experience.

"Confronted by Irradia's anguish, I lost all dignity, all restraint—all thought of myself. 'No!' I cried, wailed, shrieked, 'she has no fault, the fault is *mine*, I *confess* it, you must *stop!*'

"But His Reverence Straylish Beatified was not swayed.

"'Her fault is indeed yours,' he pronounced, 'and I will exact its penalty from you.' His hands lingered over her pale flesh, although his gaze held mine. 'Since you wish to confess, this will be your penance until I am ready for you—to witness the tortures which you will suffer eternally, and to be helpless against them.

"'With every breath in your lungs and pulse in your veins, you will struggle to oppose God's judgment in me, to resist the righteousness— which damns you—and you will gain nothing. You are bound to my will, and to Hell. Your evil cannot prevail against Heaven. Inspired by Satan's cunning, you seek to restore this maid's life with your own, but it will not avail you. Rather you will bear her pain until I am ready for yours.'

"Then in charity and sorrow he turned with exquisite care to the labor of Irradia's redemption."

I knew not how I continued. My weakness itself, and the burden of Irradia's anguish, seemed to uphold me, for without them I would surely have fallen prostrate. My eyes were open now, but I gazed only at Duke Obal. The rest of Mullior's highborn had ceased to exist for me. Only his steady glower, angry and aggrieved—only his honesty or dishonor— retained any import that I could recognize.

"My lords," I said hoarsely, "I will not speak of what was done to her." When her eyes were burst from their sockets, I screamed myself until my throat was torn, and blood spewed from my mouth. "I will say only that under the High Cardinal's hands she cried out until she could cry no more. Thereafter her limbs and sinews enacted a wailing to which she could no longer give voice. Mute, her excruciation was more terrible to me than any howl."

I drew a long, shuddering breath. "But she did not surrender my name.

"By silence she believed that she might save me. Though His Reverence asked it and demanded it, prayed and pleaded for it, soothed and wracked her to obtain it, she held my name to herself. In that baptism of agony, she stood with me, as she had promised."

Dry-eyed now, for my pain had grown too great for tears, and the hall's brilliance no longer daunted me, I met the clenched attention of my audience.

"And at last," I sighed, "the High Cardinal set aside his implements in vexation. Informing his ebon-clad servants that he would return after an hour's rest to continue her redemption, he withdrew from the chamber.

"This, apparently, signaled that their turn had come. When he had closed the door, they advanced at once, jesting with each other. One approached Irradia's table. His hands fumbled at the ties of his breeches as he moved. The other began with me.

"Drawing near, he struck me a full-armed blow, and laughed as he swung. My head recoiled against the iron of my seat. Moments of darkness gnawed at my vision, so that sight itself appeared to mortify within me, announcing the corruption of the grave.

"In glee and malice, he thrust his visage close to mine. 'You are a great fool,' he informed me. His breath stank of garlic and stale wine, rotting teeth and unrestricted appetites—'You thought yourself safe, didn't you?' he jeered. 'Hiding in a sanctuary. Sneaking into the skirts of a pretty maid. You thought—'

"His taunts died with him. Beyond him, I saw his companion climb open-breeched onto the table and Irradia. Leaning forward suddenly, I sank my teeth into the flesh of his lower lip.

"My bite drew blood. And blood drew life. Without pause or hesitation, he folded to the stone at my feet as though Heaven itself had stricken him.

"Immediately I received the benefit of his many lusts. His vitality became mine. His strength suffused my limbs. On the instant I ceased to be the weak and starving creature whom the Cardinal's ruffians had captured. Although I remained bound, I was no longer helpless.

"Shouting wordless threats to distract Irradia's assailant, I struggled to win free of my ropes.

"Curses answered me, guttural and dismayed. The man rolled from the table to his feet. Clutching at his breeches with one hand, he snatched a dirk from its sheath with the other, then lumbered furiously forward to stab at me before my bonds loosened.

"He succeeded well enough. His dirk he pounded into my shoulder with the force of a blacksmith's hammer. But it did not suffice. Irradia's tortures had driven me to madness. And I possessed all his companion's great strength.

"While his dirk thudded deeply into me, I turned my head enough to nip at his wrist.

"It was a small wound, no more—a drop of blood. I required nothing greater. He toppled, lifeless, onto the corpse of his companion, and I used what he had given me to snap my ropes.

"The dirk I must have plucked out, but I do not recall doing so. I kept it, hardly thinking that it might be of use to me.

"Then I was at Irradia's side." Perhaps it was not weakness which upheld me. Perhaps wrath and sin had struck so deeply into my bones that they became a form of strength.

"I had no garment with which to cover her. But she was clad in blood, and did not need one. Yet for that very reason I dared not touch her, although I burned to lift her into my embrace. I did not wish to slay her.

"Blinded, she could not return my gaze. For a moment, however, she seemed to know me. Her lips shaped my name, and she strove to speak. Lowering my ear to her, I heard a word which may have been, 'Forgive—' But I could not ask whom she wished me to forgive—or why. Or how.

"When she had breathed her prayer, she succumbed to unconsciousness."

At last the end was near, and I hastened to meet it. I had forgotten my fear. For the moment, at least, the prospect of my death had lost its power to appall me.

"Then there came upon me a time of darkness—a time I have no courage to describe. I might have restored Irradia, as I restored Lord Numis. I might have given her the life which I had torn from the Cardinal's servants, and raised her whole from her ordeal.

"But what then, my lords? What then? We would be prisoners still— and I would be weak again, as I am now. What hope did we have of flight? In darkness and despair, I saw that we had none. And when we had been secured anew, His Reverence would return her to torment. The screams which had brought me to madness would be no more than a foretaste of those which would surely follow.

"I had learned to love Mother Church, as I loved Irradia. Under her sweet influence, and Father Domsen's teachings, I had dreamed that I had a soul. But in the High Cardinal's oubliette I abandoned it."

That pain—that sin—was mine. Mere revulsion and death could not bereave me of it.

"With a caress of my hand, I took her life, so that His Reverence Beatified would never harm her again. Her small scrap of vitality I added to the strength I had already harvested. Then I made my escape by ascending the walls until I came to the mouth of the oubliette, and so to the open night of the city.

"Sestle I fled as quickly as I could manage." I had explained enough. My tale required little more of me. "When I learned of my lord Duke's opposition to the High Cardinal's doctrine, I made my way to Mullior. After a time, I gained an opportunity to offer him my service."

It was finished.

"In his service, my lords, I carry out my penance. My sin is plain to me, and I expiate as Straylish Beatified instructed me. I bear Irradia's pain. I seek to restore life. I resist the righteousness which damns me. And I obey Father Domsen. I take no life which has not already been claimed by God.

"Do with me what you will. I am done. Perhaps it is true that I have no soul. Irradia whom I loved asked me to 'Forgive,' and I cannot."

Bowing my head, I fell silent.

▲▼▲

The distress in the hall echoed my own. So much I had gained, if no more. Lords and ladies wrestled with emotions which they must have abhorred. Priests murmured over their beads, telling prayers I did not choose to hear.

The Duke's heir gripped my arm convulsively. "Fear nothing, Scriven," he whispered. His voice caught. "Fear—nothing."

I did not heed him. Drained of fear and strength and supplication, I regarded only Duke Obal. Above his jaw's grim thrust, a gleam of moisture or regret pierced his gaze. His expression I was unable to read. But I would not have been surprised to hear him say that I had shown myself no fit ally of Mullior—that my sin and my nature justified the High Cardinal's enmity—that a man who had slain his only friend, his only love, could not claim clemency here.

Doubtless His Reverence the Bishop would assert as much, when he recovered his wits.

Slowly Duke Obal turned away. His features were hidden from me as he addressed the hall. In a voice husky with fervor, he announced, "There is one aspect of Scriven's tale which he did not mention—because he does not know it. He has already been given a sign of Heaven's acceptance.

"Before your eyes," he told the gathering, "he has been tested by holy water. Pure water blessed and sanctified by my confessor was mingled with Scriven's wine. You have seen that he drank of it—twice—and took no hurt.

"It is not baptism," he acknowledged. "But it will suffice for me."

Abruptly he raised his fists, and his voice lifted to a shout like the cry of an eagle. "Who speaks against him now?" he called fiercely. "Who *dares*!"

Bishop Heraldic cleared his throat. Shamefaced, he mumbled, "Not I, my lord."

Around him, lords and ladies added, "Not I." Merchants and guards, officials and priests, did the same, swelling a chorus of assent. Lord Numis might have protested, but two of the Bishop's confessors stilled him.

Lowering his arms, Duke Obal returned to me. With a few strides, he crossed the rugs between us until he stood near enough to place his hands like an embrace upon my shoulders.

"'Then, Scriven,'" he proclaimed so that none would mistake him, "I say to you before all these witnesses that you are my trusted friend, and I am honored by your service. Be welcome in Mullior. Be at home. As you keep your vows, so will I keep mine. The House of Obal stands by you. While I live, you are safe among us."

In the grip of his strong hands, I straightened my back and met his gaze as best I could.

"Thank you, my lord. I will keep my vows."

He deserved better gratitude, but I had come to the end of what I could do. I had begun to weep, and had no heart to stanch it.

He was more than a good son of Mother Church. He was a man of faith.

Together the Duke's Commander and the Master of Mullior's Purse offered me escort in their lord's name, showing openly that they, too, honored me. With their support, I left the hall and the palace and made my way accepted into the night.

The Killing Stroke

When he was returned to the cell we shared, he retained nothing except his short, warrior's robe and his knowledge of *shin-te*. The years of training which had made him what he was despite his youth had not been taken from him. Everything else was gone. His birthplace and family, his friendships and allegiances, his possessions and memories—all had been swept aside. The faces of his masters and students had vanished from his mind. He could not have given an account of himself to save his life—or ours. Not even his name remained to him.

I was familiar with his plight. As was Isla. We had experienced it ourselves.

The look of bereavement in his eyes did not augur well for him. It had settled firmly into the strained flesh at his temples and the new lines of his cheeks, causing him to appear almost painfully youthful and forlorn. He might have been a small boy who had grown so accustomed to blows he could not avoid that he had learned to flinch and duck his head reflexively.

Weariness clung to his limbs, burdened his shoulders. His ordeal had been immeasurably arduous.

Still his skill, and the rigor behind it, showed in the poise with which he carried himself, in the quick accuracy with which he saw and noted everything around him. He had presumably been dealt a killing stroke, with blade or fist. Yet he remained lithe of movement, prompt of gaze—and centered in his *qa*.

So he had returned on previous occasions. That he could continue to move and attend as he did, in spite of defeat and death, moderated his air of bereavement.

His throat was parched from his various exertions. Studying us with his incipient flinch, he tried to speak, but could not find his voice at first. With an effort, he swallowed his confusion and fear in order to clear his mouth. Then he asked faintly, "Where am I?"

It was the same question he had asked each time he entered. With repetition, his voice had grown husky, thick with doubt, but his mind continued to arrange its inquiries in the same order.

That also did not augur well.

As she had each time before, Isla shrugged, glowering darkly from her smudged features.

As I had each time before, I spread my hands to indicate the cell. Its blind stone walls and eternal lamps, its timbered ceiling, its pallets and cistern and privy, were the only answer we could give.

Frowning fearfully, he asked his second question. "Who are you?"

Isla turned her glower toward me. Behind its grime, her face might have been lovely or plain, but she had long since forgotten which, and I had ceased to be curious. The shape of her mouth was strict, however, and the heat of her *qa* showed in her eyes. "Does he never get tired of this?" she demanded.

Her protest was not a reference to the young man standing before us.

"Or she?" I retorted. The debate was of long standing between us. It meant nothing, but I maintained it on the general principle—oft repeated by my masters—that we could not escape our imprisonment by making unwarranted assumptions.

The young man swallowed again. "He? She?"

That question, also, he had asked more than once.

No doubt deliberately, Isla chose to violate the litany of previous occasions. "You answer," she ordered me. "I get tired, if he doesn't."

Simply because I enjoyed variations of any kind, I tried to provoke her. "How are you tired? You do nothing except pace and complain."

"Tired," she snapped, "of being the only one who cares."

Her defeat had predated mine—although neither of us could measure the interval between them. In fact, she had preserved my heart from despair. I could not have borne my own ordeal alone. But my gratitude did neither of us any good.

And she was not the only one who cared.

Smiling ruefully, I faced the young man. "I am Asper." For entertainment's sake, I performed a florid bow. "This uncivil termagant is Isla. We are here to serve you. However," I admitted, "we have not yet grasped what aid you might need."

Isla snorted, but refrained from contradiction. She knew I spoke the truth.

A small tension between the young man's brows deepened. He may have been trying to anticipate the next blow. For him the litany remained unbroken. He had not moved from the spot where he had appeared in the cell.

"Have we met before?"

Since Isla had elected to vary the experience with silence, I continued alone. "Several times."

He did not ask, How is that possible? His masters had trained him well. He remained centered in his *qa*—and in his thoughts. Instead he observed hoarsely, "A mage has imprisoned us."

This was not an assumption. If it were, I might have challenged it. His conclusion was inescapable, however, made so by the perfect absence of a door through which any of us could have entered the cell. And by the fact that we yet lived.

Keeping my bitterness to myself, I shrugged in assent.

His sorrow augmented the weariness which burdened his spirit. In the unflinching lamplight, he appeared to dwindle.

Sadly, he asked, "What are you?"

The same questions in the same order.

"By the White Lords," Isla swore, "he learns nothing."

There my temper snapped. My own memory had been restored to me after my last defeat. I recalled too much death. "And what precisely," I demanded of her, "is it that *we* have learned?"

She answered at once, crying at the walls, "I have learned hatred! If he makes the mistake of letting me live, I will extract the cost of this abuse from his bones!"

I understood her anguish. "We both knew that neither of us would ever see the light of day again, if this *shin-te* master did not win our freedom for us.

Still I was angry. I did not allow her to leave her place in the litany.

Smiling unkindly at the young man, I performed a small circular flick with the fingers of one hand—a gesture both swift and subtle, difficult to notice—and at once a whetted dagger appeared in my palm. Without pausing to gauge direction or distance, I flipped the bladepoint at Isla's right eye.

My cast was true. Yet the dagger did not strike her. Instead it flashed upward and embedded itself with a satisfying thunk in one of the ceiling timbers.

She adjusted the sleeve of her robe.

We both gazed at the young man.

Curling his hands over his heart, he accorded us the *shin-te* bow of respect. *"Nahia,"* he said to me. And to Isla, *"Mashu-te."*

In our separate ways, we also bowed. We could not do otherwise. He had named us, although he remembered nothing.

"Your mastery is plain," he observed unhappily. "You must have answered better than I."

Opening his hand, he indicated what lay beyond our cell.

"If that were true," Isla snapped, "you wouldn't be here."

For myself I added, "Neither would we."

There was nothing for which we could hope if his mastery did not prove greater than ours.

Fortunately, he appeared to understand us without more explanation. We had none to offer. Nothing had been revealed to us. If our captor had placed any value on our comprehension, we would not have been deprived of our memories while we fought and failed.

Shouldering his dismay as well as he could, he asked the question which must have given him the most pain.

"Who am I?"

Because we were familiar with his distress, both Isla and I faced him openly so that he could see that we had no reply for him. We knew only what he had told us—and he remembered only *shin-te*.

For the first time, he varied our litany of question and response himself. Slowly, he raised his hands to wipe tears from his eyes. His struggles had exhausted his flesh. Now his repeated return from death had begun to exhaust his spirit.

That also did not augur well.

When he spread his hands to show us that they were empty—that he was defenseless—we recognized that he had come to the point of his gravest vulnerability. So softly that he might have made no sound, he voiced the question which haunted us all.

"Why?"

We would have answered him kindly—Isla even more than I, despite her hate. We knew his pain. But any kindness would have been a lie.

"Presumably," she told him, "it is because you failed."

As we had failed before him.

Despite his training, he allowed himself a sigh of weariness and regret. That, too, was a slight variation.

He had sighed before. With repetition, however, it had begun to convey the inflection of a sob. His last question contained little more than utter fatigue.

"Is it safe to rest?"

I might have answered sardonically, "We survive the experience, as you see." But Isla forestalled me.

"We will ward you with our lives," she assured him. "While you are here, we have no other hope."

He nodded, accepting her reply. Carefully, he moved to the nearest pallet and folded himself onto it. Within moments he had fallen asleep.

As before, I found no satisfaction in his willingness to trust us. I knew as well as he did that his weariness left him no alternative.

He had endured altogether too much death.

▲▼▲

Folk like myself might have said that we had already seen enough to content us. After simmering and frothing for the better part of a decade, the Mage War had at last boiled over three years ago, spilling blood across the length and breadth of Vesselege until all the land was sodden with it. For reasons which few of us understood, and fewer still cared about, the White Lords had scourged and harried the Dark until only one remained—the most potent and dire of them all, it was said, the dread Black Archemage, secure among the shadows and malice of his granite keep upon the crags of Scarmin. Even then, however, the victories of the White Lords, and the withdrawal of the Archemage, did not suffice to lift the pall of battle and death from the land. The reach of a mage was long, as we all knew. During that war, we learned how long. A hundred leagues from Scarmin's peaks and cols, hurricanes of fire and stone fell upon Vess whenever—so we were told—Argoyne the Black required a diversion to ward him from some assault of the White Lords, and of Goris Miniter, Vesselege's King.

Vess was Miniter's seat, the largest and—until the Mage War—most thriving city in the land. So naturally I lived there, within a whim of destruction every hour of my days. By nature, I think, I had always enjoyed the proximity of disasters—as long as they befell someone else. Certainly, I had always been adept at avoiding them myself. And that skill had been enhanced and honed by my training among the *nabia*.

My poor father, blighted by poverty and loss, had gifted me there after my mother's death. Though I had squalled against the idea at the time, I had learned to treasure it. When my masters had at last released me, I was a gifted pickthief, an impeccable burglar, and an artist of impossible escapes and improbable disappearances. I was also a true warrior in the tradition of the *nabia*. Faced by a single antagonist, I might leave him dead before he realized that I was not the one being slain. Confronting a gang of ruffians, I could dispatch half of them while the other half hacked at each other in confusion and folly.

Despite the visitations of power which blasted one section of the city or another at uncertain intervals, I lived rather well in Vess, I thought. Unfortunately, late in the third year of the War, some mischance or miscalculation must have brought me to the attention of one mage or another. The life I knew ended as suddenly as if I had severed it at the base of the neck. Without transition or awareness, I found myself in a stone cell with Isla and no door. When my memory was restored, I recalled days or weeks of bitter combat. I felt myself die again and again, until my spirit quailed like a coward's. Yet I remembered nothing of how I had been taken from Vess—or why. And I had nothing but assumptions, which my masters abhorred, to tell me where I was.

Isla's story, as I learned it after my memory had been returned, was completely different than mine—and entirely the same.

Her father and mother, her brother and sisters, her aunts and uncles— her whole family, in fact—had dedicated their lives to the *mashu-te,* the Art of the Direct Fist. As a young girl, fiery of temper, and quick to passion—or so I imagined her—she had been initiated in the disciplines and skills of those masters, and she had studied with the clenched devotion of a girl determined to prove her worth. The study and teaching of *mashu-te* had consumed her, and in all her years she had never left the distant school where her masters winnowed acolytes to glean students, and students to glean warriors. When she spoke of that time, I received the impression that she had never tested her skills against anyone not already familiar with them.

Still, her skills were extraordinary. It was said around Vesselege that a *mashu-te* master could stop a charging bull with one blow. I doubted that—but I did not doubt that Isla was a master. I had slipped once with her, and my *qa* still trembled in consequence.

From time to time, I had assured her that I could slay her easily, if I permitted myself to use my fang, the *nahia* dagger secreted within my robe. But that was mere provocation. I did not believe it. The truth was that I feared her—and not only because of her vehement excellence.

She had endured alone an ordeal which had nearly broken me despite her companionship.

Like mine, her life had simply ended one day, without transition or explanation, and she had found herself here. Like me, she had faced countless opponents and death, and had remembered nothing until her captor had given up on her. Yet she was whole. She was bitter, and she had learned hatred, but she was whole. I could not have said the same of myself. Without her, I would have succumbed to despair—that death of the spirit which all the Fatal Arts abhorred. She possessed the strongest *qa* I had ever encountered, surpassing even the greatest of my masters. I had never seen the like—until the young *shin-te* warrior joined us.

For three years, we had both ignored the Mage War, after our separate fashions. Now, however, we considered it a personal affront. For that reason, among others, we did what we could to aid the new prisoner.

▲▼▲

After a time, he awakened. When he did so, there was food. There was always food when we needed it. He ate sparingly, respectful of his *qa*. Then he performed the ablutions and devotions of the *shin-te,* centering himself in meditation. Isla and I passed the time as we had on previous occasions, watching him with the tattered remnants of hope.

Rest and nourishment had restored him somewhat, as they had in the past. His air of bereavement had been diminished, and the pallor of death had receded from his cheeks. After meditation, he asked us to train with him. His manner as he did so was curiously diffident, as if he considered it plausible that we might refuse—that if we aided him we would do so out of courtesy rather than desperation.

So we trained with him, although our previous efforts had not done him any discernible good.

The exercise was little changed from other occasions. Isla and I feinted and attacked, or attacked and feinted, as our inclination took us, but we made no impression on him. He altered his tactics in accordance with our assaults, varying his blocks and counters easily, deflecting us without effort. Despite his youth and forlornness, he seemed impervious to our skills, and our cunning. Behind his fluid movements and light stances, his *qa* had a staggering force. In truth, I feared him as much as I feared Isla. Although we challenged him furiously, he did us no harm. But the harm he could have done was extreme.

How, I wondered, had such a very young man become so strong? And how was it possible that he had been slain so often?

When he had thanked us for our exertions, he meditated again, perhaps on what he had learned, perhaps on nothing at all. No word or glance from him suggested that we had in any way given him less than he needed from us. Yet we knew better. We were not his equals, but we were masters, able to recognize the truth. And we could see it in the deepening sorrow which underlay every turn of his gaze, every shift of his mouth.

Again and again, we failed to prepare him for his opponents. Or for his death.

▲▼▲

"We should stop holding back," Isla muttered to me sourly. "This polite exercise is wasted on him."

She had said the same more than once.

Earlier, I had argued with her. What if by some chance we injured or weakened him? What became of our hope then? But that debate had lost its meaning, and I gave it up. Matching her tone, I replied, "I will follow your example. When I see the full strength of the Direct Fist turned against him, I will do what a *nahia* can to emulate it."

She snorted in response, but I knew that her disgust was not directed at me. The training of the *mashu-te* had penetrated her bones. She would have considered it a crime to put all the force of her *qa* into blows struck against a training partner.

The *nahia* spared themselves such prohibitions. I was restrained, not by conscience, but by understanding. If I slew him, my last hope would die with him. And if I attempted his death and failed, he might well break my spine.

I was quite certain that if I died now I would not live again. No doubt that was just an assumption. Still, I believed it.

▲▼▲

Neither Isla nor I witnessed his disappearance. In some sense, neither of us noticed it. Nothing in the cell—or in our own minds—marked the moment. He was among us. Then he was not. Without transition or summons. He was removed from the cell with the same disdain for continuity with which we had been removed from our lives.

This was precisely as it had been on any number of previous occasions.

▲▼▲

"I had thought," Isla remarked with no more than ordinary asperity, "that the *nahia* were adept at escape. I must have been misinformed."

I sighed. "Give me a door, and I will open it. Give me a window—give me a gap for ventilation—give me somewhere to begin." I had long since scrutinized the walls and ceiling and even the floor until I feared my heart would break. "The *nahia* are not mages, Isla."

"But we came and went," she protested. "He comes and goes." She meant the young man. "There must be a door."

"As there was among the *mashu-te*?" I inquired gently. "As there was on the streets of Vess? A door from those places to this? No doubt you are right. But it is a mage's door, and I cannot open it."

Attempting to lighten her mood—or my own—I continued, "However, it may be that some among these stones are illusions." I gestured at the walls. "Perhaps if you aim the Direct Fist at them all, one will shatter, revealing itself to be wood."

She avoided my gaze. "Do not mock me, Asper," she said distantly. "I have no heart for it."

That did not augur well for any of us.

▲▼▲

He staggered as he returned, barely strong enough to remain on his feet. We saw differences he could not recognize, having no memory. As before, he breathed and moved among the living. As before, his wounds and bruises had been healed. Apparently, our captor wished to spare him the obvious consequences of death. Yet his exhaustion came near to overwhelming him. A glaze of forgotten pain clouded his eyes as he searched the cell, and us.

But his thoughts had not been altered. Weary as he was, how could he have considered anything new?

When he had recovered his balance, he began the litany of our doom. "Where am I?"

We had no answer for him.

"Who are you?"

Suppressing fury or despair, Isla told me, "This must change. We are lost otherwise."

"How can he change it?" I countered. "Look at him." I was less than she, and endangered by my own despair. "He has nothing left."

"Have we met before?"

I would have given him an exact answer if I could. But the magery of his disappearances and returns foiled me. Although Isla and I could remember what we had said and done, neither of us was able to keep a count of the days, or the deaths.

"Your mastery is plain. You must have answered better than I."

Neither Isla nor I suspected him of mocking us.

This time, however, he did not ask "Why?" He seemed to understand that he had failed. Perhaps his own weakness made the truth evident.

At last he settled himself to sleep. Isla spread a blanket over his shoulders, then stooped to kiss his forehead. The gesture was uncharacteristic of her. There were uncharacteristic tears in her eyes. His bereavement had become infectious.

Her voice thick with sorrow, she said, "Asper, it must change. If he cannot change it, then we must. Someone must."

I dismissed the idea that our captor's intentions would alter themselves. "How?" I asked. Her gentleness frightened me more than her grief.

"I do not know." For the first time, she sounded like a woman who might surrender.

▲▼▲

She was right, of course. It must change. And I was a *nahia* master, adept—or so I claimed—at impossible escapes and improbable disappearances. The burden was mine to bear.

While the young man slept, she and I neither rested nor watched. Instead, I questioned her closely, searching her knowledge of the other Arts for any insight the *nahia* did not possess.

I hoped that the *mashu-te* might have some true understanding of *shin-te*.

▲▼▲

Shin-te. Nahia. Mashu-te. Here were represented three of the five Fatal Arts of Vesselege. Only *ro-uke* and *nerishi-qa* were needed to complete the tale of combative skills in all our land. And of the two, *ro-uke* was widely considered too secretive—too dependent upon stealth and surprise—to equal the others in open conflict. It was the Art of Assassination. As for *nerishi-qa* it was said to be the most fearsome and pure of all the Five. The Art of the Killing Stroke, it was called. Indeed, legend claimed that every deadly skill contained in the other four derived from *nerishi-qa*.

If legend could be believed, Isla and I had not been joined by a *nerishi-qa* master because no mage was sufficiently powerful to subdue one.

That was an assumption, however—so ingrained that I hardly noticed it. My masters had respected all the Arts, but they feared only *nerishi-qa*.

Unfortunately, Isla was well schooled in legends, but owned less practical knowledge than I. She spoke of *shin-te* masters who broke wooden planks with their fists while holding soap bubbles in their palms, but she had not been taught how such feats might be accomplished. If indeed they were possible at all. Her isolated life among the *mashu-te* had been more conducive to the proliferation of mythologies than to a detailed awareness of the world. *Nahia* was called the Art of

Circumvention. Our skills and our *qa* were rooted in use. And the masters of the Direct Fist were so very scrupulous—

If I desired understanding, I would have to gain it from the young man.

▲▼▲

As before, he roused himself at last, broke his fast, performed his ablutions and meditations. This time, however, he had slept in the grip of troubled dreams, and had awakened unrefreshed. His gaze remained dull, and the hue of his skin suggested ashes. Still he did not diverge from his pattern. When his meditations were complete, he asked us to train with him.

I refused, in Isla's name as well as my own.

He seemed to flinch as if he had received another blow. His dreams had left him weaker than before—younger, and more lost. "You say that I failed," he murmured. "Without training, I will surely fail again." He had not regained his memory. By that sign, we knew that the mage was not done with him. "You have trained enough," I informed him. "You need rest, not more exertion." More than rest, he needed insight. "And we are already familiar with our limitations.

"With your consent"—he was a master, and deserved courtesy—"I will question you."

"Concerning what?" Isla protested irritably. "Have you forgotten that he remembers nothing? What do you imagine he will tell us?"

I ignored her, and instead watched doubts glide like shadows across his bereavement. In his eyes, I seemed to see his desire to trust us measure itself against his failures, or his dreams. And he may have guessed that I desired to probe the secrets of his Art. At last, however, he nodded warily.

"I will answer, if I can."

Isla wanted me to account for myself, if he did not. But I wasted no effort on explanations. In fact, I had none to offer. I was simply groping, as my masters had taught me, hunting the dark cell of my ignorance for some object or shape or texture I might recognize.

Stilling Isla's impatience with a gesture, I began at once.

"What," I asked him, "are the principles of *shin-te*?"

Having made his decision, he did not falter from it. Without hesitation, he replied, "Service to *qa* in all things. Acceptance of that which opposes us." He remembered his training, if nothing else. "There is no killing stroke."

I stared at him witlessly. All the Fatal Arts were given to obscure utterance—it was one of the means by which we cherished our own, and deflected outsiders—but this seemed extreme, even to me. I pursued him as best I could.

"Please explain. Your words will give us no aid if we do not understand them."

Politely, he refrained from observing that we were not intended to understand. The urgency of our plight was plain.

"*Qa,*" he began, "is the seat and source of self. It is the power of self, and the expression. Without self, there is no action, and no purpose. To deny service to the self is to deny existence."

So much I could grasp. It was not substantially different than the wisdom of my masters. They expressed themselves more concretely, but their meaning was much the same.

"*Qa* draws its strength from acceptance," he continued. "To reject that which opposes us is death. Life opposes us. Nothing grows that is not contained. And life will not alter itself to satisfy our rejection. Without acceptance, there is no power."

Privately, I considered this mystical nonsense. He was worse than the *mashu-te,* I was *nahia* by nature as much as by training. I kept my opinion to myself, however. It was as useless to us as his oblique maxims. "That there is no killing stroke," he concluded, "is self-evident. No man or woman slays another. There is only the choice to live or die."

In response, I laughed softly, without humor. I might have asked him if he denied the existence of *nerishi-qa,* but I did not. I wished to circumvent misunderstanding, not enhance it.

Was not *shin-te* one of the Fatal Arts?

"There we differ," I told him. "I myself have shed blood and caused death. Do you call this illusion? Are the men I gutted still alive?"

Isla nodded sharp agreement, although I was certain that she would argue in other terms.

He appeared to regard my challenge seriously. Yet he gave no sign that it disturbed him. Rather, he considered how he would answer. After a moment, he stepped near to me and touched the place where I had secreted my dagger.

"Strike me," he instructed simply.

I hesitated. Naturally I did not wish to slay him—or to harm him. But I felt a greater uncertainty as well. That he knew my fang's resting place troubled me. As I had been taught, I varied its location frequently. And I took pains to ensure that I was not observed when I concealed it.

"The *shin-te* teach that there is no killing stroke," he insisted. "Show me that this belief is false."

"Asper—" Isla murmured in warning. Her wish to see blood spilled here was even less than mine.

I understood him, however. He might have been a *nahia* master, reminding me to affirm nothing which I could not demonstrate.

By no hint of movement or tension did I announce my intent. I had studied such moments deeply. Without discernible transition—or so I believed—I transferred my *qa* from rest to action. More swiftly than the bunking of an eye, my hand projected my fang into the arch between his ribs.

Yet my fang bit air, not flesh. Wrist to wrist, he had deflected my attack.

I did not pause to admire his counter. Following the line of his deflection, I turned my stroke to a disemboweling slash.

Again I found air rather than my target. He had shifted aside, guiding my hand so that my own motion helped him drive my wrist against the point of his knee.

My grip loosened. Before I could secure it, he knocked the fang from my fingers.

By that time, I had already directed a jab at his face, seeking to gouge him blind. But the motion was a mere formality, nothing more. With a negligent flick of his elbow, he knocked my arm aside.

Then he stood a pace beyond my reach, holding my dagger lightly by its blade. I could not see that my efforts had inconvenienced him in any way. I told myself that I might have pressed my attack more stringently—that I might perhaps have retrieved my fang in a way which threatened him—but I did not believe it. He had made his point in terms I could not contradict by skill alone.

When I had bowed to show my acquiescence, he restored the dagger to me and bowed in turn.

At once, Isla advanced. Her desperation she expressed as anger so that it would not turn to despair. With the compact force of the Direct Fist, she flung a blow at him which caused my own *qa* to quake, although I was now a bystander.

Her speed did not exceed mine, of that I was certain. However, the efficiency of the *mashu-te* had the effect of enhanced quickness. Her first strike touched his robe—as mine had not—before he turned it. And even then her fist focused so much *qa* that he was forced to recoil as if he had been hit.

As easily as oil, she followed one blow with another.

He did not deflect her again. Rather, he met her squarely, palm to fist. I hardly had time to see the flex of his knees, the set of his strength. When their hands met, I flinched, thinking that she had shattered his bones.

Yet it was Isla who gasped in pain, not the *shin-te*. Her own force had nearly dislocated her shoulder. If the blow had betrayed any flaw, she would have ruined her arm.

He waited, motionless, until she had mastered her distress enough to bow. Then he replied gravely, with such respect that if I had not seen the event I would not have known he had humbled her, "Have I harmed you?"

Glaring, she dismissed his concern. "This proves nothing," she retorted. "You are greater than we. Your skill surpasses ours. So much we already knew. You have not demonstrated that there is no killing stroke."

"Still," he assured her, "it is the truth."

"I disagree," she protested. "A master may strike at a farmer, and the farmer will die. He can neither counter nor evade the blow. Is he then responsible for it? Is it not a lie to say that he chooses his death? Is the blow not murder? The *mashu-te* teach that the burden and the consequences belong to the one who strikes. How otherwise," she concluded, "do the *shin-te* call themselves honorable?"

He was young and bereft—and apparently better content to contest his beliefs with actions than with words. Yet he did not shirk her demand.

"Service to *qa* precludes murder," he answered. "Acceptance of that which opposes us necessitates responsibility. There is no killing stroke.

"Consider the farmer. Do you contend that the master struck him without cause? Is that the act of a master? Do the *mashu-te* conduct themselves so?" He shook his head. "If you wish to say that the farmer did not choose his death, you must first consider the cause of the blow."

"That is specious," Isla snapped. "Maybe mages reason so. Warriors do not.

"No cause is sufficient," she insisted. "Despite whatever lies between them, they are unequal in skill and force. Therefore the blow is murder."

Unswayed, he lifted his shoulders delicately. "Since you do not name the cause," he murmured, "I cannot answer you. The truth is there, not in the conclusions you draw from it."

Although he had been slain several times, he knew how to render the teachings of the *shin-te* unassailable.

He disturbed me. I found suddenly that I feared for him more than I feared his skills, or the distilled potency of his *qa*. Isla was right. His words, like his actions, proved nothing. I was *nahia* to the core. I knew—as he did not—that any belief which placed itself beyond doubt nurtured its own collapse. A warrior who did not risk despair could not master it.

▲▼▲

Again, he was no longer among us. Neither Isla nor I saw how he was taken from the cell. We could not name the moment of his disappearance. We only knew that while she wrestled with her own beliefs, and I considered my fears, the object of our concern ceased to share our imprisonment.

"Asper," she said when she had recognized his absence, "we're beaten." She may have meant "broken." "We can't help him. And he can't help himself. If he can't remember what happens to him, he can't get past what he's been taught. And all that *shin-te* training has already failed him."

She had endured her own testing without aid or companionship. She had strength enough for any contest, even though it killed her. But she could not suffer helplessness.

I on the other hand—

I could not have borne repeated death alone. But I was *nahia*—oblique of heart as well as of skill. I had been trained to impossible escapes and improbable disappearances. My masters had made a study of helplessness.

I did not attempt to answer her. She was too pure—no answer of mine would touch her. Instead I turned my attention to the walls.

As ever, there was no door, no window, no gaps at all. Faceless granite confronted me on all sides. But I did not allow myself to be daunted.

Raising my fists, I cried as though I believed I would be heard, "Are you stupid as well as cruel? Does magery corrupt your wits as it does your heart? Or are you only a fool? He cannot succeed this way!" Isla gaped at me, but I took no heed of her chagrin. I was certain of nothing except that our captor needed this *shin-te* master as sorely as we did.

"He remembers nothing," I called to the blind stone. "He learns *nothing*! Death after death, he fails you. If you do not let us teach him, he will always fail you. And we cannot teach him if we do not know what he opposes!"

The walls answered with silence. Isla stared at me in shock. After a moment, she breathed, "Asper—" but no other words came to her.

"Hear me!" I demanded. "They say that the Black Archemage is malefic beyond belief, but even Argoyne himself could not be this *stupid*!"

An instant later, I was stricken dumb by the sudden vehemence of the reply. From out of the air, a voice clawed with bitterness replied, "And what in the name of the Seven Hells makes you think I can *spare*—?"

As abruptly as it had begun, the response was cut off. A soundless tremor filled the cell as though the stone under our feet had flinched.

"Asper," Isla whispered, "what have you done?" She stood ready for combat.

I swallowed a moment's panic. Adjusted the fang in my grasp. "Apparently," I said, feigning calm, "I have insulted our captor."

"Oh, well," she answered between her teeth. "If *that's* all—"

Without transition, we became aware that one of the walls was gone. Its absence revealed a corridor I knew too well—a passage as wide as the cell, leading from nowhere to nowhere, and fraught with death. Like the cell, it was endlessly lit. And it showed no intersections or doorways through which it might be entered. Still it held perils without number, threats as enduring as the light.

It was the arena in which Isla and I had been slain too often.

In the center of the space stood the young *shin-te* master, waiting. His back was toward us, but his stance showed that he was ready, poised for challenge. No sound came from his light movements, or from the faceless walls—or from the warrior advancing behind him.

The warrior held a spear, which he meant to drive into the young man's back.

I made no attempt to help or warn him. The silence stilled me. I remembered sounds from that corridor, a host of small distractions hampering awareness—the distant plash of water, the rustle of unnatural winds, the grinding of shifted stones. And I did not believe that we had suddenly been given our freedom. But Isla immediately hastened forward, perhaps thinking that she would be allowed to aid the young man.

At once, she encountered the wall of the cell, and could not pass it. The scene before us was an image, mage-created, showing events which transpired elsewhere. Apparently my demand had been heeded.

"By the White Lords!" she swore, "what—?"

I ignored her confusion. It would pass.

That warrior looked to be the same one who had slain both of us until we were entirely beaten. I saw no reason to think otherwise. I had killed him occasionally myself, as had Isla, but death had not hindered him significantly. When my memory was restored, I had concluded that he was not a man at all, but rather a creature of magery, returned to life whenever he fell by the same power which had first created him. If he had a man's features—or even a man's eyes—I could not recall them.

From a distance of no more than five strides, he cocked his spear and flung it.

Warned by the sensitivity of his *qa,* the young *shin-te* turned, snatching the spear from the air. With the ease of long familiarity, he whirled the weapon as if it were a staff, and confronted his assailant.

By some means which I could neither observe nor understand, the warrior held another spear. Flipping his weapon swiftly end for end to disguise the moment when he would strike, he attacked.

The young man countered smoothly with the shaft of his staff. Foot and knee, hip and arm, at every moment his stances were flawless, apt for attack or defense, advance or retreat. The fast wheel of his assailant's blows he parried or slipped aside, adjusting his distance from the warrior at need.

Then he saw his opening. Stabbing his staff between the warrior's arms, he slapped its shaft against both of the warrior's wrists at once. The spear spun from the warrior's grasp.

A quick thrust would end the contest, at least momentarily.

"Now!" Isla commanded sharply, although the young man could not hear her.

He did not thrust. Instead, he stepped back, holding his staff ready.

"Fool," Isla groaned.

I agreed mutely. That warrior could not be defeated by death. Still, a living assailant was always more dangerous than a dead one. That the young man seemed to have no use for his spear's point disturbed me. To my eyes, the *shin-te* carried their denial of the killing stroke to unfortunate extremes. Surely these contests were being staged to test his ability to master living opponents? If they had some other purpose, I could not fathom it.

Already the warrior had retrieved his weapon. Now he held it by its balance in one hand, bracing it along his arm so that it extended his reach. With his free hand, he warded away the young man's staff. To my eye, this method of attack seemed awkward, but the warrior employed it smoothly. Feinting forward, he flicked his fingers at the young man's eyes. In the same motion, he kicked rapidly to draw the staff downward, then jabbed with his spear.

The young *shin-te* countered, retreating. A line of blood appeared on his cheek before he knocked the spear aside and spun out of reach. The staff blurred with speed in his hands. Undaunted, his assailant advanced. An abrupt slap of the spear broke the staff's whirl. Precise as a serpent, rigid fingers struck at the young man's throat. I felt rather than saw the spear follow the blow.

The young man saved himself by dropping his staff. Simultaneously, he blocked the spear with one palm, the blow with the other. An instant later—so swiftly that he astonished me—he collapsed one arm and struck inward with his elbow, catching his opponent at the temple hard enough to splinter bone.

The warrior flipped away to diminish the force of the impact.

The *shin-te* pursued without hesitation. But the warrior landed strongly—and in his hands he now held both weapons, their points braced for bloodshed. Again the young man was forced to retreat.

I hardly saw the warrior settle both spears into his awkward-seeming grasp. The young man commanded my attention. His poise betrayed no uncertainty, and the cut on his cheek was small—dangerous only if the spearpoint had been poisoned. Still he alarmed me. Although he fought well, his eyes held a flinch of defeat. Repeated death had eaten its way into his heart. When his opponent attacked again, weaving both spears in a pattern intricate with harm, he could find no opening through which to repay the assault.

"Asper," Isla breathed suddenly, "he needs a champion."

I ignored her. I could not look away from the *shin-te* master's grief.

"The mage," she insisted. "He needs a champion. That's what he's testing us for. He's trying to find someone good enough to fight for him."

Without thinking, I murmured, "That is an assumption."

A rent appeared in the young man's robe, showing blood on his skin. He countered at the warrior's knees, but failed to penetrate the weaving of the spearpoints.

"I'm sure of it." In her excitement, she turned her back on the scene before us in order to confront me. "Forget your *nahia* rigor for a moment. Listen to me.

"Why else does a mage do this?" She gestured at the young man's battle. "A mage so beleaguered he has no power to spare? If he were not already embattled for his life, he would have no need to treat us this way. What does he gain?"

I found myself looking at her rather than at the contest. She had thought of something which had eluded me. Her assumption exposed my own. Without realizing it, I had simply believed that the motives of mages surpassed our capacity to explain them—that no guess of ours could hope to approach the truth. But we had been given a hint when the mage spoke. And she had made better use of it than I.

"Why doesn't he return us to our lives?" she continued. "Or simply kill us? Or let us remember? Because he can't spare the power. These trials are all he can manage.

"He needs someone," she stated as if she were certain, "to fight for him."

Behind her, the *shin-te* went to the floor in a flurry of spear strokes. I thought him finished, but he recovered. Scissoring his legs, he flung out kicks which cost him a jab to one thigh, but which succeeded at breaking apart the warrior's attack. For an instant, he appeared to spin on his back among the spears. Then he arched to his feet, facing his opponent.

Now he held one of the spears. I had not seen him acquire it, could hardly imagine how he might have wrested it from the warrior's grasp. Nevertheless he had restored a measure of equality to the struggle.

Although his leg had been wounded, his stance remained sure. His air of strength was an illusion, however. His new weakness revealed itself in diminished quickness, diminished focus. Pain and damage disturbed the concentration of his *qa*.

And still he used the spear as a staff—a defensive weapon. While his opponent sought to kill him, he appeared to desire only the warrior's defeat.

He had said that *there is no killing stroke*, but he was wrong. And I believed that he knew it, although might not have been able to name the truth. The anguish in his eyes did not arise from his wounds. Mere hurt could not exceed him.

I knew to my cost that the killing stroke was despair.

For a moment, I had the sensation that my mind had closed itself, shutting out thought. I felt only panic. Who else but Argoyne might require a champion in the midst of the Mage War? Black Argoyne, Archemage of the Dark Lords? All others like him were dead. And everyone in Vess—everyone in all Vesselege—knew that the White Lords were winning. They had no need of a champion.

Isla had not yet pushed her assumption to that conclusion. When she did, what would she say? Impelled by the scruples of the *mashu-te,* would she insist that we must pray for the young man's failure, so that Argoyne would receive no aid from us?

I was *nahia* to the bone. The violation of such a sacrifice would burst my *qa* entirely, leaving me empty and lost.

While she returned her gaze to the contest, the warrior again changed his tactics. Now he held his spear by its butt with both hands, whirling it about his head as though it were a bolus. To my eye, this seemed an implausible assault. Surely it left him exposed to counterattack? Yet apparently it did not. The young *shin-te* found no way past the wheeling spearpoint.

At first this baffled me. And the more closely I studied him, the more confused I became. Why did he not strike *now*—or *there*! But then, despite my panic, I glimpsed the truth. The warrior varied his stance,

distance, and pace in ways which exactly mirrored the young man's
qa. Every shift of the young man's energy or intention was reflected by
the whirling spear. He could not counter because the warrior's weapon
matched each movement.

The truth was that I had concentrated my attention on the wrong
combatant. Thinking that I must understand the young man's skills and
limitations and mistakes in order to aid him, I had missed the real point
of Isla's assumption. His mastery was not at issue. Rather, he needed to
grasp the nature of his opponent. If it was true that Argoyne required
a champion, then it must also be true that the warrior we watched had
been mage-made to mimic an opposing champion. The champion of the
White Lords, and of Goris Miniter, Vesselege's King.

"Where—?" I tried to ask Isla. But my voice stuck in my throat. I
swallowed, breathing deeply to clear my *qa*. "Where," I began again,
"have you seen a spear used in that way before?"

I feared her reply almost as much as I feared her scruples.

However, she answered softly, "I haven't." Then she added, "The
mashu-te distrust weapons. I know less than you."

Indeed. No doubt the *mashu-te* believed that any weapon diminished
the personal responsibility of its wielder. In contrast, the *nahia* studied
weapons without number. But ours was the Art of Circumvention. We
studied all weapons—apart from the fang—in order to counter or defeat
them. We did not wish to become dependent upon them. And I had
never encountered tactics such as the warrior used.

"Do the *ro-uke* fight so?" I pursued, although I did not expect a
response. I was merely thinking aloud.

"If they do," she muttered, "they do it in secret." I understood more
than she said. The *ro-uke* did nothing publicly. In Vess, however, I had
watched such masters at work. Once or twice I had measured myself
against them, when one escapade or another brought us into conflict.
Theirs was not an art of direct confrontation.

In addition, the tactics this warrior now used were ill-suited to the
stealthy work of assassination. They demanded great skill, but lacked
both quickness and subtlety.

Still they were effective against the young man. I knew how I would
attack in his place. Thrown at the warrior's foot, my fang might serve me
well. And I could guess at Isla's counter. Direct in all things, she would
attempt to catch the spearpoint—or break the shaft. But I could not
imagine how the *shin-te* would meet such a challenge.

Service to qa *in all things.* He may have been handicapped by the
strengths of his art.

Abruptly I received my answer. Amid a flurry of feints and deflections, the young man struck.

All the Fatal Arts made a study of *qa,* and I was a master—yet I saw no hint of his intent, no concentration of purpose or projection of energy, until he had carried it out. A blow like his would have felled me where I stood.

Whirling his staff, he swung it against his opponent's spear a span or two below the point. I felt the crack of impact before I truly saw what he had done.

Apparently, however, this was the opening which the warrior sought. Using the young man's force to accelerate his own motion, he reversed the spear in his hands so that its butt punched down onto the *shin-te*'s crown. Less than an instant later, his foot hooked the young man's ankle, jerking away his support. Stunned, the *shin-te* dropped to his back. Before his spine touched stone, his opponent had reversed the spear again. Both Isla and I winced as the point drove deep into the young master's chest.

Our only hope was dead before his limbs had settled themselves to the floor.

▲▼▲

"I'm not sure that was a good idea," she observed when she had composed herself. "What do we gain by watching him die? I don't think any master can beat that—that whatever it is—that creature."

Certainly she and I had both failed often enough. Pacing the cell, she continued bitterly, "It's inhuman, None of us can defeat magery. That's not what the Fatal Arts are for.

"If our captor wants a champion to fight an enemy like that," she avowed, "let him create one."

"Again you make assumptions," I sighed. "Your conclusion does not follow from your observation." I had no wish to argue with her. More than that, I actively wished to avoid speaking of my own assumptions. I did not know how I might counter her reaction to Argoyne's name. But the young man's death had restored my knowledge of despair. I contradicted Isla simply so that I would not succumb.

"That our captor uses an inhuman test," I explained, "does not necessarily imply that he intends his champion to fight an inhuman opponent. It suggests only that he cannot persuade or coerce an appropriate master to serve him." If he could have done so, he would have had no use for us, and our lives would have been left undisturbed. "Lacking any man or woman who fights as the opposing champion does, he is unable to test us fairly. This is the best he can do. With the power at his disposal."

A power which was itself being tested to its limits.

"Are you defending him now?" she protested. But her objection was not seriously meant. "Who is he, anyway?" she asked more plaintively. "Who in all the White Hells needs a champion at a time like this?"

I spread my hands. "Does it matter? If our captor cannot obtain a fit champion—and if his champion does not win—we will die. Nothing else has significance."

She snorted. "Of course it matters." Apparently she felt a *mashu-te* contempt for the ambiguities of the *nahia*. "All this must have something to do with the Mage War. Why else does a mage need a champion? Are you saying that you see no difference between the White Lords and the Dark?"

In Vesselege it was believed that the White Lords were the servants of light and life, while such men as Black Argoyne devoted themselves to havoc and cold murder. For that reason—it was believed—Goris Miniter had allied his reign and his kingdom against the Dark Lords, and the Archemage.

I shared such assumptions. If I distrusted them, I did so on principle, not from conviction.

"That is not how you reasoned with the *shin-te*," I countered wearily. "Then you claimed that only the blows mattered, not the context." More than my companion, I had been broken by my defeats. "Who we are asked to serve will mean nothing to us if we are dead."

I prayed that this thin argument would suffice. I lacked a better one—except that I was *nahia,* and my loyalties did not much resemble the abstract purity of the *mashu-te.*

Fortunately, Isla was silenced while she considered the contradictions of her beliefs.

▲▼▲

Once again, he returned from death to the cell, remembering nothing. The sight of him wrung my heart, for his sake as well as my own. The bereavement in his eyes had deepened until it seemed to swallow hope. For the second tune, he staggered as he appeared. And he was slow to recover, as though he were unsure where his balance lay.

Still his thoughts followed their familiar path. When he could summon his voice from his parched throat, he asked, as he had always asked, "Where am I?"

Neither Isla nor I attempted a reply. Instead we stared in dismay at the blood which drained from his lips with each word, dripping from his chin to spatter his robe with failure.

Then he was gone. We observed his departure no more clearly than we had witnessed his arrival. We only knew that he had been given back to us—and taken away again.

▲▼▲

"By the Seven—!" Isla cried. "Asper, what's happened to him?"

The young man's blood might have been my own. I had grown tired of speculation. I did not like where it led me. But I did not need to assume much in order to answer.

"Our mage grows weak." According to the stories told in Vess, Argoyne had fought alone against the assembled might of the White Lords for the better part of a year. "He could not spare the power which allowed us to witness the contest. For that reason, the *shin-te* was inadequately restored from death."

She accepted this explanation. "Who is he?" she asked again. "Asper, I do not know what to wish for." She was close to despair herself. "I want to live. I want to repay what this mage has done to us. He has taught me hate, and that I will not forgive. But I cannot desire victory for such as the Black Archemage.

"I need to know who it is that requires a champion."

Behind the grime on her face, her anguish was plain. Until then, I had not fully appreciated how costly the scruples of the *mashu-te* might be. During my own trial, she had saved my spirit. Now she threatened to crush it within me.

"Isla," I replied as gently as I could, "I am *nahia*. We have taken no part in this war because it surpasses us." Tales were told of *mashu-te* who fought for Goris Miniter, and of *ro-uke,* but never of *nahia.* "Who are we to stake our allegiance"—our honor—"on a struggle we cannot understand?" Honor was a word which my masters did not use lightly. "I want to live. And I want to repay this mage. Other concerns do not trouble me."

Mine was the Art of Circumvention.

I expected more *mashu-te* contempt, but Isla surprised me. She regarded me, not with scorn, but with wonder and pity. "You're avoiding the truth," she breathed. "You know who he is. And you don't want to name him."

Her *qa* confronted me as though she readied a blow.

"You believe he's Argoyne," she said softly. "And you're willing to help him. You believe we'll die here if we don't help him defeat the White Lords, and you're willing to do it."

I would have preferred being struck. Stung by despair, I cried, "Because it does not matter!" Against her scruples and her purity, I protested, "*I* matter. To me. *You* matter to me. The *shin-te* matters to me. But this war of mages and kings—" I could not explain myself to one who was not *nahia.* "It requires too many assumptions."

Her reply might have finished me. Before she could utter it, however, we became aware that the young man had returned.

▲▼▲

The blood was gone from his lips. He appeared stronger—perhaps better rested. This time more magery had been spent on his restoration. But it did not soften his loss and bafflement. Mere power could not heal the aggrievement of his young heart.

"Where am I?" Mere power could not make him other than he was. "Who are you?"

This could not go on. If Argoyne was scarcely able to heal those he tested, his crisis must not be far off. And despair was not cowardice. Although I feared Isla in several ways, I did not allow her to daunt me.

Only memory would be of any use to him. Instead of answering the young man, I faced Isla squarely.

"Stop me now," I told her. I was certain that she could do so. "If you mean to abandon your life"—and your hate—"for the sake of guesses, do so now. Or stand aside, and let me do what I can."

The young man appeared to think I meant to attack him. His stance shifted subtly, focusing his abused *qa.*

She glared at me from the depths of her begrimed face. The *mashu-te* placed great value on achieving their ends through sacrifice—in this case, obtaining Argoyne's defeat at the cost of her life. But to sacrifice my life, and the young man's, for the sake of her purpose troubled her. And if she played only a passive part in the Archemage's death, her hate would not be appeased.

Deliberately she withdrew. From the distance of a few paces, she fixed a gaze hungry with anger on the *shin-te.*

In haste, I turned to the young man. I could not know when Argoyne's crisis would overtake him.

Recognizing his apprehension, however, I paused to bow. I wished him to see that I meant no challenge—that I regarded him as a respected comrade, not as an opponent.

As he bowed in reply, he softened his stance somewhat. But he did not set aside his readiness.

"Young master," I began, "you have been imprisoned by a mage. As have we. He has deprived you of your memory. For that reason, you cannot recollect your circumstances, or your name. You do not remember us. But we remember you. We are your allies." I could not imagine why he should believe me. In his place, I would not have done so. Certainly I had mistrusted Isla long enough—until death and isolation had forced me to set aside suspicion. Nevertheless I spoke with all the conviction I had learned from my plight.

"Our captor," I continued, "is Argoyne the Black. The Dark Archemage. Somewhere beyond this place, the Mage War rages, and he intends you to play a part in it, if you are able."

I studied the *shin-te* for a reaction, but he betrayed none. His expression revealed only courtesy and grief, nothing more. Lacking memory, he could attach no significance to Argoyne's name. Doubtless the Mage War itself meant nothing to him.

Perhaps that simplified my task. I could not tell.

Stifling a sigh, I informed him, "The Archemage desires a champion. By some means which we do not understand and cannot fathom, this war has become a matter of single combat. Both Isla and I have been tested to serve as Argoyne's champion, but we failed. You are all that remains of hope for the mage—and for us.

"*You* have not failed," I insisted, fearing that Isla would contradict me, although she made no move to speak. "You have met certain setbacks." This was difficult to explain. "They account for your weariness and confusion. The magery which restores you exacts a toll. But you have not failed. The *shin-te* teach that you must give 'service to *qa* in all things,' and you have done so."

The young man received this assurance as he had all I said—sadly, without acknowledgment. Though he had no memory of the experience, he appeared to understand in his bones and sinews—in his *qa*—that he had indeed failed.

Breathing deeply to quell my alarm, I pursued my purpose. "However," I announced, "you have not grasped the nature of the champion who opposes you. The champion you are asked to defeat. And your ignorance has caused your setbacks."

At last I saw a hint of interest in the *shin-te*'s eyes. He found it easy to credit that he was ignorant—and that ignorance was fatal.

I summoned my *qa*. "The challenge before you is the true test," I told him, "simple and pure. The *shin-te* believe that 'there is no killing stroke.' You will face a master of the *nerishi-qa*. The Art of the Killing Stroke."

There I stopped. I saw in the sudden flaring of the young man's eyes that he knew more of the *nerishi-qa* than I.

Isla could not silence her surprise. Advancing, she demanded, "*Nerishi-qa*, Asper? How do you know?" At once she added, "How long have you known? Why haven't you said anything?"

"I do *not* know," I replied without disguising my vexation. "I am making an assumption." An exercise I did not enjoy. To the young man, I said, "We were permitted to watch the contest from which you have just returned. In it, you were slain. And restored by magery. At the cost of your memory. Your opponent fought in ways unfamiliar to me. I am *nahia*. Isla is *mashu-te*, I have seen the *ro-uke*. And you are *shin-te*. Your opponent's skills belong to none of these. Therefore he is *nerishi-qa*."

From the first, the *shin-te* had met death with sorrow, remembering nothing except his loss. Now, however, there was another light in his gaze. Strictures shaped the corners of his eyes, the lines of his mouth. A sensation of anger emanated from him.

"The *nerishi-qa*," he pronounced softly, "teach a false Art."

Isla rounded on him. "How so?"

"Legend teaches," I put in, "that *nerishi-qa* is the first and most potent of the Fatal Arts. All others derive from it."

The young man shook his head. There was no doubt in him. "It is false. "You have called it 'the Art of the Killing Stroke,' yet there is no killing stroke." The strength of his conviction shone from him. "The *nerishi-qa* claim for themselves the power and the right to determine death. But he who determines death also determines life, and that they cannot do. Life belongs to the one who holds it. It cannot be taken away. Therefore no killing stroke exists. There is only choice."

In my urgency, I had no patience for such mystical vapor. And Isla felt as I did, apparently. Nearly together, we objected, "We saw you die."

Direct as a fist, she added, "That champion nailed you to the floor with a spear."

"Did you choose that?" I demanded.

Uncomfortably, he answered, "I do not remember."

A moment later, however, he shouldered the burden of his beliefs. "Yes. I did."

Then his earlier sorrow returned to his gaze—a bereavement shaded by shame. "You say that I was ignorant. I did not know him for *nerishi-qa*."

I accepted his assumption. I feared to weaken him with doubt. But Isla did not.

"Or you knew," she countered, "and that's why you chose to die. You knew you couldn't defeat him." *Mashu-te* to the core, she accepted the risk of what was in her heart. "You surrendered to despair."

Anxiously I watched the young man for his response.

"I do not remember," he repeated. "Perhaps I did."

The flinch had returned to his eyes, although he did not look away. "If so, I do not deserve to be named among the *shin-te*."

Seeking to help him if I could, I asked, "Are you acquainted with the *nerishi-qa*? Would you recognize that Art?"

He considered for a moment, then shook his head. "There are scholars among the *shin-te*, preserving our knowledge of all the Arts. I have studied the texts. But they are old. And what is written conceals as well as reveals what it describes. I have never seen the *nerishi-qa*."

I sighed privately, keeping my relief to myself.

Isla was plainer. "Then perhaps," she said, "we can still hope."

"I do not know," he said as if admitting the true source of his sorrow. "Every year, my masters send one of us to carry a challenge to the *nerishi-qa*, so that we may test our skills—and our beliefs. But the messengers are always spurned. The *nerishi-qa* disdain to measure themselves against us."

I was sure that Isla retained her wish for Argoyne's destruction. For the present, however, she had apparently accepted that life was better than death. There may have been a hint of the *nahia* in her nature. Rather than merely assuming that the Black Archemage would be ruined by the young man's defeat, she hoped to witness that ruin herself—and to participate in it if she could. And for that purpose sacrifice would not serve.

▲▼▲

As on previous occasions, the young *shin-te* needed rest. Both death and restoration had been arduous for him, as I remembered well. Despite my eagerness to know what he had read in the texts of his scholars— and my belief that Argoyne's crisis was near—I urged him to his pallet.

He acquiesced readily enough. But he was not granted an opportunity for sleep. As he uncoiled his fatigue upon the pallet, a tremor shook the cell. In the distance, we heard a mutter of stone, as though the crags of Scarmin ground their teeth.

"Earthquake," Isla suggested when the tremor had passed.

"Do you believe that?" I asked sourly. I did not.

A second tremor followed the first, stronger and more prolonged. In its aftermath, dust sifted from the ceiling, filling the constant light with hints of peril. Again we heard from afar the rumor of crushed rock.

We were on our feet, the three of us, instinctively keeping our distance from the walls—and watching the timbers above us, in case they should start to crack.

For the second time, a voice spoke in the air. "Now," the mage said harshly. "It must be now."

Then the young man was gone. Neither Isla nor I saw his departure.

▲▼▲

She reacted while I stood motionless in consternation. In the wake of Argoyne's bodiless utterance, she protested, "He's exhausted! He hasn't rested!" Furiously, she cried, "By the White Lords, do you *want* him to fail?"

There was no answer. Instead a third tremor jolted us. It struck the cell harder than the first two combined, endured longer. I staggered, despite my training, and Isla fought for balance. Above us, timbers shrieked against each other. A disturbing unsteadiness afflicted the lamps.

Argoyne's peril was more desperate than I had imagined. He had expended too much of his power testing us—and lost too much time.

When the convulsion eased, I saw that its force had stricken a crack up one wall from floor to ceiling beside the door.

The door—

Isla did not see it. The straining timbers consumed her attention. "Asper!" she shouted. "The keep is falling! We'll be crushed!"

The door. At last. Argoyne's magery had failed him. Or he no longer needed it. Or our imprisonment served no further purpose in his designs.

"I think not." Between one heartbeat and the next, my dismay vanished. Some sleight of circumstance transferred it to her, and I was freed. "These quakes will cease as soon as Argoyne announces his champion."

I had already turned my fang to the challenge of the door.

Now she noticed it. "Asper—" she gasped. "What's happening? How did this—?"

"Compose yourself," I snapped, "and let me work." Her questions, and my own, would answer themselves soon enough.

I was *nahia*, a master of Circumvention. No mere door could hold me if I bent my will to escape. But could I bypass this obstacle quickly? That was another matter altogether. The more strictly the door been secured, the more time and skill would be needed to open it.

I did not care why Black Argoyne's concealment of the door had failed. Rather, I wished to know how much trust he had placed in that concealment.

"This changes everything, Asper," Isla insisted at my back. "The White Lords must have beaten him. He can't protect his keep. Why don't they press their advantage? Why risk this war on a champion when they can tear his power stone from stone?"

"Am I a mage?" I snarled without interrupting my efforts. I had no patience for her. "Do I understand these things?"

I understood bolts and locks, staples and bindings. Estimating the actions of mages required too many assumptions. Words were also a form of circumvention, however, and they could cut as well as any blade.

"Perhaps," I continued while I tested the door, "the effect of their attacks is hidden from the White Lords. Or perhaps the Archemage has other uses for his power. The truth—"

Abruptly I sighed. It appeared that Argoyne relied more upon magery than upon physical restriction. My fang found the doorbolt and turned it so that its hasp left the staple. Carefully I began to slip the bolt aside.

"The truth," I repeated as I pulled the door open, "will be revealed when we find him."

Between her teeth, Isla remarked, "Asper, you amaze me." But she did not pause to admire my handiwork. "Come on," she commanded at once. Ahead of me, she hastened from the cell. "I have a debt to repay."

I followed without hesitation. I, too, had a debt to repay—although it did not much resemble hers.

For the first time in uncounted days, we were free of imprisonment. Therefore we were also free of Argoyne's purposes, and could now choose our own way—or so she apparently believed.

I did not make that assumption.

▲▼▲

We found him with relative ease. The corridors and chambers within the keep were simply arranged, one level above the next. On each, a large hall filled the center of the structure, surrounded by a wide passageway. Smaller rooms were arrayed between the corridor and the keep's walls. A broad stair climbed from floor to floor. We might have spent days at it if we had attempted to search the outer chambers, but by tacit agreement we concentrated on the central halls. I was content to believe that the Archemage would need space around him in order to wield his power. On each level, we opened massive doors to look inward, discovered nothing, and proceeded to the next stair.

None of the passages we traveled resembled the one in which we had been tested.

At another time, I would have been fascinated by the apparent absence of any servants, retainers, companions, or defenders. Argoyne the Black, it seemed, desired no human service—or had been abandoned by it. In addition, I would have been intensely interested in the possessions with which the outer rooms were filled, as well as in the uses to which the inner halls were put. Much of what I saw served no purpose I could recognize. Now, however, I was in too much haste for curiosity. Refusing investigation, I kept pace with Isla.

Five levels above our cell, we came upon the Archemage.

In a stone chamber lit by the keep's ceaseless lamps, he sat at a long trestle table scattered with scrolls and charts, his back to the door. More scrolls curled outward from the stool on which he perched, in reach of ready reference. And still more, texts by the hundreds, were piled upon row after row of shelves propped against all the walls—scrolls in profusion, of every description, some plainly ancient, others still gilt and gleaming. Together they held more knowledge than I had ever seen, or indeed imagined, in one place.

At the sight, I experienced an eerie pang. Where the *mashu-te* valued purity and scruples, the *nahia* prized knowledge. Granted the opportunity, my masters would have cheerfully slaughtered a kingdom to obtain so much treasure.

Isla, in contrast, would have cheerfully fired the room to rid Vesselege of Black Argoyne.

Even here, our captor was alone—a small figure immersed in his robes, hunching over his scrolls as though he fed from them. Whatever his needs may have been, for food or drink, for companionship or service, he supplied them by magery. The White Lords and Goris Miniter had made him a pariah to be feared and shunned.

From the back, a nimbus of white hair as fine as silk concealed the edges of his face. And he did not turn toward us. Indeed, he seemed unaware of our arrival. Sacrificing stealth for haste, we had not opened the door quietly, but other concerns held his attention.

As they would have held mine, in his place—"Asper—" Isla breathed softly.

I ignored her.

Before the Archemage hung an image like the one in which Isla and I had watched the young man's last test. This was far larger, however, filling one end of the hall. And the scene arrayed within it lay at some considerable distance, that was obvious. Argoyne's stone walls—his keep among the peaks of Scarmin—contained no sunlit meadows, rich with wildflowers; and grasses, like the one I saw beyond the table.

I knew at once that I gazed upon the ground appointed for the contest of champions. For the blood of the young *shin-te*—or of his opponent. For the resolution of the Mage War.

From the foreground of the image, the young man emerged, striding slowly away from us as if he strolled the meadow at his leisure. At first he was alone among the flowers under a sky defined by plumes and wisps of cloud. Before he had taken ten paces, however, a row of horsemen appeared along the far horizon. Dark with distance, and silent as dreams, they galloped swiftly forward, converging on the *shin-te* as they rode—an ominous throng, fifty or more, most of them soldiers and warriors. Soon I distinguished Goris Miniter by his helm and bearing, and by the crest of Vesselege on his velvet cape. The men on either side of him, clad in flowing robes so pure that they appeared to flame with reflected sunlight, must have represented the White Lords.

Neither Isla nor I advanced. The sight of the young man, isolated among the blooms, facing a force great enough to overwhelm any champion, kept us motionless.

At last the riders drew near enough to encircle him. By some trick of magery, however, they did not obscure our view of him. From horseback, Goris Miniter appeared to address the *shin-te*, but his words made no more sound than the mute hooves and tack of the horses, the silent commands of the soldiers. If the young man answered, we could not hear it. In the image they were all as voiceless as the dead.

Abruptly Argoyne searched among his scrolls, opened another on the table, and set his hand upon it. At once the scene seemed to gain depth as the meadow unveiled its sounds to the hall. A breeze we could not feel soughed gently. Horses stamped their hooves, jangled their reins. Men coughed and caught their breath.

"Goris Miniter," Argoyne muttered, "King of Vesselege, I'm here." By magery his voice carried into the distance until it appeared to resound in the air of the meadow, echoing strangely.

Startled, many of the horsemen searched for the source of the sound. One of the White Lords leaned aside to advise or instruct the King.

Miniter raised his head. His features were plain before us—the iron will of his mouth, the lines of calculation around his eyes. In Vess he was known as a clever monarch, a man adept at ruling powers he did not possess and could not match.

"Join us, Archemage," he commanded the breeze and the sky. "This war will be decided here. Your absence warns of treachery."

"As does your presence, King of Vesselege," Argoyne answered. His tone was querulous and unsteady, the voice of an old man, wearied by his struggles and bitter about death. "I've agreed to this contest in terms that bind me. If my champion loses, my defenses fail with him. And if I attempt treachery to help him, my own powers will destroy me.

"Your White Lords are similarly bound. But you are not. You're only an ally here, not a mage. Not a participant.

"I'll stay where I am," the Archemage concluded, "in case you're tempted to take matters into your own hands."

Goris Miniter scowled at this response, but did not protest. Instead he barked, "Then we will begin! The sooner your darkness is brought to an end, Black Argoyne, the sooner hope and healing will dawn at last in Vesselege."

With one gloved fist, he made a gesture as if he meant to fling all his riders against the *shin-te*.

Only one horseman advanced, however. A warrior nudged his mount a pace or two into the ring. Among so many other men, he had not caught my eye. But when he left his place in the circle I seemed to know him instantly by the completeness of his command over his horse, the liquid flow of his movements as he dismounted, the perfect readiness of his strides and his poise—and by the palpable force of his *qa*. The might compressed within his frame was as vivid as a shout.

"'Asper," Isla breathed again. "It must be now."

Still I ignored her. Argoyne could not remain deaf to our presence indefinitely. And when he noticed us, we would be lost. We had no hope against magery. Yet I could not break the spell cast on me by the sun-blazed robes of the White Lords, by Goris Miniter's grim attention—and by the plight of the young man who had fought and died, fought and died, without knowing why.

The *nerishi-qa* was not a large man, perhaps no more than three fingers taller than the *shin-te*, and of somewhat greater bulk. Among my other apprehensions, this also troubled me. Where skill and *qa* were equal, any contest might be decided by weight of fist. Here was another disadvantage for a young man already hampered by fatigue and sorrow. In contrast, the *nerishi-qa* seemed arrogant and calm, certain of his strength.

His masters had at last accepted the challenge of the *shin-te*. And the fate of a kingdom rested on the outcome.

Respectfully, the young man bowed to his opponent. We could not see his face. Within myself, I prayed that the gaze he fixed on the *nerishi-qa* held anger rather than grief. When it did not sow confusion, anger bred force. Grief nurtured despair. And the harvest of despair was death.

The champion of the White Lords did not bow. His smile held untrammeled disdain as he advanced.

Despite this insult, the *shin-te* withheld attack. From the distance of the keep and the image, I saw no tension in his shoulders, his hips, his *qa*. Standing lightly, he waited in sunlight for the test of the killing stroke.

When it came, Isla also struck. Seemingly borne aloft by his *qa*, the *nerishi-qa* focused both weight and muscle in a flying kick which might have snapped his opponent's spine—and Isla launched herself at the Archemage. While the *shin-te* slipped the kick aside, countering with elbow and palm, she slapped the crook of her arm around Argoyne's throat, clamped her forearm to the base of his skull. Holding him so, she could snap his neck with one quick lift of her shoulders.

Instinctively he clutched at her arm. At once, she swept her leg over the table, wiping the clutter of scrolls beyond his reach.

"Isla—!" I protested.

In her turn, she ignored me.

"Now," she murmured to his ear. "Now you're mine. I hold your death, mage. I'm going to repay my own."

Carried past the *shin-te* by his kick, the *nerishi-qa* rolled in the air to deflect the swift force of the young man's elbow. Then, instead of landing heavily, he seemed to settle into the grass, his poise undisturbed. I could not hear him—the image had lost sound when Argoyne's hands left his scrolls—but he appeared to be laughing.

"Wait," I told Isla urgently. "Wait!"

Hastening to the table, I confronted her past the Archemage. I feared and distrusted him as much as she did. Now that she had grasped his defeat, however, I found that I did not want him slain. Instead I wished to see the outcome of the young man's contest.

I wished to believe that my own deaths had not been wasted.

And I wished to understand this war.

Argoyne the Black had the look of a man who had spent his life among midnights and maggots. His beard was of the same fine white silk as his hair, but beneath it lay the slick, sunless complexion of a fish. And with Isla's arms wrapped about his neck, he gaped like a fish, eyes bulging, scarcely able to breathe. Hints of milk in his eyes obscured his vision.

As she had said, she held his death in her arms. Yet he appeared undaunted. Gasping for breath, he demanded, "What do you think you'll gain by breaking my neck?"

"Our lives," she retorted without hesitation. "Victory for your enemies."

"You won't enjoy it," he warned.

"Won't I?" She tightened her grasp. "You don't know me very well."

I could imagine no appeal which might reach her. Her face held nothing for me, no doubt and no softness. Her scruples lay elsewhere.

I could have killed her there. My skills and my fang were apt for such an action. But my masters would have never forgiven me that dishonor. No *nahia* would have forgiven it.

"And you," Black Argoyne panted in return, "don't understand the tyranny of the pure. You fool, I'm all that remains of hope for this land!"

There I saw my opening. "Hear him, Isla," I urged quickly. "Let him speak. We know nothing of this war. If we will determine its outcome, we must know what we do."

She looked at me. As if involuntarily, her grasp loosened, permitting the mage more air.

"Isn't he the Black Archemage," she challenged me angrily, "devoted to darkness? Hasn't he rained down death on all Vesselege until Goris Miniter himself has been forced to side with the White Lords? How much more do you need to know?"

In the image, the *nerishi-qa* attacked again. His tactics had changed. He no longer attempted to end the contest with one blow. Instead he advanced through a flurry of strikes and feints.

As before, the *shin-te* countered, landing a blow of his own when he could, parrying when he could not. Despite the pressure of his opponent's assault, he moved easily, preserving his strength.

In a sense, the battle had not yet become serious. Both champions still measured each other, probing not so much for victory as for an estimation of their skills and weaknesses.

"You understand honor," Argoyne coughed. Hooking his fingers on Isla's forearm, he strained against her hold. He could not shift her grasp, but he gained space enough to speak more clearly. "Or you should. Every Fatal Art preaches it.

"Why do you think all the White Lords and Goris Miniter have banded together against me? Do you call that honorable? Do you really believe I'm so malign—and so powerful—that they had no choice? I'm just one mage. One man. Would every *mashu-te* in Vesselege go to war against one *nahia*? Or even one *nerishi-qa*?

"This whole struggle," he spat, "is dishonorable."

His assertion surprised me. I had not expected such an argument from a mage. Despite my experience of death, my enmity toward him wavered.

For her part, however, Isla was unmoved. Sneering, she retorted, "And what do you have to do with 'honor,' Archemage?"

"Little enough," he admitted. "Everything they say about me is true." His voice held an edge of savagery—of rage prolonged and constricted beyond endurance. Battle after battle, death after death, he had nurtured his fury until it filled him. "I study darkness. The Seven Hells are my domain." He released one hand to indicate the ring of riders in the meadow. "*They* can't bring slaughtered warriors back to life. I can. And I have rained violence on Vesselege. But not until they forced me to it. Not until they formed their alliance against me.

"Your White Lords—" In his mouth the words were a curse. "They don't just think I'm wrong. They think I should be crushed. Because my magery isn't like theirs. They want to destroy me because I look for power in places they fear. They want to destroy my knowledge. Not because of anything I did. Because of what I am. And what I know. Until they started this war, I'd committed no crime they could hold against me."

That argument I felt as well, but Isla snorted contemptuously. "They aren't here to defend themselves. Why should I trust anything you tell me?"

My attention was torn between Argoyne and the contest—between Isla's grim hostility and my own uncertain intent. Glancing aside, I saw that the *nerishi-qa* had begun to spin, flinging out kicks and blows as if from the heart of a whirlwind. His balance and the stability of his *qa* on the uneven ground of the meadow seemed unnatural to me, almost inhuman. I could not have done what he did. Even at this distance, I feared to encounter such a master.

The young *shin-te* retreated steadily, dodging from side to side to foil the onslaught, occasionally diving beneath a kick to improve his position. If he discerned any opening in the assault—as I did not—he took no advantage of it.

But the Archemage had not faltered. He pointed at the White Lords before us. "They believe they're in the right," he answered. "In the right! As if being in the right has anything to do with knowledge. 'Right' and 'wrong' have to do with how knowledge is used, not with knowledge itself."

Every word he uttered seemed to whet his fury. His tone was as sharp as my fang. I felt its edge against my heart, although Isla held him helpless. My masters might have spoken as he did.

"I tell you on my soul," he rasped bitterly, "if there were fifty mages of my kind in the world, I would not have formed an alliance with them against the White Lords. I don't want the White Lords dead. I don't even want them hurt." He strained at Isla's grasp to express his ire. "But I will not stand by while my knowledge and my life are erased as if they never existed."

She opened her mouth to voice an objection, but he overrode her. "That is not a claim your White Lords can make," he insisted. His vehemence seemed to flay at the air. "They do wish me dead. They wish my knowledge destroyed. Because they believe they're in the right.

"Oh, they're as pure as sunlight," he raged, "and just as cruel. Do you think they care about Vesselege? You delude yourself. They could have ended this war whenever they chose." His voice rose to a shout against the pressure of her arm. "They could have stopped! But then I would have been able to keep my life and my power. All the land would have seen that I attacked no one except in my own defense. And that," he cried, "they can't tolerate because they are in the right."

Then he subsided to bitterness. "They're so pure that they're prepared to see the whole kingdom laid waste to prove it. As if 'right' and 'wrong' have anything to do with war."

At the edge of my sight, I saw the *shin-te* fall under a vicious wheel of blows. At once, kicks like adzes hacked at him among the grass and flowers. Several he blocked, but one caught him a glancing blow at the point of his hip. As he regained his feet, I saw a small twitch of pain on his cheek. His stance suggested a subtle weakness in that hip—a hurt that slowed and hindered him.

My heart went out to him, alone among his enemies, but I could not help him there. The meadow might have been leagues or days distant. I could do nothing until I found my way through the maze of Argoyne's self-justification and Isla's hate.

Troubled, she looked to me. Apparently she desired some response. She had not been swayed—not as I had—but the Archemage had touched a nerve of uncertainty in her, which she did not know how to relieve.

I took hope from her glance. "Heed him," I urged her softly. "Would the *mashu-te* be enriched if there were no *nahia*? If every master of the *shin-te* were slain? If the *nerishi-qa* ceased to exist? Light must have darkness, Isla. Without contention, the Fatal Arts would have no purpose. Therefore the *shin-te* teach 'acceptance of that which opposes us.'"

When I saw my words strike home in her, I turned toward the mage. Deliberately I toyed with my fang so that he could see it in my hands and know that I, too, might choose to kill him. Studying the blade, I asked, "What is Goris Miniter's place in this?"

Black Argoyne coughed an obscenity. "The tyranny of the pure is easily manipulated. Miniter knows he'll never truly rule this land if he can't rule the mages. And he doesn't have the power to do that directly. Not without drowning Vesselege in blood. When he was done, he wouldn't have anyone left to rule. So he's playing on the purity of the White Lords. Using it to make them do what he wants. They think he serves them because he knows they're in the right. The truth is, they serve him because he knows how to lie."

Isla tightened her hold. "And you don't?"

He groaned his distress and exasperation. "Of course I know how. But I'm too tired to bother. I don't want to rule anybody. Right now the only thing I want is to keep myself and my knowledge alive."

When she eased her pressure, he added, "I'll tell you how you can recognize the truth. If my champion wins"—again he indicated the image before us—"if that poor young man finds some way to defeat the enemy of everything he believes—those self-righteous fanatics won't stand for it. They'll intervene. They'll strike him down themselves. They'll accept their own ruin to prevent me from surviving."

Darkly, he muttered, "And I still expect treachery from Goris Miniter."

Isla seemed to think that she had found the flaw in his self-justification. As if she were pouncing, she demanded, "'Accept their own ruin'? What good will it do them to strike the *shin-te*, if they're destroyed in the process?"

"Oh, 'destroyed.'" Argoyne made a dismissive gesture. "They won't be destroyed. Fewer than half of them took part in the oath of this contest—the oath which seals them to its outcome. The ones who swore will die. The rest said they would abide the result, but that's only because they think their champion can't lose. If he does, the War will go on as before. They'll say I betrayed the challenge. As long as Miniter stands by them, no one will question their story."

To my surprise, I found that I believed him, I was *nahia*, disinclined by nature and training to trust men and women who predicted the actions of others. But Isla had taught me that those who prized their own scruples did not think as I did.

Belief tempted her as well. That was made plain by the doubt which darkened her gaze, the way her teeth gnawed the inside of her cheek. Where the *nahia* studied habits of mind, the *mashu-te* served convictions. Was she not prepared to sacrifice her life to gain Argoyne's defeat? Then would the White Lords not do the same? If they were certain of their own purity, as the Archemage insisted?

However, her uncertainty led her to questions which I would not have considered important.

"So that young *shin-te* is your only hope," she snarled in his ear. "If you're telling the truth. You can't betray the oath of this contest, and you won't try, even though you assume your enemies will attempt treachery." Word by word, she tightened her arm on his neck until he again began to gape for air. "So tell me why you've done everything you can to weaken him. Explain why you're trying to make sure he loses."

His eyes bulged wildly. "That's madness," he gasped. "I've done no such—"

She clenched his throat. "You took his memory! You prevented any of us from learning anything from all those tests!"

"Isla," I put in sharply, "let him breathe."

The glare she turned toward me had the force of a kick. Still she eased her arms again, granting the Archemage air.

"Do you think it's *easy*," he panted quickly, "bringing people back from death?" With both hands he pulled against her grasp. "Do you think all I have to do is wave my arms and *wish*? You don't know what you're asking.

"If you reanimate a corpse, what you get is a walking corpse. A body without a mind. But restoring the mind— Ah, that's hard. Dreams, memory, reason, layer by layer, you have to bring it all back, or the corpse isn't fully alive. And hardest of all to bring back is the spirit, the"—he muttered a curse—"you don't have words for it. It's *qa*, but it isn't—not the way you think about it." Squirming against Isla's insistence, he tried to explain. "It's the resilience and hunger that makes people want to go on living in the face of death. When you reanimate a corpse, if you restore the memory of death, and don't restore the spirit that refuses to accept it, what you get is a madman.

"I've been fighting a war here." Sorrow mounted in his tone as he spoke. His plight might have been the same as the young *shin-te* master's. "The whole time while I tested you, I've been fighting for my life. And I've been losing. When I brought you back from death, all of you, I didn't have the time or the power to do everything. So I chose to keep you sane. Instead of making you whole. You're all useless as warriors without *qa*. So I held back memory instead."

I could see—as Argoyne could not—that he baffled her. Her anger could not accommodate his account of himself. Frightened by uncertainty, she demanded, "Then why did you restore our memories when you were done with us? Why did you bother?"

"I hoped," he admitted, "that if you were whole you might find some way to help me. But even if you didn't—even if you hated me too much to try—" He sighed, sagging within his robes. "I couldn't bear to leave you that way. You didn't ask to serve me. And nobody deserves to be crippled like that. To be alive without memory or spirit—" He shrugged weakly. "You'd be better off dead."

At another time, I might have contested this assertion. Whole or crippled, I did not wish for death. I knew it too well, and the knowledge had done me great hurt. For the present, however, I left Argoyne's belief unchallenged. Where Isla suffered confusion, I felt only urgency. I did not know how long the young man could endure his opponent's assault—or how long Goris Miniter would abide the uncertainty of his own fate.

Hampered by the pain in his hip, the *shin-te* was forced to counterattack. He could no longer afford to await openings which he would then ignore. If he failed to drive the *nerishi-qa* back, he was finished.

His weakened stance gave rise to an awkwardness which began to impede his blocks and parries. Blows which he had once deflected with ease now threatened him. His hands seemed to stagger as he warded strike after strike away. Lessened in grace and speed, he appeared helpless to save himself when his ribs were left exposed to a slashing kick. Only the concentration of his *qa* betrayed his intent.

As the kick arrived like the sweep of a mace, he flipped his legs from under him and dived backward below it. The strength of the blow and the momentum of his own fall he used to spear the fingers of one hand into the pit of his opponent's groin. At the same time, he swept his other arm around the *nerishi-qa*'s leg and rolled so that he bore it beneath him to the grass.

Before the White Lords' champion could wrench free, or scissor another kick, the *shin-te* cut with his elbow deep into the nerves at the back of the *nerishi-qa*'s thigh.

When the *nerishi-qa* regained his feet, his jaws were clenched on a pain to match the *shin-te*'s, and his own stance hinted at weakness. A new respect disturbed the arrogance of his gaze.

The time had come. Deliberately I made my choice.

"If Goris Miniter means treachery," I asked the Archemage, "what form will it take?"

Argoyne shrugged. The question did not appear to interest him.

I indicated the image before us. "Are you able to show other scenes? Can you spare the power?"

"As long as my champion is still alive."

Containing my exasperation, I pursued, "Can you reveal our surroundings?" At once, however, a more useful question occurred to me. "Can you detect movement within the keep?"

The mage snorted. "There isn't any. We're alone." His tone suggested that he had been deserted long ago.

"What's the point, Asper?" Isla did not look at me. Disturbed by Argoyne's answers, she kept her gaze on the young *shin-te* while she wrestled with her hate. "The contest is there, not here."

"But if the King means treachery," I retorted, "it will be done here." With every passing moment, my urgency grew. "He cannot interfere with the White Lords' champion.

"Can you do it?" I demanded of the Archemage.

He lifted his hands to show that he was helpless without his scrolls.

"Isla," I instructed the woman who had saved me from despair, "release him."

She turned to me hotly. "Have you lost your mind? As soon as you let him touch his scrolls, he'll put us back in that cell." She secured her grip. "He'll turn us to dust. We'll be dead before you can blink."

"No," Argoyne and I said together.

"Do you 'assume,'" she shouted, "that you can trust him?"

"No!" I yelled in return. "I *assume* that the man who troubled to make us whole again after we had failed him has no interest in our deaths!"

She faltered. The simplicity of her loathing for the Archemage did not sustain her. He had challenged too many of her beliefs—as I had as well. "Treachery" was not a threat which the *mashu-te* suffered lightly.

"Asper—" she breathed, warning me.

With an effort of will, she removed her arms from Argoyne's neck.

Instantly his hands plunged among his scrolls, scrambling for the one he sought. When he found it, he slapped it open before him. "Movement?" he croaked as if she had damaged his throat. "Movement?"

Without transition, a new scene—smaller, and apparently more distant—appeared beside the meadow and the contest. The image showed a stone passage, featureless apart from the mage's eternal lamps and the doors on either hand, and entirely empty.

Empty except for the brief flutter of a black robe at the corner of the corridor.

"By the Seven Hells," Argoyne muttered, "you're right. Conniving bastard!" He meant the King of Vesselege. "They're already inside. I can feel"—he paused momentarily, then announced—"six of them."

From his scroll and his power, he produced other scenes, all of passages within the keep, all empty—and all defined by glimpses of stealth.

Somehow the intruders eluded more direct observation.

Ro-uke.

I did not hesitate. I had made my choice. As I left the table, running, I called to Isla, "Guard the door! We must have one of them alive!"

"Alive?" She did not appear to understand me.

"We must have evidence!"

If the *nerishi-qa* did not study honor as well as killing, I did not know how to combat them. I had seen the young *shin-te* slain once. I did not expect him to triumph now.

From the doorway I flung myself into the outer corridor.

▲▼▲

Six of them— If they were allowed to reach Argoyne's chamber, they might slay him, regardless of his defenses. Theirs was the Art of Assassination. And their weapons were many.

An hour ago, I would have applauded the Dark Lord's death. But now I did not mean to see the Mage War decided by treachery.

I wished for other weapons myself. My fang's range was limited. But first I required a vantage from which I could watch over the Archemage without hazarding him. I could not seek out the *ro-uke*—I had recognized none of the corridors revealed in Argoyne's images. Therefore I must await his attackers.

A quick circuit of the passage showed only one stair rising to this level from below. That was fortuitous. I might be able to hold one stair against six *ro-uke*—although I doubted it—if they came at me singly, and did not take me by surprise.

Already, however, I had made a false assumption. And assumptions of all kinds were fatal. Because the scenes which Argoyne had opened in the air appeared distant, I had believed that the *ro-uke* were likewise distant.

As I hastened down the stair to select my point of vantage, a trident bit into my shoulder, tearing at my flesh with such force that I was thrown to the wall.

My fall became a tumble on the edged stone. I could not yet feel the pain of my wound, but only the shock of impact and the hard stairs. Later, if I lived, I would chide myself for a fool. Now, while I plunged downward, I reached out with my *qa*, measuring the trident's path toward me, gauging the location of my enemy.

When I struck the floor, he was no more than four paces from me, charging with his *ro-uke* katana upraised to sever the skull from my spine. Masked in black from head to foot, and voluminously robed to both conceal and contain his weapons, he might have been a long scrap of shadow cast by a torch held in an unsteady hand.

But the illumination in Argoyne the Black's keep shone without wavering, as endless and unmoved as stone.

Within two strides, the *ro-uke* folded at the knees and pitched onto his face with my dagger buried in the base of his throat. His sword slithered from his grasp, skidding its steel across the floor.

Now the pain of my shoulder came to me, and I knew at once that the points of the trident carried poison.

How swiftly the toxin would act I could not guess. And there were five more assassins to be considered. I did what I could, however. Retrieving my fang, and snatching up the katana, I ducked behind the foundation of the stair. There I pulled back my torn robe to examine my wound.

Some poisons were swift—others, slow. Some might be endured by a concentration of qa and will. To others I was immune. But the nature of this toxin had not yet revealed itself. Gripping my courage, I dug my fang into the wound until my shoulder bled heavily. Perhaps the worst of the poison would be flushed away.

Past its stone foundation, I saw no one approach the stair. No one advanced at my back. No sound earned from above, where—or so I prayed—Isla guarded Argoyne's door. After a moment spent to quiet my heart and my fear, I risked leaving the stair in order to peer beyond the corner of the corridor behind me.

My fang I again secreted within my robe. The sword I bore before me, ready for use.

Although I was cautious at the corner, I was not cautious enough. By ill chance, the *ro-uke* creeping toward me caught my gaze as I met hers. She was some distance from me yet. But now I had neither the advantage nor the disadvantage of surprise.

Rather than attempting to foil her by stealth—which was her Art, not mine—I stepped past the corner to confront her formally. With the katana's point directed toward her heart, I bowed in challenge.

As if by magery, she produced a sword from within her robe. This, too, was her Art, not mine. However, I was not daunted. I was *nahia*, and understood edged weapons. And I had always believed that because the *ro-uke* were proficient with weapons by the score, they were expert with none.

Soundless on the stone, she advanced to assail me.

Her first blow would have cleft me where I stood, but mine was the Art of Circumvention. I slipped her katana away along my blade, then turned my edge against her. She countered fluidly, liquid as a splash of ink.

Point to point, we considered each other.

A low slash followed, and one high. I saw that if I met her blade directly, force against force, I would open myself to her return stroke.

However, that was not my nature—or the nature of my training. With each oblique deflection, I disturbed as well the cut which came next.

Again she brought her point to mine and paused.

There I might have died, but the alteration of her *qa* gave me warning. By the standards of the *nahia*, her skills were too thinly spread. She had not the gift of launching an attack without discernible preparation.

Warned, I flinched aside as she flung a shuriken at my face. Her stroke skidded from my blade. Unbalanced by the angle of my deflection, as well as by the force of her throw, she extended more than she had intended.

At once, I stamped a kick into the side of her knee, and felt the tendons tear as she collapsed.

Alive, I had told Isla. *We must have one of them alive*! But a growing numbness had taken hold of my shoulder, and four more assassins still crept the keep. In desperation the *ro-uke* cast another shuriken, but I stepped past it and cut her chest apart.

Dark death spilled and pooled beneath her as though her black attire melted to shadows.

A moment of dizziness swept through me. Fearing for my life, I slashed a strip from her robe and bound it tightly about my shoulder. Its pressure weakened my arm, but might also slow the toxin's progress.

If mine was the Art of Circumvention, clearly I must find some means to circumvent another direct contest. My dizziness receded, but did not pass entirely, and my heart had acquired an unsteadiness which alarmed me. After a moment's deliberation, I compelled myself to cut into the fallen *ro-uke*'s robe and search her until I discovered a rope and grapnel, which a stealthy assassin might use to scale a sheer wall.

Coiling the rope, I returned warily to the stair.

In my absence, any number of intruders might have ascended to the level of Argoyne's chamber. That I could not alter, however. If Isla did not choose to defend him, then the Archemage must defend himself. I could do nothing more than guard the stair.

Among the outer chambers, I found one with its door unlocked. From within the room, with the door nearly closed, I could watch the stair unseen. Failing to imagine an alternative, I accepted the disadvantages of surprise—which had slain my first opponent—and secreted myself to wait.

While I crouched at the slim crack of the door, numbness slowly sank its teeth into the side of my chest. A renewed wave of dizziness bore with it the bitter sensation of despair.

The young *shin-te* still lived, of that I was certain. If he—and Argoyne—had fallen, some sign of it would be felt in the mage's keep. Such powers did not pass lightly from the world. But how long could the *shin-te* endure? How long could I?

Focused and feverish in my confusion, I did not notice the *ro-uke* as he gained the stair. I had seen him approach—and yet he appeared to arrive like an act of magery, without transition.

With my strength ebbing, I waited in silence while the assassin crept upward. I could not challenge him openly, and did not trust my stealth to equal his. Despite the danger that he might ascend beyond my reach—or that another *ro-uke* might come behind him—I did not move until his head had risen into the stairwell, out of sight. Then I eased open the door of my covert and hastened toward him.

By good fortune, he paused where he was, no doubt studying the hazards of the floor above. Whirling the grapnel by its line, I flung it at his legs.

Again by good fortune—for I could not claim skill in my condition—I had cast true. The grapnel caught him securely. At once, I hauled on the rope, heaving him off the stair in a rush.

The snapping sound as he struck the floor told me that he had broken bones. He flopped nervelessly at the impact, then lay still. When I ventured near him, I saw that he was dead. The fall had crushed his skull, or his neck.

Giddy with relief and poison, I stumbled to the foot of the stair, seated myself, and rested my head on my stronger hand.

▲▼▲

Three *ro-uke* remained. In a moment, I promised my weakness, I would rise to my feet and consider how I might oppose them. But first I must breathe. So that I could estimate the progress of the toxin, and concentrate my *qa* against it.

"Asper," Isla called softly from the head of the stair. "How many?"

I lifted my head to peer upward. A haze clouded my sight—apparently Argoyne's lamps had begun to smoke—and I could not see her clearly.

"Three," I told the stairwell.

"Then come up." She sounded impatient. "There are three here. One used the stair—I thought you were dead—but the other two must have climbed up the outer wall. They came at me from rooms across the passage.

"Asper, what's wrong?"

I had been foolish. A *ro-uke* must have gained the stair while I fought around the corner.

Vaguely I indicated my shoulder. "Poison."

Like the *ro-uke*, and Argoyne himself, she had lost her need for transitions. I alone still required movement from moment to moment. She appeared at my side, tugged me to my feet. "We don't have much time," she said as she urged me upward. "The *shin-te* is losing. Maybe Argoyne can help you." Rents marked her robe. Blood dripped from a cut in her scalp. Her cheek showed a bruise so deep that it must have covered cracked bones. "I kept one of them alive for you. I stunned her, but she'll recover soon."

Alive—She had succeeded where I had failed.

I could hope again. Gratitude swelled my *qa*, and a measure of stability returned to my limbs. "I am in your debt," I murmured as I amended my pace. "You are a tribute to the *mashu-te*."

"I hope they'll think so," she replied. Apparently her scruples disturbed her yet.

However, they no longer troubled me.

▲▼▲

In the chamber of the Archemage, I saw at once that Isla had spoken truly. Argoyne's young champion stood near defeat. The resilience was gone from his movements, his eyes were empty of purpose, and his *qa* seemed to flutter within him like a torn rag. He still kept his feet, still blocked and countered. And he had exacted a price from his opponent. The *nerishi-qa* fought with one eye swollen shut, two broken fingers, and a falter in all his steps. The arrogance was gone from his gaze. Yet it was plain that the *shin-te* would be the first to fall. If I had not felt the proximity of his death like an emanation from Argoyne's image, or read it in the vehemence of his opponent's *qa*, I would have seen it on the faces of the White Lords, and of Goris Miniter. Anticipations of triumph defined the sunlight in their eyes. The young master had received blows which his flesh could not withstand.

The remaining *ro-uke* had recovered consciousness. Isla and I kept the woman between us, pretending to hold her captive. Perhaps Isla did so. For my part, however, I clung to her for support. Unsteadiness surged and receded in my head, and I could not trust my legs to sustain me. Like Argoyne's champion, I would soon fall.

Without delay, Isla informed the mage, "Asper needs help."

Reluctantly Argoyne turned from the meadow to consider my plight. His obscured vision regarded me as though I had lost my place in his attention.

"No," I said at once. "His need is greater." I indicated the *shin-te*. "Send us there. While you still can. We must go now."

The Archemage appeared to understand me. "They won't listen to you," he warned.

I sighed. "Then we will not speak to them."

Isla glared a question at me, but I had neither the heart nor the will to answer her. The outcome of the Mage War lay between warriors now, *shin-te* and *nerishi-qa*, Goris Miniter and the White Lords no longer had any part to play.

Argoyne nodded, reaching among his scrolls. "After all," he muttered as he found the one he sought and opened it, "I have nothing more to lose. If you wanted me dead, all you had to do is wait for it. And it's always easy to trust warriors. That's why," he finished cryptically, "they're called 'the Fatal Arts.'"

I could not have asked him what he meant if I had wished to. He and his chamber and the stone keep were gone.

▲▼▲

Washed by morning sunlight, we stood in the meadow, surrounded by Miniter's horsemen. Isla still held the *ro-uke* by one arm, and I clung to the other, concealing my weakness as well as I was able. Five paces from us, both the young *shin-te* and his opponent had paused to stare in confusion and mistrust at our sudden interruption.

Around us, horses flinched and reared, snorting their alarm. Several of the riders prepared to charge against us until the King called them back to their places. The White Lords made warding gestures in our direction, but sent no magery to harm us.

Again haze dimmed my sight, as though the smoke of some vast and fatal bonfire had clouded the meadow. Yet I could see well enough to determine where we were. The meadow lay in a broad valley among the abrupt foothills of the Scarmin. Beyond them, crags and mountains shrouded by distance towered into the sky. And there, distinct against the high cliffs, stood Argoyne's keep.

This struggle for the fate of Vesselege took place at the boundary between the domains of magery, separated by height and stone—the borderland between the White Lords and the Dark.

Before Goris Miniter could raise his voice to demand an explanation, Isla and I bowed to him formally. Coerced to do so, the *ro-uke* followed our example.

"King of Vesselege," Isla said at once, "this test of champions has been dishonored. We've brought proof of treachery."

At her words, quick consternation echoed around the ring. Horsemen muttered and cursed. If she had announced to him that all his pain and effort had been wasted, the young *shin-te* could not have looked more bereft. Bowing his head, he slumped in sorrow or despair. However, the *nerishi-qa* reacted otherwise. He advanced a step or two angrily, as though he meant to challenge us. His *qa* was a furnace, feeding him where a lesser man such as I would have been consumed.

Once more Miniter stilled his riders. At his sides, the White Lords considered the peaks of Scarmin like men striving to bridge the distance in order to see Argoyne's thoughts.

Despite the haze which troubled my eyes, I could not mistake the King's calculation as he asked in tones of iron, "What has the Archemage done?"

"King of Vesselege," I answered, "the treachery is not his." Although I spoke weakly, my voice carried across the meadow. "The dishonor belongs elsewhere."

The White Lords' champion approached another step, outrage burning in his open eye.

"Inside the keep of the Archemage," Isla explained for me, "this *nahia* and I met and defeated six of the *ro-uke*. They are assassins, King of Vesselege. I think it's safe to assume"—she gave the word a sneering force—"Argoyne didn't send them against himself."

"Then who?" the King countered harshly. "And for what purpose? If you 'assume' so much, do you also 'assume' you know why they were there? The *ro-uke* have as much honor as the *mashu-te*. Their presence is not 'proof of treachery.'"

Turning to the captive woman, I shifted my grasp on her arm so that my mouth reached her ear.

"Speak," I told her softly. "The truth. On the honor of your Art." Within her robes, my fang drew blood from the skin along her spine. "I do not hold you accountable for the service you were asked to perform. But your life and all Vesselege are forfeit if you lie."

Bitter as a blade, Miniter continued, "And you ask us to believe that you and one *nahia* alone defeated six of the *ro-uke*? That is hard to credit. If there is treachery here, perhaps it is yours."

The assassin cleared her throat, lifting her head to the young *shin-te* and his opponent rather than to Miniter and the White Lords. "No," she pronounced. She, too, recognized the nature of this battle. And, as Goris Miniter had said, the *ro-uke* understood honor. "The King of Vesselege sent us to rid his land of Black Argoyne, the last of the Dark Lords. He wished the Archemage slain during your contest."

A hush fell over the meadow—the silence of shock and dismay. The sky itself seemed to carry an echo of chagrin like a suggestion of distant thunder. Although his glare spoke of murder, Goris Miniter held his tongue. It may have been that his soldiers and adherents were more disturbed to hear the words spoken than they were by what the words meant. The White Lords revealed no surprise. But there were warriors among the horsemen, students and masters of the Fatal Arts, and their distress was plain.

To the *nerishi-qa*, I said, "There is no honor for you here. No victory. The contest is meaningless. Let it go."

"No!" one of the White Lords returned sharply. "The challenge was made and accepted in good faith. The contest is between mages, and we are bound by it. We stand or fall by the deeds of our champions, not by the honor or falsehood of kings and assassins. Goris Miniter's actions are his own, irrelevant. The contest must be resolved."

Although the mage's lips moved, his voice did not appear to issue from his mouth, but rather from some source as distant as Argoyne's keep.

The *nerishi-qa* withheld reply. He studied me narrowly for a moment, considering my wound and my weakness—gazed briefly at the young *shin-te*—then strode from the center of the ring toward Goris Miniter. Raising his head and his *qa*, he confronted the mounted King as though he were accustomed to passing judgment on the actions of sovereigns.

"Is this true?" he inquired softly.

Goris Miniter's calculation was written on his face, plain to all who chose to see it. His eyes sifted lies and half-truths, deflections, while under his beard his jaws chewed the consequences of whatever he might say. In the end, however, the man before him was a *nerishi-qa* master, able to distinguish truth from falsehood, and he did not hazard prevarication.

"In case you failed," he answered. "The Dark Lords are an abomination. Vesselege will never be whole while one of them endures."

"Vesselege," the champion of the White Lords retorted, still softly, "will never be whole while the King is treacherous."

So suddenly that his action startled the wildflowers, the *nerishi-qa* braced a hand on the neck of the King's horse and vaulted upward, sweeping a kick which struck Goris Miniter upon the helm and dropped him like a stone to the meadow.

Among the grasses the King of Vesselege lay still, with blood drooling from his mouth, and his skull crushed.

The young *shin-te* watched in bafflement and rue, though he grasped nothing.

On all sides, soldiers and adherents shouted their fury and fear. They might have goaded their mounts to charge at the *nerishi-qa*, but the warriors around the ring were quicker. *Ro-uke* and *mashu-te*, they hastened their horses forward to block the soldiers. Doubtless they felt as the King's adherents did. For one reason or another, they had pledged their service to Goris Miniter. Yet they understood that a contest of champions had been dishonored. And without honor the Fatal Arts would fall to dust.

In relief, I sagged against the support of the captured assassin. The toxin in my shoulder had become stronger than my resistance, and I believed that I had accomplished my end. The *nerishi-qa* had acknowledged the contest dishonored. Now he and his opponent could withdraw without loss on either side. Without more death. Argoyne would live to defend his knowledge a while longer. And my life, and Isla's, and the young *shin-te*'s, would not be forfeit for our service to the Black Archemage.

Haze gathered over the meadow. Helpless to do otherwise, I trusted that the *ro-uke* would uphold me.

I could only stare in dismay as the White Lords announced together, "The King's treachery has been repaid." Their voices tolled thunder. "The honor of this contest is restored. It will continue."

Isla groaned. She may not have felt my qualms about sacrificing her own life, but she could see that our young comrade was already beaten. Only a few blows were needed to complete his death.

The *nerishi-qa* appeared to ignore the White Lords. Turning his back on them, as well as on Miniter's corpse, he advanced again into the trampled circle of the contest. When he was within five paces of his opponent, he stopped.

He spoke quietly, but the thunder which the White Lords invoked was not more clear.

"I care nothing for mages," he informed the *shin-te*. "If they are bound here—White Lords or Dark—the oath is theirs, not mine. This test lies between *nerishi-qa* and *shin-te*.

"For years we have refused your challenge, believing you fools. But you have become offensive to us. You have named *nerishi-qa* a false Art. I was sent by my masters to repay your folly, and to teach you that the falseness you repudiate is your own."

Although he had been injured, his readiness for combat betrayed no flaw. The resilience compressed in the muscles of his legs matched the hard force of his *qa*. Relaxed and quick, his hands seemed to hold every blow which had ever been struck.

"Now," he concluded, "our contest has meaning."

From the edge of the ring, the White Lords nodded approval.

A low moan escaped the young man's lips. Yet he did not withdraw. Wavering on his feet, he answered, "I must accept. This test lies between us." A maimed formality dignified his words, despite the frailty of his flesh. "Yours is the Art of the Killing Stroke. I will show you that it is false."

His knee buckled as he assumed his stance, and he nearly fell. Staggering, he drew himself upright again. The loss in his eyes was terrible to behold.

He had met despair. Already it proved itself against him.

Had I been less weak, I might have wept for him. My own death crouched near me on the meadow, but it did not trouble me as much as his. Poison filled my thoughts, and I could not imagine any help which might save him. His spirit and his *qa* had not failed him. Still he was too young for the burden Argoyne had given him to bear.

Unsteadily he braced himself to meet his opponent's last attack.

Within me, the toxin seemed to clench its jaws. The *nerishi-qa* had not yet moved. However, I could see his assault in the haze before me, precise and fatal. When he struck—

"*Shin-te*," Isla called out suddenly, "remember your Art!"

As if involuntarily, the young master turned his bereavement toward her.

"There is no killing stroke," she reminded him. Her voice rang with certainty. "There is only choice. Or despair."

I feared that she had lost her mind. Had she not contested his beliefs herself? Yet in the end it was plain that she understood him better than I did. Or that he understood her—

Empowered by the magery of her words, his limbs regained a measure of their strength, and the sorrow receded from his eyes. Years of pain shed themselves from his shoulders. As he rose out of his stance to face his opponent again, he conveyed the impression that he was being lifted beyond himself.

Surprised by the young man's movement, the *nerishi-qa* paused, easing his own stance.

Deliberately the *shin-te* bowed to his opponent. When he straightened his back, his arms hung defenselessly at his sides. Yet he appeared taller in some way, as if his own words in Isla's mouth had given him stature.

"Your skill surpasses me," he told the *nerishi-qa*, echoing her certainty. "But your will does not. No man's choice exceeds another's. You cannot make me other than I am."

Slowly he spread his arms wide, closing his eyes as he did so.

"Here I stand," he said, "unguarded. Strike me, if that is your wish. Your blow is mine. The victory is mine. If I have chosen to die, you cannot kill me. Any blow of yours can only carry out my will.

"How, then," he finished softly, "will you teach the *shin-te* that they are fools?"

The *nerishi-qa* frowned, studying his opponent's displayed form as though to determine the best target for a killing stroke.

"Strike," one of the White Lords commanded urgently. "His choices have no significance. The contest does not rest on them. Only the blow matters. Only his death matters. The Dark Lord will be destroyed when his champion falls."

Clinging to the *ro-uke*, I fought to clear my sight.

Without warning, the *nerishi-qa* struck—a blow so fierce that it seemed to stun my own heart. His fist flashed forward with all his *qa* behind it. Under its force, the cloth of the young man's robe sprang to tatters across his chest, torn thread from thread.

And yet the *shin-te* did not flinch. His skin had not been touched.

His arms remained wide in sacrifice.

With great care, as though he had found himself on the edge of a precipice, the *nerishi-qa* stepped back, rising from his stance. After a moment, he snorted under his breath.

"Look at me," he instructed his opponent.

Obediently the young master opened his eyes.

"You are indeed willing to die," the White Lords' champion observed between his teeth.

Lowering his arms, the *shin-te* shrugged. "Your skill surpasses mine," he repeated. "Yet my life is my own."

The *nerishi-qa* snorted again. "The *shin-te* are fools to challenge us."

For the first time in my experience of him, the young master smiled. "So I believe." Years lifted from his face in an instant. Without transition, he resembled a boy, innocent and unbereaved. "We learn nothing from each other."

As if at a great distance, I heard Isla sigh, "Well said. Well done."

The *nerishi-qa* did not smile in turn. Scowling around his swollen eye, he left the center of the ring to stand before the White Lords on their mounts.

"The contest is ended," he informed them. The authority of his tone allowed no contradiction. "The *shin-te* has proven himself against me. I am forced to acknowledge defeat."

Hearing him, I buried my face against the shoulder of the *ro-uke* to conceal my tears. The *nerishi-qa* had studied honor in such depth that I was humbled by it.

Yet I looked up again at once, for the White Lords had raised their voices in a cry as cruel as the clamor of a storm. From within their bright robes, they summoned their power and thunderclaps answered, rolling among the foothills and over the meadow, gathering fire. Called from the clear sky, lightning hammered downward. Isla, the *ro-uke*, and I were knocked from our feet, horses were scattered, soldiers and warriors were tossed to the ground.

In the center of the ring, the blast scorched wildflowers and grasses to char—and the young master with them.

But his death was not defeat. The White Lords who struck him down had already ceased to exist.

▲▼▲

We did not, however. Instead we stood in the chamber where we had left Argoyne, the three of us, *shin-te*, *mashu-te*, and *nahia*. The Black Archemage was not present. In his place we found three goblets brimming with wine, enough food to satisfy us twice over, and the rich silence of peace.

Like our struggles in the meadow, the Mage War had ended.

My shoulder had been healed, although it still held the low ache of remembered poison. Isla's lesser hurts had been made whole. And the young master stood intact before us, restored by a Dark Lord's magery. He had shed his sorrow in fire, and his eyes smiled when his mouth did not.

His memory also had been restored, but he neglected to tell us his name. Perhaps he thought that we already knew it.

Smiling, he raised his goblet to thank us for the part we had played in his victory. "While I live," he told us with the earnest sincerity of youth, "I am in your debt."

I bowed to answer him. "As we are in yours." I was foolishly pleased with myself, and cared not what I said.

Isla also bowed. She smiled as well. Yet the expression in her eyes revealed the trouble in her heart. After a moment, she protested, "But we didn't do anything."

The young man laughed—a happy sound which suited him well. "I also did nothing," he assured her.

Perhaps for that reason *shin-te* was called the Art of Acceptance.

But her concern was not relieved. With some severity, she observed, "You took a great risk. That blow—" She shuddered, despite her training. "Your heart would have burst."

He nodded gravely. "I believed that I would die." Then he added, "But that was a small matter. I was already beaten. Yet when you spoke my own words to I me—one of the *mashu-te*—a student of the Direct Fist—I heard them in a new way. They became"—he rolled his smiling gaze at the ceiling—"how shall I say I it? They became simple. Despair is the killing stroke. There is no other." Lightly he shrugged. "My hazard was no greater than yours."

That was true. If their champion had killed the *shin-te*, the White Lords would no doubt have slain both Isla and me, for the help we had given Argoyne.

We lived only because the young man had stepped beyond the circle of his own comprehension.

Still Isla had not named what was in her heart. Instead she asked, "What will become of Vesselege now?"

The wine seemed quick to intoxicate me. I, too, laughed. "Argoyne and the White Lords will endure each other until the contest between them takes another form. Then they will resume their struggle. As for the rule of Vesselege— Sovereigns are easily replaced. Perhaps the new King will profit from Goris Miniter's example." I drank more wine so that I would not laugh again. "I would advise him to make peace with both the White Lords and the Dark while he can."

"And what will you do?" Isla inquired of the *shin-te*.

He did not hesitate. "I have learned a precious truth. I must teach it."

She looked to me. "And you, Asper?"

I met her gaze across the rim of my goblet, concealing my mirth. "First I will drink. Then I will sleep. And when I have recovered, I will dedicate myself to the study of dangerous assumptions. There is power in them, which the *nahia* have neglected."

She fell silent, frowning to herself.

Seeing her unease, I returned her question to her. "What are your intentions, Isla? The wine is excellent, we are whole, and the sun shines on Vesselege. What disturbs you?"

With an effort, she revealed her thoughts. "I've come to doubt the teaching of the *mashu-te*," she admitted unhappily. "If *nerishi-qa* is a false Art, then so are the others. I'll have to leave my home to study among the *shin-te*."

I stared at her. The idea of turning away from the *nahia* had never occurred to me. Her scruples—her need for the purity of her beliefs—surpassed me.

"Do not," the young master urged at once. "The *shin-te* are indeed fools to challenge the *nerishi-qa*. My Art is as false as any."

"And as true," I murmured.

That challenge had been rightly spurned by the *nerishi-qa*. It resembled the hostility of the White Lords toward Black Argoyne. In the meadow surrounded by enemies, however, the young *shin-te* had learned his own wisdom.

After a time, Isla nodded.

When she had let her concern go, I sighed my relief, and drank again. In all my life, I had never been farther from despair.

What we were could not endure without honor. And the price of honor was death, in one form or another. I thought of the young man's acceptance of death—of Isla's willingness to sacrifice her life—of the *nerishi-qa*'s surrender to defeat. I thought of the hazards I had faced.

Argoyne had said, *It's always easy to trust warriors. That's why they're called "the Fatal Arts."* I believed now that I had begun to understand him.